PAPERBACK VERSION
OF THE KING OF EROTICA 5
WARDROBE:

DEDICATED TO:

# Marcus Sands
# Antonio Fleneury

*16 year friendship, alliance*
*With you both.*
*Loyalty is everything.*

PHOTO BY JOHN WILSON

# Books by Dapharoah69

THE KING OF EROTICA EMPIRE:

*The King of Erotica 1: The Throne*
*The King of Erotica 1: The Throne Special Edition*
*The King of Erotica 2: The Crown*
*The King of Erotica 3: V.I.P. Edition*
*The King of Erotica 4 the DeTHRONEment of the King*
*Call Her Queen Hatshepsut*
*Some Men Wear Panties*

Phaze Publishing

*The Diary and the Strap*

Anthologies
*Voices From Within*
*WSN Network*
*Mocha Chocolate*

£@®®¥

ISBN #: 978-0-578-05401-8

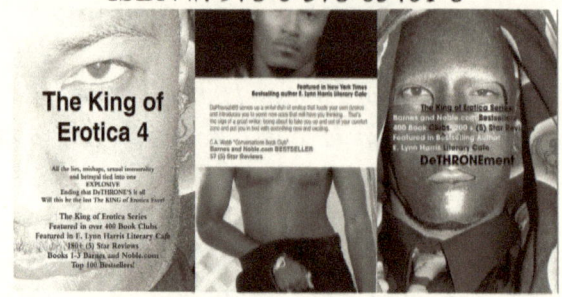

THE KING OF EROTICA WARDROBE
Published by TKOE Publications
Copyright ® Aliyaih Hernandez, Sunjaraih Wilson
Larry C. Wilson, Jr. Amuraih Hernandez, Mykhale
Rivera, Jalen Artevia Wilson

Front and Back cover:

**John Wilson and Larry Wilson**

Library of congress cataloging-in-publication data has been applied for.

# The King of Erotica 4 DeTHRONEment

# *Foreword*

## By Dangerous Lee

I first became acquainted with The King of Erotica when he was a guest on my now defunct internet radio show "Ask Dangerous Lee Live." The book he was promoting was *Some Men Wear Panties*. The title alone piqued my interest because I have a fantasy about a man wearing my panties, so I had to have him on my show to discuss the topic.

I was so into the subject matter of the book that I hadn't done much other background research on just what Mr. Larry Wilson Jr. was all about. At the time I didn't know that he was HIV positive and very open and honest about it. I didn't know about his abusive past and I also didn't know that he was bisexual. Sure, I could have assumed as much because he wrote a book about men in panties but assumptions are not my style.

I also don't think he knew at the time that HIV education and prevention is one of my passions along with writing. This gives us a connection. Through this connection I learn more about him as a person each day. His daily insight and humorous ramblings on Facebook have resulted in me admiring him. I also get to experience the love his fans have for him and how many lives he's touched with his work. I should be so lucky.

I have to admit that I know Larry Wilson, Jr. the person better than I know The King of Erotica. I have three of his titles in my possession and I have not read any of them...yet. My schedule and the fact that I am working on self publishing my first book is why I have placed his books on the "To Read" shelf of my bookcase.

However, I felt guilty having not read any of his material when I was asked to write the forward for this book. I wondered if I should turn down the offer, but who does that?

Would he be offended if I tell him I haven't read his books yet? I still don't know the answer to that as I write. Should I try to read three thick ass books before I write the forward? No, I would never get done before the deadline and you shouldn't rush good reading.

I did get a taste of his writing style when I asked him to review a short story from my upcoming book *Keep Your Panties Up and Your Skirt Down*. Along with the review he also added some ways that I could reword the story King of Erotica style. I'm sure I would have found it insulting had he not explained his intentions and I actually found his wording very entertaining and helpful. Needless to say, I did make some creative changes to the story. The King of Erotica style works!

I hope to get to know The King of Erotica better. I hear he has over two hundred five star reviews, thousands of books sold and over four hundred book club features to prove it and he owns everything. Smart man. Talented man. A Dangerous Man!

Everything I Google about writing forward states that you should read the material before writing a good forward. I don't believe that entirely. We have history and like I said earlier we have a connection and dammit I am Dangerous Lee. I can redefine the book forward!

Besides, this book is a combination of his past four books! I have a lot of catching up to do, and so do you if this is your first time meeting The King of Erotica.

Get in the mood and enjoy!
Dangerous Lee

# Operation:
# WAR: Dr.O.Be

Many of us have outfits. And we all wear clothes because it's against the crummy law to walk around in the nude, even though the doctor saw our asses and genitalia before we learned to spell dick and pussy. With that being said. After you wear your clothes they are dirty and needs to be thrown in the dirty clothes hamper. That's what my books represent. They are clothes you wore while reading and they became dirty. So does our birthday suits. You sweat it up and it has to be cleaned. What happens when we clean our clothes or put them in the cleaners or wash our birthday suits in the shower? Our garments are once again cleaned. The WAR.Dr.O.Be represents the clean outfits, so this book will have additions to a few of the stories previous King of Erotica books didn't have. You will go deeper into the thoughts of the characters and experience a little more dialogue. So you get something more than just all the King of Erotica books put in One.

This book combines The King of Erotica Books 1, 2 and 4. The King of Erotica 3 is excluded. It was just a VIP edition for the fans, to hold them over for the King of Erotica 4 so that book isn't included in this volume because none of the stories are continuations. So this is the Wardrobe. Kinda like organizing clothes on hangers in your closet. You hang some, you put your shoes neatly on the floor or on top of the shelf or you fold your clothes and put them in the dresser. You have your Easter suit and the Funeral suit. You have your night on the town outfit and a few women have Freakum dresses, skirts and fancy blouses. You have clothes you never wore and don't intend to wear. You have them because you could afford them. You have sexy underwear or you don't wear any at all. You take them to the cleaners or you wash them by hand or using the washer and dryer. This book is your Wardrobe. It represents all of that. The clothes and the closet is a part of our daily lives. A lot of folks hide in the closet, afraid to peek outside and be free of prejudice and bias. You lie about your HIV/AIDS status and you lie to your wife and family. Same goes to the undercover lesbians. Whatever suit you need to wear you will find it in one of these stories.

I want to thank God for the gift of words. Without God where would I be? I want to thank John Wilson for your love. Demetrius Mozell and Kalvin Tate, my best friends, two strong, intelligent black men who keep me grounded and keep it real with me on all levels. I love you two beyond reproach. Thanks to my Case Manager Kevin Palmer and Meredyeth T. Lightbourne for having my back and keeping me healthy and strong. I also want to thank Jhonathan Pierre for taking the pictures of me with my camera on Piedmont Park, Atlanta on Labor Day Weekend. Me, him, Michaela Todd and Sierra (Anyla Marie) had a blast. Thanks Hans Bidon for pushing me to write my autobiography, which will be completed hopefully by next year. Thanks Tai for your love and friendship and for capturing the images of my book signing at the Grand Hyatt in Buckhead, Atlanta. I want to thank my FaceBook family for loving my status updates and for showing me love. For all those who interviewed me, Joey Pinkney, Chick Lit Girl, Cyrus Webb, Meak Productions (my agency, Love you Miko Evans), Dangerous Lee, Vonetta, Kevin McNeir, Lonnell Williams, The Skorpion Show, SwaggaKings.com (Hi, Latoya!), Maddaphobia Online and Fran Briggs. Thanks for taking the time to elevate my craft. Without further ado, I wanna bow out gracefully for you all can enjoy the King of Erotica 5: the WAR:Dr.O.Be.


Love Dapharoah69

**R.I.P. Michael Jackson. The King of Pop, Rock and Soul. R.I.P. E. Lynn Harris**

# Long Live the Kings!

ITLA Pride, Atlanta 2009

Mr. Christopher Street Visionary

Multi-blogger Lonnell Williams

*Love ya' Nikki. Very special lady to me.*
*Most important Fan I ever had.*
*God bless.*
*The King of Erotica*
R.I.P. to your babies.

# Jadish Houston

Beautiful, witty, and sensually sexy, Jadish Houston was in the middle of her work-out session when the phone rang. She was naked. Sprawled across her Queen-sized bed. Her legs spread-eagled, her huge breasts bounced progressively as she worked her hand and fingers all over her sweet-smelling pussy.

*Ignore it! Ignore it!* Ring! *Goddamn it, Bitches. Hang up! This work out is feeling...so good! Every time I try to spend some time with myself somebody got to knock on my door or ring the phone off the hook...*

*Ring! Damn! Damn! Damn! Hang up! What do you want? It better be about something really important or I'm going to be one pissed bitch! I'm getting really tired of this! If I'm not babying my husband I am babying my mother! I needed my space sometimes and every day I have to be Wonder Woman, turning in circles just to POW the bitches out of my face.*

Hesitantly glancing at the caller I.D., she had to answer it because of the name that flashed in her eyes. Shit! Just her luck! Indifferent, she snatched up the receiver, drenched with sweat. She tried to set her body on idle but her pussy wasn't having it.

*Damn, I want to finish!* "Hey, baby!" came the loud, annoying voice through the receiver that made her bottom lip twitch and her ears burn. Jadish rolled her eyes, trying to maintain her level of pleasure. She gently stroked her kitty. *Meow*, it told her. *Arg!* her fingers responded because she had to put everything on pause.

*Maybe she called to wish me a happy birthday!* "Hey, Mama." She could barely say the words. She felt so good. Her soul wanted to rejoice but the feeling was cut short because her Mama was on the freaking phone.

*Mama, nice time to call, when I'm getting me a quick one!*

"How are you doing today, baby?" her mother asked.

*I'm trying to* do *my pussy if you must know!* Pinching her clitoris, she was desperately trying to hold the phone to her ear with her shoulder. Gasping for air, she slowly worked her fingers in and out of her wet flesh.

"Baby, are you there?" her mother asked.

Jadish was in another world, taking herself to extremely breathtaking dangerous heights.

Sensation whipping her into a maculation of emotions, she could hardly breathe. It was hot and sticky, even with the windows open and the rainy breeze sending chills up her spine.

"Jadish...I know she didn't put me on hold," her mother argued, sighing. Jadish's TV volume set to "low," Jaheim, a famous R&B crooner, sung "Put your Woman First" from B.E.T.

*This feels good!* "I'm just spiffy."

A smoker's chuckle. "Good to hear it," her mother went on, coughing.

Remaining upset about the phone call, she closed her eyes, riding her fingers like a horse; which was a little difficult to do, but she was doing it and doing it well. She worked her hips the way LL Cool J licked those lips. A mild explosion started to crawl along her spine, making her legs shake uncontrollably. Her toes curling with the satin sheets, she brought one of her breasts up to her mouth and used her tongue to erect the nipple. Her sweat taste so divine, better than any red wine.

*Girl, just hang up on her. Make yourself come and then call her back. Pull the phone cord from the wall! That'll work.*

"How much do you need?" Jadish asked haphazardly, rolling her eyes. She knew her mother called for money. She was worse than bill collectors.

Her Mama gave a small giggle. "I didn't *call* you for that."

*God, this is heaven! Maybe If I try turning on my side I could finger bang myself that way? Nah, not much pressure on the clit. It's all about the clit, baby!*

"Yeah, *right*. You've been my...mother for twenty five years. I think I *know* you."

A moan escaped her lips and she closed them tightly, rolling her eyes into her head. She felt her body rising and falling, as sweat popped from every pore. Her spine tingled. Heat rose. Her stomach was in knots trying to chase out the butterflies.

"Girl, now is not the time to get on my nerves. Can I borrow ten dollars?"

*Oh shit oh shit! I'm almost there!* The butterflies released Goosebumps all over her arms..."For what? And why can't Daddy give you the money?"

Feeling everything but obtuseness, she spread her legs as far as they'd go, eyeing the door knob, getting freakier by the second.

"I'm asking you."

Who cares? Go get a job, Ma! "Ma, like I said why can't you ask your *husband?*"

"Because I don't want to," her mother said more sternly.

Stupefied, Jadish spat, "You probably drained him dry." *And I'm about to drain myself dry.*

Soothingly, she spewed, "On all accounts, honey."

Jadish didn't want to hear that. *Girl, go to the door knob. Door knob, you hear me, Jadish?*

"You both get social security, and on top of that Daddy gets disability, eight hundred dollars a month. Disability just helped him get a damn SUV."

*Door knob, hmm never tried that one before.*

Her mother stuttered, "That isn't important. Can I…"

Go to the door knob NOW, BITCH! Getting a huge burst of energy, the adrenaline rushing straight to her brain, Jadish jumped out of the bed, and rushed over to the door. Pushing it back against the cheaply-constructed wall, the vibration knocked three hanging pictures on the floor, the glass shattering against the checkered tile.

"Baby, what's that glass breaking?" her Mama asked.

Exacerbated, Jadish replied, "Nothing. Just a movie. I'm. Watching…"

About to lose her mind, she turned her back to the door, and put her ass on the knob, fluttering her eyes closed as she felt the small brass ball slide inside her warm flesh. *Oh, yeah! Oh goddamn yeah! It's on and it's on tonight!*

"So, can I borrow the money, Jadish?"

She wanted to love herself. "Yea, woman you can."

"Thank you, baby."

*Jesus! This feels so good!* She gyrated her hips, tears falling from her eyes. She worked it, loved it, felt it and needed it.

"So I guess I won't be hearing from you in the next three months."

"Yea, that's about the jest of it."

*Good I should give her twenty dollars so she could vanish for six months.*

The sudden feeling took her breath away. Sensations hurdled over each other, sending her into a spasmodic tremble. She felt the explosion, pulsated along her spine, settled in the nerves of her torso. Speeding up as fast as she could go, tears fell down her face as she gripped the phone, her legs drumming together, she was pounding her pussy up against the door knob, the brass ball brushing against her G-spot. She was in love with the knob. Oh, yea. She and the knob were going to be best friends. It was a recession and a bitch couldn't afford a goddamn dildo so hey, bitch! I got a goddamn door knob and she will fuck that brass bitch until its sterling silver.

The door and the wall played a banging symphony that had her about to pull her hair out.

*Oh yea. Oh yea...OH YEA!* Her muscles contracting in her pussy, she burst open. All her love, her anguish, her misery and her joy, everything she was as a woman spontaneously recreated the freak deep down inside of her and she couldn't handle it. She could no longer contain herself.

With a joyous smile. *"Oh shit I'm coming!"*

She began coming on the door knob, shuddering where she stood. Her body appreciatively pleasured. She held her face as another orgasm rocked her sweaty body senseless, her pussy lips contracting on the brass. Eagerly, she dropped the phone, her mother shrieking and disgusted.

Once the tremors subsided, she fell to her knees, picking up the phone. Her mother was saying, "You nasty bitch!"

Jadish smiled, staring at the phone, embarrassed.

Her mother went on, clearly pissed, "You're getting some while you're on the phone with me?"

Jadish moaned sensually, rolling over on the carpet and smiling.

*"Sorry* Mama!" *Well, I'm not sorry, actually. This is my fucking house. My phone. My rules.* "You know how it is. On all accounts I feel good, to use your words. Have a good night."

Kissing through the phone she hung up.

£@®®¥

Bored out of her mind, Jadish was in the shower, thoroughly washing her hair. She thought about her husband of two years. Arrogant, selfish-ass Saxophone Jenkins was the love of her life. He was called "Sax" (his mother named him after her favorite instrument). His handsome image played in her brain cells and she held the wall, her pussy throbbing. She ached for him but that aching and the smile and the lust and the horniness quickly dissipated into a redundant frown. Sax was a gorgeous man she loved with everything in her. Yet he selfishly pressured her everyday for this and that. Iron the clothes. Cook the food. *I don't really cook*, he told her. *I wear the pants. You wear the panties. And you don't even let me taste your pussy as much as I want to*, he always whined. In fact his quips were becoming jittery and confusing.

There was nothing she wouldn't do for him. Well, there was *one* thing she couldn't bring herself to do and she didn't want to think about it. She was under the shower nozzle humming an old Drifters cut, wondering was she truly happy in her marriage. She didn't have the best marriage.

In fact she was having major problems. But could she work them out? Did she even want to? Most of her female friends were miserable with children, dating man after man trying to find that One who reminded them of their ex's, or alcoholics, bums or faggots sucking dick on the low and were gayer than a Mexican Santa Claus in a thong waving a three dollar bill at the straight clubs in Liberty City.

Lost inside her comfortable shower, she continued to hum, thinking about her husband.

And the fact her Mama used her for loot.

Jadish was drying off, wondering why her mother never really called her. It was something that used to irk her but she decided not to think about it. Her mother had her life, and Jadish had *hers*. Simply put. In fact she was thinking about her life and the direction it was going in. Her birthday sucked. Turning 25 today wasn't what it was cracked up to be. It was just another day to her. Had she gotten anything? Hell no. Was she expecting anything? Um, no! But her Mama wanted money. *Mama didn't even wish me a happy birthday. Fucked up!*

She was expecting loud mouthed Sax to come barging through the door of their two bedroom/two bathroom home and throwing his lunch sack down on the floor like a spoiled child. He would then call her name until she came running and point at it like she's a dog. Sometimes she would get on her knees and suck his dick to please him, yet as of late she hasn't been doing that because swallowing his nut landed her a trip to the clinic to get her stomach pumped. He came more than four fat men watching a hot dog commercial. And it has been pissing him off. She really didn't give a shit.

He'd then kick off his funky shoes, exposing those funky ass feet and need-to-nuke-them-socks and ask for his dinner. She *hardly* cooked. She *hated* cooking. Once he bitched about God knew what, he'd head for the Lazy Boy recliner in the well-cleaned and decorated den to watch, no, breathe ESPN. Or play Madden two thousand whatever fucking year it was on the Playstation 3 that cost more than her mortgage payment.

*He was not like that when we met.*

Suffice it to say, when Jadish's husband came home an hour later, after she put rollers in her bushy hair (staring at the door knob with a secret smile and wet panties)—"Damn I need a perm, badly!"— he grabbed a cold Heineken from the refrigerator and popped the top with the back of his cigarette lighter. Fortunately, he didn't call her name. Thank the Lord!

Turning on the TV, he flipped the channel to ESPN and crashed on the couch, eyeing the Playstation 3. He then looked at the hanging photos of his wife and managed a smile. Deep down in his heart he loved her beyond anything logical. But that love has shattered logic and revealed its surreal head because he wanted some pussy and she guarded her clit like the Russians and Iron curtains. The thought of divorce entertained him briefly. But he loved her too much to put it into action.

The thought of his wife's amazingly chiseled body danced in his head and gave him a much needed hard on. He was so horny he was about to fuck the couch. Angrily, he quickly dismissed it. Taking a hefty swig of the beer, he smacked his lips, looking at the bottle. The announcer said something trivial about the Miami Dolphins. He cursed at the TV, drank half the beer and fell asleep an hour later, dropping the bottle on the floor. The beer spilt and soaked in the carpet.

Jadish had initially heard her husband rumbling through the house. She didn't bother to get up. She just lay there, like a zombie, with a blind fold over her tired, itchy eyes. He was on his own today.

She had an amazing orgasm, an incredible work out and she felt elated. She didn't even want to move from the bed and she wasn't going to and if he crawled in the bed next to her tonight she would politely get up without kissing him and sleep on the couch.

*And my husband didn't come up to wish me a happy birthday. The hell with him. And he isn't getting any pussy.*

*Not that I ever gave him any.*

"Forever Young! *Forever young!*" Jadish sang with Rod Stewart a few days later, like some wishy-washy duet. She was prancing in front of the stereo, trying to clean the house and do something different. She wasn't a fan of Rod, but she felt like listening to something different. All she ever cared to hear was anything 2 Live Crew, even though they were played out like Vanilla Ice and his comeback attempts. OutKast was her favorite rap group. Young Jeezy and his hustling tales enthralled her. Any man talking about cocaine more than paying bills had to be some sort of entrepreneur. Or just fucking loco. Too Short and his Dick Tales made her laugh 'cause the brothah had to be camouflaging the truth somewhere in his rap music. Mama always taught her if a man bragged about getting pussy he wasn't getting pussy at all and fucking your hand ain't the business. Anything

Whitney, Janet, Tony Benet and Barbra Streisand she absolutely enjoyed.

At this particular point in her life things were looking up. Except in her marriage. Opening the curtains in her living room, she marveled at the sunshine. She was an outdoor type of gal. She couldn't remember the last time she kissed her husband let alone hugged him or had a decent conversation with him because he was too busy trying to stick his dick in her asshole and he hardly got the pussy so bam, boom pow bitch move the fuck over. Go smoke a blunt and play ball with the boys and slap some sweaty asses. When she was in his arms, her heart *knew* it was right. It felt so good. But her gut pushed her away and she begin to feel queasy and the more he insisted on fucking her the more rebellious she became. It was something she couldn't control.

He once asked her why she tensed up when he sometimes touched her and she dismissed his request with a wave of her hands and a fake chuckle. "No reason. Just don't feel good." Her words tore through him like knives. She busied herself with housework to keep from taking the conversation further. She knew she was being baited and she didn't remember seeing a shrimp when she looked in the mirror.

How did she tell him that she couldn't stand when he touched her? How did she tell him that she probably would never...

She put it out of her mind when her husband called. Quietly picking up the remote, she turned down the music. Hesitantly answering the phone, she inhaled, rolled her eyes, sucked her teeth and said, "Yes, Sax."

He implored, "Are you cooking today?"

*Well hello to you too horny man!* She closed her eyes, picking up the duster. She began dusting the shelf again. "No, *why?*"

He got an attitude. "Why won't you cook sometimes?"

She sucked her teeth. "Because I work."

"I work, too," he whined bitterly.

She rolled her eyes. "Did you call to start an argument?"

His attitude was deteriorating into a bunch of massive explosives ready to sound off. "No. I *called* to see if *you* cooked dinner."

*Whatever!* "Well *no*. You got money. Stop by McDonald's and utilize the dollar menu. I heard it's pretty...fulfilling, Sax." She was giggling and he didn't find it funny.

"I. Don't. Do. McDonald's."

*Well I'm doing the door knob tonight!* "I *hope* you don't. Then that would be called cheating."

He chocked over the phone, coughing uncontrollably. "You know what? Have dinner cooked when I get home."

"Try Wendy's, also baby," she said absent-mindedly. "They have a dollar menu as well. And then there's Checker's. Two for one price does wonders when your wife isn't cooking you a meal…"

"You're really pushing me, Jadish! Is this supposed to be love?" She put her hand on her hip. *I do love you, Sax. More than anything!*

"I'll go to Publix and buy some food. What do you want? Rice? Chicken tenders? Bullshit? A pot of piss? A container of You Ain't Tasting This Pussy Ice Cream or a bag of Male Chauvinist Vegetables?"

He released a large gush of air. "Jadish…"

She said, "Good bye," as politely as she could and she replaced the receiver.

Biting back tears.


Jadish lowered herself on the floor and buried her face in her hands. She prayed to God, trying to ignore the feeling in her gut.

*Maybe marrying him was a mistake. The biggest mistake of my life.*


An hour later, she was smoking a cigarette. Sitting on the couch. Staring at a replica of Juan Antonio De Frias Escalante's *The Dead Christ* painting she had created in Art school. A little before she dropped out to pursue being an elementary school teacher. She blew smoke into the air, separated by the spinning, dusty ceiling fan blades. Her passion for helping kids overrode her true calling for the canvas and oil-based colors. Then real life kicked in. Mounting bills, dealing with everyday people who always made her feel guilty for her talent.

Many people tried to buy her painting, which looked the exact, spitting image of the original, which was created in 1663. A local art museum in New York wanted to display her brilliant work of art but she declined.

"I paint my grief," she told the Executive Director of the Museum. "And I don't care to have people marvel at my misery."

The real reason why she didn't give up the painting was because of the very reasons why she painted it in the first place. Her bad dreams. In her dreams, a man was chasing her. He wore all black and she wore all white. He had a huge red X on a card covering his face like a terrorizing mask. He was calling out to her. *"Jadish, come back here. I just want to swallow your innocence and taste your blood."*

On her head was a cap with a tassel. She was holding it as she ran through the grass. It started to rain and her hair and clothes were getting soaked, sticking to her voluptuous body. Her high school appeared. She raced through the doors, trying to lock them. His heavy footing pushed her to the ground. Staggering to her feet she dashed towards the auditorium…Unbeknownst, her body sometimes, at any given moment of the night, spasmodically twitched in her bed. The humidity rose and the cool air sucked out her anguish. She'd dig her nails into the pillow, sweat pouring from her skin like sink water. Her body in an arch, she'd moan piteously, lost within her nightmare. The bed shook with fierce abandon, her eyes rolling to the back of her head. She'd break out in hives.

She was calling out to God in her dreams and he always sent a bolt of lightning that split the Jordan River into the Red Sea before her very eyes. Before she could cross it she saw, in the middle of the ocean floor, a woman. Being deflowered by a man who had a familiar face, but she couldn't put her finger on it.

Suffice it to say, all this went through her mind when she painted *The Dead Christ*. Some girl was losing her virginity by a horrible man. The stranger's virginity became *The Dead Christ*. Her face was black and her hair was flames. By the time she was done painting, occasionally looking at the picture of the original from a text book, her coveralls were covered with light browns, beiges, and orange colors. All over her face was sweat and black paint. It was in her hair. She was crying so hard she phoned her mother and told her she was having the dreams again.

Her mother wanted her to seek help. "Baby. They are just dreams. Ignore them."

Jadish wasn't trying to hear it. "But I have the *same* dream."

"Of the man in black and you got on white."

Jadish said, cautiously, "Yes."

"Then do what you do best, paint something, Jadish."

Jadish was sobbing so hard she couldn't breathe. Why was she having the dreams? Why was she wearing white? Who was the woman in the middle of the ocean floor being deflowered? Why was the woman's hair flames and why was she sleeping, like she was virtually unconscious?

Jadish spat icily, "I *did*, Ma."

"Then I don't know what to tell you. Maybe you need to see a shrink."

"Why do you always insist on me going to a therapist?"

"Because you are having the *same* dream over and over."

Insulted, Jadish hung up in her face and she never discussed her dreams with anybody else. It was her secret.

One she never shared with Sax.

*The hell if I go pay a shrink to listen to me talk about some fucking dreams. Are you crazy, Mama? Or am I losing my goddamn mind?*
A few days later, after Jadish annoyingly cleaned the dishes, she reluctantly looked at her despondent husband and said, "Baby, did you like dinner?"

Smiling, he said, "It was good, baby. I like the cream of mushroom you poured over the sautéed chicken. That was nice, something new."

*I bet your hungry ass do!* She smiled. She was drying off a plate. She looked over her shoulder at him. "What are you going to be doing tomorrow?"

Releasing a large gush of air, Sax closed his eyes, holding the *Sports section* of *The Miami Herald*. A glass of Grey Goose was in front of him, light ice. He decided to wolf it down and have another shot.

*My wife is full of shit!* "Nothing, why?" His eyes peered over the paper. Something wasn't adding up with her.

She pondered the thought. "Maybe we can catch a movie."

He frowned. "We'll see, Jadish. Movies are for 6 year olds. Not married people."

*Here we go! Why are men so stubborn and set in their ways?*
She turned off the sink water, wiping her hands on her apron. Taking it off, she hung it on the clamp by the pantry door, disappearing into the living room. Sax didn't take his eyes off her amazingly plump booty. It bounced when she walked. His dick was hard instantly and he pressed down on it to kill the erection.

She paused in front of her painting, looking and feeling gloomy.

*Fuck this! She's my wife and she's coming off the pussy! Today!* Sax, setting the paper down, stood up, the chair audibly sliding back. He walked up behind his wife and took her into his arms. She cringed inside, rolling her eyes.

*What is bothering you?* He thought. "Baby, you smell good tonight."

*God!* "You too, baby," she lied. She meant, he smelled good, but she *wasn't* going to have sex tonight or any other night. She felt his hardness up against the crack of her ass and it didn't do anything for her. *Am I gay?* She thought bitterly. *Is that why my husband don't turn me on?*

He was kissing her neck. The warmth of his fleshy lips felt enticing. Her insides came alive but her gut hardened her heart and she said, "*Not* tonight. I'm on my period and I'm out of Massengill."

He looked at the back of her head. "You said that the *other* night." His erection softened. *Damn it!*

*And I'm saying it tomorrow night and the rest of the fucking year!* "I know." She felt low. She kept looking at the painting.

He was carefully analyzing her. "What is it with this painting, Jadish? You are always staring at it."

She was rubbing her hands as if she was cold. "I just like it."

He was getting jealous of the painting. Ever since they have been married she stared at this picture every time she passed it.

"Do you like me?" He was feeling on her ass.

*Stop touching me. Please, don't do this!* "I love you."

He was pulling down her shorts and her panties, getting on his knees.

"Then show me how much. Push your pussy back on my tongue. I wanna make you cum, Jadish! I know you be fucking yourself with the bedroom door knob. I saw you the other night."

Her smell, her fragrance lapping the contours of her expensively-perfumed skin turned him on. He was rubbing her pussy from the back, sticking in thick fingers one by one and she winced. He was sucking on her ass cheek, spreading them and sliding his tongue all over her tight hole. She shuddered with glee. *Wow. Oh my God!*

He was hard for days. He needed his wife. He sensually bit her ass cheek, careful not to inflict pain and she melted. Deeply offended, she pulled up her clothes. It took great effort. "Did you *ask* to do that?" She couldn't catch her breath.

He gushed with anger. "Why *should* I have to? I'm your husband. That's my pussy!"

She was shaking her head, disgusted. "Yes, you are and you still got to respect me. This is *my* vagina. Not yours! You don't just go pulling off my clothes, man. Who do you think you are?"

He couldn't believe this was happening. Trapped inside this torture chamber called marriage was not good for him. He pointed at the paining. "I'm *not* the dead Christ, I can tell you that."

She averted her face, her temples twitching. She needed a cigarette. Badly.

He shot, "You can't look at me? Why are you still staring at that ugly goddamn painting?"

She turned to face him, pointing. "Grow up. Please! It's just a painting!"

Despoiled, he took the painting from the wall and brutally smashed it against a nearby lacquered chair. Shocked beyond her wildest dreams, her heart shattered with it. She was paralyzed from the neck down. She could not move. How could he do that? How could he destroy her immortality? He was now stomping it, and said, "Fuck you and the painting. And dinner tasted like shit."

Devastated, she rushed over to the broken pieces, falling to her knees. She cried so hard she cracked open. "You destroyed it, you destroyed my art!" She was trying to put the pieces back together like a puzzle. Her hair hung in her face. "You are a mad man. You have *no* feelings for me. All you care about is sex!" she stammered. She couldn't get a grip on reality.

His heart bled for her but he was tired of showing it so he held it inside. Frazzled, he went upstairs and slammed the door closed, rushed to the bathroom and took off his pants. Taking out the lotion bottle, he opened the closet and reached for the nude magazines hiding behind a pile of neatly folded towels of assorted colors.

*Damn shame I'm married and I'm still jerking off to nude magazines. Where they do this kind of shit at? America? Or just my marriage?*

Hastily opening *Black Ass Tails* magazine, he sat on the toilet and laid the magazine on the floor. He lathered his hands. And he stroked his dick into a powerful orgasm, calling out his wife's name. He couldn't take his eyes off the female with the bubble ass.

He had cut off one of his wife's pictures and put her face on the porn model.

Later that night Sax awakened when the bed began to shake. Thinking it was an earthquake; he got out of bed and turned on the light, realizing that Miami, Florida didn't get earthquakes. Quizzically, he looked around. "Then what's that banging noise...?"

He was alarmed when he saw his wife twitching in the bed, having a seizure. He didn't know what was going on. He had never before seen this. Panicking, he picked up the phone and called 9-1-1, realizing how much he truly loved his wife. *Should I call your Mom and Dad? What is going on with my wife? Oh my God! I can't lose her! I love my wife.*

When the authorities answered he said, about to lose his mind, "It's my wife, she is having a traumatic seizure, please get an ambulance to 13455 S.W. 109th Court."

"One will be there momentarily. Sir, please stay on the line."

He didn't know what to do. Jadish's body bounced on the bed, making the headboard slap the wall with an aggravating banging sound. His heart fluttered with his tightening throat. On second thought, he picked up his wife, carried her to his car and did 125 M.P.H. to the nearest hospital.

Sitting in the main lobby of the new Baptist Hospital in Homestead, he had his face in his hands, deeply depressed. What was going on with his wife? Watching his wife's body twitch and arch in the air the really scared him to death. Was this something she just developed or did she *always* have seizures? Couldn't be the latter because she never had them since they've been married. He took out his cell phone, and called his mother-in-law, telling her where Jadish was.

"She'll be fine," her mother said, not really concerned. This struck him as odd.

"Your daughter is in the hospital. She had a seizure. Maybe you didn't hear me."

"I heard you. She wasn't having a seizure. She was having a bad dream."

He was appalled. Standing up, he snapped. "What in the fuck…"

"Listen, Sax. Then you'll understand…"

"Listen to what?"

"There is something Jadish…never mind, just hear me out."

"I don't know if I want to."

A few hours later, Jadish, deadly tired, was sitting in the front seat of Sax's SS Impala. Quiet. She refused to look of him and he refused to look at her. She didn't put on her seat belt and when Sax saw it he said, "Mind putting your safety belt on? You know these Cubans can't drive."

Not up to arguments, she put it on. Humming to herself. She was trying to remain cool. Sax was manhandling the rain swept streets. Very difficult to see when it rained like this. His turmoil worsening for his wife, he turned on some Billie Holiday, turning the volume down low. Erroneously buggered about how those doctors rushed his wife out of the hospital just to make room for another patient, he had a problem with something he chose not to bring up. Did they even run the proper tests on her? His mother-in-law claimed she was just dreaming. He thought anything but. No one told him anything when it came to the results of the few tests they did run on Jadish. Felt like they were purposely keeping him in the dark. He remembered approaching the doctor, inquiring about his wife's condition. The Doctor's pompous behind said, "I know she's your wife. But Jadish gave me specific instructions. She said not to tell *anyone* her medical business." The Doctor looked an angry Sax deeply in the eyes. "…*Especially* you."

Pushing the doctor to the back of his mind, Sax said, shaking away the brief, got-him-nowhere-meeting with the doctor, "Mind telling me about these nightmares. When did you start having them?"

Jadish said, "Don't talk to me, Sax."

He averted his face, his temples twitching. "This is lunacy. You're treating me like the enemy," he said helplessly.

She glared at him, too weak to argue. "When you broke my painting *that* really hurt me."

"I'm sorry. But you give it more attention than me."

"It's a painting, Sax. Not another man."

He was being stubborn, hitting the left signal and getting over into the left lane to merge onto the Turnpike.

"The painting has another man in it, and you stare at his chest like it's a dick or something."

She was laughing bitterly. "Oh my God! It's a painting of the Dead Christ for crying out loud. Christ died for you and me…"

"Well cry out in silence and tell me what the fuck is going on? What are these dreams? Tell me. I'm your husband."

*He's right. I'm making him suffer for something I don't understand. What do I say? Where do I begin?* "I have dreams, Sax. Of a man in black. I wear white. He's chasing me through some wet grass. God always splits the Jordan River. In the middle of the turf lies a woman being deflowered by a man. Her face is black and her hair is flames."

He was looking at her slowly. "Are you serious? Are you making this up to cover the truth?"

She rolled her eyes. "Yes, Sax. I'm telling the truth."

His mind was racing. "It's just a dream, Jadish…"

"Sax. It's a dream I've been having for three years plus. The same dream. It's like my heart is trying to tell me something. You wouldn't know of them because I can count the number of times you slept in the bed with me: hardly ever. You sleep on the Lazy Boy with the remote in your lap."

"Is the girl in the middle of the turf you?"

"*No*. She's someone I *can't* see. I also had a cap with a tassel dangling from it on my head in the dream. The man has a big red X over his face. I ran into my high school. I don't know why."

"I don't know what to say. But what does that painting have to do with anything."

"In the dream the woman loses her virginity. She's asleep or something. So I painted the Dead Christ after waking up one morning from having the dream to commemorate the death of her innocence."

Sax said, "Damn. I'm sorry, baby. That's what the painting meant to you?"

Hot tears falling down her face. "Yes. And you destroyed it."

He felt like shit. *I have to patch things up with my wife before I lose her. Everything has changed.* "I'm sorry."

She touched his hand and he looked at her then turned his eyes back on the road. "Sorry don't cut it this time."

\*\*\*

Sax spent the next few weeks at work, trying to keep it together but nothing was the same. Just last night they slept together and he tried to hold her and she pushed him away and clung to a teddy bear she had ever since she was nine years old. She said the teddy used to chase away the demons. And then she looked at him. He guessed he was the demon. He slept with his back facing her. He silently cried himself to sleep out of frustration. She did the same thing. He usually greeted everyone at the packaging company; they all loved him, but not anymore. He also worked at a mechanic shop part time and he wasn't performing his jobs up to par. Customers complained. His boss complained to him. Sax looked like he could care less. He didn't fix the customer's cars to his fullest potential. In fact he barely looked at the vehicles. He did poor oil changes. Forgot to change the filters. Clocked out late for lunch and clocked back in late. Sometimes he didn't clock out at all. He ate his food in front of customers, making them angrily wait at the service desk. He would laugh then pick up the phone and call a few of his friends, talking about looking at tits and pussy at the strip clubs with his boys.

He had attitude problems, snapping on people who didn't do anything to him. He didn't give a shit. Dealing with customers he could live without. He loved people, so his sudden attitude change had everyone he worked with having meetings about him. They worried about him. He masturbated in the bathroom every day, thinking of the pussy he wasn't getting at home. He took out the magazine with his wife's pictures pasted all over the models and said, "I guess I can fuck you this way!"

At home he and his wife argued and fought. He told her he hated her and she said that she loved him. They had serious problems in their marriage but she refused to talk to him. She chose to sweep them under the rug and pretend that everything was saucy between them. After all her mother *used* to do the very same things with her father. Ignore his concerns, defy his govern and she kind of did her own thing. Her Daddy was too whim-wham to do anything about it. He figured since he had a wife and some good pussy at his disposal, he wouldn't do anything to lose it. He wouldn't speak out against it.

Her father was very paranoid about being alone. As a little girl she took notes she was now using on her own husband. Men were stubborn and her man was no exception. It had to be his way or the highway and she wasn't with the program. In the beginning she hadn't really protested against anything he wanted because she was *too* naïve to open her mouth or speak for herself. But lately she was getting tired of his childish antics and it was beginning to piss her off. Common sense told her she was partly to blame. She didn't make love to him and he was lashing out. He needed his wife and she deprived him. All he thought about was sex, sex, sex and she thought about anything but. Maybe that's why he thought about it 24/7 because she wasn't giving it to him, she gathered.

If God snapped his Holy Fingers and made every man's dick turn to dust half these men would cease to live. They'd kill themselves. Except for some of the gays. Losing a dick they hardly used wouldn't upset them at all.

Jadish made it to an age most youngsters didn't live to see. But she didn't want to live her 25th year on the planet arguing with the love of her life. If blacks weren't dying from drug abuse and being murdered as a result of negative living, they were winding up in jail, making babies just because Baby Daddy had some good sausage in his package, and trying to write bad damn checks or scam the government and credit card companies. She didn't fall into either of those categories, thank God!

Clad in Nike spandex shorts and halter top with Michael Jackson's glove glittering in the middle from the Thriller days, she settled down on the sofa, watching her husband do some pushups out on the back patio. What a nice ass. Jesus! On Monday's, Wednesday's and Friday's he always did his work outs and focused all of his energy on that. His body was off the chain. But she needed something other than that. She needed to understand her dreams.

She smiled thinking about him. She rubbed her legs and looked around the living room for her cigarettes. She couldn't find them. Her smile died when she realized she hadn't been treating him with the love and understanding a man needed from his woman.

Despite her convictions towards her husband, she loved him to death. But one thing jeopardized their marriage and she thought about this with a frown. She hasn't fucked him yet. Not once, since they've been married.

She was still a virgin.

*I'm just not ready. It's been two plus years since we've been married. I just can't do it yet, I'm scared and I am not changing my mind anytime soon.*

*Hell if I had half a brain I would truly convince myself that I know the reason why he's so selfish with me. I haven't fucked him yet, even when we were on our honeymoon. I jacked him off and that was it. He wanted me to swallow his come and I told him I didn't remember Tylenol making Cold Come Plus Pills. And I really didn't want to jack his dick! How hugely disappointed he was. But I didn't care. Who said I had to fuck on the honeymoon? This is my pussy! He said he loved me for me. Well put your dick back in your pants and put your money where your mouth is because I don't want to give up the coochie yet; I don't care if ten years go by. He wants pussy that badly he can go pay for it. Hell everything else is on sale in America from Botox shots and luxury cars to fake tits and fake asses. I heard he be in the strip clubs behind my back anyways so I'll let him keep thinking he's fooling me.*

She checked her watch. 8 PM. She tidied up the house. Well, that was until Loud Mouth started opening chips, dropping crumbs here and there. She had the clothes washed. Well, that was until he kicked off his tube socks and took off his stinky clothes, throwing them all over the house like he had a goddamn maid. His underwear was ironed and folded. Well, that was until he took off his crusty-stained draws and left them in the middle of the bathroom or their bedroom, which told her he didn't do a great job wiping his stank ass when he took a shit. She laughed about that one. A grown man with more brown in his underwear than wrappers and chocolate candy on store shelves.

By 10 p.m. she was snoring in her bed and Sax was sitting on the chair by the computer, staring at her. Withdrawn into himself. Quiet.

*I don't know how much more I can take of this.*

The next day, Wednesday, Jadish paid the bills and sent out some checks. She dusted the TV in the bedroom because he had specifically asked her to do that. And since this was her off day she decided that maybe she'd treat herself to a day at the Spa in Kendall.

She was the fourth grade teacher at an elementary school. And frankly she was getting tired of teaching a bunch of rambunctious, energetic kids. She felt like her teaching gig has turned into Babysitting 101.

She noticed the pile of dirty clothes by the washer. "Damn I just washed clothes. And this husband of mine keeps piling them up."

She sorted through them, pouting. Mostly dirty underwear. Not feeling like being bothered with laundry, she threw them in the wash, added Tide with Bleach and closed the lid. Her Mama always taught her "Don't put off tomorrow what you can do today. Laundry and dishes included."

Needing a laugh or two, she called a few friends and checked in on them while she waited for the laundry to finish. After she dried them an hour later, she folded his T-shirts; put them neatly in his drawer and she ironed his draws. "I actually iron my husband's underwear, bitch you fell and bumped your head."

She smiled to herself, walking over to the low table and picking up her wedding picture. She looked it over. The image was stunning. The happiest day of her life. *And I haven't given him any pussy yet.*

She thought back a few years, when she first met Saxophone. When he was young vibrant and polite. Back when he had it going on and then some. Back when she couldn't stand his ass.

Back when she didn't even know he was alive.

# Back in the Day

She was fresh into her first year of college at the University of Miami when she met Saxophone. The finest, sexiest man she'd ever seen. All the Hoes wanted him. She didn't. She hardly even paid the jerk any attention. He had tattoos on both arms, wore glasses that brought out his heavenly brown eyes. She loved the way the sunlight trapped them. She was twenty years old then. He drove a flashy black SS Impala on black with machined lip rims; housed inside always polished-with-Armor-all-Firestone tires. He loved his car.

She was leaving the Convocation Building, walking down the steps when she tripped over shoes she thought were tied. Plummeting towards the concrete steps he suddenly appeared out of nowhere and caught her just before her chin slammed against the concrete. She felt like Tom Cruise in *Mission Impossible.*

She had trouble catching her breath. "Thank you," she said, clearly embarrassed. The perfect gentleman, he helped her stand up. She gripped her purse uncomfortably, nervously shifted her reading glasses and feverishly shook his hand. He had a firm grip, nice ass and his nipples poked against his gray wife beater. She held her breath, not breaking away from his piercing gaze. He had a Colgate-commercial-ready smile.

He said, "Are you all right?" His earrings glittered under the Miami sun.

"Yes, yes." She wanted to die. She stood there looking goofy in a plaid skirt which came down to her knees and white blouse with huge silver and gold hoops dangling in her ears. She was the most beautiful thing he'd ever seen. She still wanted to die.

*Oh, God! I look like complete shit! I needed a perm, my nails are chipping and the finger nail polish is wearing off; my tennis shoes are brown and don't quite match the beige and black of my outfit. Shoot me God!*

He was studying her. "I thought your chin and the concrete were about to merge."

She laughed uneasily, her hands shaking. She hugged her purse. No one that fine has ever talked to her. In fact, throughout her twelve years in public school, only *one* guy had asked her out and she'd said "No!" because she thought he was playing a prank on her. Boys loved her, but she failed to realize it. She felt uncomfortable standing in front of this beautiful man! *What a hunk!*

"Yeah. Oh, thanks for helping me." She rushed past him, running down the stairs. She shivered all over. "Bye, bye."

Appalled, he spun around and ran after her. A few girls stood in front of him, trying to talk to him but he pushed them to the side and took Jadish by the arm. He couldn't let her get away. "Wait. Damn, can I get your name?"

"Jadish. Now let me go please."

He wouldn't let her go. He was incorrigible. She loved men who knew what they wanted, but she never knew how to talk to boys. Plus they only wanted one thing and she had no idea that some asshole indirectly and unwillingly popped her cherry on the night of her high school graduation party. The perpetrator was her daddy's best friend Tommy.

He got her drunk and fucked her senseless. He did all kinds of unspeakable things to her, making Jadish his love slave for the night.

The next morning she felt good, revitalized, and her body took on a life of its own. Then an hour later she wound up hugging the toilet, having the worst hangover of her entire life. Her stomach felt like flames burning hay. She couldn't grasp a thought. She didn't understand why her body was reacting the way that it did. She would think about it for months! Years! Tommy was one of the closest people to her, and he would keep the secret until he died.

Sax asked, "Can I drive you home?"

*Please. No Says Me!* "I *drove* to school. I'll be ok," she lied. She caught public transportation to school four times a week. She was an Education major. With a minor in computers. She loved money and would do anything as far as an education to achieve it. She didn't have time for men because she was too busy planning her future. Or so she tried to convince herself. There have been stolen moments she masturbated to Brad Pitt and Denzel Washington magazines, coming all over her sheets and calling out two men who didn't know she existed in the world.

He kissed her hand and her panties were wet. A few people passing by whispered to themselves, eyeing her ugly skirt. She was beautiful to Sax, she took his breath away. Now if only he could convince her.

He wouldn't let her go. "I'll walk you."

*I can walk myself. What is it with men?* "Please, I'm fine." A nervous chuckle. She was avoiding his eyes. He stared her down.

He was gently rubbing her hand. Like a fine piece of crystal.

"Come on." He was pulling her towards the student parking lot. She was reluctant. *Please leave me alone. Leave me alone, man!* "No."

He was smiling. She was melting, falling into a dark hole which had the pathway to the sunlight. She actually laughed.

*Bingo!* he thought victoriously. "Now will you let me take you to your car? How about we go on a date?"

*I don't think so.* "Man you can have any bitch you want. Why do you want me?"

He faced her, not letting go her hand. "Because I want a *real* woman. Not a bitch. And you're *not* a bitch."

She smiled, touching his cheek. She felt like she was dreaming. Six months into her freshman year of college, and finally a good, sexy black man was talking to her.

"That's a sweet thing to say."

"Where's your car?"

"By the Metro buses."

He looked at her blankly. "Are you serious? Parked where the city bus travels?"

She went in for the kill. "No, Niggah. I caught the bus to school."

"Well *not* anymore. Where do you live? I live in Cutler Ridge, a few blocks from the mall."

"I live in Cutler Manor. Me, my Mama and my ten year old brother."

"Well, looks like I'll be taking you to school and home from now on."

"I don't give up my coochie that quickly, Niggah. You men only want pussy."

He was offended. "Nah. Not me. Come with me. Let me share my little blank life with you."

She found that hard to believe. "Yea, right."

He held up his palm. "Scouts Honor." He was serious. She hugged him, saying, "Yea, you can take me home, I have no problem with that."

"You sure?" he asked, kissing her cheek. She blushed.

"Yes. I'm sure."

He led her to his car. "And for the record I haven't had sex yet, either. I'm still a virgin."

*Yes*, he thought. *A female no other man has had. I got to make this work.*

They would spend the next few years together. She never pressed him for sex, and he never pressed her. He was perfectly fine without having sex. He was kind, attentive and selfish as hell. He was also stubborn. His sign was the Sagittarius, so she understood why. They were controlling and greedy.

But not Sax. In the beginning, he used to buy her roses and take her out to eat. He had a part time job doing security at the Miami Arena. He had taken her with him when he applied for an up and coming packaging company that was looking for stocky, strong men. He got her into all kinds of concerts. She became his world. Women around campus detested her. They wanted him; he was the product of bets being taken around campus, ranging from women to the gay men who wanted him. Fags daydreamed about him. But Sax never gave them the time of day.

He fell in love with her because she was always attentive, a good listener, didn't really question him, even though he never did anything to make her feel inferior. She always wrote him little poems. She confided in him. Told him that on her graduation night she was the happiest girl in the world. But she had too much to drink and she passed out. When she woke up the next morning her body felt beat up.

"It's my fault for drinking like that. I should have known better. But for some reason I can't get that night off my mind." She said she was drunk and didn't remember anything but her most trusted friend Tommy giving her drink after drink. Sax was thinking to himself.

"I remember I woke up, throwing up in the toilet and my pussy was on fire. Dried blood was on me. The last person I was with was Tommy, my dad's best friend. But he has been in the family for years."

Sax was quiet. *Well, baby.*

*Tommy most certainly fucked you that night, crummy bastard.*

Then the day came. Sax wanted to have sex with Jadish and he wasn't taking "no" for an answer. The thought of this Tommy character beating the pussy pissed him off. If it wasn't for him Sax would have officially been her first. But he didn't say much because she had no idea Tommy fucked her while she was unconscious, and Sax wanted to hunt him down and kill him ass.

He had wined and dined her, trying to pamper her. She felt like a Queen. The way he spoiled her made her feel like heaven. She told him that and he thought, *I am pumping you up the way you fatten a turkey before you slaughter it for the main course meal. Gotta keep the pussy fed. The pussy is the main course.*

He'd do this for about three weeks straight. Shower her with gifts, tell her she's beautiful and open doors for her. She melted inside his charm. How could she say no? He then met her grandmother, mother and father. She had a big family, and they all adored her. The family took Sax in immediately because Jadish never brought a man home. Her mother especially was proud of her for keeping her legs closed through high school. While Sax chatted with them he was hoping to meet Tommy, to see the man who fucked his girl.

A few of her fine female cousins tried to fuck him a few weeks later, during a family reunion they were having, on the sly but he turned them down and told them where to get off. He let one of the cousins, an obese chick who had an affinity for Erykah Badu, suck his dick in the back of Jadish's parent's house, and that was only because she gave him alcohol and weed and sucked everything from his asshole to his nuts, toes and dick. And by the time she put her pussy in his face he was so nauseated he threw up all over her tits, some getting in her mouth and she shrieked, vowing to stab him to death.

He reluctantly met Tommy around Christmas. That was the day Sax summed him up: smooth talker, very handsome, and was a ladies' man without even trying. *Yea. He fucked my girlfriend on her graduation night. Had too. The way he looked at her when she stood up from a chair or walked around the room talking to people. He watched her with memories flooding his eyes in ways tears never could.* When Tommy tried to shake his hand he turned his back on him and went over to Jadish, putting his arm around her protectively.

Tommy read a little into it, putting up his guard. He then shook his head, deciding that he was being paranoid. *This Niggah don't know my business. I never met him a day in my life. I took Jadish's pussy. She'll never know and I'll never tell a soul,* Tommy thought with a bitter smile, somewhat jealous of Sax getting Jadish's attention. Sax met Jadish's little brother and fell in love with him after the New Year. He treated her brother like his own sibling. His name was Thompson. Sax then took Jadish's entire family out to eat, including Tommy. They chit-chatted, got to know each other and once the check came he paid for everyone's food but Tommy's.

Appalled, Tommy evil-eyed him, remaining quiet. Pulled out his wallet and paid for his own food. Jadish and her mom went out to the car early. Her grandmother excused herself and went to the restroom. Thompson wanted to go to the mall with some friends and vanished to go ask his mother. Tommy was alone with Sax. *Finally*, thought Sax with a bitter smile.

"Why did you bring us out if you weren't going to pay for my food?" Tommy asked with an attitude. He looked good in blue jeans, a T shirt and a $500 leather jacket he bought from a crack head for ten dollars. "I can't spend outside of my budget. A man should keep his word."

Sax looked at the fool. "I changed my mind," said Sax, standing up.

Tommy drank his beer. "So what if I didn't have the money. You didn't give me any warning. Real men don't do that."

*Real men don't drug women and fuck them.* Sax snapped, "And real men don't..." He swallowed the words. "You know what, fuck you. I don't like you and I never will. You perverted asshole."

Tommy brushed it off. "Watch your mouth, kid."

Sax said, "Kid? I'm a grown man, dawg. I wasn't a kid the day my dick dropped eleven inches from my nuts."

Tommy was seething with anger on the inside. "I don't *like* you, Sax. What kinda name is that?" he joked, getting a kick out of this entire ordeal.

"I was named after an instrument, you know. Your Mama's lips they used to call flutes, Pimp."

Tommy slammed his fists down on the table and all activity ceased. People looked on in silence. Jadish grandmother confusedly watched from the ante-chamber with Thompson. Tommy quipped, "*Look*, I don't know *who* you think you are. But you're new to the family; you probably won't last ten more seconds. Do you know who you're messing with?"

Gritting his teeth, Sax got in his face and said, "A pussy-ass Niggah is who I'm fucking with. Go ahead. Whip my ass, Niggah. Maybe put a drug in my drink or something and take my fucking virginity."

Tommy closed his eyes and breathed in deeply. "What are you talking about? I don't do the gay shit." *Goddamn he knows! He knows! Oh my God how did he find out? Does Jadish know? Had she told her father? This can't be happening. I covered all my freaking tracks,* Tommy thought frighteningly.

"You're right. You don't do the gay shit. You just do innocent, can't-defend-themselves females. Try that shit while I'm on the block, Jack and you'll get that ass stomped."

Deciding that he had enough, Sax picked up the remainder of his Sprite and dumped it on Tommy's head. "Cool off. Your head seems…kinda hot, dawg. And oh yea you're riding with Jadish's daddy 'cause you're not getting in my Impala. You do one thing to piss me off, loose lips will sink ships. Feel me, Playah?"

Sax left Tommy standing there, fuming.

Sax was traveling on Florida's Turnpike with Jadish. Her cell rang. It was her grandmother. "Hey, Ma. Yea, I'm good. I'm with Sax. Where is Tommy…? Oh, he's with Dad. I wonder why he didn't ride back with us? He came in the car with Sax and I. Oh, what did you say? He and Sax had a fight?"

His mouth falling open, she looked at him. He turned up the radio to the point she couldn't hear her grandmother. She hung up, turned the radio down and said, "You and Tommy had a fight?"

"Yea, anyways. Old news. Mind your business. How did you like the lobster?" Jadish decided to keep her mouth shut.

Maybe she'd ask Tommy. On second thought never mind.

Sax was heading towards the Hilton Hotel on South Beach thirty minutes later. At the time he lived with his mother so he couldn't take her back to his house. She'd call his name over and over and ask him to do this and that so he didn't feel like being bothered.

"Where are we going?" Jadish asked him, when she saw the hotel up ahead. It had started to rain really badly and she didn't like being on the road when the driver could barely see. Plus she didn't want to fuck up her hair, cost $90 and she didn't have money to burn.

He was clad in a nice red sweater and black velvet pants with Jordan sneakers. Hair cut done up right, mustache on point. He turned into the parking garage of the hotel. He didn't answer her question. Self-explanatory.

The happiest man alive, he parked in the handicap spot in the parking garage. He didn't have a handicap tag permitting him to be parked there. He didn't care, either. He wanted to fuck his woman. Jacking off had lost its aura with him. Plus he wanted to bash

Tommy's head in. The car could get towed for all he cared. He was about to smash some pussy, and best of all he was in love with her so it was extra special. His dick was hard thinking about the gushy, gushy.

Sax said, "We're here." He closed his eyes. Yes. *It's about to happen. I'm about to get some pussy!*

She was guardedly looking around. "I see. Why are we at a hotel?" She was gorgeous! Flawless make up, long, flowing white skirt with ruffles on her ass. Purple blouse with matching pumps with the six inch heels. "Plus when are you going to talk to me about Tommy? I love him like family. That's my God daddy."

"You'll see." He ignored the Tommy part. He took her hand and she followed him into the hotel in silence. Through the main lobby and past the receptionist desk they walked. She held her breath, her heart pounding. They boarded the elevator. They traveled to the ninth floor in silence. She felt like she was being lead to her death by firing squad. Wrapping his protective arms around her, so deeply in love, he tongue kissed her, his hardened dick pressed against her crotch. She felt his urgency. Her body responded. She pressed her groin up against his and kissed him deeply, running her tongue all over his perfect teeth. He couldn't keep it together.

"I want you."

She was keeping it together. "I'm not so sure I want you yet." But she wanted to kiss him again. *What is the big secret about Tommy? What is he not telling me? Something is not right. I gotta call Tommy and find out.*

He pressed emergency stop on the elevator and she screamed, covering her mouth. She pushed him, angry.

He said, "We need to talk."

"About what? Tommy? And why you two were fighting?"

"The *hell* with Tommy. This is about *sex*. Sup with the pussy, baby. I *need* you."

She threw her hands up in the air. "God, *no!*"

He wouldn't give in. His dick was hard as a brick. "It's going on three years since we been a couple. How long do you expect me to wait?"

She was stubborn. "For as long as it…"

Getting on his knees he lifted up her skirt and ran his tongue all over her panties. She cringed, falling back against the mirror.

Her eyes were wide with fear. "What…are…you…" The sensation washed over her like waves, sending tiny ripples up her spine. Pulling her panties to the side, he spread her pussy, stuck his finger deep inside her and he sucked on her clitoris. She almost fell over. He was hungry. He was feeding. Tasting her innocence. The warmth. The glory. Sucking invisible evidence of Tommy right out of there and down his throat.

She pulled up her skirt and rode his tongue, never before experiencing this type of pleasure. She twirled her voluptuous hips, tears falling down her face.

He turned on the charm. "Baby I want the pussy."

She demolished it. "Eat my pussy, Niggah. Yes!"

He turned it up a notch. "You like that?"

She turned it down a notch. "Hell yea." She pulled out her titties and when he saw them, he released a soft moan, his dick getting harder, to the point his nuts began to hurt. Staggering, he stood up, taking her tits into his big hands. He eyed her while he was suckling on her nipples, one by one. *Am I doing good?* Running his tongue over both nipples, squeezing the tits together, he slow humped her against the mirror. He wanted penetration.

Getting on her knees, pushing him back, she pulled out his dick and got to work. What a long dick. She had never seen it before. She teased the head with her slick tongue, trying to remember how the white Ho's sucked dick in the porno movies. He was thrown, in a good way.

"*Ooooh* baby. You have never sucked my dick before. Hell, yes. Ah. Shit. *Umm.* Yea. Shit…shit! Feels so good! Slurp on the dick like you want it…you been hiding the pussy. Gimme the pussy, baby."

She put his nine inches all the way in her mouth, down her throat. She did it like a pro. Inside her mind she wanted her man, her heart told her it was ok, and he was faithful to her for years. He never wavered. He looked at her like she was the only woman in the world. She should thank him by dropping the panties. Why not? All lovers fucked, right? He was so excited about getting some head he exploded with a ball bolting jolt. Cum shot in her face, stinging her right eye.

She rubbed at her eye feverishly. "Shit it burns!"

He was pleased. He stood back, watching her. "Baby it's just nut."

She stood up, her eye still tingling and burning, and pulled down her skirt. "We can't fuck, Sax."

His spirits dropped. "Why?"

*Isn't it obvious?* "I'm not ready."

He said it slowly. "What do you mean you're not ready?"

She sucked her teeth better than his dick. "I'm just not." She was fixing her skirt.

He was getting agitated. "You just gulped nine inches of dick like a pro and you tell me you're not ready. What the hell, Jadish!"

"Hell is that way," she spat, pointing at the floor. "Tell Satan to morph into some pussy and fuck him 'til you make babies. I'm not ready."

"You're pushing me away." *I don't mean it. I just wanna fuck my lady.*

Jadish was frantic. *Oh, no! I don't want to lose him. What am I doing? But I'm scared; I don't want to have sex yet. Why can't he wait for me? Girl, how long do you want him to wait?*

He was getting angrier by the second. "Are you *gay*?" His voice rose dangerously.

Deeply offended, she tucked her chin back, glaring at him with icy eyes. "No, why?"

He reached the boiling point. "Then gimme the pussy! I'm your man! *Let* me fuck! Your body belongs to me!"

*Drop dead! This is my body!* "I'm not some Ho! You don't gotta yell and be rude."

He wanted to snap her fucking neck, teasing him and leading him on. "I'm about to flip out. I need some pussy. From *you*."

"Then join the circus if you're about to flip out. Am I supposed to be scared? And I SAID NO!"

Bile rising in his throat, he pressed the "emergency stop" button again and the elevator rose. He refused to look at her. She turned her back on him, wanting to run and hide. When they got off on the ninth floor he stamped to their room. He refused to look at her. Fuck her. The hell with the cold-hearted, think-she's-all-that-tramp! There were plenty Hoes that would let him fuck. *That's the problem. They're Hoes,* he thought, about to burst into tears. *I want to make love to a complete woman. I want Jadish to make me a whole man tonight. I'm tired of jacking my dick, imagining what pussy feels like. Time for the next step.*

He rented out the Presidential Suite. It had a living room, kitchen, dining room, and two bedrooms. Saying nothing he pulled out the keys and unlocked the door.

Jadish thought gravely, *I want to go home! I don't want to be here with this insensitive man! All men want is pussy! Pussy pussy goddamn pussy! I don't crave dick like men crave pussy! That's just me. That's why I masturbate. I do it on my goddamn terms!*

When she got inside he turned on all the lights and forty dozen roses were all over the place. Some in vases, others on the bed. She nearly fainted from the surprise. She smiled so big she had to rub her forehead. Her panties were wet; her body seemed to come alive then. He looked at her reaction, getting even quieter. *Materialistic bitch!*

Candles were lit, Maxwell singing on the radio.

*"Fuck these flowers!"* he yelled, crushing her happiness in the blink of an eye. The smile died from her face. He felt like she was playing cock blocking games and he was a grown man. He didn't have time for the bullshit. He loved her. Things were suddenly complicated. *"I should burn this fucking room to the ground!"*

She held her breath, her skin crawling. "Why?"

He was pleading his case. "I want to make love to you."

She was stern. "I'm not ready." She didn't want to hurt him. He didn't deserve to be treated this way. It was unfair, she knew, but something in her soul wasn't right.

*Fucking bitch!* "Why?"

"Because I'm trying to understand why my pussy was on fire that night I got drunk on my graduation night, at the party."

He had enough. "*Why* are you stuck on that dumb ass shit?"

She felt powerless. Her man was slipping through her fingers. How did she stop it? What did she do? "I don't know. It consumes me in my dreams. When I day dream its there. When I shower I think about it. Why is that? Why can't I forget it? What is my mind trying to tell me?"

Depressingly sad, he was sitting on the edge of the bed, his head hanging low. He said, barely audible, "You don't *need* to know."

She got in his face. "What were you and Tommy fighting about?"

*This bitch won't give me some pussy but I gotta do what she says? Yea, right bitch!* "Nothing." He said it too quickly.

"You're lying. You twitch your lips when you lie and they just twitched."

His lips twitched again. *And I jack my dick when I'm horny!* He jumped up to his feet and turned his back on her. He gripped his dick, it throbbed, the thought of pussy made him smile. Huge tears fell from his eyes. It'd never happen. He'd die a virgin. Why didn't she want to fuck him? Was something wrong with him? Was it something he did? Something he said? His boys would laugh at him. He'd be a disgrace. He said, "Drop it." He wanted to get out of the room and run. He couldn't tell her and he wouldn't. He'd take it to the grave.

She pushed him and he flew into the wall. "Talk! What is going on?"

Pain shooting through his right shoulder, he rushed up to her and grabbed both her arms. "DROP IT!"

She exploded. "TELL ME, SAX!"

"No!"

*Now I don't care if I lose him. I hate liars!* "SAX!"

*I'll never tell you, Jadish. I will keep it to myself.* "Tommy fucked you! He drugged you on your graduation night and fucked you all night long while you were unconscious. That's the reason why you won't let *me* fuck. That's why your mind won't let you forget. That's why you can't stop dreaming about it, Jadish…And you're making me suffer for what he did."

*Now he lies on Tommy!* "You are lying. Tommy would *never* do such a thing. I trust him. My daddy trusts him. How messed up for you to accuse a magnificent man of rape. My dad's best friend would *never* betray me, *or* my dad. In fact I'm pissed off that you would even talk about a man you don't even know."

His mouth fell open in shock. What? Did she think he made this up? "Whatever. Look." He dug in his pocket and produced the most gorgeous, expensive ring she'd ever seen. He toyed with it, the diamonds well cut and trapping the lights. He closed his eyes. She held her breath.

Excitedly, she said, "OH MY GOD!"

He interjected. "Goodnight Jadish."

Disappointed, she shouted, "Baby."

He said depressingly, "I've always treated you good. I never pressured you. I am a virgin; I don't want to *die* a virgin. I want to fuck baby, *please.*"

Tears wet her face. *I'm going to lose him. He doesn't want me anymore. I should make it easier for him. I'm not letting any man force me to have sex if I'm not ready. It's my pussy!* She was feeling guilty. "You treat me really good. I know." She was rubbing his face, trying to hold him. He let her. He poured onto her. Felt the warmth from her hands and he wanted the fire. Fuck the heat. Fuck the sulfur. Just give him the flames. The scorch. The inferno. The pleasure. The cum.

Bursting with love for her, he hugged her tightly, kissing her with urgency in his touch. She was hypnotizing. Life. Breath. One. His fingers were clumsy and eager. Dazed, he unzipped his pants and slid up in her pussy. She froze. He froze, with his mouth hanging open from the sudden pleasure that sent warmth throughout his cock. The feeling felt unusual and weird, but good. He fucked her so fast and so hard she had to punch at his chest to get him to stop.

After about ten seconds of his constant pumping like a dog, she pushed him off, panting. *Oh my God! It didn't hurt? I heard when you're a virgin it is supposed to hurt, that some kind of lining would pop producing some blood. I am looking at his dick. There's no blood.*

She thought back to her graduation night. Tommy looked radiant. He looked so cool. "Here, have this Henny. It'll loosen you up."

And when she finished, powered by her new found adulthood and her high school diploma, she drank about four glasses of Hennessy. It tore her up. Tommy led her to his room. He lay her down and said, "You can rest here."

Then she blacked out. *Oh my God? I'm not a virgin! But how do I prove it?*

Sax was looking at her. She couldn't look him in the eyes. "I'm not ready, Sax! How could you try to force me to have sex with you? Are you not in control? Are you going to rape me?" Every part of her body was shaking. She was about to throw up. How could Tommy betray her? Sax felt really low. Did he just rape his girl? Guilt tore away at him. He didn't want to be in the room anymore. But he hid it from his face. He said, "Stop saving the pussy. And no I'll *never* rape you."

She just about had it. Men were horny bitches! Angry about Tommy's betrayal, she lashed out at Sax. "Fuck you! You're pissing me off."

He exploded so badly she shut up. "Fuck you, you selfish bitch!"

He really didn't mean it. It's just that he waited his entire life for this moment, when a woman made him a man, took his innocence, showed him how its done, nurtured him, kissed him, allowed him to be so deep in her his manhood went through another birth. Her mouth fell open in shock. His body numb, his dick losing its erection, he stuck the $11,000 engagement ring back in his pocket.

In a fit of rage he ripped every rose in his path, red petals twirling this way and that, thorns on the stems penetrating his shaking hands, blood trailing down his wrists, being smeared on the covers. He flipped the bed over, punching holes in the hotel walls. Once he destroyed the most beautiful room she'd ever seen, he went into the adjoining room, slammed the door closed and locked it, cursing her and calling her all kinds of names until he fell into a deep sleep. She sat on the edge of the bed, her face in her hands, sobbing as the room lay in ruins before her very eyes. For the first time in her life she felt alone.

# The Wedding

She was seething with an uncontrollable rage that nearly rendered her speechless.

"Look. I don't care *what* you're going through. Don't come."

The person on the other side of the phone line said, "You don't threaten me."

Her eyes laser beams. "Oh, yeah, bitch?"

She was fuming. Chandra said, "Who are *you* calling a bitch?"

It took a minute for the upset mother to gain her composure. She was pacing around her high-tech kitchen, clad in a cheap knockoff Baby Phat outfit and nine inch pumps that noisily clicked against the newly laid tile floors. She hungrily pulled on her cigarette, wanting a joint. A beautiful framed photo of her only child, her daughter, set on a niche above the stainless steel stove. She was holding onto the telephone for dear life, her breathing coming in short gasps. "If you show your face at my daughter's house you will be dealt with."

"And how are you going to do that?" Chandra asked, gripping the telephone with one hand and holding a needle with the other, pulling the rubber band around her upper arm with her teeth, feeling the tightness made her smile.

The Mother smiled like a Cheshire Cat. "I will tell her everything."

And the phone went dead in her ear.

$£@®®¥$

"Are you ready?"

*It starts! Dealing with my iron-fisted Mama!* "Mama. Yes! I've been ready. For three years now." I wasn't happy about Mama being here. I wasn't.

She gave a phony smile, the same phony smile she gave when things didn't turn out the way she had hoped. She had control issues, the very same issues that kept us at each other's necks like lions on bloody buffalos during the dry season. I really hope this special day didn't turn into an episode of Animal Planet.

Mama said, "Engaged three years and its finally happening. Well, it's long overdue."

*Everything has it's season.* I said, "No. It's happening when it's supposed to happen, Mama. I'm just a young woman born and raised in the county of Dade. Cutler Manor to be precise. I came a long way."

Mama ignored me. She picked up the broom and started sweeping some trash off to the side of the room. I watched her, keeping my mouth closed. She was clad in a very expensive pink dress, damn near knocking my white wedding gown to hell; I paid out the ass to have it created from scratch. I was talking about thought up from my brain to a storyboard sort to speak to the fabrics to the actual sewing of it, which was done by hand, one hundred man hours to be exact like I was Beyonce Knowles.

I paid for Mama's dress, too. But she did the unthinkable: she went behind my back, after I made the final arrangements and had her dress altered. Where it was long and sexy she had it cut short and some-what skimpy. I oversaw every dress and every suit worn in my wedding. I didn't want anything taking the attention off me and my fiancé's attire. But Mama did it, and there was absolutely nothing I could do about it. Her hair damn near looked better than mine, her makeup damn near looked better than mine. The way her breasts sat on her chest, squeezed in a bra two sizes too small made mine look like mosquitoes bites. Mama, she just had to try to rain on my parade.

My fiancé and I have been together since the fourth grade at Pine-Villa Elementary. We broke up here and there but we always found our way back to each other. No matter where he got his rocks off, no matter what bitch he sported for the moment he always built his stone castle with me. No one compared to me. Now those very same Hoes living in glass houses were eating my dust because now that my man and I were about to marry they couldn't kiss my pussy from his lips any longer behind my back, when they thought I didn't know. Come to think of it they kissed my ass, toes and feet, too. Little did they know I got the last laugh *and* the man. And they were all here now, sitting out waiting for me to walk down the aisle in a dress that cost more than anything they had on, combined!

I couldn't blame him for returning home to Mama, me of course. When you had flames dancing in your pussy and resin based on your titties, you'd come running back home, too. And on the flip side, no matter what man was trying to pounce on my pussy, I never gave it up to anybody but the man I was about to marry. Now sucking a Niggah's dick was my shit. No matter what brand new face

I pimped for the mouthpiece (meaning let him eat my pussy), I didn't care if I was in love with the Niggah, when my fiancé called, they were persona non grata. Peace, be gone. Every man I had left me because I found myself comparing them to my fiancé. The man I was about to marry in a few short moments. For some reason when he took my virginity I didn't want any other dick in me but HIS!

We then had to live together when we became adults. We took each other's shit. We dealt with things we didn't *think* we could tolerate about each other.

My fiancé loves sports and I hated it. But I did love playing with…balls. But the balls I loved had pubic hair all over them and gave my man the *oh, ah* feeling when I caressed them in that loving way that turned me on full throttle. I loved going to get my hair done every two weeks at La Chic Salon in Naranja, just before Homestead, and he hated getting haircuts, but he did get them because he didn't want to hear my mouth.

Mama broke the silence. "Girl, I'm getting tired. This wedding needs to hurry up so I can get my drink on and chill out."

I was looking myself over in the mirror. "My wedding is *not* the free liquor store." *This ain't Gusto's Bar and Grill, Lady!*

She gave me the once-over. "If you say so." She put the broom off to the side, by the lacquered pedestal holding a Nefertiti bust I got from Rome last year. "And what's up with this little squabble you and your man had over George W. Bush?" she asked, and I wondered how she found that out.

"Because he loves George Bush and I detested him! How many black men you know supports him? Hell he sent me to Iraq and I just got back, what, a year ago. I'm glad I didn't die! I thank God, Mama."

She decided to ignore what I just said. "Why didn't you re-enlist anyway, baby?" She threw me a bone.

My hands on my hips I glared at her. "Because. I'm 30. I did eight years in the Army. Active. I *did* my time."

Her eyes were dangerous. "You should have made a career out of it."

*Oh, God, woman!* "No, Mama. *You* should have made a career out of it."

She got quiet. I guess I hit a nerve. Today was a special day for me. I hoped she didn't mess it up, and she had such rich history messing up the very special moments in my life. When I graduated from Pre-K to the first grade, she messed it up by being caught throwing the pussy to my friend's daddy, Gregory, out in his old school Cadillac in the crowded parking lot of all places. The bitch wanted to be caught. I was too embarrassed watching my Mama give it up to "Endless Love" to ever voice an opinion. I could never listen to that damn song ever again! When I went to the seventh grade prom at Cutler Ridge Middle School, she messed it up by doing the same thing, hunching some Niggah in the bathroom at the school while Millie Vanillie's "Girl you Know it's True" boomed from somebody's stereo. *How do you pussy pop to Millie Vanillie?*

She was supposed to be serving drinks. I guess when she got thirsty she pulled on some dick until her throat was satisfied from the eruption that spurted from the black one-eyed snake. I was too mad. She did a host of other shit I couldn't think about now because I didn't feel like crying and messing up my make-up. She knew I was thinking about something. Mama smiled uneasily, standing up from the couch. Looking ravishing.

Mama said, "I couldn't make a career out of it." She looked depressed. I didn't feed into it. I gave her a knowing look. Since she was the queen-of-reminding-you-of-your dirty-panties-from-your-past, its time to flip the script.

"Because you were caught in an orgy with the First Sergeant, your element leader and their wives by some General, and you were all court marshaled, right?"

She was in denial. "Anyways. It didn't go down like that."

Yea, right. I read her papers behind her back. "Whatever."

Her eyes became a little withdrawn. "You're about to get married, baby! Miss Francine Jakes Mann-Lester. Can you believe your big day has arrived?" Mama asked.

*Flip the script, Mama!* "I know, Mama." My earrings dangled freely, gifts from whom else: Mama.

"Are you ready? Getting cold feet?"

*What the fuck?* "No, Mama. I don't *have* cold feet."

She gave a phony smile. "Baby. *Every* woman gets cold feet."

Through clenched teeth I said, "No they don't."

She was determined. "*Yes* they do." Her eyes narrowed.

I was gritting my teeth. "Mama, not every bitch gets cold feet."

She grinned. "You're in church, watch your mouth."

"I'm in my home. This *isn't* a church. Or have you forgotten?" I was getting mad. On my wedding day. Of all days to piss me off she would pick this day. I was set to marry Samuel Lester. He was a business man who took a T-shirt venture from the soul of the 'hood and took it to a level that brought him $500,000 a year. Street hustling inspirational shirts in the 'hood, being ridiculed, talked about, slammed and slandered certainly paid off. He now drove a Rolls

Royce and had a fitness video coming out. His brother, Prado, hated everything that he did. He claimed Samuel stole his ideas. I didn't believe him. He seemed to be a jealous man anyways, always trying to take what his brother earned and couldn't even raise his damn kids!

My Mama was like that. Mama got in my face and I held my breath. This was the story. Mama and I were always going at it. She still hadn't realized I cut the umbilical cord from her navel when I sucked my first dick when I was fourteen years old. She always wanted to hold my hand. I wanted to do shit on my own, but *no*, Mama was like the solar eclipse. Blocking my sunshine. Nothing was right for her. If I made straight A's she wanted me to make them the next year. I could never satisfy her yet she couldn't satisfy herself. She always bragged about me around Goulds, the town in Miami, Florida we're from.

My baby this. She made the honor roll that. Your child isn't as smart as mine. My life was reduced to a bunch of stats. I was her pumpkin when things went right. I make one wrong step she disowned me like a bad habit. I was measuring my words.

"Get out my face," I whispered breathlessly. I really wasn't up for this. I was supposed to be happy go lucky, damn it!

Her eyes challenged mine. "*I'm* your mother, and just because you're about to get married doesn't mean you're exempt from my rule."

It exploded in me. "*Bitch!*" I walked around her, tossing my veil over my face. I shook with pain but I wouldn't dare show it. I loved this woman, looked up to this woman. She survived the cold streets of Chicago. She rose from hooker to cooker, slut to house wife, low-life to a career with the federal government with a TSP fund and 401 (k) that would make anybody jealous. She was assistant Warden of a federal penal institution. She made close to $100,000 a year. Got in the church, totally reformed herself when her own parents wrote her off. And now her parents were ringing her phone off the hook, wanting money, trying to apologize. The money they were influenced by. They wanted the green that Niggahs killed themselves over everyday in the drug game.

Suffice it to say, Mama's mistakes fell on me because she was certainly making me pay for them and I was her only child. I graduated valedictorian from Miami Killian High School. That wasn't good enough. Forget that Killian was out of my residential area in Goulds. I was supposed to go to *Southridge*. I loved the Ridge! All my girls were there.

All the fine Niggahs were there, despite my having a man. But Mama wanted me to be different. In some ways she wanted me to be white, act white, date white men, *fuck* white men and *become* a white man's wife. Like hell. I loved and respected white folks but their cup of tea was my cup of coffee, for real, Chile. She once told me black men always amounted to the epitomes of the ghetto: Hustler. Pimp. Thug. Dope Dealer. Dressed for success but was broke as a joke. White men dressed like they were broke but were rich as hell.

Then after high school I graduated Summa Cum Laude from college, if that's how you said it. Shit, I been out of school for a longtime. Getting too old to be remembering al that Summa Cum bullshit. But even being in a sorority wasn't good enough for Mama.

I quit my job at an insurance firm to help my soon-to-be-husband rise to fame. That wasn't good enough. She told me I was being a fool. *You keep your job, save your money and spend up your man shit. Are you fucking crazy, bitch?* She asked me, pissing me off. She walked all sorts of cute white men in the house; they wined, dined and paid for everything that made my heart smile, even ate my pussy on call. But my love couldn't be bought. And giving me a nut with vanilla lips didn't stroke the scoop in my clit.

I loved Samuel. He ate pussy so good he sucked the memory of seeing the white men from my brain and the memory cells in my eyes, if I had memory cells in my eyes. Shit, I didn't know. Samuel, my baby, then gave me fifty percent of the shares in the company to prove to me he loved me for me. What black man you knew trusted his woman like that? Wasn't any *Waiting to Exhale* shit popping off here? That wasn't good enough for Mama.

Pushing all that to the back of my mind, it was almost show time. "I'm about to get married. Can you please leave and send in my matron of honor. I want to talk to her."

She was quiet for a moment. "That's another thing. She didn't show up."

I stared at her through the reflection, hands rising to my hips. "She didn't *what?*"

Mama smirked, her eyes sparkling. "She called in sick. She said she found out she's pregnant, that she couldn't make it to the funeral."

*She called in sick? This isn't a goddamn job, Mama. You don't just call your best friend and say* "Oh, I can't make it. Won't be in today." *Was she serious?* I was confused. "*Funeral?* This is supposed to be a wedding." I was offended.

"Funeral, wedding, whatever. This shit is crazy." There was something she wasn't telling me. I felt it crawling along my spine but I said nothing. I pivoted on my heel and looked at my watch. Three o'clock. Why hadn't Chandra shown up? She never let me down. Never in my life! "So I guess you got to stand in for me then Mama." I said it cautiously, slowly. I eyed her. "Right?" I covered my face with the veil.

She looked delighted.

"You can't talk? You were against Chandra standing up for me since the beginning. And you once told me you'd do whatever it took to stand up for me. I didn't believe you. I didn't think you were that crazy."

Mama was hiding something. She was smiling too big. "So…are you calling me crazy?"

"No. Do you want to stand in for me, Mama?"

"I thought you'd never ask."

I had to keep it together. "Well go on out, Mama. I'll be out on cue. I just want to spend a few moments alone with myself as a free woman."

She got what she wanted. So as far as I was concerned I could die right now and she'd be happy, as long as she got to stand up for me.

"Ok." She toyed with my veil and kissed my lips. I averted my face a little too late. I wouldn't look at her, and I stared at the marble floor.

"Honey, like me or love me I am your mother."

"Mother. Leave, please."

She laughed to herself, leaving me to my thoughts.

When the coast was clear I whipped out my cell phone.

*Chandra, you have some explaining to do. You don't stand me up on my fucking wedding, are you goddamn serious, bitch? We talked about this shit for months! You even helped me plan my wedding, helped me do the invitations and you helped me cook the food! We stayed up all night dancing to Billie Holiday, Whitney Houston and Janet Jackson with flour in our hair and mustard on our white aprons and sipping bubbly and smoking goddamn weed, and you stand me up, bitch? We did the Beyonce uh-uh-uh-uh ah no no dance to Janet Jackson's If breakdown and we had a blast and forgot the cake was baking and it was ruined and we still put frosting on that bitch and fucked it up over some fried chicken.*

My best friend Chandra was married to a man who neglected her, a man who detested her, a man who used to be her universe until he got caught trying to take me to bed. I pulled that bozo out the closet. I took him to her face and told her what he did. And I had a mini recorded taped confessional to prove it. She cried and attempted suicide. I was there for my girl. Men were assholes.

When Chandra answered the phone I started smiling. There had to be a logical explanation for this. "Chandra, *why* are you not in my wedding?"

"I can't, Francine. Girl, I love you, but I can't bring a storm cloud over your big day."

I narrowed my eyes, wrinkles forming on my forehead. "What storm cloud? You can tell me anything."

She had an attitude. She never got an attitude with me before. Something was off. "No, I can't. Some things are better left unsaid."

I sucked my teeth. "You're not making any sense. Mama says you're pregnant. You're carrying that asshole's baby?"

She hesitated. "Yes. *He's* an asshole. That much I will admit. But I got to go."

I smiled anyway, determined to change her mind. "Please come be my Matron of Honor. You're my air. I love you like a sister…"

She snapped, "I can't."

I was unnerved. She had never turned me down. Never. Whether we fought loose-pussy, dick-gobbling Hoes over our men, fought bitches for jacking our dance moves, our hair styles or came down from Carol and Liberty City to Goulds trying to run shit, we stuck together. We dressed in the same clothes, rocked the same earrings and hair styles. We had 'em all, from the Salt-N-Peppa look to the Janet Jackson "That's the Way Love Goes" and Jill Scott "A Long Walk" looks. We rocked the Era like fine wine. And now she turned me down? Something wasn't right in the milk I was about to drink, for real. "Why?"

"Because your Mama called me and said if I showed my haggard face at your house she'd have me thrown out."

*Oh, God! I can't stop! Why can't I stop? I keep ruining my body with drugs and I love it and hate it.* Chandra had huge tears falling down her face, the drugs tearing through her body, passing through her heart via the blood stream. She wanted more, but she felt weak and her inner voice told her to take it easy but how could she? Drugs were her master, and she had to remain its fledgling at all costs. Needles were everywhere. Her house used to a home, place of refuge, her port from the storm and now it was a shell. Her family detested her now. No one wanted to deal with a drug addict. Her use of drugs sent the town on a tizzy. No one could believe one of the most beautiful women in

Dade County was now a dope head. She had no respect for herself. She dressed like she had no sense.

The question was: How did it happen?

She pressed the phone to her ear with her shoulder, her eyes rolling to the back of her head. *Fuck your wedding, Francine! I am in love with these drugs and a bitch is feeling mighty, mighty, lettin' it all hang out, bitch!*

"Bye, Francine. Have shit to do."

# Part II

Leaving me devastated and confused, Chandra clicked in my face. The phone went dead. In my hands. With my heart. Why would Mama *threaten* my girl? What was going on? Something wasn't adding up. I didn't like the feeling in my guy, made my stomach turn. I could hear it bubbling, as my legs and arms started to get weaker...weaker.

I had to sit down. But I didn't. Everything always came back around to this heartless bitch! Yea I called my Mama a bitch! She was one and she was acting like one. Angry and infuriated, I intended to find out. *Before* the ceremony.

This bitch was just determined to ruin my big day...

The door opened and Prado, Samuel's brother and best man came waltzing in the room. He closed and locked the door. He wouldn't face me; I thought this was a little weird. But I kept my cool. The man was tall, sexier than his brother and could talk the dead alive. He threw his dick around town like Cast Away and Hoes held onto it like Tom Hanks did the volleyball with WILSON on it in the movie Cast Away. He had seven kids from seven different women (and I heard he got 3 sons from another bitch, but he refused to take a DNA test), didn't pay child support for any and just got out of jail because the State wanted him to care for his babies. They all looked like him and were some little ignorant fucks, didn't respect their elders and his sons were 8, 10 and 13 talking about how much pussy they were getting and could barely spell B-A-T-H and S-O-A-P.

Mama always said Whores had daughters first, that God punished you for all your whorish qualities by giving you a girl. Well, he got seven daughters. Guess God wanted revenge. My pussy always got wet when he came near but I hid it from my face and forced myself to go numb. Just because I was in love didn't mean I wasn't attracted to other people. Hell, I wasn't dead. I did love men. All shades. I did love dick. All shades. But it's what you did with that attraction to other people that made it a sin.

I managed to smile, with Chandra's words stampeding through my brain like wild horses. "Prado, what's up? You can't be in here."

He faced me. Quietly. Narrowed red eyes. My every instinct told me he was high on weed, he was always high on weed. Weed and alcohol was his life. That and pussy.

Macho charm on full blast. "You're so beautiful."

I actually blushed. "Thank you. I'm about to go out and get married. So go take your place."

"I'm about to." He was walking towards me, pleading eyes, sexy lips. He looked withdrawn within himself. I smelled (I sniffed the air) alcohol. My defenses quickly went up.

"Are you drunk?" I gave him the Go to Hell look. I loved his swagger, his dick print behind the black slacks seemed to move like an Anaconda through an African Rain forest and I felt my nipples standing up like the Twin Towers.

"I sipped on the Goose, that's about it."

"Grey Goose, 'ey." I smiled anyway. "Why are you acting funny?"

"I think you are a sight for sore eyes."

"You talk like you found a job."

He smiled. "I did."

I applauded him. *He listened to me. I suggested he find one, and he did. This was three days ago.* "Now you can feed your kids. I seen your son yesterday, let's just say you need to buy that boy some new clothes and shoes."

"He'll be ok. I got him, I promise."

I was observing him, trying not to look at his dick. "We'll see. Yet you're just staring at me all crazy. Is there something going on I should know about?"

He studied me a moment. The silence fell on my ears with the force of Tech 9's. "My brother shouldn't marry you."

Offended, I rolled my eyes and held my hips with an attitude. "Not you, too! Did my Mama send you in here?" My body was craving Prado. I fought it. Damn it. Get your sexy ass away from me!

He fixed his pretty hazel eyes on me and my soul stirred. My hands were trembling, my blood boiling. Damn it I gotta stop taking those vitamin B12 pills. I was a Horny Bitch in a Wedding Dress.

"No. Francine you don't understand. I have loved you since the first day I saw you."

I guffawed loudly. "Come on man, I love your…"

He interrupted. "*You* love *me*."

Ha! Fat chance! "No I…"

Caught in a whirlwind of emotions, he wrapped his arms around me and gently pulled me into his embrace. We couldn't stop looking at each other. The chemistry shattered every test tube in my brain. I wanted him, needed him and desired him. But I was about to take that much-desired trek down the aisle to become Samuel's wife. But should I marry, knowing I didn't really explore men the way most women had? Would I regret getting married? My feet felt like cinder blocks in this room yet my hips and breasts felt like ships sailing the rapturous waters of Hurricane Prado, about to give in to his lustful trances and his deviously beautiful eyes. I was butter in his arms, in ways I wasn't to Samuel. The world being snatched from under my feet, he kissed me, tenderly, slowly, passionately and I tried to break free but his dick pressed up against my groin and we bumped pelvises and I was taken off guard. My panties were sliding down my legs, literally. And these were my good panties, panties that cost me $400. If I was getting married then my pussy needed an outfit, too so I kept the receipt and I will be taking these bitches back tomorrow and getting my $400.

Hungrily, he released my titties from the oval buttons on my dress and squeezed them together with those smooth, manly hands I loved…running his tongue across both nipples. I shivered with delight, trying to block it out my mind. I was trying to will myself to push this creep off me. But I was a woman. A woman in a wedding dress wanting another man. A woman who *loved* her man. A woman trapped in a room with her fiancé's brother trying to get to my pussy...Oh dear God what do I do?

I silently told myself, *Pussy please don't fail me now.*

# Part III

My pussy failed me! Sorry to say. It told my breasts, *"Look bitch, get this free dick! What goes on in this room stays in this room."* Yet my head was like *"You're getting married! Your man never cheated on you! He is very loyal! You got a good man! You had this man even before he had money! You had him when he was down and out. When he was broke and poor, when he worked at a fast food joint. You believed in him. He is your world and you're going to spit in God's face by fucking his brother?"*

*Well hell yeah!*

The agitated butterflies in my stomach were making love to the Goosebumps on my arms to birth a pleasure so uncontrollable I almost exploded. My vaginal juices runneth over like a spilt cup of milk. I smelled my pussy in the air, electrified us both. Shivers went up and down my spine and popped in my pussy when his moist warm tongue touched my expensively-perfumed skin.

My cell phone rang and I ignored it. He got on his knees and buried his face in my pussy. Eagerly, I watched him through the ceiling to floor mirror in ecstasy. He made me weak in the knees, I could hardly speak. I slow humped his face, thinking about my future with his brother. A man I didn't love. LET'S BE REAL!

Prado was right! I never loved Samuel. Ever since the seventh grade I haven't loved Samuel the way that I had when we first met. It was puppy love. I was a little girl *thinking* she was in love. My friends were telling me that I was in love because I melted when he smiled. I loved him because he took my virginity when I was fifteen years old, giving me my first piece of dick. Dick that made me a whole woman. Dick that made me nut over and over and over and he used to make me suck his dick clean then kiss my pussy's tears from my lips. He had made me cum over and over and over in his mother's bed, while she was drunk, passed out on the living room couch with weed strewn all over the place. After all that history, his brother now drove me crazy. I wanted Prado since day one. I was just too afraid to really say what I felt.

Good dick had me blind. It had me in ecstasy. It made me listen to my mother and stay with Samuel. I didn't have anyone else's dick but his, so I didn't have another dick to compare it to. So Prado would be the prime choice. I wanted him to terrorize my pussy to the point where my asshole felt taunted and my nipples felt like slaves and my lips were contortionists and my booty cheeks applauded and my pussy was the burning bush telling Moses to free my clit from bondage before the Pharaoh was swallowed by the Red Sea.

I WANTED HIM! Show me what Samuel's dick failed to do. If it had ever failed to do anything. Dick-blind, I was against the mirror. My right leg was around his neck. His slick tongue slid in and out of my opening. I loved getting my pussy eaten. I *wasn't* going to front. What woman didn't? Eat it, baby! Suck Samuel right on out of there. Excavate the tomb my Chocolate Archeologist! Send my pussy into dress rehearsals with that motherfucking tongue. Dress that bitch as Nefertiti.

I fought to keep it together and it was unraveling at the seams. "Please, you…got to…stop, please!"

He stared into my eyes. My soul reached out for him, past Samuel. He longed for me. This man was truly in love with me, a woman he never had, a woman he always respected. Prado opened doors for me, Samuel didn't. Prado cooked for me, Samuel didn't. It was always business with anal retentive S-A-M-U-E-L! Samuel would wine, dine and 69 me. Prado would cook me a home meal, give his brother a plate, call his mother and offer to take her a plate, fry his daddy some fish and crack open his Michelob and eat last when everyone else was taken care of. Why couldn't he take care of his kids like that? I wondered for months.

"I want some *pussy*, baby. *Let* me fuck. Come on, baby. It's me...*Prado*...I *need* you, sweetness. Flow with me. The *hell* with my brother. He isn't the saint you think he is. He doesn't deserve you. I want to make a baby with you. Have my child. You *know* you want to. Let me be the man you always wanted. I *know* Samuel don't make you happy. I can see it in your eyes."

I was gone. *Get out of my head! How did he know how I felt inside? I had never told him my feelings and now he picked me apart like Tonka toys.*

"Take me baby, please," I was moaning to him. Smiling in victory he stood up, with his sexy chocolate ass, and pulled out that juicy, scrumptious dick, putting on a Lifestyles condom. The right way.

No I wasn't ready for all that yet. All that glorious dick scared a bitch into early retirement and I wasn't even married yet. I took off the condom and tossed it, got on my knees in my huge wedding dress. I tore a hole through my veil and he stuck his dick in my mouth. I nearly came from the anticipation alone! It was hot in this room. Through the hole in the veil his dick caused my mouth and tonsils a ruckus. I was freaky like that and I gripped his nature, trying to suck the Almond Joy out of his Snickers bar. I sucked, pulled, jacked and slurped. I leaned with it and rocked with it. Spat on it and jacked him some more, watching him oooh and aaah with his thuggish self all up in my face. He stuck his dick all the way in my throat, holding the back of my head and I held his thighs, trying to pull back and he thrust forward, pulling my head back on it and I kept gagging and I kept burping and he loved that shit.

His legs were trembling, nuts dangling, slapping my chin. "Suck it, baby...Let me stretch that throat like I'ma stretch your pussy."

I gave it my all, knowing this shit was wrong. I knew men. You suck for too long they were going to have thoughts of getting the pussy. He grabbed me by the arm and pulled me up. "I want to fuck."

I was Dorothy trapped in a tornado. "I want to suck.

He smiled. "And you suck a mean dick, Ma."

There's no place like home. "Well let me finish."

He licked his lips. "Beg for the dick."

Be my Todo, please. "Damn baby, let me suck on it, 'til you come."

He wiped pre-cum from his dick and wiped it on my lips. "I want my come in your pussy, baby. This is *my* pussy! I'm *taking* it from my brother. He isn't tapping it right."

I begged to differ. Samuel was good in bed. "He taps it good."

Prado protested. "Good don't make it right, Ma."

*Whatever.* "He's the best."

He narrowed his eyes, stroking his Monster. "I'm *better*," he challenged. "Does he hit it from the back while rubbing the clit?"

I stopped breathing. "No, he never…"

Prado was sucking on my neck, feeling on my booty. "Does he let you ride it while a vibrator is deep in your ass, filling up both those holes? Does he pull his dick out and make you suck your pussy from it? Does he suck on the twat after he comes in it, sucking his own juices down his throat?"

I was tonguing him, gripping his dick. "Oh, *hell* no! Is that even possible?"

A deep laugh erupted from the base of his larynx. "Does he push your legs back and beat the pussy up and make you say ahhh and drop spit in your mouth while looking you in the eyes and then tongue kiss you and make that pussy hiccup?"

"Nooo."

"Come to my bedroom."

"No. *We* can stay right here."

Prado was unbuttoning my dress. "How do you want this dick?"

*Let's see.* "Deep in my pussy!"

"You won't regret it, Ma."

Such urgency in his breathy voice. The aggression was amazingly blinding. I wanted him to fuck me good, make my pussy The Terminator and his dick Arnold and I want him to say "Cum with me if you want to live!" Oh my God!

Sure about himself, he pulled another condom from his pocket and put it on. What a dick! It was about two inches thicker and bigger than Samuel's. And my fiancé had a huge dick, slightly curved. When he put that thing on me it scrubbed my vaginal walls like a Dentist tool between my teeth. It was hot in here.

We were breathing heavily, on cadence with each other. I was rubbing his muscular arms, not too muscular. He kissed his dick off my lips. Without further ado I braced myself as he got between my legs and before he could slide up in me I pushed him out my face, stomped his foot and slapped him so hard he stumbled over the chair.

I got me a nut. I didn't tell him, and I was straight. I was about to marry the man of my dreams. I may not love him but he was a provider...and I planned on telling him exactly what happened in this room.

"See you at the wedding."

After I got myself in order, I was snatching up my bouquet, a brilliant display of white and red roses when Prado said, "You're making a mistake."

*Niggah you should have told yourself that when you were on baby number 3 without a fucking J-O-B!* "It's my mistake to make," I told him, walking out into the ante-chamber. The door closed behind me, and I heard Prado cursing. He'll live.

Linda, my childhood friend, was going to town on the organ about thirty feet in front of me. Samuel had a huge living room, den and everything else. The people seemed light years away from me. No one saw me, thank God! The sea of people looked so good, everyone I loved and hated most in the world were present. I saw the Miss Tai, a photographer related to a man I used to fuck, was capturing the essence of my big day. She had a nappy ponytail, ripped jeans and a Lenny Kravitz coat and penny loafers.

People were whispering in anticipation. I got an adrenaline rush. I smiled, tears falling down my face. I resisted temptation. As bad as I wanted Samuel's brother's dick knee deep inside me I just couldn't. That was his brother! That was nasty. I couldn't sink that low and do that, and even though I felt guilty for giving him some bomb head, I *knew* in my heart I could love Samuel if I just released my inhibitions and remained true to him. Samuel was a swell guy and well liked, well versed and he knew how to turn three dollars into shopping mall magic. I loved his money. Money made the world go round and shut the bill collector's the fuck up because money did all the talking and money paid the bills, money didn't grow on trees and right now (and hopefully forever) it would buy my happiness or put it on layaway at least so I can cash in my rain checks and I.O.U's.

I never cheated on him and I wasn't about to start. Well, not until today. Nobody told God to make Prado so fucking fine.

For some reason I just didn't feel right. It was one of those feelings that came out of nowhere. Like some unknown force was trying to tell me something. But what was it? Did I really wanna get married? Did I really wanna watch Samuel grow old? I wasn't sure if I wanted him seeing my perky tits go south for the winter, spring and fall as I age with time. Maybe I was tripping. Maybe I was scared that

Samuel would find out that I gave his brother head and he would throw me out on my ass. Maybe I didn't give a damn. Hell, I earned fifty percent of his company, so he couldn't throw me out if he wanted to. I was riding his dick and making my pussy juices spill down his nuts and the crack of his ass when he signed the document. He actually gave me twenty percent control, but I hired some hackers and they made a replica and he signed the replica and I put the original contract in the shredder. I read Waiting to Exhale. I wasn't a total dumb ass. After Bernadine, in the book, helped her man for eleven years build his brand and he left her for a white bitch, me and my pussy had a mission, and I bound those nuts to a goddamn agreement. He leave me for a white bitch or any bitch I would drain his ass dry.

Everyone had their secrets and I had mine. Who was to say that Samuel didn't fuck a bitch behind *my* back, calling it the Last Hurrah? Black men with money got their dicks wet outside of marriage, I didn't care what they told their wives. A dick whipped bitch was an obedient bitch and she did whatever Daddy said. I wasn't that dumb.

I looked ahead, my heart fluttering. The beautiful white orchids all over the place, everyone dressed in white or purple. Selected colors I specifically requested. My single life about to go down the tubes. No more bachelorette bullshit. Was I ready? Could I do this? Oh my God. My mind has gone blank. The room was spinning. I couldn't even remember my name right now. Two plus two was eleven and eight times three was six. Had I done all the things I wanted to do before I take that walk on the wild side. Once I do marry Samuel it *has* to be forever. I wouldn't be getting a divorce. It's FOREVER!

An ice swan was by the front door. Champagne was on ice. Cold feet. I was getting cold feet. I took off the veil, balled it up in my hand and stuffed it deep down in my titties. There was a hole in it, didn't want to look fucked up in my own wedding. Damn! I couldn't get my mind off Chandra. I tried calling her again but no answer. Thank God no one saw me. My handsome fiancé was at the altar. Talking to Pastor Mark James. He looked happy, serene.

He always made me feel good about things, which was one of the reasons I wanted to marry him. I closed my eyes, praying to God.

Protect me.

*If anything had been done behind my back let me find out before the exchanging of the rings. Don't embarrass me, Lord. I have been through a lot. I didn't want to turn out to be like my mother. Keep us in good health.*

*Amen.*

I opened my eyes and Chandra, disgruntled, stared me right in the face. I jumped out of my skin, startled.

My heart dropped.

# ~~Part IV~~

Chandra was heartbroken; she looked a complete mess. Nothing she had on matched. She was wearing high heels with a light blue jogging suit with the sleeves cut off, revealing her frail-looking arms. And her weave was red and beige, like some ghetto copy of Keysha Cole and that non-singing bitch was ghetto enough.

"Chandra? Talk to me." I lovingly grabbed her arms, holding on to my bouquet. It cost over three hundred dollars to make; I couldn't afford it to get messed up. "Oh my God, your skin feels cold. You're shaking. *What* did your man *do* to you?"

She was standoffish, a little nervous. I never saw her like this before. I knew something was wrong. What did her man do to her? I would kill that man, for real! "Nothing."

I was searching her face. "Did he hit you?"

She was trying to get away from me. "No."

She knew *I* knew she was lying. She was a terrible liar. My keen, observant eyes danced all over her taut body. She looked frail.

"What's wrong, girl, talk to me. I'm your sister. Your best friend."

She was stuttering. "It's hard."

"Make it easier by opening your fat trap."

She became fire. "Please, don't make me go there."

I became the goddamn flames. "Go there, let me pack some bags and we can have a picnic when we arrive."

She smiled so beautifully. Her always perfectly white teeth were greenish, and her breath smelled foul. She has never let herself go like this. She used to wear braces as a kid and she vowed to always keep her teeth up. So what made her take the backslide? I wiped the tears from her face like a big sister.

She smiled again. "You always make me smile."

*Now we're getting somewhere!* "That's what I'm here for."

"I know, but I can't tell you…"

"Please, I'm about to get married. To that man behind you, well a hundred feet behind you."

"So what, Francine."

"What is wrong?"

Her eyes grew dark. I knew that look. When somebody crossed me she got defensive and now I was not only worried but I knew something had gone down she didn't want me to know about.

She said, "I just want you happy, Francine. I always want you to be happy. But I can't live with myself. I can't do it. I can't look you in the eyes. I can't form the words. I can't hurt you. I'll die. I'll slit my wrists. I had no choice. I was forced to do it. I had no other option."

Despite her shitty breath, she smelled great; I loved the White Diamonds perfume. My fiancé bought it for her a while ago and she'd been wearing it ever since. I studied her arms really well, my blood turning cold. "Are you doing heroine *while* you're pregnant?"

She shook. I held her tightly to me. My wedding could wait. My girl didn't do drugs. She never did drugs in her life. She didn't even drink. Her lungs were fleshy and red. Not black. Something wasn't right. Oh, God! How fast were you acting to show me a picture that I wasn't seeing? I don't work for Kodak or Fuji, goddamn it. What the fuck is going on? I knew heroine marks when I saw them. There were a lot of addicts in my family, smoking and basing any and everything under the glorious sun. My Mama's brother was the biggest crack monster in Goulds, that Niggah would smoke clothes if he could fit it in his pipe.

Chandra said, "Yes, I'm doing drugs."

I was appalled. "DRUGS?" I looked around to make sure no one was listening to us.

She looked wild-eyed. "I was forced."

This was absurd. "Yea, somebody put a gun to your head..."

She was shuddering, like she was cold. "*And* to my stomach."

My mouth hanging open, I grew shockingly silent. This was a nightmare. This was some Hollywood movie come to life.

"Who would do this to you, Chandra? Who?"

She turned her back on me. She NEVER turned her back on me.

"Girl, I'm not pregnant from my man."

"What? You aren't? Who are you pregnant from?"

She clammed up. "I can't tell you."

My patience became retrogressive. "Tell me!" I whispered harshly, not drawing attention on ourselves. "Who are you pregnant from, bitch?"

She was defiant. "*I said no!*"

Time to do some wire-pulling. "Chandra, you're pissing me the fuck off...tell me! We're sisters, bitch we don't keep secrets. I'll beat your goddamn ass, Ho!"

She laughed bitterly, tears forming in sad-looking eyes. "Right." She averted her face.

I was devastated. "Why are you keeping things from me, Chandra?"

"I'ma grown woman," she spat icily. She never talked to me like this before in her entire life. "And you're not my goddamn Mama, Francine."

I bet her man was behind this. Ever since he came along everything has been thrown out of organization. I should call his ass and ask him what's going on. I couldn't *stand* him, God I couldn't.

"I know you're grown." I was about to lose it. "Tell me."

*"Fuck off!"*

All my anger snapped inside me like explosions. Impulsively, I slapped her so hard she held her face. "Fuck the goddamn games! Who are you pregnant from?"

She was in tears. Shaking feverishly. I shook with her. I felt her pain, even though I didn't know what it was. She was hiding it from me and I didn't understand why.

"Slap me all you want! Beat me, kick me I don't care, Francine! I can't tell you. Your Mama threatened me. She told me...she said she'd tell you everything if I showed up. I can't do it, girl please!"

I started to cry. I couldn't deal with this. The lies. The treachery. What was going on? I had to know!

"Girl, who are you pregnant from?"

Chandra drew in air. Looked at me. Closed her eyes. Lowered her head like someone died. "Your *fiancé*."

God just spat back in my face.

And it wasn't a very good feeling at all.

Crushingly shocked, I dropped the bouquet on the floor when "Here Comes the Bride" started playing. I was astutely floored. I put my heel on the orchids and I crushed them with my heart, a sadistic look on my face. I knew men with money cheated on their wives, I knew this shit! I couldn't breathe and I damn sure couldn't say anything to Chandra right now. What was going on? Why didn't I see the goddamn signs? Were there ever any? My sweet husband-to-be, the love and my life. Fucked my girl behind my back and got her pregnant. He put a gun to her stomach and her head? Why? Why would he do that? Prado warned me. He told me I was making a grave mistake. He was right. Oh how Prado had just tried to warn me something wasn't right about me being with his brother.

Wait a minute! Did Prado *know* what was going on? Was that why he tried to fuck me, to take me away from his brother? Was he as shrewd a manipulator as his no-good brother? He did say Samuel wasn't a saint, that he didn't deserve me. He was right, right, right! I shoulda fucked Prado! Damn it I shoulda went all the way through with it. I shoulda cheated, damn it! I always wanted to feel that Snicker's chocolate any-damn-way!

Devastated beyond my wildest dreams, small moans escaped my lips and Chandra took my hands and squeezed them, bringing them to her lips and kissing them. I didn't feel her hands on mine. I didn't feel her lips. I wanted to go out there and bash the punk's head in for hurting my girl. Friends over dick any day.

What did Mama have to do with all this? She did tell me that my mother had warned her to stay away from my wedding, that she declined being my Maid of Honor because Mama threatened her. She had some questions to answer. Making a quick minute decision, I took my girl by the hand and we fled out the back door, leaving my fiancé, my man, my baby standing at the alter as I did my version of Runaway Bride. That motherfucker would never see me again. I swore to God he wouldn't ever hear from me again.

Or Chandra.


Quietly, trapped in a myriad of thoughts, Samuel smiled to himself, overlooking the breathtakingly handsome men standing behind him. *Where's Prado?* He asked himself impatiently. He looked around without setting off any alarms. He was nowhere to be seen.

A little uneasy, he stood before two families, many generations of people who came to his gorgeous house to celebrate the union, to celebrate black brilliance. Samuel loved his wife-to-be, but he harbored something in his heart. His Mama and Daddy, married for forty-seven years, eloquently sat next to his bride-to-be parents. He looked around for his soon-to-be mother-n-law. There she was, chit-chatting with a few people in the audience, while making her way to the altar. He breathed in deep.

*Where's Chandra? I hope she stays away,* he thought silently. *She poses a goddamn threat. She shoulda just kept the pussy out my face. I didn't mean to cheat. She kept seducing me. Let me stop lying. I seduced her! I am so goddamn jealous of the friendship she got with Francine! She called, my fiancé would drop me like a hot potato just to be at her side. Over my dead fucking body!*

He wanted to be like his parents, have a marriage based on love and longevity. They didn't believe in divorce, he didn't either. So he figured by controlling her every move, controlling her job, friends, family and dreams, their marriage would last for a lifetime. You had to get rid of the other factors outside of the marriage so you could truly appreciate the union. And having a close relative and a best friend would destroy a good marriage in no time because then they started complaining about never spending time with Francine, oh you used to come around but every since you met Samuel you put us aside. Fuck that!

He wanted this to work with his fiancé, he worked so hard on their relationship and it took so much. The pussy he turned away, despite trying to destroy Chandra, filled his ego. The feelings of autonomy that beckoned for their separation tortured him. The feelings of not letting someone get close to him destroyed him. The feeling of selfishness took hold of him and turned him black inside. He had to think of himself and *only* himself. His homeboys told him to leave his fiancé alone because they were jealous. They didn't have the woman he had and they envied that. His own parents trying to force him to start a family when he wasn't ready did a number on him. Joint bank accounts didn't seem an option, sharing their names on bills was out of the question. But he couldn't live without her, nor did he *want* to.

*Yes*, he made his mistakes. Some of them he could never tell his bride. Bad decisions hung on the hangers of his internal closet; forever locked in the core of a subconscious too dark for public consumption. But he asked God for forgiveness and shunned them away and came out on top.

Temptation always knocked on his door; he'd shun it all away. He couldn't go to the store without women giving him their phone numbers scribbled on everything from his hand and scrap pieces of paper to panties and condoms. Just last week, at Publix Supermarket, on the bread aisle, some chick stuck her hand in her panties and wiped her pussy juices on his lips, gripped his dick and said, "Call me and come taste some real pussy," slid her business card in his pocket (she was a lawyer) and vanished without a trace.

Nothing would come and take away his big moment. She put up with his good and bad side, taking his shit. The times he didn't come home and the hours he put in at work unnerved her. She was there before the money. She was there when he was poor. She was there when he stayed with his parents.

Breaking his thoughts, the music began to play. It was time. He was getting upset. Where in the hell was Prado? He closed his eyes for a second and then opened them. He carefully scanned the crowd, clad in purple and white. The white orchids were glorious. He saw four women who hated his fiancé. He made sure he sent them invitations so the bitches could see up close and personal that his fiancé came out victorious.

Ah. There goes Prado, buttoning his coat, smiling, looking like GQ Magazine's next cover model. GQ. He was smoother than Samuel, more suave. Good with the ladies. Once Prado got up to his brother he shook his hand, hugged him and said, "Sorry I'm late."

"Just take position…and why do you smell like pussy?"

He gave a boyishly devilish grin. "I can't wait for you to marry your bride. I just saw her. I've never seen her look so gorgeous. You are one lucky man." He smiled to himself.

As if on cue everyone rose. Here Comes the Bride. He waited five minutes. Nervously, he checked his watch. No bride made an appearance. He breathed in deeply, the huge fans blowing cool air all over the place. He held his breath when a scent filled his nose; a scent only one person wore. His blood boiled and his temples twitched. His heart dropped. White Diamonds! His soul ripped from his body. He closed his eyes and a small moan escaped his lips. The Pastor instantly picked up on the negative vibe and he raised his hands, the talking and the music died in an instant.

His parents blinked rapidly. His mother, looking like the Queen from Eddie Murphy's *Coming to America,* held her neck, fidgeting with her pricey pearls. Chandra got to his fiancé. Oh goddamn no! *Where's my fiancé?* He suddenly felt itchy all over, his eyes running over with tears. He tried to suck in air and keep it together but he couldn't. Prado was alarmed.

*Damn, does he know I tried to fuck Francine?* he thought. *He can't find out. Yes, I love my brother but he is a sneaky sonofabitch and I want to tell Francine what he's been doing behind her back. She's so beautiful, so fine. She should be marrying me. A real man!*

He kept his mouth closed, he wouldn't volunteer any information.

Their worlds were shattered into tiny pieces of oblivious turmoil. Distraught, Francine and Chandra hopped inside a taxi cab. Francine was crying so hard she was about to crack. She held Chandra as tightly as she could and promised to protect her.

The male taxi driver, weather-beaten and dingy looking, stared at the two through the rear-view mirror. Lighting a cigarette, he thought to himself, "Lesbians!"

As the taxi turned onto the Florida Turnpike, North, Francine vowed to cut all ties with Samuel. She wasn't going to call him. She didn't want her things. She would let Samuel go on through his life wondering why he was stood up at the altar. She would go with Chandra to another city and start over. She had enough money in her bank account. Her name was on all of Samuels bank accounts as well.

She could spend whatever and not be brought up on charges. She would be ok; she would get through this. No matter how much it hurt. Samuel would pay. One way or the other.

Chandra said, tears streaming from her eyes, "Don't let me go, Francine."

Francine squeezed her tighter. "I won't."

When she closed her eyes and burst into heavy sobs, Samuel checked his watch, looking into his brother's eyes. Prado had a satisfied smirk on his face. Both families and their friends were starting to get restless, impatient. After thirty minutes passed, people started complaining. Was there even going to be a wedding? Samuel went to his bedroom and slammed the door in a fit of rage, vying to find Francine and Chandra and demand an explanation. Prado followed his brother to the room and let himself in. Samuel was on the floor by the bed, his face in his hands. Prado said, "I don't understand why she left you at the altar."

Samuel responded, "Fuck her."

Prado got a hard on, thinking, *Yep. My tongue got to Francine.*

He poured himself some Hennessy and leaned back on the sofa, ESPN flashing in his face, with a satisfied smile.

Francine and Chandra got out of the cab at a nearby hotel. She walked up to the front desk, feeling like a fool in her wedding dress. People were looking at her, some shaking their heads. Francine looked at them all, smiled and said, "How are you all doing?"

*"Fine."*

*"Good."*

She smiled again. "Now stop fucking staring at me you dumb motherfuckers before I shoot all you ugly bitches."

They turned away.

Huge mascara rings were around her eyes, she could not stop crying. She could not get a grip.

Should she call the police? Should she do something? Where did she go from there?

Or should she just stay away?

"A room for 2," Francine told the receptionist. "And please, if one is available we don't want to be disturbed."

Francine settled onto the bed and hugged her girl until she cried herself to sleep. Chandra seemed to be at peace. She looked at her diamond watch and saw that it was getting late. She picked up the phone and called Prado's cell phone.

He answered. "Who is this?" he asked. "I don't normally answer restricted numbers."

It took a while before she said anything. "*Shh*, Prado. It's Francine."

His face beaming, he said, "How are you?"

Francine was severely depressed. "I'm good."

"Are you coming back?"

"No, Prado. I'm *never* coming back. Chandra and I are gone."

"Come back. At least tell him face to face. He's a wreck."

"…You know what I can't do that. It's best if I stay away and cut all ties. Nothing can be salvaged. Nothing."

"You should still tell him, Francine. That's one of the things I love about you."

"You. Love. Me?"

"Yes. Always have. You are a good woman. You have your flaws. We *all* do but you never struck me as the type of woman who run away from her problems and pretend they're not there. I love my brother, yes I do but he's an arrogant asshole who my parent's praise."

"Prado…I. Love…"

*Girl! Don't! Don't go there! You are hurt and you are vulnerable and you are feeling things you shouldn't feel. That's what happens when you suck another man's dick behind your fiancé's back and think you could get away with it. Shit blew up in your face. Things happened, like they were unfolding right now. Now you feel like shit! Now you wanna die! Now you want revenge!*

She couldn't tell him the words. She couldn't tell him that she loved him. That she always has. Or did she? Was she finding a way through her hurt? Was she trying to hold onto a piece of Samuel by thinking she loved his brother? She did know that she *once* (years ago) dreamed about Prado and wanted to be his wife and she wanted to have his children. But that was a fantasy she kicked herself for. He was broke, a thug at heart and lived life on the edge. He sometimes sold drugs. She LOVED the dope boys. They turned her on. They knew how to defend their women and keep them safe. Samuel wasn't that hard. But he had drive, stamina and money. Bottom line being a thug and beating a man's ass over his woman didn't stop bill collectors from sending collection agency's after you.

Her voice trailed off. Hanging up the phone she said a silent prayer. *Prado I love you but God help me to forget this man. And Samuel. Payback's a bitch in pumps and I'm about to give her my wedding dress.*

When her eyes opened she was standing before the mirror, studying herself. The image played into her eyes like a tennis match. Her dress still looked marvelous. Her heart was heavy. Her friend was destroyed inside, pregnant and cold-hearted.

She smiled evilly. "Samuel, want to get married?" she began, looking at her sleeping friend.

"…Then a marriage you'll get."


Fatigued, Samuel was in the bathroom, washing his face. He didn't have the nerve to go out and tell his family he wasn't getting married. Damn. How could this have blown up in his face?

Francine's mother had come into his room and demanded to know where her daughter was.

"She got cold feet."

She seemed amused. "I knew it, I knew it. She'll be back. She loves you, Samuel." She kissed his cheek.

"And so do you. You love me, too."

"Don't get it twisted. I love your dick. And nothing else. See you at the altar," And she sashayed out of the room. Samuel turned off the water and pat dried his face. He felt like a shell with nothing inside. He wanted Francine.

He couldn't live without her. A few short seconds later his cell rang. It was Francine.

Relieved, he said, "Baby, where are you?"

"I got cold feet. I had to leave, I just couldn't…but I'm coming back. Yes, I'll still be your wife."

*So Chandra didn't get to her. Yes. Yes. Good. Good, the bitch listened and stayed away. I should have known. Francine's mother told me she already warned her not to show her face at my house. Damn, I wonder if I could tap that ass again before I marry her daughter.*

He snapped for Prado. "Go tell everyone the wedding is back on," he said with elation. His testicles swelled with bravado. "Sorry for the delay. Francine is coming back."

Prado looked concerned, confused was more like it. *She's coming back to marry him?* Shaking his head, he decided to leave it alone. Whatever she was planning to do he would support it.

He loved her that much.

Francine was in back of the cab. She had done her make-up over, but she took off the veil. She didn't want one. She wanted Samuel to see her pretty face, her beautiful eyes. She wanted him to take her hand and profess his love for her. Then she was going to destroy him.

Lighting a cigarette, she told the cab driver, "About fifteen minutes North and we'll be there. I'll tell you what exit to get off when it gets closer."

She smiled whimsically.

Prado was in the bathroom, sitting on the toilet. He wasn't having a bowel movement but he was in a lot of pain. He loved Francine so much and now she was coming back to marry his selfish ass brother.

*I thought I got to her! I love you, Francine and I have to stand by and watch you walk down the aisle and pretend to be happy with him because he got money and how could I fault you? I love money just as much as you do and I can't even fathom the idea of being broke. Yet all the money in the world can't replace the emptiness I feel right now.*

He stood up and stretched. What should he do? Should he keep quiet and let his brother keep the girl or should he fight for her? He decided not to even bother. He would rather consolidate his feelings and call it a day. He'd go get some new pussy from one of his many whores saved in his phone and come on their pretty faces. He'd go fuck a few of his homeboy's wives and imagine he was fucking Francine. He'd roll a few blunts and smoke them until he passed out. Yea. Hell yeah. That sounded better than fighting over a confused bitch. When she married Samuel he knew he'd hate her for the rest of his life. He thought she would keep it real. If she loved Samuel why did she give him the best head of his life? He was still on fire. His dick hardened thinking of her moans, he could still feel her breath on his skin...her scent terrorized his nostrils to the point of insanity.

*Fight for her, Prado! Hell, no! This isn't A Different World! I am not Dwayne Wayne! I will not run in the assembly and express my undying love for her like Dwayne did to Jasmine Guy on that memorable episode when she was about to marry another man. I am not a pussy! Fuck these whores! But she's not a whore, Prado. She's your Queen. Nah. She will soon be Samuel's wife!*

His cell beeped a few times and he answered. "Where are you, Prado?" Samuel asked.

"On my way to you."

"Good. Good. Get out here. The wedding starts soon."

Prado dropped the phone in the toilet. And flushed it.

Wiping away tears. "Can't cry over a female. Gotta keep it Gangsta."

# Golden Masks
## Part I:
### Roll Call

Clad in a black suit with silk black tie and golden gloves, The Facilitator looked himself over in a small compact mirror he'd taken from his mother's purse early this morning. The mustache was gorgeously trimmed. Sliding the mirror into his inner coat pocket he smiled and blew his breath into his hands, sniffing. Smelled well! Movado watch sparkling. He was dripping in diamonds bought with his brother's drug money.

"Hello, how are you?" The Facilitator of the Event asked the beautiful young woman.

*Damn, he's fine!* she thought crazily. *Nice ass, killer chest, black snake skinned shoes and his eyes looked like they changed colors.* "I'm fine, thank you." Her eyes sparkled. She ran her shaking hands over her green velvet dress. Her floral hat was divine and a bit sinister, since an ex-con made it.

He winked lewdly.

"Your name?" he asked, barely above a whisper, trying to be sophisticated.

She licked her lips. "Deep Pussy." *I should have shaved the beaver. Oh, well. Too late now. I really don't give a shit!*

Opening the laptop, he cued up the profile roster. He looked at her gorgeous face and the screen. She matched.

"You may enter."

*It's about time!*

"Thank you."

He said, "Remember, follow the rules."

*Well damn, is this The Matrix?*

"Yes sir," she said, rubbing his dick before she disappeared down the hallway, towards paradise on earth.

I need dick in my life.

Maybe it'll knock this tuberculosis infection right out of my system.

\*\*\*

"How are you?"

The Facilitator looked over the overly handsome tall man with the well-trimmed goatee and thin mustache connecting to a thin beard. Calculating eyes hidden behind rapper Rick Ross-type shades.

"Oh, I'm fine."

*Who are you hiding from?* "And your name?"

*I hope no one catches me here. Gotta keep it gangster.* He thought about it. "Little Dick, Deep Asshole."

*Homosexual on the low. That's why he's hiding. And he's married, nice wedding ring, pimping. I don't understand why men get married just to turn around and cheat on their wives? Anyways. It's not my problem. I am not the one to be worried about what the next man does with his wife. It is not my concern and frankly my dear I don't give a fuck!*

The Facilitator checked his profile. "You may enter. Remember, *follow* the rules."

"I got you, pimp daddy," he said, his voice full of southern twang. His gold teeth shining, he vanished down the hallway, towards the double doors. He told himself he wasn't going to tell anyone he was HIV positive. Why should he? The man who gave it to him *never* warned him, and he felt it was unfair to have ended up this way. He had one goal in mind.

*I'm going to infect as many people as I can and I will never show my face again.*

He vowed it on his soul.


*Well! This woman is what James Brown would call Super Bad. I might how to make this one mine. Damn it looks like she has good pussy!*

"You look *new*," gushed The Facilitator with a huge smile. His eyes sparkling.

"I am." She was elegant in a satin Gucci dress, with long shaved legs. Her earrings shined from the soft lighting, her four inch patent leather stiletto heels gleaming. She licked her lips, tasting her lipstick. Her nipples erect, she stuck out her tits.

"And you are?"

She gushed, "Take It in the Ass Only," covering her mouth like a school girl.

The Facilitator checked her profile. "You may enter."

She gave an attitude of model Naomi Campbell standards. "Thank you." She bit a fingernail coyly. "No one will touch my pussy, *right?*"

He looked around discreetly, coming around the podium. He got on his knees and kissed her pussy. Smelled so fresh. Standing up, she smiled, pinching his cheek. He said, "No one will touch it, but damn I just wanted to kiss it."

She wasn't impressed; in fact she shoulda pissed in his face. She gave an innocent laugh, like the girl next door. "Can I go now?"

"Remember, follow the rules."

"Whatever, man. I don't follow fucking rules."

She smiled, silently farting as she went down the hallway. Too much pasta last night. *Damn, I have to take a shit. Oh, well. Too late for that. They still can't touch my pussy. I mean business, too. Somebody's getting a…shitty dick today! I've always wanted to be a painter. Should I be Picasso? Leonardo Di Vinci? Or Van Gogh? Ok, pussy. I'll be all three. Call me Picasso Leonardo Gogh. Yea. That is perfect.*

*I don't care.*

*That's the way it's got to be*

***

In came Anaconda Snake.

"Man, *you're* Anaconda Snake?" The Facilitator was gawking at the visitor's profile. It was a page long, with his photo and stats.

No Teeth smiled. Fat and handsome. Stinky and had the gall to spray on clouds of Cool Water. Smelled like Hot Shit. "Yes I'm is."

The Facilitator sneered. "Yes I'm is? Man, it's yes I *am! Where* are you from?"

He was scratching his pubic region something terrible, herpes bumps on his top lip. "I'm from Da City."

"You have got to be joking. Da City where?"

"Liberty City!" he snorted. "Where da *Hoes* at?"

The Facilitator said slowly, "In the back."

No Teeth was clapping his hands. "Can I enter?"

The Facilitator said, "Follow the rules."

Wobbling down the hallway, he said, "*Fuck* the rules. Where's da pussy?"

When he got to the double doors The Facilitator picked up his Nextel phone. Chirp, chirp. "Yea, Man?" said the Receiver.

The Facilitator said, smiling, "Send Free Willy home. Make sure he leaves amicably. Send him out the back door. He is *not* the guy on his picture I have in front of me. Rule violation."

He slid the phone in his pocket, listening to some people sing an inspirational song he loved through the other set of double doors. His father was having morning worship. But the Facilitator, the Pastor's son, was having a different kind of worship today.

The kind that celebrated the human flesh and his thirst for lust.

Can the participants handle it?

In came Sloppy Pussy. The Facilitator wanted to fall over and die.

*Who let the dogs out?* "This is crazy," he said, looking over her wrinkled business suit. She weighed 100 pound soak and wet. Looked stale and pale. "Damn, bitch, do you eat? Alley McBeal weigh more than you do. And your hair...shit, *what* hair? Can you say Grace Jones, Conan the Barbarian?"

She was offended but she let it roll off her shoulder. She was used to being dissed. "Don't hate on me."

"Hate on you? Are you serious, sticks and bones?"

She was making noises with her teeth. "I don't *know* about this."

The Facilitator was laughing inside. "Then take your buck toothed ass home."

She looked like a zombie. "Dang, why you gotta be so mean?" Her feelings were deeply hurt.

"Because I think of football every time you smile."

She was confused. "Huh?"

He gave her a content look. "You know." He made a field goal sign with his arms. "It's good!"

She flipped the bird, scratching her pussy something terrible. She looked uncomfortable. "Damn, I can't stop scratching. I knew I should have stuck with Summer's Eve."

He laughed so hard he chocked. She said, "Ah, whatever. Can I enter?"

He leaned into her face. "No."

She was desperate. "Please!"

"Sorry. Your pussy is *too* sloppy. Don't meet the criteria. And you sent the wrong picture over the net. I'm looking at your entry now. This is actually Janet Jackson with short hair with a hat shielding her face. How could I have been so blind? Please leave amicably. I do work for the police department, and I am the sergeant."

She left, pissed and disgruntled.

"I didn't want to come anyway," she said.

In came Married with Children. Her sexy self brought her husband.

The Facilitator asked, "And your name, sir?"

"Suck Some Pussy," he said, evilly eying his wife.

"You and your wife may enter. Remember, follow the rules."

He shook the Facilitator's hand, hugging his wife, going down the hallway. Smiling to himself, not knowing he had syphilis and was HIV positive. After all, he'd been ignoring the signs for three months...

Towards the double doors they headed.

"When we get in there," he was telling his wife, with an attitude. "You don't know me and I *don't* know you. We're happily married, but this is our chance to fuck new people and new faces, then we go back to our boring lives."

She didn't seem interested. *Unhappily married, yes!* "Whatever."

He snapped at her like a fish. "I'm deadly serious!"

She wasn't having it. "Man, *who* are you supposed to be with that trashy dick you got?" she asked, playing his game.

He opened the double doors. "My point exactly."

"Whatever, man."

"Bitch shut up and let's go have some fun."

"My name isn't Samantha Fox. I don't move my body all night long."

"Oh my God I didn't come here to argue!"

"Then why won't you shut the hell up?"

He wanted to slap the shit out of her. "*Because* I have to go home to you and Lord *knows* I wish I could leave your dumb ass in this church."

"The feeling is mutual, Creep!"

"Blah blah blah. To the left, to the left, bitch!"

"That's what my pussy told your little dick! Go to hell!"

*And I'm fucking raw, no condoms...*

The Facilitator smiled when one of the Ushers opened the door to the Main Assembly Hall. He tried to remain inconspicuous. Didn't need anybody finding out his true intention for attending services today. Church was in progress, you could hear the singing bursting into his ears.

"Brother, we kinda hear you in here."

The Facilitator said, "No problem, I got you."

"Thanks, brothah," he said with a wink.

"I'll keep the tone down. You just go back in there and do your thing."

The Facilitator slipped a hundred dollar bill in the Usher's pocket.

"I got you. Save some of that pussy for me."

And the doors closed.

***

In came Flawless Fancy.

"You're so fine," The Facilitator said, blushing, "that I'm not checking your profile." He kept his voice low.

Her slender fingers carefully dancing across each glowing pearl around her slender, swan-like neck. "I'm a transvestite." She was on a natural high from taking her hormone shot (two doses over the regular limit).

He did a double take. "Looking like *that?*"

"*Yes*, honey. They call me Flawless Fancy!"

"Well gone, with your bad self. Goddamn, you look just like a bitch. You may enter."

He/she grinned with perfect white teeth, all transplanted, of course. "Thanks."

The Facilitator asked, "You g'on let me fuck?"

Flawless Fancy beamed, tossing his/her hair behind his/her head. "Are you gonna break me off some loot? Sucking dick is a business. I can write that shit in as charitable donation on my taxes."

"You give it to me like you're a woman, moan like a woman and make me *think* you're a woman I will give you what you need."

"I'll stick to what I want. I'm not cheap. Can I go now?"

"Why are you in such a rush?" He looked around discreetly. "Let's go in the back closet. Give a niggah some quick head. If you're so good, how long will it take for you to make this dick spit? You already look like a bitch and talk like a bitch…"

"You're cute. But I don't have time to mess with the hired help…"

*Go to hell, whore!* "*Hired help?* I am the organizer of this event. Don't get testy with me, all right?"

"Call me Miss Ross." Flawless Fancy faked a yawn, smacking his/her lips.

"Remember, follow the rules," The Facilitator said.

"…As long as they follow me!"

And Flawless Fancy was off to see the Wizard behind the double doors.

***

I was 5 feet 4 inches with a Lil' Kim-type body without the plastic surgery. Men always said that I looked like Toni Braxton but sexier. I knew that already. *Duh!* I was too pretty for my own good.

Keeping well onto my secret, one I couldn't bring myself to think about, I walked up the long concrete walk-way towards the filled-to-capacity church on a very glorious Sunday. Palm and oak trees were all around me and the enormous old building. The sun was hot, the air was crisp and I smelled the scent of rain and well-cut grass. The sky was cloudy, some black clouds on the horizon.

I was tired from club hopping all night Saturday and didn't get home to my house from South Beach, until about 5 a.m. in the morning. I got some sleep, but I had to get up at ten a.m. to come to Sunday School. I couldn't miss it.

I grew up in church, like the average American child from the ghetto, but as of late church was really not for me but I went to look cute and to look at the fine men who were playing possum in their marriages. Silly wives. How can bitches be so goddamn dumb, stupid and blind? Your husband was fine as shit best believe Melissa tasted her clit from his lips, fingers and scrumptious dick.

My parents used to own a church, both serving as Pastors. They were very respectful and respected. That was until I did something naughty and it crashed the church to hell. Someone caught me playing with my pussy in the Pastor's Chambers and the rumor mill crushed my parents' organization to shreds. I gave up on praising God for the next few years. I didn't want to have anything to do with Holy stuff. But something in me wouldn't let me give up. Maybe it was the faith of a mustard seed that never grew past a tree.

I told them freaks were in the church. Hello, world. I'm Freaky Deaky. There was a Bible verse I always read when it came to whores in white and virgins in black having communion amongst each other. **Isaiah 23:** *Talks about how God shut the gates of the port city Tyre for 70 years because of its "whoredoms". It also stated that after 70 years had passed Tyre would return to its old ways but this time the profit from all the bad behavior would go straight to the people of God for "good food and fine clothing"!*

Now, in the five years I have been going to *this* church I never came to Sunday School. Never! I didn't have the desire to attend them like I used to when I was a promising, easily impressionable teenager. Why would I want to study with a bunch of people I saw in the neighborhood? Just didn't thrill me. I did come to the Main Service. And I never returned for the Evening Service at 6 P.M. That was just too much goddamn church for me. I really didn't care for fellowship at the present time. I had my reasons. And I wouldn't change my mind. When I first started going here, I was 18 years old. I was young, dumb and full of cum. I knew these horny Niggah loved fresh pussy. I came to find some moneyed grown men to take home.

I searched for dick like free money back then. I was not going to lie. But the Word of God hit me and I changed my mind. I actually got saved and tried to do the right thing. Prior to attending this church I had gone to one in Carol City. I was around, say, 13 years old. I attended bible study, which took place after Sunday School. Mama didn't really force me to go. She kinda did her own thing, celebrated God in her own way. After she lost her church she had a new attitude, and it wasn't pretty. She still blamed me instead of blaming herself. As much as she masturbated when she thought I was asleep what made her think I wouldn't twitch the ole clitoris after hearing her say, "This feels so good, oh my God!" I got tired of smelling her pussy through the AC vents every night when Daddy was at work.

She hardly ever talked to me; she was too busy doing her thing with my Daddy. They had their own lives. I had mine. Oh, well. Case closed. Moving on. Next. So I never bothered her. She basically let me come and go as I pleased.

I fellowshipped with certain members from this church. I went out of town with my peers from my study groups to Orlando and Atlanta for Bible Bowls, which we always won. I must say I had a good time.

But if men had come at me before I got saved they really hounded me once I was dipped in that cold water. I nearly had a damn seizure. Despite that, I tried to put my heart into it. I truly did. But when I seen how faulty the organization actually was, men screwing the sisters and the preacher secretly taking dick up the ass, I fell out of love for it and basically did what everyone else did: never took it seriously. I never screwed anyone from this church as of yet.

But today was going to be a little different.

## £@®®¥

Inside the double doors of the Main assembly, Pastor Troy Darling delivered a powerful sermon. One of the Ushers, Ronald, pulled the hundred dollar bill The Facilitator gave him from his pocket and put it in the collection plate before it was to be sent to the other members. He smiled to himself. He had a pocket full of cash and he never dipped into his *own* funds to give to the Lord. Everything he has ever given came from the whores at the strip clubs. And he wondered why God blessed the strippers with nice cars and houses and he still lived in his mother's basement, had to pay child support for five kids (which weren't his, but his so-called Baby Mothers wouldn't tell him that because of their love of the cash) and was in early stages of colon cancer and didn't have the slightest clue. Ronald eyed Pastor Troy Darling, who had charm and was poised to lead the organization into the rest of the year with style and decorum. He was clad in a purple suit and suede shoes. People loved him instantly. He had the type of voice one instantly identified with.

"God is the rock. He is the way." Sweat poured down his face. He used a wet handkerchief to wipe himself. His wife, Sister Darling (with her nosey ass), sat behind him on a high backed chair, fanning herself, sipping water. Her keen eyes surveyed the church, secretly laughing at the few women who dressed like a hot mess, yet she forgot about the huge hole in the back of her panties.

Pastor Darling saw a man he wanted to fuck, over by the back door. He tried to ignore the urge in his nuts, but his dick was hard and he shook the thoughts away. Rumor has it that ole boy had the best piece of ass in the church. Half the married men fucked him and threatened to kill his family if he ever talked. He might as well get him a piece of ass because he wasn't touching his wife with a ten foot pole.

"My son, who could *not* make it today, is the rock in his girlfriend's life. He understands that you can't have sex until marriage. He understands that his girl *has* to be in the *Word.* The Word being the Word of God! He doesn't participate in the game of sinful flesh. He doesn't lock himself in a room and masturbate. No sir! He studies the *Word* of God!"

All sorts of hats bobbed in the sea of people, women dressed nicely and young and old men looking good. Sister Darling was pleased.

"Without God there is no rock. No life. No air to breathe. You see, many people sin but those very same people don't repent."

*"Speak Pastor!"*

*"Hallelujah!"*

A few dedicated church members jumped off the pews and begin to clap, cry out to God and chant. They publicly disclosed their embarrassing sins before the organization, asking for prayers and for help. A big two hundred forty pound woman dressed like Halle Berry was clapping and tossing off her pumps, making an unnecessary scene because nobody paid her ass any attention. She was shaking her hands in the air and her eyes on "…De Lawd!"

Pastor Troy Darling noticed some familiar faces; faces that never missed a Sunday were missing from church today. He began to worry. He made a mental note to call the missing members and see why they missed church. Attendance played a big part in the growth of God's

Word. And that was $300 he couldn't get today. Pastor Troy Darling snapped at the Ushers. That meant a very important part of service was about to ensue. Three handsome young men, who dressed for success instead of dressing for God, moved in front of the door so no one could get in or get out.

"Many people convince themselves they are the rock in their spouse's and sibling's lives. But they are mere pebbles I used to thumb into the lake behind Morning Star, when I used to belong to that church, right here in Goulds!"

Hand claps. Songs of praise rose from the sweaty lips of God's people, or so they convinced themselves.

Pastor Troy did his little dance across the stage, about to lead the church into communion. His mind was on how much money he was getting out of their dumb asses today.

He saw a pretty suit he wanted to buy at the Dadeland Mall last week. He also wanted to put a down payment on a new Cadillac because the old one, he had for three months, a gift from church members, he decided he didn't want anymore.

He also had picture-less profiles up on various gay websites, anonymously meeting men, having his way with them behind his wife's back.

Then he justified it by frequently coming to church on certain chosen Sundays bashing homosexuality and anybody participating in it.

He couldn't get on his knees and ask for forgiveness, but he can get on his knees and suck dick to his heart's content.

"Homosexuals will not go to heaven by the way of Jesus Christ! They WILL BURN IN HELL! They will not see the kingdom! They will not be shown the way!"

And his organization praised his antics. So many people jumped off the pews that it was ridiculous. The Down Low brothers were clapping and stomping their feet, eyeing the out-of-the-closet punks evilly, daring them to have a slip of the tongue.

*Yes, you dummies! Listen to me,* he thought. *I'm bisexual myself. I don't believe half the shit I'm saying! Maybe it's time to get some more money out of you dummies! Get you to scribble in those check books and toss that cash! I should buy a debit machine so you can swipe your credit cards! That doesn't sound like such a bad idea! After all tricking you dummies is a business.*

His heart was black. It was not pure. He didn't know his son, calling himself The Facilitator, was hosting an Orgy in the back of the church.

# Part II

My gut told me church today was going to be an event. And if I could be real with myself I'd admit I barely got up out of bed this morning. I had to force myself to get up. When my alarm clock sounded I wanted to hammer the bitch quiet. But I couldn't find my hammer. I did find my huge dildo and I threw it at the clock. It fell off the dresser and it came unplugged. I savored the sudden silence. But then my pussy came alive at the thought of the dildo, sitting on the floor. Feeling all alone and deserted. So I got up, picked it up and worked my pussy until I felt my vaginal walls creaming all over the crummy bastard.

My body felt like it was beat up. My head pounded excruciatingly. I hope it wasn't because of my medical condition. A secret I was keeping to myself. I tried to cook some breakfast, shaking my ass in the wee hours of the morning to some Sly and the Family Stone (Thank you for lettin' me be mahself, bitches!) but when the eggs and grits were done I felt nauseated. The thought of eating made me want to puke. I had to hold my stomach and settle down on the floor in the corner of the kitchen. My face in my hands I started to sob. I couldn't breathe because I never thought of death or thought about dying until my doctor gave me the worse news of my life. I never thought the day would come. I was like most people. Thinking I was going to live forever, that getting old was for other people and that I was invincible. But God was showing my ass full throttle.

Imposing death was really getting to me. My life had actually subsided to this. My life flashing before my eyes a hundred times a day. I needed to clean my apartment; I never let it get messy. But I had a busy week. I worked for the Precision Response Corporation (PRC); located down the street from the Cutler Ride Mall. Gay Central I called it. If the men weren't gay they were on the DownLo. Secretly tapping booty hole when they had girlfriends or wives. Men were a trip sometimes.

*I got to stop clubbing on Saturday nights and trying to get my ass to church on Sundays!* I had shaken my ass for hours at Club Metropolis. I sucked some dick in the bathroom. I forget his name. But I knew the name of his dick. It was "Penis," and it had two cousins that hung out with him all the time, named "Testi" and "Cles." Pronounce it testicles. I charged him three hundred dollars for my services, since he was a so-called big baller and shot caller. He gave it to me with a grin. Then around 4:40 a.m., on my way home, I met another Niggah. He was short, fine, had a Caesar cut and was slightly bowlegged. We made small talk. He offered to pay me for some pussy and he ate me out in my Honda Accord right on Ocean Drive. I bust three nuts on the jerk's tongue and I promised to take him back to his hotel room, since he was visiting from Birmingham, Alabama and he'd never been down south. I tried to tell him that Miami Bitches didn't play the bushes. Trina and Jackie-O weren't the Baddest Bitches in the South. While the world, Hollywood and the hip-hop community in a whole lusted after South Beach and the Hoes it catered to, they didn't know about the true Down South Bitches. Bitches that put it down. I was talking about the Perrine Bitches. The Goulds Bitches. I represented Goulds to the tee. The Princeton Bitches. The Naranja Bitches. The Homestead and Florida City Bitches! The Liberty City and Carol City Bitches!

My new fellah had drive and charisma and he loved talking about my wet napkin between my legs. I charged him two hundred dollars for my conversation and for licking my pussy into remission and boy could eat some twat. I actually dug in my purse and opened the Crystal Louisiana hot sauce, coated my clit with it and told him to pretend its catfish and use that dick to spread the tartar sauce. That shit tingled, but it made me nut. He didn't see me sliding his green-paper-and-credit-card filled wallet from his deep pants pocket. Hell, how could he know?

Once I put my visors up he leaned the driver's seat all the way back, putting the steering wheel up as far as it'd go. He had my face down on the car floor and my pussy in his face. He paid me up front, which was all gravy because it kept his mind off his wallet. I slipped it into my bra. I had huge titties so he wouldn't notice a thing. Us Goulds Bitches would get you if you got caught slipping.

After an eternity, the windows fogged up and the humidity grew to startling intensities. I expertly pulled myself up and slurped on his scrumptious dick while he tongued my pussy. I got a head rush, all the blood rushing to my brain, mixed with the pleasure of a very wet, slick, skilled tongue gave me an adrenaline rush out of this world! The 69! In the car! My skirt up and around my hips, I felt my thighs trembling. Gripping either ass cheek, he tongue fucked me so fast and hard I was popping my pussy on his tongue with fierce abandon. He sucked my asshole and ran his tongue back to my wonderful opening. I shivered.

I felt the Honda rocking, I didn't give a shit. Why pay close to a hundred or more bucks getting a hotel room on the beach when I could fuck in my car for free? He pumped my hot mouth until he came down my throat. I swallowed his hot load. He seemed to come forever. It was thick and sweet. I didn't think about HIV/AIDS, didn't look like he had nothing. He was too damn fine, plus he was married. That shit had to mean something, shit! I felt his huge dick throbbing in my mouth and it made me wetter and I felt myself letting go as I fell over the mountain, plummeting towards the earth with no parachute…my walls pulsating on his tongue, which was deeply embedded in me. I exploded. I had to suck on his nuts to keep from screaming. He twirled those hips, grinding on my car seat. He smelled so good downstairs.

Once it was over I felt drained. It took great effort for me to fix my clothes and sit up on the passenger seat. He pulled up his pants, not all the way, and let the dick sit there, looking all good. I couldn't resist. I grabbed it and stroked it softly. He looked at me, smiling. He was boyishly handsome.

I had said, "Baby, see Wet Willy's over there, do you mind buying me a drink and then I can take you home to my world and fuck you to sleep, show you what them Birmingham Hoes don't have? I'll drive you to the airport."

He had tried to kiss me. I wasn't having it. His hazel eyes shined bright under all the South Beach lights. "I'll be right back, Shawty," he said, hoping out my car, and pulling up his FUBU jeans in public. Who the fuck wore FUBU. Wasn't that shit played out? And look at that dick! And his wedding ring shined brilliantly. I didn't care. He wasn't my man. Hell he could go back home to his wife in Alabama when it was all over. I just wanted some fast cash!

Sexy man he was. Would he understand what I was about to do? When he crossed the street, running in front of luxury cars like he'd lost his mind, I turned on my engine, rolled down my driver side window for some much-needed air, asked the Niggah in the Cadillac Escalade could I cut in front of him and he and his boys whistled at me when he allowed me to do so. I zoomed up to my victim, blew the horn and said, "You got enough cash?" Damn, he didn't look as good as he did in the car. Something was off. His head was too big and he had buck teeth, oh my God!

I smiled sweetly. Men were on my jock, elbowing each other, nodding in my direction. He checked for his wallet. "Where's my…"

I dangled it in his face. "Have a safe flight back to Alabama. Oh, I got your wife's number in my cell phone, you call the police I call your bitch! You've been punked!"

And I drove off, speeding up Ocean Drive, turning onto 5th Street, heading for the Macarthur Causeway, going home to count this loot.

I shook the memories away as I stared at the huge white and beige church. I earned close to three grand last night. When I got home I ordered four thousand dollars worth of clothes from Prada, Gucci and Sean John, entered his credit card information and had the items shipped to an abandoned address up in the City, next door to my girl Stacey, who I called and put on alert.

"Girl, I got you, can you order me those Beyonce shoes."

I was alarmed. "Beyonce got shoes?" *Gots to get me a pair.*

"That's what I heard, girl. And I want that dress she flaunting in the Deja Vu Video."

I was laughing. "I got you, girl. And that's a corny ass video. Looks like outtakes from the Baby Boy video."

"I love it. But we're all waiting for Miss Jackson's Call on Me video with sexy-ass Nelly. They showed a V.I.P. Peek on BET tonight, girl, she is *hot hot hot* with that Massai Tribe outfit and the Mohawk. I got the Mohawk!"

"No you don't, girl! You got the Mohawk already? I might get it, too! It'll go good with my snap-and-you'll-miss-it skirt and my rhinestone pumps, Chile!"

"Shit, order me some Apple Bottom pants while I'm thinking about it. Did you do one day delivery?"

I snapped my fingers. "You damn right!"

"Girl, *you're* so crazy."

I hung up the phone. Now I could pay my rent and car note and buy some feminine products because I was on my period when homeboy ate me out in my car. I wondered when he was going to realize my blood was all over the lower part of his face when he went to Wet Willy's to get me that drink. I wasn't going to say anything. And he actually wondered why I didn't kiss him.

Chile, please. I was a freak. But not that freaky!

"Time for Sunday School," I said, trying my best to forget last night. I had a feeling this would be one Sunday…School I'd never forget.

"Ain't that right," I whispered to my coochie before I had entered the double glass doors. I had feelings of unease. When I entered the building, the strong smell of Pine-Sol and Comet knocked me speechless. "Well, somebody over did it with the cleaning." I had a very messed-up look on my lightly made-up face. A little lip gloss made my dick-sucking lips fuller. Breath mints I sucked on, because I had forgotten to brush my teeth and I still had nut on my breath. It didn't smell bad.

I had perfect teeth and no damn gingivitis. So that was a good thing.

"Why look at you. Tell a Niggah what's good with you, sexy red."

"Brother Lloyd Troy. Nice to see you. I guess you're the emcee today."

Brother Lloyd Troy, The Facilitator, said, "Time for Roll Call."

Popping my minty fresh gum, I paused in front of the podium out in the empty Main Lobby. A few pictures of the Whorish pastor were on the wall. I was chuckling to myself. Rumor has it that he was into men. Whatever floats your boat, Jack, was what I said. Over on the huge billboard were about thirty 3x5 color photos of the Church Trip to Atlanta a few months ago. Yea I went. And I popped my pussy up there, too. Hey. You know how I do! But I wound up with a yeast infection and I raised hell on that fuck Niggah.

"It's always a pleasure to see you. You're looking rather, tempting."

"I could say the same thing about you. I love the suit. What do you have on underneath?"

"I'm free balling, you know that. You know it's about to go down."

I was shaking my head. "All right Young Joc. You know you're only twenty-one, you don't know shit about going down now *do* you?"

"Aw, the assumptions begin. And don't say my age too loud. I told some off-brand bitch I was the police sergeant when I'm not even a cop! You know how we do! Aren't we being a bit presumptuous, Sister Jackson?"

"I don't think so."

"Careful, we can't get freaky in the Main Lobby."

My eyes sparkled. "Oh, yea. Forgot about that. I got four glasses of Remy tearing me up, I'm horny as hell, my nipples are hard, my pussy is wet and I'm ready to pop, pop, pop, get it, get it, so what's up, where do I go?"

He scratched the side of his mouth. "Down the hallway, the double doors past the Preacher's chambers. You're the last arrival. But don't be too loud out here. They're having communion inside."

"Chile. Don't nobody care about no communion."

"Well, apparently they do."

"They also care to fuck each other and talk about others. I don't even know why I joined this church. Ain't your daddy a faggot?"

He grinned. "Hey, that's his business."

"I guess so. And the more he gets on his platform and bash gays for no reason, the more he's pulling himself into question."

"Girl, whatever."

"And I don't care about fake bread and that stale tasting wine. Plus your Daddy is a Ho. He has your Mama fooled."

"That's his problem. The man taught me everything I know."

Dressed to kill in my best Sunday outfit I started down the hallway. Until his voice stopped me. "Whoa! Wait, hold up. Come back here Sister Jackson. I don't see your name on the list."

*I wonder why?* Disgruntled, I went back over to Brother Lloyd, who looked me up and down. He was definitely the Preacher's son, the one holding the Special Event in the church. I heard Hallelujah's and Amen's bursting from the closed doors to the main assembly. They didn't have a clue what was about to go down in the back of the church.

Mama always said the biggest freaks were in the church. And the Special Invite Only event proved it.

I pointed to my name on the list, which he kept carefully hidden under the Church List. Damn. Sixty people were in attendance in the Special Sex Session Area. I should know. He checked me off, and the number 60 was next to my name.

"Freaky Bitch is the name you chose?"

I eyed him, licking my sexy lips. "Yes, Mr. Facilitator. That would be *me*. And I guess you're Mister King Kong Dick of the South. You better be packing the beef with the name you gave yourself."

"I am. Trust me. You'll see soon. Go ahead. Proceed. Remember, follow the rules. And once the party gets started, I'll give you what you need."

He picked up the lists. He put the Main Assembly list in the drop box. And stuffed the sex list under his arm. Turning off his lap top, he locked it under the podium, stuffing the key in his suit jacket.

I walked past him, twisting my romp. My hand in mid air, my floral hat was angled on my head, my sexy dress classy and black.

"And I'm sure you will."

My heels clickety-clacked down the hallway with sounding echoes. Towards the double doors.

To do what I need to do then take my sleepy ass home to my own bed. I smiled when I heard all types of moaning float into my ears.

I smelled sex in the air.

# BEHIND THE DOUBLE DOORS

Candles of all sizes were strategically placed everywhere. Oriental carpeting held the finality of spent bodies dying for pleasure. Hanging oil paintings of yesterday's rulers looked down on the orgy. Ferdinand the Great watched as two men were fucked by women wearing strap on dildos. Elizabeth frowned down on a woman spreading a male's booty cheeks and tasting the chocolate syrup from his pulsating hole. Chaka Zulu smiled down on a sexy black/Caucasian male who pulled out of another male's ass and came in the mouth of a burgeoning whore with sagging tits and a God-awful overbite. She would *never* tell anyone she had Herpes. Fruit was used inside the pussy of another eager whore who had lice in her hair. Lust rampaged from sweaty bodies like skis on slopes. Human beings so lost within their desire to feed the flesh have rendered them speechless. They dance together in unison, golden mask to golden mask to golden mask to golden mask. Tongues tasted lips, ass and pussy. Dicks whipped orifices to brand new heights. No one wore protection. The four room moderators, walking around looking like minions, used rawhides and whacked sweaty ass cheeks like they were slaves. Candle wax was poured all over sweaty backs. The sensual smell mixed with the power of the air conditioner set them ablaze. A few married women *never* thought of their husbands. A few married men never thought of their wives. Straight men released their inhibitions and did every homosexual thought that came to mind. After all, this orgy only took place once a year.

## Part III:

"Take off your clothes and your hat and put it in the cubby hole by the restroom."

Candles were lit everywhere. I could faintly hear the morning worship from the other side of the wall, which only made me feel more adventurous. This was a small, cool room. Very intimate. The Transition Center. Reluctantly, I took off my clothes. Eyeing him weirdly. "Panties and bra too," the man said demandingly, clad in a black robe and gold mask on his face. Very crafty golden mask. I like,

I like! I did what he said. His gorgeous hazel eyes glittered seductively, his full lips luscious and tempting. He had big hands and big fingers. Oh, yea! I loved them big. There was another set of double doors ten feet before me. He helped clothe you before you entered paradise.

I heard people being fucked from the other side, a cacophony of moaning and obscenities and dicks loosening pussy and ass. To my complete surprise, I heard a whip cracking down on flesh. Crack. Crack. Crack. Yes! I could hardly stand it!

I had to open the double doors and look inside. Walking past Your Royal Dickness, I opened the doors and my mouth fell open. A pleasurable, strawberry smell over came my nose and cool, moist air hit me in the face. The Garden of Pussy. The Lake of Titties. The Ocean of Dicks. Wow. I saw four tall, life-sized black men walking through the orgy like Gods with whips and Golden Masks on their faces. They had huge afros. So 1970's. Their dicks swung gregariously. My pussy was so wet it felt like someone turned a faucet on in my clit.

They monitored activity. The different sized candles. The men who were having their way with other men. I saw a woman fucking a man with a strap-on dildo. The hanging oil paintings were divine. Elizabeth! Ferdinand! Was that Chaka Zulu? Oh my! I wanted to go inside. But Your Royal Dickness took me by the arm and pulled me back. One of the Room Monitors saw me. He smiled, adjusted his mask, and whipped some booty cheeks as he stepped over them and headed my way. He raised a finger. Come here, bitch. Your Royal Dickness closed the door just as he was reaching for me. I was holding my breath, face to face with the door.

Oh, shit. *Spank my ass with that whip Daddy!* Crack. Crack. *Yes, do it again.* Crack. *AGAIN!* Crack. *Spank my titties with the whip!* Crack! *I'm Harriet Tubman! I tried to escape slavery and hid in a pig pen!* Crack! *I tried to taste a sugar lump from the sugar bowl!*

Crack, crack, crack! "You can't break the rules and go in there without a mask on. I should send you home."

"I just had to see."

"You can't let anyone see your face. The Golden Mask protects you. No one is to know your identity, but me and the Facilitator."

I turned to face him. He was in my face. It turned me on big time. He said, "Put on this black robe."

Unhesitant, I put it on. He gave me the once over. The walls in my pussy jumped. "And your name is?" He talked like Barry White.

I could barely breathe. "Freaky Deaky Bitch."

He narrowed his eyes. "And the code?"

"To be dicked down froggy style."

"Open Says Me." He said with a smile, perfect white teeth.

"Why thank you, Big Daddy Good Dick."

"You're granted the Golden Mask." He went on. "Faces and names will remain anonymous. What adheres in this place will remain a mystery. You will not speak of the events in here outside these doors. The lives you will destroy are unconscionable."

"Yes, Sir!" I saluted him. Sucking my teeth.

He wasn't fazed. "What is your real name?" he asked.

He's breaking his own damn rules. "Doesn't matter, now does it?" I asked annoyingly and he got the point. Feeling ill at ease, I put on the Golden Mask. I had my hair in a tight Chinese bun. I had snap-and-you'll-miss it length hair anyways. I normally wore a wig. I had on a Shirley Temple wig last night. I felt freaky. I was about to fuck in church. I knew this was wrong, but half the church were having sex with each other so why not?

I lived once. So I was going to enjoy my life.

After all, I was dying of cancer! I had to undergo Chemo in a few weeks, so I might as well die in style because I was *refusing* to take it. I hated doctors! I never told my mother and I didn't tell a soul. When I found out three months ago I had cancer its like I ceased to stop living. I recreated in my mind everything I'd done wrong and then realized God was about to bring me home, to judge me. I was going to hell anyways so why not speed up the process. I was going to burn in hell for eternity. So I might as well start dancing in the flames with this secret orgy.

The both of us stared at the doors in pure shock when some man yelled, "Bitch! You got shit all over my dick!"

"So *what*. You aren't *touching* my pussy!" a lady screamed at the top of her lungs.

"You coulda cleaned your *booty*! I should fuck you up!"

"Shut up!" she stammered miserably. "Let's just say you get your dinner early. Lasagna and shrimp pasta with a side of brown rice!"

We couldn't help but laugh, this was too funny.

Mr. Golden Mask kissed my cheek. "Proceed past the other set of double doors. Remember the rules. What goes on in here stays in here."

*What is this, elementary school? I'm grown! I know the rules!* "I got you."

"Marriages could be destroyed."

*Ok, damn it you're pissing me off!* "I got you, pimp."

Before I could turn around he pulled me into his manly embrace and took my pussy into his hand like a baby bird with broken wings. I loved direct men, men who took charge of a woman and made her swing to his rhythm. He expertly and eloquently stuck his fingers inside me and kissed me passionately, his expert tongue darting with mine, secretly fencing. Golden Mask to Golden Mask. Repetitiously bumping his hand against my pelvis, I twirled myself on him with urgency. My breath caught in my throat. The pleasure was immeasurable.

I lifted his mask and saw Lloyd's brother, Mack. He was twenty-eight, three kids, faithful Proverbs wife at home who tended to his every need. I tongued him, getting lost on his sexy lips, letting him taste the fruit of my labor. He swapped another man's cum from behind my top teeth. I would never tell him. Men got over on women all the time. Hmm, I get the last laugh!

I wondered how good he ate pussy. Just because he kissed good didn't mean he ate good pussy and just because you ate good pussy didn't mean you could fuck. I found that out the hard way.

I broke free, sank to my knees and took his eight inches into my hot mouth; I held his hips as his passion searched the confines of my mouth for my tonsils. I deep throated him, even though he didn't have *much* to suck on. But it was thick and full and it turned me on. I played with his nuts, fingering his anus, pulling him out of my mouth and sucking his hole off my fingers. Smelled good. The man was clean inside and out; I liked that. He smelled like Cool Water cologne down here in Australia. Turned me on some more, women loved handsome men who smelled good. With a sense of ease, he tenderly grabbed my head and banged my mouth so hard and fast.

"...*This feels good...!*" He thrust himself inside me. I loved every single minute. Such the horny woman I was, I played with myself and fingered him at the same time and he said, "I gotta piss," and he pissed right down my throat. Reluctantly, I swallowed every drop. I had never done this and I was glad he didn't have a huge load. I felt hornier, knowing I did something I never thought I'd do. It wasn't half bad, but I wouldn't be doing that again.

Before I could take him out of my mouth Lloyd appeared behind me, getting on his knees after placing on the mask, and he dug his tongue in my womanhood from behind, spreading my cheeks, spitting on my hole and finger banging me while his tongue searched for Pearl Harbor. I was in ecstasy. Horniness burning Mack senseless, he continued pumping himself in my mouth, pressing both my fingers deep in his ass. Humping my fingers, he held my head, tears racing from under the mask. "Goddamn, Ma! I never did this before. It feels good, Ma! Don't stop, put those fingers deeper, deeper, oh shit, Ma!"

Someone took my hand out of his hole and when I saw the robed figure get behind Mack and immediately slid his nine inch condom-clad stick deep inside of him I was breathless. Mack, a look of shock on his face, tried to break free. But the robed figure held him tightly. He grinded into him. Fucking him fast and hard and Mack finally broke down and Lloyd entered me, banging me in the doggy-style and I was floating…approaching the mountain, about to fall over. I *knew* how to make myself come; it was a skill of mine.

I would never forget any of this; I would always remember this, my first orgy. I never had sex for free, but this sexual experience was unlike anything I ever felt. Mack pumped my mouth as the stranger tapped him from the back. His body on the verge of breaking down on this new found pleasure, he looked up at the ceiling, his legs trembling. "Yea, baby! Yea…take it from me…*daaamnnn*…I have never done this before! This feels good…."

He knew he had good dick. "You like it, Dawg?"

Mack was in la-la land. "I love it, baby!"

He pounded Mack harder. The pleasure was too much for him. He moaned so loud and begged so much he forgot his own name. He reached behind him and gripped homebody's amazing ass, pulling the dick deeper into him. His knees were drums. I reached up and undid homeboy's robe and it opened, revealing a killer body, magnificent muscles. He had tattoos all over his stomach. *Thug Life. Mama's Enemy. Daddy's Mistake.* And *305* on his upper chest. He had huge, erect nipples. I was about to shake out the room. I wanted him!

His voice was deep, sexy and full of baritone. "Now do you love it? You wanted this shit, didn't you? Prancing around church for years like a little bitch and nobody tapped this! Now I'm claiming it and I'm tapping this shit. You hear me?"

He was about to quiver out of his skin. "Yes!"

I crawled behind him; Lloyd still deep inside me, following me like two dogs stuck together, and I ate out the stranger, sucking his nuts from the back while he tagged Mack.

"Damn, Ma!" he said. "Damn, lick me all over, Baby… You freaky like that?"

"Hell yeah," I said, Lloyd hitting my G-spot and I almost had heart failure. There was so much candy in the room I didn't know what flavor to taste next.

I threw the pussy back on the dick for dear life.

"Did you know your Mama is being screwed by three men behind those double doors?" the Stranger told Mack.

Mack didn't care. "No, man!"

A toothy grin. "She's 50 but she still got that fire, like her son! She always talking about somebody in church, telling people she don't do any wrong but where is she right now?"

Ecstasy had him trapped like a confined maniac.

"It feels so good! I don't want to talk about my Mama!"

"Lloyd, your brother is inside being smashed by all kind of men?"

Lloyd was lost in my pussy. "Is that right...?" He was panting, trying to catch his breath, the pleasure breaking his body down. Lloyd looked pleased. "...I know you getting this ass next."

"You know it, Niggah!"

"I want it *now*!"

*"You get it when I say you get it."*

"I want it now!" he begged like a bitch.

*"What* did I say?"

"I need it, Daddy!"

"I'm *not* your Daddy!"

*"Please!"*

"BEG FOR THE DICK!"

"Please, give it to me. Now! I need it, I want it. I want it all day and all night! Don't make me take that dick! You know I crave it daily and nightly. When I'm at work I crave it!"

"CONVINCE ME!"

"I don't know how to, Daddy!"

"Then you don't want this dick."

I wished I had a camera. This type of shit you documented and sent to HBO. This was crazy! I never knew anything like this ever existed in this world. It seemed so la la land. So contrived. So make believe. This was something out of a fantasy. And I couldn't believe I was a part of it.

I didn't want this day to end. I wished it could last forever...

# ~~Part IV~~

Lloyd was in paradise, not showing any signs of leaving my pussy alone.

"I got you, gangster," he told Mack's Golden Mask Partner.

"I'm the boss! You hear me? I run it how I see fit. I got the best dong in the building..." He looked at his partner. "Who it belongs to?"

Mack was gone. No inhibitions. *"It's yours!"*

"Hold that booty open. Jasmine, go put his dick back in your mouth, let me see that shit."

Obviously he was in control. I did what he said, even though my name wasn't Jasmine. Where did he get that name from? Lloyd seemed a little exhausted. I didn't care. I took Mack back into my mouth. He was a little limp, but in no time I got him up again. He held my head.

"Did I tell you to let that booty hole go, bitch?"

Mack let go my head quickly and spread himself back open.

"...And you better not let your dick fall out home girl's mouth!"

"You like that, Daddy?" Mack asked seductively.

"Oooh, shit! That's what I'm talking about! You got some good ass!"

"Hell yea, Daddy!"

"Where you want this nut?"

"In Jasmine's mouth!"

Lloyd staying deep inside me, the robed man pulled out of Mack's rear, moaning loudly, snatched off the condom and pulled me to his dick, coming in my mouth. I played with it, put Mack's dick back in my mouth and gave him head with another man's nut. And when Mack finally bust, the robed man fingered Mack's hole fast and hard as he pumped juices into my mouth.

Like a wild beast, Lloyd was thrusting deeper into me, reaching his orgasm, and when he bust, the Trojan condom catching the pleasurable seeds, he lay on the floor, rob open, his sexy, 6 pack abs body glistening from the glow of the candle light.

He was short of breath. I was short of breath, still transfixed on what actually had happened. Hell, I didn't even make it past the other set of double doors and I had no need to. I'd been fulfilled right here where I was.

I heard moaning and cursing and pussy being smashed and dicks being pulled on and slurped and I stood up, spit the nut on the floor, grabbed my clothes and disappeared into the bathroom.

Turning on the water I washed my face, gargled with the Listerine by the toilet, enjoying the burning sensations. I rinsed again, put on my clothes, tilted my hat on my head, checked myself in the mirror and smiled. I ran my tongue across my teeth.

When I left the bathroom Lloyd grabbed my arm. He wanted some more. I'd had enough. My pussy was through dealing for right now.

"No, Sir," I said, snatching back my arm. "You know the rules. What happens here stays here behind these doors."

"Damn, Freaky Bitch."

I waved a finger at him, kissing his cheek. "It's Sister Jackson. Freaky Bitch I left in the bathroom."

"Damn, Ma!"

"Your Mama is on the other side of those wooden doors, having the time of her life. Seems to me your daddy *isn't* doing his job."

"My daddy hasn't touched her in months."

"She wants that young Thug Dick."

"And she's getting it."

"I'm out this bitch. Peace."

Smiling victoriously, I opened the door, didn't look back and gripped the gold mask in my hand, as a souvenir.

I sashayed up the long hall way, my high heels clickety-clacked against the fake marble. I put my hand on my hip and gripped my purse and the mask. I quietly entered the Main Assembly, grabbing a Song Book. I sat in the back and prepared for church services, my heart pounding.

I felt bad. Really bad. I searched the ceiling for God to strike me dead with lightning. I sat down next to a man I'd never seen before, closed my eyes, put the mask in my purse and clapped my hands when Pastor Troy Darling got behind the podium. I'd just missed communion. I wasn't going to eat the bread and drink the fake wine anyways.

"Come with that power now, Reverend!" I screamed out, tears falling down my face, feeling ashamed for what I just did, the way the power of my flesh took over me. I was no better than the whorish Pastor, so now I couldn't judge him because my stone castle turned into glass.

I heard a series of Hallelujahs and people who shared in my fake passion to hear the preacher speak with the usual smooth, powerful sermon he always gave. I was scared of death! I was scared of hell, and right then and there I made a vow, *Lord, from this day forward I leave the slut behind and I will prepare myself for the judgment!*

And this time I meant it. I was going to give what's his name back his wallet in person. Ask for his forgiveness, stop that shipment and call my girl Stacey and tell her I was sorry but I didn't want to die and go to hell, even though it might already be too late. But I still had time to try. I was going to give a testimony.

I stood up. All the clapping deceased. I took off my hat, cleared my throat and I began.

"Church, I have a confession to make. I'm dying of Cancer. I *don't* have much longer to live." I had never received so much love in my life. I cried so hard I doubled over on the floor, holding my chest, begging God to forgive me.

I didn't know I actually had the Holy Ghost.

A couple weeks had gone by and I still couldn't believe I actually had an orgy in church. And I am not going to lie I haven't been back. My phone has been ringing off the hook. I changed my number when I realized it was Lloyd from church, leaving all kind of messages on my machine.

*Can I see you again? Your pussy was fire! Let's have a one on one. Fuck my wife. I want you!*

So much for his little quote, what happened behind these doors stayed behind these doors? The truth of the matter was I felt ashamed. I shouldn't have done that in God's house in the first place. It actually turned my stomach. I found myself getting lost in my grief by taking Hennessy shots to the head and smoking trees. I spent four hundred dollars on weed and alcohol alone. And with my telemarketing job at PRC, this put me way out of my budget.

I was in the kitchen cooking a small pot of gravy for my biscuits when the phone wailed. Wondering who it was, and needing to put my bills in the mail box (I should get automatic bill pay through my Bank of America account). I untied the apron from my waist. I cursed myself for getting flour on my black pants suit. I then walked past the love seat and sofa and snatched up the phone. Looking in the mirror (how the fuck did flour get on my fifty dollar weave job?) I said, "Yes."

"May we speak to Mrs. Jackson, please?"

"Chile, I am *not* married to a man. I'm married to my pussy, *yes*. Well, maybe you can call me Mrs. Sexy. *Anyways*, speak now or forever hold your piece and I am not talking about your gun."

She laughed easily. *Whoever* it was made me crack a smile. I didn't have many bitches for friends. In fact I couldn't think of one woman I was friends with. The fact of the matter was that Hoes *weren't* to be trusted. I screwed married men like the Seattle Zoo so I *knew* other Ho's would take my man. I smelled my gravy. Such a lovely smell for a Tuesday morning.

"Girl you are a trip. This is Bianca. From the doctor's office."

*Oh, Boy.* "Oh, hey, Girl! How are you?"

My gravy smelled so good I tell you.

"Listen. Doctor Hamilton needs to talk to you."

I got quiet. Cancer. I was dying of Cancer.

More and more every day I felt like I was suffocating. I couldn't believe that my life has panned out to this. "Ok, about?"

She was quiet. "Just come in, Mrs. Jackson."

*I'm not fucking married.* "When?"

"Now."

"Jesus, *why* now?"

Goddamn it, now I couldn't eat my biscuits and gravy.

It took me forever to find a parking spot at Baptist Hospital. People parked every which goddamn way, even in the fire zones. I happened to see an old lady backing out. "Bitch, hurry the fuck up!" I was steaming. She flipped the bird. "Hurry up. Ho! You can audition for the Efferdent commercials later!"

The old hag said, "Bitch, fuck off!"

"Fuck you, Ho!"

She honked twice: Fuck You! I honked three times. Fuck. You. Bitch! I got me a parking spot.

"Hey, Bianca!"

She set some files on a cluttered desk. She looked at me with a smile.

"*Hello*, Mrs. Jackson. The doctor will see you now."

I sighed, giving her a gloomy look. I wondered what this was all about. He could have scheduled my chemotherapy session over the phone. It was bad enough I was dying, even though I didn't look or feel any different.

*Lord, please don't give me any more bad news!* "Ok, I'm going."

"You look like you're headed to the torture chamber."

*Yes, bitch! Does seem that way no don't it?* "Feels like it, Chile."

"It'll be all right."

*Shut up, bitch!* "I'm dying and you say it's all right."

She said nothing. Dismissing her comments, my heels clickety-clacked towards the doctor's office.

"Yes Doctor," I said, as if the Grim Reaper was about to cut me in half. I entered the office and closed the door. He seemed pressed. I didn't want to disturb him. Just tell me what you needed to say so I can get on with my life.

He looked up from his desk with a smile. "Hey."

I wasn't in the mood to be cordial. "Sup, man?"

He was smiling. Big time. I was getting mad. I didn't like men toying with me. Fucking me, yes. But toying and clowning? I didn't like Parker Brothers or *Chutes and Ladders*.

"I'm dying. And you're smiling."

His eyes sparkled. "It's a beautiful day Mrs. Jackson."

*Was he serious?* "Really?"

He uncoiled from the chair and walked up to me. "I have some good news."

"Jesus is coming back?" I said sarcastically, closing my eyes to hear what this so called good news was.

"Charts got mixed up. You don't have cancer."

I kept my eyes closed. I had to suck in air. This couldn't be happening. *Run Run Run!* I ran out of his office before he said April Fools.

And it was the month of July.

I drove home in silence. I couldn't believe what the doctor had told me. No wonder they were smiling at me like that. They know they fucked up. Kill 'em with a smile, 'ey bitches? They mixed up my charts. I should kick their asses, got me thinking I was dying of cancer. I must admit a huge burden has been lifted from my shoulders. What a relief! I should sue their asses! Scaring me like that!

I looked at the sunshine differently. I smelled the air differently. I turned on the radio, lighting a cigarette. And then I heard it. The commercial said, "Want to go see Janet Jackson on B.E.T's 106 and Park? Go online and send in your request..." I, Melissa Jackson, will be going online to send in my request.

New York, are you Freaky Deaky?

# The Strap

I was twenty-eight years old, with a Playboy-pin-up body: 36, 24, 38 would be the exact measurements. I had doe-shaped eyes, was caramel-complexioned and my long, Indian-like hair made women jealous because it wasn't weave or extensions. And with all those attributes, I still had low self-esteem.

"Hey, Jasmine," said my co-worker Estella, a Cuban woman who got on my last nerve. I've been working here for two and a half years and never have I encountered the likes of her until recently, when she was hired.

I turned my back to her, frowned at my reflection in the Pepsi soda machine, rolled my eyes so hard I thought I snapped a migraine, sucked my teeth and then faced her with the phoniest smile known to man.

*This bitch needs to croak.* "Hey, girl!"

I hugged her tightly, wanting to vomit. The minute my body touched hers I had a knee-jerk reaction, but I played it off as best I could. I was already mad somebody broke into my locker and read my goddamn Diary. They didn't take my money or credit cards. Thank God for that! They just stole my Diary, which detailed my life at the moment, well over the past two years. I felt violated, that someone in the office knew my business. I never discussed my home life at work, which was probably why someone felt compelled to read my damn life I had jotted down in words.

Now someone knew I sucked on my dildo because I hadn't sucked my husband's dick in months! That burned me up. Now someone knew I fucked myself with bananas and when I came I ate them, swallowed them to my sheer delight. Now someone knew I looked out my bedroom window, at my neighbors, the Wilma's, and watched them fuck almost every night while I masturbated, being a peeping Tom, while my man was out doing God knew what!

"How have you been doing?"

I hated that crazy Cuban accent. "I been fine, we missed you around here! How was Cuba?" *Why did she smell like a dead damn cat?*

Her eyes glowed. She loved talking to me. Why? I didn't know. I wish I could find the reason and send the shit to hell. No other black woman in this building gave her the time of day. I guess I was just nice and didn't want to seem rude. That would be me: Miss Polite…with a big booty to match. I was not trying to think of my ass. It hasn't been touched in months. It probably has enough pollen and dust on it to send America into a Sinus Fit.

"Girl," she went on, looking tore up from the floor up in this Goodwill purchased business suit, which seemed a mockery because the dick-sucking bitch drove a flashy Benz. And I drove a 2005 Acura Legend. "I took some money over to Cuba. I'm trying to get my Mama from over there so she can get a job and work, supporting my father."

I tucked my chin back. "Get her a job where?" I tried to alleviate the sarcasm from my voice.

She gave a god-awful smile. "Here, of course. I might be supervisor by next quarter."

*Over my dead body,* I thought bitterly. "You know you need a Bachelor's degree to work here, Estelle."

She brushed lint off my jacket sleeve. "You are so caring, Jasmine, which is why I like you."

"Did you hear a word I said, pretty girl Estelle?"

She blushed, running her crappy hands through her sunset-colored hair. "She thinks I'm pretty. Girl, lunch is on me today. And I heard you. My mama got a Bachelor's in Survival and I got one in Hustling. I can show Rick Ross a thing or two about Noriega owing me a hundred favors."

Jessica, my co-worker, gave me the evil eye, walking past us, sucking her teeth, pooping her gum. "Now you know you selling out talking to that ditzy bitch," she mumbled in my ear, turning to face Estelle with the nastiest look on her face. "Hi, Estelle! You looking fucked up as normal!" she gushed, all girly, giving her the once-over and then sashaying all that big booty out of the break room. Estelle flipped her the bird.

"Never mind her," Estelle told me. "When I become supervisor she's the first one I'm firing."

"She's a hard worker."

"And so are you. Plus, rumor has it that she used to Pussy Pop on stage at the Club Rolexx. How's your husband."

*Jessica was a stripper?* "Oh, we're great! He *treats* me good and *always* takes care of home." I felt uneasy. Why was she asking me all these questions?

"Good, good. Let me know if he doesn't treat you good." She looked deeply into my eyes. "I'll have his balls for supper if he doesn't." I shivered when she said that. "Better yet, cancel the lunch date. I got an appointment with someone. We can grab lunch tomorrow or so. Is that ok, Jasmine?"

"Fine by me, sexy." *Sexy? God, shoot me!*

She was wearing too much red, too much lipstick, too much make up, too much eye shadow and was just too damn happy. She should be. Out of all the black bitches and Niggahs working here at Sky's Limited, architectural offices for some of the world's fanciest, richest architects, Downtown Miami, she was the only one hired on the spot. No interview. No background check. This bitch could be a serial killer Castro released from prison and let come to the U.S. And our own black people here couldn't find a job if they were felons. I was shocked my co-worker Richard Liam, Jr., Notre Dame Graduate, got hired with his checkered past.

All Estelle got was a pat on the back because of the sob story she gave. "I've only been in America for five months. I barely made it over here alive. Nine of us were crammed on a tiny boat with no food. Ad my husband died the minute we touched land, after the Coast Guard tried to stop us."

I should know what she said. I pressed a small glass up against the wall in the break room on the other side of the office, with about ten other blacks doing the same thing and we all dropped our glasses when we heard, "Welcome to America! You have a bright future with us!"

"What?" said Seymour, fat ass, weighing about as much as Monique but she was no Monique, the Comedian. "How did she...what did he just say..."

Devastated, I shook my head in the negative and grabbed a broom. "Cubans are just getting over."

Jessica said, "They turned down my brother the other day and he got three degrees in architecture. And this Ho jumps her fat ass off the boat and just waltzes in here and gets pat on the back?"

Lamar Samuels, sexy Niggah, about 6 feet 8 inches of pure body, steel and brains, said, "Your brother was over qualified, Jessica."

"And this bitch is under qualified," she said. "And did you see what she had on going into the interview? She wore a short, barely there mini skirt. Her huge titties were stuffed in the little girl halter top and some fucked-up black pumps. Tell me home girl had on some panties, because, as tight as that skirt was, I didn't see the lining."

"Let's get back to work," I told them, since I was the supervisor. "And thank God we have jobs."

With a *humph* and more obscenities mumbled under their breaths, they reluctantly got back to work. It was when I ducked down to pick up a glass that didn't shatter that I froze in place, stuck where I was, the breath catching in my throat.

"Oh, Estelle...suck that black dick, bitch...yeeea, I knew you wanted this job! You can't tell nobody ok Mami!"

I heard her slurping on the dick, pulling and teasing. I heard the chair squeaking. "Oh I won't tell a soul, Papi, you gotta big dick Papi...Want some of this Cuban pussy, Papi?"

"Close the blinds and suck my dick, bitch, until I nut all over them mammoth titties. I'ma show you how us Dirty South Niggahs get down in Miami, ever had some Overtown Dick, bitch?"

"*Oooh* la la!"

"You g'on swallow my nut, sexy?"

"*Oooh* yes, Papi…I swallow all the time, Papi…"

"You better not waste one drop, cunt! Now suck on the dick like you want it. I'll beat your ass with those 11 inches you gripping!"

*Goddamn! Eleven inches? Wow, little boss man Kevin, five feet 8 inches, packing Grade A beef like that. He gotta be lying!*

Wanting to know what eleven inches looked like, I daydreamed about it. I was jealous she was getting some and I didn't have any in months. I locked the break room door behind me, letting it close silently.

I ignored the tingling in my breasts.


When I got home I was suddenly depressed. I wanted to pick up my purse and run back out the door before my husband found out I was home. There was soft lighting everywhere. Every blind and curtain was closed. I inhaled and remained quiet. Nobody was home, probably.

Why did I lie to Estelle and say my man treated me good? That he took care of the family? Maybe because of my pride. Maybe because the Cuban bitch had it so good and I had it so bad that I didn't want to look stupid and foolish in the face of a woman I hated with a passion.

Tears fell from my eyes like midgets pushing rocks over a cliff. I lowered myself onto the red velvet sofa and balled. I was already hot in my business suit and these red pumps were killing my tired feet. I needed to cut my toe nails and I hadn't time to do that because I had four kids who would be kicking down the front door like they were from the samurai in about four hours.

Looking up, and trying to swallow the painful ball in my chest, I rocked back and forth. This was how it was going to go. This was my everyday life, which I wrote in my diary. I was going to start dinner for my husband of four years. James Rodriguez, the asshole who had a Puerto Rican Mama and a Black Venezuelan Daddy who seemed to control our lives. They were always here eating our food from the fridge and considering that I was the one making all the money, my man didn't work, I had no say. I was raised, ever since I was a little girl in Savannah, Georgia, to always care for my man. When he had a job you cooked, cleaned and washed all the clothes. And when he *lost* his job you cooked, cleaned and washed all the goddamn clothes. That's what I've been doing, even for my Daddy ten years back. Because Mama, Bertha, has been handicapped for sixteen years. Thank the Lord I *didn't* have any siblings. If I did have them I probably would have had to cook and clean for them as well.

I hated my own image. I hated myself. I hated *everything* about me. But the fellahs at work have been whistling at me, blowing kisses and leaving explicit notes and cartoons on little pads doing the nasty. I've been ignoring it, because, out of all the fine men at work (and don't get me wrong, I was turned on by a few of them) I didn't quite know who were leaving the notes. I didn't want to assume. Plus I was unhappily married and I never cheated on my man. When your man had good, out of control dick, no matter if you got it twice a week or once every eleven months, as in my case, you didn't cheat or walk out on that.

He wasn't eleven inches, like my boss, but he was a good nine plus inches, three and a half inches in diameter, filled my pussy to capacity like water filling a glass. How did I go from a self-assured female, running the streets of Georgia during my teens, having men and hoes on my jock, smoking weed, and getting my drank and freak on every Friday night, to being married, cooking for my husband, raising my kids, being slapped around and letting my in-laws run my household?

I glanced at pictures of my loving babies. I only stayed in this marriage because of my children. They loved their father, who was good to them. I didn't want my kids hating and detesting me because I broke up their happy home. I leaned back on the sofa, hadn't fucked in almost a year and stifled a yawn. I needed a drink. I knew I had to go put dinner on. I was a bit surprised my husband wasn't in the living room with me barking orders. He would normally sit on the Lazy Boy when I came home. He knew my routine. He knew what time I got off work, what time I got there and if anything was off, even by a couple seconds he slapped my ass up good.

Bitch, do this. You didn't clean the kitchen right. Last night you fucked up dinner. Our kids hated the lasagna you made. Next time don't make the shit from scratch. You're a stupid bitch! Why did I marry you? Do I gotta whip your ass, bitch? Who's your man? I need about nine hundred dollars. Yea, I been job hunting, but you are going to hold it down with the bills until I find one.

And I'd look like a doe-eyed fool, crying softly, and adhere to his demands. I let my man bring me down because *he* was down. He stopped me from being with my friends. He forbade me from seeing my own family. I cut my parents off. Because I loved this man.

He used to work as a teller at the bank. He was a successful man, with a Bachelor's degree in business. Graduated, top honors, from Harvard University. Belonged to a fraternity.

When we met, on Bayside in Miami, Florida, we were both visiting Miami then. I was 20 years old. He was 21. We fell in love instantly. After all the one night stands I had through college at Xavier University, the different ways men ate my pussy, used toys on me and fucked me so good in the ass it felt like I had two pussies, he was something refreshingly different. He dressed classy, smelled good and treated me like a lady. I had big titties, and wore a revealing outfit that showed parts of my body. Hell I was in Miami. I wanted to flaunt my body! That was my mindset back then. Men looked at him with contempt. Some fellahs tried to lure me away from him by dangling keys to Bentleys, Rolls Royce's and Cadillac's.

But when James gazed at me, he dissed his boys, rushed over to me, took my hand and said, "You are so goddamn sexy. Can I buy you a drink?"

"Sure," I had said, not taking my eyes off this sexy Black man with the heavenly eyes, full, sexy lips and he had an ass and a dick print behind those loose jeans that set me on fire. My pussy was like "Hell yeah!" And my asshole was like, "How sweet! Fresh meat!"

He was the hottest man in Miami. He didn't buy me a drink. In fact, he took me to the Gucci store and bought me the sexiest dress on the rack. He whipped out his VISA platinum card and when the $1,200 price rang up on the register in green letters I just looked at him, my hand on my throat, wide-eyed. "I don't need a bag," he told the tall, white bimbo-looking cashier, who had wet panties herself starting at him.

I blinked rapidly. "That's for me?" I had asked. He kissed my hand, never taking his eyes off mine. He was three inches taller than me. I felt like melting. "There's a dressing room in here somewhere. Go take that flashy shit off and put on this dress. On the way grab some of those Gucci pumps and I'll buy 'em. Just lose the Hot Pussy Outfit you got on. You're a queen. You're my lady. I'm claiming your ass as of right now."

I had never run so fast. And that's the day that changed my life. I had changed my school, did my last two years at Harvard with my man. I went from pussy popping at the clubs to keeping it under control. My man taught me that the true power wasn't in my pussy but in my mind. We studied together and we spent so much time together. He was easy-going, very easy to talk to and he actually listened to you. I never had the urge to cheat on him or do things behind his back. I was addicted to him; he was the very air that I breathed. He was the first man I actually fell in love with.

All the bitches tried to fuck him. He always told me who they were and I beat their asses to a goddamn pulp. He never kept things from me.

And when we made love he fucked every hole on my body. When he asked me to marry him I had said yes. I was in love with him, the late night talks we had, the times we ate out, sometimes I paid. He went back to Georgia with me to meet my childhood friends and my parents. I showed him around, giving him a view of my old stomping grounds, my elementary, and junior and senior high schools. He soaked it all up like a sponge. I knew everything about him and I bared my soul to him. Everything, I left nothing out. He was my soul mate. He then took me to his hometown in Houston, Texas, where he was born. I met his parents. Then he took me to Los Angeles, California, where he was raised and would eventually finish high school.

We got married a few years after we graduated from Harvard together. Our wedding was huge. His parents paid for it. I felt like I was Cinderella. My parents were there. I felt like a Queen. I felt like life was so good. We honeymooned in London. I had never been there. We would spend three weeks there, nights full of romance, good foreplay, good fucking and immaculately-tailored food.

How could it go wrong? It did. After our second year of marriage things deteriorated. Building our home from scratch in Miami, after joining the Church of Christ in Coconut Grove, started to come apart at the seams. After all the parties we threw we shunned everyone away. The times we made love all over the freaking world (I could still feel his tongue and strawberries deeply embedded in my ass and pussy in Polynesia) became distant memories. Getting joint bank accounts, putting our names together in unison on everything from our cars to our bills, went to hell.

He started getting demanding. His parents started coming over once a week, then twice, then three times, running shit. He started hitting on me when his job was going downhill, and because I loved him I did nothing. A few women filed sexual harassment charges on him, which was settled out of court. He stopped keeping himself up. He had a full beard, didn't look as sexy as he used to. He stopped going to the gym.

I was scared of him. Then I found out he used to be in the blood gang since he was nine years old. Then I found out he'd been to jail repeatedly as a teen. Then I found out he raped four women, who were adults at the time, when he was 15 years old. Then I found out he had a temper so out of this world. Then I found out he went to therapy for five years to get it under control. Then I found the pills he was taking to keep himself calm. That explained the reason why he was having mood swings. He wasn't taking his pills like he was supposed to. Then I had our children. And he became more of a male chauvinistic pig, but I wouldn't dare say to his face.

Then he lost his job. No more parties. No more trips. No more home-cooked meals, no more freaky sessions all over the world, bills mounted, our mortgage was $1,500 a month and now everything fell on me. The kids' daycare, the kids' food, clothes, my man's needs and his car notes, I was responsible for. I had to pay close to $1,000 for his F-150 truck with the pounding bass and his Bentley he hardly ever drove. He started staying out late. He treated me like a bitch. He used to spit in my face. But I wouldn't give up on him. I almost turned my back on God.

Enter the present scene. I was crying on the couch, afraid to move. I wanted *out.* I wanted to pack my bags and go! I was a sexy bitch! I could have any man I wanted! But I needed my husband! Our history was ancient!

Fed up with this marriage and this life, I stood up. Snatching off my jacket and blouse, my titties sprung free. I rushed past the low-table holding our wedding picture and stared at myself in the mirror.

"Where's the bitch that used to have a back bone?" I asked aloud, hot tears snatching the color from my face. "Where is she? My man hates me! Where's the woman that never let a man hit her? Why am I such a punk bitch?" I searched my eyes, looking deep into my reflection and I shivered.

I nearly fell over when I seen the rose petals on the marble floor. They trailed from the front door, past the low-table, up the hallway and into the bedroom. I saw candles flickering all over the place. The soft glow was dancing on the walls. Why hadn't I noticed this before?

"Oh, God! He has another female in here! In my home! In my bed! Where are my children?"

I sniffed the air, hoping my nose caught a scent of another bitch's perfume. Badussy better not be tramping in the air (booty, ass and dick).

Seeping with anger, I pivoted on my heel, snatched off my business skirt, and me and my Victoria's Secret panties, which went up my ass, sauntered quietly down the hallway. I passed my children's rooms. I peeked inside. They were empty. "Shit, they're not home from school yet. Why am I tripping?" I paused at my bedroom door.

I nearly fainted.

There were more rose petals leading to the bed and the bathroom. My man was barely dressed, his chiseled body so immaculate. My pussy was on fire. He was slow dancing with himself to Marques Houston's "Naked." The song had just started.

He faced me, looking good in his silk boxers. He was hard and ready. I wanted to hold it. Jesus! What an ass! I used to love tonguing his body, while he lay on his stomach. I used to spread his ass cheeks apart and tongue him so good and so nastily he'd come all over the sheets. I shuddered, leaning against the wall. Our bedroom was beautiful; we put over $23,000 in this room. Remote control windows and doors. We could run a bath from the touch of a button. African-American paintings hung everywhere; ceramic statues of Queen Hatshepsut and Nefertiti were on pedestals on either side of the bed. Vincent Van Gogh's *Four Cut Sunflowers* painting hung by the closet door.

Candles were on the dressers, night stands, stereo. I melted. I was in tears. What was going on?

"You're doing all this for another woman, James? In my home? Are you asking me to leave? Are you…"

As soft a summer's breeze, he walked up to me and placed a sexy finger over my lips. My eyes fluttered closed, like butterflies. "No. Baby. This is for you. I love you. I'm sorry for all the mean things I've done. I checked into therapy to help me with my temper problem; I prescribed a refill on my pills. I go to therapy on Saturday, will you go with me?"

I was an open book. "Yes, baby. I'm your wife; I'll do anything for you." *Oh, God! You must have heard my prayers! Thank you, Lord! Thank heavens! I know all our problems aren't gone, but this is a start!*

"I don't want you giving me money anymore. I also got my old job back at the bank. Those broads who filed sexual harassment charges on me are being indicted for fraud. The papers from my lawyer are on the dresser, you can read them. I told you I was innocent."

I was silent. I hugged him. "Baby, that's great! Incredible!" I was so overwhelmed. I couldn't contain myself. My titties and pussy was on fire! I leaned back and tongued my man, passionately, slowly. He kissed me with a longing I never quite experienced. He missed me and I missed him.

"Baby we're gonna fuck five times a week for now on, if you want it six times a day just tell me and we're going to fuck all over this house. I'll send the kids to fucking boarding school if I have to."

"Ok, baby, for real?" I asked.

He kissed me. A peck. He had so much love in his eyes. "Yes. For real."

"But what about your parents."

I cringed. He hated when I brought them up. He smiled. "You won't have to worry about them. I told them house visits are no longer an option. And if they disrespect my wife I'm going to cut their asses off at the knees."

"Oh my God, baby. Finally, peace."

"Yes, peace."

He had a red rag tied around his head, like Tupac. My Thug Niggah at heart. I never had Thug Dick. I always had the Cautious Dick. The Gentleman Dick. The I Missed You Today Dick. The I Had a Hard Day at Work Dick. I had every type of dick from my husband, but never the Thug Passion Dick. The Straight Dick in Your Pussy 'Til I Nut Dick.

He walked backwards, away from me, slowly dancing to Marques Houston's sexy, sensual voice. I used to masturbate to Marques Houston's sexy ass!

Marques was singing from the stereo. "I know I cheated on you before." I never knew James could dance, he ran his sensual hands up and over his hips, taking his dick in his hands, rubbing himself, swaying his ass, turning elegantly, moaning sensually, cooing and oh and ah-ing and it drove me crazy.

He looked at me through the reflection in the mirror. He winked at me and bit his lower lip.

"I cheated on you, baby," he said, words that destroyed my gut instantly. "But not with my body. Not with my tongue. Only in heart, baby. I'm going to be honest with you."

Relieved, I walked up behind him and hugged him from the back. "Thanks for being honest."

"I cheated at heart, with my thoughts. I never acted on them. Baby, it's like this. I don't know how to tell you." He faced me, stroking my face, hugging me, placing his hands firmly on my ass. I closed my eyes, thankful for the attention. It may be another eleven months before this happened again. "Baby, I am bisexual. No, I never been with a man but I've thought about it. I been through a lot in my life. There's one thing I didn't tell you. I went through a lot as a kid. As you can see I'm sexy and handsome. But my looks has brought about perverts in my life that used to come around my family. And I never had help. I joined the gang to escape, but wound up going through similar things with them. I became temperamental and started fending for myself. But my feelings for Niggahs never left, and when I married you I wasn't totally in love. I was battling the dl life, even though I never touched a guy, and the straight life."

My heart opened to him. I appreciated the honesty. "Baby, I love you. That's all that matters."

"I want to ask something of you, if you don't want to, you don't have to."

"Yes, baby. You're my husband."

"I want to fuck you. Good, baby. Thug Dick. I know you want it."

"Oh, baby. You read my mind."

"I want the asshole and I want the pussy."

"Yes, Daddy." I shuddered with ecstasy. I felt myself taking off my panties. He picked them up, smelled them. Ran his tongue over them, sucking my wetness down his throat and he put them in my mouth.

"I'ma fuck you in the ass first, and you better not let these panties fall from your mouth, you hear me baby?"

I moaned my answer.

Getting behind me, he got on his knees, my ass all on his face and he tongued my hole, which was tight, exhausted from a day's work and I needed to shower. He didn't care. He spread my cheeks open with urgency and buried his tongue, which was long and thick, in my asshole, becoming one with it. I moaned so loud I almost went blind. He slapped my ass repeatedly, the sound of hands on ass sounding off in the room. and he took one of the candles, poured the hot wax on my cheeks, licking my ass all over. I fell on my knees. The thug in him surfacing, he pushed my face to the floor. Spreading my ass open, he mounted me, carefully sliding his thick dick inside my tight hole.

I shook with delight. Oh God this felt good. The pain was there but the pleasure overcame me. "Hold that ass open, bitch."

I did so, quick, fast and in a hurry.

"Dem panties still in 'ya mouth?"

"Mmm hmm!"

He fucked me so good, giving the Long Dick; I felt his balls bouncing on my ass. My face hurt on this floor but my man wrecking shop in my asshole was worth it. I felt my pussy tightening; the flames were licking at my clit.

"Rub that pussy, baby."

Oh yes I did, sir! I rubbed my pussy so fast and so deep I damn near fell on my titties. I felt my tits bouncing, and my man gripped the edge of the bed and slammed that dick into my ass, the panties fell out my mouth and I couldn't help it.

*"Fuck me baby, fuck me bay yes, yes oh my God I'm bout to come baby fuck meee oh God!"*

He banged me harder, long stroking me until the breath caught in my throat. I shivered uncontrollably. I couldn't help myself.

And I came all over my hand.

"Suck that shit off your fingers."

I refused to.

He pulled his dick out my ass, picked my ass up and tongued me, taking my come-clad hand and sucking my fingers, sucking up all the white love and kissing me, pushing it down my throat.

"Don't fucking hesitate, swallow it."

"Wow, baby. You're a maniac," I said playfully, swallowing my own juices.

He then pulled me to the bed, and he lay on the rose petals. There was a strap-on dildo, of moderate size, by a plate of fruit. I was a little thrown.

Wide-eyed. "Baby, what's a strap on for?"

He looked so sexy, so embarrassed. "Baby, fuck me. Fuck me good, baby. If I can't cheat on my wife then my wife needs to please her man. I want to know what its like. If you don't do it then I'll find someone who will" And he meant it.

I was a little quiet. But he was right. I didn't want my man cheating on me. I knew how it went. I saw what Terry McMillan went through, I watched Oprah. I didn't understand. Terry's ex man looked gay, talked gay, how could she not have known? At least I'd know what my man was doing if he wanted me to do it. Plus I always been curious about how men would react if the woman had a dick and they had the pussy. So this was actually a fantasy of mine.

He lay on his stomach, twirling his ass to Marques Houston.

"Put on some Pac, Baby. 'All Eyez on Me.'"

I did so. We had a 100 disc changer, Pac was disc number ten.

Strapping the dildo on my waist, he slow humped our silk sheets. He looked like he was trapped in a lustful dance, a trance, which turned me on, watching my man's ass cheeks tremble. Damn he had a nice ass. I took out the baby oil, squirted it on his back, ass and legs and spent twenty minutes massaging him, making him feel good, sucking his dick at times, eating his asshole…he moaned so loud, so elegantly. I loved when he moaned. I really loved making him feel incredibly good.

"…I want it baby…"

I straddled his waist and slid the dildo deep in his ass. He froze, gripping the sheets, tears falling down his face and I slowly gyrated in his tunnel, sucking the back of his neck, my hair hanging in my face.

He twirled his hole on the plastic dick, moaning so sensually. "Feels so good, baby feels so good baby I love you baby you're making me feel so good!"

I pounded that hole the way he fucked me earlier, getting acrobatic with it. We fucked doggy-style, I slapped his ass, pulled him up to me, hugging him from the back and I gave it to him so good.

"Jack that dick, Niggah!" I demanded, releasing my inhibitions.

He whacked off, long stroking that thick dick. I felt him shiver; he threw that ass back like a pro.

"Baby, I'm 'bout to nut!" He screamed out as his hole pulsated on the dildo and cum shot all over the head board. I felt so powerful I was about to lose it. Damn now I want to do this all the time, no wonder a man sexing a woman was so thrilling to him. I felt an ounce of that thrill right now. I pounded him faster, harder until his orgasm subsided and I fell on my back, the dildo pointing towards the ceiling fan. I was sweaty, spent and I fell asleep.

Dreaming.

When I woke up hours later my man was fully clothed, reading a book of poetry by Langston Hughes. He had showered, was freshly powdered and he smiled at me.

"Hey, sleepy head." He kissed me.

"Hi, baby."

"I missed you. You fell asleep on me." He had dreamy bedroom eyes.

"Was I dreaming?"

"No, baby. You weren't." He rubbed the back of my neck. I loved his touch.

"So this is really happening?"

"Yes. I gotta go to work in about five hours, I should be sleep. But I bathed you while you slept. I clothed you."

I sat up, looking at myself. My hair was in a tight bun. He did my hair? My toe and finger nails were cut nicely and done up with clear polish. Wow. I was stunned. And he put on my pajamas; I smelled like my Apple lotion I loved wearing.

"Thanks, baby. I must have been knocked out. I didn't feel a thing."

"I know. I carried you to the tub and I bathed you. I then toweled you off. You looked so angelic. You must have had a hard day at the office. I then carried you to the bed, dried you off, did your pedicure and manicure, put on your pajamas when the nail polish dried and I just watched you sleep. Then I felt myself getting horny so I pulled out some Langston Hughes."

"But you hate poetry."

"I love it now. I read some of Legendary's shit on Myspace. The Niggah is bad. And they talk about Zane and Afro erotic. This Niggah is dope."

"Yes, he's fire." I felt myself getting aroused.

I stared deep into his eyes.

"I love you baby, I will never hit you again. I promise. I will be a better man, a better husband."

"I believed you, Baby."

"I also made an appointment for us to see a marriage counselor, if that's all right with you."

He looked a little standoffish, anticipating my answer. I was just glad he didn't think our problems diminished like a light switch. He was taking responsibility for his actions. Who was I to shit on that?

"Yes, baby, just tell me the time and the place."

"Thank you, baby, for putting up with my shit and not leaving me. Most girls woulda been gone."

"Most girls, yea. But I'ma woman who loves her husband. For better or for worse, richer or for poorer, until death do us part. I took vows."

"And so did I." He handed me an envelope. "This is yours."

"What is it, baby?"

"Open it," he suggested amicably.

I opened it and pulled out a shit load of hundred dollar bills.

"Baby...what's this?" My breath caught in my throat.

"All the loot you gave me, paying my car notes, taking care of me and the kids. That's $12,000 you need to put back in your account. I got a little loan from the bank when I got my job back. Don't worry about my monthly payments. I got it; it's my burden to bear."

I hugged him. Truly appreciative. I never loved him the way I did at this moment. "Thanks, James."

"Take off your pajamas, baby."

"Why?"

"Can't your man eat some of that passion fruit between your legs?"

"Oooh, baby...yes you can."

"I want you, baby. Let's make love until I go to work. I wanna make you nut over and over and over. I got eleven months to make up for. And don't worry; the kids are staying with my parents for the next two weeks."

I took off my pants then panties. "Why?"

"So we can reconnect as husband and wife. And they can eat up my parent's food, the way they ransacked our home and ate up our shit."

I laughed with him. "Good deal. So two weeks all to ourselves?"

"Yes. Well, we both have to work. But when we get home, I'm cooking for you, baby. *Whatever* you want to eat."

"I want to eat you."

"My asshole is kinda lonely."

"Ha ha ha."

"And when you go to work do me a favor."

"Yes, baby."

"Thank Estelle. Because she paid me a visit and told me you weren't happy at work. She felt kinda bad calling off the lunch date she told me she booked with you."

I grew quiet. What?

"She read your diary and found out you weren't happy at home. Because of Estelle, I realized I had a good wife and she said I was a pussy for hitting on you and treating you so badly. She returned your diary. It's over on your dresser."

He pointed at it. I was patronized at the moment.

It was Estelle?

"Thank her for me. She saved my life; a complete stranger saved my marriage. Her brother is the marriage counselor we're going to see this weekend."

With tears in my eyes, I hugged him.

"Baby, I'm thirsty," I said. "Do you mind getting me some water?"

"Moet coming right up."

When he left the room I called Estelle's cell phone. I had everybody's number at the office, since I was one of the head supervisors. She answered.

I was very silent.

Estelle said, with a tired voice that cracked, "You're welcome. You don't have to thank me."

"Yes I do!" I tried to keep it together. It was next to impossible.

"No you don't. I hate praise. You've given me love and treated me with respect at work when all others look down on me. I know I did some things I shouldn't have to get a job. But I got eight kids who must eat. So I gotta keep them fed. I did what I had to do by sleeping with the boss. But you show me love. So I returned the favor by confronting your selfish ass husband by taking him your diary and making him read what he was doing to you. Sometimes the truth is better told in words. So I take it things are back to normal."

I cried so hard my hand shook. I dropped the cell phone.

"Let it out, girl. You have been through a lot. But God will carry you the rest of the way."

And the line disconnected.

My husband came back in the room, handing me the Moet.

"Baby, why are you crying?"

He looked at the cell phone.

He seen Estelle's name.

He put two and two together.

"Baby, I got a better idea for this glass of Moet...sit up."

And when he poured it all over my breasts, the cold contents making me cringe as it flowed down my stomach and between my legs, mixing with my pussy juices his tongue and mustache played Twister for the next hour.

I had my husband back.

Thanks to Estelle. The Cuban.

# Down, Set, Hike

Look here. I loved sports. Particularly football. Sure, I was a woman, and women were traditionally tied to getting their hair and nails done. Paying for pedicures and girl stuff. Hand bags were very equipped essentials that made being feminine such a treat. Most women loved men and dick, lusted after a cute new face when he moved into town and loathed PMS. But as much as all that kept my interest, I loved football. I loved men in football uniform. The tight pants, tight asses, the knee and shoulder pads and the cleats turned me on. I hated the invention of Nut Cups. They protected the scrotum sack of the players from forceful injury. They hid the dick prints. The helmets somewhat hiding handsome faces reminded me of S&M. The sweat, the power and the force kept my pussy wet. I loved the sex appeal.

The hormones raging on the field were mind blowing. Estrogen in the crowd with wet pussies and hardened nipples trying to make some eye contact with testosterone in helmets through silent communication was what I lived for. That was until I met Sidney, my worst nightmare.

It all started when I was seven years old, cheering for South Kendall Eagles on Eureka Park back in the day when Teddy Jammed with the singing group Guy and I lived for the DJ's for the latest Uncle Al jam. I was a cute, curvaceous thang. I was zonked on watching old footage from my father playing football for South Dade Senior High for four years, being the star quarterback. I got off on watching him throw the ball. Handle the ball. Control the ball. I was nailed to the couch every time I pressed play. It was a past time of mine.

Every boy on the 90 pound team wanted me, even back then. I used to get off on Niggahs being in uniform. They had a certain zeal, a certain cockiness that turned me on, even back then. Mama always fell over when she seen my little brother, James, strap on his helmet, beat on his pads screaming, with the rest of the football team, *"Eagles, get ready to roll! Eagles get ready to roll!"* And they'd hit their pads like a Janet Jackson Rhythm Nation video. They were in sync and full of hope and promise.

And my panties were wet. When I turned thirteen, attending Southridge Senior High as a freshman, I tried out for the cheerleading team. I could dance, having taught myself watching every video ranging from Paula Abdul, Janet Jackson to Michael and James Brown. I had the natural agility to look at something and move with it in less than ten minutes. Maybe it was the Caribbean blood in me, the Nassau, Bahamas, where I was born and partially raised, until my parents migrated to Miami when I was four years old for a new and better life.

It was hard trying to convince the Captain of the Cheerleading team, Miss Prissy Bitch, to let me on. When I auditioned she took me on an emotional trip. She hated my turns, even though they were done expertly. She hated my big boobs and ass; because they were bigger than hers and she knew the boys came to the prep rally to see the girls shake shake it like a salt shaker. Plus she was a white bitch with blue eyes and blonde hair and fake boobies, even in the ninth grade. She had money, drove a Benz to school. Her Mommy was a lawyer and every Niggah in the school wanted to fuck this silly, dizzy Ho just for her money. Her reputation for sucking half of the football team's dick preceded her. But she didn't care. She wore that dried semen on the bottom of her chin like a goddamn badge of honor. I was a tomboy in school. I hated lipstick and earrings. I hated pumps and dresses. I didn't see the point. As far as I was concerned, let those Niggahs wear pumps and dresses and let the women wear pants and shit. I refused to be reduced into what society felt a female should be. I had a nappy afro. I never got a perm, despite my long hair. I kept braids in my hair. Cornrows, very fancy looking ones with beads on the ends. I wore black everything. Black shoes, socks, panties, bra and pants. I was Pro Black. I read black literature, danced to black music despite being a fan of Paula Abdul. I stayed mostly to myself. And every time my pussy got wet from looking at a hot Niggah I would just force myself to go numb.

I was in the FBLA, Future Business Leaders of America, on the Airforce Jr. R.O.T.C. squad because I had military goals, and a part of the Spartan Patrol, making sure students weren't skipping or caught roaming the halls without a hall pass during classroom hours.

I made the team eventually. The white Girl, Jane, couldn't deny me for too much longer because the other girls selected wanted me. I went to every football game, becoming fascinated with the sport. I attended the scrimmages, the practices…I had my eye on the middle linebacker, sexy ass Sidney, from Los Angeles, who had just moved to Miami with his biological mother after his father died in a physical plant explosion.

Why didn't I like the quarterback? Because he didn't do shit but throw a goddamn ball. The middle linebacker did all the crushing, squishing players on the field. He had a lot of sacks, and I loved a man who could "hit" and "sack." Told me he could "fuck" and "Get me in the sack," get my drift.

I hounded Sidney for half the school year. He had a girlfriend, Tiffany, who was a bubble head black girl who talked and acted white. Rumor had it that he screwed her everyday while his parents were at work. He'd sneak over there after practice, stinky and all, and fuck the daylights out of her.

I was jealous. I wanted him to fuck me, but of course I would never tell him that because all the other Hoes were doing that for me, and getting the dick for me. I heard the rumors, and I used to get wet the way women in school said he serviced the pussy.

He was in my Biology class. Being the direct girl that I was, I waited until the time was right to pounce. Timing was everything. It was in the month of December, three weeks before Christmas of 1995. My teacher gave a pop quiz and I wanted him to be the first to pop this pussy. I came to class wearing a nice blouse and tight jeans, high heeled black leather boots and my hair was corn rowed, hanging down to the middle of my back with sea shelled beads emphasizing my original style. I had arguably the biggest booty in the entire school.

I walked up to him while he chatted away with three members of the team, our classmates. The conversation ceased when I stood before him. He was handsomely clad in his football jersey and black jeans. I smiled sweetly. He and his boys looked me up and down, their eyes never leaving my ass.

I licked my lips, try'na be cute "Excuse me, Sidney. I know you don't know me, I'm Nivea. I was wondering do you have an extra pencil, because I don't have one and we are having a test today."

He licked his lips, his light brown eyes sparkling from the classroom lights. He was a dream, so goddamn sexy. His chest was that of a grown man and I saw the bulge in his pants, he had a grown man dick. Good God! And I was still a virgin, keeping my pussy in the closet like Michael in his video.

A few bitches tapped each other, pointing at me, whispering. They gave me the evil eye. I turned to a group of them, while the teacher answered her cell phone during working hours, and said, "Do you skanks have a problem? Is there any reason you Hoes are all up in my grill counting my goddamn teeth?"

They shied away, staring at anything but me.

"That's what the fuck I thought, bitches!" I went on with a sassy attitude, my pussy getting wet as hell. My panties were drowning and my clit didn't have a life jacket.

Sidney said, "Damn, Ma. Calm down. It's cool. The big one is my sister."

"Oh, sorry," I told him, knowing damn well I didn't need a pencil. I wanted him. "Which one is your sister again?"

He pointed at her. She wore a blue leather skirt and a RuPaul T-shirt.

I waved at her. *Bitch next time shut your fucking mouth!* "Sorry. I just hate being stared at."

"You cool," she said, running a shaking hand through her fucked up perm job.

*I know I'm cool, bitch!* "So Sidney, can I get that pencil?"

His boys stared me down, whispering to each other. I wouldn't look away from his eyes. He had a way of looking at you, keeping you slavishly chained to his eyes. He studied you as he looked, and electrical currents shot through my nipples and pussy like fire on gas.

"Yea. I got an extra one. But you can't have it."

"Why?"

"Because I want your phone number."

"But you got a girlfriend."

He was shaking his head, like "Bitch, get a clue."

He said, "So. I can have friends." Self-assured, I liked that. "Talking isn't cheating."

"And neither is eating," one of his friends said, number 23, with dread locks pulled into a pony tail. He slapped palms with number 11. Like the little boys they were.

"Only if your eyes aren't bigger than your stomach," I told number 23 and he got quiet. "They say when your dick is small you eat a lot of junk. Maybe you shoulda ate your veggies Gerber baby. Anyways, can I get the pencil?"

Sidney was enjoying this. "I already told you no."

"So how am I going to write down my number with no pencil? I don't have laser beams in my eyes. I am not Superman."

"Thank God," he said, handing me the pencil. I scribbled my number on his folder. He took my hand and kissed it, the feel of his lips turning me on like lights.

"Call me now, don't wait three weeks either. I know you Niggahs."

Sidney knew he couldn't run that game shit on me. I wasn't the line of scrimmage. "Oh, trust that I'ma call you."

"Yea, right. I'm going to my seat now."

"What, you don't believe me?"

I pat his shoulder. "No I don't."

He took off his jersey, number 36, and put it on me. It smelled Downy Fresh and so Tide with bleach. Mama washed her laundry with Downy and Tide, I knew the smell. I fell in love with his scent, and his cologne. Manly.

"Wear my jersey today. Take it home. Now I have a reason to call you."

"But your girl." As if I cared about the bitch.

"She can't get mad because my cousin is wearing my jersey, right?" He winked at me.

"I got you."

I turned to go sit down just as the teacher got off the cell phone when he took my arm, standing up, pulling me to him and gave me some tongue. I sucked on his tongue, closing my eyes as he held my ass, squeezing it. I pulled away, breathless. Girls were clapping and Niggahs were dog barking.

"Quiet the hell down!" snapped Miss Tonsils. "What's going on in here?"

"Nothing Miss Tonsils!" All the students said, keeping Sidney and I confidential. I wonder why my teacher's parents put Tonsils in her name. Sounds like a bad porn movie.

"Then shut the hell up. Let's get ready for the test. I hope you all studied."

"We did!" we all said in unison.

Flaunting her curvaceous body wrapped with a green and yellow floral dress, she stood up, opening her leather brief case, taking out papers. Sidney stood up and walked three rows over to me, making the white boy who sat next to me get out his seat. Sidney said, "This is my seat now. You can have my old one; I gotta keep my eye on Nivea."

He didn't protest. He picked up his book bag and exchanged seats. "So let's get to know each other."

"*After* the test."

He smiled, leaning up to me a little bit. "After the test," he repeated. I looked at his dick. He moved his shirt and let me see the huge brick throbbing behind the jeans.

I melted.


He walked me home that day. I had loved wearing his jersey and watching the bitches get jealous. I didn't care. I hung out by myself anyway. I found out that he stayed around the corner from me. I had never known that. I stayed on 190th Lane in the Hollywood Square, HUD Housing. He stayed on 190 Terrace. I never knew that. This thrilled me even more.

"So why are you sweating me?" he asked, challenging me. I liked that. He carried my school books. He had brown eyes and a low fade cut close to the scalp. Four gold teeth to the bottom. Five tattoos all over his arm. King Kafra. Nefertiti. Tut. Aesop. And a face of his mother. Very ethnic, I liked that.

"I am not sweating you."

"Yes you are." It was hot out, and I was sweating, the humidity damn near killed us. We walked past the Driver's Ed parking lot on the side of the school, heading for the projects.

"What do you call it?"

"Me going after what I want."

"And what do you want?"

I paused, looking him right in the face. "Dick." He smiled, holding his big bulge. "I want to get fucked for the first time."

His eyes widened. "You're a virgin?"

"Yep. I'm sick of listening to Let's Wait Awhile. I want it to be too late. I want to do it to some Pop that Pussy, some old school Throw that D!"

He laughed with me, covering his mouth, pointing at me. "What do you know about Throw that D? That's Two Live Crew, isn't it? I think so. My mom is at work. We can go to my crib. Let me get that pussy, baby."

I was scared, but I wasn't that scared. I was about to let this Niggah pop the cherry.

"Only if you eat my pussy first."

"I'll suck the walls off it, baby."

"I doubt if you're that good."

He gave me the once over. "I'm the best."

"You're probably a virgin!"

"I'm going to fuck you like one."

He put his arm around my shoulder and led me to his house.

My Lord. His room was rundown and tacky. Smelled like old tube socks and dirty draws. Old blue carpet with beer stains. I smelled it. He had Lil' Kim on his wall with stains all over her face. Come stains. Tupac hung on the open closet door. I wanted to puke. I felt like I was in a cheap hotel. His clothes barely hung on the iron and plastic hangers of all colors. A funky teddy bear was on his twin bed with a comforter that rivaled anything I saw the homeless sleeping with. Roaches scurried in and out of his shoes. His lamp didn't work, he relied on the lights from the ceiling fan which had 4 blades and was turning and rocking like it was playing pinball.

And this sick bitch had the gall to say, "Welcome to Casa De La Sidney's, where the pussy gets popped and the dick spits cum." He was so goddamn ghetto. For real.

"Oh my God! You're so goddamn stank."

I was disgusted. My titties wanted to suddenly become baby kangaroos and go back into the Mama's pouch.

His eyes sparkling. "Why thank you, baby."

He turned on "Throw that D" by the Two Live Crew. Oh, God! Strike one for no romance, even though I requested the song. I didn't actually *mean* it! This was not how I envisioned my first time. *Am I making a mistake?* I asked myself. When he moved towards me with his dick while I lay on his bed I was a little nervous. Yea I talked shit but I kept forgetting what Mama always told me, "Be careful what you ask for. You just might get it."

How true that was.

He approached me and we started kissing. I was reluctant, of course, because his breath was starting to lose its luster. Goddamn. This was a mistake. But my pussy was wet and I wanted him to fuck me so I could see what all the hoopla was about with his dick, and with sex in general.

Homeboy had skill. I rubbed his tight ass. Damn nice. His breath was even funkier now but he sucked on Tic Tacs on the way home so it was tolerable. My pussy responded in a way that even surprised me. He played with my pussy, digging in my pants, making me suck his fingers. I sucked on his neck, and then his ear and he moaned, tilting his head to the side. He got down on his knees, pulled my pants off and buried his face in my pussy. He tongued it, kissed and came up, saying, "I don't eat pussy. I just remembered. But you are sucking this dick. I'm the man. Deal with it. You want to wear my jersey then suck my number 2 pencil."

"I guess so." I was flabbergasted. But I did what he said.

I took the rest of my clothes off, slowly, looking around his room, wanting to puke. I looked very annoyed, very disgusted. I wanted to jump out the window, through the glass and everything but I couldn't. There were a few friends of mine outside his window, across the street and they didn't see me come in his crib and I didn't want news of Sidney fucking me getting back to school. I didn't want to be called a Ho.

He smiled sweetly. He was a cocky bastard. Determined to please me, he put his dick in my mouth. I had trouble sucking it because a) it was big and b) I was too driven. I tried to do the skills I saw on the porno but my teeth kept grazing his dick and he didn't jump or squint.

"Yea put your teeth on my shit," he said aggressively. "Suck it, baby." He had an incredible body. Smelled like football but I didn't care. He had huge nuts, and I ran my tongue over them, some of his pubic hairs getting in my fucking throat. *Arg! Ugh!*

He needed to shower, for real. I could smell his musk and asshole. Like he took a shit and didn't wipe correctly. I was about to gag but home boy thought it was because of his nature calling the confines of my mouth trying to find Ace Ventura.

"Yea, I love when the Hoes gag. Suck my dick, I wanna feel your spit trailing down my nuts an asshole, bitch."

I said nothing. I lay on his stinky bed. These SHEETS WERE FUNKY! My titties bouncing, he leaned back, his huge dick falling from my mouth. He got between my legs, with no finesse, and pushed my legs all the way back. He pushed up in my pussy so fast and hard I screamed from the pain. I was getting wetter down in my bushy terrains and it felt like flames. He pounded me like a demon, tearing into me. I was crying, digging my nails into his back.

"Damn this some good pussy!" He said, possessed. I truly didn't know who he was anymore. "Feels better than my girlfriend's. You wanted this dick, right?"

"No…"

I was sobbing. The shit hurt. I felt embarrassed and felt like an idiot! Sex wasn't shit! Where were the fireworks sluts talked about all the time? If dick felt this bad then I didn't understand why women craved it so much. They craved pain?

He kissed me and my lips didn't move.

I thought I'd be reasonable. "Get off me Sidney, please."

"No. I'm taking this pussy you gave it to me."

*Oh God help me Jesus, please!* "I know but it hurts."

"Me and my dick feel good, girl, now take this dick."

He fucked me harder, bouncing in my pussy like we fucked on a trampoline. I had to hold his ass to try to take the pain. I was falling off the bed. He didn't care. He grinded my tunnel.

Then out of nowhere this pleasure overcame me and my body jerked, my loins were burning and my spine tingled. It felt so good. I couldn't explain it. I felt my groin slowly bumping to his. I tried to find his rhythm, match his beat and now his dick felt sensational. He was giving me a feeling I *never* felt before. He slowed up when he saw my reaction and he tongued me passionately and I responded, thankful for him making me a woman, a whole woman, a real woman. I held his back, making demands. "Damn baby, shit, this feels good Sidney."

"You like this dick baby?"

"I love it baby…leave your bitch."

"This my pussy. And she has my pussy, too!"

"But I got that good pussy!"

"Ooooh shit I love when you talk about that pussy!"

The bedsprings squeaked nosily and this turned me on further. We moved as one. Rose and fell. Kissed and breathed each other's air. He got slower and more skilled; I was amazed at his control. Now he seemed concerned about me instead of himself. He watched my face, studied my reactions, sliding his grade A beef into me. I felt every inch, looked into his eyes, my pussy getting wetter and wetter.

He sucked on my titties, running his tongue all over them like the pro he was. I shivered. I never had this pleasure before.

I felt a building in my loins and it got stronger and stronger and I started shaking and he kissed me, winking at me, my pussy locked up and it started contracting and the feeling made me moan out his name Sidney! Sidney! *Siiiiiidddnnneeeyyyyyy!* What is happening to me?

He said, "You're coming, baby?"

"Women come?" I asked, my body trembling as the feeling took me up, up and away from this down, set, hike match with the star football player, hitting me in the right spots, sacking my pussy for the first time in my life.

I started crying again and he moved into me deeper and a little faster and the feeling came again, and I felt my pussy talking again as I got wetter. I moaned like there was no tomorrow.

"Damn," he said. "You're coming again, baby?"

"I guess…so…Oh…God!"

I came and came and came.

My body spent he wasn't done. He flipped me over with his dick still in me and he fucked me from the back, my clitoris getting a shaft shot. Damn, yo! Felt incredible. He was hitting spots I didn't know I had, and how could I know I had them? I just had sex for the first time.

Seconds later he pulled out and held in his moaning as he came all over my ass cheeks, spurting all over me like hot rain drops. With the skill of a porn star, he gently rubbed it in like lotion, almost admiring it. He taste some of his nut and kissed me with it. I must admit, tasted kinda sweet. Sweat trickled from his face and onto my body. It was hot as hell in here. I could barely breathe and I really smelled his ass now.

Smelled like shit in here, for real. When it was over I was out for the count. He watched me sleep and when I awakened, I was in my bed, hugging my teddy bear, wondering what in the hell was going on.

Disgruntled, I sat up in my bed, looked around and I smelled pasta through the door. The clock read 9 p.m. I was in a cloud of confusion. "How did I get home?"

Getting out of bed, in my school clothes, I looked down and saw blood all over my pants. Blood from where? Oh, God! What did he do to me? My house phone rang and I screamed to Mom that I'd get it. It was Sidney.

"Damn, I didn't fuck you good enough. You're up already."

"So it did happen?" I asked, thankful my room didn't smell like his.

"Yea."

"How did I get home?"

"I borrowed my mom's car when she showered and I carried you to it, put you on the back seat and drove to your house. Shit, took me ten minutes to find the right house key on your key chain. I finally found it, carried you to your bed, played with the pussy a little bit but when I seen blood I left your ass there and went home."

"Oh my God! I DON'T REMEMBER ANY OF THAT! How did you find my house?"

"Easy. Your friends told me."

"My friends who?"

"The ones who were outside my window, watching us."

"Oh God Sidney, they watched us?"

"Yea. You're the big topic at school. Down, set, hike. You do like football players, right?"

And he hung up.

I crawled in a ball on my bed and cried myself to sleep.

# Joints, Beer and the Cheating
# LOVERS

Oblivious to any rational thoughts, my boy and I rode around good ole Miami, in a deep silence. I had a bad craving for some weed. I always had a craving for weed. I smoked on excess of three joints a day, and thinking about it I needed to stop by Whopple Store in Goulds, just off of US1, and buy some Swisher Sweets so I could roll a few blunts.

Maybe I should use a Dutch Master. Nah, I couldn't even begin to make a choice. My mind was messed up. Really fucked up. But I did want to smoke. I didn't feel like swinging by my cousin Robert's house to pick it up. I was a little adamant about going. Seemed like twice a week SWAT was busting down his door. I was angry, I felt betrayed and unwanted. And it all had to do with my wife.

My loving wife. The Slut! Devastated, I was driving on I-95, bumping Pretty Ricky. I really didn't want to hear any music. I didn't feel like breathing, shitting or eating right now. My stomach was in knots. I fell out with a receptionist at Lender's bank a few hours ago. I told the bitch to take my wife off my bank account and she looked at me like I was stupid and said, with an attitude, "I need her here."

I frowned. "For what?"

"She has to sign off on the document."

*Sign? This isn't a prenup, bitch!* "But it's *my* account."

"And it became your *wife's* account, in conjunction with you, when you signed her on it. So you have yourself to blame."

This *Ho* really wants me to stomp her ass. In the bank! "Where's your customer service?"

"Sir, I'm talking to you with respect."

"Oh, now I'm 'sir!' Last week and a few months before that you called me by my first name. Now it's 'Sir?'"

"Please, sir, the bank is crowded and we have to get a move on."

"Ok, then, take my wife off my account. Today."

"Sir, it's against regulations—"

"—*Listen*, bitch!" Everyone in the bank looked at me. All activity ceased. "I don't know what kind of fan club you ugly Hoes are running, but it was my account years before I married the cheating bitch! Take her off. Or I'll close this account right now!"

Ten minutes later it was closed.

Now I'm driving my SUV, mad with the world. I hadn't felt this way since the day my daddy died.

"Why are you so quiet," my boy asked me. I remained silent. "Homeboy?"

I looked at him, red-eyed. "Yo."

"We're going to get through this."

"I don't know."

"We will."

"I feel dead inside."

Two hours later.

"My wife left me," my homeboy Kevin told me, like I didn't already know this shit.

"I know homeboy."

I loved his gravely, smoky voice. But I'll never tell him that. "Why the attitude?" he asked.

"Because you said that eight times in five minutes. And let's not count the number of times you said it while we drove around Miami in your SUV looking like zombies!"

"Damn, Clive! My wife cheated on me."

He huffed and puffed like he always did when he got aggravated.

"Goddamn, man!" he went on. He was full of drama, drama and more drama. I led a drama free life, you feel me?

I had my own problems. "I'm getting high," I said. "I can't help it. I got to get this shit off my mind; I got to get it out of my head. This isn't cool!"

He flipped the bird. "I'll tell you what isn't cool, you tripping."

I guffawed. "*You* are, too! Anyways. Pour me some Hennessy,"

I suggested and he flipped the bird at me again. I returned the gesture. He looked deep into my eyes. I felt chemistry building. "Pour your own shit. I'm not your bitch." He glared deep into my eyes. "And I never will be your bitch!"

"Ok. But first I have to tell you something."

"What?" He looked frustrated.

"My wife left me."

My friend laughed at me, bitterly. And I get pissed. "She wasn't good for you," he informed me, and I ignored him. Sometimes he could be the biggest asshole on the face of the earth. "My wife wasn't either. Our double wedding blew up in both our faces!"

His smile and laughter died to anger and a frown that shook me a little bit. He sipped his Hennessy, puffing on my joint.

I gave him the most confused look. "Why do you always talk down to me?"

"I'm your boy; I tell it like it is."

"And I guess that's what you're doing?"

"Yes, Clive, that's exactly what I'm doing. We both live in the heart of the ghetto, in sunny Opa Locka in Miami. We have no life. You're married, but your wife was caught sucking on another woman's pussy. A woman who *happens* to be *my* loving wife! And you're getting an attitude with me?"

Clive said, "Some friend you are, Kevin. And pass the weed; you're hogging it all up. I paid out the ass for that bag."

"I'll pass it when I'm finish!" My boy wanted to cry. I could see it written all over his beautiful face. He was a thug at heart and dressed the part and always carried his Glock. He'd shoot a Niggah quick. We've been to jail together and went to jail for each other. We had the same jobs, hated working for the man and hated politics and the President.

"Come on Kevin! I need to get higher than I am. All I have is a buzz; I'm not a goddamn bee."

He unzipped his stylish, red Echo jacket and passed me the almost-gone joint. Ten minutes ago, when I first got to his house (his stuff packed up in boxes from All Over Moving and Supply) my joint was six inches long, and he gives it back to me damn near an half of an inch. I wanted to kick his ass. Kevin and I have known each other since high school. We met when the both of us tried out for the junior varsity basketball game. The coach, fat-ass Mr. Samuel, refused to put us both on the same basketball team. He said all we did was talk and run trains on the bitches and he didn't want a "bad influence overshadowing the ethical diversity of his fucking basketball team!" I thought the team belonged to the high school.

I couldn't stand him. And back then basketball was my life, my heart. It was all I ever did, all I ever watched on TV. Michael Jordan and Erving Magic Johnson were my idols. I had everything Michael and Magic on my walls (posters, trading cards collected in my dressers, video games, sneakers). I used to play one-on-one with my Daddy, the Beloved, Late Reverend Henry, until he passed away of a heart attack (after fucking my Mama half to death, and when he had his thunderous orgasm, he died right on top of her).

I could still hear Mama's screaming through my bedroom walls after the sex ended. "MY BABY! MY BABY! WAKE UP! PLEASE, BABY, DON'T LEAVE ME WITH THREE SONS! BABY!"

I was stunned. I held the telephone, high off weed and I was paralyzed. I couldn't move. And when the ambulance wailed onto our drug-infested, dope-dealer-central block, everyone crowded around my house when my Daddy was wheeled into the ambulance, breathing mask on his face, dead. The Emergency workers had grim looks on their faces. I stood there in my P.Js, crying so hard I cracked open.

My boys held me together as the red and blue lights from the ambulance and police cars colored my face. I loved Daddy; he was attentive, warm and sincere. He loved people. He didn't have a hate bone in his body. He knew that bible. He loved my basketball skills. He always supported me in my games in junior high school, high school and college. He was my biggest fan.

Kevin and I were the same height (5 foot 9), the same age (28) and were from the same 'hood (where we lived now). We always had each other's back. We both married in the same church at the same time in front of four families. My wife was best friends with his wife. They grew up together and went through thick and thin together.

Liana, my wife and Beatrice, Kevin's wife were inseparable. The warning signs were there in the beginning, when every time I came home from work she was always there. Even after she got married, she wasn't home from her honeymoon for an hour and she was already tearing my door down to get to Liana. Girl this and that and we went to this and did that. I always left them alone and went over to Kevin's house when she came over. I figured they wanted their privacy.

And now this. My wife cheated on me, when she was in love with Kevin's wife, even before we married. An hour and three blunts later, Kevin and I were watching Method Man on the movie *How High*. One of my favorites. We sat in his living room. The big screen flashing in our faces the way those police lights flashed on me when my Daddy died. I was sad now, feeling vulnerable. I loved my wife; we had a good home, even if it was in the ghetto. We had goals of having our own business. She was my world. I was faithful to her in every sense of the word. I never flirted with the Hoes behind her back. I always put her first. And she did this to me and Kevin and his wife. Heartless bitch. I held in my tears. A thug never cried. I closed myself off to the love I had for her. My boy lit another joint. I was already bouncing around Mars, looking for red sand and he wanted me on Jupiter. Higher. So I went *higher*. When I took the joint from him my hand grazed his. Vulnerable, he looked at me. He was so handsome. Of course I had to keep it G-rated, couldn't tell him that. His baggy pants were under his ass and his Timberland-clad feet were propped up on the *Vibe* magazine-cluttered low-table.

"All right punk, you aren't got to touch on my hand like that. I don't do the freaky-deaky shit. Just get the Dutch and puff puff, my Niggah."

I squeezed his upper thigh and he chopped me playfully. I took the joint. "Niggah, I don't want to touch you."

"Yes you do," he challenged me. And I accepted the battle.

"That's what your wife is for."

He was high, drunk and sad. I felt bad. My heart sank, and I hid it from my face. I wasn't a Ho-ass Niggah, but Kevin loved his wife just as much as I loved mine. We were dedicated Niggahs, turned down pussy for our wives, turned down money and cars.

"I'm sorry," I said, apologizing. He hugged me, held me tight.

"Please, don't let me go," he said, shaking. I felt him trembling.

I held him back, welcoming his arms. I felt good in them...He leaned back and kissed my lips. Softly. Looking into my eyes as I inhaled Hennessy and weed from his sweet, moist breath.

He looked sexy. I fought myself not to think that way. He had a big ass and a nice body. Very young-looking. I leaned up to his quivering lips. Gave him a kiss. Something to remember.

"If our wives can fuck then their husbands can fuck, too," he said, taking off my pants. I had on silk boxers, with weed all over it.

Like a starving lion, he took out my dick and started slowly chopping me up, sucking the pole the way he wanted his sucked.

Hating distractions, I picked up the remote and turned off the TV. He pulled and noisily slurped. My boy gave head before because his teeth didn't graze my shit. I leaned my head back, opening my legs. I had on a brown jacket. I took it off; he kept my nine inches deep in his hot mouth.

"Suck it…!" I told him, grabbing the top of his head and fucking that pretty mouth. He gagged and chocked but he kept swallowing the dick. He moaned like a bitch. I slapped his ass, whack, and put my right hand in his pants, playing around with a butt that had never been fucked. I pulled my hand out, sucked on two fingers, and put my hand back on the ass, massaging that tight hole. He twirled that ass on my fingers as they slowly entered new territory. His eyes wide, he moaned louder, taking my dick out his mouth and I slapped his face with my big dick.

"Put it back in your mouth! Did I tell you to take it out?"

"No, baby…."

I was a beast, taking out my anger on his body. "I want to feel the back of your throat!"

He sucked me so slow, so good. I pumped his mouth. My nuts bouncing. My masculine moans filled the house. After I came on his face I stood up, turned him around, slapped that ass and made him get in the doggy style position. I spread his cheeks apart and sucked the middle like my favorite candy, giving him my thick tongue.

He went crazy. "Oh, Niggah that feels so good. I shoulda did this shit years ago. You're making me feel like a bitch!"

I ate him out like he was one of my females, he tasted so good. He tasted better than any woman I've ever been with. He turned into a bitch. "Who's my bitch?" I asked him, demanding an answer.

"I am, dawg! I'm yours!" He only wore the do-rag and boots. His birthday suit was a bit sweaty. His sweet ass was in my face.

I then slid up in the hole, giving him all nine inches, slowly; expertly…his hole was so tight, so hot. He, wide-eyed, looked back at me. He couldn't believe it felt like this, so good. I can't believe I never thought about fucking my homeboy. He felt so good.

I fucked the shit out of him. He was a thug. And I told him to take it like a thug. He whimpered, cried, and begged me to stop. He said it felt *too* good. He couldn't handle it; he said the pleasure was too much.

I grinded inside him harder, putting one leg on the sofa and tagging that ass. His ass jiggled, he was loosening…He fell on his face. I kept tagging it. I was controlling the out-of-control-bull. I was watching myself slide in and out of him so fast it made his head spin. I slapped his ass, over and over and over. We were drenched with sweat.

"You love this shit?"

"Yea, Daddy!"

"You belong to Daddy?"

He looked like he was having panic attacks, turned me on even more. "YES!"

"You ready for this nut?"

His eyes rolled to the back of his head. "Yes I am!"

I wasn't convinced. "You aren't ready for this nut!"

He was whimpering. "MAH NIGGAH I'M READY!"

We were yelling so loud we didn't give a fuck if anybody heard.

I shot my ball-jolting load deep inside him, letting him feel my dick pump my preemies. His walls were still tight on my dick, and he began throwing that ass on my shit, and I damn near buckled at the knees. I had him hooked. I was going to have sex with him every day. He didn't have a choice. I was addicted to his ass, and he had some good ass at that. When I pulled out the front door opened and our wives walked inside, puffing a joint. They were holding Budweiser beer cans.

"Yea, girl, he mad 'cause I sucked that pussy," said Liana.

Beatrice beamed. "Anyways, fuck them! They always together! They never have time for us."

"Girl, it smells like sex in your house."

Beatrice looked at her, clad in a skimpy skirt and a Lenny Kravitz T-shirt. "No it doesn't, probably my carpet in the living room. It's mildewing. My man wouldn't cheat on me. Even though he walked in on us, he wouldn't hurt me..."

They turned to face my new Niggah and I kissing. Their mouths fell open in shock. We lay there, smiling. I loved the reaction. It made me smile again. My boy looks at me and says, "Light up another joint. They were just leaving. Revenge is a bitch, isn't it..."

I smiled victoriously at my cheating wife. "Let's go to Saturn this time."

Beatrice walked over to us, silent. She sat by her husband. She was taking this all in. I thought she was in a state of shock. She kept rubbing her eyes, looking at us, pinching her skin. She looked pale. I knew she was in pain. The joke was on her. How did she like that? How did she expect us to react? Were we supposed to give a fuck when she'd been fucking my wife for months, probably years? My heart went out to her but the Thug in me wouldn't let it go too far. He took off his wedding ring and threw it across the room. It smashed into their huge wedding picture hanging in the dining room, and the glass cracked.

"BULLSEYE!" he screamed evilly, staring at her with the most wicked smile I'd ever seen.

He went on. "Got something to say? Feel like bashing me? Are you hurting? Am I twisting the knife in your back deeper, the same knife you used on me?"

"Baby..."

"I'm not your baby. I'm not your husband. You can try to take my house, bitch, it isn't going to happen. You committed adultery first! Now bitch try me!"

I touched his arm, looking at him sweetly. "Calm down. No sense in fighting. We all hurt each other. We're human. We're acting like children. And we're making hasty decisions based on hurt and pain. Calm down."

When I pulled on the weed, she said, "Can I get next on the weed? I need it."

I looked at my boy and laughed so hard I fell off the chair.

# Purple Panties

My purple panties were fabulous, gripping my Grade A ass like they loved me. I gave my best puppy dog look, clad in a long, huge-belted trench coat standing in my living room. I looked so Beyonce Knowles "Ring the Alarm," but I wasn't angry. My name was Rosaline Cowart. I was known as "Roz." I was full of love and I wanted to be full of my man's you know what I was saying.

"Baby, you *work* too much," I told him with my Ima-bad-girl voice.

He loved me so much, so deeply. It danced in his gorgeously brown honey-dew colored eyes. He was sexy, super fine and he had a heart of gold but I didn't love myself and I didn't believe in gold and I just wanted good dick, which was why I dated him. I never anticipated getting feelings for a man who treated me like royalty in the beginning, until I started getting demanding and misunderstanding everything he ever said or did. I wanted to show him these sexy purple panties, so I could play the Black Kim Bassinger or was it Sharon Stone? from *Basic Instinct*, to show this young Ho Beyonce Knowles how to properly do it without all the SWAT members in her crazy, stupid, rushed video. He looked me over. I knew he loved me but sometimes I didn't know. We've been having problems lately, and now it seemed like we argued over toothpaste as well as other trivial things. We argued over who was going to walk the German Sheppard. We argued over who was going to take my Mama dinner. She was in a wheel chair and couldn't get around like she used to. Blame it on the car crash three years before. And my Daddy was too busy running around, at 60, still making different families with these young, can't control-the-pussy hoes. He has four families so far. His dick was legend. Women talked about his twelve inches in the hair salons from Miami, Florida to Savannah, Georgia.

"I don't work enough," my boyfriend said exhaustedly, clad in his Publix supermarket uniform. Goddamn the attitude was starting to get to me. Why couldn't we be happy, like in the beginning? I know I told my share of lies. I know I haven't been completely honest with him but what woman was completely honest?

He cut off the goatee, Publix Supermarket regulations, which was a dumb ass regulation. His mustache had to be at a moderate length, barely there I called it. No earrings and my man loved his jewelry. He was the Stock Manager in the downtown Miami store.

My brows rose. "You don't what?"

"Have you been taking showers effectively?" he asked off-handedly.

I was deeply offended. "What do you mean?" I asked breathlessly, trying to control myself, trying to keep it together like the girl singing group 702 and those singing bitches from Vegas haven't been a real group since, well, you get the point.

He gave a tart smile. He shot icily, "Because if you have, you would have stayed in the shower long enough to clean the wax out of your ears so I wouldn't have to repeat myself. No wonder Q-Tips went down on the NASDAQ."

*No he didn't!* "Fuck you, Pierre."

My words seemed to have knocked him in the gut. He winced a tad. And I didn't goddamn care! He stared deeply into my eyes with his famous sexy gaze. The one that set me on fire. He said simply, "You wish…"

That made my blood boiled, how nonchalant he was. I was hurt beyond reason. I didn't deserve this shit. I said, "And that's beginning to be a problem. I want to be fucked, baby."

He rolled his eyes. "I don't *have* any babies. I don't remember seeing you go through nine months of labor, Missy. Your *ex* fathered all your children, who you barely see and barely know. No *wonder* he has custody of them…and that's all we ever do is fuck. We get mad we fuck. Happy we fuck. Cook, we fuck. Come home from a funeral, we fuck."

My nipples were hard. I loved when he got mad, he got aggressive and that If-I- ever-Crossed-your-Mind-Brian-McKnight shit went right out the window. I said, "And is that so bad?"

"You don't *know* me."

"I know you like the back of my hand."

He had challenging eyes. "What size boxers I wear?"

Now see, this was the kinda shit that made me mad. Why did he challenge me like that? "You wear draws."

His eyes lit up. "Wrong. Draws gives me a rash. What size do I wear?"

I shot from the hip. "A nine."

His mouth hit the floor. "A nine?" he spat vehemently. He couldn't believe his ears. "I said boxers, not *shoe* size."

He was appalled. Right now he couldn't stand the sight of me and the only sight I wanted to see was his dick going in and out of me until I came out the gushy stuff. He had some good dick!

"Anyways, this is pointless."

He got in my face. "What's my favorite color?"

"Blue," I guessed.

"Black. And my favorite entertainer?"

I felt stupid. "Toni Braxton."

He rolled his eyes and released a large gush of air. "I can't *stand* the bitch. Whitney is my favorite entertainer."

OK. So I didn't know him like the back of my hand, which is probably why I barely look at my hands. "We need to talk."

He sneered. It made my heart jump. "All you *do* is talk, Inspector Gadget."

I tucked my chin back. "Inspector Gadget."

"Yea." He walked up to me, his hands in his pockets. *Hold me! Touch me! Kiss me! Do something, Niggah!* I craved his touch. He hadn't touched me in a few months. Always working, and when he got home, he crawled into bed. Funk and all, and snored so loud my ears packed up and left town. "What's with the trench coat?"

"I'm cold."

"Hearted, tell me about it." He shook his head, sneering at me. Clearly not wanting to play my game, he checked his watch.

"Why are you acting like this? Are we about to argue again?" I asked him, getting unnerved really quickly. "I'd rather fuck baby. Let me suck on that dick a little, come on baby. *You're* so uptight."

"Why should we? It'll be pointless. I tell you what. *Your* favorite color is pink."

Ok he caught me off guard with this. What kind of *game* was he playing? "And?"

"Pink because your favorite spot on your body is your pussy and pink reminds you of that and your favorite food is shrimp, grilled shrimp with extra Lawry's Season Salt and Louisiana Hot Sauce, which is more for flavoring. And you are a Leo, you hate Valentine's Day, your wear your bra one size too small cause you like the way your pretty titties look in it, you hate chocolate, you detest peanuts and your favorite entertainer is Patti Labelle."

I got real quiet. And my pussy was WET WET WET! I could see the tears biting at the bottom of his eyes, but he didn't want to be or look like soft so he said, "Damn it must be dust in here 'cause my allergies are fucking me up."

He didn't have allergies. My temperature rose. "I hate you," I said out of anger and he just winked at me, grabbing his car keys from the low-table.

I've been with Tay for three years. He was so attentive and sincere, well he was in the beginning, when we met at the Red Lobster. I was just getting out of a ten year relationship, not looking forward to divorce or fighting over custody of my children.

But I was facing it, and being in my early forties, when your shit was supposed to be together, this just made me sick to my stomach. A white bitch destroyed my happy home. All because I wouldn't go down on my ex husband and suck his dick. He figured all wives all over the world suck dick, so baby you aren't an exception, he told me and I showed him what part of my ass he could kiss. Truth be told, he pissed from his dick so why would I want to suck on the Piss Carrier?

"I know. You hated me for months."

I narrowed my eyes suspiciously. I said, calmly, "Why do you say that?"

He paused at the front door. His head hung low and my heart hung lower. Something was eating him alive. I wanted to know what? What could it possibly be? He looked sad, like every light in his mental house went dark, power outage.

"I gotta go to work, Roz. I'll see you when I get off at 11 PM."

I gave a faint smile, my heart melting for him. "Ok."

He turned to face me. Tears fell from his eyes. Now I knew something was wrong. I rushed up to him, my patent leather boots itching my feet.

"What is it, baby, tell me. Why are you crying?" A knot formed in my throat. My chest felt tight. I couldn't breathe.

He held my face. "Have fun tonight."

"I won't be gone long, baby."

"I know. How is my god brother doing?" he asked sarcastically. *Shit, what made him ask about his god brother?* "He's doing all right."

"Good, tell him when he gets back in town I want him to call me. Pierre."

The color left my face. "Get back, what are you talking about, baby? And your name is Tay."

"I know. You called me 'Pierre' a few minutes ago. Pierre is my god brother's name. Not mine."

I covered my mouth, trying to find a quick lie to cover my ass. But no words formulated. "Baby…" Words failed me.

He smiled evilly. "I know he's out of town. And you've been going over to his house every night, baby. Screwing his wife with your plastic humming toys. Wasn't my dick enough? I didn't eat you right?"

My world exploding painfully, he went on and on and I felt like complete shit. I wanted to run and pull my hair out. I hurt this man. How could I?

He went on. "You told me you were hanging out with him and his wife. You said ya'll played spades to kill the time. Those were lies. I followed you last night. I saw your lesbian lover eating your pussy on his couch. I didn't know I had a gay girlfriend and no I am not happy. I didn't even know she licked pussy! I wonder if he knows. I'ma find out, believe me I am! Next time close the door all the way and make sure it's locked."

"I can explain…"

He held up his hand, shutting me up. His eyes were blood shot red. "I should cook her some chicken and throw a party that she took my lady from me."

"She hates chicken. She loves lasagna."

"And buy green streamers and throw a party—"

"She loves the color gray, and she hates a crowd."

"Maybe I can buy her some damn crotchless panties; I know she's a size 9."

"No, she's a size 6."

"And I can buy her some of those nine inch pumps; I think she's a size 5."

"She's a size six, and she hates heels over four inches."

"*Voila!* And there you have it. You know more about her than me, you can't even get my favorite color right. I was testing you; you stupid motherfucking cunt bitch!"

Before I could get over my shock for falling in his trap, incriminating myself beyond repair, he pushed me on the couch and I shattered like glass. I felt like I was on fire.

"Oh, God baby! I'm sorry! I can explain."

"Explain *what?* Tell me about it while I'm at work. When Ken's Moving Service get here tonight show them my things so they can pack it up and I'll be gone forever. Oh," he went on, faking a smile, "…I love the Purple Panties! Those are the same panties I bought my homeboy's wife for their wedding. And now *you* have them on, but of course you didn't know me at the time. That was also a dead giveaway, slut!"

Angrily, he slammed the door closed behind him and the force made me jump.

My man busted me.

# Rayne in the Bedroom

"Honey, I want to live out my dreams!" she said.

"Then live it." He said, nearly whispering. He was handsomely clad in a velvet top hat and a smoke-colored suit.

"Is she coming?"

"Yes."

"Really?"

"*Yes!* Are you mad?"

"No! This is girl number three. All in a week's time period!"

"Yes. It is," he said simply. He puffed on his cigarette in sync with his lady.

"But what about the photographs on the night stand?"

"They can stay. She just wants to be paid."

She smiled with her man. Let the fantasy begin.

Ah, the British accent worked wonders.


An hour later.

She stood five feet four inches, fire engine red hair that draped down to her amazingly well crafted buttocks. She prided herself on her good looks. She was only 19 years old. What did 19 year olds know about the power of the pussy? *Easy, when you have the mental capacity to match, the sky is the limit, and the sky can get between my legs and go Bone Appetite, too.*

*If I had half a brain I'd admit that I'm thirty nine years old! I look good for my age. I told this jerk I was 19 because, on his online profile, Sex me right now.com, he only wanted girls from ages 18-21. And I needed the money. He offered me five hundred dollars. Cash. No C.O.D. or I.O.Us.*

"What is your name?"

She gave him her best Marilyn Monroe imitation, trying to stop herself from doing something she'd never done: prostitution.

"I told you over the phone," she said intently, elegantly moving about the bedroom.

He astutely studied her. She looked like a seasoned professional, but she wasn't. She was amateurish, and she didn't know what to say or do. *I can always leave! I can tell him I left my cigarettes in the car. No. He had cigarettes on his dresser. I could say my son needed me? No, I already told him my sons were with their grandmother. My shit-talking mother. Oh, God I can't let her controlling ass find out!*

Unfortunately, she felt unnoticeably lost in here with all the gilt framing, the frescoed ceilings, the expensive Oriental carpeting and the red walls of which some of the most elegant art hung. Felt so Renaissance in this room. This was a very different world from where she came from. The Bronx.

Cool and collected, he pulled on his Salem Light cigarette, looking poised. Too poised to be a man, but he was a man, an immaculately handsome man. *That* she couldn't deny. Over his heavenly eyes were thick Bandi shades. *Why the shades indoors? The little sunlight coming through the windows was somewhat shielded by the lavish curtains and vertical blinds, barely opened. What are you hiding? Mama always said just because you wear glasses doesn't make you smart, especially when they're shades.*

"Tell me again," he said smoothly and she took his cigarette and stubbed it out in the ash tray on the night stand that held three 5x7 framed photos of a very gorgeous woman clad in a summer dress. She had full curves; she was smiling into the lens like she hadn't a care in the world. She didn't want to smell smoke, not when the room smelled like roses.

She looked him square in the eyes. And said, "Rayne."

He loved the way her lips moved. "You mean rain? As in the morning weather when a Paris mist drifts to Miami after three a.m.?"

She rolled her eyes, especially unnerved at his British accent. *This fucker is crazy! I've never been to Paris and I've never seen it. Isn't that where people fuck in the streets while tourists pass by? And why does it sound like he's speaking British? Paris isn't in Great Britain, or is it?*

She really didn't give a shit. She drove her need-a-tune-up-and-oil-change '83 Mazda hatchback all the way from Miami Lakes. She fought 4 p.m. traffic on Florida's treacherous Turnpike, where Cubans seemed to crash into each other like toppling Lego's. And once she got to his three story estate in the boonies, located in the Redlands she parked her car by a huge fountain and told herself one thing: she was there to fuck and get paid for it. The hell with all the Jagged Edge "Meet me at the Alter" fantasies. Ain't nothing going on but the rent! And a bitch like her had a mortgage payment a car note, food to buy, and an overdue light bill

She had a three year old son at home who wanted to eat and wanted this and that. She barely got by on welfare. She had a job interview at the Super Wal-Mart just off of Okeechobee Boulevard. But that wasn't definite. She had a thirteen year old who wanted a Play station 3 that was about to come out later this year, he wanted a bike; he wanted new clothes to impress his new girlfriend and his girlfriend better take her fat ass to her parents and have their asses fork over some cash to make shit easier on her. She was against him having a girlfriend, but she let him because, with how grown these sack of shit children were these days, he'd do it anyway, he'd rebel. She certainly had, at his age, and now she was getting back what she gave her mother in spades.

She thought she could hold off the Playstation 3 until a month went by when she got her two child support checks, which were peanuts, but she couldn't. Her baby fathers were in prison; they were best friends, actually, locked up for trying to rob a Farm Store and got away with a hundred dollars and a five year prison sentence. She didn't write and she didn't accept their collect calls. Fuck 'em. Fuck 'em to hell! Dumb motherfuckers! Killed your freedom over minimal cash.

She then held her son Melvin off further by telling him, "Make straight A's in school, I'll get you a Playstation." Melvin, a very good kid with brains of steel and a sexy body already making the girls swoon, brought his report card home a few weeks later with so many A's on it she had to run in the bathroom, turn up the small stereo on the niche next to her tampons and half empty douche bottle, turn on the shower and just boo hoo boo hoo because she couldn't raise kids on her own.

Her children needed their jailbait daddies and them trying to run shit from jail wasn't happening, because her kids needed them their physically to teach them how to be men, how to treat women and how to handle tough situations life threw in their path. She could only do so much as a mother, she didn't know how a dick worked, how to use one or how to teach them to be men. She had titties and a pussy, and women were a man's rib, according to the good book so how could a rib show a rib cage how to be ribs?

He broke the silence. "Did you hear me?" He stood in front of her.

"Hear what?" She lay back on her elbows, her hair framing her angelic face.

"My Paris comment?"

"Yes, I heard you. And I don't know what you're talking about. But its Rayne, R-A-Y-N-E."

Amused, he looked her up and down. He had a thick Yosemite Sam mustache, very gorgeous body and was clad superbly in a smoke-colored suit. He set her on fire. She looked him over. *Why are you so quiet?* she wondered. Feeling a tad bit uneasy, she got undressed. She slowly peeled off her rose-colored blouse then her satin bra and lace panties. She left on the hooker/cooker heels. His keen eyes widened from such a lovely sight! She wanted some music, but decided against it. *I was getting paid for a service, not a concert*, she thought smartly.

She was getting tired of all the beating around the bush. "All this ass and pussy in your face and you just stand there? I'm not your wife. She'll be home soon. Let's get it on Marvin Gaye Style."

"Marvin's too 60s, 70s," he said knowingly, massaging his hard on. She looked down. He wasn't massaging much. She was a size queen. She loved the motion in the ocean.

*Should I fake a back ache?* she thought cryptically. Her mind raced. She kicked off her stilettos and settled on his bed, looking confused but luxurious. She loved the yachts floating, drifting, sailing. Who wanted a speed boat? Who wanted a row boat; she didn't need it rowing gently down her stream. Oh, no she didn't! And life was damn sure not a fucking dream! She didn't want a canoe with an oar; just the oar was fine by her.

"Do you mind some lesbian action?" he asked and her heart dropped.

*What is it with men and the two women fantasy? I'm not trying to become a "butch" anytime soon.* "No. I'm strictly dickley."

"Mind if I just eat you? I do not really want sex right now. It's a fantasy of mine."

*Thank God!* "Why yes. Eat away."

He got on his knees, crawling like a lion. Spreading her legs, he dove between them, smelling her pussy. He ran his nose over her well-trimmed pubic hairs, separating her walls with quivering hands. He was anxiously running his tongue up and down her pink sanctuary. She shivered from his touch. *Wow! Wow, he's very good at what he do!*

He sucked on her clitoris while she played with her nipples, bringing her ample breast up to a hungry tongue and she licked it gently. Tiny explosions set her off. She bumped pelvis to tongue. Rising and falling. Tasting her pussy from his fingers. Yummy.

He turned her on her stomach, putting a pillow under her tummy. He tasted her from the back, tenderly massaging her ass. She cooed into the pillow, wanting to pull her hair out. The slurping noises filled her ears the way his tongue filled her. She felt the explosions creeping up her spine, her thighs and her knees. They popped in her pussy so fiercely she felt her body arch and her torso moved at breakneck speed on his tongue, as if it was his male hardness. She burst open like a pissed off river, coming on his tongue, moaning so loud it filled the room.

"Oh, *God! Suck* that pussy! Oh, God…I'm *coming!* Oh my GOD!"

Her body shook like pistons, she was wiggling this way and that, gripping the covers inside closed fists…The earthquake was inevitably over, the ocean was drained.

A satisfied smile on her tired-looking face, she turned over, her breasts shaking like mountains crumpling. And she held her stomach, tears falling down her face. She felt spent, alive, and wonderful!

"WOW!" she said to him. That was the best head of her life. No one had ever sucked her pussy with such urgency, such passion. Pleased by his performance, he began unbuttoning his coat and dropped it on the Lazy Boy, by the computer.

"You're amazing!" she went on, warming to her new lover.

A shit-eating grin. "Still don't want any lesbian action?" The piercing eyes narrowed.

Rayne smiled sweetly. "No thanks. What you did was enough."

He pulled five hundred bucks from the top nightstand drawer and handed them to her. "This is for you. For fulfilling my fantasy."

She took the money, and forced herself to get out of bed. He walked up to her and tongued her, taking off the shades.

He had green eyes, like the woman in the picture.

"I love your eyes!" she gushed.

"I love your pussy," he said, his voice devoid of the British accent.

It was a fake! He took off the top hat. His hair was stuffed under a black hair net. Off came the net. His hair fell around his face. He then smiled as Rayne, shaking her head in disbelief, began walking backward. He took off his Italian shirt and his tits were duck taped to his skin, making them look small. Rayne covered her mouth, clearly stunned. Off came the tape and the tits popped free.

They were more gorgeous than *Rayne's*! Lastly, he swiftly kicked off his boots and unbuttoned his pants. The sock fell on the floor with her heart. Rayne wanted to die. "Oh my God! You're the woman from the photographs on the nightstand," she said in shock. Her knees drummed together. "You're not a man. You don't have a wife. You lied!"

The Woman smiled at her. "My name's Clever. Thanks for the fantasy. I posed as a man to get what I wanted. Me and my imaginary man is proud to be of service," she went on. She inhaled Rayne's pussy from her top lip, giving her a natural high. She was picking up the hair net and the top hat, slanting it on her head where it covered her right eye. So theatrical.

Clever didn't care to see her again. *Get out, bitch!* "Now will you please leave? We're expecting another young woman. Her name is Elizabeth. I have to put back on the male disguise so I can fool her." She looked dead into Rayne's sad eyes. She felt nothing for Rayne. "The way we fooled you. Good bye."

*Get out, prostitute! I already paid you. Leave!* While Rayne sat on the edge of the bed, confused and deeply embarrassed, Clever snatched up her male disguise and sauntered into the Ladies room. Gently closing the door behind her.

Rayne had never run so fast in her life.

"Honey, I want to live out my dreams!"

"Then live it," he said, clad in a velvet top hat and a smoke-colored suit.

"Is she coming?"

"Yes."

"This is girl number four. All in a week's time period!"

"Yes! *Yes*!"

Smiling intently, she looked herself over in the mirror. She enjoyed talking to her split personality, all in her head.

"But what about the photographs?" she asked nonchalantly.

She changed her voice to the British accent.

"They can stay. She just wants to be paid."

She smiled at the male disguised reflection.

"Let the fantasy begin!"

Ah, the British accent worked wonders.

# On the Low-Low

I was in love with my dude, Terrance Jo'Shawn. And I wasn't going to apologize for it. Being in love with him reminded me of when I used to shoot pool with my step father. I knew he wasn't my real daddy but the things we did together reminded me of heaven, and I wanted to always stay there, shooting pool, listening to his directions of the game. How to hold the stick. The strategy. Learning your opponent, getting his weaknesses and using it against him. And the day I laid eyes on Terrance, all the rules of the pool game, and what my now ex-step father taught me was the gospel.

Who thought a rambunctious, 27-year old ex thug would ever admit something like that, considering so many other factors were in the mix to reprieve Jerry Springer. But this was more Oprah material than anything.

Terrance was very original. He made me laugh, cry and smile. I couldn't quite understand or wrap my mind around him. I mean, this man was far more superior than I. He was a lot stronger than I was. The things he survived and lived through I commended him on. If I would have went through being raped, a brief crack cocaine use and hating my mother I probably would have gone insane. But the man I loved and admired bounced back from the odds, wrote his own epiphany and prevailed above the naysayers and the haters.

He was conceited. Not in a stuck up way. We were both 'hood. We *kept* it 'hood most of the time, despite our careers and our professions. It took him forty minutes to get to work. It took me twenty. I made $30 an hour working for a cell phone company. I was one of the well-trained Branch Managers.

My dude had a Bachelor's degree in Business from Morehouse College and worked for a small time business that catered to up and coming lawyers. He also sold bootleg CDs and DVDs. He had been doing this for a couple years now. He made nearly two thousand dollars a week from *that* alone.

He was a one man shop. And I always admired him for the way he hustled. His business savvy was superb. He had flyers and business cards. His bootlegs were of high quality, high definition; complete with cover art and all. He pushed more copies of DMX, Letoya Luckett, Beyonce and Janet Jackson's new joint 20 Y.O. than Janet, Jermaine, Beyonce, Letoya, DMX and Virgin Records combined.

He sold damn near 800,000 copies combined just from the click of his laptop and the trunk of his car. Ten dollars a pop. He knew the shit was illegal, but he didn't care. He was so smooth with his shit, always covered his tracks and never got caught. I hated the fact that his vocal cords were deeper than mine. I talked like Morris Chestnut from the movies. He talked like Mekhi Phiefer mixed with the rapper

DMX. That real 'hood voice that made your skin crawl and any Niggah's dick hard, straight or not. My dick had been getting hard from his voice for 15 years, since we played on the basketball team at Northwestern Senior High School back in the nineties.

I been wanting this Niggah since then but we got so wrapped up in life and its forever changing bullshit that we decided to just shed it all away like a bitch's period once a month. The sexual tension and chemistry have always been evident with both of us, but we ignored it and never talked about it. DJ battles twice a week was our life back in the day. Living in the "Subs" during the Summer with my gangster Grandma who pushed more dope than Scarface and got more dick than the twenty year old bitches; and we lived with our mothers, who resided on the same street, NW 22 Avenue and 53 Street, when not with Grandma.

Back then our lives were all about smoking Black and Mild cigars and wearing baggy jeans, unlaced boots and do-rags covering our wavy hair. We were driving whips (cars) at the age of fourteen. We had matching blue Chevies on chrome rims. We were getting phone numbers from the bitches and playing the Hoes. Getting pussy was a ritual. Our Head Sessions never left our minds. The weed and alcohol influenced us. Being the envy of nearly every Niggah in the 'hood, who wanted in our circle, was our life line. We never stayed home. Worrying our parents to death we didn't try to do but was the end result. The streets loved us and we loved them. School, work and sports drove us. Practice and football and basketball games we would die for. Life was a party for us back then.

Now, all these years later, we were about to have another type of party. He always talked about himself, but not in a way that seemed condescending. You felt a sense of urgency and pride when he spoke. He changed you when he spoke. I, on the other hand, hated talking about myself. I was the one who normally offered solutions. I wanted to solve problems all the time. I thought I knew all there was to know about everything. You couldn't really tell my stubborn, thick-headed ass shit. I was more intimidated by the unknown and I worried about myself more than anybody I knew. We also sold a little weed on the side. Because Niggahs couldn't get enough money. Every black man had a little (or a lot) of Niggah in them, no matter how they tried to denounce it or cover it up by blasting the usage of the N-Word. We both came from the slums. We both had unfortunate beginnings. And because of that, and all the murder we saw as kids, all the rapes we witnessed, all the financial hardships our mothers and fathers endured, we had thick skin. My motto was: If it's about that paper, than I was there to chase it.

We fought and fucked all our lives. I knew him most of my life but refused to get close to him. I always had his back. We were like brothers. I watched him fuck bitches. He watched me fuck bitches. We watched lesbians fuck each other. We fucked bitches together. Well, all the time to tell you the truth. Every day was a different Hoe. But I kept the feelings at bay. If I had half a brain I'd admit that I was in love with him, that my feelings were already involved. But the 'hood side of me, the gangster side that liked totting guns and tossing bullets and smoking weed, always overshadowed feelings. We were rolling blunts by age 8. We were experienced in shooting everything from .357 Magnums to M-16's before we turned twelve.

An ex crooked cop taught us one day when we were walking home from school, a few days after the annual Martin Luther King, Jr. Parade in The City. We saw him under one of the Under Passes, Downtown Miami. Crack heads were some of everywhere. Must have been about that time for another re-up, I figured. We sold crack so I had a pocket full. My intent was to sell all I had, which was $400 worth, and get my ass home. My boy had about the same amount in product in his underwear. Clad in matching Malcolm X shirts and baggy jean shorts with brand new black Addidas shoes, we were about to hop on the Metro Rail. Terrance and I never went anywhere alone. Not with all the perverts and Niggahs out to get our cheddar. Our only defense was mace, our fists and knives.

That was until we met Officer James. We noticed he was putting a dead body in the trunk of his Monte Carlo. KRS-One was rapping from the stereo. He had on black cargo pants and a police shirt with his badge swinging from his neck. I remember it was hot as hell that day and my boy was like, "Yo! That Niggah *killed* somebody."

I looked. And my mouth fell open. Trying to prevent us from being killed, I grabbed my boy's arm and we slowed up, narrowing our eyes, scooping this Niggah. Goddamn. We shouldn't have come this way. Nervous, we had tried to turn the other way, hoping the nearby bushes would obscure our presence but his keen eyes caught us and he screamed, "Hey! Get ya'll black asses over here."

"Hell nah, Niggah," Terrance said, about to run. He was scared out of his mind.

I kept it 'hood. I wasn't scared at all. I was curious. "Let's go see."

"He might pop us, Norman! I am not with that shit, my Niggah."

"Let's go!"

I took him by the arm and pulled him with me. When we walked up to the police officer, we had our shoulders straight, little chest out and back straight. He smiled at us. We didn't smile back.

"Sup, dawg?" my boy told him. "What it do, pimpin'?"

I just nodded.

"I'm Officer James." He shook our hands. "Firm grips, I like that. Where are you boys from?"

I looked at this handsome 6 foot tall Niggah. Gold teeth. Looked like he just cut his dread locks off. They were strewn all over the dead body, trunk and the ground. He was sweating profusely. Money and huge bags of cocaine took up most of the trunk.

I told him we were from The City. He smiled. "Really. So am I: 17th Ave and 83rd Terrace to be exact."

"My mama stays…"

Alarmed, I popped my boy in back of the head. "Shut up! Before you get us popped and our Mamas, too."

Officer James said, "*You're* loyal. I *like* that. Ya'll ever shoot a gun before?"

"Nah," we both said. We didn't. But with competition out in the 'hood, it was only a matter of time before we needed a gun. The thought actually made me smile.

Going into the back seat, he handed me a .357. I took it with trembling lips and hands. I had a heat right in my possession! Wow!

Absent-mindedly, he handed my boy an M-16 from the trunk. And he spent an hour teaching us how to shoot cans and rotten apples. Near-by concrete bricks. He taught us breathing techniques. Proper stances. How to hold it, he was very skilled.

After our session he gave us the .357. I held it like I was a big man. My boy wanted the M-16, but we decided against it. Couldn't hide a damn M-16 on the Metro Rail. Metro Dade Police would have our asses locked up faster than you could say I'ma kill the President.

"All right Officer James. We're out," I told him, putting the gun in my back pack. My boy shook his hand.

Officer James saluted us. "One thing. I'm Fat Daddy. The muthafuckah in the trunk was Officer James. Remember that in life what is obvious sometimes isn't."

We had never run so fast in our lives.

Suffice it to say, I changed my mind more than he did. He normally made up his mind and carried out his decisions. Our daylight vision seemed more spectacular than women.

The vision of his naked body finally lying before me drove me crazy! After 15 years of wondering what it looked like without the wife beaters, the baggy jeans, the boxers, the boots, the fucked up sneakers and the do-rags had me breathless.

My arms were sore from all the working out at the gym earlier. I worked myself to the bone. And a bone was what I now had as I tongue kissed this sexy ass Niggah. Slowly. Looking into his eyes with such passion made me weak. We were two fucks to each other. I was keeping it real. I rubbed all over his amazing chest, taking his nipple into my mouth. I was suckling on it like chocolate. I have wanted this man forever. And it took forever and a day to get him. We were both homeboys. Both devoted to other people. Both tired of those *very* same people. But I didn't think about that. It kinda hurt too much to think about because I knew I was a flaw Niggah for ever doing what I was about to do. So was he. But when two people had come bubbling in their bodies like hot lava all a Niggah wanted to do was fuck and release. The *hell* everybody else.

We had months of build up inside each other. I wanted to be his bottom forever, but bottoms were supposed to be the more submissive ones. And yet I turned out to be the thug aggressor.

I picked up the motion lotion. "What flavor is it?" he asked.

I smiled. He smiled back. "Cherry."

"I like cherry, dawg."

"I like it better on you."

"All right, Norman. I hear what you're saying. Trying to run game on a Niggah?"

I kissed him. "Whatever, man!"

I popped the top and put some on my finger. I tasted it for effect, staring deep into his bedroom eyes. I put some in my hands and rubbed it on both nipples and his nuts. I put it all over his dick, and left the head free of it. I massaged it on his chest, his dick, jacked him off a little bit. He grinded in my hands. Oh shit, Niggah. Yea. Like that dawg. You know how to handle that dick, playa. Shit, my Niggah.

I then put my lips a few inches from his nipples and blew.

"*Ooooh* shit! The shit is heating up, dawg! Oh my God, Yo! This is fire, pimp!"

I kissed his lips. "You like it?"

He bit my bottom lip playfully. "Do that shit on my dick!"

I took him into my hand, sucked the head only.

His eyes sparkled. "Oh my God, Yo! Handle that shit!"

I gave him some tongue. Used my thumbs to manipulate the back of the head. Gripped it and blew air on it.

"Ow! I love it, dawg! It's heating my dick! *Shiiittt* dawg, goddamn!"

"I love how you're grooving to my rhythm, my Niggah."

He pulled me to his lips. "I can't wait to be inside you Niggah."

I could wait. No sense in rushing. I waited months for this day to get here.

I flipped him over, moaning with him. I moved with him. Spread him open. His ass was amazing to me. Such a tight body. On point Niggah. Most tops didn't like their asses to be fucked with. He was *different.* He was totally under my control. I tasted his chocolate. Took an ice cube from the tray by the bedside, ignoring the fact that candles were lit everywhere, like our own private Lantern Room, trying to shun Barry White's deeply sultry voice from filtering into my ears, and I slowly, tenderly ran the ice from his back, *doooownnnnn* to his ass cheeks, licking, kissing and probing my tongue between his cheeks, tossing his salad without remorse. And this Niggah shivered, demanded and begged me to never stop.

He suddenly pushed up from the bed, the muscles in his bi and triceps flexing, turning me on even more, and picked me up. He snatched the do-rag from my silky waves. My light brown eyes shined from the flames of the candles. He gave me some tongue.

"You ready for me?" he asked.

"I was born ready, Niggah."

"You know this is such taboo."

"I know. What we're doing is so talked down upon by society."

He looked deep into my eyes. "*Fuck* society. I want you. I *need* you. I wanna *breathe* you. I want you to feel these ten inches."

"I'ma Thug Niggah. I'm down for whatever."

"Talk, talk, talk," he teased boyishly, keeping it Gangsta, the way I liked.

"*Niggah*," I began silently. "Take me…"

He smiled again. He always smiled. I loved his smile. "I got you, pimp."

"And you better handle this shit, my Niggah."

"I'll handle it like I did those free weights at the gym."

"Aww, when I broke you down."

We were tonguing again, this time more passionately than the last. We were now in the darkness, except for the moon shining on us. I suddenly felt submissive because his aggressive side came out like Mufasa in *The Lion King* trying to save Simba from the stampede.

His wife was at work. She wouldn't be home for another three hours. And I planned on sexing it up with this Mekhi Phiefer looking Niggah for the next hour and thirty minutes. I was a freak. I wasn't an amateur by a long shot.

We were hugging and feeling each other. Trying to become one. We whispered nasty shit into each others' ears. What I'd do to his dick. What he'd do to my ass. He told me I felt better than his wife. I told him he felt better than my wife and my mistress on the side. We bumped and grinded. Barry's voice was a little distant. I shook all over; I was about to nut all over this Niggah.

We hunched standing up. Yearning each other. Feeling each other. Dying for each other. I had to take a piss, but I somehow willed it back up into my bladder.

"*Niggah*. I want you," said Terrance.

"Niggah, take me, dawg."

"You want this, dawg?"

"Shit my Niggah I'm from the City, what the fuck you talkin' 'bout?"

"Get on your knees and handle this shit, let me feel the back of your throat."

I didn't hesitate. Now I wasn't a hoe ass Niggah. I was strictly on the low-low with my shit when it came to Niggahs. I had a very strict, intact reputation as a ladies man, despite my marriage. I kept my wife dick whipped. I gave her enough threesomes to last a life time. She always wanted to suck on pussy so I never protested, because I got off on hoes sucking and eating each other like the free buffet.

I took him into my mouth. I pulled on the dick like the Hoes pulled on mine. All lips and tongue. No teeth. In fact I folded my lips over my teeth. He leaned his head back, moaning for me to hear, talking shit, telling me what to do and I hated following directions. We moved like waves meeting the ocean shores. My tongue was one set of footprints. My lips carried us over the golden sand. I played with his nuts just a little bit, ran my tongue over them, holding up his incredible member.

Homeboy was packed better than sausages. I loved every inch of it! My heart hammered with his. Impulsively, I took him back into my mouth, making suction noises with my tongue and lips that reverberated throughout the house. I felt his heat swelling harder. I felt his passion. His burn made me tremble. His legs drummed together. My knees were killing me so I sat on the sofa and grabbed both his ass cheeks and controlled his hips, and his didn't lie. Fuck Shakira. That non-singing tart had nothing on my boy.

"Niggah, get on your knees and put your face on the chair," he told me. "NOW!"

"Well, *shit!* Slow down."

He pushed me. I liked a man roughing me off. Anything feminine or in-between about a man turned me completely off. I like hard edged shit. I pushed his ass back and we started wrestling and shit. All over the bedroom. We somehow pushed each other out into the living room. We kissed from time to time until he turned me around and went up in me and my eyes got wide. Yeah, Niggah.

"You like that shit? I got your feisty ass now, huh, Niggah?" he asked me and I slowly backed it up on him. Letting my opening get used to all the beef he had and homeboy had good dick. I gyrated while he tore my shit up, hugging me to him tightly. I rolled my eyes to the back of my head. I died for his heat. I rose with him like waves. I kissed his fingers with love and adoration. He put his hand on my back and made me touch my toes and he grabbed my ass like a saddle and pounded me until I screamed out in pleasure. He bounced off my walls. Absorbing me. Tears ran from my eyes. "Oooh shit!" was all I could say, sounding like a Ho. I felt like one. I loved the feeling.

"This is my ass! I have been waiting forever to hit this shit."

"Fuck me, Niggah."

"Yea! You have that *bomb* shit, dawg."

"What's my name?"

Before I could say his name, we heard keys. We froze in shock. My heart stopped. The color actually left his face.

"*Oooh* shit!" he said, nervous. He began to shiver.

Not wanting to be yanked out the closet, I ran into the room and got my sweats and ran into the guest bathroom like my life depended on it. I didn't know what my boy did. I turned on the shower and got inside, taking the soap and sped like hell cleaning myself.

*Oh shit oooh shit oh shit!*

I heard her voice. "Hey, Baby," my sister said to her husband. My Niggah on the side.

"Hey, baby. How are you?"

"It smells good in here," she said happily. "You got Barry White playing. You got ice cubes by the bedside. You look sexy, so right."

"All for you, baby."

"All for me?"

"Yes my love. But we can't do anything right now."

"Why?"

"Because, I want you to go into our bathroom, turn on the shower, clean up and come back out to me. So daddy can make love to you."

"*Ooooh* daddy! You don't have to tell me twice."

When I heard the door close he came in the bathroom with me. He locked the door. I was terrified. I couldn't let my sister find out I just let her husband fuck. My sister had no clue about me, plus she and my wife were the best of friends. What was I doing? I knew I was wrong.

"I gotta go dawg!" I told him, turning off the water, drying off. He pulled me to him.

"Not until I get this nut."

"Dawg." I was getting mad. He kissed me and I suddenly got soft.

He was inside me again, no protection, beating me up, fucking me like a savage. Two thugs. Two dope dealers. Two fathers. Two friends. Two mutual homeboys who loved Niggahs on the low. Two Niggahs being unfaithful to our wives. Despite that, I melted. After an eternity he exploded deep inside me and when it was over he kissed my lips and said, "Now I got the first nut out the way so when I fuck your sister the second nut will take a lil' minute to get here."

"Keep our shit on the low-low." He winked at me.

"Get out of here dawg, before she gets out the shower."

I had never gotten dressed and ran so fast in my life.

# The Hotel, the Elevator Prelude

August 2, 2006: 8 PM

*Amjad M. Khan, 63, of Troy, a certified public accountant and former chief executive officer of American Home Health Care Inc. ("AHHC"), of Warren, admitted submitting fraudulent claims for non-reimbursable expenses to Medicare on a cost report and supporting documents filed in 1997 and 1998.*

I turned the radio. Young Joc "Its Going Down" would do. Anything was better than hearing, for the umpteenth time, about Amjad. I was sick of hearing about this shit. Greedy ass Niggahs. For real. He needed to get what was coming to his ass. For real.

Niggahs like me bust their asses to have something plausible, and then you hear about this shit and blacks wonder why white people wouldn't hire our asses if we had bad credit, debt and too many goddamn kids. Afraid we'd steal their shit!

Anyways. I was sure. About one startling thing. I didn't want to sleep another night, alone, in my bed. My mummified bed depressed me. A bed that has been my coffin, my source of comfort when I was masturbating more than relating. And the orgasms I had! I love to cum. Some were good. Some were horrible. I had a bed that has been my place of comfort for years. My crazy place of somewhat cautious solitude was getting tired of me crying like a pregnant bitch every night. *Cautious* because I barely brought anyone to my home to sleep with me. I usually met up at a hotel/motel, Holiday Inn or Motel 6.

Turning my flashy Porsche onto rain-swept Jefferson Avenue, feeling elated and a bit brisk about my future (chummy, let's be real), I was approaching the 250 room Courtyard Marriott, in the Millender Center. To see someone. A special lady. On my back seat lay the most expensive red roses Detroit had to offer. Cost me $500. And I had a suede box in my damn jacket pocket with something that cost me $9,000 carefully hidden inside. The smile colored my face at that instant just thinking about it.

Why did she want to stay here in this hotel? I asked myself. Her house was getting renovated. I told her she could stay at my place, since she's been breaking in my bed for the past year. She wore my T-shirts and sprayed on my cologne and wore my boxers. I once made her wear my boxers backward, lining the hole in them with her asshole and I fucked her so good she came out her pussy without touching herself.

She watched my TV and threw her clothes here and there. It felt good to have some feminine shit in my home. Brought it to life. But she declined.

"Baby. Thanks but no I don't want to cramp your space," she told me and before I could protest she put an elegant finger on my thick lips and shut me up. "You're absolutely wonderful, baby, but no I'll stay in a cheap hotel until it's all finished. In about two weeks it'll be finished."

I didn't say a word. *The Courtyard Marriott is not cheap! In fact it's about $119 and up. Located between Brush and Randolph Street. A wonderful view of the city. I know this, I fucked many bitches here. I hope I didn't run into any tonight! Very clean hotel. Had air conditioning and a mini bar. I especially loved the mini bar. Maybe I could take my lady there tonight! Or we could go* *through Greek town. Maybe not, maybe it was too late for Greek town. But there were some nightlife options available. Maybe I wanted to do too much!*

I pulled up to the entrance doors. Getting out after putting the car in park, I looked around; wanting to whip out my cell and make sure my girlfriend was at this hotel. I heard from some chick at the office she was staying here. But she wasn't sure. Why did I have to find out from a bitch at work where my girlfriend was staying? And this wasn't the place she initially told me about, now that I thought about it deeper. Why would she do that? Why was I looking for problems? I wanted to surprise her, so I put the phone in my pocket and stood to the front of my ride, stretching. Felt really good. I reached in and grabbed my wallet from the dash, put it in my pocket and grabbed the roses. I was going to go park my ride in a parking spot away from everyone else's car because I didn't need any accidents. People opening their car doors, slamming it into mine because they were jealous I drove a Porsche.

I was startled when a little guy jumped in my ride, put it in drive and high-tailed it to the valet section. I didn't even know the hotel had a valet section, must be some new shit. Underneath the stars and a full moon, I looked angrily at the valet when he wobbled his ass up to me with his hand out. I started to give him the roses. But they were for my lady. I tucked my chin back. "I never asked you to park my car."

He was chuckling, his Adam's Apple bigger than mine. "It cost fifty dollars, sir." He had yellowing teeth and beady, sinister eyes.

"You're not getting fifty dollars," I told the midget-of-an-employee, clad in his little valet suit, throwing around his little words like they hurt me. I'd kick his ass tonight.

His eyes got big. "Do I need to call security?"

"To suck my dick? Sure. Be my guest. You're not getting fifty dollars. As a matter of fact *give* me my car keys."

My blood boiled. I was opening and closing my hands into fists. My dick got hard; it always got hard when I was mad.

"...All I did was get out my car to see if this was the right hotel and you hopped in my Porsche like you're escaping from L.A. and sped in my shit to the valet section."

"Company policy, you must," he said defiantly.

"Fuck your company and its policy. I'm from the streets, pimpin'. You don't want to fuck with me."

"You're not from the streets. You work at that fancy rich computer company. You're one of the execs."

"Anyways, can I have my keys Leprechaun Two?"

"Wait right here while I get my boss," he said smugly.

"Fuck your boss, dude!" Under the huge concrete structure were a lot of classy looking people, mostly white. And they were mean-mugging me. Some shook their heads. I flipped the bird at a white-washed black couple dripping in diamonds. They were appalled.

"What the hell are you staring at?" I asked them, very audible. I didn't give a damn about what they thought of me. I got loud when I was uncomfortable. What I hated the most was the way they looked at me, like I didn't belong, and I made $150,000 a year. And I happened to be a man of color. Nah. *Fuck* that. I was a Black man!

Completely tired of the bullshit, I slapped the little bitch so hard his teeth clicked together. His face turned ashen as he stood there, tears welling in his eyes (Oh, Lord!), holding his cheek. And he was supposed to be a man? I would have punched him but he was gripping like a little bitch so I bitch slapped him. I was giving this five star hotel some Commando action. All I wanted was my keys! You didn't fuck with a black man's goddamn ride! Nobody! My Mama couldn't even drive my car, well, that wasn't quite accurate. Let me stop lying. I snatched my keys from his vest pocket and made my way to my car.

"Don't mess with me today. And tell security that!"

On second thought, I let it stay parked where it was.

The Niggah in me told me to do so.

And once he spoke, it was murder she wrote.

Main Lobby: 8:09 PM

I entered the main lobby of the hotel and walked up to the receptionist desk.

"I'm here to see Josephine."

The skinny white woman, clad in the cleanest hotel uniform known to man, simply looked at me with too much eye shadow and blush on her too made up face.

"What room is she in?"

*Well, damn, where's the good service I'm used to?*

"Room 567."

"Is she *expecting* you?" She popped her gum, her earrings dangling. She had pimples across her forehead.

"Yea, she *is*." I was getting agitated, and real fast. I was already late to work, and why I detoured and came to this hotel to see my girlfriend still behooved me. In fact I really wasn't late. I got off early today, at about two p.m. I had a doctor's appointment. But my job called me back in around 7 p.m. And I wasn't in a rush to get there. I already proved myself to the company; I was a heavy weight so I wasn't going to get fired anytime soon.

"Go on up, then. You didn't have to tell me."

"Some customer service."

"You're not a customer. You're a visitor."

And just like that she turned to her computer screen and it was like I wasn't even the room.

"Well suck my dick, bitch!" I mumbled for her to hear, and I grabbed my sack and went on my way.

I made my way through the posh Lobby. Smelled like strawberries in here. Gorgeous chandeliers, amazing carpeting, the huge, larger-than-life ceiling to floor glass doors revealed a huge pool. It was a pool party going on, salsa boomed into my ears. You didn't hear much salsa in Detroit, Michigan. I wished it would snow, quite honestly.

I looked at my watch. It was after 8:12 p.m.

When I got to the elevator I pressed the clear oval button, sticking my manicured hand in my pocket, gripping the roses. I pulled out the little ring box. Yep. I was going to ask her to marry me: the woman of my dreams. My rock. My salvation. My territory. My better half. I was contemplating. Should I just turn around and leave and go to work? I worked damn near 18 hours a day, 6 days a week. I barely got any sleep. I was tired now. When I got home all I had time for was a shower, a TV dinner, and some ESPN before I drifted off to sleep. Sometimes I fell asleep when I was jacking my dick, Vaseline bottle on the floor, spare towel at my side as I doze off into Z's Land. That's my life.

To my sheer delight, Josephine sometimes stayed over, and she sometimes got to my crib before I did. I loved it when she'd cook dinner and have it piping hot on the table. But when it looked like I crawled through the door when I got home from work, she'd video record me, poking fun at me, she'd give me some good head while I filmed her (we did this many times) and after she swallowed I'd damn near drop on the floor from exhaustion and sleep like a baby. I always woke up in my bed when the alarm clock went off.

I had to hire a maid to clean my house four times a week. That was until Josephine started keeping the place clean. She saved me 400 bucks. My light bill was about a hundred dollars. I was never really home to run anything. I barely touched my stove. The oven was *never* used. I was twenty-three years old so I never cooked anything. I never used the guest rooms. I never had visitors. My parents flew up from Miami, Florida once a year. They had their own lives. And I had mine. As far as relationships, I lost them all because of my work schedule. I hadn't time for love. I just fucked and got somewhere. A few times I'd invite women to my house for a little night cap when I got off work. Yet when they saw the huge two story home and my Porsche, they automatically thought by giving me the pussy they had rights. They thought they had words of validation to make me turn my life upside down and do what they wanted. They even went as far as to say, "This is your pussy daddy. Yea. Fuck me. I *belong* to *you*." And I would roll my eyes and be like "Yea, right. You probably said that to every Niggah you fucked." Of course I said it in my head.

No time to think of that now, because I was getting a hard on. I had on a tailor-made suit. The pants couldn't hide the eleven inches in my boxers. Nor was I trying to hide it.

I jammed to some Pitbull. Miami rapper. I didn't know he got play in Detroit, home of Eminem.

Damn what's taking the elevator?

I met Josephine at work. I've known her for three years. She tried forever to get me, said she was a real woman who did real things. She was heavy into the church. I was not. I believed in God and I believed Jesus died for my sins, but I've been sinning out the ass, which was why I never pursued this sexy woman. She had big tits, a huge booty and when she wore those tight business pants it seemed her pussy ate them all up, you could see that fat monkey for miles. I always got hard when she smiled or when those tits thrust forward when she walked. She barely wore make up. She always wore Elizabeth Taylor perfume. She always wore those impossibly high heels. She put Beyonce to shame in the body and looks department. Her hair was a series of curls hanging down to the start of her butt. She was perfect.

What attracted me to her was her class. She never got involved with office fodder. No one knew anything about her. She seemed to have appeared from thin air. No one bothered her, since she was, after all, one of the bosses. She graduated from Howard University. She was the easiest woman to get along with and when I did work my nerve to talk to her, and I could remember this clearly, I walked up to her.

"Dinner. Tonight. At 8 p.m. I'll pick you up," I said confidently. "I'm not taking no for an answer. I promise to behave. Hell we can even decipher Revelations in the Bible together to keep our mind off sex."

She tossed her hair behind her and cracked the most gorgeous smile. She looked at me like I was the most handsome black man on the face of the earth. I was, shit. I was 6 feet tall, about a buck 90 (190 pounds), dark-skinned with a huge dick, debonair to the max and GQ quality from the 305, Miami. We went out. We made love on the first night. We have been stuck together like glue ever sense.

She completed my sentences. She stood up for me, even when I wasn't there to defend myself. She kept the personal shit out of the office. I was just one of the guys at work. But she always bought me food or cooked for me and I felt special. She loved watching me eat, especially when I ate pussy. She made it so much fun! She helped pay my bills, even though I told her not to. She instantly learned my favorite color, Blue, and my birthday, November 17, and my sign, Scorpio. She met my parents and my youngest brother. I had three siblings, no girls.

I met her parents when she took me to Cancun, Mexico. They lived there for the past six years. Retired lawyers. She came from a long line of money. She was very polished, very moneyed, in a down to earth kind of way. She always heard me out, helped me with situations beyond my control, and always showed me a positive way to things. If I forgot to take chicken out to thaw, I got mad. But she'd look at me and say, "No problem. We'll eat out. Tomorrow just take it out. No problem." If bills were too much she said, "Pay some of them in the middle of the month. That alleviates the burden of paying them all on the first of the month." My mortgage. "Well…$1,100 is not so bad when you could pay half in the middle of the month and the other half at the beginning of the month. You can actually save money."

She was perfect. I heard the *ching* of the elevator. Happily, I gripped the roses, about to rise on cloud nine. That gentle cloud that rained on you, made you feel like you were in a much-needed shower after a grueling day at the office. The cloud that was under your feet when you danced, walked and cried. The puffy white cloud that told you that everything was going to be all right, that it was good to let go the past, embrace the future and you couldn't embrace it if your arms were filled with bags and things from the past. The past was over and done with; you had to move beyond it.

With a smile I was about to go on up to the third floor to surprise my baby. I was going to give her the flowers. I was going to get on my knee and ask her to marry me. She was going to say yes! I would love to be Mrs. Josephine King. We were going to have a lavish, all expense paid wedding. In the Virgin Islands.

And hope they didn't burn to the ground because we were promiscuous blacks. I was smiling. I would get her pregnant. She would have all my children. I would die for her.

"Goodbye to the Bachelor Days," I said as the silver elevator doors slid open with a tisk. I closed my eyes, inhaling the lovely scent of the elevator. I knew my woman had been in here earlier because it still reeked of her perfume. That gentle, feminine smell that got a rising out of me and I wasn't talking about the sun. I held my breath, letting her essence take me up and out of the hotel, hoping I could find her room along the way. Opening my eyes it took a moment for the beautifully polished ceilings, the gorgeously breathtaking lighting pouring into his eyes like spilt milk and the ugly scene on the red carpeting before me to really kick in.

The muscles in my high cheekbones were sporadically jumping as anger washed over me from that shitty, puffy white cloud. The cloud that told my gut, which was in a thousand knots, that an amazing trick was played on me; the puffy white cloud that turned into a storm cloud and lightning lit the core of my brutal betrayal and the thunder boomed in the pit of my throat so powerfully I had to ball his hands into tight fists and breathe in and out with the force of a dying man desperately trying to breathe. My world exploding in my face, I dropped the flowers and the ring. My face shaking.

My heart exploding.

Elevator: 8:17 PM

Josephine beat me doing the knee thing.

Heavily engrossed in her head game, she was deep throating a tall, chocolate male who looked strikingly similar to my daddy. His head leaning back, he was in control of this sick game. His cornrows were beautifully braided and I wanted to snatch them out. They stopped all hotel and party activity. They didn't know we were watching. He was fucking her slowly in the mouth, swinging those hips like Justin Slayer, the Porn star…

"Suck on it…yea!" he demanded, gripping her head. His baggy jeans crept down his muscular legs. His boxers covered his big booty, but his velvet rope was all in her mouth. Spit trailed all over the place. Her tits were bouncing, and her lacy bra barely held them together. She was fingering her pussy; it dripped, in ways it didn't drip for me.

"Shit. I'm about to come!"

She shivered with delight, and that's when I dropped the bomb.

"Josephine." Was all I could say, my heart torn asunder. For two reasons.

In complete shock, she froze. Wide-eyed, with his dick in her mouth. The Justin Slayer clone looked at me with the *"Oh, shit. I'm sorry!"* look on his face. He lowered his head, stepping back, his huge dick falling from her mouth. He shoved it in his boxers, pulled up his pants, and leaned back against the mirror, looking sad and withdrawn into himself. He felt dirty. And he should feel that way.

I couldn't take my eyes off my love. I was so in love. So in love SO IN LOVE SO IN LOVE! "Will you marry me?" I asked her with a cracked voice, getting on one knee. I held my middle finger in the air, my hand shaking. I gripped the roses so tightly the thorns tore into my skin and blood dripped all over the expensive tile, but I didn't feel it. Now for the second reason why my heart was torn asunder.

"And brother, my little brother, my Mama's third oldest child, will you be my best man?" I told my brother Kingston. With tears in her eyes, Kingston, feeling torn and guilty, snatched me off my knee, hugging me.

*"Big brother, please, I can explain…I'm sorry, please, she came on to me, she paid for my plane ticket to fly here, she seduced me, she told me you and her were through…"*

I felt nothing.

Angrily, I pushed him so hard his body slammed into hers. She moaned piteously, clearly scared of me. She'd never seen this side of me; I was always Mr. Rogers Neighborhood around her. Would you be mine? Devastated, she rushed up to me, "Baby, I can explain," and I slapped her so hard across the face with the flowers she fell to her knees. Petals drifted towards hell like snow. I grabbed her by the hair and yanked her semi-naked ass into my face.

"Fuck you. Lose my number. Fuck you, bitch! FUCK YOU!"

Everyone was watching. Their hearts went out to me. I should know. They all stared at me with sympathy dancing in their eyes. I was on fire. It hurt so badly. My God take this pain away, take it away. I could hear my bed calling for me. *Come home, baby. I'll comfort you. Yet again. I'm here for you. Come back to be mummified!*

And I had never run so fast in my life.

I forgot the ring. And I left the flowers. Hoping my blood on the floor reminded them of what they both lost.

Me.

Forever!

### Disclaimer from dapharoah69

Many people I've spoken to have opened up to me after I told them of the abuse I went through as a kid. Many people have told me why they turned out to be the way they were, being molded as kids to be something even they grow to detest. Many people have asked me how could I be so open about my past. I'm open because I am no longer scared. I'm no longer going to allow ANYONE to force me to be silent to spare people who have bitterly and gravely hurt me in this lifetime, and every time my fingers brush the keyboard, oh how they shake with fear. Because Larry wrote this short story at the request of someone I know, who wanted his story told. I changed the names.

This is for you, and you know who you are. He had come to me one day when I was taking a break from writing. A complete stranger, someone I had never seen before. He introduced himself and I had an attitude at first because I'm very anti-social and I don't really talk to people I don't know because you never know their true intentions. But he was cool. He told me had read some of my work on Thugworld, a website I use to post some new material. Again I thanked him. But it seemed he was building me up to ask me something. I'm a straight-from-the-hip person so I asked him, "What do you want?"

"I want you to write a story about me."

"Why should I?" I asked him, getting upset because it seemed everyone wanted me to write a book on their lives.

"Because I don't like being bisexual."

"Well, what turned you that way?"

Over dinner he told me his story and I agreed to write it.

Since then I have gotten a lot of letters from people about this story. They thanked me for finally talking about a bitter taboo in the black community, hell in communities period. Because this reached into every culture on earth. No culture is exempt. Abuse from within the family. Online, in forums and on Myspace women and men from all ages and creeds have written me personal detailed accounts about family members who did them over sexually. I was even stunned. I saved 'em all. I read them all the time when I come up with ideas for a new story.So read the story that follows this page with an open mind. While *some* people feel people are "born gay," I say "BULLSHIT." This was my opinion, of course. Some people are molded at a very young age to turn out the way that they have.

I should know. It happened to me.

# Dapharoah69

Sometimes I didn't know what to do with myself. I would hesitantly look in the mirror and see myself for who I was. When I was out and about I lived behind a mask because I was *too* afraid to let anyone in to take a look at the museum of problems I had. They hung like photographs on my skull that appeared to be blotch marks to the general public, being anything they wanted it to be. Now a complete stranger lustfully spread my ass cheeks apart and demanded that I hold them open and I did. I loved being controlled. I loved when a man took charge and told me how he was going to tap the booty. I appreciatively looked back into his eyes and what mirrored back shattered the mask. It fell to invisible pieces and turned into a caricature of who I was when I looked in the mirror. The both of us were sweating profusely while we had sex in a local department store. He was sticking me as fast and hard as he could. Why he was trying to fuck me like we were making a Dawg Pound porno confused me. He grabbed my booty and I felt fingers embedded in my skin. Those silky deadlocks swung gracefully. It was after two a.m., and everyone has gone home.

We were in the huge storage closet; there were no cameras and we fucked all over a mattress we took from the Furniture Department. Before the store closed we hid in this closet until everyone, even the managers went home. And now it was dark, hot, with a little bit of light and I've been taking him every which way he gave it.

He slapped my ass. I hated it and I really hated being bisexual. I thought sex with a man was sick, but I couldn't break free and I've tried to break free but the more I tried the more it swallowed me whole. I *knew* you had a choice, free will church people called it, but *no* one had the upbringing I had. I was forced to do things with people I *didn't* want to do them with. Things *too* advanced for young eyes. I went through that, by someone I trusted, someone I used to love, admire and look up to.

"Goddamn, this *ass* is jiggling!"

I guess I had some good booty because he moaned like he was being shot and that was turning me off. I met him today, when he came in to order a huge swimming pool. He looked broke as a joke so I really tried to avoid him but the customer was always right so I had to adhere to his requests. I was the Assistant Stock Manager, made pretty decent money. Willing to help the man, I went in the back and he followed me, since me and James, a co-worker who took fifty smoke breaks in a ten minute period every damn day, were the only two working. When I located the pool I was startled when the stranger got behind me, rubbing my ass. He was a straight thug and looking at him you would *never* guess he got down.

"You got ass," he told me with a sneer and a smile. "Can a niggah hit this shit?"

Um, no! What was it with men? When I did give them a piece of my Klondike bar they thought they possessed it. When in fact they were merely getting a piece of what they could never have because it was mine. I didn't know if I wanted it myself. Before I could answer he cut me off. "I've been *watching* you. Having my eye on you has turned me on."

And now we were fucking. Getting bored easily, I crawled forward and his hardened member fell out of me. He was grasping for me, his hands slipping on my sweaty arms. I turned around with a smile. He challenged me. Hating myself for what I was, I sucked him up the best way I could. His eight inches filled my mouth. I swallowed his first load and now homebody wanted the second load deep inside of me. With H.I.V. on the rise I didn't know about all that. I wouldn't stop sucking him up. I loved making a man feel good. It gave me power beyond my wildest dreams. They way he moaned and looked at me set me on fire.

His prison tattoos, all five of them, shined from the little light coming through the opened back door. After an eternity of foreplay, he cringed, giving me a helpless look.

"I'm 'bout to nut!" He stood up and came all over me. It sent me over the top. Before I knew it I was coming also.

"Nah, Niggah. Let me see!" he said, flipping my tired, worn body over and watching me burst all over my stomach. He got on his knees and licked it all up, swallowing every drop. This was nothing like...my first nut. My cell phone rang.

"Is dat your man callin' you?" he asked, brows rising. He was joking but he was serious.

"Naw. I ain't got nobody," I lied. I had one night stands coming and going out of my room like clockwork. And *why* was I talking ghetto?

"That's what all da men say. When I saw you in this store I was like he has to be mine." He stored his number, all three of them, in my phone. "You got ass of fire. And you better not give my shit away," he went on. I really noticed him now. He had a scar under his right eye and on his chin; his pants dipped to the start of the V-shape on his groin area. He had a small gut. He had a lot of ass. I liked it.

"You sure you want to be with me," I asked, watching him put on a Scarface shirt. I smiled. He laid on top of me and gave me some tongue. I tasted the weed and alcohol on his breath and I didn't care. I liked my Niggahs rough. My cell kept ringing. It was my Mom.

"It's my Mom, dawg."

I answered.

"Where are you," she asked. "I'm sitting in my car outside of the store..."

My dude heard. "Oh snap, dawg," he whispered low enough for me to hear it. "...Don't look like you got the power no more."

We laughed quietly. Something in me told me if I crossed him I'd be a dead man. "I better get out of here," I told him, hanging up on Mama cursing me out.

"Good thing you left the back door cracked when they turned on the alarm," he said and I agreed. "Alarm ain't even on now."

"Go shopping then, Niggah."

"Don't worry. By the time 4 a.m. hit I'll have a U-haul truck full of stuff."

I left after kissing him. It was hard leaving him because I had the feeling that since the dick was good and the vibe was good that I'd never see him again. I hoped that wasn't the case but my heart told me with three of his numbers in my phone he was going to be a keeper. I went out to Mama's car. Once I got in she let me have it, cursing me out. When we turned out onto the street, I saw my Niggah's silhouette over by the store, with his hand on his dick and a shit-eating grin on his face.

I deleted his numbers out of my phone.

I would never talk to him again.

Two hours later. Mama sipped the last of her Bacardi when she looked at me, cupped my hands and said, "Baby, I'm your Mama. What's up? *Why* are you so depressed?"

I looked at my mother, Henrietta Hampton with the bitchy attitude and sighed. I was 23 years old, holding my mom's hands like I was a bitch. When was I going to grow the hell up?

"Ma. I'm fine." My heavy, brawly voice did somersaults off the beige walls hung with silver-framed photos exhibiting fifty years of Black History. She and my dad (he was a carpenter and at work now) built a life together. They met when they were kids. I remember Daddy told me that they knew they were meant to be together when he stopped a white man from trying to kill her. She'd accidentally stepped on the white man's white shoes in Savannah, Georgia and he pulled out a pistol and tried to shoot her in the face. Dad, who was getting in a car with his parents, noticed it and he jumped out and ran at the white man full throttle. When his little body smashed into the white man's legs, the gun flew through the glass window of the convenience store and the white man fell on his face. A cloud of dust circulated around him. Mom was so shaken up she passed out and woke up in a hospital with both of her parents and my dad and *his* parents hovering over her with the police.

The racist cops chewed on toothpicks and looked at them like they were pigs with human dicks in their asses. After ten minutes of making statements like, "The white man claims you stole his wallet and stepped on his shoes and tried to flee," "We might be back to ask you more questions," the cops left mumbling "Niggers" under their breath. Mama told me Dad looked at her and kissed her cheek (making their parents oh and ah). He whispered in her ear, "I'ma be your protector." And for fifty years his life was dedicated to making Mama happy. But he made my life a living hell. He has been abusing me ever since I was a child. Back then abuse was suppressed and hidden deep within the family. You never invited an outsider. You never told a soul. I wanted to die! I figured it was my fault. I was molded as a kid to dress up in Mama's clothes and dance in my father's thespian act while keeping a straight face.

Though we haven't been getting along like we used to (because of my anger) we would get along if he stopped trying to tell me what to do and stopped occasionally fucking me. It has gotten to the point where I started loving what he did. When he raped me the father in him ceased to exist and I fell in love with the demon over the next few years. I hated the feeling of caring and loving a man who gave me life but he slowly took my innocence and turned it into a mass of confusion and I couldn't let go or break free because I figured I was to blame. He was so fine I couldn't say no. I was so fine he couldn't say no. Together every bitch in town took bets on who was gonna take us to bed. We have been offered money, cars and high-paying careers. Some woman, yesterday, told me she wanted me and my daddy to double penetrate her. I was like *damn* I wanted to but not with dad. So I fucked her solo and came in the pussy. I wanted to make a baby. I loved the hoes but secretly I loved the Niggahs too.

Dad (Earl) was a tall, imposingly incredible man with a heart of gold but he had a blackened soul. Everything was a deal, a bargain or a hustle with him. If your read Ice Berg Slim, Dad had a lot of that instilled in him. He cheated on Mama countless times, pimping women when he was twenty years old to keep a roof over my family's heads (without Mama ever knowing because he pimped in Chicago and we resided in Georgia). He did whatever it took to keep Mama happy.

He never killed anybody and he never stole from nobody. We got what we got 'cause of a man being a man. He was a good Dad, taught me things about life, all the things a real man taught his son was there. But the *only* thing I hated was when he sniffed cocaine, drank his booze and his hands started wondering my body. I loved my Dad, and back then he was *God* to me. He was a man I looked up to and tried to imitate. I talked like him with that Georgia Peach Slang, slurring words like I'm tipsy.

I copied him. He taught me how to flirt with women. He taught me how to fuck by fucking me. My dad used my love for him to cripple my independence. I was the one who didn't depend on him. I had a job at thirteen years old, bagging grocery and he hated that with a passion. He wanted to be the only man working in the house. He wanted all the recognition.

To dispel that he caught me off guard one day and changed the course of my life. He was dressed superbly in a suit. Shit, when I looked at him I was like goddamn he's fine as fuck, but that was dad. He asked me, "How do I look," and I said, "Dad you look good!"

He locked the door and asked me to sit by him and I did with the quickness and he asked me had I kissed a bitch before and I said "Naw, Dad, don't know *how* to kiss."

He had loving, invitingly dangerous eyes. He was a man who got what he wanted. All of me loved pleasing Dad. I played football as a kid to make him happy and won several trophies that are still gleaming, years later, on his dresser next to Mama's photos.

"Now comes the next phase in me teaching you how to be a man. I gotta teach you how to please women. *That's* my job."

I was ignorant, so ignorantly naïve. I didn't know any better. I believed everything that came out of his mouth. If he woulda told me Madonna was really Janet Jackson with a blonde wig I woulda believed him. He slowly leaned up to me and I reluctantly leaned up to him. I stared deep into his eyes; eyes that said do what Dad said. He knew best. "Stick your lips out son." I did. We kissed. He gave me the tongue and I flowed with him. My dick was hard he stroked it. "Bitches love to kiss and love when they can stroke the dick like this son." It felt so good. I was breathing hard, hugging him. He stripped off his pants and told me to give him head and I did and he screamed at first and I jumped up.

"Use your lips. Not your teeth. Bend your lips over them and do it, like this." He leaned over and gave me head and lightning shot through me. It felt so good I looked at him and was confused. Damn, if I had a son did I teach him how to be a man like this?

He sucked me until my body tensed and I came and I didn't know what was going, The feeling was so intense tears raced down my face and white shit pumped out my dick and my body went into spasms and Dad looked at me and said, "That's your first nut. You never forget your first nut. *That's* what my Daddy taught *me*."

He put on his pants and darkness befell his face, leaving me a shattered soul.

Now Mama pours another shot of Bacardi. She stands up from the couch and smiled into her reflection in the mirror.

"Son. Talk to me."

"About?"

Her eyes cut into mine from the reflection.

"Tell Mama about your...first nut."

And she killed the drink at the same time my heart did a back flip.

*To be continued…*

# Zephyrhills

Hello. My name was Jabari. And I had a story to tell.

Bottles have been around for thousands of years. Some people have even wrote messages on papers and placed them in bottles, tossing them in the ocean or lake, hoping someone on the other side got the bottles and read the messages for whatever reason. Even though I've never done that, considering I never believed hope floated, but Zephyrhills served a different purpose for me. It not only represents water, something pure, power, and natural and needed for survival. But it represents that very same purity being held captive by a plastic bottle to be consumed at the consumer's discretion.

This was by no means an attack on Zephyrhills. Because there are plenty of water companies out there: Evian, Dasani, and so on and so forth. But sometimes sex is like water.

Pure. Powerful. Natural.

Trapped in a bottle we call the human body.

I knew many people, as well as myself, who used sex to *trap* someone into a) relationship b) using it to control someone c) getting them to do what you wanted d) blackmail and e) using sex as a form of validation.

I knew I was guilty of all the above.

I have a friend named Kenny. I will change his name to protect who he was. He's from Miami, Overtown. Born and raised. He grew up alone all the time. Mama always worked. Daddy was barely there. He went through emotional abuse. His uncles always told him he'd amount to nothing because they were crack heads who basically threw their lives away. They tried to destroy his dreams before he even realized he had dreams. He didn't have much self-esteem. He was a loner. He barely spoke to people, despite being popular. He smoked weed every day. Half the time in class he was high. Just a real laid back person who caused no problems. He was an all-around good person. But he did one thing that tarnished his image in his own eyes. And that was use sex to trap his girlfriends into doing whatever he wanted them to do.

Kenny and I met when he moved down to Goulds when he was about sixteen years old. I was also sixteen, in my junior year of high school. Southridge Senior High. He transferred from Edison High School. We called our school "Da Ridge." A little slang to keep it 'hood. I hated Da Ridge, mainly because of Mr. Hooper's dumb ass *always* messing with me. And the Principal, ex-coach Norris, my God.

Those two alone made me want to jump off a cliff.     I remembered him well.  Clad in all black and some fresh black Etonics, he sauntered through the crowded hallways, quiet, meek and his swagger had the ladies swooning almost immediately.  I was also quiet and meek, but around my friends I was humorous and always cracking jokes and dancing.

His locker was next to mine.  I was putting away my Government text book, getting ready to go home for the day.  It was after 2:15 PM.  I had left class early so I could get to my locker, beat the crowd and make it to the school bus and at least get a damn seat.

A few girls smiled and winked at him.  He spoke back, and left it at that.

"You, pimp sup with you?" he asked me like he knew me for years. I slammed the locker shut, looked over my red shirt and extended my hand.

"Sup man, I'm Jabari...I don't remember seeing you at this school before."

Before he could say anything I heard my name being called.

"*Hey, Jabari!*" Bertha screamed from across the hallway by the cafeteria, which I never ate in.  Come to think of it I never went inside it either.  He ignored my friend but I looked over his shoulder at her, nodding and she mouthed, "Who is he?  He's fucking fine!"

"Anyways.  I have a lot of friends.  I never seen you before, man," I hinted.

"You haven't. I just transferred down here from Edison."  He had a deep, gravelly voice.

"Oh, shit.  Edison.  I hate that damn school."

He laughed.  "We all right, Niggah."

"Ya'll suck.  Especially ya'll sports department."

"We're pretty decent."

"Yea, yea, yea."

"Don't be a hater Niggah."

"Anyways what's your name?"

"Kenny."

"Nice to meet you.  I gotta catch the bus home so I gotta kick rocks."

"Are you catching the school bus or the city bus?"

I felt really comfortable around him.  He held on to the strap of his back pack.  He studied me quietly, summing me up. He looked at me from head to toe whenever I looked away or made sure no teachers came around the corner, catching me out of class.  The coast was clear.  Just a bunch of trophy cases holding dusty ass trophies.

"The school bus."

He looked over the small index card in his hands. Clean nails. Clean hands. Both ears pierced. Brown eyes and a low-fade cut close to the scalp. Very masculine and cocky, like me. "I catch bus number 200."

"Shit, dawg, that's my bus. It's packed, too. My advice to you is to get there at least five minutes before the last school bell ring releasing us from class. Or else you'll be standing up."

"Well we better get on now, huh Jabari?"

We looked into each other's eyes for a brief moment. "Yea, dawg."

He had four gold teeth to the bottom and five gold ones to the top. He looked and smelled clean.

"Well let's go. I'll follow you. I don't know where the fuck I'm going."

We started for the hallway leading to the back of the school.

When we turned the corner, passing more lockers and a few students rushing out of class before the bell rung, going here, there and everywhere, my friend Tonya appeared in front of me. She was so fine. She wore hot pink and her pants were so tight her ass looked like a part of them and she had the biggest titties. Kenny smiled at her, staring her down.

"Where you going Jabari?" she asked, giving Kenny the evil eye. She already had a son.

I kissed her cheek. "The bus."

Her eyes sparkled. All my friends loved me. "Niggah, you better get on. And who is this Niggah? I never saw him before." She didn't give me or him time to answer. "Are you new here? Where you from, boy?"

"Overtown. Edison High School. My name is Kenny. And yours?"

She shook his hand and said, "Tonya. Kiss my hand boy, I don't know where yo hand been mah Niggah."

He kissed it.

"Damn, soft lips," she said, flirting. I looked at my watch, on the verge of cock blocking.

"Soft hand, Ma."

"You got a phone number?"

I said, "Girl you date my cousin, that's fucked up." Jokingly of course.

She dismissed my comment with the wave of her hand. "Your cousin got other bitches. And Taquana is saying she's pregnant from him."

"Girls will be girls," I suggested, smiling, pinching her cheek. She and Kenny exchanged numbers.

And the Zephyrhills syndrome began.

Kenny and I got along almost perfectly. We got close over the next few weeks, which poured into months. We went to the movies.

I met his family. We hung out. He sometimes came over to my mom's house to chill. We played video games together. We flirted with chicks at the malls.

We fucked women together. We confided in each other about everything. We stayed on the phone all damn night, talking about the future, life and our pasts.

We each told each other the darkest things about one another. It brought us closer.

In school I rarely flirted, because it was all about school work. Mama was on my ass like a cord plugged in the wall. She had a tight hold on my progress reports, report cards and classroom behavior. She never sat back and let the teacher do everything. She played a very hands-on role. She wouldn't hesitate to put that extension cord on my ass, I feared her to death. I fucked a lot of people, but I kept it on the low. I never kissed and told. Not even to my best friend Mark Birds and Theodore Sampson. I had sex with a lot of people in my neighborhood, the Pine Island Projects.

Three months went by and Kenny and Tonya were dating, very discreetly. Three women claimed to be pregnant from him. He didn't care. "I wore a Jimmy. Plus that ain't my goddamn baby."

Tonya heard about it but she didn't care. She was still seeing my cousin, who was cheating on her left and right, but she wanted Kenny and she got him.

She used her pussy for her own sick pleasures. I was still a little wet behind the ears then, but that was slowly drying up.

Kenny was sociable, well-liked and popular. He was on the basketball team, doing real well. He made about ten points a game, three assists, a few dunks.

Nothing major but major enough. He made decent grades. But he fucked a different chick almost every night, even bitches from other schools. Sometimes he'd tell me to meet him somewhere and we'd hook up, go over to some chick's house and run a train on her. I couldn't always do that 'cause Mama worked. I was the product of a single parent house hold with 2 little brothers (and an older brother who ran the streets and sold dope) so I had to be mom's eyes and ears and belt while she worked.

He'd call me on the phone when he was getting it on so I could listen. I used to jack off, stuck in my own world.

One day before the Martin Luther King Jr. holiday, he came to me when I was just walking out my mom's front door to catch the number 70 city bus. I caught this bus only when Mama didn't feel like taking me to Melvin's house, my cousin, so I could catch the school bus. I used his address to go to Southridge anyway because I didn't want to go to Homestead Senior High or South Dade.

"We gotta talk," he said.

"About what?"

"Tonya. You know we're dating, right?"

"Yea."

"She thinks I'm being unfair."

I locked the door, stuffing my keys in my book bag. I looked good today, got little sleep because I stayed up on the phone with my friend Hanna, listening to her problems.

We slapped palms. "Unfair about what?"

"I'm running her. We fucked a few weeks ago," said Jabari, a little sad.

"What?"

"Yea."

I noticed a Nissan Altima in my Mama's drive way.

"Who's car?" he asked.

"My brother's. He slings big dope. He let me borrow it for today. Come on, fuck the bus. My Niggah is going to Da Ridge in style today."

"Cool, dawg."

"So ya'll had sex and then what?"

I got in the flashy car. Definitely carjacking material. I put on my seat belt and watched him do the same, putting my bag on the back seat. Open condom wrappers were all over the place. My brother could get mad all he wanted; I was driving to school today. Plus he slept all day. He got up around 5 p.m. I'd have the car back by then.

"I told her I make the rules. I gave her good dick, and the bitch gotta do what I say."

"So you were trapping her?"

"Yea. She doesn't want me to go to your cousin and break his heart. He's already sweatin' a Niggah when I be in the halls. He a big Niggah but he can get knocked on his ass."

"You're something else. And your way of talking is different. 'When I be in the halls?'"

He laughed easily. "It's like this. I grew up with no self esteem. My Mama never raised or respected me. If it wasn't for my grandma on my mom's side I'd be dead. So women are that to me: instruments to be played. I get high self esteem when I fuck 'em and control 'em. Tonya works at K-Mart part time. I make her give me half her little check."

"That shit isn't *cool*, Kenny."

I turned the key in the ignition and drove out the drive way, turning onto Moody Drive 268th Street, heading East.

"I know. But you don't understand. Tonya isn't the only bitch I'm fucking. I fucked her older sister Tangie, who goes to F.I.U. I fucked the one girl Bertha."

"You fucked big Bertha? I heard she got that shit."

HIV. "Nah, she cool. She got a deep pussy. She told me you hit it?"

"She gave me some head and swallowed the future NBA star but that's about it."

"*Anyways*. I fuck bitches to control them. Trick them into getting what I want. See my threads. They bought this shit. These hoes down south are dumb bitches."

"And what about you? You say you're trapping these clueless hoes but aren't you allowing yourself to be trapped?"

"Yea." I turned left onto Allapattah, 112 Avenue, and heading North. "I don't know. Its like I feel wanted and needed when I fuck. When they do what I say I feel ruthless and powerful. I feel like water, free to roam and devour any lake or damn along the way and make it over flow."

"That's not healthy dawg."

"You've done it too, Jabari. You told me of your childhood and shit, which I sympathize. But you've fucked bitches and Niggahs for control and to fit in, too."

"No, it's not like what you're doing."

I went around a cement truck that was traveling too slowly; well, I was traveling too fast. Well past 70 m.p.h. on a 45 m.p.h. road. Bushes and trees were on either side of us. A few bus stops we zoomed by. It was muggy and hot today and he didn't have on the radio or the AC.

"Denial, my Niggah. It ain't no fun when it's about you." He lit a joint, sucking in the smoke. He felt it in his lungs and his eyes watered. He was taking it to the head.

I was getting frustrated, because he was right. We were young then. Very naïve. But the more experience in the sack we gave in to, the more we got people to do what we wanted, the more it built up our self-confidence. And that was dangerous because the minute the sex was over we fell hard. Back to earth. We were sad, lonely and depressed.

"Whatever."

I slowly braked at the red light by the Cutler Ridge Mall. I gripped the steering wheel, my legs wide open, his joint between his lips. He looked at me with a grin. "Jabari. Didn't you fuck Gio and got her to take your math test for you?"

"Yea, and?"

"Didn't you fuck Linda and she gave you twenty dollars?"

"Yea."

"Don't you always fuck Linda and get twenty dollars, in addition to the ten dollars a week your Moms give you?"

"Yes?" I failed to see the connection.

"Then boom. There it is. You fuck to get what you want. That's the only relationship you have with Linda. Sex for money. Tricking we call it these days. So don't come down on me."

He was right.

I'd graduate like this. Using people to get what I wanted through sex. It grew inside of me, manifested.

Kenny was so far gone into using sex to control women that one shot him in the back when he was caught climbing out of her sister's window a little after we graduated.

He didn't die, but present day, 2006, eleven years later, he's still handsome, smooth but he's in a wheel chair. When he was shot it didn't change who I was and what I was doing. I got worse.

I was the quiet Niggah. Rarely talked. Joked around. But I was the biggest freak. I was manipulating married people, getting what I wanted, people years older than me. I was going with Hanna and at the same time I got in a relationship with Lisa Lane Waters and used her. I didn't have sex with Lisa; I fucked Lisa who I called myself being in love with. She had two sisters and three brothers. But I used my charm, looks and smooth voice to con her into doing this and that for me.

I was ruthless. I didn't accept the answer "No."

I got Lisa to do threesomes, let other Niggahs fuck her while I watched. I fucked her and let Niggahs watch.

I got her to be videotaped, just her face and our sweaty bodies fucking into oblivion. My face was never put on there.

It was all about power and control. I didn't love her. I had swore into the US Army, with the intent of marrying Lisa. I made big plans. Wrote them out. She was, at the time, a sophomore at Southridge. I had got low test scores on the ASVAB test. But scored high enough to go there. My first choice was the Airforce. But I scored too low. So I was like fuck flying high. I wanted better test scores. I scheduled to take it again. I met a sergeant while at the M.E.P.S. center in Miami. He came up to me, age thirty, cocky and somewhat built, married and he extended his hand. "I'm Sgt. Glad. And you are?"

"Jabari."

"You play ball?"

I felt the chemistry. "Very well."

"What about golf. You good with controlling the stick?"

"Very good." I had on sweats. I had a big ass, and my ass always got attention. I smiled at him and asked, "What do you do here?"

"I work here."

"Oh, *yeah?*"

"Yea."

"Listen. I'm free tomorrow around four p.m. Come through to my Moms crib. I need a favor."

"You got a number?"

I gave him the house number.

He stored it in his cell phone. He was in uniform.

"I'll holla at you later."

"Make sure you do."

I walked away, silently plotting.

The next day he called around 4 p.m. Moms was at work.

"Can I come through?"

"Yea."

"Can you ride somewhere with me?"

"Yea. I'm grown."

"Oh, shit, big man. Fresh outta high school."

"Yep."

A knock on mom's front door got my attention. I had just gotten out the shower. I wrapped the towel around me and answered the door.

He smiled, the army man. I shook his hand, wet all over. I was the only one home.

"Come on in."

"Sure," he said, coming in and I closed the door. We were alone.

Face to face.

He set his wallet, keys and cell phone on the glass end table. "So why did you call me over here."

"Who gives out the testing?"

"What testing?"

"The ASVAB?"

"I'm one of the officials."

I smiled. I got all the way in his face and kissed him. He wrapped his arms around me, taking the towel off. I sucked on his neck, getting his clothes wet. I didn't care. I was a lion. I had fire. I wanted more fire. Our skin felt like flames.

Backing up from him, breathless, putting on the towel I said, "Get me a good score on the test. And you can have me. Anytime, anyplace."

"Consider it done." I looked down, he was hard for days. The look in his eyes was wild and sensual.

I slid his cell phone under mom's couch when he wasn't looking. I may need to use it.

I got a good score on the test.

Mr. Glad smiled at me when I got my scores.

"I am still going to the Army."

He was kind of mad. "But I just got you good scores?"

I changed my mind. "Fuck it. Throw that shit away. I'm going to the Army."

Angry, he ripped the test in half. "So that means I don't get to hit it?" he whispered.

I said nothing. "Yea, we can still do that."

He perked up then. "Cool Niggah, cool. We gotta keep this on the under."

Yea, I gotta go. I borrowed mom's car to come here. She hates me gone with her auto for a long time. Call me."

"I can't find my phone. I know Vanessa is about to kill me."

"Who's that?"

"My wife."

*Vanessa's her name. Check mate.*

A few days later Mr. Glad came and picked me up in a government-plated car. We drove to a hotel. After he checked in we spent the next 6 hours rolling across the bed, and it never dawned on me about his wife. I rode him, got in the doggy style position; let him get it from the side. He filled me up beyond limitations. I had a girl friend and I didn't give a shit. All I cared about was me, getting mine. I was playing a game. The first one come wins. I didn't care back then. I didn't want to keep him, and I didn't have good self-esteem. I used him to build me up, take me away, make me come and once it was over, I left my come soaking in the sheets as I slipped out the room, taking out his cell phone.

I called Vanessa. I told her, "I just slept with your husband. If you don't believe me watch this."

I went back into the room and set the phone on the night stand. I began sucking on him, and he slowly awakened from a deep sleep, the snoring turned into sensual moans as he moved in my mouth. I was on my knees and he took the back of my head and slammed it down on his dick. I loved rough shit.

"What's my name?" he asked.

"Mr. Glad..." I said, filled with pleasure.

"Suck my dick...yea, my wife can't suck it like you. She always wants me to eat her out but she can't slob my dick...turn over Niggah." He got up and flipped me over, spreading me open.

"Take this tongue."

"OH HELL NO!"

He froze, looking around. He looked scared, he was shaking.

"Who was that?" he asked?

"I don't know." I got up and pulled up my pants. "I'll talk to you later."

I rushed out the door.

"YOU'RE SEXING A MAN ON ME, NIGGAH?" his angry wife screamed through his cell phone, and I smiled all the way to the bus stop.

Mission accomplished.

I never saw Mr. Glad again, and I didn't feel a twinge of remorse. I got off on controlling a thirty plus year old and I was only 18. It fed the void in my heart with negative images and distorted thoughts.

I never dared to call him, and when I went to the M.E.P.S. center to check on my test scores, from my first test, I asked about him.

Staff Sergeant Miller said, "He moved away. His wife caught him screwing a man at some hotel down here. It's all over the M.E.P.S. Center."

I smiled, shaking my head. Eyes sparkling.

"Any word who the dude was?"

He was sad. "Nah. Wish I knew. He destroyed a happy home. He got four sons, one is dying from cancer. I know it happened to him while he's young, but it happens. Life. I wish I cloud find the Niggah who slept with Mr. Glad so I can tear his head off."

"Mr. Glad wasn't at all innocent in this."

"I know. But now Vanessa has to raise those boys on her own. She filed for divorce. It is definitely over."

I lowered my head. "Damn. Fucked up."

Guilt was fucking me up. I hurt Vanessa, why did I even call her? I wanted control, and the control has come back to bite me.

"Want to hear the best part, Jackson?"

Sadly, I looked up. "Sup."

He got quiet. "You got tears in your eyes."

"I hate when kids lose their fathers. My dad wasn't there for me."

"I feel you. But anyway. One of his sons committed suicide."

I got so quiet I cracked open. I wiped tears away and said, "I never meant for this to happen."

He stared at me, blinking twice. "What are you saying?"

"It was me. I slept with Mr. Glad. And I didn't intend for this to happen." I had never run so fast in my life. That's the day I stopped using sex to get what I wanted. Well, for a few years anyway.

# The King of Erotica 2

## The Crown

INSTEAD OF PICKING UP A GUN WHEN ANGRY
PICK UP A PEN.
THE POSSIBILITIES ARE ENDLESS
PUSSIES CARRY AND BRANDISH GUNS
REAL MEN BRANDISH A GOOD BOOK

# Booty-Do

My name was Princess Webster. And I was having the time of my life at a banging party in Florida City, Florida. It took Ed a few weeks to convince me to go. I didn't like a crowd, and I liked being to myself. If it *wasn't* about money then it didn't make sense, was what I said. My business was *my* business and every time you met new people they wanted to *know* your business, especially down here in Florida City, the boondocks. Against my better judgment, I remembered last week. I was helping my mean-ass Daddy clean his gorgeous, sporty Chrysler 300M. He was absent-mindedly buffing and waxing and I was consciously using Windex to clean his windows on a perfect sunny day. I hated living on Lucy Street because black folks always got in your business without a care in the world. West Homestead Elementary School loomed about a hundred feet away from me. Across from that was the "New Buildings," a housing projects with more drama, whores, sluts, dumb asses and a few good people to keep my away from there. My home girls lived in there, and they were always snatched in some female baby daddy shit that was uncalled for.

Ed called my cell phone and told me he was having a party. I rolled my eyes in disgust.

"Are you coming?" he asked excitedly. He loved entertaining people. I loved entertaining myself.

I thought about it all of three seconds.

I shook my head. "*Nah*, Ed. I have things to do."

"Aw *come* on, Princess! You'll be the life of the party."

I cracked a smile. I appreciated the flattery. But my Daddy didn't. He glared at me and squirted some water from the hose in my lightly made-up face. Now see he was fucking up mu blush and foundation. What if some cute men drove by? Daddy was cock blocking. The water was so cold I jumped out of my skin, dropping my phone. Damn it! I hope it wasn't cracked. It was the iPhone. I paid out the ass for it. Damn, Daddy! Now I was pissed. I gave him the middle finger. He stared at me, daring me to get lippy. Believe me I wanted to. Fuming, I kept my mouth closed, guardedly picking up the phone. I couldn't live without it.

Getting myself back together, I said, "Ed. I don't know about coming to your party. I should go…maybe I shouldn't."

"Like I said. You'll be the life of the party."

I smiled, despite my unease around Daddy right now. "Ed. The shit talker."

"Nah, girl I'm the smooth operator."

"That's funny. I didn't know you looked like Sade."

"*Whatever.* Are you coming?"

I thought about it again, holding the phone to my ear with my shoulder, squirting window cleaner all over the windshield and wiping it off with Bounty paper towels, since they lasted longer.

*Here goes.* "Yea. I'll go."

"*Sweet*, Princess," he said too excitedly. *What are you up to, Ed?*

"See you there," he went on.

"Just let me know what day," I was scratching my tit. "And call and remind me. How's Georgia doing?"

"She's out with her cousins. They are some *cool* Niggahs, too. They just moved to Miami. Well, they've been living here for a few months now. They're addicted to South Beach."

"That's one sorry, expensive ass beach. What is it about that crummy beach everybody loves so much?" I asked rhetorically. "Smells like piss half the time. I'd rather go to Cocoa Walk in the Grove." I kissed through the phone.

Daddy stood in my face and kissed my forehead.

"Forgive me?" Daddy whispered.

I squeezed his shoulder. I loved Daddy.

"Bye, Ed."

"Talk to you later, Princess. And come to the party."

A couple weeks later, after postponing it several times (money issues), Ed had his party. He had a huge, fabulous house on Redland Road, about ten minutes from my house. So the two DJ's he hired for the festivities played their music as loud as they wanted, without the neighbors calling the police every five minutes, because his house sat on 8 acres of land, surrounded by monstrous trees and bushes. The bass from the speakers nearly knocked my hairstyle out of place. Creep paper, confetti and balloons were everywhere. I loved the "Get your Freak on" theme. This was an adult party. You had to be over 20 in age. There were bouncers clad in black, long-sleeved (too tight) security shirts at his door. Huge, burly Niggahs with asses bigger than horses and dicks longer than ropes pat you down like they just came back from Iraq. Free drinks for the ladies. Five bucks for the fellahs. Since I knew the game plan I didn't drink at all. I had the same plastic red cup for two hours, holding the same ole beer. Looked like a prop in my hands. I needed to throw this shit away. I remembered when a short, handsome black man with huge dread locks brought me the beer. I wasn't here ten minutes and already the jerk magnet on my body sent out invitations. He was too pushy, too direct. Every fifth word was "My Niggah." And his vocabulary made me sick to my stomach.

It had turned me off, so I accepted the beer (I could have gotten for free anyways, so he didn't do me a favor) just to get his dumb ass out of my face and told him, as politely as I could, "*Look.* I came to party. Solo. That means *without* a man."

To my dismay, he called me a stuck-up bitch and walked off. *Typical.*

"Your Mama's a bitch!" I yelled behind him, tucking my chin back. He turned, grabbed his dick, wiggled it at me and stormed off. He was very immature. I mean I had my immature days but damn, not like that! He was too damn old to be doing junior high school shit.

This was the play. Men wanted to get the ladies' drunk so they could fuck 'em every which way. I knew the play all too well. I did it plenty of times myself. Getting drunk and then I come off my pussy like it's free. Now, if I wound up in *anybody's* bed I would *know* how I got there.

The party was in full swing. A blanket of lust and sensuality lay under such a glorious Miami, Florida moon. The air was cool and crisp. There was a little wind, but nothing alarming. I got tired of carrying my red cup so I gulped the beer. It tasted like Corona. I tossed the cup in the trash. The women looked nice tonight. There were the usual melee of ghetto Hoochies clad in their daughters shorts and skirts, shaking it through the crowd. Talking loud, popping gum and those huge bellies wiggling over their waist lines like that shit was cute.

A few lesbians, pretty women at that, tried to get with me but they got somewhere after I told them, "I don't do the same ocean water I came out of, you feel me?" They respected that. I had my gun in my purse if they wanted to get rowdy.

Ed, clinging to his wife Georgia, danced up to me. He looked so cute. She kissed my cheek and I hugged them both. My very good friends. I knew them for ten years. My Dad was in the Marines with his father, they actually retired together. So we were family.

"Enjoying yourself, girl?" Georgia asked me, her Asian/black ass pulling on her mouthwatering joint. She had red eyes, and could hardly stand up. I liked her Baby Phat pants suit; she was rocking it with some rhinestone stilettos. The accessories, the chain belt and the matching chain earrings brought out her eyes.

I took her hand and cupped it lovingly. She was like a sister. We have been through it all together. Two abortions, two heartbreaks and bad yeast infections forever tarnished our female resume. I was there for her when she first met Ed years ago. He was a different man then. He used to cheat on her, beat her and talk down to her. He was a prick and I tried to shoot him plenty of times. He used to hate women, yet he dated them like he loved them. He didn't even have respect for his own mother. Back then he was a big time gangster. He would shoot you in a heartbeat. But once my father got a hold of him, and showed him a better way of treating women, he got his act together, married Georgia and never cheated or beat on her again. He needed a role model because his own father was too busy chasing skirts and putting his Mama through hell to be bothered with his seed. Bottom line Ed was big and all mighty, but he feared my father. We withstood it all.

I brushed lint from his jacket sleeve. "I'm having fun," I said, noticing a tall guy trying to get his grind on with a white girl over by the pool. Beach balls were flying here and there, water splashing, half naked adults finding solace in their watery heaven. I shook my head. I hoped he was careful. That white girl, Pauline, was a robber. She'd rob his ass in a heartbeat, all while keeping it classy. She robbed so many men that she lost count after twenty.

Ed said, "Dance with me, girl." He possessively took me by the arm.

I pat his shoulder. "*Nooo*, dance with your wife." I kissed his cheek, taking my arm back. Georgia nodded her appreciation. She *knew* that deep down Ed wanted to fuck me; all those men wanted some of my apple pie. "I'm going to check out the scene. See ya'll later. There's money to be made out there, girl!"

"Girl don't be tricking all through my house," she joked, kissing my cheek. We squeezed hands fondly, and then I went on my way.

The instant I turned around two men were in my face. Startled, I jumped out of my skin, patting my weave. One took my hand.

"Hey, baby." He had gold teeth, dirty shoes and an oversized coat. *Bitch let me go!*

The other man grabbed my other hand. "Are you here with anybody?" His T-shirt was too small and his jeans were so tight you could see the size of his nuts. Suddenly I didn't like Planter's anymore. He reminded me of a Shabba Ranks and Johnny Gill music video: out of air play. There was nothing slow and sexy about those men.

Before they could say anything else I danced to Khia's "Look Back at it." Shaking it like it just didn't stop. I pranced past them, snapping my fingers, released a "*Heeeeeey*!" as loud as I could, twirling my head and out into the sea of dancers; shaking my ass all over the place. Everybody rushed out to dance. This was the jam! I was in a crowd of horny women, all shaking their asses, trying to get the men to notice. One fat girl, clad in tight pink patent leather, did the "Walk it out" dance, looking more like someone pulling a pink Now and Later candy from the pack and actually struggling with it.

I laughed to myself, went over to her, gave her a high five and said, "Girl, you doing that damn dance! And your hair is cute!"

She hugged me. "Girl, thank you."

Her hair looked like shit.

Thugs were everywhere. Lifting glasses of booze in the air, they rocked back and forth, looking gangster. I loved it.

I smelled liquor and weed in the air, a dizzying cornucopia of aromas blending easily with different body fragrances, colognes and deodorant.

Feeling it, and feeling good, I pulled my dress up to my thighs and kicked off my heels. I was jamming. I was throwing my weave like Britney Spears. Wait a minute. She was bald now.

It wasn't everyday I got to jam and have fun. Since I worked as an undercover prostitute, content on the money I made and not caring about people, I cut loose. I didn't have to worry about ducking and dodging the police, even though five of Miami's Finest were my regulars.But tonight was different. I wasn't going to lure any prospects from Ed's party. I wasn't going to disrespect his house. Most people didn't care, but I was a woman who respected her friends. Now I was thirsty. I wanted some water or something. That beer didn't do it for me. So I made a last minute decision to go take advantage of the free drinks. Why not? I lived for times like this, when you could just let go and live a little and *not* worry about problems or bills. Just forget your damn name, honestly. I was going to take full advantage of Ed and his party.

Putting back on my heels, I walked through the dancing crowd.

Marijuana and alcohol putting her on cloud 9, Georgia lovingly looked at Ed, kissing his lips.

"The party is live and in charge, baby." She was on top of the world. She was happy to be married to an ex-gang banger who now worked for FP&L, making honest money. She was a hair stylist, charging her clients as much as $200 for their hair styles.

He sipped his Heineken beer. "Yea, that's true, even though there are people here we didn't invite."

"Ah, baby," said Georgia, licking the white residue from his cute nose. He loved when she did that, made him get a hard on.

They kissed.

"Let the people have fun." She tasted the cocaine in her mouth, which upset her because Ed told her he'd stopped, yet there was white residue on his nose.

Aggravated, because he just remembered he had a ton of bills to send off tomorrow, Ed replied, "Hell, I have been doing that all night." He held her tight, looking down into her pretty eyes, suppressing a smile. Felt like he could see Japan.

His baby, his love.

He could not live without her. He wished he could take back all the heart ache and grief he once brought to her life, but he chose to leave it where it was. In the past. Where it was now buried.

Over by the bar, just in front of the back door, a short man asked the tall, gullible bartender for a small cup of Hennessy. Light ice. Top it off with Coke soda.

The Bartender looked him over. He got a bad vibe. He looked good, but he spelled trouble. "Sure, coming right up," said the bartender. He worked for Ed for some side cash. He owed Ed a favor. His regular 9pm-5am job was on South Beach, at one of the popular clubs. But business has been on the decline and he needed something quick, fast and in hurry so he didn't lose his seedy condo on Miami Beach. The people at Ed's party weren't really his type of crowd, but when someone paid you $300 for five hours work, you jumped at it. He poured Hennessy in a plastic red cup, threw in four ice cubes, and topped it off with Coke soda.

Handing it to the short guy, he said, "Five dollars, player."

The short guy handed him a ten. "Keep the change."

Sipping the drink, he guardedly turned, slowly walking over to one of the tables by the dark corner of the huge house. Sitting down, he cautiously looked around; making sure no one was watching him.

Then he put his plan into action.

With the skill of a brain surgeon, he opened one of the small plastic bags he pulled from his left pocket, no bigger than the little bags the dope boys sold weed in, and he dumped the GHB into the drink. Smiling sinisterly, he eyed one of the women. A short, Cuban woman was shaking it with some girl like there was no tomorrow.

Working up enough nerve, he tossed the small bag on the ground, used a dirty finger to stir the drink, making sure the date rape drug dissolved properly. He rhythmically snapped his fingers, dancing over to the fine woman. When she seen him she was instantly turned on. Eli's body-clinging gold dress was irritating her skin. She reached out and shook his hand. She loved black men.

"Is that drink for me?" she asked, grinding her butt all over his groin.

*Bingo! Free pussy tonight!* "Yup." He handed it to her.

She had to use the bathroom. "Give me a second, Papi. Be right back. I gotta pee."

"I'll be right there, Senorita," he said smoothly.

He could not keep his eyes off her bouncy breasts.

Eli's friend took his arm and said, "Dance with me 'til she gets back. You're cute, Papi."

Holding her ass, they danced the night away.


"Hey, Princess! What are you getting from the bar?" I looked at my good friend Eli Rodriguez. With her pretty self. I called her the Latino bombshell because she was a very *sexy* woman.

"I'm getting a Hennessy and Coke," I told her.

She waved her hands feverishly, thrusting her drink at me with a smile. "Here. You can have mine. I just got it not too long ago."

I accepted the drink, sipping it slowly. Yummy.

Eli, her hips moving to the playing salsa, told the bartender, with a voice of butter, "I'll just have bottled water. With no ice."

He couldn't take his eyes off of her.

"No problem, sexy," he told her, trying not to admire her amazing curves. Yet he had to look anyway. It was in his nature.

Resoundingly, I felt their chemistry. She rubbed his hand like a spoiled child. "And pour it in one of those red cups. *Thanks* Papi."

"No problem, pretty lady."

"And he's a flirt…"

"I can be more if you want me to."

I was laughing at those two.


I felt good; sipping the drink opened me up.

This was just what I needed. All that salsa music died away and the DJs were playing my cut. I didn't know who sung this jam, but I loved the beat.

*Take it to the floor. Now drop, drop, drop bring it back now.* Yes, I was feeling this dance song. It was straight 'hood! It was when I bent over to touch my toes and shake, shake it, that a man got behind me, holding my ass, and smacking it. Whack. I loved it.

I turned to face him. He had huge diamond earrings. His face was so angelic. And his hazel eyes stopped my heart. I ran my hands over his bare arms. I was being hypnotized by his presence. Never have I met a man who initially made me feel this way. He was dressed in Phat Farm gear. A hat angled on his head. Well-trimmed, smelled nice.

"And your *name*, Ma?" he asked, barely able to keep his eyes open.

I studied him. "You're *not* from here, are you?" I asked him, noticing he was drunk and high. He could barely look at me.

Eli sipped her water, making her way out of Ed's bathroom. She made sure she cleaned up behind herself. The house was packed with people, dancing and having a good time. Four brothahs utilized the dining table for their noisy, cussing game of dominoes. Slamming the game pieces to the point where the table shook. She gyrated past the low-table, the dining room, and out the back door. She stopped and asked the bartender, "What is your name?"

He wanted to lie. But he decided against it.

"Dan."

Desperately sticking out her breasts, she went in for the kill. "You're cute. Can I get your number?"

Taking a sharpie marker from his pants, he gently pulled out her plump tit and scribbled his number just above the nipple. He then kissed it, sending electricity through her body. She stared at him.

"That's an erasable marker, so the more you sweat, the faster my number disappears."

She licked her rosy lips. "Really?"

He looked deep into her angelic eyes.

"*Really*. So I think you shouldn't dance that hard. By the time the song goes off, my number will vanish into this air."

Leaning over and giving him some tongue, she had an idea. "How about writing it on my pussy and *eating* it off."

There was activity in his boxers. "I leave at about 3 a.m."

"I'll call you," she said breathlessly.

He was stuttering. "I'll come find you."

"I should feel so special, 'ey Papa?"

"...Whatever makes you happy, sexy lady. And your name is?"

"Oh, I'm Eli. *Cuban*, baby!"

"I'm looking forward to kicking it with you."

He looked past her and noticed the short man he served the Hennessy and Coke to staring at her with the most evil eyes. He shuddered. Not liking the feeling in his gut.

Eli took her friend by the arm and playfully pulled away from the fine black man she was getting her groove on with.

"Ok, girl I'm back. I'm cutting in." She killed the water, feeling the cold liquid trailing down her throat. "Shit, that hit the spot!" She handed her friend the cup, dancing to rapper 50 Cent's "Just a Little bit."

"Thanks for the drink," she told her new friend, kissing his cheek.

He studied her. *Yes. She drank all of it. Now all I need to do is get her to my SUV, and when she starts to fall asleep I can take her home and beat the pussy up. I can't believe how easy that was.*

"Want another one?"

"No, I'm straight," said Eli with an attitude.

Before she could hug her new friend and kiss him, Dan took her by the arm and said, "Mind dancing with me?"

"*Oooh*, Dan! Yes! I thought you would never ask."

Dan looked at the little guy and said, "Yea, I'm cock blocking. She's mine, you lose. *Peace*, pimp."

And the little guy stormed out of the party, arms folded, cursing under his breath.

*Goddamn!*

*I don't get to have sex!*

In a drunken stupor, my new friend responded, "Nah. I'm from out of town."

I suddenly had an interest in him.

"What's your name?" I asked him.

"Thomas." He had slurred speech.

"I'm Princess. *Nice* to meet you, playboy."

"Princess is a pretty...name..."

He hugged me and almost fell over. I didn't know what to do. He was heavy, yet I used all my strength to hold him up. I decided not to leave him in this state. I helped him into Ed's house, past Niggahs kissing face with women, rubbing on their asses and all that. I helped him up the stairs. I was five feet 9; he was about five-eleven, maybe six feet tall. He was moaning piteously. Damn he was lit pretty badly.

Once we reached the top of the stairs, the coast was clear. Upstairs was off limits for partygoers anyways. I was family. The stipulation didn't apply to me.

I took him to the guest room and locked the door, helping him lay on the bed. I nearly dropped him on the floor. One of the heels of my shoe snapped off and ricochet off the TV. I just laughed, rubbing my forehead. Then it happened, a run up my stockings made me curse under my breath. I shouldn't have worn panty hose anyways, that shit was played out like Vanilla Ice, the rapper. Two huge framed pictures of Bob Marley hung above the head of the bed. Black carpet. Red furniture. Very deep neo-soul feel in this room. Huge plasma TV mounted in the wall, 70 inches of pure beauty. A huge fish tank. I loved fish tanks, every time I came in this room I just admired it, afraid to touch anything. Showing off my sincere side, which I hardly shown to anyone, I took off his shirt and tossed it on the Lazy Boy. What an amazing chest. I looked him over, my eyes raking his body like Daddy rake leaves.

Turning on the tube (ESPN, *figures*), I sat on the Lazy Boy and watched him writher all over the bed. He was rubbing his head, his eyes slammed shut. He said he had a head ache. I debated. Should I help him?

No. Girl, *yes*! Do *something*. I didn't know him. We're strangers. No you're not. His name was Thomas. And he was the most beautiful black man you have *ever* seen!

Rape him, girl! No, bitch! Girl, get that dick, shit it's free! No its not, Chile. You crazy! Get on his dick and ride it reverse cowgirl style. I guess get a hat, too, 'ey? Shit, he's out of it! He won't remember it in the morning. No, girl I can't! Scary, bitch! You're just scary!

Against my better judgment, I took off his shoes. He had on crisp white socks. Feet smelled good. Like lavender powder. Taking off his socks I noticed the pretty feet. Very nice. I liked this, a man who took care of his body. His toe nails were a little long. I opened the night stand drawer and took out the toe nail clipper. I spent ten minutes giving his toes special treatment. I felt good doing it. Why not? I would rather be here then at the party. Wanting to go the extra mile, I went into the bathroom, wet a wash cloth with warm water, turned it off, kicked off my heels, sat next to him and placed the folded rag on his forehead. I dabbed it all over his face, his chest, like I was dusting his skin for prints.

He had the most *gorgeous* smile. "Oh, Ma. That feels good."

I kissed his cheek. "No problem."

I noticed the wedding ring on his finger. So he was married. My eyes racked his killer chest. Damn! And he had huge, gorgeous nipples. I rubbed his pecks, massaging him. Hell, men took advantage of women all the time. It was time for me to take advantage of a drunken man.

*Get that dick, bitch! Oh God, conscious, shut the fuck up! You better get it, or I'ma give your ass plaguing migraines for the rest of your natural life.*

*I'll just make a doctor's appointment and swallow pills until they vanish, so do what you gotta do. Damn, you're a scary Ho!*

I was getting sleepy, very drowsy. I tried to keep my eyes open but I couldn't. I was getting dizzy, my vision blurry. What was wrong with me? I felt good, though, my body tingled. I felt hands on me, the softest hands. They were on my face. A kiss. I was kissing Thomas. He dabbed the rag on my face. We tongue kissed again, his hands massaging my shoulders.

"Lay down, Ma," he said. "You tried to take care of me. And even though I'm fucked up, let me take care of you." I felt safe. My panties were going down. I felt his tongue all over my pussy. Before you know it I was out for the count.

Ed was silently looking over Georgia. She wondered what he was thinking. Judging from the look on his face he was worried that someone was going to break something in his house. He was very anal about things like that. Last year someone broke his favorite statue. Some drunk happened to accidentally push it over while he chased ass all over the place and never replaced it. And thinking about it he smiled. Because Princess pieced it back together like it was never broken. Yea. He smiled bigger.

He loved that girl…

# Was It a Dream

Groggily, I awakened from a deep sleep when I heard my alarm clock. Sitting up, I looked around wildly, not knowing where I was. The clock read 9:56 a.m. I felt good, actually, the warm Miami sun shining through lacy curtains, making shapes on my body. And despite my body feeling relaxed, pleasantly relaxed, I couldn't quite shake the shade of wearifulness that had me on the verge of collapsing back into hibernation. My weave job was fucked. That was just great! Another $100 gone down the drain in one night. I swear sometimes I had to remind myself that money wasn't going to grow on trees any time soon. Benevolent, I asked myself, "Where am I? That is not my clock." I felt weird, like I was trapped in a surreal world where nothing made sense.

Black carpet, big screen TV. Turned off. Bob Marley pictures on the wall. Oh. I was in *Georgia's* guest room. I smiled uneasily. I wondered she was. With the feeling of wanting to monkey around, I got out of bed, a terrible wringing in my head. Feeling vulnerable, my eyes were burning. I was butt naked with a nasty after taste in my mouth. I smacked my lips, narrowing my eyes for effect. Did I fuck or something? Because my body felt good and my pussy felt incredible! In fact my pussy has never felt this incredible in my life!

Racking my brain for answers, which was more of an empty tree trunk with echoes bouncing around haphazardly, I went into the bathroom and took a much-needed shower. Ed and Georgia always said I could make myself at home when I came over and I never had. I had every intention of doing so. I loved using my friends' houses to do my thing but I didn't want to overstay my welcome or seem selfish so I wound up taking my black, sexy ass home and crashing in my own bed, using my own shit. Well, goddamn, I meant Daddy's shit.

Not today. Again, I wondered where Georgia and Ed were. They were probably fucking. They fucked more than porn stars. I wondered how I got up in this room. I knew I had a good time at the party last night; I guzzled the beer like Kool-aid, and then the Hennessy and Coke didn't make matters any better. That's what did it, produced this conduit of problems seeping into every chamber of my body. Stepping in the shower, I felt good. The warm water fell all over me, snatching my uneasiness and spreading it all over my skin, waking me up even more. I smiled really big, staring at the tile. I felt sensational, despite the lingering effects of the alcohol wearing off like an old pair of blue jeans. This was just what I needed. I was so discombobulated I didn't even know what day it was. I knew I had to go to work at about 4 p.m. So I was safe for right now. I didn't jeopardize my job, even though I worked at Burger King in Naranja, Florida, on U.S.1, and 268th Street. I used that as a smokescreen to hide my real profession, prostitution. Money was money and if I had to flip burgers to make some extra doe than boom, that's what I would have to do.

Georgia had a plethora of hand creams and body wash. They were neatly organized in a swinging iron tray under the shower nozzle. The bitch had the best of it all. I liked that. My eyes gravitated to the Dove Body Wash. I grabbed it, took the foamy sponge, popped the top and squirted some on the sponge. I cleaned myself thoroughly. I *hated* the smell of Dove, plus the liquid sometimes irritated my sensitive skin but I didn't feel like being dirty another moment and I damn sure didn't feel like getting out the tub. Rubbing the sponge all over my breasts, I felt tingly. I rubbed my pussy. Yup. IT'S ALIVE! I had a *Weird Science* pussy, not a Frankenstein pussy. Like the old school movie *Weird* Science, my pussy had a mind of its own. It could be Kelly LeBroc one day or it could turn into a damn toad the next and sit there.

I was held spellbound by the horniness that catapulted from every opened pore on my body.

Attentive, I leaned against the light blue tiled wall, free of mildew, and started rubbing my wet opening. The pleasure shot through me like bullets. My hair was wet, now I had to get rid of this weave...I shuddered as I slid the sponge over my dripping pussy, carefully manipulating my clit. I took y time nurturing my clit. My clit made me feel so beautiful I was about to die inside. Life didn't get much bigger than this and for those who think I need to find a new hobby can suck my ass, go to sleep, wake up and suck my ass again.

My legs drummed together as steam enveloped me, taking me up and out of the bathroom with the force of a gusty wind. It produced powerfully breathtaking images of last night in my skull, causing them to explode in my brain...from some unknown force in my soul. Something that tried to make me remember beckoned me, wanted me to remember. It needed me to...remember. I was floating, rising and falling like a feather, making loops around the sudden urgency to be touched, to be loved, to inevitably be fucked good, long and hard...

I saw a fine man, clad in Phat Farm gear. His face I could not make out, but he had the most incredible smile. His name was Thomas. And he was taking off my panties...trying to get to my pussy. No, Thomas. You can't get to my twat. No, baby. I was trying to take advantage of you. I cut your toe nails, damn it. You were supposed to be intoxicated. Now you're trying to get between my legs. Hadn't you spent enough time between your Mama's legs when she was pushing you out of her pussy? There's no place like home, huh? Thomas tasted the wetness, sucking my panties until they no longer smelled of good pussy. He tossed them, opening my legs, tasting the sliced peach, reminding me why I wished I was born in Georgia, so I could be called a "Georgia Peach." I would be sweet to taste, sweet to the touch and *sweet* to all the human senses.

His "touch" was heaven. It lifted my clouds and presented the Red Sea, which spilt open and revealed a man eager to have me, eager to love me, eager to pleasure me. Over rapturous waters I was the feather again. I was rising, falling and floating towards the cliffs of desire. Rocky ledges and bumpy roads. Winding paths and drifting seas. I smelled liquor on his breath. He *was* intoxicated.

His "sight" tore into my soul, sliced my retinas in half, revealing my optic nerves which made the pulse in my thighs pop with jubilancy. His tongue and hands moved over me effortlessly. I was ungrateful because I was too out of it to really get into it, but I felt my torso twirling like wind chimes. He was about to make my pussy regurgitate.

His "smell" opened chambers in my heart and soul I never knew I had. I felt the wind of pleasure pick me up; turn me on my stomach, while his fabulous, baby smooth hands spread my ass cheeks apart. Like God peeling away petals, telling a sick planet earth he loved it, he loved it not and his tongue dove into my hole with such abandon I felt like putting up no vacancy signs all over my body, just so he would never stop licking, slurping and tasting the chocolate.

From my hole to my pussy he was tasting perfection, tasting what took Daddy ten minutes to release and took Mama another nine months to make. A man has never taken his time with me. A man has never made me feel gorgeous. A man has never taken away my problems. A man has never made me forget the outside world. *God please don't let this end! God I never knew what it felt like to be treated like a Queen. A man always rushed, rushed. Now he was taking his time. My pussy felt like a garden of roses and now I wanted a garden of tulips. Two lips on my pussy.*

My "hearing" increased the instant he slid his passion deep into my soft place. Maybe his dick became the eager archeologist, roaming my tomb, searching for Nefertiti; trying to find out if she was buried in the Valley of the Kings or in the trunk of the baobab trees. Unshapely, my promiscuity got the best of me. I saw myself. I saw Thomas tapping my pussy from the back. His beautiful ass cheeks were jiggling in a manly way. His back was strong and firm. His hands were planted firmly on the bubble of my ass. He mounted the horse in my pussy, feeding it the apples which lined the veins of his dick like grapes on vines, like intersections on road maps.

The sponge brought me sheer pleasure as I felt my toes curl, nearly causing me to slip in the tub and break my head open...on my knees I was, humping the sponge, my buttocks jiggling like Jell-o...the water turning me into a seductive tsunami, of which I begin to rise and fall like Anne Rice Vampires, full of power, devoid of reason, homely and deformed, seekers of blood. My eyes remained on the bed. Thomas was lying on his back, guiding my throbbing pussy on his incredible dick. My tits bounced like Michael Jordan was trying to win Chicago Bulls the 6th Championship with his tongue out. It took a moment before I realized that Ed, Georgia's husband, was sitting on the toilet before me. He was naked, sweaty, able and willing.

*What the fuck...?*

He was jerking his juicy dick, his nuts jumping up and down, making my pussy wetter. I was stunned, but my sense of "taste" caused my tongue to grow a mind of its own. *Girl, don't do it. Bitch, shut up. Georgia's my best friend. I just wanna suck his dick. Damn.* I leaned over, my wet hair all over his muscled thighs and I kissed the head of his passion. His eager hands inherited my head. Feeling like an eager slut, I took him deep into the contours of my mouth while Thomas, from last night, in my mind, brought me to orgasm. I shook and shivered in the tub, Ed rubbing my face, talking to me, loving me, telling me he'd been wanting me for years, that what we did would stay between me and him, that he loved how I worked the tongue, bringing his dick the needed joy it so wanted forever.

I came and I came, manipulating my pussy with the sponge. I moaned pleasantly, loving this freaky episode. He closed and locked the door. He picked me up, sat me on the toilet, and he stuck his tongue so deep inside me, triggering my G-spot. I rode his face and his tongue hit something in my pussy because my bladder tingled and I had to pee. He sucked my clit while I took a piss. I didn't give a shit. He wanted a dirty bitch I gave him some salty piss. He took some of it and rubbed it on my nipples, suckling the right one, carefully biting it in a way that brought pleasure and not pain.

Pushing my legs back, he munched the pussy like some bubble yum. Hmm. Work the tongue baby. Wait, wait, *damn* it. *That* hurt. Don't use your teeth. Take your time. My pussy lips were like wet toilet paper. Wipe gently—*oooh*, shit. Now that felt good, Ed. Suck my pussy. *Yea.* Yea, yea YEA YEA YEA AH YEA AH SHIT. Lick me, taste me, suck me you fine motherfucker. Suck my pussy like it's Georgia's. He sat on the floor and guided his throbbing member deep inside my pink walls. We grinded on the floor. I took the Nike hat from his head, slanted it on my head and rode his scrumptious dick. My booty clapped on his thighs. But all I could see was Thomas. Loving me, wanting me and desiring me, and suddenly my body shut down.

What was I doing?

Georgia was my home girl. I couldn't fuck her man! I was a woman of assured probity, at least I thought so.

*Girl!* Oh, no! No! NO! *Conscious, please, don't start. Yea, girl it's me! Hey! Get the dick, get the dick GET THE DICK! Fuck Georgia, this was not about her. Yes it was! She's my best friend. No. Georgia as a selfish bitch who was sitting on good dick and never offered to share it with you. Friends share. Yes, conscious. They do, but they don't share their significant others. Fuck it I'm going to grind on Ed's dick until my pussy screams!*

Deeply ashamed and simply unprepossessing, I hopped up and snatched a towel from the niche. Running into the bedroom, I picked up my clothes and heels. I couldn't breathe; I could still feel him inside me. I wanted and needed Ed back inside my pussy. I wanted him to replace Thomas, to beat him out of my system because I just admitted to myself that I *love* Thomas with all my heart. No, I didn't. Girl, yes you did! I'm confused right now. Nothing was making sense. I had to go. I didn't know what was going on and I didn't want to know. All I knew was that I didn't want to hurt my girl; I couldn't stay here and feed into Ed's infidelity when my heart ached for a man I could hardly remember, or would probably never see again. I started to cry. My insides opened so wide I almost fell into myself, in search of myself, trying to *find* myself. It was just me, myself and I; we got each other until the end. Men weren't shit; well, Thomas was my soul mate, my angel.

He was perfect. God, would I ever find him again? Ed spun me into his face. God, he brought sexy back. The hell with singer Justin Timberpussy. He grabbed both my tits with fire in his eyes, ready to say *fuck the world. Yea, I was doing the unthinkable!* The mood was right and I wanted her, his eyes told me. He didn't pull a "wardrobe malfunction," leaving singer Janet Jackson before the world, gripping her own tit.

I wanted him so damn bad. But should I go through with it?

"Where are you going? You can't run out on me, girl. I need you."

I would not meet his demanding gaze.

"What about Georgia? I can't do this to her."

He tried to turn on the Rico Suave charm.

"Look. I *love* her. *You* love her. But I want you. I need you. Please, baby. Make love to me."

"I can't! I just can't!"

"Just open yourself…uh, and let yourself be free."

"Ed. This is not *General Hospital.* And I said 'no.'"

He was pleading. He wanted me. He reached out for me. I grabbed both his hands and pulled myself into his arms and when I realized it was the business woman in me, the prostitute who was all about money I made up my mind.

"Two hundred dollars and we can fuck all over this room. Georgia is my girl, but business is business."

He smiled victoriously, pulling me into his embrace. We kissed, rising on tidal waves of lust together. We crashed on the bed, wetting the ocean shores. We built sand castles with tongues, fingers and whispering sweet nothings that didn't mean anything in each other's ears as he guided his rod into my green pastures and we spent an hour rewriting Psalms 23 all over the sheets, making me come over and over and over, while I dug my nails into his back and his hips quivered between my legs the same time his dick throbbed between the pink walls.

"I'm gonna nut in this pussy," he promised and he exploded deep inside, grinding me to oblivion as my moans filled his ears, but wasn't powerful enough to fill the room and when he fell on top of me I hugged him, stroking his hair, kissing his lips, looking into his eyes.

"Where's my money?"

He produced his wallet and gave me five hundred dollars.

He was standing by the bed. I weakly stood up and yawned.

"When can we do this again?" he asked, deeply in love with me. Oh my. What have I done?

I felt like shit. I just fucked Georgia's man and made him pay for it. "Never, Ed. Georgia must never find out about this."

I was nervous. I was ready to run out of the room the minute the time was right. I tried putting on my clothes but he took them and threw them across the room. He took me into his arms, sucking on my neck, making me so weak in the knees the left one slammed into his nuts and he was on the floor, like a helpless lady bug, holding his sack, whimpering.

I snatched up my clothes and fled from the room. Stomping along the hallway, I accidentally knocked their wedding photo off the wall. It fell on the floor, the glass shattering. Fuck the picture! I gotta get out of this house! I gotta get far, far, far away from this hellishly induced scene.

Destroyed inside, I was running down the stairs, fumbling into my clothes, and hurriedly put on my heels. I was reminded that one of the heels was broken when I fell flat on my face, by the coffee table. Ouch! That hurt. On my feet I was, racing through the kitchen. I came to a screeching halt, quietly grabbing the island counter, inhaling deeply and holding my breath.

Georgia was on the phone.

She was talking so loud, and the radio was going a mile a minute. I was shocked. She was home? Oh, God! What had I done to my girl? I wanted to cry. I was shaking all over. I hated to admit it, but Georgia could fight. The bitch was notorious for whipping so many asses Playboy might, just might call her for a job molding the ass it sold monthly across the U.S. and all over the newsstands.

She didn't see me. I was looking at her from behind, with the news of her potential separation from her husband drying in the form of his saliva all over my pussy, neck and nipples.

But I'd let it dry, because I'd die before I hurt my girl.

She turned down the radio. "When are you going to fix my sprinklers, John? And what is that smell? I have a really sensitive nose…" Georgia joked through the phone, her hand on her hip, stirring some black beans.

The kitchen smelled like the Chef's quarters, made my stomach growl.

*Shit shit shit! She heard it. She froze, paralyzed. Oh, God what do I do? Think think think!*

Before she turned around I ducked, hiding behind the counter. "John, yea I'm here. Thought I heard something, anyways you gonna come over and taste my black beans and my famous ribs…? What do you mean? Yes, I used my mama's recipe!"

I crawled to the opposite island counter, by the start of the living room and I carefully and quietly stood up and tip toed out of the kitchen and into the living room and I had never run to my car so fast in my life. Half naked, I hopped inside, and did 65 mph heading for my Daddy's house, crying the entire time. In love with a man I'd never see again. Thomas. And. Princess.

My sweet, sweet Thomas.


Georgia was opening the oven to check the status of her mouth-watering ribs when she thought to herself. She loved Princess like a sister, would do anything for her. They confided in each other, stuck up for each other. She trusted this woman with everything in her soul.

Her heart burst with joy at the very thought of Princess. The realest woman she'd ever known. She was down to earth and cocky, was a hustler and knew how to get her money.

When she heard a strange noise she'd turned around and hadn't seen anything. She dismissed it as nothing. Then a familiar smell overcame her nostrils. She'd sniffed the air, smelling what…seemed…like Dove. Dove soap, yea. Dove. Had to be Dove. Dove was her favorite soap. She used it everyday for nine years plus. Ed hated Dove with a passion. She tried to get him to use Dove for years instead of that god-awful Zest soap but he was stubborn.

So she didn't sweat it, fuck it. But when she opened her counter to take out the salt, she looked in the small mirror hanging under the counter and froze when she saw Georgia crawling out of the kitchen.

She didn't know why, but something wasn't right.

And she intended to find out.

Humming the tune "Secret Lovers" in her head, she picked up the phone and called John back, her friend. Stirring the beans, she realized she didn't like the feeling in her gut. She tried to ignore it.

"I'm back. What were we saying now?" She held the phone to her ear with her shoulder.

"Oh, yea you wanted the recipe for my mama's ribs. What? I'm cranky? I need a massage? Nah, my husband will do that. What does that got to do with ribs? His job is to make sure I'm ok not yours. Ok?" And she said more sternly, "I don't cheat on my husband and he would never cheat on me…"

And she believed that with everything in her. Ed would never deceive her. Never.

She could almost guarantee that.

A few days later Daddy and I nabbed a table at Applebee's restaurant by the super Wal-Mart in Florida City. I sat down and started flipping through the menu, on the verge of taking advantage of the two for one drink special. I wanted the strawberry daiquiri.

"Are you ok, baby?" Daddy asked, handsome in a black suit. Earlier today he had attended a real estate seminar hosted by a city slicker by the name of Bobby Taylor. I personally thought it was a get rich quick scheme Daddy fell for because he bought two books from the man. *How to milk Home buying and Investing in Real Estate.* Price tag? Fifty dollars per book! Could you say "Daddy you're a dumb ass?" A hundred dollars for some bullshit he could have downloaded or looked up, for the price of running America Online once a month, without spending a penny. But Daddy always dreamed big.

"I'm ok, Daddy. What about you?"

His Fossil watch was nice. It had a black face and three little diamonds. I paid $150 for it from Macy's at the Dadeland Mall, with an extra 20 percent off. In fact Daddy was dripping in diamonds, with his wrists and ear lobes getting the pleasurable frostbite it deserved from his only daughter.

I gazed at him. "I'm ok." I had so much on my mind. He opened the menu, carefully looking it over. I watched him. He was a very handsome man. If I was true and real with myself I'd admit that Daddy was fine as hell. But I didn't look at my Daddy in such a whorishly incestuous way. I couldn't stop thinking about how I betrayed Georgia. Shit burned me up day and night.

"I wonder what I'm going to drink tonight," I mumbled.

Before I could say anything Daddy told me with a smile, "Strawberry daiquiri is *your* thing. Real men don't drink…fruity drinks, I want something with punch, some Batman shit. Pow! Bang! Boom!"

We laughed easily. A few people at the opposite table looked over at us, laughing as well. Daddy was quite the comedian.

"I hear ya. You should order vodka."

As if on cue a tall, sensual looking blonde paused at our table. Her work uniform was crisp, with a few bills peeping from her pockets.

She gave a smile and a warm, "Welcome to Applebee's. I'm Stacy. How may I help you two? Do you know what you'd like to drink?"

I looked at Daddy. He looked at me, grinning.

"I know what I want to order. I want a strawberry daiquiri, the two for one, and the appetizer entrée. I'm not that hungry. And Daddy will have the steak and shrimp dish and he would like to drink some Parrot Bay."

"Very good," Daddy said, taking my hand and kissing it. He always made me feel like a woman, letting me know if I met a man he better pamper me like Daddy and take my bullshit in stride. "But then again, you always order for me."

"Daddy. Every time we come here we always order the same damn meal."

"The same *darn* meal. Don't curse at me, young lady," he said sternly. "I'm your Daddy! I'm *not* your best damn friend."

"Best *darn* friend, Daddy. *Don't* curse at me."

He gave a warm, defeated smirk; his eyes lighting the entire restaurant. "I got you."

Stacy smiled, telling us she'd be back with the drinks.

Annie Lennox's "Sweet Dreams" came on. Daddy snapped his fingers and tapped his foot on the floor. He loved this song. He extended his hand and I shook my head in the negative.

"I don't dance in public," I told him and he stood up, stuck his chest out, and snatched me from the chair. Pulling me into his arms, we did our little strut to the middle of the floor, just in front of the bar, having fun. I warmed up. It wasn't so bad. I just didn't want eyes on me. I didn't want to think about the fact that I was in love with a man I couldn't see and that I fucked Georgia's husband. Amongst cheers and jeers, Daddy and I did our thing, wowing the crowd. My phone vibrated in my pocket. Taking it out, doing the salsa with Daddy, I looked at the caller I.D.

My heart stopping, I decided not to answer it.

*Why aren't you returning my calls? What is going on with you, Princess? This is so unlike you. A bitch could be bleeding to death. I could be getting raped and you wouldn't know it because you're too busy for me.* Angry, Georgia, hanging up her cell phone, looked at Ed. He was managing the high octane precision of his brand new Mustang, 2006. *This man is always spending money on shit we don't need.* His hands galloped over the steering wheel with the grace of a NASCAR driver; maneuvering in and out of rush hour traffic.

He was perspiring. The AC wasn't doing much.

"Damn it! I *knew* we should have taken the 836 West, instead of the 826."

She smirked. "I *told* you. But *no*…you didn't listen."

He leaned over and quickly kissed her cheek, pretending she was Princess. "You didn't tell me anything…."

"Yes I did." She was defiant.

He glared at her. "Now is not the time to get smart. I'm trying to get us home."

Rolling her eyes, she sucked her teeth. "I can always call a fucking cab."

"Baby, please. Not now."

"Why are you rushing home anyways?" she asked, taking off her Baby Phat jacket. She was a knock out in tight pink pants and matching pink blouse that left one shoulder bare and barely covered her amazing breasts. She was accessorized with bangles, leather belts and huge chandelier earrings that trapped the sunlight every time she looked around.

Ed swallowed hard. "I got things to do."

*The only thing you're concerned about is your dick. Can't even stop whacking off three times a day and you got a wife.*

Her brows rose. "You got things to do? Such as…?"

He was uncomfortable. "You know…uh…yea. I'm going to play ball with the boys."

Wrinkles forming on her forehead, she was deep in thought. "*What* boys? You haven't played ball in ages."

His cell phone vibrated. His heart racing, he ignored it.

*Damn! What if it's Princess and she wants to give up some more good pussy? Goddamn it, why did I have to be stuck in traffic with my nagging wife?*

Georgia was upset. "Aren't you going to answer that?"

Guiltily, he looked down at it. Taking a deep breath, he then glanced at her with a discreet smile. He tried to play it off. "It's nothing. It's probably a bill collector."

She grimaced noticeably. "Our bills are caught up. And since when did you start putting your phone on vibrate status?

*Why is she asking me all these questions? She's suspecting something. I can't let her find out about me and Princess.* "Since last night. I need a change."

Her heart rate quickened. "This conversation isn't making *any* sense."

Determined to find out what's going on, she took his phone and flipped it open and he flipped out, snatching it back from her.

He spat angrily, "Do I go through your phone?"

She was appalled, thrown by his reaction.

"Well, no."

Fire was in his eyes. "Good. This is my phone."

*Something is not right with you!* "But I pay the bill."

His hands dangerously tightened on the steering wheel. "But you're my wife."

Damn. Defeated. *What is it?* "Ok, I respect your privacy."

"Good."

She remained quiet as two things went through her mind with the force of wrecking balls: 1). He never put his phone on vibrate and 2). He has smelled like Dove soap ever since the day Princess crawled out of her kitchen. *What am I not seeing?*

She forced herself to go numb. She would not think about it. She didn't like the feeling in her gut. It was the same feeling she got the day she went in her guest bathroom and saw two things.

Georgia's earring by the toilet.

And Ed's boxer briefs, soaked and wet.

\*\*\*

Daddy and I were eating when he looked at me and said a few words that made me choke.

"When was the last time you talked to Georgia?"

*Oh, God! The "G" word! Are you serious, Daddy?*

"Dad." I was coughing, my eyes watering. He handed me a glass of water.

*Damn it. How could I betray Georgia? I should go and just be a woman and tell her I fucked her husband. Would she cut me or shoot me?*

*Or both?*

"I haven't spoken to her in days." I quickly took a hefty swig of my drink, suddenly getting nervous. What made him think about her? And why were my hands trembling?

He was watching me, actually studying me.

"You can't go two hours without talking to her." A beat of silence. "And now it's been days. Unusual, if you ask me. Are you and Georgia having problems?"

*Yes. I fucked her man. And she didn't know it.*

I avoided his eyes. "Nah. We're cool, Daddy."

He used his butter knife and fork to cut up his meat. He looked like a private school veteran giving a class on etiquette.

"*Cool.* Is that what they say these days, 'cool'?"

I felt really uncomfortable. "Daddy, what's wrong?"

He dug into his pocket and produced my missing earring. I smiled, reaching out for it.

"My fucking...I mean..." He glared at me. "I mean my earring. Dad, where did you find it?"

"I didn't find it. Georgia did. By the toilet in her guest bathroom."

Grabbing my stomach, I jumped up to my feet, heading for the toilet.

I threw up the minute I laid eyes on it.

Two months had gone by since Ed and I had sex in his guest room. Two months of pure hell! Nothing went right. I cried every night for Thomas, a man I was deeply in love with. He was a man that changed my soul in some unexplainable way. And to add insult to injury, my soul went through withdrawal because I could never see him and didn't know *where* he was. I searched phone books. I was looking for Thomas and found over three thousand Thomas's, which depressed me even more because I didn't know his last name. I didn't know a thing about him, his birthday, nor where he was from. He could be from out of town for all I knew.

I could have asked Georgia, but I was scared of that house. Her husband would be there, and he would probably press me for pussy. I should tell her, like any real friend would do. But what if she didn't believe me? What if she blamed me? What if Ed turned it all around and told her I seduced him? At any rate, he really wasn't her husband if he's tip-toeing around on her. I was sure I wasn't the only woman he had sex with behind her back. I thought the Old Ed was reformed. Now I knew better. Once a cheater always a cheater.

I did proposition him, turned my guilty pleasures into a business transaction. If I came clean to Georgia then where would I be? Without a good friend, so I decided to keep my distance. Plus she told me people were at the party who were *not* invited, so there went the notion of Georgia actually *knowing* Thomas. That house became garlic to the vampire in my heart, the blood-sucking, selfish bitch who sucked Georgia's husband's dick, a man I didn't want around me with a ten foot pole. I had lost respect for him and I truly cared *nothing* for him. And if I had half a brain I'd admit that I lost respect for my damn self. I was just as much to blame as he was. The truth hurts because I couldn't even think straight right now.

Suffice it to say, Georgia found my earring in her bathroom. Maybe I was overreacting. There was no way she'd figure out Ed and I fucked. And I doubted if he told her. Ed was loyal, especially when it came to things he wanted. He wanted this pussy. So I know his lips were sealed. So what she found my earring. Didn't prove she *knew* anything.

She has been calling me left and right and I always made up excuses as to why I couldn't hang out with her. I had to work. I just got off work. I gotta do overtime. I gotta close tonight. I gotta open tomorrow. She took it all in stride. But there was only one problem.

I never stood her up before.

And Ed. *God.* Your Royal Britches has been calling me for months. On my cell I declined his call. When he came by the house I slipped out the back door before he could come and talk to me. I didn't want to tell my Daddy we had sex because Daddy loved Georgia like a daughter and I already knew what he would do to Ed's skull. Not to mention he'd have my head as well, because he raised me better than that. Daddy always taught me not to be a home wrecker, yet I wrecked so many homes with my prostitution that it was pathetic. Selling pussy was a business; just ask the porn industry. I was the type of prostitute that had a big clientele. I only messed with men who had money and drove flashy cars. They had to pay up front. Here were the menu choices. For head lasting thirty minutes: $50.

I only ask that you wash it and have it delightfully fragranced. I didn't suck a stinky dick. Yea, I kept a stop watch.

An oral session lasting an hour: $100 plus tax and gratuity. If you were a two minute brother, that's *your* problem.

When you come (meaning have an orgasm) then the session's *over*. Anything beyond *that* we could talk about. Just make sure your wallet is *available* with green bills, *not* debit cards. My sexual exploits became tax write offs every year camouflaged as Volunteer Services. To simply eat the cooch (my word for 'pussy') ranged from $50 to $150, depending on his cleanliness. Believe me…men paid out the ass to eat my cooch. The Cooch Eaters were mainly chubby men who couldn't get it up or lacked the proper skills to pay the bills. To have sex in the cooch for half an hour: $100 flat fee. To get the ass for half an hour: $200. I always worded it "half an hour" because, to the consumer, it seemed like he would be getting his money's worth when I advertised my product. I didn't like sucking dick so I said, "For head lasting 30 minutes," because it seemed shorter. You got me? OK, keep up, damn it.

Anal sex was dangerous, so the fee was a little high. I supplied the condoms. I gotta protect my investment.

I followed my menu to the tooth and nail. I never deviated from it.

If my clients were good enough, I kept index cards with their information and stored it on my palm pilot, a digital organizer given to me by Georgia for my birthday a couple years ago.

I saw particular clients probably twice a week and we kept it simple and discreet. We always met in my room.

Daddy worked at a doctor's office, filing papers. Twelve to thirteen hour days kept his ass at bay. So he was hardly ever here.

I had enough money to get one of those expensive condos being built all over Dade County, but I decided to work from Daddy's house, and lay back and leave the driving to my pussy.

I wasn't about to give these greedy, trying-to-take-over-Miami Cubans my hard-earned money.

Right now I was glowing from the good dick I was enjoying. It was 8 a.m. to be exact.

A very fine, sexy man was tearing the pussy up. Kenny, 23 years old, from East Harlem (and just moved down south to Miami) was a stone-cold freak and I was hoping that he became one of my regulars. I was punching his chest as he took my legs and put them behind the backs of his elbows and grinded into me. His hardened friend brought me pleasure beyond this world. His dick took my mind off my problems. And I had a big problem. One I couldn't shake.

I was in denial. It was one of those problems I didn't know what to do with; I didn't know *how* to handle it. One of those problems you hid from everyone in your life because you didn't know how they'd handle the news.

So I pushed it to the back of my mind when I looked at us fucking from the reflection of my bedroom mirror, loving the eighth wonder of the world. The sexy God and I were bumping pelvises together, hoping to create a spark in my pussy my clitoris could learn to live with. And if it pushed my electric bill up a few dollars it would be well worth it because he wasn't getting this pussy for free.

Now we were kissing and hugging. Cursing and whispering. He had his way with me…using huge cucumbers and bananas to sex me…and sucked coconut juice off my pussy while I was on my period. I wouldn't tell him. I was selfish like that, couldn't help it. Money was money, and bill collector's still rung your goddamn phone while you were on your period so PMS became my motto and every time that day of the month came, I worked *three times* as hard. This was my "secret weapon," because we all knew men loved running and playing women like the Sweet 16 in college basketball soon to be the Elite 8. So being that men have run game on me before, getting a Niggah to go Downtown and eat sushi while Aunt Flow was in town made me laugh inside. You know, get' em before they get you.

Hell if he couldn't figure out coconut juice was white and not reddish white then that's on *him*. Kenny and I were fucking while my Daddy was fixing the shelf in the living room, dancing to some Sam Cooke. I could hear the wooden floors squeaking. Dad was heavy-footed. "Twisting the Night Away."

Now he was singing so loud he'd wake the dead. It didn't bother me at all because he was less susceptible to hearing Kenny hang Head Shots on my pink walls. He had a late day, so Dad wouldn't be leaving for another hour or so. Normally, I'd wait for him to leave; but I wanted Kenny with a passion, so we did the old school sneaking around thing. Being the adventurous, rebellious woman I was, I took a chance. And with that in mind I think back to when I met him.

Mr. Good Bar. Kenny.

*I was coming out of the Dadeland Mall, looking hot to trot in the most expensive dress and high heeled pumps Macy's had to offer. Huge bangles on either wrist, I had six necklaces—of all sizes—around my sweaty neck. A huge medallion rested on my titties. My hair was looking flawless.*

*I was getting in my Nissan Altima when I heard "Goddamn, girl! You're so fine!" coming from behind me. He had the smokiest ghetto voice I'd ever heard. I didn't mind his tacky line. I was wondering if my outfit would reel in the men and from the looks of it I hit the jack pot. Now could I cash in my earnings?*

*Of course I blushed. I quickly wiped the smile from my face and gave my famous mean scowl. A bitch like me had to play hard to get. Even though I was notorious for giving up the pussy to a fine ass man, when I saw a tall, sexy chocolate man approaching me, like a lion on a lioness before the actual beast penetration, clad in Gucci, I was wet. Goddamn it, now I got to change my panties. I was tired of changing panties five times a day. I hated my panties sticking to my cunt every time a fine man looked, breathed or winked at me. Maybe I should buy some Depends, put the diaper on before I put on my panties, so when I got wet, the diaper would get soaked and not my goddamn panties! I pay good money for my undies, $50 a pair from Victoria's Secret.*

*When he smiled, I looked him over. Cadillac Escalade behind him, another man in the passenger seat. He wasn't so pleasant. I rolled my eyes. He got bitchy, saying, with a whiny voice, "Kenny, she think she's all that. Her name is probably Booty-Do."*

*Kenny held up his hand, not breaking away from my gaze. My mouth ajar, my hand was on my neck. I looked past Kenny, sashayed up to the Escalade and said, "Excuse me. My name is what?"*

*"Booty-Do. Your stomach sticks out further than your Booty-Do. Bitch you ain't all that!"*

*I hated when people called me names my parents didn't name me. Infuriated, I jumped in the SUV and yanked the Niggah by his huge earrings. I tried to snatch them out. So what my stomach stuck out further than my ass. I was pregnant. What did he expect? He reminded me that I had a problem. A problem that would change my life once nine months passed by. What would my* father *think? Knowing I didn't have a clue where the Daddy was? Thomas disappeared off the face of the earth. He came into my life just to help me make the little angel in my womb.*

*With that in mind I eyed this sack of shit inside the Cadillac. I wasn't scared to get grimy and dirty with these no-good men. They thought women couldn't fight, but I had a trick for this man today!*

*I was fuming. "Who are you calling a bitch?"*

*Angrily, he slapped me across the face. My teeth bit down on my tongue. I winced. Damn that hurt. Fire in my eyes, I spat in his face, scratching his cheek. He opened the passenger side door and tried to jump out. I grabbed his huge chain and wrapped it around my hands and pulled the bitch like I was bucking an out-of-control horse.*

*"This bitch is crazy!" he said aguishly, wiggling, and flinging his arms wildly. Dadeland Mall security caught wind of the fiasco and flashing lights were*

*headed our way. Alarmed, Kenny grabbed me from the back, kicked his door closed and looked me dead in the eyes.*

*"Damn, baby. I need a woman like you. Ready to fight like that? Calm down, Ma. He's cool. That's my brother."*

*I was huffing and puffing, fixing my hair.*

*I said, "So I take it your name is Kenny." I tried to calm down. I kept glaring at his pussy-of-a-brother.*

*He squeezed my left arm gently. "Yea. And your name is?"*

*I breathed in deep and got it together. I brushed off my outfit, making the transition back to being a lady in the streets. "Miss Webster. They call me Diamond." Diamond was my prostitute name.*

*He kissed my hand. His brother was cursing and making a huge scene. He acted like a female. What real man you know fought pregnant women? Sad. People were starting to gather around, but up here on Kendall and 88th Street, where the mall was located, those people were the stuck up type. They had money. Drove fancy cars. And I didn't like the atmosphere up here. I was from further south. Florida City. I wasn't used to snobbish people sizing me up.*

*Security parked next to Kenny and me. An out of shape white, Texan-looking man got out, pulling up his pants. He grabbed his walkie-talkie. He said, "What seems to be the problem over here?"*

*I looked at him and said, "Go about your business and stay out of mine."*

*Kenny pulled me behind him and said, curtly, "We're fine. Really. We were just leaving." He glared at his brother. "Weren't we?"*

*He remained quiet, rubbed his neck. He got back in his brother's ride and closed the door. The next second he blasted rapper Young Jeezy "The Inspiration" so loud we couldn't hear ourselves talk.*

*I had to strain to hear Kenny. "He's mad. He just lost his wife and his job. So he isn't in a good mood." He looked at me a little more fixedly. "She left him because he called out another woman's name in his sleep, and was actually having sex with her in his dream. She couldn't deal with it, and she packed up and left him."*

*I felt sorry for him. No wonder he was acting crazy. Losing your woman and your job had to be doing a number on him.*

*"It's cool. Look…I'm on my way to a D.J. party in Richmond Heights," I told Kenny. "You got a number I can reach you?"*

*"I can do better. How about we tag along. We need a diversion."*

*I took his phone from his hip, put in my name and number.*

*"Ok, sounds like a plan. Follow me."*

Now a few days later Kenny and I were in my father's house, playing around with fire. If my ex-Marines Dad found us in here playing "House" he was going to shoot us both.

I loved playing around with the fear of being caught, living on the edge. So I had given Kenny specific instructions: Come to my bedroom window. Because the back of the house was shielded by huge oak and palm trees. And since you wanted to do something different bring some props with you. I was open to anything, within reason.

He followed orders. I loved when a man listened. There was a big difference between a man who listened and a man who listened when he wanted some pussy. When he crawled through my window and got naked and I laid eyes on his *Playgirl* Centerfold-type body, he politely gave me three hundred dollars to bounce in the cooch, eat my pussy, get some head, and we got right on down to good ole sex. I was glad he remembered I didn't have sex for free. Some men thought they were so damn fine that women would just waive the fees. Not me, honey.

I had told him about my services when we left the DJ Party. I was a tad bit uncomfortable. After getting to know each other a little better, we'd gone out to *Flannigan's* and grabbed a bite to eat. Georgia was on my mind the entire time. Yea, his whiny brother came along. He got his own table, refused to sit by me. I didn't give a shit.

I also told Kenny I turned tricks. I did what I had to do to make my money. He seemed amused, telling me he spent half of his paychecks at the strip club anyway.

And now pushing all of that to the back of my mind, I examined his dick, making sure he didn't have any bumps and scrapes. Looked good, of course. He was somewhat offended, but he remained quiet. Didn't care how he felt anyway, I was the star of this show.

I then did a rush job on his dick, trying to suck it as fast as I could so he could come as fast as he could and we could get on to doing something enjoyable. I didn't like giving head, not even with Georgia's husband. I guess part of me wanted Ed, too, which was why I sucked him up with the energy and desire that I did. I shook just thinking about it.

But Kenny was so happy somebody was sucking his dick that he didn't care that my teeth kept making him jump and his blood run cold. I saw the anger in his eyes, but he swallowed his pride and savored the smoother moments I gave him with my mouth.

"Ouch, shit you *bit* me again, girl!" I loved his gentle voice.

I rolled my eyes, wishing he could be going down on me. "I didn't mean to."

He huffed and puffed. "Are you sure you know what you're doing?" He eyed me evilly.

A flick of my tongue on his bulging mushroom head silenced him. He smiled. "Yea, I do. *Don't* talk shit." I didn't want to give him head. He was *too* anxious.

He shook his head in the negative.

"Don't bite my shit."

I bit it purposely and he yelped like a dog, trying to get away from me and I gripped his nature so hard he froze. "You *better* be happy…" I sucked on his nuts and his eyes rolled to the back of his head. Oh he loved that. "…Somebody is sucking you up."

He narrowed his eyes, kissing at me, admiringly rubbing my cheek. "Girl I got a lot of Ho's."

*Is he calling me a Ho?* "Then *why* are you here with *me*?" I got an attitude.

"Because I felt—*lick right there baby, yes suck my balls, God, yea*—sorry for…you."

*Can you believe the nerve of this man?*

"Sorry for me?"

I was wet. I didn't want romance. I just wanted to have a good time. And homeboy from New York had one of the prettiest dicks I'd ever seen! I never knew dick could be so pretty. They all looked so, I didn't know, little, big, or some-what all right. Dick, for me, was nothing but different shapes and sizes, and I never thought one could actually look appealing. Yet *his* penis was a light shade of caramel, blended with some Swiss Mocha. Slightly curved, thick and huge, about ten inches. Definitely a perfect ten on the old school scale.

I couldn't shake Thomas. The length of his dick was incorrigible. The way he felt blew my mind. The way he looked at me turned me on, even in thought. The way he appreciated me caring for him when he was *too* drunk to walk changed my life. The way he moved deep inside me recreated my pussy. The way he became the human Van Gogh, the famous painter, and painted his magnum opus inside my womb with the skill of the Great Creator himself pushed me towards the Bible.

The night we made our baby.

My Dad walked to my room door and knocked. I was licking around Kenny's testicles.

"*Yes*, Daddy?" He didn't stop my party.

"I'm on my way to work," he said, Kenny losing his erection.

Kenny looked at me. "Are you crazy? Is the door locked?" he asked, whispering.

I sucked the head and got it back up, and he pushed the pillow on his face to shield his moaning.

*Man, shut up! Be a man and stop being a pussy.*

"Love you, Daddy. Talk to you later."

"I can't get a hug?" he asked. Dad always hugged me before going to work, we were very close. Daddy never hurt me, always provided for me and my family.

I wrapped my breasts around Kenny's dick, spat on it, lubed it really good and tit fucked him. He went crazy, his legs trembling; he tossed the pillow and was whispering all kinds of bullshit in my ear. How he wanted to marry me. Yea, right! How he would die for me. He wanted me to be his bitch. Yea, I heard that before.

"Dad, I'm naked." It wasn't a lie, of course.

"I'll call later, baby. Have a good day," he said, walking off, the floor squeaking like rats on cheese.

After Kenny came, he said it was his turn to please me. He ate me out slowly, expertly, talking to me. He was telling me how cleaned my pussy was. How good it tasted. I instantly came all over his tongue; no one had ever praised the Cooch quite like he had. Were all New Yorkers this smooth, this in tune with tongue to pussy interaction?

His cell phone kept vibrating, getting on my nerves so I gave him a very cold stare and then said, while his head bobbed and weaved, "Your girl calling you?"

He laughed, sucking my clit. He spelled out his answer.

I. A-M. S-I-N-G-L-E.

Not believing him, because he was too fine, probably had many bitches, I rolled my eyes, shivering, holding on to his head. My legs began drumming together as this man took me into orbit. I had some good head in my time, but never like this.

"Then why is your phone vibrating out of control."

His eyes sparkling, he spelled it out with his tongue again, all over my pussy.

P-R-O-B-A-B-L-Y M-Y B-R-O-T-H-E-R.

*Probably his brother.*

And with that in mind I picked up the cell phone, placing it on my left nipple. When it vibrated again, it sent tremors throughout my breast while I pulled the right tit up to my lips and began suckling my right nipple until it got erect.

Kenny held my upper thighs, munching the Cooch. He then separated my pussy walls, sliding a cucumber up in there, tearing me up sensually, driving me crazy.

I shuddered with glee. Then came the coconut juice, which was a treat. He'd peel bananas, fuck me with them, eat and feed them to me like a bird putting food in the baby bird's mouth. A sharp pain shot through my abdomen and I knew it was Aunt Flow knocking, but I didn't care. I felt it. He poured more coconut juice on my pussy. I still couldn't believe my period still came on when I was pregnant.

I could feel my blood mixing with the milk. He didn't have a damn clue. So I didn't say anything, but when he tried to kiss me I faked a yawn. On my breasts and vagina he made a salad with the offending vegetable and fruit. Adding tomatoes and crisp lettuce, he said he had to use the food because it has been in the ice box at his brother's house for about three days. He'd just gone grocery shopping when the Government gave him his food stamps on an American-flag-clad debit card. I loved the originality. But I was even more impressed that a man who drove a Cadillac Escalade, a $55,000 vehicle, paid off, was on government assistance.

Now we tongue kissed. I melted like butter on a flame into his skin. We rose and fell together, my hair plastered to my face. The humidity reached intense levels.

I was moaning uncontrollably as his huge bat tried to find the batting cage in my pussy. He dug and dug, like Osama Bin Laden was hiding deep in my cervix.

We kissed again; I wrapped my legs around such stern hips. He bounced off the pink walls, slip and sliding me into pure promiscuity. I felt like a silly fool, the way he dug me out. The way he looked me directly in my eyes and told me "Do you like it?" set me on fire. The look on my sweaty face told him "Yes!"

I had four powerful orgasms before he exploded again, the finality of his Magnum condom capturing his fiery seeds all in one whop. He pushed his dick all the way inside me and paused, as if out of breath. I could feel it pumping and throbbing, his body pressed against mine, the heat enveloping the both of us. His eyes fluttered closed. Then he rolled over, his amazingly chiseled body spent, and he then started gathering up his clothes. Stuffing them under his arms, he walked into the bathroom and turned on my shower without permission. I watched him quickly take a rinse off using my wash cloth and soap. I didn't appreciate that at all. He looked peaceful.

Trapped in my own thoughts, thinking about his brother, I sat on the edge of my bed, smoking a cigarette. He tried not to look at me.

When he was done, he dried off, put on his gear and didn't as much as look at me. He didn't kiss me. *Well fuck you, too!*

He hopped out my window, closed it and jumped in his Cadillac.

Why it hurt me I would never understand. His phone vibrated. Oh, yea. Let me see if those Ho's were trying to get at him. Why I suddenly felt territorial was beyond me. Kenny was not my man.I looked at the caller I.D. When my eyes locked on the name flashing in the screen all the breath left my body. I couldn't stop smiling. I couldn't think straight.

The name read: Thomas.

# THE PHONE CALL

I stared at the phone.

Praying to God I wasn't seeing things.

I opened Kenny's phone and started scrolling down, looking for Thomas's name. My heart was racing so fast I was about to hyperventilate. I couldn't think straight. All those days I was miserable without him, wondering where he was. I wanted to know what he was doing. Was he healthy, dead or alive? All those lonely days turned into even more miserable nights. I cried myself to sleep, cursing and hating myself. The showers I took, trying to erase his scent, his lips, his tongue and his immaculate touch, but I couldn't erase it because I didn't even pick up the soap. I couldn't even mentally erase his touch because he was some unknown body sculpture. He chiseled hieroglyphics all over my body. Symbols of Egyptian warriors engaging in various hand gestures shimmied away on my pussy and I'd cling to my pillow, afraid of my own sheets. I'd tell myself, "God, why am I going through all this torment?"

I was a woman who lived by the mood. A woman who got into prostitution because men always made me feel beautiful. When I was younger, I used to listen to Too Short rap songs and he always preached "Don't fuck for free" and I listened and took his advice. The pornography business was a multi-billion dollar empire, Bill Clinton got his dick sucked in the Oval Office, and Monica Lewinsky has become a millionaire by saving his dried sperm on her dress so why shouldn't I make men pay for it? Hollywood stars were always paying for it, look at Heidi Fleiss, Hollywood's ex-madam who got busted by the law for selling her whores to Hollywood's Elite Circle of power players. I worshipped her, so I started charging men when they wanted to have sex with me. I got deeper and deeper into it, becoming lost within myself. I naively told myself that I'd do it for one more day, one more hour and one more night…only to fall back in it every time I thought about the money. Every time I thought about my vanishing self-esteem I spread my legs and let a man suck my clit until I came. The love I claimed I had for myself and my body was never a reality, yet I didn't love myself or my body until I met Thomas.

Now I didn't *want* that life. I didn't want the money, yet I had clients who came to see me on the regular. How did I stare a potential $2,500 a week in the face and turn it down? How did I turn down good dick? Good dick was just as addicting as crack, as a matter of fact it was a-dick-ting! However, wanting to be with Thomas overshadowed it all.

When I found Thomas's name in Kenny's phone, I clicked on it. When Thomas's picture came up he was smiling. Oh my God! The smile the smile *the smile* THE SMILE! Perfect match! Dropping the phone in my lap I found my angel, the same man who slapped me at the mall, the same man who said my stomach stuck further than my booty do. Before I could write down his number Kenny snatched his phone from my hands.

"Why are you looking through my phone?" Laser beams in his eyes make me shudder.

I tried to think of a lie, wiping tears from my eyes, sucking in sex-clad air. "I didn't look through your phone."

He tilted his head to the side and gave me the blandest look. Made me stir on the bed in an uncomfortable way. "Damn, *why* are you lying? I stood at your window watching."

"Let me ask you something. Do you happen to know what name your brother called out in his sleep?"

He stared at me, shaking his head. "You don't even like my brother. Why should I tell you? And why are you getting personal?"

*He's the way to your man, girl keep it together. I can't lose Thomas again, I just can't!* "*Calm* down, damn Kenny my Dad's here."

"You need your *own* crib; you're too grown to be living at home, sneaking men into your Daddy's house."

*Ok, now I was getting offended. Just because the Niggah had good tongue and dick didn't give him the right to diss me in my own goddamn home!* "And you need to get off welfare,"

"For your information, this card doesn't belong to me. It belongs to my bitch."

I knew it. I just knew it, he was a damn snake.

"So you do have another woman."

"Look, the game has never changed. Adam and Eve made the game, and it hasn't changed since then. Get a clue. I just wanted to fuck. Let's be real, girl. I knew you were Diamond when we met.

Every Niggah down here said they paid for your pussy. They talked about how good and tight it was. I had to find out. It's good as hell. But I paid you, so the transaction is complete. If I want it again I'll pay for it. Nice meeting you and when you see me on the street make like you don't know me. Got that?"

I felt like a fool. "Fuck you, asshole! Who are you supposed to be?"

"At least I'm not a prostitute."

And before I could say anything he hopped out of my window and I tried like hell to forget he ever existed. But I couldn't forget that his brother's name was Thomas. His brother was my soul mate. And I'd never see Kenny again. I cried myself to sleep, telling God that if I couldn't have my baby and my man I would just die inside. It felt good to be in love. It felt right wanting to be in Thomas's life. I knew I was his missing rib. Deep down he had to know his wife wasn't the one. I was the one. Maybe I was just crazy. Quite honestly, I didn't know if I was coming or going.

And I didn't want to know, either.

My cell phone rang a few hours later. Waking me from a deep sleep. Rubbing my tummy, giving Thomas's baby some real love, I looked at the clock with an exhausted smile on my face. It was after 3 p.m. I was about to be late for work. But I decided not to go. I didn't want to see or be around people. I got out of bed and answered my cell; it vibrated on the night stand.

"Diamond." It was Kenny. I was mad instantly. "Hey, girl."

*Calling me like everything is all right. When you had good pussy, they always called back.* "What do you want?"

"I know we'll never see each other again, which is all good. But you asked me a question and I will answer it."

"What question would that be?" I couldn't keep the contempt from my voice. It made me shake with anger.

"I never understood it, but my brother said the woman he fell in love with never told him her name; not that he could remember."

I got quiet. My heart was racing. *"And?"*

"I don't know *why* I'm telling you this; my family prides itself on keeping family business between family."

"Yet you're on the phone with me."

"I know, shoot me. I can't even stand your ass, going through my goddamn phone. And I thought you were a cool broad."

"I don't have time for this."

"Well make time. I have something to tell you."

"That you're an asshole?"

"You know what..."

I was getting defensive. "What, jerk?"

"Well *listen.*"

'Listen to what."

"Diamond..."

"Maybe this wasn't such a good idea."

I didn't like the sinking feeling in my gut.

"My brother called out for her in his sleep. He told me all he could ever think about was this woman. He doesn't remember her face or anything. He said he was drunk when they met. The same night she helped him up to the room because he was too drunk to walk...I talked to my sister-n-law, who is bitter over the entire thing. And she told me he called out for Princess Webster all night, and was actually making love to her in his sleep." I didn't hear anything else because when he said my name I dropped the phone.

The line disconnected. I grabbed my coat and ran out to my car, devastated. Kenny's brother was my soul mate.

I have a white friend. Her name was Veronica Simms. She was a tall, gregariously ugly Ho who thought she knew it all. I called her a *Ho* because she called *herself* a Ho. And she was proud of it. Veronica and I did everything together. We shared our men. We never talked behind each other's back. We cooked for each other. We talked all day on the phone and always had each other's backs. Worse case scenario, she acted black. She was like a black woman trapped in a white woman's body. She was bipolar, or so she said. I didn't think so. I knew what bipolar people did and said and she didn't fit the description.

I didn't consider myself a bitch because Ho's got paid and bitches got played. Bitches fucked for free. I was for a) rent and b) available for a limited time. I was a reliable prostitute, undercover of course because I still lived with my father, even though I was 21 years old and my Daddy would kill me. My new prostitute name was Booty-Do. Because my stomach stuck out four inches further than my Booty Do. Well, actually I was punishing myself. Thomas called me that the day we met, *again.* The day that would prove to change my life because the man I have been searching for was right in my face. We were in a fight, cursing each other, causing security to come and try to calm things down. That was Satan keeping his rib from finding her home.

Now I was sick to my stomach. Now I was very insecure about my body. I was *very* down on myself, whoring away while being pregnant with another man's child. Did I care about the safety of my child? STD's? HIV? Potential ailments that could erase my baby's bloodline before it developed and in the process destroy my own?

As a child I always had issues with my weight. I used to read Aesop's Rhymes to keep myself cool and calm growing up. I read Aesop every night before I went to bed. My parents were welfare-stricken during those times, before Dad joined the Marines. Dad got us out of poverty. So my parents couldn't afford much of anything, except food, and boy did I eat when I was mad, angry, happy or sad. My room I shared with my older brother, Big Scooter, who would die three years later from a hit and run driver who was never found. We were very close. And when he died I withdrew into myself. The world was suddenly lonely and cold.

I used to have funky posters and stars ripped from magazines on my red and green colored walls. My friends swore my down that I was Haitian because of it. Whatever. My bed was much too small for me. When I slept I always fell on the floor when I turned over. My clothes I outgrew two weeks after getting them. My feet always had corns because my shoes were too small. Nah, I just grew into them quicker than the average child. My hair barely grew and was barely there. Snap and you'll miss it, and you had to squint to find it. My Daddy called me a fat bitch who needed to stop eating. My Mama called me fat and ugly. They would do this for years. It would ruin my self esteem. It would be the reason I went out and got some dick. I wanted to be accepted by people. I wanted to feel beautiful like the women on TV. I wanted to belong, to fit in and to feel special.

And on top of that I was black as tar. Blue-black my enemies called me. All the light-skinned, skinny-need-to-eat-bitches always talked about me. At face value I never showed my true worth. I never let them know they hurt my feelings and made me feel low. Hell, if my parents used to do it then why shouldn't I let everyone else? Veronica and I used to work at an Auto Parts store in Homestead months ago. She was the only friend I had. She treated me good and always had good things to say about me. We've known each other since the eleventh grade, attending pissy-smelling Homestead Senior High School. I had a new name for Homestead. It was called "Pregnant *instead*," because half those girls were pregnant before their junior year, popping pussy more than popping corn at the local theatres and half of them sucked dick in the back of the theatre as well. I called them "shones." A fancy word for WHORE.

Back then I was quiet and to myself, never thought I'd have a female friend. I didn't bother anyone, did my school work, lived for the Prep Rallies, and went home. Half the bitches only hung around you to jock your style or bite your dress code. That was until Veronica waltzed into my Home Economics class trying to run shit. A white girl talking tougher than the black girls intrigued us.

We kind of hit it off real big. Despite trying to be bossy, she had a heart of gold. She was very upbeat and outgoing. I was introverted and much of a homebody. She had just moved to Miami from Lebanon. I had never heard of Lebanon. She said that's where she was born, and where most of her family remained.

That became evident when, a few days ago, she came to my Dad's house, banging on the door, screaming at the top of her lungs, "Girl, turn on the TV! Conflict is erupting in Lebanon! I'm concerned about my family over there..."

I was thankful my Dad wasn't home. Despite his love for her, he would have cussed her out for banging on the door like the police.

Exhaling audibly, I opened the door for her, gave her the evil eye and invited her in.

"Girl, what are you talking about?"

Quiet and tears falling from her gray eyes, she turned on the TV and picked up the remote, turning up the volume. On the news a reporter, in Lebanon, was talking about the violence over there. My heart went out to Victoria. She hung onto the reporter's every word.

I told her to sit down. She didn't want to sit.

"Crying isn't going solve the problem, Victoria."

"I know. But I feel so empty inside. I wish all of my family were here and not just me."

I gave her a lingering look. "They *can't* come over?"

She sadly thought about it. "I don't know. Quite honestly I don't think they *want* to come over."

"Can't they get visas or passports or whatever that's called?"

"I'm pretty sure they can. Believe me I've spoken to them and practically begged them to come to the states to have a better life. But they are so stubborn."

"They're probably scared, girl. Moving and change isn't very pretty sometimes." I looked at her, hurt on my face. She was studying me. "It's not."

"Suddenly I don't think we're talking about my situation anymore. What's up, girl?"

I looked away from her. "Nothing."

She was concerned. "Is it the *baby*?"

I looked at her in shock. "*What* baby?" I tried to suck in my gut, but her eyes fell down on my womb so fast I held my breath.

She smiled. "The one you're carrying, we *all* know you're pregnant, girl."

I started to cry. "Oh, girl, I'm in love, I don't want to be a prostitute anymore, his name is Thomas and he's the most incredible man. He's my air, my soul mate, girl I will die without him."

And Veronica not only believed me she held me, because she knew, deep down, I never talked about any man the way I was praising Thomas. I would never get to see him or be with him again. Because Kenny, the man with the key that led to him, was gone out of my life forever. I had to call Georgia.

I needed her right now.

While some women who faced the empty nest syndrome, a depressed state felt after their children grew up and left home, tried to cope and find new and exciting things to do with their lives, I felt the Lost Love Syndrome. Thinking about my lover Thomas made me feel whole. He gave me some good love, then he just up and left me, leaving me to fend for myself. Feeling like an imbecile, it took me a little minute to gather my composure, and it took extra effort for me to tell Veronica not to tell my business to anyone. Georgia was on my mind. I needed to do something and fast. But I didn't know how to tell her. But I knew I had too.

Veronica's lips were like holes in the bottom of cups—couldn't hold juice, milk or water, got to tell everybody everything and the minute somebody wanted to whip her ass for running her big mouth, she wanted to dial my ten digits.

After telling Veronica I'd call her later, I went out to my car and attempted to call Georgia.

On second thought I hung up the phone.

I parked next to Georgia's bad ass Toyota Camry. It had deep dished rims and a killer stereo system. I wondered if Ed was home, I haven't been over here since the day after their hugely successful party.

When Ed did what he did, when *we* did what we did…I could *still* taste him on my lips, I could still see the sexy image that dangled like a carrot on a fishing hook before the library of my brain.

I shook the images away, and knocked on the door.

Georgia answered and embraced me, happily, when she saw me. "Hey, girl! I have been trying to call you for *months!*"

"You have?" I knew she was, but I thought she found out I had her man and she wanted to call me to set up a date when she could shoot me and I was too goddamn scared to find out so I kept my distance.

She stared at me. "Yes. You didn't see the missed calls on your cell?"

"I got a Metro PCS, the lowest cellie on the cell phone totem pole, Chile, you know how they do, mess everything up."

She knew I was lying. "Come in! And I been telling you, girl, I can put you on my Cingular plan so you can lose that Metro Piece of Shitty-ass phone."

I gripped my purse and walked inside, the cool AC hitting me in the face. "Girl, whatever, don't be talking about my phone."

I walked up the hallway, passing framed photos of her and Ed's family and made my way over to the lavish sofa.

Georgia turned on the TV, looking dashing in vest with pleated mini skirt, huge earrings and flawless make up. Breathtakingly gorgeous, and she knew it. I could *never* be that pretty.

The entertainment shelf had beautiful engravings of roses, beautifully polished to a shine. The low-table held four crystal bowls, with intricate carvings. Potpourri filled them to the brim.

The three baccarat-crystal chandeliers were just dashingly breathtaking, made my Dad's house like an episode of Scooby-Do.

"So what brings you by after all these weeks, girl?"

I looked at Georgia, trying to keep the tears from my eyes. I lowered my head, and, alarmed, she rushed over from her chair and sat next to me, taking both my hands. I was shaking my head. I didn't want to be held or touched. I just wanted to be left alone.

She said, "Talk to me, girl. We been through hurricanes and tornadoes together, what is it?"

*Say it, Princess, tell her you fucked Ed. Tell her you are just as messed up as he was for deceiving her.* "Is Ed here?"

"You want to talk *alone*, come on." She snatched me off the sofa, pulled me up the stairs, kicked open her bedroom door—and, to our surprise, Ed had his pants around his ankles, whacking off to a porno playing on the huge plasma TV. *Asian Bubble Butts Volume 2.*

Startled, he jumped up, pulling up his pants, frantically trying to explain himself.

Georgia was fuming and clearly embarrassed.

"Get your nasty ass out the room so I can talk to my girl, God you men can't keep it in your pants for *nothing*, can you?"

He gave me a discreet look, zipping up his pants and flying out of the room, embarrassed and we were laughing.

"That husband of mine," she said to herself, closing the door. She pointed across the room. "Girl, have a seat on the sofa by my closet. And tell me what's wrong."

Before I could even lift my foot I blurted it out.

"I'm in love, girl."

She laughed, waving her hands, "*Yea*, right! What's wrong, girlfriend?" she said, not hearing a word I just said.

I said it more cautiously. "I. Am. In. Love."

She rolled her eyes. "I know you're in love with *money*. I *got* that. *Houston*, we're gonna have some big problems if this bitch don't tell me what the hell is up with her."

With a huge smile I blurted, "I AM IN LOVEEEE!" and she fell silent, slowly sitting next to me, staring at the side of my face like I was Marvin the Martian.

I tried to hold my smile. *Hold* it, girl, hold it! But I *couldn't* because the tears fell and I shuddered because suddenly the world was so cold and I didn't want to raise my child alone, he or she had a right to know his/her father and I deprived him/her of that, it was all my fault and I would never find him again because I fucked it up with Kenny and I could just shoot myself for that, the one golden ticket to Thomas.

She was clapping and laughing happily. This was the best news. Words she thought I'd never say. "You're in love. You? The woman who said she'd *never* fall in love, the woman who played men like Chess and an episode of who sunk my Battleship?"

"Yes." I looked at her with so much pain on my face and she took my hands. "I am in love. But he doesn't know I'm in love with him."

She searched my face, looked deeply into my eyes as only she could do, she had it down pat, she knew when I was lying and when I was telling the truth, I hated she knew the keys to my kingdom. "You got it bad. You. Are. Gone. Chile. Wow, are you serious? Who is he?"

"Girl he's gone, gone forever, we had a passionate night, he made love to me, while he was drunk, better than any sober lover I ever had, he changed my life, made me look at myself. Oh girl I can't live without him."

She was squeezing my hands, crying with me, kissing my hands, telling me it'll be ok. "Girl in life friends come and go."

"But I wanted him to come and go with me."

"Season's change, my love. You know this. It isn't summer all year round, winter turns to spring eventually, it's inevitable."

"But why does it have to be that way?" I asked angrily, jumping up and pacing the bedroom, kicking off my shoes, enjoying the comfortable feel of her plush white carpet tickling all between my toes.

Georgia's house phone rang. "Hold on, girl. Hold that thought." She went over to the caller I.D. She picked it up. "Sup, man. What do you want now, *more* money?"

I looked at her while she engaged in her phone conversation.

She looked pissed. "What? You still haven't found a job? You want money to buy food? Don't you have a food stamp card? Yes you do, I got it for you. Listen, I got you a car and I got you some money, lined you up with a job, look, cousin, I am family, yes blood is thicker than water, but god the fuck damn Niggah get off your ass and help your motherfucking self I am not the ATM machine!"

And she bammed the phone down.

"Damn, girl, that phone call was intense."

"Girl, my cousins have been living in Miami for a few months. One had a job, lost it and the other just gets on my nerves."

I couldn't keep my mind off Thomas.

I covered my face and leaned against the wall, shuddering. She went on and on about her cousins, the hell with her cousins.I didn't know what it was but some unknown force pulled me off the wall, took my hand and before I knew it I silenced Georgia when I opened her door, walked down the hallway, to the guest room, opened the door, smiling at the black carpet, the Bob Marley photos…I lay in the bed, rolling across it, rubbing my pussy until I shuddered, crying for Thomas, wanting him, I was crying so hard I came on myself just thinking about him, my body on fire, trying to find the flames of finality so I could have a fulfilling relationship, but that would never be, could *never* be. Thomas was out there, somewhere, going through a divorce. He was probably doing what his brother did: fuck all the girls, kiss them and make them cry.

I was crying, and he kissed me from head to toe.

"Princess! Girl, get over that man!"

I stood up, wrapping the sheets around me, like a cloak that protected me and my baby…my subconscious revealed the carefully placed memories in this room. I rushed over and closed the bathroom door, didn't want to remember Ed's memories from the toilet and beyond.

"Why did you come to this room, girl?" Georgia was carefully observing me, not getting the big picture.

I looked at her with a sweet smile. "I *love* this room."

She studied me carefully, looking around, trying to figure it out.

"I see that, girl. What's going on?"

"I made my baby in this room."

She looked me up and down, taking the sheets from me and lifting my shirt. "OH MY GOD! YOU'RE PREGNANT!"

I hugged her. *"Yes!"* Then I fell silent, because I didn't want to say the words, I didn't want to say "And I'll be raising my child alone. Another black single mother in America to get frowned down on talked about and ridiculed."

"How many months are you?" she asked, in a state of disbelief.

"A little over two months."

She pushed me on the bed, got on top of me, playfully and tried to tickle me. This was my girl; we always wrestled and had fun.

"And you didn't tell me?"

"I didn't want to make it a big deal."

She was skeptical as hell, over analyzing the entire ordeal in her head, probably, I knew her like a book.

"You didn't want me knowing you might be going on Maury to find out who is the father. *Billy you are NOT the father, Frank you are NOT the father!"*

We were laughing so hard I damn near fell out of the bed.

"Sam you are *not* the father," I said, warming to our subject with a smile. "Jarvis, you are damn sure not the father, you're too fucking fat! Larry, you're *not* the father...you're too gay. Veronica...this is your 19th time on the show...Harris is not the father. You're a whore!"

"But Maury, my son has Larry's nose! Look at the screen Maury, it's a mistake it's a mistake? He has Larry's eyes!"

God, we were tearing our stomachs up, laughing.

She went on.

"And you don't know where the father is?" Ok. The spotlight was back on me. Damn, I was trying to evade it.

"*No*, girl. No clue. And before I could get his number out of his brother's phone, he snatched it and has been AWOL ever since."

"Have you tried *calling* his brother back?"

"Yes. Repeatedly. But he blocked my number."

"Crummy men!"

"He was an asshole, really. A big one."

Her phone rings again. "Damn it," she said, waltzing over to it like a spoiled brat. "It better not be my cousin again."

She looked at it. She said. "Oh, *good*. It isn't him." She answered with a smile. "Well, well, well. Tina. Sup, girl...yea, I know right...Divorce isn't cool at all," said Georgia sadly. "What? You're trying to milk him, girl he has to live, too. I know, but did you actually see him cheat on you…I know, girl what was her name then?"

Her eyes lowered to the floor. Then she looked at me with her mouth open.

"What?" I asked her. "Is it somebody I know? Who are you talking to anyways, Georgia."

"Oh my God! Princess Webster is my best friend; you mean to tell me your husband called out Princess Webster's name in his dream?"

The room was spinning, I had to sit down.

Why was I smiling, why was I smiling.

"Oh, God, girl! Are you telling me my Thomas, the man of my dreams, my soul mate is your *cousin?*"

Georgia said, "Tina, get over to my house, now. Princess is here. And she's pregnant with Thomas's baby."

Georgia's head snapped away from the phone. Tina had clicked in her face.

"Princess, this is crazy. You met him at my party?"

I tried to smile. "Yea. He was drunk. *Very* drunk. I was feeling it, dancin' and groovin', Hennessy and Coke pulverizing my blood stream, girl." They shared a chuckle. "He approached me. I felt the chemistry. *Strong*, girl. He could barely stand on his own two feet, Chile. So I led him to the guest room because he was not stable. I wiped his face with a wet rag, trying to nurture him. By then the drink had started to have an effect on me."

She was really having a hard time with this. She was trying to put two and two together. "I can now understand why you stayed away from my house, girl what you must have been going through, thinking you would never see him again, getting real feelings. Honestly, he didn't love Tina anyways; he only married her because everyone around him basically coerced him into doing it. It was all for show. He worked his ass off for Tina, and yea, Tina and I are cool, but she can be a bitch. Take his money, buy this and that, saw other men behind his back, I knew it, everyone knew it but we didn't want to break Thomas's heart."

Why was I upset? "She did that to him, that incredible man?"

"Yes. Then, after months of playing the field, someone robbed her in an alley in New York. She almost lost her life. She was stabbed and left for dead. Through the miracle of God she survived, she knew deep down that was her punishment for creeping around on her faithful husband. And you would think going through the darkness would make you a better person. She and Thomas got worse. She talked down to him, didn't appreciate him. She stopped the cheating, but the night Tina said he called out your name, she told me he was moaning your name, telling you how to take it, that he loved you, that he wanted to divorce her and spend his life with you."

I had to sit down, this was overwhelming. All I knew was that I wanted Thomas, I had to have him and I didn't quite know if I could have him. Maybe this was a fantasy; all this was in my head. I did screw his brother; this union with Thomas would never work. How could it? With so many factors against me?

"Girl, I need time for all this to digest. Life isn't to be played around with, girl."

She smiled easily. "I can see you and Thomas together. He's fun, loving. He's one of my favorite cousins."

I still couldn't believe it. My nerves were bad. "Why didn't you introduce him to me?"

"Because his older brother Kenny is a jerk. I wouldn't introduce that dick head to anyone, Chile. Girl, I helped them move down here. I got Kenny a Cadillac Escalade; one of my friends at the car dealership owed me a favor. I even got one of my home girls to get him a food stamp card, in her name so he could keep his fridge stocked and he calls me every other day for more money, won't go get a job."

*So much for the lie, Kenny. Your bitch got you a food stamp card, 'ey? You probably didn't even get to sniff the Cooch. I hated men who lied on their dicks.* "And he's a piece of shit." I told her Kenny was one of my clients, I also told her about his cell phone, and when I saw Thomas's number I thought that was the key to being led back to my love, but it blew up in my face.

"Kenny always prided himself that he never had to pay for pussy."

I laughed with her. "Girl, first time for everything."

She fell silent, like she just remembered something. She had a very disquieting look on her pretty face. "Some man got arrested at my party."

"What does that have to do with anything?"

"Well, the bartender claimed there was something fishy about the short black man, that he was stalking your friend, I forget her name."

"*Who*, girl?"

"The Latino bitch. She's in jail, too."

"Oh, she gave me the drink." I blinked twice. "Why is she in jail?"

Georgia stared at me. "Shit, the Henny and Coke, you just said that."

"Yea girl what's up? Are you getting at something?" I was starting to feel queasy. Tina was on her way over here, and she better not come with the noise either because I will whip her ass.

"He put GHB in the Henny and Coke he gave to your Latino friend. She saw him put it in there. She told the police when she saw him lace the drink, he came over to her and she took the drink, pretended that she had to go to the bathroom, and she gave the drink to a friend of hers…"

I was talking really slow, the room spinning.

"Girl, she *gave* me that drink."

"Yep. She then befriended the bartender, bought a bottled water, had him pour the water in a cup identical to the one she gave you and had little man thinking she actually drank the drug-infested liquor."

My hands were shaking. I was having a hard time with this. My Latino friend and I were really cool, but not anymore. What real friend would do something like that? But then again the bitch has always been jealous of me. "No wonder I felt out of it, got sloppy and everything while I was dabbing a cold rag on Thomas's face. The night of your party Thomas and I made the baby I am carrying, I love him, I don't know girl, he was so drunk and I had a date rape drug in my system."

"At first we had no proof of an actual drugging taking place, but the miniature plastic bag the GHB was in was found by my bar. And the cup on Henny was in my guest room, apparently girl you didn't finish it all. The cops ran tests on it and viola, GHB was all in it, girl."

The room was spinning, faster. I moaned piteously, trying to stop the migraines from taking over my brain. "I need a minute to be alone, would you mind, girl? If I stayed in here?"

"Take all the time you need. I'll go put us some corn dogs and fries on, you hungry?"

"Girl you know I love food."

"Shit, you're eating for two, now. Goddamn it, Thomas got a baby on the way."

"You say that like he doesn't have any kids."

She kissed my lips; I loved my sister at heart. "Girl, he doesn't, you are about to give him his first biological child."

When she left I savored the moment. Yes, that's because I was his soul mate.

I waited until the door closed behind Georgia before I made my move. I went over to the caller I.D. I saw Tina's name. Had a "305" area code by the number. Must be the house phone. I picked up the phone and made a call.

"Yes, how are you? Me, I'm fine. Thank you..."


Thomas was getting out of the shower when his wife came into the bathroom and threw some bills in his face. The envelopes hit him on the forehead and snow flaked towards the wet tiled floors. Angry, he said, "What is your problem?"

"I thought you paid the light bill."

He rolled his eyes, drying off his nuts, dick, ass and lower part of his track runner legs. "Whatever, you pay it. Aren't we getting divorced?"

She put her hands on her hips. "That's why I'ma clean you out in court."

He laughed so hard she tucked her chin back.

"Well let's spend some tax payer money. Because I'm not giving you shit."

"You aren't shit."

"I should have never married you."

She withheld the knowledge of another woman being pregnant with his child. She told herself *I'm not telling him. He doesn't deserve to know.* "Whatever, Man. I am so glad I didn't have your child."

He lowered his eyes to the floor. He always wanted to be a father. He loved children; they were his pride and joy. Something about a child that comforted him, allowed him to escape the real world and see things simply through the angelic eyes of a child. And now he would never experience that because Tina destroyed his will to want to father a child.

He looked up at her. He wrapped the towel around his hips. Walking past her, he said, "I don't want a slut having my child anyway."

Infuriated and getting tired of Tina, he opened the top dresser drawer, pulled out a pair of boxers, put them on and slid into a T-shirt.

When he turned to go over to the closet Tina got in his face. She wasn't happy. "Look, *motherfucker.* I'm going to be real with you. You don't want a slut having your child then why did you marry me?"

"Get out of my face. I'm not about to stand here and let you turn this nonsense around on me."

"Oh, you're going to stand there. Listen, Thomas. *I'm* fertile." He frowned. He stared at her. "In fact if you touch me I can get pregnant. I just didn't want to have your child." She walked over to the dresser, opened it, and then pulled out the secret compartment. She wiggled the birth control pills in his face. Her eyes sparkled while the sparkles in his eyes died. He shook with rage, his hands fists.

"So you lied to me."

She laughed playfully, tossing the pills in the trash. "Don't need those anymore, since you won't be fucking me…"

Impulsively, he grabbed her by the neck and started squeezing, as hard as he could. She grabbed his hands, but he squeezed harder, death in his eyes. They fell on the bed tussling. His anger got the best of him.

"Die, bitch!" His face was shaking; she was losing air, losing it all. She kicked her feet as hard as she could, trying to get away from him. He put all his weight on her, spit in her face, let her go, stood up and said, "Go to hell, bitch!"

"Have you lost your mind?" She was in fear, for the first time in her marriage she feared him. *What have I done?* she thought to herself. She shook her head, rubbing her neck.

Getting out of the bed she opened the closet and took out a few suit cases. He watched her, torn up inside. Her world spinning she had to sit back down so she sat on the edge of the bed. He kept staring at the small trash can, her words flowing through his brain. She took birth control pills. Bitch!

Taking the birth control pills from the trash, he extracted the remaining twelve and rushed over to her. Panicking, she tried to run. He chased her all over the room, flinging her arms and screaming but he was a beast. Jumping in the bed, she tried to crawl to the opposite side but he grabbed her feet and pulled her to him He grabbed her sweaty neck, forced her mouth open and pushed the pills down her throat. She spat a few of them in his face. He punched her in the jaw and she kicked him in the balls. Falling to the floor, he moaned piteously, quickly getting up to his feet. She got on his face and started punching at him. He slapped her so hard she fell to her knees.

"I HATE YOU!"

His words shook the room. She stood there, blood on her lip, breathing hard, hair disheveled. She closed her eyes and covered her face, falling to her knees in shock. He hated her. This bothered her more than she thought it would.

He cried to himself, silently. He wouldn't dare sob. He reached out to her, his hands shaking, attempting to hold her, become one with her but he withdrew his hand and turned his back on her. He didn't love or trust her anymore. He didn't care if she lived or died. He was tired of being her fool.

His cell phone rang. Answering, he said, "Hello."

"How are you, sir?"

He narrowed his eyes. "Who is this?"

"I'm calling you about a position that is available at the Motel 6."

He wasn't interested. "Is this a survey?"

"No, sir. Your name was given to me by a George Harper. Said he went to school with you. We are looking for a manager."

"I like the job I have now."

"Would you like to reconsider?"

"No, thank you."

"Well we want you."

"So does everyone else."

"Stating pay is $35,000."

He sat on the edge of the bed.

"When do I come in?" *And who the hell is George Harper?*

"Now, can you make it in, say, fifteen minutes?"

"I'll call you when I'm on my way."

"I'll call you. And good luck."

The line disconnected.

Tina was in a myriad of thoughts. First her husband called out another woman's name, in the bed they shared during the course of such a rocky marriage, and then he showed his ass, talking down to her, jumping on her. Where did he get off? She didn't believe in calling the police so that was out. Her jaw hurt, she made herself regurgitate the pills. That's what she got for playing with his emotions. She knew she was wrong for what she did. Thomas, deep down, was a good guy. And she was turning him into a bitter fool.

She didn't have to put up with his shit. If she wanted to she could have him thrown out of the house, but her civilly caring side didn't let her. She had to admit that she didn't love him, she only married him because the dick was good, the money exceeded $29,000 a year, he pampered her, bought her anything she wanted, let her do what she wanted and she had become so accustomed to the "finer things in life," diamond rings and jewelry, getting credit cards in his name, that she lost touch with what really mattered in a marriage: the Union. She dated other men behind his back. She fucked other men behind his back. She didn't think anything of it. Why should she? She had loyal friends. Her friends always covered for her. She had no desire to stop, that was until Thomas called out another woman's name in bed.

Part of her was crushed that she never got to give him the child he always wanted. She told him she was infertile, that if she carried a child she would die. Buttered him up. Got into his mental. Made him believe her bullshit, and gave him some pussy to set it in stone.

But the truth of the matter was she didn't want a baby, and she damn sure didn't feel like pushing one out of her pussy. She didn't want to deal with the needles, or appointments, shitting for two, the baby showers, the gifts, having a bunch of Hoes all up in her house, all up in her face pretending to be friendly when they all wanted to fuck her man. But none of that mattered now. She was waiting on a delivery. A friend of hers bought her one of those organizers, and she was really looking forward to getting it, so now she could properly keep notes and schedules, and all that good shit.

Yes, Georgia was sweet to get her the organizer, such a sweet gesture. Something good actually came out of her gravely defunct marriage: Georgia, who she was very fond of. She couldn't say the same about doggishly whorish Ed. He tried to fuck any and everything on two legs.

"Now I wanna gut the motherfucker" She was fuming, her blood running cold. "Getting another bitch pregnant? Oh, our marriage is so over. I can't believe this shit. I should go whip the Ho's ass; she's over Georgia's house right now. Damn it, I can't believe this shit!"

There was a knock on the door. Answering it, tossing blonde weave out of her face, she cracked a smile and signed the clipboard the UPS man handed her. He was kind of cute, shit. He looked her over, slowly taking in her presence. She had a nice body, baby making hips. Easy on the eyes. He had to will the penis from erection prematurely. Didn't want to appear out of control. Eyeing him, she took the package, kissed his cheek and closed the door, opening her package.

The organizer looked really nice.

I approached the Motel 6. I was sort of nervous. Shaking uncontrollably, I brushed lint off my clothes and looked in my compact mirror, making sure I looked decent. Lipstick was off the chain. Make up, all right, nothing overdone. I smelled really nice.

I wanted to run, though, for what I was about to do. I was going to do something I have never done in my life. And quite frankly, I needed to get on with it. Sometimes in life you gotta go after what you want and don't let anybody stop you or stand in your way.

I worked up enough nerve to knock on the door. When Thomas answered and he saw me he frowned and said, "What do you want?"

I stared at him. My prince, my baby. So much love and respect burst deep inside me. I stood in one spot, hot tears falling down my face. He cocked his head to the right, wondering what was wrong with me.

"Are you ok, Diamond?" It hurt him to say the words. It hurt him to be nice to me, to see what was wrong with me. He had to force himself to show me compassion.

I just hugged him, threw my arms around him and started sobbing uncontrollably, I let go; I couldn't help it. I loved him, would die for him, and looked forward to having his baby. He'd hate me, call me names because I was a prostitute; well used to be a prostitute. I didn't want to be one anymore, I wanted to be faithful, be in love with someone who would treat my body like it was supposed to be treated. I reverted back to the little girl I was when I was teased, called all kinds of names, fat and unwanted. I vowed then to work on myself and my body to make myself look hot and sexy and I started selling my pussy to fit in and to belong and to feel special. I thought men were only here to give me good dick, give me some money and then get the hell on.

Thomas changed my life. In one night. I felt his hands go around me. He held me close, smelling my hair, rubbing my arms. I felt the chemistry, the same chemistry we felt when we met, when he approached me at Georgia's party. Oh God I melted into him, kissing his lips gently, then it built to a tsunami of kisses and tongue lashes that left us breathless. He was rubbing my back, our tongues fencing for the next Olympics…I vowed to never let him go. But I had to tell him who I was. We slowly pulled away from each other. He shuddered, a pleased look on his face. I forgot I ordered Tina the organizer, and pretended I was Georgia. Had to distract her. I forgot I used Georgia's phone to do the ordering, after I called Tina and made sure she stayed home. I made sure she didn't come over to Georgia's. I forgot I told Georgia I had an emergency, that I would be back to her house shortly. I forgot I called Thomas's cell phone, told him Motel 6 was interested in interviewing him for a job, just to get him out of Tina's house, so I could tell him who I was.

The sparkles in his eyes arrested my attention and kept it. He smiled really big, hugging me. "You don't have to say anything. I'm glad you came back to me, Princess. Goddamn it you've been right under my nose and I didn't know it, until now."

"How did you know?"

He kissed my lips. I knew at that moment I was going to be his wife. That we would never be separated again. "The smell of your hair told me everything, smelled the same way it did the night we met. Oh, God I can't believe this."

"Well believe this. I'm pregnant with your child, a little over two months. And if you want a DNA test, I'll give it to you. The night we made love at Georgia's house was the night our baby was conceived."

He hugged me, picking me up and spinning me in a circle. He was jubilant and ecstatic, I fed off it. I had my King back.

"But what about Tina?" he asked me. "We're going through a divorce."

"Let's just leave town. Pack up and go, start over somewhere else."

He thought about it. "Yea, we can do that. How soon do you want to hit the road?"

I looked at him, hugging my future husband. "Right now."

"I thought you'd never say it."

Georgia was in her closet, taking the suit case down from the top shelf. She could hardly reach it, so she used her tippy toes. When she grabbed the handle, she pulled it down and it nearly fell on her head. Inside the suit case was all of her high school memorabilia. She cherished it. While in high school her mother loved her acting. She majored in Drama and excelled. She loved it so much she wrote a play. In it she pretended to be on the telephone while cooking dinner at the stove. She was a lonely woman who had just lost her husband. Her teacher loved her play. Pulling it out Georgia wiped some of the dust from the document, smiling bitterly. Tears fell down her face.

She opened it to the first page.

# Act 1: Scene One:

## THE PRETEND CONVERSATION.

[Georgia was cooking black beans at the stove]

"When are you going to fix my sprinklers, John? And what is that smell, I have a really sensitive nose…"

[Georgia joked through the phone, stirring some black beans].

"I'm back. What were we saying now?"

[She held the phone to her ear with her shoulder.]

"Oh, yea you wanted the recipe for my mama's ribs. What? I'm cranky? I need a massage? Nah, my husband will do that. What does that got to do with ribs? His job is to make sure I'm ok not yours. Ok? I don't cheat on my husband and he would never cheat on me…"

Dead inside, Georgia put the papers back in the suit case, frowning. "Princess you fucked my man. I know you did. I saw you two in the shower together…"
    She closed her eyes and would continue to play the game.

# Cream in my Coffee

When my fine boss walked into his expensively-designed office he took one look at me, smiled to himself, and closed the door. He always loved looking me over, as if his eyes were scanners and my taut, voluptuous body was a carefully created document. He really needed to stop looking at my ass because if he asked for some I was going to ask him to pay my rent, lights and phone bill. And I didn't want him going to pay for it himself. Just give me the money, Hello! He was 6 feet tall with an athletic body. He had a very sexy smile. He was sort of LA Lakers Kobe-ish. But he looked more like Michael

Vick. Croppy hair. Smart chin. Thick old school the Jackson 5 nose. He had a knack for using his hands when he spoke. So that told me he'd use his hands to split the peach between my legs. He had creamy milky skin. His eyes were reminiscent of a black panther, seriously. Cat eyes, in a very masculine way. Like Tyson Beckford, but he made Tyson's eyes look like puddles of dog shit. He was well trimmed and well groomed. Every day. And he didn't have a nappy hair line.

"*Sup*, Brandy, how are you?" he barely said above a whisper. He was having one of those long days at the office, you know, when nothing went right. Maybe it was because it was Friday the 13th. April 13, 2007.

"I'm cool. What's wrong with *you*?" I played around with the stretch bangles on my wrists I ordered out of the Victoria Secret catalogue that came in the mail last month.

I was the queen of catalogues and the Home Shopping Network. I was tired, been up since 5:30 a.m. I normally got up at 6:30 a.m. but this morning I had given my car a quick wash because I was tired of the neighborhood kids writing "Wash your car!" on my windshield every other day; I vacuumed my living room, did some dusting, dancing to Patti Labelle at about 6:39 a.m., and then I cooked a small pot of grits and eggs that I never got to eat because I turned on the news and got lost in the ways of God's dying world.

"I don't know. People don't know how to follow directions."

I smiled at him, standing up and giving him a much-needed hug. We weren't lovers. God, no! But I have often thought about how good his love making might be. Especially when I go to bed at night, my "cold cocoon" I called it. I really thought about his loving then. Especially the dick. My clit was throbbing right now but I swallowed extra hard and tried not to think about it.

"Are we talking about people that work for you?"

He sat behind his desk and threw files by the computer, rubbing his temples. "*Yes*. People that work for me."

I looked at him more intently. "Um, people that *you* hired?"

He started smiling, "I know. I wrote my *own* Scarlett Letter."

I was smiling. "Sure did."

He kissed at me. "They are messing up faxes. Coming in late. Calling out for stupid reasons...Showing poor customer service. Clarisse was taking minutes for the Builder Architect Meeting earlier today and guess what the bitch wrote?"

My brows rose. I always loved hearing about Little Slutty Clarisse. To put it bluntly, she had sex whenever/wherever she chose. She didn't care if she was stuck in traffic, she'd get her bump and grind on in broad daylight, and she didn't care about the police. If it was about a) money or b) dick oh she was so there for the taking. Realest woman you'd ever meet. Very down-to-earth, like ocean shores. "What did she write?"

He looked me over for a minute. "Well, physically, to the naked eye, she was taking notes about our merger. The building that is in production, the way they wanted the blueprints done up, zoning, permits, clearing, the whole nine. But in her mind and what she actually wrote were two different things. So I'm reading over the minutes, because I type them up myself."

This surprised me. He wasn't strong in the clerical field. I liked it, though. "You don't get the secretary, Melissa to do them?"

"Nah, I love typing, keeps my mind clear." He stood up, deep in thought. "Want some coffee?"

*Hell to the no!* "Sure." I hated coffee, but how could you tell this sexy, brilliant man "No?"

"Anyways." He poured the coffee in a mug with his daughter's face on it. She's about eight years old, with her snaggle-toothed ass, but she was cute. "I'm typing, *right?* And she wrote, 'So I went down on him, sucking his big ole dick, and I tasted pre-cum, tasted like a Klondike bar, I felt like a...lesbian!' and so on and so forth." He looked embarrassed. I was laughing.

He handed me the coffee with the weirdest look on his face. I laughed harder, covering my mouth, stunned. In a good way. I could see her writing that. I thought about the long talks me and Melissa had about men and their strokeless attributes. "Thank you, so what else she said?"

He smiled. "Let's just put it this way. By the time I was done reading the story I locked my door and masturbated."

"Oh, God TMI." I sipped the coffee. *Yuk!* Nasty shit! I hated black coffee, where's the cream and sugar?

"Too much info, I know, we're adults here, deal with it sweetness." He sat on his desk, holding the coffee mug as if his life depended on it.

The tone of his voice changed. "Are you ok? I'm sensing something else is bothering you."

"My baby mama." He narrowed his eyes. "She called me today."

*Here we go. Making my ears bleed talking about his retarded baby mama, the bitch who hated the very ground he walked on.* "Oh, God. More money?"

He stared at me. "How do you know?"

"She's a Ho, I warned you about her before you married her. She thinks her pussy is laced with gold, when I heard it smells like baby shit."

We laughed, he damn near chocked from the coffee. "Gurl, you so wrong for that."

"I hope you bought some Tic Tacs," I said, frowning. *I hate bitches that don't douche and keep their bodies clean.*

"Why do you say that?" He set the mug on the desk, by the conference phone.

"Because, if you went down on her, she shoulda tasted like...sewage."

He laughed again, an easy-on-the-ears laugh, one that made you smile, and one that soothed you. I could look in his eyes and tell an incredible weight has been lifted from his shoulders. He had a younger brother.

I forget his name right now. My boss raised him because his parents died in the military, a horrible chopper accident many years ago. He was about 18 at the time, so he raised his only sibling, beat his ass, got him out of school and worked two jobs to pay for him to go to college. His brother was in school to be a lawyer and when he thought about joining the Armed Forces my boss, Daniel Lynn, kicked his ass all across the city of Miami.

"Are you *crazy?*" he had said, very hurt, very angry. "Our parents died in that shit, I don't wanna loose you, too. You're all I got." And Joseph Lynn, his brother, never thought about it again.

Daniel said, "My baby mama doesn't smell like sewage."

"Maybe you do, then."

"You got jokes. But back to my baby mama. She's a bitch."

*Who cares!* "You shoulda thought of that when you were rolling all through her pussy like you was looking for the needle in a haystack."

"Good one." He stretched, and then opened his jacket.

I was trying to calcify the situation, when he got hot headed he got crazy, stubborn and I was pretty much the only person who could calm him down. He was in love with me but never actually told me. I knew because once a week he took me to dinner and he bought me roses. He sent little notes to my office. "You're beautiful. Lunch is on me." He was very thoughtful. He told me I reminded him of his mother. I told him I reminded myself of my mother Darla Way, Puerto Rican bombshell married to my ex-gangster father Johnny Way, award-winning freelance photographer. But Daniel's situation was one that was very complex.

He hated his Baby Mama. She hated him. They used to love each other, back then they had everyone fooled. Thinking they had a rare type of love, until one day he came home and saw, in his bed, another woman sucking her pussy. Every picture he was in was turned face down on the shelves, dressers and niches throughout the house. Crushed, he went postal, whipped both their asses. He did 6 months in jail. Once he was released I went to pick him up, bought him some new threads, and drove him around town to take care of his personal business. He called his lawyer a few weeks later and filed for divorce. He couldn't prove she was unfaithful, and since they co-signed everything from the bank accounts to the cars he was stuck with not only child support, but he had to pay her car notes, and she drove some thug called "Big Baby Gangsta" around (or Big Baby Gangsta flossed (showed off) in the car, always harassing Daniel) to the point Daniel wanted to kill him.

Sometimes Daniel was calculatedly stubborn, a bastard in other words. He was class-conscious, and therein the problem lied. He had his own set of morals, and always pushed his beliefs on other people. Wherever he went chaos was the end result, which was why I didn't give him any pussy yet, didn't want him going Downtown and breaking the store windows from my pussy. Hell to the no!

"I just don't understand people these days," he went on derisively, standing up and walking over to the window, that overlooked Bayside Miami, a very profitable tourist spot that charged you damn near five percent of your paycheck just to park. Then he said more fixedly, "They say, well women say, they want this and that and don't really know what they want. We've become so shallow that we look to musicians to help raise our children, to give us some type of outlook on life. You know you're fucked up when you study Old Dirty Bastard's words just to find out how you like it: raw or fake."

We shared a few giggles. But I felt him, really I did. Whenever I get my heart broken, I pop in Whitney Houston's "Saving all my Love," "It's not Right, but it's Ok," "Heart break Hotel," and she's kicking crack like she kicked rocks, and maybe that was the same damn thing.

"Hell, I said, "I heard music calms the beast."

He looked over his shoulder, hands in his pocket. He had a nice ass. "It does, but it doesn't get rid of the beast, I tell ya'."

"Ain't that the truth?" I set the coffee down on the low-table, I couldn't drink this nasty shit anymore. If I kept sipping this poison I wouldn't live to see twenty-three. And I'd be hitting that magical number in three weeks.

He faced me. Studied me. Blushing, I averted my face and couldn't wipe the smile off. Damn it. My pussy was wet. So I squeezed my legs together. So tightly I thought my water broke and I wasn't pregnant.

He had dimples in his cheeks. Never noticed it before. "I like you," he said throwing me off guard.

I circled the right dimple with my index finger. "I hate you."

He gently took my hand and kissed it. "Whatever."

"I don't know what you're insinuating," I told him, the climate changing. He wouldn't let my hand go.

"You're so stuck up," he joked with a boyish grin.

I flipped the bird, looking flawless in my black pinstriped skirt suit. My hair long and real, curly, the right side of my hair pulled away from my face to show off my Asian-like hazel eyes.

"Whatever."

"I'm tired, I'm horny, I'm mad at my baby mama, and I wanna kill her boyfriend. Driving a car with my name of it, and I can't do a thing about it. I have no time for presumptuous B.S."

He sat back behind the desk, took off his jacket and undid his lavender-colored tie. Matched his shoes. I remembered seeing his feet before. His second toe was longer than the big one. He had big feet. Pretty feet. Clear toe nails. Big hands. Clean nails. Low-cut nails. His middle finger was bigger than the index finger and the thumb was thick. Mama always told me those were signs that a man had a big, thick dick. I never believed in superstitions. But with my pussy quivering my clit was telling me to make like the center of a Tootsie Pop and "find out."

I could hear his suit rustling. It was so quiet in the office; the silence was popping in my ears. I kept crossing and uncrossing my legs. I was very uncomfortable. I kept having...visions of this man eating my sugar Puss. For real. I had to squeeze my legs together to keep my pussy from gawking like a goddamn parrot.

I looked him over while he took a quick phone call. He handled his business. My eyes handled theirs. I was eye-fucking him. I was descriptively encoding the essence of his being into my brain, since it was like an IBM computer. Ciphering something that would be gregariously deciphered later.

But the downside. He was an arrogant S.O.B. Four-dimensional and talkative. But he actually had something to say. I heard he was a playah-playah. But this pussy was the playah slayah. Seriously. I was a take-it-back-ho in the bed. A straight freak-a-lic. Work it, these hips won't lie when it hypnotized the Anaconda.

"Ok, I'll call you later," he told someone on the phone, bringing me from my thoughts. Damn it, don't disturb me, I was trying to...assess the possibilities here. I smiled to myself. He picked up the remote and turned on Bob Marley. He loved Bob. Always listened to Bob once a day. The stand out track, "One/Love, People get Ready" from the 1977 *Exodus* album, his favorite of all-time. I knew he wanted me to know that information. Woman's intuition. And he told me one day last month over dinner at IHOP.

With that being said, since I was far from being some independent PMS-ridden feministic bitch, I, forsworn with a secret crush on him, amply tuned into his world with a flourish.

Leaning forward in the chair, I relaxed. I was about to head back to work. Lunch break was nearly over.

"We're both adults, right Daniel?"

He didn't get me. "Yea," he said cautiously, looking me deep in the eyes. "You haven't really touched your coffee."

I challenged him. "Can't drink it without...cream and sugar, and Lord knows I can...swallow some...coffee."

He caught my innuendos superbly. Standing up, he walked around the desk, with a strut stank of masculine charm. He was impossibly fine! Damn it! I didn't mix business with pleasure but after business, when we clocked out, it was such a pleasure to mix thoughts and world events with him over dinner. He leaned against the desk. The screen saver, on the computer monitor, turned into Janet Jackson slapping Mariah Carey in celebrity death match.

"Obviously, this conversation shouldn't be entertained in the office," he told me matter-of-factly. "Don't wanna be filed against, you know, for sexual...harassment."

I ducked his chauvinism. "I feel you." I stood up and stretched. "I gotta get back to work." He hugged me, for a long time. It felt good to be in his arms, to smell his cologne, the SMELL turned me on. My nose always found me good men with good dick in my life. I'd date a man who worked for the Garbage Company that smelled like Zest soap and Cool Water over a man in an expensive suit that smelled like dirty shit. For real.

To my complete dismay, I started for the door. I put my hand on the door knob, looking down. I had to play hard to get. I wanted to fuck. I was like Janet Jackson in Poetic Justice. Let's cut the bullshit ok. Now what do you really, really want from me.

"Stop back by after work," he told me, I heard sadness in his voice. Like he didn't want me to leave.

*Fuck him, I wasn't staying. Yes, bitch, yes you are. No, I was not, I gotta clock back in, but he's the goddamn boss.*

I was stuttering. "Ok, for coffee?"

"Yes. Cream and. Sugar, right?"

Hesitantly, with my mind telling me to leave, I faced him. He was in my face, our noses damn near touching. He reached past me and locked the door. Against my better judgment, risking losing my job for some goddamn dick, I kissed his lips, a peck, slowly pulling away. He was feeling on my booty. I was measuring the length of his hard dick, using my fingers like centimeters on a ruler.

*...One, two...*I got greedy so I diverted the centimeters into inches......*Three, four.* I kissed him, giving him some tongue. ...*Five, six.* I licked his top teeth; bit his bottom lip, pulling him to me. ...*Seven, eight, nine...ten.* Ten inches. A ten inch dick, hell to the yea!

He gripped my face like a fine piece of crystal just super glued back together, and our faces and lips bobbed and weaved like my grandmother's needle shaping patters on an artistic quilt. I pulled myself to him, kissing, our tongues dancing. I was Ginger Rodgers, he was Fred Astaire, of course the restored with color, ghetto versions.

"I love you," he said. "I want to be with you; I can't...breathe without you."

I put my hands in his pants and held his dick. *Yea* its mine. I just claimed it. I knew the bitches in the office were going to be hating on me, because I was in the boss's pants and they didn't even get to hardly see him with them on when he was on the clock. Tough shit. "My bed is...cold without someone in it, I'm...tired of playing with my...pussy all by myself."

He backed away from me, slowly, taking his time. I loved his sense of urgency, his control. He unbuttoned his shirt, and revealed such an incredible chest. Lovely nipples, I had to place my hands flat on his chest and just look into his eyes. He handed me my coffee.

"Hold the coffee, baby."

Pulling out his dick, through the unzipped hole of the pants, he started gently stroking it. I drank some coffee, held it in my mouth then, feeling adventurous; I got on my knees and took the head of his passion into the confines of my strong jaws. His eyes rolled to the back of his head, moaning silently, nothing too loud.

Just right.

He matched my rhythm as the warm coffee tingled the head of his dick, giving him a warm sensation. I never slept with anyone from the office, I thought about it a few times. But I never acted on it. I didn't want to go through the sexual harassment thing. I didn't want to lead anyone on. I didn't have time to teach grown ass men how to be classy, they shouldn't act like little boys. You didn't hear Boyz II Men on the damn radio that much anymore. Fellahs get a clue!

My male co-workers took bets on who was going to fuck what woman at whatever time. That's why I never went to parties or the clubs the job set up for employees to network and get to know each other. I took my black ass home and did my thing behind the four walls of my bedroom.

Now I was sucking my boss's dick, riding dirty to say the least. I played with his balls, gently cupping them like the contents of my coffee cup and basically brought him sheer ecstasy. He looked down at me with narrowed eyes. His male hardness sliding in and out of my mouth set me on fire. I gripped it, jacked it hard and fast, spitting on it and using my baby soft hands to smooth my saliva all over his incredible member until is glistened.

"Jack it, baby…yea, baby, just like that."

I looked up at him, loving the way I was making him feel. He was at my beck and call, my mercy, dependant on me. "You like that, baby?"

"Yes, baby." He shuddered.

"*Oooh*, you taste so good in my mouth."

"Let me feel your throat."

I tried with all my might to put his entire package in my mouth, I started to gag, he had too much dick, but he smiled and gripped my head and fucked my mouth, gyrating his hips like Van Gogh paintings on canvases…he appreciated the feeling I gave him, he didn't try to make me choke.

Reaching into my panties, just under my loose skirt, I started rubbing my pussy, bringing myself pleasure. I closed my eyes, enjoying the feel of my lips and tongue on his shaft, lifting the dick up and putting his nuts in my mouth, bouncing them on my slick tongue.

"Oooh baby, *yeeeees*! Yes, baby, damn…"

I opened my eyes and rubbed my pussy juices all over his dick, and took him back into my mouth, tasting pussy on dick ever so gently. Tasted good. I was the master at giving head and a wizard at taking dick. I didn't do it much, but sucking dick was an art form to me. You took your time. You got into a Niggah's head and his soul through conversation. You opened him up mentally then you used your tongue and lips physically.

He jerked, and his hips moved so fast his dick fell from my mouth. He instantly grabbed his dick and started jacking it, "I gotta cum." He stood over my coffee and his ass cheeks locked and his hole started pulsating as he came in my coffee, his head leaned back, sweat all over him. I watched with a smile from the chair, crossing my legs, looking like I didn't just do anything naughty.

"Damn, daaamn, damn, baby." He was trying to control his breathing. He looked at me lovingly, like I was an angel visiting earth for a little while. He put his dick in the coffee and stirred it, smiling with sparkling eyes. His lips formed an "O."

Handing me the coffee he said, "Cream and sugar."

I stood up, gripped the mug and I wolfed it down. Smacking my lips. "Ah. All gone. So, what does this mean?"

"I got court with my baby mama tomorrow, would you like to join me?"

I kissed him, wrapping my arms around him. "I wouldn't miss it for the world. But only on one condition."

He ran a shaky hand through my hair and just looked in my eyes. I could see the love dancing across his handsome face.

"What would that be?"

"Bring along Clarisse. So she can take down…minutes."

"You are a goddamn fool," he joked, hugging me so tight we would rock and dance to Bob Marley until the CD ended. Fuck work, and fuck clocking back in.

I got a new man now, and I was going to appreciate the fact that we were friends for two years before we were lovers. Which was a good thing? Because I knew all his flaws. I saw his good side and his bad side. I know what makes him happy and sad. I know all of his fears. I know what drives him and what doesn't. deep down inside I told myself that I enjoyed being alone but now that it was changing, I welcomed it because I needed a good man in my life. I tell you one thing:

If his Baby Mama comes with drama I will stomp the Ho. Seriously.

# Fate Williams

Red,

*What's up! I want to be in your world because I really feel God put us together. I'm writing in text form, the way I do when we text with cell phones, because its easier to say what I have to say and its quicker to write. I have tried nothing like this before but I want to be happy so I'm willing to do this for the first time in my life to be in a relationship with someone I care about, which is YOU. I want us to just accept each other for who we are. We are soul mates. We will last and finally get it right because we want to and because we are ready to start over fresh with no judgments of any kind, please.*

*When I come to you I will trust you and I do trust you. I have and will make sure I put all my baggage behind me. No more comparing you to my Ex. I may not hold psychic power but we just feel right when we look at each other and when we kiss oh God! When we kiss it's like we just met for the first time. I love kissing you, OH YEAH! You're my girl and I want you to be there for my son...You are the aggressor! You are my life! I love when we're lying in the bed playing and my son Renaldo just burst into the room when you're trying to get my coochie!*

*I love that smile of yours. You're beautiful inside and out. And even thought we're both strong women and have soooooooo much in common we are still sooo different in sooo many ways. For example:*

*I love food. You love junk! I'm a fem. You're a stud. Your mannerisms are different. I would like for you to communicate with me more about your feelings. Please, please stop taking me so seriously. I love that you know when I'm playing. I will never hurt you, Red! I love you Pooh Bear! And please no secrets! No lies! And no people who want to fuck numbers or pictures and for you to let yourself love me. Don't hate because I'm like you. Embrace me more because you wouldn't accept me as your girlfriend if you didn't think I was special.*

*Thanks for going to therapy with me, to help me deal with my past. This truly allowed me to open up about my life and work on myself, and that made me a better person. A better mother. And a better lover. We are both strong 'cause we have to be. All we had is and was our moms. The difference is that you wanted to be strong like mine and what we have in common with our "strongness" is that we are raising 11 year old boys that we want to be strong. Just please take your time with me, please! And have patience with me even in games because I love you very much and I will like to show you what real love feels like. And baby my humor is only in fun and sometimes when I'm nervous and this is a part of my soul. I won't make it seem so serious, Boo! I just love playing with you. I know my part as your lady, the main parts. Who is the woman and who is the man when it comes to the boys but anything else I don't know because I'm just trying to get to know. I hope I really get to have my second child with you. However God wants it.*

*Sincerely yours,*

*Miss Fate Williams*

Uneasy, I sealed the letter with a kiss, wondering did I just make the biggest mistake of my life. Should I have written this letter? Should I throw it away and speak from the heart? I shouldn't take her back; I shouldn't even entertain the thought. She lied to me. This *beautiful* person, this woman who looked like Gerald Levert deceived me. I loved the way she looked and how she carried herself like a classy thug. She's my studsband (female husband). She smoked weed, drank alcohol and fought like the Niggahs. When you spoke to her you'd swear she was a man. But she lied. About everything. Our entire relationship was a lie, orchestrated by a very insecure, selfish bitch! Yes, I was a lesbian. I loved pussy just as much as I loved my own. I was a very feminine woman; I loved women who looked like men. Because it was like I was having my cake and eating it, too. I got to have a woman who knew how to be touched, cuddled and held, yet I kinda had a man also because she looked like one, dressed like one and acted like a straight "Butch." I remembered when I first realized I liked women. It was in high school. I had a big crush on a girl name Lianna. I was with my boyfriend at the time, my son's father, but I never stopped fantasizing about her. I used to masturbate thinking of her touch; and her lovely smile. I was too gullible to approach her. I never did. And I never would.

I could still remember how I met Red. It was at Club Goodfellahs, in Perrine, Florida on Gay Night (Sundays). I'd gone there solo because I didn't feel like giving my friends rides home, especially if they wanted to leave and I didn't. Everyone started arriving well after 2 a.m. I was dressed in Gucci, right on down to the imitation socks. My weave was immaculately long and curly. I was going for the Tyra Banks look, very *America's Top Model.* I loved that show. I gotta catch the next season. I had sat down at the bar. I didn't want to be harassed. I smiled at the short, white female bartender, who kept giving me the once over. It was mighty dark in there, smoke looming here and there. The green wrist band was making me feel uncomfortable because my outfit was pink and this green stuck out like a sore thumb. I had a lot on my mind that night, thinking about my past and my Daddy. *Daddy.* I couldn't get him off my mind, nor could I get my son off my mind. It was very hard to do.

"And what will you be having, pretty lady?" the Bartender asked me, shuffling her long dirty-looking blonde hair from her face. I smiled and shook her hand.

"Could I get a Rum and Coke, light ice?" I was Jamaican, so my accent was noticeable. A few lesbian Hoes were all on my jock so I grabbed my titties and wiggled them playfully, feeling it tonight. A bitch was out and about and loving it. My son was with my mother, and I was glad he was because Mama and I fell out today. She told me she was going to call Child Protective Services on me because I was a gay woman raising a son on my own. I looked at this cunningly stupid bitch and told her, *"Bitch, try!"* I couldn't believe after all the hell she had put me through in my life, she was trying to fuck up my adult life in the process.

She challenged me. She stood up from the Lazy Boy in my living room and said, "Oh, I will. My grandson doesn't want your lesbian lovers around him. He goes to church. He believes in God. He doesn't want all that damnation around him."

"This is my house and he's *my* son. I went through eleven hours of labor with him. I take care of him and feed him. You don't do jack shit but claim grandmother parental rights over him. It's all in goddamn name only."

"You're a pussy sucking whore and I'm ashamed to have you as my daughter."

I blew a gasket in my brain. "Get out, now!" I was slightly taller than my Mama. I was 5 feet 11. I weighed 180 pounds, chunky but a nice chunky size. I still had on my medical uniform. I was a medical assistant, making $20 an hour at Baptist Hospital, been there for three years and I was tired of being single. My son's father, well, my eyes welled up with tears thinking about it.

"I'm not leaving without my grandson." She snatched up her purse from the low table and she walked to his room. I was right on her ass.

*I'll rip your clit through your ears, bitch!* "Leave, mother!"

"RENALDOOO! Where are you, baby?" She was determined to get to my child.

She opened his room door. My son, with his handsome self, spitting image of his Daddy, was at the computer. He quickly sent a screen to the bottom of the page. I said, "Mama. Good bye. It's time for you to go home. I'm not trying to be rude."

She ignored me. "Grandma is taking you home. You don't need to be living with filthy slime."

He looked scared. "Grandma," he said, lowering his head. He was holding back what he really wanted to say. "That's my Mama; please don't talk like that about her."

She dismissed his comment with the wave of her bejeweled hand. "I'm sorry, grandma don't fake it for nobody, baby. Your Mama licks pussy, simple as that now LET'S GO!"

I snatched her ass by the hair and dragged her ass into the hallway. I was viciously slapping her face, kicking at her.

"You bitch!" I was so hurt, so disrespected in my own home I snapped on her. I never hit her. She was clawing at my legs, my thighs…she managed to pull herself up and she scratched my face and I spit in hers.

"Don't. You. Ever. DISRESPECT. ME. IN. FRONT. OF. MY. GODDAMN. SON! I'm gay because *of your* molesting ass, cunt! Tell him how you use to sneak into my room, Ho and make me do things to you!"

Mama froze and just looked at me. We looked like two train wrecks, breathing hard. Hard-eyed, in defense mode, fight mode. Picture frames shattered on the floor. My statuettes on the floor, broken. None of them could replace what Mama had done to me thirteen years ago, when I was a little girl.

"Yea, bitch!" I screamed at her. "Let's talk about it."

"Talk about what?" Mama stared me down evilly. "I never touched you. Why are you making things up just to have your way? All you do is lie; you will always be a fucking liar!"

"I'm lying, Mama?" I intimidated her now. She remained quiet. I said, "*Aw,* you're all quiet now! Tell my son how you used to sell your body…and bring those untrustworthy men into our home."

Recollection bit her eyes but she kept a straight face. "Don't believe it, grandson. Your Mama turned those men on behind my back! She let them crawl through her windows; she even got thrown out of high school for sucking damn near every football player's dick on the team."

"You're lying! I never even slept with a man in high school," I said, defending myself. I couldn't believe this. "*Why* would you lie, Mama?"

"Mama did you do those things with men?" my child asked sadly. "Grandma told me a long time ago you were a Hoe." My mouth fell open in shock. "I just never…"

I snatched his little ass by the shirt collar and yanked him into my face. "Now you listen. For starters, watch your mouth and your tone; secondly your grandmother is a stone cold liar. We couldn't afford to pay bills. My Daddy worked three jobs. She wanted revenge on Daddy because his work ethics kept him away from home. My Daddy slaved away to feed us. And this bitch, selfishly I might say, received money from military people passing through our house day in and day out. She was feeding her sick, sexual need. When she was done with them she sent them, drunk and high as skunks, into my room and they had sex with me. I had no choice. She was always in the room, coaching me. Suck it like this, fuck them like that, and learn how to take the dick. Son I am talking to you bluntly. Your grandmother put me through hell."

He snatched himself out of my arms, turned on my mother and stomped her foot. He then ran into the room and slammed the door. He was screaming all kind of shit, my heart hurt, it killed me to tell him about my life, my past like this. But I had no choice.

"Get out, Mama. Get out; I don't wanna see you again."

"I'm not going anywhere. You can't just turn on me. I'm your mother. Back then I did what I had to do to survive." She straightened her jacket and ran her hands over her hair, trying to look presentable and I snatched her wig again, slapping her ass, fucking her up and she ran into my body, bear hugging me like a wrestler and the both of us slammed into the wall, falling on the sofa. She got with me. Mama taught me how to fight so she gave me a run for my money but I had a change up for her funky ass that turned her dollar punches into three goddamn quarters. We fought and just held each other; we wouldn't let each other go. One of us had to give.

"Tag out, bitch!" I yelled at her, spitting in her face and she sank her teeth into my breast and I screamed so loud we both fell off the chair.

"You tag out, bitch!" She retorted.

This was ridiculous, fighting my Mama was wrong. God frowned on this but did he frown on those men destroying my innocence? Where was God? Why did he allow this to happen to me? Fuck the book of Job! Why did he let those men destroy a little girl?

I let her go and openly sobbed; we both were at the point of no return. She never accepted my lifestyle; she never accepted responsibility for molesting and sexually assaulting me. She never admitted to herself that she actually tried to sell me for crack. She never admitted that she used to dress up in my Daddy's clothes, cutting her hair like his, spraying on his cologne and trying to make love to me, her only daughter, when I was 15 years old. She was delusional, paranoid. I tried to urge her to go to a mental institution, but she blamed herself for my Daddy's death. He died in a car accident. I missed Daddy. He always protected me. I never told Daddy I was being raped by men while he worked. I never told Daddy Mama snuck a different Niggah in his house every night he worked and fucked her in the ass or pussy or mouth, in his bed, while he slaved away trying to give us a better life.

Struggling to stand up, I turned my back on her. She then stood up, breathing hard. Mama wanted to hold me. My head said "No," but my heart allowed her. I needed to be held. I let her.

When she wrapped her arms around me she kissed my face and old feelings of lust awakened in me. She rubbed my arms the way she used to when she raped me. When she tried to kiss my lips I angrily pushed her on the floor and I said, "You are not going to do this to me again! I'm standing up to you. You're a sick bitch!"

Like Lucifer himself, she slowly walked around me, looking into my eyes, smiling maliciously.

"You praise your Daddy, don't you?"

"Yes. I miss him. He would have never approved of what you did."

She laughed bitterly. "Renaldo. Let's go," my mother said. I seriously doubted if she hurt my son. I knew in my heart she would never hurt him, why, I didn't know, call it a sixth sense.

"He was a good man, your father," Mama said off-handedly.

I was silent for a moment. "*That* we agree on."

"With a dark heart," she snapped.

I was quiet now. Then I exploded, walking in her face. "Don't even try to denounce my Daddy's good will. He was a caring man, a good man."

"So am I. I'm caring. I provided for you."

"*Yea*, by sending men to rape me, Mama?" I was shuddering. So much pain enveloped me. I felt betrayed all over again. I relived my childhood standing in my living room as an adult; a successful, college degree earning adult. "We never talked about this; we both have lived our lives trying to pretend this didn't happen, because we try to live a lie. Worrying about the public scrutiny. Fuck the black community! All Niggahs do is hurt each other, bring each other down. Fuck that. Fuck you!"

"Your Daddy worked very hard," she said, scaring me.

"I know," I said slowly, suddenly guarded.

"He never wanted you, girl."

I was cautious. What was she talking about? Through clenched teeth, "What are you suggesting?"

"Your Daddy wanted things done a certain…way."

"I know that. Even though he worked he gave you instructions, have this and that cleaned, feed my daughter at such a such time, wash all the clothes, iron my clothes and give me my pussy when I get home. I know all about that Mama. He was a provider. And you shitted all over that."

"He controlled everything in our home. Everything was approved by him."

I narrowed my eyes. "What do you mean everything was…approved. By. Him?" I didn't like the feeling that suddenly overcame me. "Tell me."

She smiled wickedly. "Those men that came and went out of your room wasn't sent there by me. Your Daddy sent them; in fact he collected the cash before they even arrived to our home."

I had to sit down.

The room was spinning. My Daddy. My sweet Daddy. I started remembering what he used to say to me when he came home. *"How are you doing, baby? Rough night? Couldn't sleep, baby? Why is that? You help Daddy around the house, don't you? You are so pretty, so smart. You g'on make Daddy rich one day."*

*He was getting rich off pimping his only daughter! How could he? I can't deal with this. I gotta get out of here.*

I made my mother leave. I grabbed my knife and chased her ass outside. My son appeared out of nowhere and said to me, "I'm going with grandma. I don't wanna stay here anymore, Mama I hate you!"

And I thought I was losing my son. No time for that. All I could think about right now was Red. Maybe I was fucked up for putting thoughts of women before my son's well being. I seriously hoped he didn't need therapy. I damn sure needed it. I was dealing with a lot. I didn't know how to really handle finding out my Daddy pimped me.

I remembered Red sat next to me at Goodfellahs and paid for my drink. After the preliminaries she bought me another one, looking spiffy in a suit. All the gay men tried to holla at her. She said, "I'm a butch, female, lesbian. I don't do men." They still tried to holla. She looked better than any man in the club. I loved her instantly. She was very polite and patient. We danced and talked about life. I told her I had a son. I reluctantly told her that his father died during a drug deal gone badly. A few tears fell from my eyes. Graciously, Red wiped them away. She was from Opa Locka. She was Haitian. I cringed when she said that. I didn't date Haitians. I was so sorry. I had *nothing* against them but that was just not my cup of tea. But she was persistent; she didn't act or look Haitian. I gave her a chance. Her biological name was Lolita Harvey. She had an eleven year old son named Jameson.

Around 4 am she asked me to go out to eat at Denny's. I loved that place. Denny's was the hang out spot after you left the club.

While there you were supposed to swap numbers, flirt, and get your groove on. I drove in my Dodge truck behind her Dodge Intrepid. We both had Dodge vehicles. It took everything in me not to just make a U-turn and go home; I was too scared to go any further with Red.

But I did. Something pulled me towards her. I didn't want Red in my life, in my family business. I was going through a lot. I wasn't settled emotionally. It wasn't fair to bring her in on my abusive past. So I made a vow to keep it hidden from her. I'd make shit up. Tell her my life was peachy teen. We got the corner booth and ordered a country breakfast. Red paid for it; put it on her platinum card. I was hurting for my son, hurting for my lost innocence; I was hurt about what Daddy had done. Part of me didn't believe what Mama had said. But part of me did. I had to wear an invisible mask. I couldn't let Red in my world. We just met. It would be months, if ever before I let her in my universe to see how fucked up it was. But I wanted someone to talk to. Someone to lean on. A shoulder to cry on. Someone to stroke my hair, tell me that everything would be all right. I knew deep down that was a fantasy. But it didn't hurt to dream.

I wound up crying and Red comforted me. We kissed. I hesitantly gave her some tongue. I didn't care about giving her public affection. Everyone in there was gay anyway, so g'on and get your swerve on…I told myself.

I wound up in Red's bed half an hour later. I didn't even remember getting the doggy bag, because I couldn't finish my food. I didn't remember getting in my truck and following her to her house all the way in Opa Locka, not too far from Ali Baba Boulevard in Miami. I didn't remember how my panties wound up in her mouth and she ate my pussy. I felt tongue, lips and lacy panties all at the same time. Drove me wild. I never fucked on the first night. But getting some head was *not* fucking. This was the dental part of the package you got with a friend with benefits.

She spread my pussy with big hands and tongued my clit, bringing me to utter ecstasy. I shook on silk sheets. In the darkness, with just the glow of the TV beaming on our bodies I was revitalized. We bumped pussies. Aggressively, she got on top of me, one of my legs bent back, and our pussies gyrated on each other, sending me shivering and coming all over the bed.

The dildo. I sucked it then beat her pussy with it, like a belt on an ass cheek, taking my time, sucking her barely-there titties, spanking her ass, relinquishing control. She sucked my pussy until I came again, then she got the double ended dildo and I got in the doggy position and she slid it deep in my wet cunt, then she slid the other end inside her flesh and our ass cheeks bumped and jiggled while the plastic toy, eleven inches long, brought us to Pleasure Ville.

I still thought about my son.

After that night we were inseparable. We didn't become friends; we dove right into a full fledged relationship. After the months peeled away to hours wasted on sex, sex, sex, I realized I didn't know a thing about her and she didn't know a thing about me. We then talked about it because I vowed to keep my pussy under lock and key until we got to know each other. She was all for it. So we talked and related more than we had sex. I loved it. We knew each other's favorite singers, foods and colors. We knew each other's birthdays and favorite holidays. She helped me wash my truck. I knew when she went to work and when she came home. She was a pharmacist at the local drug store. She was much loved at work. I had to drive for forty minutes to Baptist Hospital everyday from Red's house. She tried to get me to give up my apartment and fully move in with her but for some reason I declined. I wasn't ready. I changed Renaldo's school.

Over pasta at the Olive Garden a week later I told her about my mother and what she did to me, how my son felt. I couldn't lie to her. I couldn't look someone in the face and blatantly lie. I had to slay in the bed I made. I couldn't sleep at night if I lied to someone.

Red met my son and he liked her instantly. We got really close. Then she told me she had an eleven year old son, who looked just like her. I told her she had already told me about Jameson at the club the night we met months before. She just laughed. We combined families, moved to North Miami Beach, never to see my Mama again. I changed my cell number, and my life was so fulfilled. I used to love the way my son and Jameson would come into the room, when Red and I watched TV, and disrupt her from getting my pussy. We'd play it off like we were wrestling. Our sons hit it off. They got really close really fast. They protected each other, went to the same school and did everything together. I really felt like I found my soul mate. Jameson was a handsome young man. We clicked instantly, just like my son and Red had. He always asked me questions, loved reading books, and loved the Cartoon Network. He liked his fried chicken cooked with Oregano and complete seasoning only, and Louisiana Hot sauce.

My son liked bar-b-que everything.

One day I was home alone. I was going through all my old stuff, trying to throw away what I didn't need any more. That included old photos. I had too many. Exhausted, I came across a picture with me, Lianna and my baby Daddy from high school. I was close to Lianna, I loved Liana but I never had her. She was in love with me, but we never did anything. And when her parents found out their daughter was a lesbian all I knew was that Lianna was withdrawn from school and no one had ever heard from her again.

I was sad and depressed, such a sweet girl. I had one other picture of Liana. She was wearing a red dress, her hair piled atop of her head. She had gained a few pounds in the picture, but her beauty was so radiant it was breathtaking.

Red came in the room and looked at me, and then she said bluntly, "I'm taking our sons to the store for ice cream. Want anything?"

She was a darling. "I'm ok; I need to throw half this shit away."

"Ok, we'll be back."

I stood up and gave her a firm hug. Gripping a hand full of my ass, she gave me some tongue. We always kissed like it was the very first time. "I wanna do something for our sons…put like a little family tree thing together."

Red said, "Ok, that's hot to death."

"Ok, I need your Mama's name, and your son's father's name and all that good shit."

"Ok, when I get back I'll get you everything you need."

"Ok, damn we're damn sure saying 'ok' an awful lot."

Red looked deep into my eyes. "I love you."

"And I love you."

Red got serious on me. "I will never hurt you, never lie to you, baby. I will die for you."

I felt appreciated. I truly missed my son's father, and he was the first and only man I ever wanted. I loved him, when we were together everyday was a holiday. I remembered rumors circulated around our high school, Miami Central Senior High, that he slept with Lianna. I didn't believe it of course.

He was too busy selling dope and talking to me on the phone. I knew that couldn't be true. Then I got pregnant. I kept my son, and Mama tried to make me abort him. I told her to fuck off. My life was on the upswing…*that* was until my baby Daddy, Dunn McKinney, was murdered. I never thought I'd love again. So I turned to women again and the rest was history.

"Ah," I said, hugging her tighter. We held each other. "For some strange reason I believe you."

And we kissed.

I was nearly done throwing shit away. Took me twenty minutes and they still weren't back. I didn't worry; she did call me and said she was stuck in traffic. Go figure.

I opened Red's closet and put my photo albums on the top shelf. One fell down.

"Shit!"

I suspected it was hers. Breathing through my nose, I picked it up and decided not to be nosey. I was gonna put it back.

When I reached up to slide it on the top shelf, some photos fell out.

I squatted on my knees and took them up but the instant I looked at them the breath caught in my throat.

I held my neck and sat down, staring at the photos in disbelief. I opened the book and right before my eyes I found out all I needed to know.

Lolita Harvey wasn't Lolita Harvey.

And I didn't need to ask her who her baby Daddy was.

Lolita Harvey's real name was Lianna Gregory.

My long lost friend, the woman I was secretly in love with from high school.

And her son's father was the same man who fathered my son.

Dunn McKinney.

The high school rumor was true!

Oh, God! *Renaldo and Jameson were brothers!*


When Red came into the room an hour later she handed me some flowers. I just looked at her. I looked at the floor and she instantly knew something was wrong.

"Baby," she started and I turned my back on her, my heart split in two. "Baby!"

"What?"

"Talk to me."

"About what?" I was seething with rage.

"Something happened. What is it?"

I smiled bitterly. "Guilty conscious, 'ey?"

She waltzed around me and gripped my shoulders. "We can talk about anything."

I wanted to spit in her face. I hated a lying ass bitch. If I could keep it real then damn it so could she. She was my love, my life. I opened up to this girl, told her about my abusive past. Did I tell her as a means to keep her? No. But at the same time she never really touched on topics from her past.

"Sure. Let's talk. Then I'm taking my son home."

"You are home."

"HOME!" I didn't mean to yell. She blinked several times, backing away from me. "Home, down in southwest Dade. My apartment. I should have known I couldn't trust you."

"You can."

"What high school you went to?"

"Miami Southridge. I told you that. You know that?"

"Really? And I guess you're going to tell me your name is Lolitha Harvey right? Or is it Lianna?"

She stared at me, her mouth open.

"Can't talk, Ho? You lied to me! Do you even remember me? Do you?"

"No, I don't. What are you talking about?"

I smiled graciously, taking apart the flowers and ripping them to shreds. It rained rose petals in the room, a room I didn't want to share with her anymore. This was how it always ended. Bitterly. A motherfucker couldn't be honest to save their lives. What was it with black people and honesty?

"You don't remember me, Lianna? We went to the same high school."

She stared at me, taking a few more steps back. "I don't..."

I approached her. "Your son's father, what was his name?"

"Jack Stephens."

"More lies. Your son's father I dated in high school. Rumors were flying that he fucked you. I never believed it."

She was in tears. "No, no...Are you telling me...you are..."

"Yup. Yup. It's me. You were fucking my man behind my back in high school. We were really close. And you mean to tell me you didn't recognize who I was at the club when we met?"

She got really quiet. She lowered her eyes and sat on the bed, folding her hands. Part of me wanted to hold her. But I couldn't hug a liar. "Yes, I knew who you were."

I was stunned. "So you played games with me."

She looked up. "No..I mean it looks that way."

"Why?"

"I have my reasons."

"Why? Tell me. Or I'm gone forever."

She pleaded, "Please don't leave. You have a piece of my son's father with you. Your son. I know he's the father."

I was hurt. My blood turned cold. "So everyone knew but me?"

Her eyes lowered to the floor. "Yes."

It took a while to gather my thoughts. I was rubbing my arms. "Why hide it from me? I'm going through enough shit, Red."

"I had to." She averted her face. I was getting angry.

I sat next to her and glared at her. "Tell me, everything. What *aren't* you telling me?"

She said it hastily. "It's about your mother."

I cringed inside. My Mama. She didn't *know* my mother.

My eyes wide, I breathed in deeply. "What about her."

"I can't get into it…" She turned away from me and I walked around her, getting in her face. I was on the verge of whipping her ass.

"Talk to me. What about my Mama?"

She looked scared, her teeth clicking together.

"I can't talk about it, Fate."

My eyes were slits of malice. "TALK!"

She retaliated. "Mind your business. It slipped out. Disregard what I said. I was making it up, just to get a reaction out of you."

"Why are you lying to me, woman?" I was about to lose it. "Open your goddamned mouth and talk before I snatch it out of you."

"Don't threaten me, bitch. Just because I bounce in that pussy don't mean you can whip my ass."

My brows rose. "Bounce?" I mocked, laughing. "The dildo bounces in this pussy pot, you strokeless bitch." I was getting her upset. She always spilled her heart when she was mad. She didn't realize that.

Red had an attitude. She got like that when you tried to force her to talk.

"Mind your business, Fate. Some things are better left unsaid."

Forcibly, I slapped her so hard she looked at me in shock.

I didn't give a shit. "…Talk…"

Angrily, she rushed me, grabbing in a bear hug. We slammed into the wall, pictures falling on the floor. We were going at it. Punching me in the face, I grabbed her by the afro and snatched the Ho across the room, kicking her in the lips. Blood on my shoes, she catapulted up to her feet and I Karate chopped the Ho in the face. Wincing, she fell to her knees, disoriented. Yea, bitch. Didn't expect that One, Two Chop did you? She looked up, breathing hard and I stood there, breathing hard, my hair disheveled. The bitch fucked up my hair do. Silly, Ho!

When I looked up at the ceiling she attacked, jumping to her feet and punched me in the gut, ripping my top, my tits springing free. I rushed her and we fell over the bed, my head hitting the nightstand.

"Nobody hits me, bitch!" she was screaming and I bit her tit, jumped up to my feet and pushed the nightstand over on the bitch.

Spitting on her she pushed the nightstand like a beast and she grabbed my foot and pulled me down to her. She held me so tight I couldn't move.

"FATE!"

"I hate you, bitch!"

Red wouldn't let me go.

"Your mother is the reason my son's father is dead."

I was breathless, I was getting a headache. I had to stand up. She had to be lying. Blood on my face, I went into the bathroom and wet a wash cloth. She was behind me, tears in her eyes. I looked at her through the mirror. On her face was regret and remorse for hitting me. I didn't know how I felt about the bitch anymore. No one got saucy with me. I should grind my foot in her ass. Nah. She might like it too much. Bitch!

Mama never...wait a minute! Mama did hate him. But she never really *met* him. I *never* brought him around the house. And when we did see each other I had to sneak out the window.

"My Mom don't know my baby Daddy, Red."

"Yes she did."

"Why do you say that?" I was wiping blood from my face, running warm water over the rag, wringing it out.

"He was killed during a drug deal."

"I...I know. He was the only man I ever loved."

"Same here. He was the only man I ever had. He was selling crack to someone and the person was short of money. When he asked for all his money a gun was drawn and his life was taken, like it meant nothing."

"And what does my Mama have to with this?"

"...Um..."

"Red, please. Just say it..."

She looked at me. "Your Mama pulled the trigger."

I looked at her for a long time before I did anything.

She was trying to hug me. Pushing her away I glared at her and said one thing, "I need some time alone. I'm going back to my apartment, and I will call you when I'm ready to talk or see you."

I walked past her. "If I ever wanna see you again," I went on, slamming the door behind me.

I locked myself in my apartment for days. I couldn't believe it! I just couldn't wrap my mind around it. I burned on the inside. I couldn't eat or sleep. I cried so much, tears failed my eyes the way words failed my tongue. I tried reading the Bible to understand it all, but it was like I was reading empty pages. Nothing registered. I let my son stay with Red. For some reason I couldn't separate him from his brother. No, we haven't told them they were brothers yet. I didn't know how to. I didn't know what to say. Why would Mama kill my man? Why would she? Hadn't she robbed me enough in my life? Hadn't she allowed people to hurt me, shatter my soul, shit on my self-esteem? When would this shit ever end?

I couldn't live without my man. I loved him so much. But did he love me? He slept with Red in high school. She looked dangerously different than she looked in school. I could have passed her on the street and not know she used to be sweet Lianna. That chubby sexy girl I wanted with a passion. I guess I got what I wanted.

Why would my man cheat on me? Wasn't I enough? Didn't I please him? I gave him pussy gave him the ass and gave him head when and where he wanted it. I never protested. I had his child. I thought I was the only one with bragging rights.

How could Red deceive me? What was her purpose for finding me? Leading me on? Was it all a lie? Was it really because she wanted her son to know my son? Combine my dead man's seeds? Was that it, or was there more to it? What did I do? If I was another woman in America going through this would I react the same way? I couldn't watch TV, I couldn't brush my teeth. My hair weave looked like shit. I smelled like it.

Several times over the next few days people knocked at my door. I didn't answer. My phone wailed like drunken sailors. I didn't answer. I didn't go in to work. I was probably fired by now. I didn't check the mail. I didn't get horny. I thought about Mama.

Before I knew it a few days later I was in the shower, took a long one, did my hair, got dressed and hopped in my truck and drove to Mama's house.

When she answered the door I stared at her. Dead inside. She looked radiant. A party was in progress. It took a while to realize it was her birthday. Oh, well. I wasn't here for celebrations.

I wanted to whip her ass! Shoot her the way she shot my man! I shook with rage, my blood boiled.

I got all the way in her face and told her one thing.

"I know."

She turned her back and said, "Everyone meet my daughter. Isn't she grand? Welcome to the party! Come on in!"

Otis Redding was singing. Everyone here was over 40. I felt like I was in a nursing home. They were dressed to kill. Dancing and sipping booze. Conversations ranged from Vietnam to Bush lusting over oil.

"Hey," they said. Some danced over to me and gave me a hug or shook my hand. I was very polite. I smiled at them. Then I glared at Mama. I took her hands. I spat "You look ravishing mother," so icily she shook.

She was trying to read me. I shut the radars off in my eyes, giving Houston a fucking problem.

"Thanks, baby."

"I know you killed my son's father."

She laughed nervously, snatching her hands back. "I don't know what you're talking about."

I gripped my Chanel purse under my arm. I was beautiful in a Baby Phat shirt with spaghetti straps and tight blue jeans dangerously riding my ass crack.

If I couldn't beat her, join her. "Would you like something to drink? I know I need one."

"Baby I can explain…"

"Wait here."

Dying inside, I snapped my fingers, swallowed my anger and danced across the room. Her old friend George grabbed my wrist and kissed my hand.

"Hey, George."

"Hey, sexy! Been a long time."

"I know. They make Viagra. And I'm not the supplier."

Kissing his cheek, I waltzed over to Mama's bar. Years of whoring like the second coming of Jezebel got her the most fabulous two story $450,000 house in Miami-Dade County. Foyers and a four car garage, even the guest house was an actual house in the huge back yard, complete with Olympic-sized pool and TV screens built into the walls.

Stubbornly, I looked over my shoulder. She was dancing and carrying on like I didn't just drop the bomb on her. And that was her life. Getting away with everything. She dissed felons, but she did felonious things throughout her life. She used to rob people, sell drugs and use them. Prostitute. Check. Whore. Check. Adulterer. Check. Married a man who fathered me and pimped me. Check. Check. Check.

I looked at the short, old woman with a gray stinky wig and pink dress. Her dentures reminded me of Mr. Ed. She looked lovely nonetheless.

"Hey." I just looked at her. Never saw her before in my life.

"Hi," she said. "What are you drinking?"

"Make two Rum and Cokes. Light ice in my mother's."

"Who is your mother?" she asked me, getting right to work with the skill of a well seasoned bar tender. I was impressed. She had a big ass and big titties. She still had that "Umph" that made men go "Whomp!"

"The birthday lady."

"You're her daughter? Fate? I finally meet you?" Setting the rum bottle down, she walked hurriedly around the bar and engulfed me, kissing my cheek. "Oh ho ho hoo! Your Mom and I go way back. Back into time, Girl! We grew up together. We went to school together married together and had babies together."

*Whoopee Do bitch!* "Glad to meet you. And you're name?"

"Call me Janis the Pearl!"

*What kinda name is that?* "Aw, cute name. Glad to meet you."

She turned to dig in her purse and I grabbed the drinks.

Mama approached me and took her drink. I handed it to her with a smile.

"I met Janis the Pearl."

Her eyes were evil. Her smile, affectionate.

"Aw, isn't she wonderful?"

"Does she molest her children like you? Since you two married together and had kids together."

"Listen, I will not be talked down to in my own home. Get over the past. That man was no good for you. The best thing he ever did was give you a son and got missing."

"YOU KILLED HIM, BITCH!"

People heard. The music died away. She looked around nervously, and kissed my cheek. "...And scene! You remembered your lines for your theatre class. Good job, baby."

And these dumb ass people clapped and whistled.

"*Regular Angela Basset, honey!*" Some lady clad in a yellow dress yelled dumbly and I rolled my eyes.

Another woman said "*And you look better than she do.*"

"*Angela Basset isn't no Halle Berry,*" said Yellow Dress acidly.

"*You're right she acts better. You brought up Angela not me.*"

"*No she don't act better! Do Angela got an Oscar?*"

"*Nope and she didn't have to make her pussy feel good to get one either.*"

"*Whatever, the Ho isn't no bigger than the Tina Turner role she played.*"

"*Listen, damn it…*"

"Hey hey hey," said George, looking silly in a tight gray suit that showed off the shape of his nuts and dick. It made my stomach turn. He hugged both the flaming hot women, smelling like clouds of White Diamonds and moth balls.

"Crank up the music," he said drunkenly. "Turn on some James Brown. Otis is a boring muthafucker. I don't like docks sitting or bays goddamn it!" The party roared back to life.

I looked at Mama harshly. She looked at me.

"Drop it girl! We all have pasts. I am not perfect. I did what I had to do. I know I fucked up. Call the police if you're sick in the head. You're trying to blame me because you let men rape you! You were a mistake! I hate you. In fact you don't even need to be raising your son! I'm calling the man so I can get custody." She leaned up to me and kissed my lips. I looked down, her nipples hardened. I could smell her pussy in the air. She was wet for me, yearning me, wanting me. Her breath came in short gasps. I closed my eyes and tried to will myself out of the room and wound up telling myself what I won't do.

I handed Mama her drink. I sipped mine, tears falling down my face. I couldn't compete with her. I didn't know what to do. How do you stand up to your Mama? Who made you? Molded you? Destroyed you? This family had secrets that would never get out and I was too afraid to do anything about it. But my job was to protect my son. Give him the protection I never had as a child. I was never secure.

She killed her drink, smacking her lips. "Be a good little bitch and put the glass in the sink. And when the party is over be back here so you can massage Mama to sleep. I bet you still got some good pussy *don't* you. Mmmm hmmm." Her tongue darted in and out of her mouth like a slithering snake. "*Don't* act like you don't want it, bitch! I made you. You were put here to be my slave. Admit it. I own you. I possess you. You can't even fuck anyone else without thinking about Mama. Can you? Huh? I don't have emotions. They were killed when Mama let the white man rape me and make a baby. Those crackers stole my baby and told me it died. But in my heart I knew it was a lie! Mmm hmmm. Yup. My Mama sold me to those crackers. Yes, sir. She was afraid of losing her six penance. My Daddy was a punk. He let those people hurt us. He ran away first chance he got. Left a letter. That said, 'Fend for yourself, I got my own life.' Then I had to clean their houses and cook their food. Think she helped me? Nah. She was a scary bitch! I wasn't protected, so why should I protect you?"

I hurt for her. I knew this was true had to be. When Mama was telling the truth she gave it to you raw and uncut. She looked you in the face. She had a rough life. But I had to pay for it. I hugged her and quickly pulled back. I felt like water and she was electricity. Shocking. "Mama. I can't do this. I got to go."

Hurting deeply, I dumped the drink on her and I got in my truck, never to see her again. I actually smiled all the way to my apartment. When I got there I pulled out my pad and wrote Red a note.

*What's up! I want to be in your world because I really feel God put us together. I'm writing in text form, the way I do when we text with cell phones, because its easier to say what I have to say and its quicker to write. I have tried nothing like this before but I want to be happy so I'm willing to do this for the first time in my life to be in a relationship with someone I care about, which is YOU....*

Now I contemplated taking her back. Yes, she lied. But we *all* lie sometimes. Small lies and big lies. How were they any different? A small lie could break up a happy marriage. They have little minds of their own. Depending how you looked at it. Yes, we got in a huge fight. I still couldn't believe we fought like cats and dogs. People in love didn't fight or hit each other. When you had to hit your lover it was over. The number one hit on the charts fell to number two. It didn't matter if it was gold or platinum. A hit was a hit and once it lost its luster you chopped it up to the game. Red and I were human *before* we were lesbians. I couldn't believe she would go through those lengths to have me back in her life. I had to believe her intentions were good. But when was lying attached to good intentions? I sealed the letter with a kiss. I stood up, put it in an envelope and walked into the kitchen. I grabbed my car keys, locked my front door and walked to my truck.

When I got to Red's house forty minutes later she opened the door and she looked as fine as ever, thus a little sad. "Yes. Who is it…?"

When she saw it was me she became animated, grabbed me and turned in a circle.

"Baby! You're here! Come in, baby…welcome home! I have been trying to call you for weeks! I tried calling you tonight! Something bad happened."

The blood leaving my face with a depressing moan, I thought about my son! MY SON!

"Where is my son?" I shut down. Fell to my knees. Please don't tell me my son…

"Mama!" I froze. I stopped crying, sucking in air. "When did you get back? I missed you, Mama. Red told me her son is my brother. She told us yesterday over cake and ice cream. We actually have the same Daddy, can you believe it?"

I slowly looked up at Red. She extended her hand. "Our family is whole."

I took it, handing her the note. "Read it later."

She kissed my lips. "Ok but seriously haven't you heard?"

"Heard…what?"

"Your mother…it's about…"

I flashed with anger. "What did she do this time?"

"She died tonight."

I just stared at her, immediately looking at my son. He looked like he could care less. He grabbed his brother's hand and they went to play the Playstation 3 game console.

I looked at Red.

"How did she die?"

"I don't know. People are saying she…dropped dead at her birthday party."

Crushed and devastatingly hurt, I hugged Red, clinging to her. It hurt to know this. To find this out seemed a dream.

Red cried with me, kissing my face, wiping away my tears; whispering sweet nothings to me…

It hurt that my Mama was dead. Part of me allowed myself to mourn. I burst open and sobbed so hard I cracked open. Mama was Mama. She wasn't perfect.

Something had to have happened to her in her life that made her hurt me.

She was acting out. She told me the story of her life. Our last moments were spent talking about her bitter and painful past.

I would never find out because.

I poisoned her Rum and Coke when Janis the Pearl turned to dig in her purse. I had blended rat poison and weed killer together at my apartment and concocted a nice little mix.

I then poured some in a small empty test tube from my son's science game.

The bitch would never hurt me again. I had to protect me. And overall. I had to protect my son. Plus she killed his father.

No way in hell she could ever get away with that. She got away for years. I would see to it she was buried in an expensive casket and given the proper burial. Sweet dreams.

Mother.

# Freaky Deaky

"Goddamn it! *Don't* drop my shelf!" I told the short, stocky white boy who worked for Hermit's Furniture store. "I paid a thousand dollars for that case. I need my case. Damn it watch my goddamn walls!" He rolled his eyes, mumbling and I rolled mine, bitching. "I don't care about you huffin' and puffin' like you're a Backwood cigar. *Listen,* man. Set it over there by the living room sofa! What? I paid for the assembly and the delivery, and you're going to give me $75 worth of delivery service cracker boy now hop to it!"

Jesus! Good customer service was hard to come by these days, especially when you're black and a woman. And add the third strike for being a black woman.

He looked at me like he wanted to fight. "Ma'am, it doesn't look right over by your sofa."

*The nerve of this creepy asshole!* "Do you pay my bills?" I spat nastily. Ugly with Coke-bottle glasses, the kind that made his eyes look like marbles, he left my shelf alone, wiping off his finger prints with a rag. And he had some big ass fingers. "Well, who would want to?"

I tucked my chin back. "Don't get smart, do you pay my bills?"

"No, Lady!"

My hands rose to my hips the same time my brows rose.

"Watch your tone of voice in my house…"

"I'm grown," he responded. What man argued with a woman?

I started shooting from the hip. "Are you *fucking* me?"

He gave me the once over, smacked his gum, rolled his beady eyes, sashayed over to his power drill by the end table and said, "I don't do fish," more sassily than Halle Berry in *Cat Woman.*

"Well *don't* tell me what looks good in my house. As a matter of fact get out, your services are terminated, thanks for bringing my shelf."

"What about my tip?"

I snatched up my huge purse, took out my wallet, turned my back to him so he couldn't see me shuffling through my cash, I was funny about my money, and when I was done scribbling with my pen I turned, smiled, walked up to him and handed him a note. He read it out loud. "Tip for the day, I need to get some Oxy pads to terminate the oily pimples all over my face. *What* is this? I said a tip, *not* a tip."

"Ok, you can leave now." I was pushing him out the door, and his body odor wasn't making things civil, either. "You sound Chinese, *same thang, same thang*," I went on, trying to sound Asian. "…Repeating the same things over and over, I asked for a *tip*, not a tip, confusing me, guy. Have a nice day!" I gave him a huge shove and slammed the door behind him. He called me a "Bitch," and left after cursing through my door for about thirty seconds.

Anyways, I didn't feel up to all that today. White people were crazy anyways. Yea, baby. My shelf looked magnificent. The same way it looked when I saw it at Hermit's Furniture Store a little after the orgy I had at church. I went into my room, opened my bottom drawer, pushed my panties to the side and took out the Golden Mask. Open Says Me. Images flashed in my mind. From a few weeks ago.

I had to lean against the wall because the power of the memories took my breath away, of when I defiled God's House with my own sick, selfish pleasures. That morning my flesh was so weak I couldn't think straight. When I sashayed down the hall of my church, my heels clickety-clacked with sounding echoes towards the double doors that led to paradise. Coming face to face with Big Daddy Good Dick, or whatever his name was. I was smiling, my body coming alive. I was to get Dicked Down Froggy Style.

I remembered being breathless, so hot and bothered I didn't want to be left alone. I could still feel the pleasure that overcame me when I entered lustful terrains, even though, back then, I thought I was dying of Cancer, only to find out, after the orgy, that I really didn't have a sickness.I kissed the mask, went back into the living room, opened the shelf, and set the mask inside it. After closing the glass door and locking it, I took a few steps back, lighting a Black and Mild cigar, puffing smoke through my nostrils, bursting from my sensual lips and just admired how it sparkled. I would cherish this mask for the rest of my life.

No one was allowed to touch it.

What did *Rollingstone* magazine know about journalism? I was reading the latest issue I just got in the mail, hoping Janet Jackson's ultra-sexy ass would be on the cover. Instead I had to settle for Led Fucking Zeppelin. Led Zeppelin? Oh, please! Janet did have an album coming out on September 26, 2006 called 20 Years Old, which was now being marketed as 20 Y.O. I had just gotten home from B.E.T's 106 and Park this morning. I was an unnoticeable part of the so-called "Livest Audience in the World" propaganda that I had heard about for so long. I knew three year olds who were graciously more audible and raunchy. I hated B.E.T. anyways. Same ole commercials, same movies old movies at that. Shit you only owned on VHS shit you never even contemplated getting on DVD. Same award shows, really who wanted to see Mo'Nique do the Beyonce booty dance fifty times a fucking week? Seriously, B.E.T. was once a step forward for black people. Now they market Justin Timberlake more than Janet Jackson. A step back.

B.E.T's 106 and Park was definitely *not* as good as the Free and AJ Era, two enormously enigmatic and energetic VJ's B.E.T seriously needed to bring back to hype the fledgling music video countdown show. I was jet-lagged, tired, and my body felt like it was beat up. I got some good dick while in New York. New York Dick. It was something extraordinary giving up some Down South Pussy in the City that Never Slept. Just constant partying, drinking, weed-smoking and a feel-good atmosphere not seen in Miami. I wanted to go to the raves, pop ecstasy pills and twirl some glowing lights all up in my face. But I was too scared to do that shit. I saw a documentary that showed more youngsters winding up statistics attending those dangerous raves and I decided against it.

I needed to clean up my house. I had bills to pay. I was already behind on my light bill. And I still owed another $40 on my water bill. I wished FP&L supplied my electricity because Homestead Lights were rip-offs. They fucked you out of your money. Seriously. I worked at the Precision Response Corporation, known as PRC on the Direct TV account. I made nine bucks an hour. Good money, but my bills ate my good money to hell. I had to return to work later on today. It was hell getting three days off so I could go to New York. I was still marveling at the Golden Masks Orgy I attended in the back of my church.

I checked my phone messages. The box was full. This many people hadn't called me in years. I wondered why. And it wasn't because Fidel Castro might be dead. The shit was all over the news. Maybe now Cubans could stay their funky asses in Cuba! Sliding out of my Nautica jacket (even though Nautica was so defunct from the fashion scene) and kicking off my G-Unit sneakers, I let my hair down from the loose bun and flopped on my bed. I missed home. I was hot in this jean outfit. So I stripped down to my panties and matching bra. There, I felt better. I pressed "play" on the machine and just let her rip.

Angela. *Girl I saw you on TV! You go bitch! I can't believe you met Janet!!*

Jake. *Oh my God! Girl, you represented for Miami! And Janet was ravishing!*

Bob. *You lucky bitch! You got to hug the sexiest bitch on earth!*

Paul. *Your Grandma told me you were on TV with Janet Jackson. I didn't believe her. And when I seen you in the crowd hugging Janet oh my God! I pissed in my pants. You better have gotten my autograph! Everybody in the Hood is praising you. You're a star, Melissa!*

Sitting up I pressed "stop" on the machine. I'd had enough. I turned off the ringer on my phone. I didn't want to be bothered.

I was still in a daze. Meeting Miss Jackson. How many bitches from the 'hood could say they shook hands and met Janet Jackson? I was the first and only one. I sent in my request to attend online when I heard Janet was going to be on 106 & Park Friday, July 31st. I think it was July 10th I had found out. I had gone online at Miami Dade Community College Homestead Campus and sent in the request. Being from Florida City, a ghetto-within-a-ghetto, I never thought I'd be selected, especially with Michael Jackson's little sister coming through.

How wrong was I? I saw Janet Jackson in the flesh! Oh my God! Being a twenty-three year old mother of one, even though DCF recently took my child because my Baby Daddy lied on me and said I rarely fed my five year old son, you would think my teenage fascination with Hollywood people would apishly halt. And it did for the most part. When I was a teenage girl I had LL Cool J on my wall, and every other rapper of the moment. My girl Latonia used to masturbate to his posters. I haven't spoken to her in ages.

I met Ludacris on South Beach last year. I was happy but not excited. I met a certain slain rapper when I was a little girl when I won a contest at my elementary school, West Homestead Elementary. I never knew I'd meet him, and when I heard about the short story essay I had to write detailing who I wanted to meet and why I never knew the actual first prize would be to meet who you wrote about. Hey, I was from the Hood, the ghetto. Ghettos didn't get any love.

But when the future controversial, slain rapper, I'll leave nameless, walked into my classroom, without a camera crew and goons surrounding him, nor the media, they didn't have the slightest clue, I died! All my friends fell over in excitement, running up to him, hugging him, I died again! I was like OH MY GOD! He instantly knew who I was. My ecstatic teacher, Miss Sharps, who had a wet pussy just goo-goo eyeing him, pointed at me.

"That's Melissa Jackson right there," she said excitedly, pulling out her mirror, fixing her hair and putting on a thick coat of lipstick, ripping the bottom of her dress off so it could be shorter.

When he smiled I knew I'd be strictly dickley for the rest of my life. Even though I wasn't having sex nor thinking about it. I was only about five years old.

With the grace of a ballet dancer, he walked up to me, gave me a hug, gave me his latest CD and said, "How about posing for a picture with me. I read your essay. Very talented."

I didn't get excited. I was just happy that a star was in the Hood. My classroom door was locked but when the school heard the future slain rapper was there you suddenly heard a roar outside the door, kids kicking and screaming his name. Teachers were running from other classrooms, trying to get inside. I felt lucky.

When my teacher took our picture, and one with the class, the superstar rapper kissed my cheek and slipped out the back door in full Thug apparel, into an awaiting SUV, and disappeared as if he was never there.

I didn't get excited.

But when Janet Jackson shook my hand at 106 & Park and gave me a hug, I hyperventilated, clad in my sexy tight black pants and plain T-shirt bearing her face. I lost it. I cried so hard this black girl next to me had to hug me to calm me down.

"She touched me! She touched me!" I chanted, shaking like I was the Queen of Tremors.

I watched excitedly, hanging onto her every word. I loved the ripped jeans, the colorful high heeled boots, the slanted red hat, the huge hoop earrings. She was so stunningly gorgeous, nowhere on her was a trace of the 60 extra pounds she'd shed over the last few months, when she was the butt of a thousand jokes.

Those same people were now biting dust. Janet Jackson was back.

After admiring her and drooling for the next hour and a half, she signed my T-shirt and new promo poster handed out to me when I got there. I would cherish it. I also told her I entered her Design My CD cover contest. She only smiled.

But before I was to go through all that with Janet, on the previous Thursday, I flew to New York via my grandmother, who knew how much I looked like, loved and admired Janet. When I told her I was selected to attend the live taping she told everybody. Grandma paid for me to go, my hotel for two nights, my plane ticket round trip and my food. She gave me 400 dollars.

"Go rep us Miami Bitches," she said, no teeth in her mouth, bald head (because she just beat cancer). She was just the most humorous, uplifting soul you'd meet. I did just that. Represented.

I was still on a dick high. I got my first taste of New York dick on the plane. I met a handsome man with the charisma of Billy Dee Williams. He said he was from New York. He sat by me. I wore a long dress and some red pumps, my hair long and real. No weave going on here.

I was trying to ignore him but he pulled out one of the magazines from the back of the seat and was like, "Doesn't Bill Gates looks ugly?"

And I smiled, saying, "His money isn't ugly."

"And neither are you. Sup, Ma. You're traveling alone?"

I didn't appreciate him trying to get all in my business. In fact it pissed me off. "Yea, *why?*" He gave me a long, lingering look. I felt like the Dow Jones on Wall Street. "Because I think you look good."

*Get out my face, I am not feeling you!* "So do you, pimp." Why did I just lie?

He saw the lust in my eyes. "What that pussy smelling like?"

Time to pull his card. "Roses."

"Shit, can I see?"

"You can smell."

I took his hand and put it between my legs, looking around making sure no one noticed. I took out my huge blanket and covered the lower half of our bodies. He slow fucked me with those hairy, thick fingers. I grinded on them.

"Taste my pussy..."

He put his fingers in his mouth, closing his eyes, moaning softly. Hmmm. Good.

"I know," I told him.

"Sup with tasting this fat dick?"

I licked my lips, but when he unzipped his pants and I saw Pee Wee Herman waving at me I was like, "I'm straight."

"Sup, Ma?"

I was deeply offended. "I don't do little dicked men. Sorry."

He huffed and puffed and changed seats.

Oh, well. Was I supposed to be offended?Nah. Didn't think so. Fuck you, too! Little dick man.

Then I got a nice surprise. I sucked this Juelz Santana-looking Niggah off in the small bathroom on the plane. His name was Naygee. He was sitting in front of me, gave me the eye from the Miami International Airport, to the plane and when we got 40,000 feet in the air I started really eyeing him, loving what I saw. I loved men. Men were my weakness.

When we were flying over Georgia, he turned and asked me could he use my phone because his phone died and his sister, who was knocked out sleep next to him, wouldn't come off hers. I said sure. He called his phone from my phone; I didn't know it until I got a text message from a number I had never seen before. I read it.

*Meet me in the trap. It's going down. The Niggah in front of you.*

I smiled. Homeboy was 6 feet tall and just handsome.

I went to the bathroom first. The plane wasn't full and almost everyone was sleeping. It was after 11 PM that night. When I got there I waited, debating. I didn't know him but my pussy *wanted* to get to know him. Seconds later the door opened and he came inside, not smiling, closed and locked the door, unzipped his pants, pulled out that huge Spanish dick, and went up in my mouth. I loved his scent, his taste. I ran my hands through his pubic hairs, sucking on them, then putting his dick back in my mouth.

"Help me get that nut, Ma. Swallow my shit, bitch."

He fucked my mouth real good.

"That's my wife out there, not my sister," he said, watching me play around with his dick, his nuts swinging back and forth. He looked so good. I was so gone. "Play with that pussy, leave your panties on, just rub that pussy and let me smell it tramping in the air."

I did what he said. After all, this was his Freaky Deaky Show.

The bathroom was small and compact, but I was so flexible I got on my knees, crawled all the way up to him and deep throated his dick, smelling my pussy mixed with his nuts and dick and cologne in the air, which brought the freak out of me. I was holding my breath half of the time so the length and thickness of his penis wouldn't make me gag or wanna vomit. He then sat on the toilet and pumped my wetness until he came down my throat. He was lost in my rhythm. He looked at me like he loved me. Real Thug here. Spanish Fly. With some black in his blood stream. His Nextel phone rang. Playing the "Getting Some Head" ring tone. How fittingly coy. I put his dick back in my mouth, surprised it stayed hard. Most men dicks went limp, but his stayed rock hard. He had a pretty penis. He answered the phone.

I slurped really loud, the saliva from my mouth and the force of my jaws creating a very noisy tune.

He smiled.

"Sup playboy. I'm getting my dick sucked by Freaky Deaky."

"Damn let me hear," said Playboy through the phone.

He put the phone down to my lips and the head of his dick. I gave them the audible, smiling like the bitch I was at heart.

"*Oooh*, yea! She sounds like a *bad* bitch."

"Wanna video of it?"

"Hell, yea. And send it to me."

He decided against it. "Nah. Go get your own bitch." And he hung up.

"Suck that dick, Freaky Deaky. Suck it like you want it...want Daddy to take dis dick out your mouth?"

"No, Daddy Freaky Deaky," I said, sucking on it a little bit better than I had earlier. I gave him pleasure in spurts. Rule number one in Sucking Dick 101, never do your best skills first. Issue the skills out.

"Pull dem titties out and tit fuck this dick."

I was amazed. At his frankness. I never titty fucked a man before. Shit, what pleasure was I going to get out of it? Suddenly I was selfish; I didn't want to do this weird shit! There was a knock on the door.

"I'm taking a shit," he said aloud, and the person went away, mumbling. His eyes sparkled, the light from the bathroom soft and sweet. He leaned forward and took my right nipple into his mouth, suckling on it hard and thuggish. I loved it. I held his head, running my tongue over his low-fade with the green Tupac-like rag tied in a knot around it. His earrings glittered. Leaning back he took both my tits, spit on his dick, and used my tits to smooth saliva all over it. He long stroked the tits. I positioned myself where the head of his dick went in my mouth when he slid my titties down on his dick. He loved it. He said, "Damn, Ma. Be my bitch. I'ma leave my wife to have a Freaky Deaky bitch like you."

Ignoring him. I played with his balls, sticking my finger deep in my ass, finger banging myself for a few minutes, enjoying the feeling. My pussy was dripping. I then pulled my finger out, putting it under his nose, he took a whiff and was in heaven, smiling, throwing them hips at such a fast pace. Those nuts bounced, you hear me? Feeling nasty, I stuck my finger in his mouth and he sucked my asshole right on down his throat.

"Are you Freaky Deaky?" I asked him, putting my hands up his shirt and fumbling with his chest. I squeezed his chest like he squeezed my tits, watching his nuts dance.

"I'm Freaky Deaky," he responded breathlessly, his second nut creeping on the come up.

"Take off your shirt. I'm tired of crack head DMX looking me in the face." Unhesitant, he took the shirt off.

"Now bang my tits, Niggah."

He used my titties to begin his crusade. Seconds later he moaned softly, being discreet, my tits jiggling all over the place and beautiful thick cum spurted all over them. His orgasm seemed endless. He shook and trembled, the silkiness of his pleasurable moans set me on fire with enough flames to suffocate Puff the Magic Dragon and evaporate his sea.

When it was over he leaned over and licked up his nut. He swallowed it, and then tongue kissed me. I loved the way he kissed. "Freaky Deaky Session is over," I told him.

Then he stood up, zipped up his huge baggy jeans with the huge cowboy glittering belt, fixed his green rag on his head, put on his shirt and he went back out to plane and sat by his wife, totally ignoring me. I sat behind him and played with my pussy, hiding my lower body under my blanket. Put on my earphones and watched the Nutty Professor, and melted into an orgasm. I got a text message.

*What happened in the bathroom*
*stays in the bathroom.*
*Erase my number when you read this message.*

Bitch, I thought, staring at this creep from behind. I never saved your phone number to begin with.

When the plane was flying over Virginia I got another text message.

*Meet me in the trap. I want some more head.*

Smiling to myself, I thought.
*Freaky Deaky Sessions starts again!*

# Black Paintings

When I got to New York I put my Freaky Deaky ego on the back burner. I was ecstatic about being there. This was a place I said I would never go. When I went to Times Square I took some pictures of the buildings and passing cars. I went to the Statue of Liberty. It was so beautiful. Why couldn't Miami have something this breathtaking, besides the huge hand statue dedicated to the Holocaust victims down the street from South Beach? I asked a few strangers to take my one-time use Kodak camera and take some solo snap shots of me in my Apple Bottom outfit. My ass was big. Men drooled at the booty. They couldn't touch the booty. If they had a little dick and was fruity no can touch the booty. Period. Fuck you if you didn't like it. I was a real bitch and real bitches did real things.

I was all about the name brand. With my Sony CD Walkman in my pouch with my wallet, and my ear phones pumping Case, R&B singer, into my ears, I was definitely into the groove like Madonna minus the "Hung Up" bathing suit.

In contrast to Miami, New York was just too much. Too many goddamn people. Too many men. Too many cars. Too much cursing. There were so many people smoking I thought I was in the middle of the California fires. There were fine, sexy men everywhere I looked.

I like. I like.

While in Downtown Manhattan, I met a man who looked just like "ER" actor Mekhi Phiefer. I wanted to suck his dick through a straw. A girl could dream, damn it. He had ocean-green eyes, caramel-kissed skin that glistened from the sun radiating on the sweat trickling all over his sculpted body, deep waves soaking under a black do rag, bling bling out the ass, a bunch of dope in huge pockets stitched on low-hanging baggy jeans showing off a silk-clad ass that had my pussy feeling slutty like Britney Spears, wanting to come off that Boom Boom with the Ying Yang Twins.

I was at the store, I forget the name of it, buying some shoes and he came up behind me, pressing his penis on my ass. *What the hell is going on? Why is this motherfucker all up on me like free concert tickets?* He was cocky and confident. He made it seem like a natural thing.

I was pissed for one. I paused, held my breath, my attitude surfacing in record time and dug my nails in the dress. I turned to face him. I said, "Get your dick off…" When I saw him, a sexy thing, I was like, "*Damn*, baby, sup with you?"

"I knew you'd change your mind when you took a look at this."

*Arrogant New Yorkers here we come.* I tucked my chin back playfully. "You're arrogant."

He licked his lips. "Naw, Ma. Confident."

I felt tremors in my legs. *I'll take Put his Dick in my Mouth for $600, Alex!* "I see."

We were the same height. Five feet eleven inches. He took my bejeweled-with-flea-market-gold-hand and kissed it, making my panties wet and my nipples hard. "I'm Melvin. From the Bronx."

*I'm Melvin from the Bronx,* I mocked happily. His nicely long nipples poked against his wife beater. My mouth watered. Damn!

"I'm…I'm…Melissa. From Florida City." His eyes sparkled. "You're a Down South gal." He cupped my hand.

I smiled sheepishly. "Yep."

My eyes dropped to the escalating lump in his pants. Damn, getting bigger by the second. If this was Wallstreet everyone would be rich! Why my mouth suddenly watered beats me. Felt like I was talking with a whole bunch of spit in my mouth. I looked at the expensive gold rope chain around his thick neck, a scorpion medallion glittered. Hung just above his belly button. He had "Mel's Hell" tattooed on his neck. And he had a huge red and black dragon tattooed on either arm. We couldn't stop staring at each other.

Freaky.

"You're a sexy woman."

"Thanks."

"Where's Florida City?" he asked and I pat his shoulder, looking him over.

"In Florida."

"Well, duh! You buggin'!" he joked, smiling. "I mean what *part* of Florida?"

"Miami. The southwest region."

He liked his lips. "Interesting."

*Can you lick my twat like that?* "I see."

"I love your twang. I can damn sure hear it in your smoky voice."

"Yea. That's what my man back home says." I didn't have a man. I always told Niggahs that. They seemed to get locked nuts when I said it.

He got competitive. Most New Yorkers were that way. "So you got a man?"

"That I think I'm g'on love forever? Um, yea."

He took both my hands, pressing his hard dick against my pussy, bringing my hands back to grip his ass while he played around with my hair. I dropped the dress on the floor. Some white woman sneered at me, whisking around the rack, picking up the dress. She put it back on the hanger and hanging it on the clothing rack with the other dresses. She had an attitude. I ignored her.

I was on fire. He kissed my forehead. "Does he treat you the way you need to be treated? Cook for you, cut your toe nails, caters to you?"

The woman stood on the side of me, her hands on her hips. I watched her from my peripheral vision.

"He's all right."

"Ma'am," said the store employee. We ignored her and didn't break eye contact. But home girl got bold. "Ma'am! I am talking to you."

Not letting my new flame go, I happily looked at her. I wouldn't let her break my funk.

"Yes?" It was getting cold in here.

My Dude lowered his head, suppressing a laugh.

"You can't drop our expensive clothing on the floor."

"I got arthritis. My fingers locked up and I dropped it."

He started laughing, chocking on his saliva. I chuckled, too. White people were so uptight.

"That's before or after you and your fling here bumped pelvises in the aisle around little children?"

My mouth falling open I turned into her face and said, "For one bitch you watch your goddamned tone! I'm not these New York bitches! I'ma Miami bitch and I'll fuck you up with my razor under my tongue, Ho! And I don't see any kids around here."

"Whatever, listen I'm gonna call security—"

"Call Ghostbusters too, bitch, I don't care."

"*Listen,* you Flee Market Outfit wearing tramp…"

I stunned and excited shoppers when I, without warning, snatched the bitch by her airbrushed-looking hair and she fell on her face. Homeboy took me by the arm when I tried to dig my heel into her ear.

"Nah, Ma. I got this."

Helping the shockingly disgruntled bitch off the floor, he pulled three hundred dollars from his wallet and handed it to the woman. "That should pay for the dress. Keep the change. Gift wrap it, please."

Taking the money, the white lady with "Bertha" on her tag said, "I will do. And when you want a real woman, drop this Miami Trash," and she and her blonde hair spun on her heel and waltzed to the register with the dress.

I was burning up. "Lemme whip that Ho's ass."

He was trying to hold me. "Ma. Calm down. I definitely like your fire."

I rolled my eyes. "Whatever." He held me again, tightly, kissing my lips. "I'm not your Mama. Stop calling me that."

"Let's cut to it, Ma. When can a Niggah get the pussy?"

*What's with the Ma bullshit?* "Damn, and he's direct,"

"Life is too short to fuck around."

"No, some dick is too short to fuck around. You shoulda been on the plane with me."

We laughed easily. The chemistry building in us was breathtaking. I felt like a magnet. I was naturally drawn to him.

"So can we get out of here?" he asked, matter-of-factly.

"You live in the Bronx, right?" I was a little scared, I didn't know if he was a rapist, had AIDS or was a good boy next door type of man. I'd soon find out.

"I'm from the Bronx. I live here in Manhattan." I loved the way he talked, his arrogance, his confidence was refreshing. He had a lot of class, rarely seen in a thug Niggah. He had a very deep voice, like Busta Rhymes. I liked that. He looked me deep in the eyes, never wavering. I felt like the only woman in the store.

"Cool. Well, I don't just give up the pussy when I first meet somebody and I'm going back to Miami tomorrow. I'm only here to attend 106 and Park so I could see Janet."

He smiled. "Cool, that's straight. How about I buy you that dress you're holding, and wine and dine you, and make sure you get to your Janet thing. Would that be cool?"

"Yea. That's straight, gangster. But remember, you ain't getting no pussy."

"I promise to behave."

Walking towards the unprofessional Bertha, who was explaining the situation to her co-workers, who were all white, I paused in front of her when she was about to put the money in the register. She grimaced and I stared her down, seething. I wanted to beat her ass. Goddamn it. Whoop her ass, MELISSA! NOW! WHOOP HER MOTHERFUCKING ASS! YOU'RE A DADE COUNTY BITCH!

Exploding, I snatched his money out of her hand, spitting at her. It hit her dead in the face. I slapped her so hard store cameras caught visuals of her falling on her elite circle of friends.

"You aren't getting me or his business. He's nice. I'm *not*, Ho!" And we left the store in silence.

"Damn, you Miami Girls are the shit," he said, taking his money back.

"Nah, we're gentle creatures. Until you piss us off," I went on, snatching the money. He gave it to the whore. It's mine now. You can't reclaim money. Not with me you wouldn't!

Hugging me he led me up the crowded block, making small talk. I shoved the money in my bra. I know it was a little played out to put money in your cleavage but hell I didn't feel like opening my purse.

He wined and dined me at four o'clock in the evening. I felt special. He drove me all over New York in a Lincoln Navigator, all paid for, with the spinning Spreewell rims. He had a killer booming system. He smoked his "Hydro (weed)" with the windows down to spare me. I used to smoke weed. But I haven't touched the shit in ages. He bought me Letoya Lucket's new CD. "Torn" was one song I wouldn't be listening to because I was tired of it. Home girl definitely was positioned to give Beyonce's scream-singing ass a run for her money because "Déjà Poo" wasn't hitting on shit.

When I got to his apartment, I was surprised to find it very spacious and clean. It looked more like a Bachelor Pad with all the technology to go with it— PS2, stereo with DJ speakers, Ella Fitzgerald and Fabulous on his wall. Being courteous, he poured me some Dom in a skinny flute glass shaped like a dick. How nasty! I loved it! I had never had Dom Perignon. He put on Letoya Luckett. We listened with open minds and very horny souls. Her CD was marvelously crafted, liked it a lot. But I liked my prize catch better.

Despite my better judgment I wanted him so bad. But I didn't wanna give him the impression that Miami Girls were easy. Easy to piss off but not easy to bed like sheets clinging to a mattress. Buy them a dress and drive them around like your name was Miss Daisy and viola! Instant Pussy Access.

Ain't happening. He showed me around his place. Definitely a reflection of him. He loved to run his goddamn mouth, that was for sure. I wanted to put my pussy on his lips and tell him to shut the fuck up and sniff. He lived on the tenth floor. I stood out on the balcony and looked at Manhattan. Gorgeous. The sounds of the horns blowing relaxed me, but my booty hole was tingling something fierce. The people talking were mind boggling. The air blowing and the tree branches rustling created tranquility in my head. Peace.

"Melissa." I closed my eyes at the sensual sound of his heavily smoky masculine voice. Going back into the apartment I froze when I seen him lying on his couch, naked, with whipped cream spread all over his dick and hips. His nipples were mouth watering. His feet were gorgeous. He looked like a Tyson Beckford pin-up. There was some strawberry cheesecake on the low table. Every blind and curtain was closed, keeping out the rest of the fading sunlight; and a few candles were lit. Soft jazz played. I thought it was Letoya. Winston Marsalis, I knew his material. I was nailed to the floor.

"Sup baby."

Black paintings were all around him. "Hi." I couldn't speak. I couldn't find the words. I walked over to him and towered over him, looking into his beautiful eyes, invitingly gorgeous eyes that dared me.

"No pussy, my Niggah. I don't know you like that."

He played around with his nipple. Smiling. "Get to know me like that." He made his dick jumped and I quivered.

I was getting weaker by the second. "No."

"Suck the whip cream off my dick."

"Hell, yea…I meant, no, hell no, Niggah."

"Come on, baby. Hold out your tongue."

I did. Wondering what he was up to. He rubbed his finger on his asshole, took some pre-cum from the tip of his dick and some whip cream and he stood up, pulling out my left titty and rubbed it all over my nipple. He lay back down.

He said easily, "Suck it off your nipple, baby. Damn get freaky for me."

I cupped my breast, pulling it up to my lips. I ran my tongue all over his essence and the whip cream, swallowing what exploded inside me once it touched my throat.

"Taste good, doesn't it?" he asked, looking boyishly handsome. I was on fire for real.

"Yea. But no pussy." Reaching out, taking one of my legs, he pulled me to him, put his face under my dress and he stuck his tongue deep in my wet pussy, not moving his head, just the tongue, which was long and thick. Goddamn! I tried to force myself into a state of unwanted bliss, actually trying to go numb but I couldn't. He squeezed my ass cheeks, a little painfully, and used those thick lips to torture my clitoris, which awakened with an aching it had never experienced and sent shivers up and down my spine. He would do this for a long ass time. I stood there letting him rock the boat and work the middle with his experienced tongue like I was slow dancing with an invisible man. I had to hold the arm of the chair to keep balance. Damn he was hungry.

"Come on, Ma…" He kissed my pussy and lay his head back on the cushioned arm of his black leather sofa, like he hadn't even moved.

I went crazy. I took off my dress, revealing a birthday suit for his ass. I was top notch, a dime who was top of the line with a big ass booty, good pussy and deep throat skills to pay the bills. Let's show this Bronx Bred Niggah some new shit.

I took the small candle from the table and told him to close his eyes. "Oh, I finally got you, huh, baby?" he said.

"Shut up. Close your eyes," I suggested.

He did so. I got on my knees and slowly took his whip-cream-clad-dick into my mouth, sucking on it slowly, locking my jaws, using my tongue expertly.

"*Goooodddaaammmnnn!*" was all the poor boy could say.

"I am home sick," I told him, sucking on his nuts, running my tongue across gorgeous-smelling pubic hair and skin. "I'm gonna suck Florida City out the head of your dick, spread it all over your shaft and nuts so it'll feel like I'm at home."

"Goddamn, bitch," he said admiringly, his dick jumping in my mouth. Home boy was about to lose control.

I sucked it good, swallowing the cream, playing with his balls, working the cream into his skin. He smelled good, tasted good. The air smelled like strawberries. Running my fingers over my pussy I wrote my name with my juices on his forehead. M-E-L-I-S-S-A. Spelling it out soundly as I did so. Taking the candle I stood his ten inch dick straight up and wiped hot candle wax along the shaft. He bit his lips, arching his back, his huge nuts dangling and he was like, "Oooh my God that feel so good, where in the hell did you learn that trick?"

I worked the head of his dick, letting the wax harden on the shaft. I used a delicate finger to wipe hot wax on his nuts while I punished the head with my hot mouth and tongue. He rose with my head, veins popping all over his dick from out of nowhere. He moaned so elegantly, turned me on. Oh Baby. Fuck that dick. Feels so Good. You're the best. I never had wax on my dick. I love you Miami Women. Marry me. Yea. Rub some wax on my asshole. Yea, baby. Hot! I feel good. I was swallowing whip cream, pouring the rest of my warm Dom Perignon wine on him, fucking up his white rug, tasting his sweat, watching my titties bounce. I played with my pussy. Careful not to bring myself to orgasm. I moaned with him: Yea Baby you got some Good dick! Imagine this is my pussy on the head of your dick. Take it, Niggah. And you call yourself a man?

Trapped in La La Land his nuts jerked, his thighs locked, his toes bent and I felt his dick contract, then he suddenly burst with cum, spurted straight up in the air, all over his nipples, chest and abs and as quickly as I could I put his dick in my mouth, the entire dick and swallowed the nut and the hardened wax all in one gulp. He moaned out my name, dug his fingernails into the chair, fucking my mouth slowly, tenderly, twirling his hips, tears escaping his eyes. He opened them. He had to get a visual. Cum everywhere.

"*You're* Freaky Deaky, baby?" I asked him, challenging him. His manhood was compromised. He got dark.

"You fucking right, bitch!"

"Are you Freaky Deaky?"

"*I'm Freaky Deaky!*" His voice filled the apartment.

"Ok, watch this. You gonna do what I say?"

He was like a determined college student wanting to get the grade. "YES BITCH!"

"Then shut up while I do this."

I sucked his dick again, slurping my spit off his shaft, playing with the head with my tongue, stronger, smoother, more forcibly. He jerked, grabbed my hair in closed fists and fucked my mouth. I squeezed his inner thighs, bringing him pain while bringing the head of his nature pleasure. His toes went haywire.

"Jesus Christ."

"Ain't sucking your dick, leave him out of it," I said, with his dick in my mouth. I sucked and sucked, trying to find the golf ball in his nuts and suck it out. I moaned sensually, said "Oh, yeah Daddy you like the way Mama suck this dick don't you?"

"Yes, baby, yes, baby…damn, you suck a mean dick baby, damn!"

Seconds later, like I expected, he locked up again.

"This shit has never happened before, I'm coming again! Yea, I'm 'bout to buss again bitch!"

And he released a "Grr" sound when he started coming in my mouth and one I received it all, I got in his face and he opened his mouth and I spit cum in it and he swallowed his own shit, while I tongued him, trying to find spare babies to swallow my damn self, my skin needed nourishment. I ain't playing with cha. I was Freaky Deaky.

"Stick your finger in your ass, and fuck that asshole, Niggah," I demanded. I wasn't through with him. His eyes wide with a smile, he said, "Damn, I love you, bitch I met my match."

"Hurry up, your asshole wants to be tortured."

"You ain't said nothing but a word."

He slid his lubricated finger in his tight asshole, his tight walls sliding on it made me quiver. He fucked himself good, fast and hard. I sucked on his hole, fingers…nipples, one by one, running my tongue over them like a snake across well-cut grass. I wiped up his excess cum and put it in his mouth. "You Freaky Deaky," I told him. "Swallow your nut, Niggah and fuck that asshole. Shit, let me help you." When he was done swallowing his own seeds, sharing them with me, I turned him over on his stomach, got on my knees and spread his ass open, sticking my tongue all up there. He smelled so good. He was so clean. I slapped his ass, wiping some of his cum on his asshole and sucked it off, licking the ass cheeks, fingering the asshole with two fingers. He went wild. He fucked my fingers, throwing that ass back. I saw his nuts and I sucked on them, working my fingers deep in his tunnel, grinding this New York Freaky Deaky Niggah. He was in a state of pure pleasure, never before experiencing what us down south bitches could do. He moaned obscenities, riding my fingers. I sucked his essence off them. Made him do the same and I used the cheesecake, put a huge glob in his asshole like moon beads, wiped cheesecake over his ass cheeks, nice ass this Niggah had.

And began my licking. Taste really good. I sucked on his asshole until all the cheesecake melted down my throat. I smacked my lips, standing up . I asked him to "Fuck me in the ass, baby."

"Thought you would never ask." Wiping cheesecake on his dick he slid up in my ass, without a condom, and fucked me good and long. He bounced up and down in my ass, the leather chair wet from our sweat. We were sliding all over it. He pulled my face back to his and kissed me, grinding that good dick in my ass, trying to recreate what my fingers did to his. I felt sensational. I threw that booty back, the popping and squishy sounds filling my ears. I was turned on. I sweated so badly it got in my eyes and I couldn't see. This Niggah fucked me so good I began coming all over myself. He felt my asshole throbbing. He spread my ass cheeks, got up in there and just went to town. Before long he pulled out, stood up over me and came poured down all over my hair, neck, face, lips, ass and thighs.

"Oh shit, bitch. Oh, shit."

And he lay down on the chair and fell asleep. Holding me tightly to him.

With his dick deep in my ass.

And now I was home, reading *Rollingstone* magazine with Led Zeppelin on the cover.

I smiled, thinking about Janet, New York and the sex I had. I got a text message. I picked up my cell phone. I smiled. *Meet me in the trap. It's going down.*

I text him back. *Niggah I'm home. In Miami.*

He sent another one back. *I know. I'm on the plane headed for Miami right now. Pick me up at the airport.*

I smiled really big, dropping the phone and spent thirty minutes speed cleaning my house, washing my clothes and calling in to work.

"I won't be in today. Hold over in Georgia. Gotta wait three hours for the next flight. I know you want me at work. But I can't control the airlines. They had a bomb scare…uh yea, Boss! You didn't see the news. Oh, ok, I'll call when the plane lands in Miami."

Click. I hated lying, but Dick was on a plane coming to see me. He was in for the time of his life. I hopped in my black Impala and hotrod up the block, signaling right onto 4th Street. A yellow cab passed me, going up my block. I did 85 MPH to the Florida Turnpike, heading for the Miami International Airport.

# Her Big Break

The world beneath her rhinestone pumps, Bernice Sinclair entered the elegant hotel. Full of promise and her attitude in check. Her hair was luxuriously done at La Chic Hair Salon in Naranja, Florida; across the street from Popeye's Chicken, earlier today. She paid Miss Parish a whopping $200 to get a perm. Then she got extensions. Miss Parish curled her hair and used bobby pins to keep it atop her small head and she didn't leave until every strand was in place. She had on nine inch stilettos, with rhinestones on the back. Her panty hose seemed to trap the glorious light from the baccarat crystal chandeliers looming all over the high ceilings.

She was a go-getter and she tasted the big time. A woman who'd been stomped over all her life, never getting what she deserved, she wasn't about to let that happen again. *Because I won't let it. I got a game plan, and I hope it works!* She ran her hand up and over her hips, her portfolio hanging at her right side, like a purse. She had a glass of Grey Goose in her blood stream, some weed pounding through her lungs and she could not get out her head her motto:

*I'm not leaving here until I am picked for the fucking job! I'ma Dirty South Bitch from Florida City! My Mama's a crack head and my Daddy's a failed Pimp with no money, no house and no car to show for all the bitch slapping he's done over twenty years. He's a has been and still begs for change at the Citgo gas station on 127th Avenue and 268th Street. I can't wind up like that! Fuck that! This bitch got a pussy and a brain! And I want the big time!*

She passed four hundred hopefuls in the Main Lobby. The place was resilient! Dreamy! A world inside of a world unknown to the inner cities. A place only seen on TV and graced the pages of Architectural Digest! You could feel the excitement charged with the cool air. It crawled up her spine and made her nipples hard. She had to resist rubbing her titties. The anticipation made her horny and when she paused at the receptionist desk, she had to hold it because a mild orgasm shot through her like rockets. She closed her eyes, moaned to herself, squeezed her legs together as tightly as he could, and regained control.

"Are you all right, Miss?" A pimple-faced, donkey-looking white woman asked and she smiled.

"Yes, I'm fine. And the try-outs are being held where?"

She pointed down the long, chandelier-clad hallway, hung with paintings. "Follow the arrows. But they don't start up again for another hour."

*That's what you think, bitch!* "Why thank you for your kindness."

"Honey, you're kissing the wrong ass. I'm not the one you need to be sucking up to."

"With teeth like yours, Mr. Ed, I can certainly see why. Thank you, bitch!" And she pivoted on her heel, sauntering towards her destination. "Slut!"

The receptionist ignored me and went back to business as usual. The Hopefuls, from all walks of life, beautiful, full-figured women, anorexic-looking broads mingled together; a few chubby bitches who hadn't a chance in hell shared champagne, listened to Sean Puffy Combs' music; got to know each other, took pictures with their digital cameras for memories and Bernice wanted none of that.

*I'm going to show you bitches what I'm about to do!*

Taking out her ID, she flashed it to the security guard in front of the closed ballroom doors. There was a sign on the side of him.

### BEAUTIFUL MAGAZINE TRY-OUTS

She smiled, spreading her long, gorgeous legs. She didn't wear a bra or any panties. And the guard noticed. His hard-on was the end result. She tossed the free curls behind her head, "FBI, I'm here to check out the validity of this try out."

The blood left his face and his hands were trembling. He stuffed them in his pockets, trying to play it off.

She went on with her prank. "I would appreciate your full cooperation."

She flipped her Toy's 'R Us bought badge closed and was granted access. The sexy Niggah looked nervous. "Go ahead. We don't want any trouble."

She read "Donald Rolle" on his name tag. She knew a few Rolles out of Goulds. *I wonder are you related to them?* she thought.

She touched his cheek. She looked down and seen the product of her gesture. He was rock hard. "I don't want any trouble, either. Not a word the FBI is in the building. I'll have your goddamn job and your balls floating in my martini on my next fucking break. Got that, Jack?"

And she went inside, smiling to herself.

*You dumb ass! How stupid can these Kindergarten Guards get? That's not even a picture of me on the badge. Oh, well. Plan worked. I am number 300, and I just skipped every bitch out in the fucking lobby! Kudos to me!* She held in her amazement. The ballroom looked like Cinderella was preparing for a grand entrance. Candles lit here and there, oriental carpeting. Plush leather settees. Fancy couches. Cameras set up everywhere. Amazingly crafted photo opts here and there.

Usher sang "Burn," her favorite song. *A further omen that this is for me!* A huge banner was sprawled before her very eyes, hanging behind a sexy, breathtakingly handsome black man, seated behind an African desk.

BEAUTIFUL MAGAZINE TRY-OUTS.

He seemed untouchable. Having one of those gangster looks. All business. Tailored out the ass; impeccably barbered. Looked like he took years preparing for this moment. The suit was silk, he wore $15,000 worth of diamonds in his ears, freezing his wrists, and a gold and platinum Scorpio medallion rested in the middle of his fabulous chest. His shirt was open. He seemed frustrated. Carefully placed memos lay before his eyes like Earth before God. Huge red X's were drawn across a few women's faces. *They failed,* Bernice thought. *Hoes I don't have to worry about.* She remembered seeing some of the faces mingling in the crowd. Her expectations rose.

"I'm here for the magazine tryouts."

"Are you the FBI woman?"

"Yes. With a fake ID to match. I am a go-getter, I go after what I want and I'm not going to bullshit you, my brother." His eyes flashed sexily. He loved the way she talked, looked. He loved how she got inside a try-out that was closed down for lunch. He was actually waiting on his food to arrive. He looked back at his hired help, black men from the Hood, and snapped for them to leave.

"Take twenty. I want to talk to this one alone, since she wants to impose like she's the FBI."

He gave them a knowing look. Snickering, they left.

She was young. Check. Sexy. Check. 36-24-36. Check. Ambitious. Check. "Are you going to say something, Mr…"

"Hanson."

Stars dancing in her hungry eyes, she licked her lips, clad in a black pin-stripped business suit. She had her portfolio in her hands, well manicured fingers, ghetto-looking acrylics. *Why these hoes love acrylics,* he wondered.

She read his mind. She snapped each nail off. She had well-cut regular nails, with just clear polish. He was impressed. He remained silent. He ignored the bulge in his slacks. He already fucked thirteen bitches in the tryouts, crossing them all off the list. Good pussy, good head didn't equal good photo opts and sell millions of magazines, especially one trying to get off the ground. Or so he told them. He was looking for a challenge. Someone with class and wit.

Some business sense. He rubbed his small goatee, deep in thought. *Are you going to get X-ed? Or are you going to the next round?*

*Yeah, Niggah, I'm reading your mind.* She was prepared to do whatever it took to get to the top. She would knock any bitch, fuck anybody, male or female. She would pull a J. Lo. A Jennifer Lopez. You had tons of record labels turn you down but ten minutes in Tommy Matolla's office and you walked out with not only a record deal but a full aerial assault.

*Yes she gave up the pussy for that deal, probably played tennis with the cracker's nuts! And I'm going to do the same thing if I have to!* She had a baby face, was barely 18, and he had to wonder was there any truth to the rumor that chicken sold in the grocery stores had hormones in it. Judging by this girl's banging body, that had to be true. She looked like a black Pamela Anderson with Trinidadian eyes and a Jamaican accent that set him and his loins on fire.

He studied her, quiet, observing the way she talked, the way she sauntered into the posh hotel ballroom at the Doubletree Hotel, Downtown Miami, where the old Omni Mall used to be. He could hear the brakes from the Metro Mover sing into his ears. This was a by invitation-only call for *Beautiful Magazine* that was up and running and needed a fresh new model-like bitch for the cover. The first cover. This was a big deal. Every girl had to pay $500 to the organization, send in snap shots and essays on why they should be picked. You had hungry-for-fame girls there who pawned jewelry, come up off their welfare and child support checks to pay the fee, just for the chance at stardom. Mr. Hanson banked over $300,000 dollars in Miami alone, not counting the fourteen other cities they trampled through before getting to the last stop in Miami.

All together they banked over 8 million dollars. He was prepared to pour thousands into marketing. *Beautiful Magazine* was like *XXL, Maxim* and *King* Magazines poured into a blender with skillful writing, a kick ass executive team from the University of Miami, and a skillful, sexy creator, Billy Songs, from Opa Locka, Florida who was an up and coming rapper with dreams of making it big. All the dope he slung and all the money he made he poured into his passion, to have his own publication, certainly looked like it was paying off.

Mr. Hanson said, "Lock the door. Can you do that for me? And put the "do not disturb" sign on the door knob. I'll give you an interview, if you can tell me why I should pick you to be my cover girl."

She gushed with zeal, wetting her panties. *I got the spot! I GOT THE SPOT! Why else would he ask me something like that! Oh my God!*

*Mama will be so proud! Hell yeah, this is dedicated to all the bitches from the hood, the Pine Island Projects in Naranja, who told me, while in Job Corps on the Homestead Airforce Base, that I wasn't going to amount to nothing! Suck my clit, bitches! Looks like I proved you so wrong! I can't believe this is about to happen. Ok, Ok, can't get excited. Control your breathing! Keep it grown and sexy.*

"I should be picked…"

"Whoa Lil' Mama. Lock the door. As a matter of fact, go to the bathroom, practice what you're about to say. Judging from your answer, I will X your sexy ass."

"Well, goddamn, brother."

She made him laugh. She was the first woman to make him laugh all day. Shit, all year. Plus one, he thought.

"Go on. Practice. You got two minutes to prepare."

He pulled out a stop watch and started it. Keeping her cool, she turned to the right and went into the bathroom, closing and locking the door and whipping out her cell phone. She called her girl Jamilla.

"Hell, yeah girl! He's going to pick me! I can feel it. He gave me two minutes to prepare. Tell all the girls! Shit, find my Mama and tell her I'm moving on up to the East side when I get a piece of this goddamn pie! And tell Daddy the beans don't burn in the goddamn kitchen anymore! To give up the pimping, his daughter is going to take him to the top! I got to go!" She hung up, looked herself over in the mirror and went back out to Mr. Hanson.

When she paused before his desk the buzzer went off.

After Mr. Hanson took a few test shots of her with his $2,300 dollar Motorola camera with the huge lens looking like a telescope, he set the camera on his desk and said, "Ok, why should we pick you to be our first cover girl?"

*This is it! Don't blow it, Bernice!* "I should, fuck it; I *am* the Face of the Magazine. I am a go-getter, prize winner and I want the brass ring. I will do whatever it takes, I will do the grind work, I will promote this publication, promote myself and make *Beautiful Magazine* not only a startlingly good magazine, but a force to be reckoned with."

"Damn. Confident."

"Yes I am."

"You got the job."

"What?"

He stood up, walked around his desk and paused in her face. "You got the job. Your pay will be about $20,000." She was speechless. *Ka-ching! Ka-ching!* "Not to mention some endorsement deals we'll set you up for. We have a press run of a million magazines, pre-ordered all over the world. We have a Myspace.com page. We'll do another featuring your test shots I took today. I'll get right on it. Move over *Suicide Girls*! We got to set the world on its ear. We're taking a chance on you."

She stood five feet eleven. He was 6 feet one. He took her into his arms, studied her. She was wet instantly. He sank to his knees, lifted up her skirt and stuck a finger in her pussy.

"Goddamn, you don't have on any draws."

"I like to let it all hang out."

"Pussy smells good."

"Always does."

"Really tight."

"Haven't been fucked in ages."

"Are you going to resist a city Niggah like me?"

"Why should I give it up to you?"

"Because I'm in it."

"Yea, your *finger*. But I can put this shit on pause at any given moment. How do I know you won't fuck me and X me out, like you did the other Hoes?"

He smiled then. *Smart bitch!* "I just gave you the job."

"I have nothing in writing yet, Gigolo."

"You'll get it in writing."

"Do I have your word? Come on, Niggah! I have nothing, trying to get something. My parents are low-lives. I want it all. Don't bullshit me."

*I see a lot of myself in her*, he thought to himself, amazed by a woman so young being so direct.

"Like Scarface, you got my word."

"Then eat my pussy like it has never been eaten before."

He leaned up to her velvet box, spread her walls and licked around the surface; his hot breath teasing and pleasing. She shuddered in her pumps. He tongued her juices, let his mustache tickle the clit and he rubbed his goatee hairs all up in her twat. She held his head, leaning back against the desk.

"You want me in this pussy?" he asked rhetorically.

"Hell yes." She shuddered, her huge booty on the edge of the desk. She spread her legs open, pulling them up, her knees bent towards her. Her high heeled pumps brought the freak out of him.

"You smell so good."

"You feel so wonderful."

He tongue fucked her, her breasts shaking under her blouse. She unloosened each button, seductively, showing control under strenuous circumstances. When her tits popped free he went wild. He stood up, unzipped his pants, his huge dick springing free and she got on her knees and took him into her wet mouth, her tongue quick and slick. He never took his eyes off her. She pulled, slurped and noisily moaned her approvals. She enjoyed her power, enjoyed bringing him satisfaction.

"Damn. You're a dirty bitch, I like that."

"You do?" She looked up at him, grabbed the rest of his liquor, poured it in her mouth, tossed the shot glass, ignoring the shattering; and she took him back in her hotness, the alcohol pleasurably stinging his entire shaft.

He screamed out in delight.

"Goddamn, pull on that shit, suck it, baby...*make it spit*, make it spit."

She pulled on it harder, increasing the suction in her jaws...He humped her mouth, unloosening her hair, it fell all around her angelic face.

"Fuck it. I want the pussy! I can't stand it! You suck on my shit I'm gonna wanna hit."

Aggressively, he pulled her up to her feet, unbuttoned her blouse and jacket, tossing it on the floor. He pulled off her skirt. Tossed it. "Leave the pumps on. You look so damn sexy. Get on my desk, on your hands and knees; let me see that pretty pussy all up in my face...damn, you shaved?"

She did what he said, getting into the position. He stuck his dick in her raw dog, slowly, sticking both thumbs in her ass. She let out this moan that set him on fire. She never had anything in her ass, but her new boss wanted it so hey, he signed the goddamn checks, he called the shots. She was so wet and tight. She took all ten inches like a pro. She rose and fell with him, jumping on the tidal waves, surfing, traveling and skiing across pleasurable turfs...He fucked her senseless, her ass jiggling on his dick. He thumbed her asshole as hard as he could, leaning forward and spitting on his thumbs for some extra lubrication. She moaned and called out his name in sheer delight.

"Goddamn baby, yes, ahh shit...! Damn, take my shit!"

He gave her what she wanted. He crawled on top of the desk, his hired help peeping through the ballroom door, slapping palms and videotaping the two, and he turned her on her back, put her legs behind both elbows, entered her slowly, expertly and banged her until the sounds of sex filled his ears.

He smiled down at her, biting his bottom lip, looking her dead in the eyes.

Giving her the best plumbing job of her life.

She shivered and trembled, tears falling from her eyes, his amazing ass opened and closed as he entered and exited her as fast as he could. Never in her life had her pussy been stretched to such limitations. She felt him in her gut, but it felt so good.

"I'm 'bout to cum!" she sing-songed, feeling her toes curl in the stilettos and her muscles began contracting, her wetness increased and she sucked on his intimidating nipple as she shook from the desk to ecstasy. He pounded her harder, faster, deeper, filling her up and he hit a spot in her pussy she never knew existed and she had multiple orgasms, which she never experienced before and she cried out, "*Stop Stop Stop it feels SOOO GOOD NIGGAH!*"

Suckling on her left nipple, biting it teasingly, he released the beast, coming deep inside of her, speeding up like a runaway train, claiming the pussy, marking his territory. He moaned seductively, a soft release from the pit of his vocal cords that not only drove her crazy but set her off. He sucked on her neck forever, hard, making it hurt, putting a huge hickey on her body. Making sure Niggahs on the block took notice.

He fucked enough Hoes for the day. Exhausted, he rolled off her and lay, spent. He gazed into her eyes, his chest and stomach moving fast. Uncontrollable breathing. "I want you to be mine. You have a wonderful future with *Beautiful Magazine*. Let's get the papers signed."

"I can't believe this is happening." His minions pressed stop on the recorder. Little red lights on the other twelve cameras carefully hidden in the room suddenly went black.

Once the papers were signed the competition was over. All the other hopefuls were sent home. How disappointed they were. They cursed Bernice and screamed obscenities at Mr. Hanson. Security was called. The ladies were escorted out of the building. Bernice could picture the world bowing at her feet. She got a deal!

She was going to be somebody. She waltzed up to the ugly receptionist and said, "You're right. Your ass was the wrong ass to kiss. I'm the new face of tomorrow."

"Whatever, lady. It'll blow up in your face."

"Like it blew up in yours?"
"Whatever."

# Bernice

It was three months after she and Mr. Hanson had rough sex at the Doubletree Hotel that she went townhouse hunting with Jamilla and Antoinette, her two most trusted friends. She and Mr. Hanson had been in constant contact. They talked about everything. Became good friends. He told her he was unhappily married. That his wife didn't treat him with the respect he deserved. Considering she was now pregnant. And wanted to file for divorce and take everything he owned. But that was his problem. Nauseated from taking too many Tylenol Sinus pills, Jamilla opened her black windbreaker, revealing a tight Paris Hilton halter-top and gut-stricken midriff. Kicking off her black Nikes.

"Girl, I don't know about this one," said Jamilla in disgust, looking around the amazing townhouse recently build by the brand new Publix Supermarket in Naranja, by the Waterfront housing complex. She frowned at the double glass doors, which was just thrown together haphazardly. She hated the size of the living room. Sucked. The bedrooms weren't big enough for roaches. No wonder those home makers were losing money, according to the newspapers and she read them religiously. People who bought these cheaply built, expensively priced homes were foreclosing already.

Bernice smiled, clad in a simple green pants suit. Her hair pulled back from her face. She ran her hands over the cream-colored walls.

"Why don't you know?"

Antoinette was admiring the staircase. "Girl you can hang some paintings right along this wall, leading up the stairs, Chile," Antoinette suggested. "And you can get some…dick…right about there in the middle of the stairs girl, towards the top. You have a lot of space to have sex."

"Yea, I'll consider it, Antoinette." She looked at Jamilla laughing. "What's wrong with the townhouse?"

"Well for one these glass doors. They look weird."

Bernice said, "I like them. They're unique."

Jamilla stuck her tongue at Bernice. "They're fucked up. And two, there's barely a front and back yard. Snap and you'll miss it.

Shit, I would hate to break a plate in this bitch. Nine houses down up unto your neighbor will hear it soundly. And where are the black people? All you hear is salsa music and fucking Spanish!"

"You do have a point."

"Plus they want $240,000 for it," said Antoinette. "These goddamn Cubans come over here on a boat and jack all the fucking prices up on shit. Changed the Cutler Ridge Mall to the Southland Mall. That's some Castro shit. And I heard they're trying to change 'Goulds' to 'Cutler Bay.' We gonna riot on their asses! Just crazy. Why would you go to the Hood, tear down every tree, build houses on it and charge a bitch $300,000 for a house in Goulds? The ghetto? Yea, right, bitches! But outside of that I like the condo."

Jamilla snorted grotesquely. "You have no sense of style, Antoinette. Don't influence Bernice into getting this funk box."

"Girl, whatever," said Antoinette. "She can do better. She should move to Georgia. $300,000 would get her three homes and a shit load of land. She could build a thousand staircases and get some dick then feel like Jezebel Cinderella, Chile!"

Bernice implied, "All right, women."

"I'm just saying…" Antoinette looked impishly. "She needs to look around before she signs any commitments."

Bernice smiled. "Good. Then it's a wrap. I'm going to put $15,000 down on it and then pay it off when I start getting royalty checks from *Beauty Magazine*."

"When are you getting your check?" asked Jamilla. Antoinette was on her cell phone with her man.

"Soon." Bernice's life was about to change. "Very soon."

A few days later, Bernice got a phone call.

Grim-faced, she answered her cell phone, pacing around Henrietta's living room in Liberty City, Florida. "Hello." DMX growled like the dog he was from the 60 inch plasma TV built into the wall.

"Sup, Bernice."

It was Mr. Hanson. She smiled, getting butterflies in her stomach. "Sup, man?"

"Where are you?"

"My friend Henrietta's house. Where are you?"

"I was back home in Detroit, Michigan. The wife has filed for divorce. Trying to take all I own by saying I was being unfaithful. She even got big gun lawyers. But she can't prove it because I covered my tracks with you."

"We only fucked once."

"Duh, Bernice. Unfaithful."

She laughed with him. Her heart warmed up. She knew he was a stone cold playa. She knew his type. She knew he fucked other Hoes in that competition in every city they went in. Men with big dicks swore they had the anecdote to make a bitch stupid. She needed to take the hair rollers from her hair. But she decided against it. She was staying with Henrietta for a few days. She thought she told Mr. Hanson that when they spoke three days ago.

"So what are you going to do?"

"Well, remember I asked you to give me Henrietta's address so I can send you a few recent pictures of me?" he asked jubilantly. Too jubilantly.

Her eyes narrowed. *So I did tell him I was here.* "Yes?"

"Well they should be delivered there any time now."

"What should be delivered..."

There was a knock on Henrietta's front door. Henrietta was at work. Sliding into house slippers, closing her terrycloth robe, she, mystified, walked to the door. "What did you send, Mr. Hanson?"

"Stop calling me Mr. Hanson. I'm not your damn teacher."

"What about for Sex ED.?"

"Oh, I got you."

She answered the door and Mr. Hanson took her into his arms, sticking his tongue down her throat, picking her up, kicking the door closed. Stunned, she couldn't react, but she melted into his embrace, her heart thumping out her chest. Her pussy wet instantly, she wrapped her legs around him, her robe coming untied. Her titties pressed against the fabric of his silk shirt, which put a tingling in her nipples to the point of erection.

"I want to fuck you. Cover Girl. Can I get this pussy before it hits the big time?"

"Hell, yeah... But what about your wife taking you to court?"

"She doesn't know I took a flight out of Detroit."

Laying her on the sofa he dove in her wet pussy, tonguing her speechless. That quickly turned to deep moaning. His head bobbed like a ball on water. The heat from his lips and tongue set her on fire.

Spreading her legs open she held the arm of the chair, arching her back, her breasts dancing to their own tune. *Maybe I can have him when his wife leaves him. He has long money. And an even longer dick. He has everything. Plus he's my new boss. Why not?*

"Damn, baaabbbyyy! Yea, my Niggah eat that shit baby, yes."

Sitting up he unbuttoned his shirt, taking it off. Fabulous chest, goddamn! Unbuckling his pants, he pulled a Trojan condom from his wallet, setting the wallet on the low-table. He pulled out his dick and she sat up, taking it into her mouth, suckling on the head slowly, pulling on it and he humped her face for dear life, getting lost in her rhythms. Becoming one with her. He was obsessed with her, hadn't stopped thinking about her since the magazine try-outs. When he fucked his wife he imagined he fucked Bernice; he found himself calling out her name every night but she wasn't there to answer him. He accidentally called his wife "Bernice," when she had come home from the mall a few weeks ago, but thank God she didn't hear him. Because she was flapping her jaws on the phone with her sister in Reno.

He leaned his head back; his heart pumping blood through his veins at breakneck speed. Kicking off his shoes, he got nasty.

"Let me see those deep throat skills…open your mouth! Fuck this dick with that hot mouth…*yeeeaaa*! Take this dick, Ho. Get nasty for Daddy. Likes the way you slurping my shit. Suck my wife out the hole of my dick and swallow the bitch whole. Lemme see the bitch try…to…swim. Out. Of. The. Acid. In. Your. Stomach with my nut…*yea*!"

She sucked, slurped and pulled, tears running down her face. She loved his juicy dick. She wanted it in her ass. She wanted to get kinky with it, role play. She'd be the doctor and he'd be the Medical Board. Yea. That was hot.

She squeezed her nipples. Releasing his nature and playing with herself. She kept sucking on his dick with a technique called "No Hands Barred."

His orgasm beginning to bubble in the base of his nuts, he pushed her back, lifted her legs, put on the condom and went up in her asshole. She screamed out from the pain. He didn't even lube her up. Pushing her legs as far back as they'd go, he fucked her long, hard and fast. She got lost. She fell in the dark pit. She felt his passion. Got swamped with his heat. His technique. Fell in love with his skill. His stamina. "Play with that pussy while I get this tight ass…"

She rubbed her love, as fast as she could. Fuck the slow shit. She wasn't in the mood to play around. She started fucking herself. Her eyes tightly closed. He gave her what she wanted. Good dick. She screamed vulgarities that even had him like, "Damn, Ma. My dick feeling good like that?"

"Give me that dick!"

"I'm giving you this dick. Beg for it."

"Give me the dick give me the dick GIVE ME THE DICK PAPA!"

"I'm giving you the dick giving you the dick giving you the dick." Farty sounds filled the house as her ass got loose. She was reaching her climax, and before she knew it she was coming, snatching his dick out her ass and shoving it in her pussy.

"Damn, Ma!"

"I'm cumin'!"

He slow grinded in her wet tunnel, bringing her to a heightened pleasure. She lay spent when it was over.

"Where's the bathroom, little Mama?"

She was in a daze. "Upstairs."

He kissed at her. "Can I go wash up?"

"What, I didn't hear you..."

They giggled. "Can I go take a bath or something? I hate feeling dirty."

She was rubbing her nookie. "Sure."

He kissed her lips. "You are a passionate woman."

"And you're a passionate man."

"I'm all right," he said, craving a cigarette.

She kissed his pretty feet. "You're the best..."

He left, forgetting his wallet. She couldn't take her eyes off it.

They were making love in the shower. He gave it to her passionately slow. He made her come four times. This time without the Trojan condom.

After the shower she asked him, "Why is it taking so long for you guys to get me started on the cover shoot?"

He got really quiet.

She studied his face. "Baby?"

"Next week you're booked. Just a lot of minor details adding to big problems."

"Like what?"

He turned her around, and got on his knees, eating her sore asshole.

She began rising up to the clouds. "What was that I said? I forgot," she said, bracing herself for some more Married Man Dick.

A few hours later she cooked him a burger and some fries. Henrietta wouldn't mind. She'd pay her back for eating up her food, and she'd wash the dishes she messed up. No biggie. She was fully dressed in a skirt and his silk shirt. He had on one of Henrietta's husband's shirts. He didn't care. A shirt was a fucking shirt. As long as it was clean.

"So when are you going back to Detroit?" Bernice asked, handing him a plate with steaming fries and two bacon and cheese burgers.

He smiled at her, kissing her lips. "Soon."

"Soon like when?" Her plate was bigger than his.

*Jesus, bitches loved asking questions. I wasn't married to you Ho, damn. But I do love you. At least I think I do. Or is that I love the way you fuck? Oh, well. I had time to decipher this whatever it was!* "Well, damn! Do you have enough food?"

*He thinks he's slick, trying to be evasive!* "Yea. Anyways, when are you leaving?"

"Tonight," he lied. He had other bitches to fuck.

"Tonight?"

*No.* "Yes."

"When did you get to Miami?"

*A week ago. And the pussy and ass I got. Phew. Should be a crime to be this slick.* "Two days ago."

Her voice got dark. "And you're just showing up here today?"

He felt an argument coming on. And. He. Wasn't in the mood. "Yea, Bee."

"My name is Bernice. Not Bee. What's up with this?"

*Damn it. This is what happens when you give a bitch good dick. They turned into the Exorcism of Emily Rose, took a goddamn Priest to pray the bitches off.* "Are you going to start tripping?"

"Yea. How many other Hoes you fucked when you got here?"

*Bertha. Simone. And a couple Niggahs, too,* he thought bitterly. "Look, I got a wife. I don't need a lecture."

"You need your ass whipped."

"By *who?*" He was laughing so hard he chocked.

"This Naranja Bitch! We do it big down in the dirty south, Niggah. This isn't Detroit."

"Whatever. Just shut the fuck up before I rearrange your teeth."

"With what? Your dick?"

*Too bad she was a good fuck. I had a lot of bad pussy in my lifetime but she was the best fuck I had. A rookie at heart. A man didn't let go good pussy. Not until he got bored with it, molded it. Had a Ho sick in the mind without it. In it to win it but Lil' Mama was going to lose me.* "Bernice. I like being here with you. Please stop." His blood was boiling near the danger zone.

*Bullshit!* "Why should I?"

"Because I'm not trying to go there with you."

*Let's go there Niggah.* "Go there, I dare you."

"Look, I like you. I'm trying to keep it civil."

*Is this a war, damn it? Civil, as in civil rights? Do I look like Coretta Scott King bitch?* "Man, look. I'm getting really aggravated, and fast."

"And I guess what I feel just don't matter?" he shot icily, made her shiver. But she played it off.

"It does matter, but…"

"But, *what?* All you're trying to do is get a reaction out of me, typical little girl, elementary school shit. And how old are you?"

"Whatever. I want to show you this condo I'm getting. When you give me the $20,000 I'm going to put a down payment on it."

He was confused. "Twenty grand? From *where?*"

She laughed. "*You,* silly."

He rolled his eyes, uninterested. "You're getting $5,000. I never told you you're getting 20 grand."

The room was spinning.

He couldn't be serious. "You *can't* be serious."

"I'm as serious a heart attack."

Her eyes clouded over. "But you said I was…" She was stuttering, her heart failing her.

*I lied to you, bitch! You got good pussy but it isn't worth twenty grand. Maybe fifty dollars but certainly not twenty grand. Dumb bitch!*

He was at the boiling point. "I never said that."

She exploded. "YOU DID!" The house shook. Angrily, he threw the plate of food and it shattered on the wall, falling all around her.

Stunned, she stared at him. "Get out." She was scared.

He laughed. "Bitch, with pleasure. I got another bitch to go fuck before I board the plane. I shouldn't have showered, so she could suck your asshole off my dick."

And he was gone.

She eyed his wallet on the low-table, smiling through tears. How could she have been blinded by the man? Why did she get pulled in? She was embarrassed. She felt dumb and stupid. All of her dreams were exploding in her face. The smell of food made her wrench all in the sink. She was nauseated, she hated to be betrayed. But she had no one to blame but herself. Letting a complete stranger screw her, even without rubbers. Was she stupid? What if he gave her a STD? She could never show her face ever again. And that was her problem, thinking with her pussy instead of her brain. Hadn't that caused her enough grief in her life? Hadn't she learned from her mistakes that were gentle dress-ups for bad decisions that would follow her for the rest of her natural life? Would she ever wake up? Life was bigger than sex and money.

"But that's ok. I signed a contract. I signed for twenty grand, or did I?" She got his wallet, opening it.

Three platinum cards. A shipload of hundred dollar bills.

"I will get my money. One way or the other."

# Part 3

A few weeks later, after her physical examination at the doctor's office, Bernice got a call from her home girl.

"Sup, Antoinette." She was not in the mood. In fact she felt crummy and shitty.

"Girl, when was the last time you been on the internet?"

"Last month sometime, *why?*" Her eyes were blood shot red from crying for days and days on end. Over Mr. Hanson. Over life. Was this damn *Beauty Magazine* shit even going to fly. *They got 500 dollars of my money! What if this was a fucking scam!*

"There's something you should know."

*There goes my condo!*

*My townhouse I should say. The one Jamilla hated and Antoinette loved!*

"What, girl?"

"Bernice, you know I love you, right?"

She felt queasy. "Yeah, girl."

"And I'd do anything for you."

Now she felt uneasy. "What is this?" Bernice was suspicious. "Are you trying to ask can you come to Hollywood with me?" *Yeah, right! Me? Hollywood? Fat chance! Mr. Hanson stole 500 bucks of my hard-earned cash! I sold my pussy for that money.*

Silence. Then, "Well…"

Bernice smiled, playing it off. *I can't let my friends know I won't be a star!* "Yea, girl, you're coming. How about you become my PR or agent. You damn sure know what I like and what I don't."

"I'm flattered."

"You better be."

"But back to the reason I called you."

"Let me guess. Your man ate you out again on the roof of your house like he did last month. I can't believe he actually did that, girl. On the roof? In the rain? In broad daylight? That took guts." She actually cheered up a little bit, rubbing her stomach, staring at herself in the mirror from the unmade-up bed.

"He doesn't have big nuts for nothing. And this ain't about him."

"Ok, so what is it?" Bernice asked.

"Let's just say your *Beautiful Magazine* spot is the hottest thing in the world."

She got so excited she jumped off her bed at her friend Stella's house and screamed for all to hear. "I'm on my way!" Bernice said happily, jumping up and down. All her girls, eight of them, burst into the room. In pajamas, turning on some music and celebrating with her. *It wasn't a scam! It was a dream come true! Thank you Jesus!* Bernice was elated that she was actually going to be a cover girl for a national, well global magazine! She was definitely headed for the good time.

Antoinette said into the phone, not believing what she saw on the screen before her very eyes. "Bernice log onto the link I'm about to send you on your AOL account."

Bernice turned on her laptop computer, telling her other friends, "Wait, I'm 'bout to pull it up. Ya'll going to be so proud of me. I'm classy! And I'm about to launch a new magazine! One my people can be proud of."

"Did you fuck to get the job?" asked Samantha, whose mind was always on dick.

Bernice lied, "Hell no! I used my business sense, girl. Ain't that type of party?" *Hoe, stay outta mine! If I fucked or not its my pussy, can't help that your shit was ruined before you even got out of the ninth grade.*

"That's my girl," said Jamilla, pulling on her joint.

Antoinette said, "Oh, girl, what's done in the dark comes to the light."

"I know, Chile. And with my success the darkness is about to end. I am the light." *I shouldn't have treated Mr. Hanson badly when he came to Henrietta's. I should call him and get him his wallet back. I'm pretty sure he's wondering where it is. He did call me last week and ask me did I see it and I said "No."*

"Yes you are," said Antoinette, turning off the computer. Even Antoinette's mother, in a state of shock, set on her daughter's bed, speechless. She whispered to her daughter, "I need a stiff drink. Fuck it; give me the entire bottle of Grey Goose."

Antoinette buried her forehead in her open palm, shaking her head.

When Bernice opened the link in her email and paste it in the search engine, she clicked 'Go' and it came right up. Her sex tape, filmed in the ballroom. Everyone's mouths fell open in shock.

Jamilla, chocking, dropped her blunt.

There was Bernice, sucking and fucking Mr. Hanson.

"Oh my God! What is this?" asked Bernice, frozen.

The audio followed.

*"Goddamn, you don't have on any panties."*

*"I like to let it all hang out."*

*"Pussy smells good."*

*"Always does."*

*"Really tight."*

*"Haven't been fucked in ages."*

*"Are you going to resist a city Niggah like me?"*

*"Why should I give it up to you?"*

*"Because I'm in it."*

*"Yea, your finger. But I can put this shit on pause at any given moment. How do I know you won't fuck me and X me out, like you did the other Hoes?"*

"Hell nah!" said Henrietta, laughing, slapping palms with Jamilla.

"Dirty bitch!" said Coquette Bautista. "You are amazing, girl!"

"Look at that ballroom, shit, Mr. Hanson is fine as fuck! Can I make a video next, Chile?" said Germaine, the lesbian.

"Look at the bitch's hair! Can you say *Fabulous! Fabulous! Fabulous!* faster than Eddie Murphy dressed as Mama Klump?" joked Jamilla.

Devastated and embarrassed, wanting to crawl in a ball and die, she snatched the power cord from the wall. The monitor went blank. She gritted her teeth, her eyes laser beams.

All her friends stared at her.

"The bitch is about to go postal," said Germaine.

"Let me go put up my knives," said Jamilla, laughing and stomping her feet. Finding this all funny.

"Your *business* sense, 'ey?" said Coquette, laughing. "You dirty bitch! How much did he pay you to be exploited on the net? You didn't say you were doing porn!"

"No, no, I can explain…" Bernice started to cry and her girls didn't play the bushes. They fired question after question.

"Where's your money? You can sue!" said Bernadette. Miss Ghetto Fabulous with nine kids from nine different men and she was only twenty-eight years old, "You didn't sign a media release!"

"I damn sure didn't!" Bernice said. "I'm suing."

"Where are the papers you signed? Did Mr. Hanson give you a copy?" asked Jamilla. Bernice hung up on Antoinette. She didn't need to hear it from her.

"Yes he did." She pulled them from her purse and Jamilla snatched them. Reading.

She got really quiet.

"Jamilla!"

Jamilla handed her the papers. She read them.

Oh, God!

"Did you even read them before you signed?" asked Bernadette. "You should have had a lawyer present."

Jamilla said, her heart going out to her girl, "Those were media releases you signed. Meaning those are actual contracts. They will stand up in court. And there's not a damn thing you can do about it. *Beautiful Magazine* is a porn magazine. I'm pretty sure this man fucked other girls before you came in there and did the same thing. This man lied to you. Your face will be splashed on millions of porn magazines all over the world as their premiere magazine. You're right. You're on your way to the big time. And your first check will be cut in a few months, according to these documents. So while they're making millions off you, with a website already generating multiple hits worldwide, in a matter of days, you got to wait to be compensated. So much for your big break. They're taking a chunk out of your ass. Looks like you've been pimped."

Her world of luxury, fame and fortune crumpling about her, Bernice lay on the bed, sobbing and screaming curse words into the pillow. Jamilla, Bernadette and the rest of the girls left her to herself, closing the door behind them.

When the door closed she got a burst of energy. Whipping out her cell she called Mr. Hanson.

"You have reached the rejection line," said the answering machine. "Obviously you aren't going to find who you're looking for. If he or she gave you this number to call. Then you've been royally fucked. So hang up and go wipe the shit from your face."

She turned the phone off. "Are you serious? I can't believe this is happening."

Her life was over. She just paced the room, deep in thought. Her mom would laugh at her. Her Daddy would ridicule her. They already thought she was a loser. Never been to college, and barely graduated high school. She attended the Job Corps, learning a trade. Sad. And her big break blew up in her face. Like the bitch receptionist at the hotel had told her. Dark clouds loomed overhead. Zapping her happiness. Taking her zeal for life and crushing it. Her chest burned. Acid bubbled in her stomach. Giving her heart burn.

Then it hit her. *Oh my God! How could I forget!*

Opening her purse she pulled out his wallet. Looking through it she pulled out a list of numbers scribbled on a small post-it note. She made a call, pressing a series of buttons after she dialed the number.

He answered. Good. Let the games begin. "Mr. Hanson. You sneaky son of a bitch."

"I take it you seen your porno on the web. Exciting isn't it?"

"You tricked me."

"And other bitches, too. There's nothing you can do about it."

"You are a creep! You just *ruined* my reputation!"

"You ruined it yourself. I liked you. But you got too much lip."

"Whatever. You're not going to get away with this."

"Oh yes I am. And my wife ain't going to get away with trying to take my house and cars and money."

"Oh, yeah?"

"Yea."

"I hope you rot in hell. She will find out that we fucked. I'll tell her."

He laughed sinisterly. "You sound a) naïve and b) insecure. You don't know my wife's number, my address or anything for that matter. I'm not even from Detroit."

Her heart stopped. She couldn't' breathe.

He went in for the pleasurable kill. Felt better than her young pussy. "I'm from, well, *you* know how that goes. That's none of *your* business." She closed her eyes.

Holding in her rage.

Bernice sucked in air. She would not be made a fool of. "We'll just see about that." She fell silent.

"See about what bitch? You need to let me come get some more of that pussy and stop acting so whorishly retarded."

She opened the post-it note, smiling victoriously. "Tell me. Is your wife's name Georgia?"

He stopped smiling. "What, how do you know?"

"What, do I got your dick in a bunch? Is her cell phone number…well, *you* know how that goes? Bye, I'm 'bout to give her a call."

He had heart failure. "Wait, Bernice!"

"You get me off the fucking web. You get me off now or, well, *you* know, I *call* your wife. I got her number on a post it note I just took out your wallet, you asshole!"

Click.

A few hours later her website was down temporarily.

"Ok. Good. He listened."

But that wasn't enough.

She wanted revenge. All she could think of was her friends ridiculing her and laughing at her. She'd be the butt of a thousand jokes. People would laugh at her.

Angry, she called Georgia.

She answered.

Her voice was shaky. "Is this Georgia?" Bernice asked.

Georgia poured a cup of coffee, sitting at her dining room table in Portland, Maine. "Yes, who is this? I don't know anyone named Bernice from a 305 area code. Isn't that Miami?"

"Yes. I'm calling because your husband used and abused me."

Georgia chocked on her coffee, smiling, a trembling hand finding her neck, as she toyed with her pearls. "Speak, go on. You can tell me."

"Ok. He got me to pay him 500 dollars for some *Beauty Magazine* try-out. And he tricked me into thinking it was a classy publication when in fact it's a porn venture."

Her eyes were wide with anger. "What? He is using Beauty Magazine for porn?"

"And he fucked me on the day of the try-outs. And not too long ago he claimed he flew from Detroit to come see me when I was staying at a friend's house. We fucked then, too."

"Can you prove this? You know I'm filing for divorce, and I'm trying to prove he cheated on me so I can clean his ass out. I'm a scorned white woman. I know I'll win."

"*Yes*. I can prove it."

"How?"

"I found out at the doctor's office that I'm pregnant with his child. Two months pregnant, to be exact." And she smiled dangerously, smoking a cigarette. "I'm keeping the baby."

"Well, Bernice is it? How about helping me clean his ass out. How would you like to own *Beauty Magazine* and you can turn it into something more classy?"

She smiled through her tears. "Most *definitely*. But, wait? He doesn't own it. Doesn't a man from Opa Locka own it, some so-called used-to-sell-dope rapper?"

"No, my dear. *He* owns it, I funded him the money to get it started. I didn't know it was really a porn venture. I tell you what, prove to me you're carrying his child, and I'll make sure *Beauty Magazine* is yours. Deal?"

"Yes, ma'am. Deal. And I got something even better."

"Oh, yea? Credible?"

"Yes. My cell phone records conversations. And I got our conversation lock, stock and barrel. Would that help?"

"Girl where in the fuck did you come from? You're a goddamn angel."

"With devil's horns."

OK BITCHES! BERNICE IS BACK!

"That's fucked up, Girl," said Bernadette, running into the other room, tuning on the computer, setting up her DVD burner.

"How much are we going to sell it for?" asked Germaine, her hands itching. "I got about four hundred blank CD's. I can go to Liberty City by the USA Flee market on 79th Street and sell some there. I know Niggahs will eat it up. We can call it Her Big Break!"

"Ten dollars a pop," said Jamilla. "She's our dog, but hey, I got rent to pay. And she has been living here for free for too goddamn long, eating my damn food and using my water and shit…"

"Hey!" said the girls.

"Let's set up shop. But we can't tell her," suggested Bernadette.

Coquette had a change of heart. "She's our girl. We can't do this to her. She needs us."

"Yes. She needs us to make her some money," said Jamilla.

She went on. "I'm going to set up an Ebay account. Lord hot damn we all going to make some money. Let's beat *Beautiful Magazine* at their own game."

"Amen to that!" said Bernadette. "We gotta give Bernice a cut."

"She gets twenty percent," said Jamilla. "I swear to God. We'll get her some loot."

Everyone pinky swore. "Let's put our girl on the market."

"Her Big Break! *He-eey!*" They all singed together, turning up Jay-Z.

Jamilla clicked on the website. It wouldn't load.

"Girl, don't you have DSL?" asked Bernadette.

"No, I have dial-up," said Jamilla, aggravated.

"No you don't," said Henrietta. "You got DSL! I went with you when you ordered it from Bellsouth."

Jamilla sneered. "Then why isn't the page loading?"

"Because Mr. Hanson took that shit off the site." Bernice had a packed bag in her hand. She looked good, hair done up, the Gucci outfit slamming. The make-up knocking Halle Berry right off the commercials.

"What?" said Jamilla, looking guilty.

Henrietta kicked the DVD's under the bed and Bernadette picked imaginary dirt from her nails.

"Yes. You guys were supposed to be my friends. And you were actually going to sell my porno all over Dade County."

"And the Palm Beaches," said Germaine, quickly regretting her words.

"Shut up, Girl!" said Henrietta and Jamilla slapped her in the back of the head.

"Don't worry about it. I'm moving out."

"Why?" asked Jamilla.

"Because you bitches betrayed me."

"Aw you just mad because you sucked dick to get a deal that was bogus."

"Jamilla, that's your opinion."

"That's a fact!" said Germaine. "And I have been trying to eat that pussy for years. And you meet that man and he tasted the passion fruit in an hour flat. World record time."

"*Whatever.*" She pivoted on her heel and was gone.

"The hell with her," said Jamilla.

Hornier than two toads, Crucial Williams, a gorgeous vamp, rushed into the law offices of Gregg, Gregory and Craig's on South Beach around 8 a.m. this glorious Miami morning. March 25, 2006. She turned on all the lights, killed the alarm, sent the security guard's fat ass home after giving him the rest of her Dunkin Donuts and she flipped on her laptop. Dressed to kill in a snap-and-you'll-miss-it black pinstriped skirt suit with African bangles, she looked over the paintings hanging around the fancy office. All black art. She loved it. Tapping her foot to some Lyfe Jennings booming softly from her radio, she stuck a number 2 pencil in her curly hair and smiled to herself. Sighing and still a little tired, she wanted to go home. She partied hard the night before. You didn't turn down her best friend Etta's parties, which she seemed to throw once a week. She quickly checked the lavish bathroom with the fancy Jacuzzi and bathtub, sprayed some air freshener to get the smells of yesterday out of there, opened the blinds by remote control, keeping the vertical blinds a little angled so not to get too much sunlight and she whipped out her huge vibrator.

"Shit, I'ma get me a quick cum up before the boss gets in. He always call before getting here, probably getting used to his fancy Razr phone." She left the panties home. Who needed the hassle? Panties were just indiscreet cock blockers and she didn't feel like being bothered by any barrier between fingers and pussy. Not today. Especially after last night. She didn't have the sex-sational night of passionate lovemaking like she'd grown used to. Her lover seemed preoccupied and thoughtless, her movement like sharp razors on concrete, just wasn't getting anywhere. And she went to bed, angry and frustrated, having to suck her thumb through the night to keep from throwing her lover out on her ass! Sitting behind her desk, she pushed her skirt up past her hips with a flourish, and what voluptuous hips. She damn near pissed on herself from the anticipation. She turned on the vibrator, which lubricated itself, some new fancy shit her cousin bought her from Tokyo and sent to her Federal Express. His whorish-ass was in the United States Airforce over there, fucking anything with two feet, trying to convince her to pay him a visit. Chinese men with narrowed eyes and an even narrower dick never got her past the thinking stages.

*Time to get to work!* She rubbed her pussy with long black nails, careful not to cut herself…sucked the wetness from her fingers, tasted like salt, the smell sent her haywire, and spread her velvet box with mountains of pubic hair in the V-shape, sliding the dildo so deep into her body she had to arch her back. What a wonderful feeling! Feeling adventurous she opened the vertical blinds so people in the other buildings could get a sneak peek and she got a burst of excitement, putting her stiletto-clad feet on her desk, spreading her legs as far as they'd go, and working the vibrating plastic toy, angling it so it hummed against her achingly sensitive clitoris. She bit her lip, grinding on her seat. The leather felt like the hands of a man…the grooves pressed against her back; felt like those massaging balls.

She could feel orgasms about to make their gentle but explosive debut already. *Not yet! Can't cum yet! Plenty time for that.* She had to admit that she'd never done this before, masturbate in the office. Hell, if she had half a brain, she'd realize her pension was in jeopardy, her 401 (k), the welfare of her only daughter Jessica, age 15, who was getting more and more into boys, and she was risking the best career of her life. Hell, if caught there would be news reports. Newspaper headlines. Public scrutiny, though she really didn't give a fuck about public opinion. They were freaks anyway, half of which were probably fucking themselves with dildos right this instant.

Before this very life-changing, challenging job as a paralegal, she worked at Winn-Dixie Supermarket in Naranja, Florida, thirty minutes south of where she was now. But she got fired after fucking the boss, his son, and everybody in the stock department when she was married, which prompted her divorce from a very bitter and angry black man who tried to shoot her, but to no avail. He wound up with full custody of his daughter, and when she rebelled, Jessica, by running away, going back to her mother, they arranged another court date and he signed over custody back to the mother, Miss Crucial Williams, from the Bronx, raised in Miami, graduated from Miami Edison High School.

*Seemed like yesterday!* Staring at the janitor across the way, in the opposite breathtaking building, who stopped mopping the floor when he saw this sexy vixen going to town, she licked her lips at him. Pulling the dildo from her pussy, sucking the depths of her womb from the damned thing, she moaned again. Sliding it back up inside of her, she squeezed her legs together, bringing her feet up and over to the side so the rest of the business men and women, who gawked at her in surprise, shock, disgust and excitement could get a good look at the huge dildo spreading her pussy to kingdom come. She caused quite a stir in her body. Her loins were on fire! Her ass was pretty, clean and tempting. Her feet ached monstrously. Trying to maintain control, her chair was rolling back from the desk.

Standing up, pulling her little friend from her body, she placed it on the desk in the upright position, climbed on it, lowered her body onto it and rode it like a cowboy, her knees two inches from the desk.

Her weave fell from the bun and framed her beautifully made-up face. "Fuck me, Daddy!" she screamed out in delight, smiling like a Cheshire cat. She closed her eyes and suddenly it was actor Mekhi Phiefer under her, beating that chocolate stick into her Candy Shop, tasting the Jolly Ranchers of her walls, the Snickers of her clitoris…and the Willy Wonka of her sweat.

About to lose his mind, the janitor quickly closed the door to the office across from her, unzipped his pants, pulled a chair up to the window so she could get a good look at his juicy dick, and he started masturbating, not even lubing his hand.

His legs shook.

His eyes were wide and congratulatory. He didn't even realize people from Crucial's building were forming at the window, mainly women and a few gay men, pointing, admiring, about to have information overload in the eyes. He focused all his attention on the slut across from him who was trying to drive him up the wall.

He pulled his pants down to his ankles, as he kissed at her, winked, smiled boyishly, how handsome he was, and the bouncing of his nuts between such chiseled thighs sent her over the edge.

She slammed her pussy on the dildo, her hands pressed firmly flat on the desk. It was a feat to keep balance, but she loved things that were hard to attain. She was sweating all over, her heart racing, feeling her salty walls slide up and down on such a fantastic creation.

She licked her lips, flipping the button on the toy to "very fast," and she lost control.

"Oh shit, baby, fuck me, *Mekhi*...MEKHI! Yea," she went on breathlessly, opening her eyes and being enraptured by her friend across the way, "...jack that dick, Mr. Janitor! Fuck me FUCK ME! Yes, fuck me long, hard and good! I know you can read my lips, you sexy bitch! Yes, fuck me fuck me, oh shit, yea..."

The toy hummed and hummed until the battery died, but she didn't lose a beat. She leaned forward; the toy angling and she continued to ride it, her titties falling free from the white lacey bra, bouncing all over her chest. She sat up, riding her toy, taking her left breast into her hand, thankful for the "wardrobe malfunction," and suckling on her swollen nipple, sending electricity up and down her spine, exploding in her toes. "Shit, my God this, this shit right here feels...so....good!"

She had enough of the desk. Back in the chair she went, opening her legs, sticking the toy up her tight, virgin ass. The pain was great but the pleasure that swarmed her like bees on honey more than made up for it. She went crazy. She grinded on the dildo, sending it deeper and deeper inside her. She felt uncomfortable. "Ain't lubed enough." *That's it!* Taking it out she sucked on it, tasting her ass, thankful she was a clean bitch. She spat on it repeatedly, taking the mushroom head of the toy and running it back and forth on the opening of her rectum, careful not to push it inside.

Then into softness she went, playing with her pussy while she banged her hole.

Her skin tingled. "YES!"

She rode it, cowgirl style. She felt powerful, invincible. She smiled when the police showed up to arrest Mr. Janitor. She had a gut instinct to stop, but she kept going. They were arguing, unfortunately she didn't hear when was being said. Mr. Janitor pointed at her, she laughed, using her left hand to spread her ass, and she rammed the toy deeper, deeper…sending an earthquake though her sweaty, tired body.

The cops were uninterested, the white female handcuffed him, leading him, kicking and screaming, out of the office. The other cop, white male, early twenties, slid the chair back behind the desk and when he turned to face Crucial. She smiled at him, fucking herself harder and smoother with her toy. He paused, wide-eyed, his dick getting hard instantly. Whipping out his walkie-talkie, he attempted to push the button and she winked and kissed at him. He thought about it. Locking the door, he said something into his radio, smiling lustfully at her, and then his blue eyes sparkled. He hurriedly got the chair, unzipped his pants, and he started pulling on his little weenie roast of a dick.

*How pathetic,* she thought happily. *Serve and protect, 'ey? Yea, right!* Ok, it was time to signal Mt. Saint Helen. Spread-eagled now, she rammed her toy deeper in her ass. Her fingers were soaked; she played with herself faster, more passionately, biting her lips.

Replaced was a pleasure she'd never felt. She'd never been fucked in her ass before. Never even thought about it really. She was a black woman; she didn't think black girls got kinky like that. She thought that was a white woman's trademark, their thing to do, their way to hook a black man, by letting him fuck her into remission with their Donkey Kong dicks. And now she was doing it, and it felt WONDEFUL! GREAT! *Shit, what have I been missing?*

Mr. Police unbuttoned his shirt, his walkie-talkie and gun holster falling on the floor, and he fingered his nipple, spitting on his hand, jacking his dick. He spread those legs. He didn't notice more and more people crowding the windows, all of them laughing at him. They wondered what he was looking at, what was he so focused on. He smiled, licking his lips, his legs trembling. He exploded with a ball-busting jolt! He squirmed in his seat as his torso moved up and down faster and faster and faster. She ran her tongue across her full lips, tasting the candy-flavored red lipstick her lesbian lover California bought her for their third anniversary last week. She had on this lipstick when she ate her woman out just after dinner the same night, smearing red lipstick all over her pink, sweet smelling pussy. She could damn near smell it now. Conventionally pretty, she pushed those thoughts from her head, and she stifled an imposing orgasm. The phone rang. Damn it!

Putting up her toy she answered. "Boss, that's you?"

"Yes it is. Today is interview day. Got the files ready?"

"I know, boss," Crucial said through the speaker phone on her cluttered but organized desk.

She loved interview day.

"You know what that means?"

"Yes. Hold all your calls, unless it's one of the interviewers calling to cancel."

"This would be career suicide because no one turns me down."

"I know, boss. I know all too well."

"I bet you do. How's your mother?"

"She's in L.A. shooting a commercial for dentures. She's pretty as hell, but I can't say the same for her teeth."

"So she got the gig? $1,200 for the spot. Extra cash she could use for her knitting class."

"She loves the commercial, but I doubt if she spend it on knitting. Hell she got a closet full of goddamn quilts, now."

"I need another assistant," said James, cruising the Macarthur Causeway, which linked Miami to South Beach. Beautifully constructed buildings were on either side of him, across a huge stretch of glittering water under the Miami sun. The top was down, his dick was hard, his nuts pulsated with vibrancy because he was on the verge of getting blue balls. No pussy action in a matter of months, too busy with work, paying bills, battling his Baby Mama in custody battle court (she didn't stand a chance), and warding off bill collectors, the same people he paid off days ago.

"Well, hopefully today you'll get one, James. Like you got me"

"Well, let's hope you're right."

An hour later, James Stewart entered his lavishly-expensive office on South Beach and sat behind his desk, silent. His glittering watch rented for show, he dusted the lint off his silk suit and smiled at his reflection in the mirror before him. Mr. Narcissistic. Knowing he had a shit load of emails, he leaned back in his high backed, cushioned chair, fixed his silk red tie and sighed.

Another day of interviews. He had to admit that he'd been too lenient on potential prospects. Yes, he was a cut-throat lawyer, but he needed cut-throat employees. This was how it was going to go. There were twelve interviews scheduled for today. He was going to test each and every applicant. He didn't care if they had felonies or not. To tell you the truth, the more checkered the past, the more he had to work with. Bianca Samuels. Ted Franks. Stephanie Johnson. Donald La'Shay. Fanny Daniels. Archie Bunker. Henry Jameson. Sampson Burkes. He smiled. He wondered how many he could fuck before the day was over.

Being the boss worked wonders.

# Invading MySpace

I met him on Myspace. I was checking out the men in Atlanta, Georgia, just *hoping* one was cute enough to spark my interest or at least get my fingers dancing across the keyboard by telling him the most sensual things about myself. I never knew that the very first black man I saw would do the trick. I just hoped he wasn't gay. Seemed like every man in Atlanta was either gay, bisexual or fucked men on the low and having chronic denial about it. They act like a sister didn't know.

I went to "Advanced Search" first. I went through the Process of Elimination. I didn't want a smoker, breath would be funky, and I didn't care how many Tic Tacs he sucked on or how much Scope he gargled. Smoke was smoke, and it would be in everything from his car to the clothes he wore. I didn't want a bisexual man, or a gay man. Double strike, mind you. I wanted my man to be just that: my man, I didn't want to leave for work and have to worry about him throwing on some Madonna and prancing around my bedroom clad in my thongs and bras. I didn't want an alcoholic, they didn't know how to act, and I knew where most of their paychecks would go: on goddamn liquor and the only liquor I wanted them drinking was my liquor, pronounced "lick her" from here to Kingdom Come when we're between the sheets.

I didn't want Hispanic men. They laughed too much for my taste. I liked my men to be serious, with a hint of humor, kind of like Oregano in my fried chicken. You can't really taste it, but it heightens the taste, feel me? Asians and anything that wasn't black didn't have a chance with me. He had to be at least 6 feet tall. I was a petite woman, five feet 2 inches with the most gloriously worked-on body. I took pleasure in how I looked and how I dressed. But the main reason why I loved tall men was because I liked to feel protected when we went out in public. What was a small, leprechaun-looking man going to do for me if trouble arose? Defend my ankles? Please!

After a minute of searching, I found him. Mr. Right. Well, I should say Mr. Right At this Moment. He was 6 feet 3 inches, Jamaican and Haitian, and he dressed immaculately nice. Who knew Haitians and Jamaicans mixed this elegantly well? I might have to send my home girl Danielle his profile and let her check it out. Nah. Couldn't do that. When women wanted something they spared no expense to get it, and Danielle was a jealous woman. She'd take any and every man I wanted, and I'd fuck her up today if he told me she got at him with a message, so I would keep him my guarded little secret. Intrigued and turned on by him, I checked out all of his profile pictures, carefully combing my eyes across his beautiful face and chocolate skin… they were very classy, nothing to showy or promiscuous, his nipples and chest were covered up, he smiled in every one of them, he didn't smoke nor drink. He was straight as an arrow. His profile was very tasteful. I liked it a lot. Since I didn't like adding friend's cold turkey on my profile, I shot him a very brief, to the point message. Hoping it would do the trick without the use of fireworks and explosions. Hell, I didn't need a man that badly.

Or maybe I *did* need one. I missed the company.

Of a good man. And good men didn't exist.

## Hello, beautiful Stranger;

**Hey, how are you. Hope I'm not a bother. I find you interesting, I'm 40 years old and I find men on Myspace interesting, go figure, lol (laugh out loud). Check out my profile, if you like what you see I would greatly appreciate it if you hit me up and let me know what the deal is.**

**Much Love,**

**Stacie Mender.**

After sending it, I then sent the friend invite. I felt like I was sending off for a job interview. The letter seemed so formal. So, you know, in your face. Did it sound desperate? I didn't want to come off seeming like I couldn't find a man in person. But he was 10 miles away from my zip code in Marietta County. He was single, so why not go for the juggler? Before I could log off, my heart pounded just waiting for his response, I looked at his pictures one more time. Fanning myself. Phew. *Hot!* Quicker than Bounty paper towels soaking up spilt milk, he sent a response. This was the Cash 3 winning numbers. The jack pot! I damn near fell on the floor. Covering my mouth in shock, my hands begin trembling. Why was I in shock? He was just a black man, probably a dead beat, with three kids, Baby Mama drama and a few diseases. He probably didn't have a bank account, lived with his Mama and never met his Daddy. Probably been to jail, or even worse, prison. Maybe I should just erase his reply, he probably found me to be desperate or one of those fire-in-the-pussy Hoes that probably hit him up every day.

"Oh, *God*, I shouldn't have disturbed this man," I whispered nervously, my throat constricted…standing up in my sexy black lingerie and pulled out a Benson and Hedges cigarette, lighting up and by the time I took a puff I realized I had a Nicoderm patch on my upper arm, been wearing them for about six months, haven't touched a cigarette in that long, and I was taking the back slide, all over a man. I stubbed it out in the ash tray on the nightstand and looked at the picture of my son Billy, framed in silver. He died last month, car jacking in Portland, Oregon. I was still distraught over that, because we were on bad terms when he was gunned down over those pricey rims I warned him not to buy. In fact the last few weeks of his 23 year old life I begged him to come back home, but I was hardly there for him because I worked all the time to keep a roof over his head, and being that he was well-fed and well taken care of, he needed his mother and I wasn't there. I did it all on my own. I never married his father, because he was too busy chasing Hoes all over the place, and had eight other children from eight other women who all hated me with a passion, and I hated them, well, maybe hate was too strong a word. Tears wet my face as I sit at the computer, pick up the remote and turn on some Al Green *Good or Bad, Happy or Sad,* and I sing along, *I, I, I*…rhythmically snapping my fingers, bobbing my head, moving the cursor to the "inbox" link and clicking it. I saw his beautiful picture. I smiled, tasting some tears and opened his response.

# Beautiful Stranger,

Hello, pretty lady. You seem like a real genuine woman. I read your profile. You like Al Green. I love him, but I've been getting deeper into Gerald Levert, since the brother just passed away. I don't respond to women on here, all they want is sex, sex, sex, and never bother to ask how a brother's day went.

But your message struck me as odd, because you are a very sensual woman and your message was very refreshingly different, but it's all good because you have become the first woman I've responded to.

I know it's a bit presumptuous, but I'm free this evening, I don't do Myspace all the time, I come on here to promote my spoken word CD "Fire in my Eyes." So if you would do me the honor of going to dinner I would be flattered. I know we just met, sort of, and freaks are on Myspace. So if you want to meet me at a discreet public place then that's fine as well.

My phone number I will include after this message so you can call me with your answer. Much love, and once again you are a very pretty woman. Is your personality an identical twin?

Hope to find out soon. Thad Johnson.

Thad. *Thad* was his name. I *loved* the name, damn near original, different. I racked my brain, trying to see if I met any Thads…*Chad*, yes. But *Thad?* Very original. Thad, Mr. Thad Johnson. Mrs. Thad Johnson, Mrs. Stacie Mender-Johnson! Sounded like a *ding ding ding* winning situation to me, sh…it! I damn near fell over in my chair, smiling. I hoped he wasn't a player, but he didn't seem that way. Yet since when did words someone typed online packed emotion? Why was I thinking of churches, wedding bells, expensive-Pawn-ready-engagement rings, champagne, dick, honeymoons and thresholds? Maybe I was losing my mind! How did one find out his true intention? He said women hit him up all the time tying to fuck him. I wasn't trying to "fuck," I needed a friend, a good friend, a man I could talk to, be down with, and be there for. Be his companion if it came to that. Slowly grow old with. My wet mid-section wasn't the issue. I didn't need sex for validation or to get in fit in then get out. Nah. Those years were gone. And what animatedly-colorful years, *Ow*, baby! I had good pussy. So I sat on it like gold. Dick was the fire to test the gold lining in my vagina; I was talking about the type of good dick that didn't come with Nutrition Facts, a stench or side effects that landed a bitch like me on the doctor's cold-ass iron tables, dreading STD's.

But my dildo has done the honors for the past year. Of testing the gold trim in my pussy…and really done the honor when my son died. I swore. My dildo pulled me through. Yea, I had the Bible, read the Bible and dissected the Bible; I could even open the Good book and remind myself of the tear-stained pages that attempted to get me through my ordeal. Yet failed miserably. But my dildo was here with me. Kept me sane. Rocked me into a deep sleep, so deep alarm clocks and buzzers failed to wake me up on time for work.

As much as I didn't want to think about that dark time in my life, I remembered his funeral, I was a wreck. Thank God my friends helped plan the funeral, I was indecisive. I cursed the workers from the funeral home out because they kept harassing me about what color suit my son was going to wear, since half of his pictures (when he was living) were taken with a purple, feather-clad fedora, should he wear it while being lowered 6 feet into God's Ice Box of an Earth. Should his friends be allowed to give testimony? Who was going to write the poem? I didn't have the mentality to deal with all that.

On a muggy, rainy Saturday, his funeral day had arrived. I wanted to stay home. I couldn't go to his funeral. I didn't want to feel the sunlight on my skin, and I didn't want to breathe. I felt like I was being robbed and had been robbed every time I drew in God's resilient air and my son couldn't do the same anymore. I remembered our last conversation. We argued big time. I wanted him home, because he wrote me a letter stating that he joined the ridiculously formed Blood Gang. I was in an outrage. My son was never abused, never talked down to, never ashamed by me. I gave him the world; I just couldn't give him all my time.

I was a nervous wreck, scared for my child. "What do you mean you joined the Blood Gang?" I wanted to throw the lamp across the room and dance in the solace of glass shattering. "Have you fallen and bumped your damn head, boy?"

He sucked his teeth, pure bitch fashion. "I'm 23 years old! I don't fall and I bump my head in pussy, I'ma grown man."

"Stating that you're grown is supposed to be the Kryptonite to Superman's S on his chest, right?"

"In English, please."

"How about in Japanese?"

"I don't know what that Kryptonite shit meant."

Wide-eyed, "Watch your mouth."

"I *am*, standing in the mirror, holding the phone, smoking my joint, listening to you babble."

"Babble? I'm your mother, and I never raised you to do drugs."

"All the kids are doing it."

"At least I know you're a hypocrite."

"Meaning, Mama?"

"I thought you were a grown man, yet you are following little kids."

"Stop playing your mind games on me, it doesn't work anymore."

I said "Whatever."

"Hold on, the AC is too cold, let me turn it down."

I was brutally defiant. "Where are you living up there? And I don't want to hold on."

"What?" he screamed; his voice an echo. I heard some soft banging noises, like he was opening some closet doors. "I didn't hear you."

"Am I on speaker phone?"

"Yes, Mama, I need both my hands."

"TMI, Niggah!"

"Too much information, now you sound like Sting and the Police."

"This is getting us nowhere."

He took me off speaker. "Mama, deal with it, I live once in my life, I don't want my Mama trying to embarrass me before the world because she can't let go of her son and let him try to grow into a man."

I was infuriated. I couldn't believe he would talk to me in this fashion! My *sweater* didn't even itch across my ample breasts in that fashion so I would be *damned* if a Niggah that came kicking and screaming out of my pussy, putting me through ten hours of the most painful labor of my life was going to talk down to me like red carpets all over Hollywood! "Watch your mouth. You aren't too grown for me to kick your ass."

He laughed bitterly, made my skin crawl. Angrily, I rubbed the Nicoderm patch, hoping it released enough nicotine to keep my eyes off the cigarette pack on the dresser, by my perfume bottles. I kept eyeing it, trying to keep myself calm. OK, gurl, he was a hurt young man lashing out. I had to deal with it, good or bad he was my son.

"I am too grown, and I will call 5-0 if you put your hands on me."

I was hurt. "You'd call the white man on me?"

He was silent. "No, Ma, I am not a snitch, but damn you got to cut the umbilical cord at some point in my life."

"The way your Daddy cut yours then left me to go make other babies with other women to cut their cords?"

Suffice it to say, he became less bitter and more sympathetic, yet he still had an attitude imprisoned in the soul of his voice. He was a very intelligent, handsome young man, just like his Romeo-and-Juliet-looking Daddy, no good piece of shit. "I'm sorry, Ma. He shouldn't have left you out to dry. I know you love me, you did keep a roof over my head."

Ha! "You remembered, goddamn shocked that you do, thought you had selective amnesia for a second…"

"I respect you, Ma."

"Then why are you making me suffer?" I spat without thinking, trying not to sound venomous.

He went in for the kill. "Because you were never there for me. You always worked, never spoke to me, and were too tired to speak to me. When I was 14 I lost my virginity. I tried to talk to you, because I didn't know I was not supposed to fall in love and marry the first piece of pussy, I meant cunt, I meant coochie that I got. But you told me you were *too* sleepy. You'd just gotten home from work. I was deeply hurt. When I was jumped on after graduation I called you at your job, and *yea* I understand you're a police dispatcher, but I needed you, yet you were too busy. But you always found time to go to Christmas parties and outings with your co-workers, yet I'm your only child and I was at home, crying myself to sleep because my Daddy abandoned me, cut the cord early, and you abandoned me, and still haven't cut the cord yet."

"I did what I had to do; do you want a druggie mother? An alcoholic mother? A mother who is an abuser, stripper?"

"I respect you, Ma. I'm glad you're strong. But I joined the gang to fit in. I love it on the West Coast."

"Son, *please*, I *beg* of you, get out of that gang, don't they kill you if you try you demolish ties with them? Kill up your whole family?"

"I don't know, this *isn't* the mafia."

"I got to go, don't have time for all this."

"Ma, I love…"

"I'm mad at you!" And I hung up in his face. My son was murdered not too long after that.

Maybe that was why I was having such a hard time dealing with his death. I couldn't accept it because of the unresolved feelings he had towards my never being there for him. Because of the things I told him. Because I gave him such a hard time. Because I was actually mad at him when he died.

Maybe that made it easier for him to die, thinking I was mad at him, which probably made him think his own mother didn't love him anymore. This tore me up, I began shedding tears the way snakes shed skin…shaking with fear and trembling…I needed those cigarettes. I picked up the pack, extracted one and quickly threw it on the dresser.

I looked at Thad's easy-on-my-itchy-red-eyes picture. Calmed down some, sat down and I checked my inbox again.

He'd sent his phone number. I snatched up my cell phone and called him. I let it ring once, goddamn it I shoulda pressed the "blocked number" feature so his caller I.D. wouldn't register my name and phone number. It'd show up as Private Number. Before I could hang up he answered, speaking with the smokiest, most ghetto-flavored voice I'd ever heard, packed with the ingredients that electrified my favorite strawberry ice cream. My mouth agape, I started stuttering, a duh a duh a duh I got the wrong number.

Click. Before I could turn off my phone he called back, damn it I hope he wasn't a stalker, I hoped I didn't make a mistake, calling him. And why did he call me right back? Wasn't that too soon to call me back, shouldn't he wait for me to call *him* back? Wow, what did I get myself into?

I answered, lighting a cigarette, puffing it so strongly I snatched off the patch, fuck the goddamn patch, the hell with all the goddamn patches!

"Yes, yes, yes, hello." I strained to sound like a white bitch. All airy and shit, air-headed. I had "As if," "Not even," and *"Like, totally!"* on standby in the dusty chambers of my lips.

"Hello, how are you, ma'am?"

Oh, God! And he got manners! He spoke *before* he asked for Stacie. Phenomenal, and emphasis on the word "men" in phenomenal. "I'm fine, like, totally fine." Oh, God, shoot me, I was making a complete fool of myself.

"May I ask with whom I'm speaking?"

"Donjanabi."

He chuckled. "Donjanabi? Unique name."

*Flirt!*

"Thank you, it's African for good punani!"

He chocked through the phone, laughing.

"May I speak with Stacie, please?"

"As if, not even, like totally not cool, dude!" I wanted to laugh; I stuck my fist in my mouth, about to run out of the room. A forty year old woman acting like a kid. I never thought I'd see the day. I know the stock in the gold trim of my pussy just took a nosedive by 23 points on the Dow Jones.

"Why you say that pretty lady?" he asked.

God! He's. Saying. All. The. Right. Things! "I don't know," I went on, tossing my hair all girly, looking silly.

I stomped my toe on the bed post and I was hopping up and down in grave pain.

Damn, that shit hurt. I couldn't help but laugh when the pain subsided.

He said, "Are you ok?"

I said, "Yes."

"So I want to just forget all the preliminaries. Let's grab a bite to eat. Hell, let's go now, what do you say?"

*Hell nah! Are you serious? You can be a stalker, a rapist. You can try to kill me; I don't just meet men and go out with them! Hell no!*

*You must have fell and bumped your head, like I said I don't need men that desperately and you're trying to call me a damn liar! if I say "yes" it would confirm everything I just said.*

"Sure, let's do it."

"Where do you live?"

I gave him my address.


I heard the doorbell an hour later.

I was looking myself over in the mirror, loving what I saw. A very sexy woman, yay! I closed the magazine *Black Confessions* and I tossed it on the low-table. Thankful I went for my Pap Smear test on time this month. Now I didn't have to worry about it.

I was wearing a boat neck sweater I ordered from the Victoria's Secret catalogue and black pants. High heels, and a bunch of accessories. I looked flawless. No make-up, didn't feel like being carbon copies. Tonight. Let's set the tone. Let's be real and original.

I was walking towards the front door when the thought of my son hit me like bricks. I rested my hand on the door knob, twisted and the man stood before me, a sight for sore eyes. He looked better than his photos. He wore a thin leather jacket, nice sweater, and loose jeans with black leather boots. He was meticulously groomed; I loved the way he smelled.

"Come in."

"Thank you." He handed me a box of Vera Wang perfume and a dozen white roses. I was wet instantly, yet I tried to keep my mind off the bedroom, I didn't want to play ring around the sheets and matters with him just yet.

He followed me into the high tech kitchen.

"You have a lovely home."

I put the roses in a vase, turned on the tap water, opened the Tylenol and put two in the water, and in went the stem of the roses. Mama always taught me that roses would live longer if you gave them Tylenol. I never believed her, but I've become superstitious and now I do it.

"Thanks. I do what I can."

"You do it well." He gave me the once over, without seeming perverted. "You are absolutely amazing."

I tucked my chin back with a smile. "Damn, it's like that?"

"Yea, Ma, it's like that!" Thad sat at the dining table, looking over the ceramic bowls, the non-stick pots hanging on hooks, dangling over the three island counters, the fake plants. The tiled floors. Everything in my kitchen was where it was supposed to be.

"Stacie, so are you ready?"

"Yes. Let me grab my purse, wait here."

I went up the stairs, to my room, grabbed my purse and pivoting, I froze. I could not get my son off my mind. I missed him, truly felt guilty. I needed him, he was my baby. This burned me inside. A mother losing her son. I didn't want my son thinking or dying thinking that I hated him. I loved him so much and before I knew it I dropped the purse on the floor, fell to my knees, snatched out my wallet, pulled out a picture of my son and I held it to my heart.

"I love you, my son Mama loves you. I miss you; I can't believe you died on me, baby why did you leave?"

I was whisked off my knees and pulled into Thad's embrace. I fought him, this was my pain, not his, he just met me but he wouldn't let me go. "Beat me, Stacie, I don't care, beat me, scratch my eyes out, fight me and I'll still hold you, get out all of your anger, and properly mourn your son…"

I punched him repeatedly in the chest, he didn't wince because he was a real man, and real men were wired differently from immature so-called thug men.

He held me, rubbing my shoulders. He rocked with me, back and forth, our groins pressed together. He looked into my sore, red eyes, our lips finding the metal for the magnets on our tongues and before we knew it we were kissing, while he hummed a Sam Cooke Cut. Only you send you. Darling you send you. Thrill me.

Our tongues danced in complete harmony; as I tried to turn every romance novel I ever read into a reality, I took off his jacket, wanting to feel his skin. Off came his shirt. He took his time, he didn't show a sign that he wanted to rush. We kissed and kissed, trapped in a lip lock, my nipples erect, my desire wet and willing, throbbing and pulsating. I felt him pressed against me, the urgency breath taking, we kissed and we kissed, until I couldn't breathe.

I backed away, squatting down and picking up my purse. He snatched it, threw it across the room, pulled me to him and said, "First, I'm going in your fridge and cooking you a meal. Two, we are going to sit at your dining table, and enjoy it. Three, we're going to watch an old school movie, I'll pick it. Four, I am going to run you a hot bath. Five, I will turn on jazz on your stereo and watch the TV in your room while you spend quality time with Stacie, you need it. Six. When you're done with your bath I will dry you off, carry you to the bed, and give you a deep body massage for an hour, with lotions and oils. Then I will strip naked, hold you and we will sleep the night away. I don't want to have sex with you. I want to pamper you, spend the night with you for your companionship, your company."

By the time he was done I looked at him and said, "So when you want to get started, since you invading my space, lol."

"LOL, laugh out loud, 'ey? We can get started now."

"Well, follow me to the kitchen. I got a feeling you won't be going home for a long time."

"Do you want spaghetti or lamb chops, I know you got some lamb chops."

"Guess we'll find out, Thad." He made do on everything he promised. All *that*, and *no* sex.

Guess there are some good men in the world.

# Jadish Houston 2

Saxophone Jenkins
Special Day 2006

*Hello, baby! How are you doing today? I hope this little "note" found you in the best of health and good spirits. I know you're fed up with the fact that you haven't boned your wife yet. Bitter pill to swallow, I know. But this is only temporary. I compiled a little list, which I'm typing right now. You have to do everything on the list so lie back in the tub, relax, smile and be to yourself and your thoughts. Forget about church today, even though it's Sunday. We need alone time. Please don't fight me on this. While you relax, I want you to think about your past. Do you remember how we first met? Do you remember the first words we said to each other? I can remember when you first smiled. I nearly fell down the stairs at the Convocation Building on the University of Miami College campus. Do you remember that? Do you remember our bond? Reflect. The glow and the warmth of the candles should dig silence in your head, allowing you to open-mindedly engulf everything you feel for me. The incense and the gentle smell should open the deepest part of you, a part you thought was forever sealed, and you should let what comes out walk out so you can examine it and hope it makes you a better person. It should allow you to flow with what I'm doing for you. The bubbles in the tub and the warmth of the water, mixed with some edible oil should make your skin soft and collaborate with your being able to allow yourself to let your special Day*

*engross you. I went all out for this day, pulled out all the stops. I know you work*
*6 days a week and you come home drained and tired. Today is your day, baby.*

*Let go your inhibitions. Let go of your problems. Forget that people exist in*
*the world. When you hear my voice let the universe cease to exist. The only two*
*people that exist are you and I. The bathroom is the Meditation, Release Room.*
*Utilize it. Let go of imposing bills. I'm cutting your phones off. The special*
*request goes as listed below:*

1) *Open the envelope titled: Mr. Jenkins, leaning against the wall on the front of*
   *the tub. You should be facing it.*
2) *Secondly, listen the Zhane songs "La La La," and "Off my Mind." Listen*
   *to the words. That's how I feel about you.*
3) *Then listen to Mary J Blige's "Beautiful Ones." And "All I have to Say."*
   *"Beautiful Ones" embody everything I feel for you. When I hear this song I*
   *think about you.*
4) *Then put in the PM Dawn CD and listen to "Die Without you" from the*
   Boomerang *soundtrack. This used to be my "cry" song. When I was*
   *depressed I'd play this to cry to.*
   *I know in my heart you are my soul mate. Life is too short for all the*
*fighting and arguing and fussing and alienation.*

   *By now you should know you have a beautiful best friend who thinks the*
*world of you and would do anything for you.*


*Sincerely,*
*Jadish Houston. Your wife.*


Feelings of ecstasy surging through me like out of control waves, I
smiled, pressing print and watching the paper spit from the printer.
Neatly folding it, I went into the bedroom, sprayed some perfume on
it and sealed the stationary inside a scented envelope.

Yes, it was set.

When my husband comes home, everything will be perfect.

Tossing my short, croppy hair behind my head, I stood up from
the chair and tugged on my tennis skirt. My tits were bare. Quite the
little slut today, I frowned because I never really felt this way about
my husband. Considering we haven't made love yet, I know he had a
lot of anger towards me. But like most wives, I wanted to believe that
he loved me enough to get over that anger. After a couple years of
marriage, I was exhausted from fighting with him. I was tired of
putting off the inevitability of sex with your mate. I knew I was to
blame. What man wanted to be married to a woman he couldn't fuck?

I unscrupulously ran my hands over my dripping kitty cat and wiped it all over the envelope. Thank God I wasn't wearing any panties. My man would love me tonight, but first I had someone to go and see. There was something that I wanted to know, and I couldn't put it off a moment sooner.

I grabbed my car keys and hit the door.

When I turned my car onto the turnpike, I huffed and puffed because I immediately saw two major traffic accidents, all involving these non-driving Cubans. Damn it! I couldn't turn around. Damn it! I brought my car to a halt and put it in park, turning off the ignition, saving gas. I was getting mad really fast.

On the radio was the weather report. Partly cloudy. *Yea, I know. I'm looking at the sky right now, dumb announcer. Chance of rain, got that. I do see rain drops on my windshield, damn who paid your payroll?* My cell phone rang, startling me. My heart hammering, it took a minute to calm down. It was Daddy. *What the hell does he want?* Exhaling audibly. "Hey, Pop," I said excitedly. He knew I was faking the funk.

Cautiously, he said, "I'm doing good. Where are you?"

I narrowed my eyes. "I'm trapped in traffic on the turnpike."

He grunted. "Damn, baby. I needed a ride home."

*Call Mama! Isn't she your wife?* "Dad, I can't control the traffic."

"I know, baby. I didn't mean to sound like I was coming down on you."

*Oh, yes the hell you did!* "No problem."

"I guess I got to find another way home."

The guilt trip starts. "Call my husband, Daddy."

"Well I'll be damned. Why didn't I think of that?"

We kissed each other through the phone, something we always did.

"Call me later, Pa."

"Love you, baby."

"I love you, too."

"And be careful…"

I flipped my cell phone closed, staring at a cement truck.

I thought about my God Daddy. Tommy.

# Tommy

I have photos of all my lovers. I either took the pictures with my own camera or they gave them to me. I have four photo albums filled with them. Sexy, beautiful black women.

With huge red X's over their faces. Those were my Ex Files. There were Ex Files in my year books. From junior high to high school. I still have them, put up somewhere in the storage closet. People smiling, laughing, and frowning in their pictures. With big red X's over their faces. Meaning they got the Mark of the Freak. I fucked them and left them. They were forever branded with the big red X. Ten ladies from the cheerleading team with small red X's on their magnificently gorgeous faces.

We didn't speak or know each other during school hours. But during the freak-comes-out-at-night hours, from 8 PM until 2 AM, we got it on fiercely, like two dogs. I had an orgy with four of the cheerleaders, and two women from the track team also stopped by and got busy with me. Being that I was the only man, I tried like hell to handle all that pussy. I did a superb job. That's how my father raised me. Being from Alabama, he raised me to fuck 'em and leave 'em. He did my mother that way. She didn't seem to mind being dogged. And even though she was my mother, if she didn't help herself why should I waste my time? Growing up, I didn't understand it, but I did what Dad said. He used to bring grown woman over to the house when I was twelve and he pushed them on me. So I had a crash course in Fucking 101. The best of the best taught me what I know now.

Dad and I hardly spent time together, because when he wasn't working he was fucking bitches from here to California. Getting them pregnant and leaving them. At last count Dad has twenty-three children. And he did nothing for them. Presently, Dad and I occasionally speak. But I felt nothing for him. When I thought about him I thought of pussy. And that's bad. Now that I was a man I had a problem with commitment. I was more committed to taking bitches to the telly (Hotel) than making them happy. I loved fogging up those mirrors. Once my Grade A beef knocked 'em out with one shot for the rest of the night I'd write "The freak was here" on the mirror, put on my clothes and drive my ass to my crib. But the high school days were on my mind right now. The Ex Files. The female softball team. Eight of them. We were hungry and searching for the next nut before the squirrels came out to play with the roosters every morning. So full of testosterone I was. So full of emptiness when the bitches drained my nuts dry.

Two females on the cross country track team. Big red X's. Three from the water polo team. Big red X's. Women's basketball team. Nine of them. Big red X's. Male basketball team. Eleven red X's. All one-night stands. Fuck now, forget me later.

Prison: four big red X's. I only took photos with the ones I did something with. Had to survive in jail. No way was I going to get killed or stabbed. So I did what I had to do, slinging this dick for food, protection and continued coverage. I kept it discreet, even had a few corrections' officers, and got out with no bumps and scrapes.

Throughout my twenties, before I got locked up, and even after that, I only dated people for one reason: to see how many I could actually date and get away with it. The only thing that separated me from my low-life father was the fact that I didn't father kids. I didn't want kids. Seemed women these days only wanted to have your babies so they could get a certified check to go spend on their new men and I'd kill the bitch. So why put myself in that position?

Once I fucked females I crossed their faces out with a red marker. They ceased to exist in my world. If I got it in one hour, one minute, one second or one week, I crossed them out. Too quickly. No respect for themselves. No hesitation. If they could fuck me at the drop of a dime then how many other people did they drop dimes for? Biggie Smalls said "It was all a dream," for me it was all a game. I used my strong sex appeal to get my lovers in the sack. I set records for myself. I never had to pay for it. Never had to really beg for it. My body alone and my handsome face and brown eyes did that for me. I sometimes fell in love with a few lovers. But the love wasn't what you thought it was. It was a love for sex. A love for having powerful orgasms. A love for the chase. A love for the thrill. When I cut them loose, I didn't weep, shed a tear or ask for them back.

Almost everyone have Ex Files. One night stands thrive on this. Meaningless sex has gone public. If meaningless sex was on the stock market, this would be a wicked world, more wicked then it was now.

But there was one photo I didn't put in my photo album. I couldn't do it because I felt bad enough as it was now. How could I betray a woman that was my best friend's daughter? I had to get the pussy, she was banging. The sexiest woman I'd ever seen. It wasn't about my homeboy, who I respected with everything in me. This was about testing the pussy before anyone else did. Yea. I was a grimy Niggah! If he found out he should kill my ass. But getting the panties was worth it. I fell in love with her the day I hit it. I couldn't get her off my mind. Day in and day out I thought of her and what she may be doing. I was proud of her when she graduated college. I'm in the college photos with her, sometimes the red marker beckoning me to X out her face. But how do you X out love?

Back then, she was so stuck up. She saved the pussy like it was gold. And knowing that I was the first to beat the pussy up fulfilled me in ways I couldn't explain. Her husband, Sax, hadn't even tapped the pussy yet and he's married to her. I felt so sorry for him, knowing I was the reason he wasn't getting any. I couldn't stand the Niggah anyways, talking shit to me. Insulting me in public. I will never forget he dumped Sprite soda on my head at the Red Lobster. I wanted to shoot his Ho ass!

I thought about this when there was a knock at my door. I wondered who it was. People didn't really visit me. I put on a baseball cap and answered the door.

I blinked once. She blinked back. Jadish Houston hugged me, "Hey, how are you, God Daddy?"

I cringed inside. Have to save face. I could hardly breathe.

"Come on in, girl."

She walked past me like a good dream. She was fine as all outdoors. I had to will my dick not to get hard. When good pussy was around you, your dick had a mind of its own. I had to act like a grown man right now, and not a little boy. I closed the door, tugged on my NY Yankees sweater and said, "Want something to drink?"

She gave the sweetest smile, standing in my need-to-clean-it-living room, trying to look innocent. "Yes. You got a Coke?" She sat on my sofa, crossing her legs. She leaned back, eyeing me suspiciously. I didn't quite understand why she was sizing me up, but I liked it. I loved attention.

I went into the kitchen and opened the refrigerator. I needed to go grocery shopping. Pulling out a bottle of soda, I closed my eyes and breathed in deeply. I could smell her on the air. I had to stand at the sink to keep it together. My nature stood at attention. I wanted Jadish, God I wanted to fuck her again. I couldn't get my mind off...

"Are you ok, Tommy?" she asked me, walking up behind me. Her hands were on my shoulders, softly massaging them. "Where's the soda?"

*Please don't touch me, girl! I won't be responsible for what I do.* I squeezed my eyes closed tightly, feeling like I was being taunted.

I turned around and gave her the soda. She unscrewed the top and took a hefty swig. Smacked her lips. Looked me deep in the eyes.

"How was your day, haven't heard from you in a long time, Tommy." She drinks from the bottle again, rolling her tongue across the top, making me shiver. Wide-eyed, my mouth open, I pulled my sweater over my hard on. She looked down at it, smacking her lips again. "Something wrong with your dick or something?"

I couldn't believe she was being this direct. She hardly ever *used* that word. She was a good girl and I liked her being a good girl.

"My day was good, and I'm just fine."

She looked at the junk on my dining table, the lotion bottle, the empty beer cans, and the cigarette butts overflowing in three ash trays, the uneaten KFC (Kentucky Fried Chicken).

She softly bit her index finger. "I have a question, and I want you to be honest."

I was stuttering. "Yes, Jadish, I have never lied to you."

"...You look tense. Have a seat at the dining table."

I didn't move. I was a block of cement.

"Come on," she went on, setting the soda on the table, and pulling out the chair. "Sit." I stood there, staring at her. She pushed me in the chair, I just looked at her. "You love me, right, like a daughter?" she asked, and the question threw me through a loop. My head was ringing, my ears doing the same thing.

"Yes. You're my god daughter." She straddled my leg, gripping the Coke, taking it to the head. Her small Adam's apple bobbed with each satisfying gulp. She smacked her lips, got on her knees, unzipped my pants, pulled out my dick and began chopping me up. Oh my Lord. I went wild. Her lips felt so good, so right. I *knew* she would eventually come back to the dick that popped her cherry. She was wiggling her head, tossing her hair, running her tongue along the incredible inches.

She took the lotion bottle, lathered up her hands and began jacking my dick. She stroked it just right, the way I loved. She didn't rush, she took her time. Her soft hands drove me crazy. I pulled my pants down to my ankles so my nuts and legs had fighting room. My toes curled in my Nike Airs. She sucked my balls, jacking just the head of my passion, looking me deep in my narrowed eyes. Sensations tempting me to bend her over the sofa, my mouth hung open from the pleasure.

She said, "I remember when we fucked on my graduation night, baby…You had some good dick, Daddy…"

I empathized with her, knowing I was a scum bag. "Baby, I didn't mean to. I wanted you. Yea, baby, suck them nuts, goddamn baby." I held her head, guiding her lips up and down on my dick.

"You were…" Slurp, slurp. "Good, Daddy, the way you beat my tight pussy, the way you fucked me in the ass. It felt so right and so good."

I was stunned. I thought I doped her up good. I was a little nervous. What if she told her father? He'd shoot my ass, and I was scared of that Niggah. What if her husband found out? Now that I think about it, I think Sax does know.

I was in love, I wanted her, I needed her. "I can do a repeat right now."

"Let me get your first nut out of the way." She sucked me really good; she upped the ante, pulled out all the tricks. Damn. She sucked my dick like she loved it, like the world was about to explode. She tasted my nuts, spat on my dick, made it super wet, the way I loved and she gave me that hot mouth. I had my hands over my face, my hat falling on the floor. My hips were out of control. I felt the heat rising, mixing with the cold air, creating in the base of my testicles a tornado, spewing my seeds into a rage. I was about to come and I said it amidst a plethora of moaning, my loins locked up, she sucked harder and faster, making my nuts bounce on her open palm. Damn! I loved being a man! I loved pussy! Damn I was addicted! Come spurted from the hole of my dick and I started screaming when she bit my dick like it was a Vienna sausage, sank her teeth deep in my skin, she punched me in the nuts and I was trapped amongst the worst pain in my life. Blood was everywhere as a terrible stinging sensation shot through my body, why was she doing this? Why did she attack me?

She felt betrayed; I could see the hurt on her face. "You *drugged* me, bitch! *And* you raped me! I didn't *remember* that shit, I lied, leading you on! You're the reason why I haven't even fucked my own husband yet, why I caused him so much grief, because I tried to understand why I woke up a day after my graduation with my asshole and pussy throbbing and hurting!" She slapped me so hard my head slammed into the edge of the sink. I held my head, moaning piteously.

"You will pay, motherfucker!"

She took the frying pan from the dish rack and all I remembered was blacking out on the floor when she brutally beat me in the head with it, screaming in a fit of rage.

X'ed out in my own Ex Files.

Jadish walked out to her car, running her hands up and over her skirt. She felt like a huge burden, a huge weight, was lifted off her shoulders. She felt she could breathe, the chains of the unknown snapping free, releasing her from bondage. She felt whole, like a real woman, and not a zombie, coming and going throughout her life because she didn't understand why she felt the way she felt after her graduation. She knew something wasn't right with her body, she knew it then, but couldn't prove it. And now she knew the truth.

Tommy lost her trust forever.

She called her father.

"Hey, Dad. Where are you?"

"With your husband. He says hi."

"Tell him I love him."

"She said she loves you, Sax," her Dad said, his voice a little distant.

She heard her baby say, "I love you, sweetheart. See you when I get home."

"Dad, give Sax the phone."

"Damn it, why can't you call him on his own fucking phone?"

"Because I pay your cell phone bill."

"Low blow."

"And I pay Mama's bills."

"She's your Mama, you're supposed to."

"No," said Jadish, getting in her car and leaving Tommy's house forever. "You're supposed to be paying her bills."

He avoided the imposing argument. "Here's Sax."

"Hey, baby," he said, faking.

"Hello, Sax. When are you coming home?"

*Does it matter? Am I gonna get to fuck?* "In about an hour."

"Make sure you do."

He sucked his teeth. "Whatever, and do the same thing, hug, kiss, maybe a little rubbing, cuddle, watch TV, and go to sleep. Wow, I'm really looking forward to that."

She smiled, turning up R. Kelly's old school cut "Your Body's Calling," from the 12 Play album (his best album) on the radio. She snapped her fingers, bobbed her head and said, "I'm looking forward to it, too, baby."

And she hung up.

# Leave it to Beaver

I, Baxter Douglass, immediately jumped in the shower when I got home. Sharon, a fine ass dime piece, called me on my cell phone and told me those life changing words.

"When are you coming to get this pussy?"

"Shit, you don't gotta tell me twice."

I've been waiting on this pussy for fifteen days. I was the type of Niggah who got the panties within seconds of meeting women. I wasn't trying to be serious. Hell, I had fourteen baby Mamas from here to Beaumont, Texas. I beat all their asses, too. I used to pimp nine of them, had those bitches slangin' pussy like the shot put at the Olympics. One of my Baby Mama's worked at Target Superstores in Beaumont. She put me on child support. Called my phone, talking all kinda crap. "My new man called your son *his* son and your son called him Daddy!"

"Don't get homeboy fucked up!"

"Die, Niggah! You *better* have the money in the mail or that's your ass, faggot!"

"Watch your mouth!"

"You are tutti-frutti! All the threesomes we had with Niggahs, to please your appetite! What about when I spanked your ass with a dildo! Talk about *that*!"

I was steaming. "All right, Ho! You're *pushing* me!"

The truth hurt, but my sex life and what I do in the bedroom and inside cars in the bushes was on the low. I never discussed this and she pulled my card.

What she said had me upset. Ate away at me. I hated lippy bitches. I had to do something about it. No one stepped on my manhood.

No one!

Angrily quiet, I booked a flight online, cheaptickets.com. I paid out the ass. I didn't care. I had money to burn. I packed a small bag and printed out the confirmation page. Folding it, I stuffed it in my wallet and locked my crib. Hopping in my car, I headed for the freeway.

An hour later, I was in the air via Continental Airlines.

When I got to Dallas/Ft. Worth Airport, I had a rental on standby. Took me thirty minutes to find her crib. I smoked two blunts and intoxicated myself with a few natural Ice beers.

I stopped by a liquor store and bought a pint of vodka and killed it before I made it back to the rental car. I called her and she answered with an attitude.

I could remember when she used to be the sweetest girl in the world. I told her I wasn't sending her any money. By now I was plastered and zonked.

She talked shit; I was parked under a huge tree in front of her house, watching her pace back and forth around her living room.

Her man was in the background running his jaws.

I saw him now, barking over her shoulder. Some thug dude. Rag on his head, pants sagging. Unlaced Timberland boots. Smoking a blunt.

"We getting' dat money, Niggah!" he kept rapping. "I need some new threads, Punk!"

My eyes clouded over. Showtime.

I knocked on the door.

"Tammy. I give you enough money!" I said into the phone.

"The police gonna put your sorry ass in jail! Hold on, lemme see who at the door."

I pounded on her door.

"Who is it? Stop bamming on my door like you the muthafuckin' police—"

The door swings open and my fists slams into her face. She falls back into the wall, her ponytail flying from her head, landing in the fish tank and her cordless phone hitting ole boy in the head. I had on black gloves, Goose Down jacket and unlaced Timberland boots. I tied her ass pussy ass up. Ole boy jumped in my face and I bitch slapped him, and brutally punched him in his stomach.

"My son called you Daddy, Niggah? No, I can't have that." I was standing over him, with a boot-clad foot pressed on his face, bending his nose. "You want to buy some threads with my cash, Niggah?" He tried to plea bargain. I reminded him I wasn't a judge, I didn't look like a Prosecutor and I wasn't on parole.

I tied a sock around her mouth, dragged ole boy in the room, closed and locked the door and showed him how RuPaul got fucked in the ass. When I was done I pissed on his punk ass, and went out into the living room and beat her so bad she dropped child support on me real fast. I grew up being emotionally abused; my Daddy beat me so badly I couldn't walk. He always told me to get revenge on anyone who screwed you over, and if it came down to it get revenge on bitches before they get it on you. I was raised tough. Had to fight every day of my life.

I told her, "I will send you some loot. If you spend my hard earned money on your boyfriend, the fish g'on order a Happy Meal on the house and get chicken, you feelin' me, bitch?"

She was a good little girl. She followed my directions. I should know: I paid two Niggahs to keep tabs on her at all times. I was gangster like that. I heard she left her boyfriend; he was now turning tricks, dressing in drag. I always said I had the type of dick that turned men into bitches. Pushing all that to the back of my mind, I had to get to Sharon today. Unfortunately, I didn't have that much time. My apartment in Kendall no one knew about. I sold dope from here. Everyone thought I lived in rundown, pissy Perrine, not too far from Bell Short Stop, a convenient store that had seen better days. I had one couch, a pit-bull roaming around inside, and my drugs stashed in the walls. I met Sharon a few weeks ago at the Super Wal-Mart in Florida City. I had just gotten off work, as a Pharmaceutical employee at a drug store, South Beach. My lesbian co-worker, a woman named Red, had been on my mind lately. She actually fell in love with a chick named Fate Williams, rumored to have been abused by her own mother.

That night I drove to Southwest Dade to see my mother, Veronica, because she said she needed some cash. Her social security check was late, and she only had fifty dollars left on her American Flag-clad food stamp card. I loved Mama; I had to look out for her, since I was her only son. She tried her best to help me release the anger I have on the inside. She didn't understand how I could go from being a good kid to being a rebellious man with a gun-toting problem. Blame that on Daddy not really spending time with me. Blame that on watching Mama struggle when my Dad…I couldn't think about it now.

I did have an education. Thug by day, schoolbooks at night. I always made good grades, but I loved fast cash and ass. When I was eight years old I knew I'd have the profession I have now. I used to watch my uncles cook crack on the stove. They used baking soda to confuse drug consumers. My uncles were straight gangsters, would shoot you dead without losing any sleep. The number of people they snubbed would leave one in awe, in a bad way.

They drank liquor 'til the sun came up. That's how we do down in these parts and they smoked weed.

Once I gave Mama three hundred dollars, which I already knew she was going to blow away at the BINGO in Naranja, across from McDonald's, I grabbed my keys from her dining table. Kissing her cheek, I fondly squeezed her aging hands, giving her a loving look.

My head lowered, I slowly walked through her moth-ball-smelling living room I was raised in with my late father, Earl, who died at the hands of my Mama's oldest brother. Dad cheated him out of a thousand bucks during a crap game. Driving in my Cadillac Escalade was uneventful. I shed tears for my father, who was a good man. Unfortunately, bad things befell him. I felt guilty about his death. I blamed myself. I was fifteen years old. Just lost my virginity and was on my way to tell my Daddy about it. Mama always told me to save my dick for marriage, but I wanted to fuck like my peers were doing. School wasn't about work, it was about pussy, football games and having a good time, or so I thought. I wore nice clothes, had big money, by robbing motherfuckers left and right. I also did my crimes solo, never told a soul. But one robbery left someone dead, and I kept quiet about it.

With all these unwanted thoughts swirling around in my head like clockwork, nakedly I get in the tub, the hot water washing over my tired, sore body. I rest my palms flat on the light blue tile, the last of the Miami sunlight fading to hints of a half-moon affair.

I felt elated, about this girl, Sharon. When I met her she was shopping at Wal-mart. She wore the tightest pink sweatpants I'd even seen.

She had big titties elegantly hiding behind a ruffled top, with a huge medallion dead center. She had rosy cheeks, a friendly smile, soft skin trapping the flare of store lights and perfect white teeth.

She walked like poetry, and I was straight hip-hop.

I just had to approach her. Soft as all outdoors. "Excuse me, Miss. May I get your name, I'm Baxter, but you can call me Bax."

"Nice name." She shook my hand. Then I kissed it, my protruding, luscious lips falling on soft skin with the aplomb of honey bees on petals. She seemed to get wet between the legs. They shook a little, I pretended not to notice.

She said "I'm Sharon."

You are so gorgeous. She looked like Meagan Goode, the actress. I couldn't breathe. "Are you single?"

"Nope. Gotta man."

"Damn he's lucky. He lets you shop solo?"

"No. He's in here, he just went to get some grapes, and things for the salad we're having tonight."

"Well damn, can I come over for dinner?"

"Sure, why not."

I gazed deep into her eyes. She licked her lips. The sign I needed. I slid my hands in my pockets.

"Seriously?"

"Yea, just as long as you don't come up in my house all rowdy, Niggah."

We laughed like old friends.

"So, I'ma be straight. I just wanna have sex."

"You gotta work for this lovin', baby," she informed me.

She looked me dead in the eyes.

The chemistry would shatter test tubes the world over.

I wanted to fuck. She wanted to fuck.

My dick was rock hard; I had on brown Dickies pant and my white pharmacy coat, opened to reveal a Bob Marley shirt.

My hair was a Caesar's cut, nicely trimmed along the edges, leading into a very thin, geometrically daring mustache, beard and goatee.

"So when can a Niggah hit?"

She brushed off my coat. "Give me your number. I'll call you."

Now it was going to happen. I was in a pair of jeans, T-shirt and Jordan sneakers in twenty minutes. I dabbed cologne on my nuts, wrists and neck. I didn't put on briefs or socks. Elated, I turned off my cell phone, locked up my crib and took the turnpike to her house.

She lived in the Redlands, way out in the boonies. When I pulled up to her house I saw her fixing food, setting plates on the table. I smiled easily.

Cutting the engine, I popped a few Tic Tacs into my mouth, and walked up to the door. She had an amazing spread. Six bedroom four bath home. Well-tended lawns. I knocked on the door and she answered, clad in a robe. We stood there staring at each other. I was on fire. I just wanted to fuck. I wasn't trying to wreck her happy home. No promises. No woman, no cry type shit. Bend over, give me a shot of pussy, let me get my nut and I was out.

Licking her sensual lips, she opened the robe and bare tits stared me in the face. I was rock hard. She had on ruffled panties. Looked real cute on her. Grabbing her ass, I pulled her up to me and gave her some tongue. She sucked it tenderly; I opened my mouth wide so she could do so.

I picked her up, kicked the door closed, ignoring the little shiatsu dog. He barked so much I kicked him across the room, laying Sharon on the couch. The dog runs upstairs whimpering. Little bitch, stay up there. Zebra skinned rugs. Matching throw pillows. A breathtakingly gorgeous bar by the back door, soft classical music playing.

She runs her hands across my waves.

"The Atlantic Ocean up there, 'ey?" I asked her, kissing her breasts. My tongue sensually circling her nipple. I used my fingertips to trail her arms, her thighs, her stomach, her legs and her inner thighs. She cooed playfully, arching her back. I squeezed the titties together and run my tongue over both nipples, my head going side to side. I was straddled over her on the table. I gave her an eternity of pleasure this way. I pulled out my dick, and put it in her mouth. My pants barely covered my ass, but I didn't care. She squeezed her titties on my pulsating member and she tit fucked me. Felt so good, I humped her breasts, never did this before. But I liked trying new things.

I decided I had enough after I came all over her mouth, face and breasts with a ball busting jolt that had my toes on lock. I massaged my juices into her skin, giving it that rich texture. She told me to eat her pussy. I said why not.

I started licking around the Panty Region, hair was all over the place. I liked pubic hair, so I ran my tongue all over her panties. Every so often I had to keep pulling hair from my damn teeth. I wanted to eat pussy, not floss!

"Baby, oooh wee, tassstee me, babbyy!"

"Want Daddy to taste this pussy?"

"Yes!"

With one hand, I slowly pulled off her wet panties, trailing fingertips over her skin, giving her butterflies in her stomach, like the magician I was. When the panties come off her legs are closed, she's teasing me so I opened her legs, put my face between them and I froze.

She had so much goddamn hair!

I thought it was Groundhog's Day. She had hair all over the goddamn place. I was mad! I couldn't even *see* the pussy. How could this fine ass woman have jacked pussy hairs like this? I got some choice words for her: Hygiene, bitch! I was fuming. I went through all that hell, of getting ready and shunning much needed sleep. I drove out half my gas tank coming to the Redlands, thinking I was getting some quality pussy and I wound up with a ferret with too much hair! Were you fucking serious, woman?

Wanting to puke, I inserted a finger inside her warm flesh anyway, determined to get this hairy pussy and my hand fell in like a penny inside a wishing well, nothing gripping the sides. Her pussy was ruined! God! I hated ruined pussy!

My eyes were laser beams. "Baby," I told her, mad as fuck. "I forgot my rubbers in the car, I'll go get them."

"My brother has some in the room."

"Your brother?"

"The one who was at Wal-Mart with me, I told you he was my man. He's really my brother, he's mentally challenged."

*So is your pussy!* I wanted to say but I refrained."

I got my own, give me a second." I gave her some tongue, keeping the act up. She smiled so sweetly, damn she was beautiful! But her pussy was sloppy, slaughtered as we say down south.

I buckled my pants, grabbed my wallet and keys and went outside, looking back at her. "Give me a second." Closing the door I ran to my ride, hopped inside, and turned the key in the ignition and hot-rod out of there. I was more disappointed than I was angry.

I wasn't about to handle all that hair.

I'll leave it to beaver.

# The Legendary Necklace

Love. Tell me something about it that I didn't know. Love was patient. Well. Sometimes. It was understanding. Well, that was until you put sex in the mix, then you loved fucking and not the *nature* of love anymore. Love didn't boast…well, that was until you found a helluva sexy black man to show off. Then he became your trophy. You polished his good dick. Kept him satisfied. Put him on the shelf until the sun rose. Took him out in public. Dressed him up like Ken dolls. Let him drive your Nissan Maxima all over Dade County with a killer stereo system that you could hear blocks away. Took him to all the parties. Bitches were jealous that you had him and *they* didn't. Then when the moon got off the recliner and trekked her sexy ass across starry skies, back on the shelf your "Trophy" went.

Which brought me to my boyfriend of three years? Legendary Bridgewater. I've loved this man from day one. He was attentive and inspiring. He had goals outside of the ghetto, where we lived at the time. He had passion, and we all knew that without it you truly didn't have the desire to live. He loved my mind; he loved the way I thought. He appreciated the black woman that lived deep inside me. Taught me how to talk as opposed to cursing. This was a first. Because the black men I was used to dating, fucking and yea, "raising like little boys," completely lost my trust. They tried to run game on me. Tell me our relationship was one way and it turned out to be another way with other women thrown in the mix to make Jerry Springer rethink his defunct career. He showed me true love. He cooked for me. He gave me expensive things without trying to "buy" my love. He never tried to change me, if anything, he tried to do a Beyonce: "Upgrade" me to living a better life.

He had a quiet sex appeal about himself. He didn't make trouble. He had no idea how sexy he was. But let me paint the picture for you. He had the creamiest skin of chocolate with almonds. In fact I loved his...nuts. Hazel eyes that trapped everything from the sunlight to bedroom candles with such aplomb it left me breathless. He was 6 feet 8 inches, two diamond earrings, eleven tats (of Nefertiti, Ramses the III, Akhenaton, Queen Hatshepsut and a few other Egyptian pharaohs, he loved Africa); his huge booty made even the homosexuals swoon when he walked by with a swagger stank of the type of aura the dope boys truly appreciated; and he wore a size 17 shoe, and yes, his dick was over half of that, thick, long and full.

He was the sole reason I stopped thinking all men were dawgs. Not "Dogs," but D-A-W-G-S! Straight up mutts! He called me whenever he stepped out; I always knew where he was. When he wasn't working he was home, being with me, or working out at the gym, or cooking, reading, studying, since he was trying to get his major in, shit, I forget, couldn't think of it right now. He opened doors for me. If men stepped to me in public, trying to flirt, he remained quiet. He didn't get mad. He wasn't outspoken about it. He didn't disrespect me, himself or embarrass us. He left the dialogue up to me. And of course I always said, "Look, this is my man right here, so I appreciate the love, but please don't disrespect my dude."

I always got a "No problem, Ma." And they still tried to get at me when he turned his back looking at shirts or admiring the scene around him. That's when I got stupid, and it took Legendary to pull me off the Niggahs.

And vice-versa. If women stepped to him, I left the talking to him. He never got upset, embarrassed me, or tried to hug me and slip another woman's phone number in his pocket; I knew all the little tricks. I felt totally comfortable and safe around my man. It has gotten to the point where I would do anything for him, give him anything he wanted, just to keep him home with me. I trusted him and I trusted his judgment, something most young girls couldn't and wouldn't understand. We spent so many days and nights getting to know each other. I knew him inside and out. I knew what made him happy and what made him sad.

We moved out of the ghetto about eight months after we started dating. We lived together, learned each other's habits, what we could and couldn't live with. He was neat and easy going. Very organized. He cooked and cleaned better than I did, which I truly appreciated 'cause a bitch wasn't about to play Martha Stewart Living anytime soon. We went through so many channels to get our first home on Campbell Drive, in a newly built community, fresh with a brand new elementary school and all, by Malibu Bay. I loved it, despite the $1,200 a month mortgage tag, but we made it work. He was a church-going man. A little shy; he didn't take too kindly to people calling him "sexy" or "fine." In fact the more people told him that the more inferior he became. Which was all gravy to me because I was a dime piece myself, 19-24-36, little tits in other words, but enough junk in my trunk to stop the garbage men twice a week, when they collected my trash. I even told them I had a man, and like the old school cut went, "What your man got to do with me?" they would ask me, meaning every word.

I would have answered the lingering question, but one day, when Legendary came home early from work—he worked at the Fort Lauderdale Airport, made good money—and stepped out of his Chrysler with the Bentley front frame, the men suddenly got really quiet. He offered them cold Zephyrhills waters, shook their hands and didn't show an ounce of jealousy. I admired that about him. Quite frankly, his nonchalant attitude scared the garbage men so badly they never stopped by my house again. And the sex! God, the sex! It took us a month to finally fuck. And it was really driving me crazy, because, *yes*, I fucked on the first date. I was a grown woman, and real women didn't put time and restraints on the inevitable. I jumped in the hay and popped my pussy until I came. Had to test drive the stick shift before I committed to buy. Had to ride the clutch. Simple as that. I didn't want to be committed to a strokeless, dickless man. Size was everything to me. Yes I was a Size Queen. The motion in the ocean was for simple bitches. Not me. As long as I could ride it then damn it the rest was history. I didn't do dicks that were 7 or below. Just not my cup of tea. But in my case. It wasn't my cup of dick.

He said that he had his share of wham, bam, thank you madams. That he didn't want to rush with me. That every time he started a relationship with sex, that's what it became: a *relationsex*, not a relationship and that always concluded into being a relation*shit*. And he didn't want that with me. I didn't want it either. So he spent time talking to me, taking me out, spending quality time and asking me about my goals. He wanted to know my dreams and what I was going to do to achieve them. That was high on his priority list. I told him I wanted to be a published author like my favorite author Teresa D. Patterson, who wrote a too fabulous book called *It's your World Black Girl*, which I absolutely, positively loved! I liked her better than raunchy ass Zane. Now don't get me wrong, I loved Zane, thought she was amazingly talented, but Teresa was it for me.

So he bought me the priciest computer from Best Buy electronics store, a Gateway, with laser printer and he persuaded me to write. So I have been doing that everyday. Writing on my computer, and he has been my best and worst critic. Since he was an avid reader, currently reading Eric Jerome Dickey's *Liar's Game* (his favorite author), he couldn't wait to read my stuff.

I remembered when we did finally bump and grind. It was after my mother's 50th birthday party. I was helping Mama clean the dishes, everyone had gone home. Mama loved Legendary, she said she might even adopt him, I was like "Mama you can't adopt a grown man."

Curtly, she looked at me with love in her eyes. She was cute in her pink apron. She was battling osteoporosis and social security was fucking her over so I had to look out for Mama. She put the left-over Mac and cheese in the fridge. "Yes I can. Plus he's very loving. He's certainly better than any man *you* ever had."

"I know, right?" I was wiping the counters, clad in black coveralls. I had changed out of my slamming Gucci dress, because I didn't want to mess it up. I was Miss Prixy when I wanted to be— too cute for my own goddamn good.

She eyed me, sipping some wine. Looking ghetto fabulous for her age, Mama had a body that would make Halle Berry turn gay. "And God knows I wondered when you were going to get it right."

I rolled my eyes, and my heels clicked across the fake marble floors. I sat at the dining table, using my fingers to dig up some icing from the cake. Yummy. "Mama. Don't start."

Exhaling audibly, Mama sat across from me, handing me a cold beer. I loved beer, just like I loved my man. "Seriously, you had two yeast infections, an HIV scare, three miscarriages, four abortions and one delusional ass Niggah trying to shoot you before you found Legendary."

Now see, I was upset. Why did she go there like that? That hurt for Mama to say, but Mama represented the truth and she was one way everyday. She wasn't some-timing like most of my friends and family.

Before I could start an argument, despite my respect for her, Legendary entered the kitchen from one of the bedrooms, leaned to kiss Mama's cheek, and then he kissed me. He said, "Baby can I talk to you, alone please?"

Mama stood up. "Ya'll can talk in here, I gotta go shower. Lock my front door when ya'll leave, I do stay alone."

"Got you, Mama." She hugged me and kissed my lips. I was still mad at her. After squeezing my hand fondly, she vanished upstairs and a few minutes later I heard her blasting Tyrone Davis and the shower came on after that. Mama showered for an hour or so.

He made me stand up. I studied his face, he looked bothered. I asked, "What is wrong, baby?"

"I'm just pissed."

"Why?"

"My ex girlfriend, Kizzy Lyons, called me, threatening to take me court for child support, and I don't have any kids by her," he said discerningly. "I really don't have time for this type of discomfiture."

I wasn't that bothered by it. Women always tried this tactless shit on men. "Then why would she threaten you? You dealing with her is disconcerting enough."

He was steaming. "Because my dumb ass put down I was the child's father on the birth certificate. Back then I guess I was being fanciful, instead of being realistic. Caught up in the idea of being a good father to someone's child and trying to do the right thing."

I always loved his honesty. He held nothing back, no matter how much it may hurt. "Baby, just take a DNA test. The answers lie in the results. Then we could forefend the bitch forever."

He was deeply depressed. Heartbreakingly, I kept quiet. I hated to see him in any type of pain. "I told her that, but she refused. Then I had to go through the hysterics."

*I'll stomp the bitch!* "You can set up a court date." I thought about it. "Want me to shoot the Ho?"

We laughed playfully, but I was deadly serious. Either that or I'll cut the Ho with my rusty razor. "Nah. I don't need my woman fighting my battles. I feel clabbered enough."

I was uncomfortable. "This seems so laissez-faire."

"Unfair is more like it…" He smiled faintly. "…You can kiss me."

I softened up; suddenly Kizzy Lyons was a distant memory. The chemistry built dramatically. I saw longing in his eyes. "But that might lead to teasing and temptation and we haven't fucked yet."

He gave me some tongue. Leaned back and looked at me. Eyes glowing. His dick rock hard. I squeezed it, then quickly pulled my hands away. Damn it I needed him in that sexual way, it's been a month. I kissed him again, this time we kissed long and hard, rubbing and feeling. He pulled off my coveralls, ass naked in Mama's kitchen.

I could hardly breathe. "What about Mama?" I asked breathlessly.

He kissed my left breast. "She had her Dick Fun over the years, time to give you some Dick Fun."

I was nervous. Mama was a nut case when you did freaky shit in her house and you weren't helping pay bills. "Wow, baby. Are you *serious*? Not in Mama's kitchen."

"I love your Mama but fuck her kitchen. Give me my pussy right here, right now or wait another goddamn month—"

He didn't have to tell me twice. He lay me on the dining table, took a huge piece of Mama's birthday cake and smeared it on my pussy, asshole and titties, diving in and having a bite of the good stuff. Yea, he tasted good pussy. I damn near died, he was incredibly breathtaking, and never did I dream he was this sensual and poignant with his tongue.

"Your…cake taste good," he said softly, moaning as his tongue divided thy pink walls and conquered thy clitoris with the zeal of Shakespeare and that untalented fuck was dead. Shakespeare stole his plays, but my man inherited good pussy eating skills from the sands of time, which separated him from the rest.

He ate forever. I was shuddering, shaking, going through a cornucopia of feelings, a plethora of emotions. I didn't know if I wanted to die or cry. My feelings were a bit inconspicuous at the moment.

He pushed my legs back, ran his slick tongue from the pussy to the asshole, tongue fucking my rectum until I shuddered with pure bliss. I was moaning as quietly as I could. All I seen was his head bobbing.

He got bored easily, so he turned me on my stomach and spread my ass cheeks and put his face all up in my hole again, running his tongue across my chocolate like he was auditioning for the Charmin

Toilet Paper commercials. He felt so good, so right. He sucked my pussy, spreading my legs, lifting me to my knees, pushing my face down. He leaned back and admire the eighth, ninth and tenth Wonder of the World. He spanked my ass repeatedly, in a way that enhanced his performance, my ass jiggling like Jell-o.

Without further ado he got his big ass up on my Mama's table and slowly slid his hardened nature deeply inside me, pausing, letting it sit there for a few minutes, so my tight pussy could get used to the feeling of a tomb raider trying to unearth the Nefertiti in my freak bone. He kissed the "Akhenaton" tat, and he tongue kissed me passionately, his amazingly experienced hips coming alive. He felt SO WONDERFUL! His long strokes took my breath away. He was very good at what he did. My rainfalls wet him all up. He moaned softly, his lips by my ear, sucking the back of my neck, pulling me up to him as he tapped that ass from the back, I was gyrating myself all over him, wanting him, needing his energy, feeding from his urgency, he was touching my pussy in ways my soul appreciated.

I felt the rise of smoke in my loins, the feel of elation stunned me. I was jubilant and beautiful, sultry and demanding. I felt myself drifting as I began exploding all over him. He laughed in my ear, "Yea baby, let's get it together," and he began coming deeply inside me. Together we moaned and exploded. I was hoping we were going half on a baby. Shit, I wasn't going to lie. A man with dick this good deserved a baby.

When we subsided, moaning and sweaty, Mama said, "Now get ya'll asses off my goddamn table, go rent a hotel room and Legendary, take my girl's hand in marriage. You aren't gonna be giving her *yeast* infection number three, you hear me?" she asked with a satisfied smile on her face.

My heart dropped, Mama caught us, but she winked at me in a way that told me that everything was all right.

He helped me get off the table, my pussy sore, maybe because I haven't had any activity in my tomb in a long time. Once I put on my cargo jumpsuit and he put on his Sean John attire, I kissed Ma goodbye, and when he tried to she said, "Now I watched you eat pussy and cake, don't think you g'on give me a pussy kiss. Just don't flow like that, Jack. And I saw you licking her all in the ass." Oh, no! He covered his face, I covered my ears. Jesus strike me dead, NOW! "Didn't I tell you she was a shitty baby when she was little. All she did was shit, shit, shit!"

Oh my God! He was so embarrassed; I couldn't stop laughing with Mama. He tried to laugh it off, but we both could tell by the look on his face that his stomach was in knots.

"Now ya'll go home. And before you leave, I need a hundred dollars each, because ya'll fucked in my goddamn kitchen. I will never eat my cake quite the same. And Legendary, do your new Mama-n-law a favor, write on a scrap piece of paper how you did the hurricane tongue with the cake so I can pass it to my man on the side, I gotta try that shit!"

She was slapping her knees, laughing so hard. I tried to hold it in, and when he looked me in the face, I burst open, slob falling from my mouth, I couldn't breathe. Now he was mad. After he broke her off proper, we had never run so fast in our lives, laughing like school kids all the way to his Chrysler.

We would spend the next ten months love making. He was gentle, very loving, he loved foreplay, loved giving me head before I sucked him off. He made it interesting, fun and exciting every time. When he kissed my clit and sucked the walls of my pussy I felt beautiful, like I could conquer the world. He never stopped until I came. He was smooth. He spoke to you without seemingly trying to prove himself. He always told you that you tasted sweet, and he described it. Like last night, when he ate me out, he told me I tasted like watermelon. That was because he had dumped diced watermelon all over my enticing body parts and he gave a new name to the word "foreplay" that led to floor-play.

I wasn't a fan of the Sucking Dick Club. But when I gave him head, he truly *loved* it. He'd rub my face; look at me like I was the most beautiful woman in the world. He was creative, sometimes leaving on his Timberland boots. Sometimes he turned on some old school music and sung to me while I polished him up. He was nasty and freaky without coming off as predictable and tacky. When he slid up in me, he did it with zeal, taking his time, studying what worked for me and always asking me questions.

"Baby does that feel good to you...how do you like it when I stroke the Kat like that? You love my dick, baby? Take this shit, pretty lady..." Drove me crazy!

I was happy when he decided to take his ex girlfriend to court and demanded a DNA test. I hated the fact that her five year old, cute little boy had to be pulled in the middle. He looked nothing like Legendary. The court, over a couple weeks, ordered the paternity test. Shockingly, she listened and obeyed the judge's orders. When the test came back the following week, it turned out he was *not* the father, totally freeing him from her clutches forever. She bitched and moaned in court, saying that Legendary was the only father her son, Legendary Bridgewater, Jr, had ever known. That he had his "father's name." How could he just walk away? I felt so bad. The child shouldn't *have* to suffer, so he offered to adopt his "son at heart," and I supported him. Because it was what he wanted? Another court date was made, and a few months later Legendary, Jr. legally had a father.

I would grow close to him. He'd come every weekend and spend with us. We built an amazing relationship. He liked me, and I thought he was a sweet little black boy, full of promise and life. He loved Bugs Bunny and Disney movies, I would constantly be at it with his mother, who thought she could come in my crib, because Legendary was her son, and tell me how to run my shit. My man had to pull me off this Ho a number of times.

That was two years ago. I was going through his wallet this morning, while he was in the shower, and I was going to take forty dollars because I didn't feel like going to the ATM. His money was mine and mine was his, everything was jointly owned. When I took out two crisp twenty dollar bills I noticed his wallet-sized photos. I looked really pretty in my pink dress in one pose, so I flipped to another of me with a black leopard-print pants suit. I remembered that pose; I took it last year at the Dade County Youth Fair, by F.I.U., the college. But the third picture made me freeze up with rage. He had a photo of his ex girlfriend, the bitch who cheated on him and gave birth to another man's baby.

"What the *fuck*?" I asked myself, and I heard him turning the shower off, humming an Aretha Franklin cut. I was fuming. I stood in the door way, just waiting for the door to open. I had never heard of him speak of his ex. In fact he told me he hated her, that he never wanted to see her again, yet he had her photo all up in his wallet, how did you explain that? Did he forget to take it out? Before I jumped to conclusions I would ask him.

The only contact he had with Kizzy was talking to her about his son. And once the subject ended, he hung up. He never went to see her, and the faith I had in him was tugging at my heart, telling me not to flip out.

I didn't know what to do, really. I never really had to question him. When he went to see her concerning his son he always called or offered that I come along, but I trusted him, so I let him deal with the clueless bitch. He was a good father. I loved that about him.

I heard him going through the cabinets in the bathroom. I put my hand on the door knob and slowly opened the door. Steam erupted into the bedroom; I fanned steam away, and looked at him. Dripping wet, his sexy body made my pussy wet. I wasn't even going to question him anymore. He would never hurt me, how could he hurt me, he was faithful to me, catered to me and his child. His co-workers loved him. I adored him.

Just when I was about to close the door he opened the medicine cabinet, took out a few bottles of Tylenol pills, and opened a secret compartment. He took out a folded piece of paper. My mouth fell open in shock, I didn't know he had a secret compartment in the medicine cabinet; guess Niggahs really did have secrets, no matter how Mr. Rodgers they seemed.

Sitting on the toilet he read silently, hot tears running down his face. He was wiping them away.

My heart bled, what had my baby in tears? What was going on? Was it the letter from his Dad? His Dad did die a long time ago.

Maybe he was reminiscing about the old days, wishing his Dad was here to share in the joy of raising an adopted son.

That had to be it; he always talked about his Dad. I closed the door and let him be to himself. I put his wallet up and decided to drive to the ATM machine and withdraw $40 of my own money.

And give my man his time.

When I got home his car was gone. I looked at my watch. It was well after 9 a.m. Yup. My baby was at work.

I couldn't get my mind off my man. His secret pain. The way he always put on a brave face, yet never really talked about his dead father. Most black men I knew were so bravado about their secret pain, because they thought society would frown down on them for showing even a hint of emotion. So faux paw in my opinion, yet I didn't want to push myself on him. Legendary was the type that would come to you when and if he wanted to talk or vent. He did have a stubborn streak in him that I hated, but for the most part, I could tolerate his flaws to the T.

His Mama was in the Airforce for twenty-eight years, retired in Germany a Master Sergeant. She never came back to the states. He said she had no desire to come back to such a repressed country that would bash Janet Jackson, a successful black woman, over a white boy yanking our her titty at the Super bowl Halftime Show a couple years back; yet praise Bush for cheating to get into office, and praise Madonna for tongue kissing Britney Spears in front of children at the

MTV Awards some time ago. He said her beliefs meant a lot to her considering she didn't like Janet Jackson or her music. But the way the world bashed the "black woman," and was now praising the slut Anna Nicole Smith, former Playgirl Playmate who was found dead in Fort Lauderdale, Florida further told her that America was no longer for her. His father had been dead five years at the time she retired, and she found a new man shortly after that. One with money, status in the Marines and treated her well. He was always close to her, but when she married the Marines Fluky, he lost that connection with her. She changed her address and phone number, and he never really cared about it, really, said he wasn't a little boy anymore, that as long as she was happy and was being treated like a Queen she could live her life, considering she gave birth to him when she was 13 years old and lost her life trying to raise him, and a good job she did.

All wasn't lost; he did have her email address. Once a week they sent each other emails. He used to show me all the emails his Mom sent about Anna Nicole. That's how he found out his mother detested her. We were all sick of hearing about the bitch, to tell you the truth. This chick had problems that even dead-ass Marilyn Monroe wouldn't want any part of. In a myriad of thoughts, I went in my bedroom, tossing my purse on the unmade up bed. I was tired. I had to go to work at 2 p.m.; I worked at Publix supermarket as the lead Customer Service representative at the service desk. Been there for about four years.

My baby must have really been pissed because he always made up the bed before he left for work. I couldn't get over the letter he was reading, I wanted to be nosey, yet I didn't wanna go snooping around his shit. That was his secret pain, all his own. Who was I to jeopardize that? Yet I was a black woman more than a human being so I went into the bathroom, opened the cabinet, took out the bottles of pills, opened the secret compartment, which was cleverly camouflaged to look like the rest of the cabinet and I pulled out the letter.

I closed my eyes and sighed, I shouldn't be invading his space, which was wrong of me. Yea. My heard pounded, my blood turning cold at the thought of betraying such a good man.

I attempted to put it back, and when my eyes locked on "I will always love you, Legendary, you're my life, my strength…" I froze like a block of ice.

The letter wasn't from his father. It was from Kizzy Lyons. His ex.

"What. The. Fuck. Is. Going. On?"

# The Letter

I had to lean against the sink to keep from falling on the floor. All sorts of anger surged through my body. I felt like a hot air balloon about to drift through cloudy skies, blocking my sunshine. Incomputable, I was thinking. Inconsequently, I couldn't reason. My eyes hurt; in fact the more I looked at this letter, the more animosity filled my lungs, killing off my air.

When I worked up enough nerve, I sat on the toilet and read the note, dated December 12, 2004, way before we met. Thank God for that. It was on scented Strawberry Shortcake stationary. What grown bitch wrote notes with Strawberry Shortcake? Grow up, bitch! I thought to myself. The strawberry aroma now smelled like a faint hint of peach. Dying with time, or just fading every time my secretive man locked himself in the bathroom, reading this shit every goddamn night. When I did open the note I couldn't look at it. I was about to crack open. I was hurting myself. Was I right for snooping, going through my man's shit? Was this truly invading his private space, regardless of the situation? Mama always said when you look for something bad enough you'll find it. But I have already gone to the point of no return, so I might as well finish what I started and read the goddamn note.

Ok. Breathe. Girl. Breathe. It couldn't be. That. Bad. Damn *shame* I had to pump myself up to read something that may or may not end my three plus year relationship with my knight in tarnished armor—tarnished because the motherfucker lied to me. If he lied over the author of this letter then what else did he truly lie about?

That's what I was afraid of finding out. God shoot me now.

Without further ado, my heart pounding out of my chest, I opened the note. And began reading…

# Dear Legendary,

I love you more than words can express. You are a good man with a good heart. I understand you don't trust me right now, because you think my cousin Harold is actually a man I'm seeing behind your back. But this couldn't be the furthest from the truth. You are the only man I have ever loved. The only man I care to love. I am so thankful you have been a father to my son. I really appreciate that, as a single black woman in such a racist country most women gotta lay on their back just to make ends meet, but you help me so much, you give me money to pay bills, you sometimes cook and clean for me so when I do get home from work all I really have to do is relax. You're selfless and compassionate; you make love like a tyrant. I'm glad we waited about a month or so before we fucked, it was definitely worth it. I won't make this letter too long, because I hate writing, but every night before I go to bed I'm gonna write you a letter, telling you how I feel. I love you.

I seal this with a kiss.

Kizzy Lyons,
Your Baby Mama and your Soul Mate.

I was in tears, quietly crying to myself. The letter was an old one, and definitely confirmed what kind of man he was. Yes, he was selfless, yes he was compassionate and caring, yes, and even with Kizzy he didn't just jump into sex. I smiled, actually smiled. But that was short lived. I stood up, intending to put his letter back, and I paused. Trying to keep it together I looked into the man made cubby hole in the medicine cabinet and I saw more letters, neatly folded. I also saw photographs. I was simmering now.

Taking out the pictures, I carefully and guardedly looked at them. They were of Legendary and Kizzy at the Dade County Youth Fair. Oh my God. There they were at the Red Lobster having dinner, looking snappily jazzy in church clothes, to tell you the truth. Wow. There they were at Disney World, with their son. My heart ripped in two, they looked like one big happy goddamn family! I understood he had a past and he was with other people, but goddamn did that mean you keep this memorabilia under the roof I shared with you? I paid bills here not that dizzy Ho! I felt threatened now, what didn't matter to me months ago now mattered to me at this moment. Had he truly moved on beyond Kizzy? Did he still love her or was he in love with her?

Depressingly sad, I slowly thumbed through the rest of the color photos, in a rut. What do I do? He obviously was holding on to the past; trying to cling to a woman who was trying to ruin his ass and put him on child support. Despite the court's ruling, he did adopt Little

Legendary, so the financial burden was still on him, he self-inflicted this on himself and I had to go along with it because I loved him.

I started to put the pictures away when I heard a noise down in the kitchen. Shit, he was home. I didn't care, I wasn't going to act like a scared bitch in my own home, and after all I split the mortgage once a month. Feelings of autonomy eating me alive, I looked at the picture of Kizzy handing Legendary a gift, another picture of him opening it, and another picture of him admiring his gift, which totally pissed me off. My man had lied to me. What did he lie about? *Hmmm.* Putting the photos and the letters up as neatly as I could, I closed the cubby hole, replaced the Tylenol bottles, closed the medicine cabinet and went out into my bedroom. Trying to breathe in and breathe out, I was counting to ten like I was taught in Anger Management class when I was 14 years old, after bashing my ex boyfriend's head in with a bottle when he took my virginity and spread rumors around high school that I was an "easy bitch!"

As cute as a puppy dog, he walked up the hallway, humming happily, a huge smile on his face. He was carrying the most beautiful bundle of red roses. I wasn't a rosy bitch right now. When he got up to me he gave me a huge hug, the cackle of his leather jacket popping in my ears, he smelled so good, I loved his scent, and I looked forward to smelling my good-looking Niggah every day. But today I didn't want to smell him; I didn't want him touching me. I was hexed about Kizzy's picture in his wallet. The letters. The photographs. The "special" gift she bought him.

His face was beaming. "Hey, baby," he said, kissing my lips. I didn't move mine. They were blocks of ice. I forced a fake smile.

Wrinkles formed on my forehead. "Sup with you, baby?" I asked him, eyeing the roses. I wanted to slap him with them. "Those for *me?*" *Or for Kizzy, you lying motherfucker?*

"Yes." A huge smile. Like he won the lottery. "These are for my beautiful, *lovely* girlfriend."

He handed them to me. I took them and tossed them on the bed. He just looked at me, really studied me.

"Baby, what's wrong?"

I faked a yawn. "I'm just tired; my period came on early this month." I was lying, was I any better than him?

"Poor baby, anything I can do?"

I eyed the necklace around his neck, I loved that necklace, and it was very valuable to him. His father had given it to him when he was younger and when his Dad died he didn't even let his mother touch it.

A smile. "Yes." Then more contently. "Can I wear your necklace, to ward off the evil spirits in here trying to get me sick? I don't feel too good."

Anger washed over him, but he did a good job of hiding it.

"Now you know I don't let anyone hold this necklace, I don't even take off, even when I shower."

I didn't understand his attitude. Over a necklace? "*Please*, baby? Once upon a time you said you'd do *anything* for me."

Catch-22 dancing in his beautiful eyes, he closed them, sucking back his anger. "I *did* say that."

I tested him. "And you are a man of your word, right?"

He opened his eyes, a little sad. "Yes."

"So by you telling me I can't wear the necklace basically shows me that you are actually a goddamn liar."

He hated being called a liar, especially when he was a man that claimed to never lie about anything. Well, I knew that was a lie.

"Baby, I didn't lie to you."

*He is lying with a straight face! Liar! Fucking asshole! Just tell me the truth goddamn you!* "Well," I went on, walking up to him and snatching off the necklace, "you shouldn't mind if I wear this piece of shit necklace!" I spat more angrily than I intended. He was shocked, his mouth hanging open, wide-eyed. I was just getting started. "*What?* Say something, goddamn it! Say something! SAY SOMETHING!"

He was upset, deeply. He grabbed both my arms and shook me. "You just broke the only connection I had to my Daddy—"

I rolled my eyes. "—the only connection—?"

"—how could you do a Niggah like that?"

*The guilt trip speech. Shove it up your ass, I am so freaking mad at you!* "I'll tell you why," I responded with an attitude, slapping him across the face, wide-eyed myself. Niggah didn't scare me! When were these Niggahs going to realize that just because dick beat pussy didn't mean we were pussies? "Let me read that letter your Dad wrote you, the one you read in the bathroom all the time."

He got quiet. Really cautious, measuring his words. His hands were shaking, so he put them in his pocket. "I can't let you read that, I am very private when it comes to things related to my father."

I was shaking my head. "*Why* is that? If I'm the woman of your dreams, the woman you wanted to one day marry, why all the secrets? *Why* all the lies?"

"I have never lied to you." He didn't even convince himself with that one.

My brows rose so fast I got a migraine in one second flat.

"Really?" I was twirling the necklace, with the little heart-through-another-heart medallion. *"Never* lied." I was twirling it faster. "About nothing?"

"Can I have my Dad's necklace back?"

I challenged him. "Take it from me."

He didn't want to fight with me I could see it on his face. "Baby, please! Just give it to me."

I was toying with it and he winced trying to keep it together. What was it about this necklace?

"No."

"Baby." He was getting angry.

I wanted to slap him. "What?"

He breathed in. Then breathed out. "Give it to me."

I was defiant. "No, man."

He reached for it and I pivoted. "This is ridiculous."

"Ha. You *lied* to me and *I'm* being ridiculous?"

He felt violated. "I don't have to take this."

"Then don't because, baby I don't have to take this either."

I threw it at him, hitting him on the chest. It fell to the floor faster than a leaf. I calmed my nerves a little bit. "You're sleeping on the couch tonight; you will not get, look at or sniff my pussy until I feel comfortable around you."

I walked over to the nightstand, snatched up my purse and walked towards the bedroom door. "I got someone to go see, I'll be back around 8 p.m., don't wait up for me because I damn sure won't be up thinking about you." I leaned down and picked up the necklace. "I'll take it to get it fixed."

He tried to hug me and I kicked him in the balls, walking around him, angry as hell, and I slammed the room door behind me, keeping to myself the small black velvet box on my bed, next to the roses. He was going to ask me to marry him today, and I couldn't stop the tears from falling as I hoped into his Chrysler, and burned his gas to hell, speeding up the block.

Headed for my Mama's house.

Disoriented, I got out of my car and killed the engine.

Didn't look like anybody was home. I walked up to the front door, a little cold because the air was chilly. I could hear the leaves of the palm trees rustling, a quiet sound that relaxed me. I put his necklace in my pocket and rang the door bell.

No answer. I lowered my head, sucking in air, ringing the door bell again.

How could he lie to me? Keeping all those old photos of him and Kizzy, in my house. The nerve of him! All the pictures of my old boyfriends he made me put in a safety deposit box at the post office, he raised a stinker just at the thought of me going back in time and reminiscing over the photos, yet he locked himself in the bathroom reading notes from his baby mama?

Chile, please. Make my booty squeeze! What did I look like? Punk bitch of the Year?

"Yes," came the soft voice. I held my breath.

Gathering my nerve, I then looked Kizzy deep in her pretty eyes. Despite my anger, I managed to smile. She smiled in return. Easily, I said, "Are you busy? I *need* to talk to you."

Kizzy said, "Sure. Come on in, I know you're cold, girl."

Not as cold as his Daddy's necklace in my pocket. The necklace with the untold story attached to it, a necklace that was in one of his photos, with "LIE" written all over it.

# Souls Connected

She offered me some hot tea, which seemed to do the trick. I get cold very fast; the slightest hint of wind would break me out in Goosebumps.

I was sitting on the sofa, looking around her magnificent house. It was a very articulately-decorated house. Furniture with clawed feet. Soft reds and pinks flowing into breathtaking purples. Soft purples, more like lavender. Lavender was Legendary's favorite color.

"What brings you by?" she asked, clad in an African Kimono. Her hair up in rollers. She didn't have on a hint of jewelry. She sipped her tea and said, "Want me to turn on some music or anything?"

I said "No," rather quickly. She blinked a few times and lit a cigarette. She smoked Kools. I was trying to keep my cool as well.

Setting the huge coffee mug on the low table, next to a picture of Legendary and her son clad in a breathtaking black suit, I never saw the picture before, I said, "So how have you been doing? For some reason you been on my heart."

She smiled easily, searching my face for any sign of flaw. She listened to my words, trying to see if any betrayed me. I was very guardedly cautious.

"I've been good."

"That's good to hear." I leaned back, crossing my legs. I was rubbing my right foot, showing the sign of relief all over my misconstrued face. "How's your son?"

"He's your step son, so its ok to refer to him as 'step-son,' I have no problem with it."

Now I smiled. "Really?" Eyes sparkling. "That means a lot. I am very fond of Legendary, Jr."

"And he's very fond of you." A beat. "He told me you spanked him last week."

OK, I got quiet. This was the part all the fake Kodak moments went out the window and the Ho turned "Cindy Lauper," meaning her true colors was about to shine through brighter than her chandelier lights. "Yea. Nothing abusive or anything…"

She held up her hands, tucking her chin back. "No, its ok. He's a hard headed ass child sometimes. I firmly believe in a village raising a child, like in the old days, before the government stepped in and fucked up American Families."

I inhaled, and then exhaled appreciatively. I thought I had to get Kung Fu on this classy bitch.

"I don't know about American Families, but on Black Families, we are suffering the brut of prejudiced rage."

"Tell me about it, girl. My friend Estelle lost her two boys years ago. Both 14 at the time." She got really quiet, and the silence weighed on my ears like comedian Bruce Bruce was running on my back in a tutu.

I sat up, and said, "Anything happen to…them?"

Her eyes were filled with tears. "Yes. They were identical twins, forced to split up. They were from right here in Miami, girl."

"What part of Miami?" I found myself asking.

"Richmond Heights."

"Really, I am very familiar with the Heights."

"As a matter of fact, they lived in a little house across the street from Bethel Church."

I frowned at the mention of Bethel Church. Whore Fest U.S.A. Hated to say it, but it was.

"I know a few people who live in that area."

"Girl, you ok with me." She stood up, stretching. "I think I'll turn on some music, how about some old school James Brown."

"Fine with me." I was lightening up. She was acting like a woman with class, so I would reciprocate it. I reached over and took one of her Kools. "Do you mind?"

She dismissed my comment with a wave of her hand. "Girl. Go ahead, I can't smoke all those damn things." She sat next to me, looking me in the face. "But about the two brothers. No one in their immediate family wanted to take them in. They were very responsible young black men, good in English. Were on the verge from graduating high school two years earlier because of their I.Q."

I actually smiled. "I loved English in school. Hell, now I'm thinking back to high school, when I thought I had it all figured out."

"School was a blast. But for the two brothers they wouldn't get the chance to finish…Through some sheer luck the boys were reunited. The judge ordered that they remain together. So once they were reunited, in Chicago, they started going through grief. Don't ask me how they wound up in Chicago's system, still a mystery to me, Chile. One of the boys, Trevor, was found dead in the kitchen's pantry a few months later."

She was getting chocked up, I was covering my mouth in shock. Oh my God! I didn't come here to hear this, I had a chip to get off my shoulder, but suddenly I just realized that there were people in the world with bigger problems than me.

"Who found him?" I asked and she looked at me, shaking her head.

She sipped the tea, sitting on her legs like a little girl. "His brother found him a few days later. They both worked in the kitchen, dish washers. That particular orphanage is notorious for kids getting abused. He went to the kitchen's pantry, because the main cook asked for thirteen cans of creamed corn. And when he opened the door, walking inside—it was one of those huge, organized closets— he turned on the light and the cook, who would be on the news telling the world what happened, dropped a huge hot pot of chicken when James, Trevor's brother, started screaming, a piercing wail that made every kid in the Chow Hall stop and stare, without moving. His brother's throat was slit from ear to ear. With a letter next to him, in his handwriting, stating that he couldn't live without his mother, that he wanted his family back, that he didn't want to live, that he loved his brother but he loved his mother more than himself or his brother."

"God, girl, suicide?"

"Yes."

"What did James do?"

"James didn't want to go on living, he became rebellious, cold-hearted. He blamed his mother, since her drug use was what got the boys taken in the first place. He abandoned education, and the last I heard he's finishing a five year prison sentence. He stabbed one of the line cooks. He said the cook tried to rape him, so he stabbed him in defense."

"Poor boy. Whatever happened to the letter his brother wrote? His suicide letter."

"Well before the authorities got there, he took the note and photo copied it, keeping the original, and putting the photocopy by his brother. He was distraught; the letter was the one connection he would forever have with his brother. Even when he went to prison, the state allowed him to keep the note. They sympathized with him. He didn't have a mother or a brother. He would read this note over and over, the note pulled him through. Made him want to get better."

"But he was in prison." Like my man, holding on to notes of the past. The images from the photos went through my brain: of the two of them at Red Lobster. He was *so* in love with her.

"Yes. He was reduced to a state number, but present day he is about to get a degree in criminal justice."

"Wow, girl. That's great."

"Yea. He attended school in prison. And now that he is about to get out, he is coming back home, to Miami. He remembered his address and wrote his mother from prison. She kept in close communication with her son. Being that he's the only living, healthy and breathing child she has. He plans on reuniting with her, since he's a grown adult male now."

"Does she still live in Richmond heights?"

"Yes."

"I would love to meet him."

"That could be arranged."

I stood up, taking the necklace from my pocket. I held it up, looking her deep in the eyes. "Keep it real with me. Because my man has been lying to me. *Why* didn't Legendary let me wear a necklace his father gave him? The necklace he has been holding onto ever since his father died is plaguing this relationship. Yet in *one* of the photos he has of you, from years ago, you have the very same necklace on *your* neck."

She was quiet. Her eyes were bouncing all over the objects in her living room. She stood up and faced me, real classy about her shit. She smiled, shaking her head. "Legendary's father didn't give him that necklace."

It felt like Zeus, the God of War, was sucking the air from my body. "What? He told me the only reason he didn't let me wear it was because he didn't want it getting messed up, that he wanted to honor his father's memory."

"Wait right here." She walked over to the entertainment shelf, bad ass shelf. Top of the line everything, thousands of DVD movies lining eleven different polished red cherry wooden shelves. She got on her knees and opened the bottom counter, pulling out a velvet box. She said, "Come here, girl." I walked over to her, slowly, my heart torn into pieces. His father didn't give him the necklace. Then who gave it to him? Where did it come from? I should have known better. If he'd lie about the letter then he'd lie about the necklace.

I helped her stand up. She nearly fell on the shelf. Slowly, she opened the box. I saw a series of receipts.

"I keep all of my receipts," she told me, pulling out one in particular. There was a photograph taped to it. She handed it to me, lowering her eyes to the floor. I saw the tears fall. Oh my God, why was she crying?

I looked at the receipt, from Kay's Jewelers. For $780. A necklace. The heart charm was $345. I looked at the photograph.

It was of Legendary. Kizzy. And their son.

At the Red Lobster.

I was pissed. "So you bought him the necklace?" I asked her.

"Yes. I had just had a miscarriage. I lost my baby. I was in the hospital for about a week, girl. Devastating affect this had on me because I was finally going to have his child."

I hugged her, gripping the necklace. "I am so sorry, girl."

"I bought him the necklace, said that the necklace would be our bond, that we would have shared a beautiful baby girl together. I was in my sixth month of pregnancy. I really wanted to make him a father. He wanted that very much, more than life itself."

In grave pain, Kizzy shook in my arms. Maybe I shouldn't have come here. No *wonder* he read the old letters and kept the pictures. No wonder he got antsy when anyone touched the necklace. This was a gift from her to him, when they lost their baby.

He never disclosed this information to me, and I could certainly understand why. It was probably all too painful for him, a man had his pride, a man hated to cry in front of his woman. He did tell me there was something about him and Kizzy's relationship he wanted to tell me about, but it was all together too painful.

I held Kizzy, I let her vent. "Girl, it hurts *so* bad!" Her nose was stopped up, her arms dangling at her sides. "I wanted my baby. She would have been so pretty, so…beautiful…she would have. Been. A. Ballerina. She would…have had a room filled with dolls, girl! But one night… I was drinking. I got so drunk I couldn't *think* straight. Legendary and I had a huge fight. I was saying things I didn't mean, girl. I punched at him, and my fist missed his face. I spun around and fell down concrete stairs. That's the night I lost my child. And he blamed *me*! *Oh, God...!*"

I was an emotional wreck. "Kizzy, girl." My heart beat for her, become one with her. I knew at that moment we would be great friends for life. I hurt for her; I certainly knew what it was like to lose your child. I had a miscarriage a few years ago, with Hank, my ex. I lost my baby after the first two months; my womb wasn't strong enough to carry it to term.

I didn't eat or sleep. I stand here now, crying about the death of my child, my innocent little baby. A baby I was looking forward to meeting. I loved my unborn child with everything in me, and when I lost it, I wasn't right for months! I hated life, dreaded going out into the sunshine. I couldn't do it. My family helped me through. I lost forty pounds, looked like I was Nicole Richie, I was throwing up the food I tried to eat. I wanted to die, die for my child.

I now understood, it all made sense.

Legendary wasn't mourning his father's death.

He was mourning the death of his child.

A child that would have made him a father.

Officially.

At that moment I had an entire new respect for my man. I would never doubt him or his judgment, again.

When I got home Legendary was sitting on the sofa. Naked. Soft lighting. He looked withdrawn into himself. I sat by him, looked into his eyes. I said, "I'm sorry. I shouldn't have doubted you."

I handed him the necklace. He cupped it, kissed it and said, "Would you put it on my neck, baby? Then I'll tell you about it. Why I lied and said my father gave it to me."

He turned his back to me and I put it on, kissing the back of his neck. My hot tears fell down his back. He faced me, hugging me. "The necklace..."

"I know. I know about your daughter. Kizzy and I had a heart to heart. I'm sorry about everything."

He hugged me, and we rocked with each other until we fell asleep.

# Man inUniform

What was it with women these days? They said they wanted a decent man. A man who wasn't full of himself. Someone who could tie his own shoes, break down a car and fix his toilet while dancing through flaming hoola hoops. They wanted a caring man; a man who never had a run in with the law; they wanted a man who *wasn't* a whore. They wanted someone who knew his shit around the bedroom as well as the boardroom. They said they wanted a strong black man who knew how to treat a lady; someone with a Lesbian's Heart, meaning he could be as sensual and elegant as a woman, yet he could be rough and tough in the sack. They wanted a man who drove a BMW or a Lexus coup, had his own house, a 401 (k), medical and dental, and a wallet the size of the Great Wall of China. They wanted a swell guy who had people skills, public relations experience—meaning knew how to carry himself in public. Females wanted a fellah that bought his auntie, sister, daughter and Mama roses twice a week. A man who knew how to cook, clean and quite possibly sow the buttons back on his dress shirts when they popped off.

I was all of those things, Super-Goddamn-Man, and I was still autonomously alone. Nursing Paul Masson brandy, a broken heart—broken three times over from the same woman—and a body that wanted to be held, consoled, and appreciated. Decidedly withdrawn, the phone broke the silence. Answering, I knew it was Mama. Funny how men professed to being men, yet when the rip tides your ass through hell you had Mama on speed dial. As always, Mama was her usual want to-be Oprah-Winfrey-meets-Dr.-Phil self. She thought she knew everything because she had a little money and dined with white folks. She must have forgotten that her life was crazier than mine.

"Baby, not all women are bad," she told me with so much love and understanding in her voice. I wasn't trying to hear it. I leaned forward on the sofa in my living room. Picking up the remote, I turned on some sad music. When you're heartbroken you only listened to sad, love music.

"Yes they are."

She was defiant. She said, "So what are you saying about your mother?"

*Trick questions. Sure, Mama. Make this all about you.*

I puffed a cigarette, knowing I hated smoking, but the cig calmed my nerves.

"Mom, this *isn't* about you!"

She guffawed. "You coulda fooled me. I raised you better than that."

The candles flickered silently, giving off scents of strawberries. They always soothed me, yet the shit wasn't working tonight.

I sipped the brandy. Good bourbon.

"Mama, please…"

"You get on my goddamn nerves…"

"Whatever." My voice was tired and strained from cursing out my co-worker, Officer James, down at the Metro-Dade Precinct. Because I gave him forty dollars to play the Florida Lottery for me. He not only forgot to play the lottery, he spent my money on a bitch at the Samurai Chinese Restaurant, somewhere around the Falls area.

"Don't whatever me, Son."

I was getting saucy. "I'm grown."

"Then act like you are. Crying over a bitch."

My eyes were laser beams. "She was my *wife*, damn it!"

I was a cop, mind you. I was supposed to protect the cruelly cold Miami, Florida streets with professionalism and zeal. But I couldn't protect my wife's pussy from being violated by a willing participant, her lover Sean. He used to be my best-friend and my partner on the force.

Mama said, "Get another wife! I swear. I know I raised you better than this…"

*Woman, please! Not tonight, I am not in the mood to be lectured by you.* I narrowed my eyes, clad in a tank top T, socks, and brown police pants barely covering my ass. They were unzipped, and I could see the glow of the candles reflecting from my black silky boxers. "*You* raised me?"

She was a little hesitant, as she should be. "Yes. I raised you. I worked three jobs to take care of you. You were my only son."

"True. I am your only son; your only child for that matter; but I hardly consider hooking, cooking *and* tricking three refutable jobs. In fact you couldn't even file income tax off hooking."

"That's a low blow; I did what I had to do. We're not going through this again, are we? I'm done explaining myself to you. You came out of my pussy not the other way around!""

"You could have got a *responsible* job." I was getting heated. "But you didn't. And while we're on the subject, do you know how hard it was to go to elementary, junior and senior high school, knowing half of my homeboys' fathers *paid* to sleep with you?"

"Oh, God! Lennox, *how* old are you?" my mother spat icily, sending chills up my spine. I knew I was out of pocket for talking to her this way. But I didn't want a woman who barely had a decent relationship outside of Prostitution 101 giving me advice. That was my own fault. I shouldn't have answered my phone.

I was guarded. "I'm 28 years old."

She laughed pleasantly! Could you believe this?

"Grow up! *Let* go of that little boy shit! Your problem is that you want your way when you want it and *how* you want it. Your no-good ass father couldn't stay out of jail and stop pimping women; your father wasn't as responsible as I was. He ran the streets, trying to be Scarface Noriega the Third! *Yea* I stripped and did what I had to do to keep food in your mouth and cool, crisp sheets on your body. That's more than what I can say about your Sperm Donor, you little arrogant asshole!"

It tore me apart to hear her sniffling. She was trying to hide it and a huge part of me wanted to hold and console her. I loved my mother and I respected her regardless of her past. I shouldn't be doing this to her. Good or bad she was my Mama.

Bitterly, she went on. "You weren't saying that when you had shrimp and lobster for dinner while everyone else in the Poke-N-Bean Projects had Top Ramen noodles, praying to God every night it turned into shrimp pasta!"

"*Mama!*"

"*Lennox!*"

We were very quiet. My heart was beating rapidly. I felt really low for doing this. Trying to blame her for my problems. I didn't want to admit that I was actually 28, would be turning 29 in a few days, March 15, 2007, and I hadn't gotten my life together. I couldn't keep friends. I kept chasing them away. I couldn't keep a healthy working relationship with other cops. Being that Mama was Cuban and my father was African-American and Trinidadian, my temper flared when it wanted to. I had cold cuts in my blood, so in all actuality I didn't even know who the hell I was.

"Son, talk to me."

I ignored her.

To my complete dismay, I eyed the pistol on the low-table, next to Cedrick the Entertainer's *Jet* magazine cover from some time ago.

Wedding photos of my wife and me hanging in pricey frames all over the place. I looked at the picture of me and Mom; I was wearing a cream-colored tux with lavender silk tie. Smiling so big I couldn't see straight. Thinking that marrying Danielle was the best moment of my life. Mama hugged me, smiling bigger than I was. She was happy to be a part of my Big Day.

Mama said, "Son...this is breaking my heart..."

Whatever. All of the pictures made a sudden drop on the Dow Jones of my soul. The biggest drop of my entire existence. I was embarrassed and ashamed; I could barely show my face around the neighborhood. People knew and people talked. They were in my business like my business belonged to them. They speculated and dissected every aspect of what happened. The fellahs talked about my ordeal in all the barber shops from here in Liberty City to the Greenroom Barber Shop in Goulds. Putting the phone down on the couch, leaving Mama to talk to herself, I realized that I needed to get away. Leave town for a few weeks and not tell anyone where I was going. Surround myself with people who didn't know me. Perhaps go to Istanbul, fuck it. I never have been there. Plus I didn't have to worry about people being in my business. But I couldn't go as of yet; I had a ton of bills, mortgage needed to be paid. I had a decent job and I didn't feel like putting in for leave. I didn't feel like dealing with the paperwork. Not today. Leaning back on the sofa, I closed my eyes, rubbing my temples. In a couple hours I had to be leaving out of here for work. I couldn't stop daydreaming about walking in on my beautiful wife—a woman I would lay my life on the line for—SERVICING MY BESTFRIEND SEAN IN MY BEDROOM! I needed some alone time. I was retarded for calling Mama about my problems anyway. What grown man did that?

Picking up the phone I uttered, "Mama, I got to go."

"...Lennox."

With an attitude that rendered me speechless, I hung up. Anger exploding inside me, I jumped to my bare feet and threw the liquor bottle through the living room window. Glass shattering, the liquor rained down on everything from my mahogany-colored entertainment shelf, my plasma TV, and the carpet. Material possessions meant nothing to me right now. Like a zombie, I walked over to the small mirror hanging by the start of the hallway. Nefertiti was on a pedestal next to me, along with my wedding picture. I breathed in so deeply my lungs and chest seemed like hot air balloons with no sign of landing. I ran my hands over my wavy hair, perplexedly sad. I could remember my wife bought that Nefertiti statuette for me. There was an Egyptian Festival that came through Miami, Florida, and she knew how much I loved Akhenaton and Nefertiti, his wife in Egyptian Literature. I was fascinated with Kings and Queens, even though these days white people were trying to say they had olive-colored skin and were white. Yea, right, bitches! Didn't think so!

The images of my wife's infidelity bit at my skull. Danielle gripping Sean's organ; slurping, sucking and pulling. Intricately rolling her tongue across the head of his passion. Their heat rising and cool air falling, creating tornadoes all over my satin sheets. Neither one of them, two people I left alone countless times, saw me standing in the doorway, my hand on my pistol, my heart broken. I had feelings of nausea, but I swallowed it, backed into the shadows of the hallway and watched her perform. I had just gotten home, thankful for the comfort of my own crib, thinking about my bed, my dogs (feet) were killing me. I had run a hot bath in the guest bedroom, wondering where my wife was. She'd normally have dinner cooked. I had sniffed the air, and it smelled of perfume and other things, but not food, so I was a little disappointed. But I didn't trip; she was probably in the bedroom, watching the Lifetime Channel, television for Women with absolutely NO GODDAMN LIFE!

When I reached the top of the stairs, I started down the hallway, passing framed pictures of my Mama as a little girl, my daddy and Mama when they married, even though it lasted two years. I was smiling, longing my wife, wanting to find her, massage her and eat a little pussy. After all, my lips needed their daily supplements.

When I got to my room I froze in shock, not believing my eyes. My mouth agape, I covered it to stop myself from screaming. The curvaceous breasts shook when she crawled on top of him and he, gripping her amazing ass, lowered her wet opening down onto the rod that would comfort her. He became her Pslams 23, rejecting her wedding vows, vows I thought she made whole-heartedly (or was it for show, since half the bitches in attendance she couldn't stand?) with the flick of his experienced tongue across very erect nipples. Her face turned into green pastures every time she and Sean locked lips, her hair framing her angelic face, forever disguising the women I sought out for eight months from the love contained in my heart.

Holding the headboard, she tossed her weave from her face, held her breasts like doves with broken wings and I saw all the explicit details, his huge organ playing the flute of her vagina, the wonderfully created music deafening me every time she said,

"You fuck *better* than my husband."

His eyes sparkled. "…Oh, yeah, baby?"

"Hell yeah, and you got...some good dick, baby. Goddamn, baby, shit feels so good deep inside me."

"Yea, baby, praise daddy."

She laughed coyly. "Oh, yea I'm praising Daddy! Lennox will never be big daddy!"

My heart burst, the wind knocked from my gut.

"The hell with him," Sean, a man I loved with all my heart, my brother in name, a man I knew for twenty years, had said, with no emotion for me in his voice. He actually betrayed me for some pussy, a twenty year friendship gone down the tubes. Like it never existed. Words couldn't describe how I was feeling at that moment.

I closed my eyes, taking out my cell phone. Quietly, I slipped into the hall closet, leaving the door ajar, my eyes clapping on two bodies, sweaty and taut, loving, teasing and admiring. Rising and falling, becoming the Pacific and Atlantic Ocean, intertwining two gloriously seasoned shores into one breathtakingly sinister picture only Lucifer could imagine.

I called Sean's cell phone. It rang, sitting on my nightstand, the photo of me and my wife laying face down by the telephone. He looked at it, smiled, put a finger over his lips and answered with a belligerent, "*Hey*, buddy, where are you?"

I wanted to cuss him, spit obscenities at him. "Close by, thinking about coming home early tonight. I'm hungry, where are you?"

"Busy at the precinct?" He kissed my wife's lips, and then she crawled, like a pussy cat, down to his penis and took his member into her mouth trying to pleasure him orally. He locked a huge glob of her hair in closed fists and started humping her mouth. The pleasure dancing across his face made my stomach hurt. It took everything in me not to just jump out the closet and shoot them both, but timing was everything.

"Well I could swing by Checkers and get you something to eat," he said, a moan escaping his lips. Holding the phone to his ear with his shoulder, the muscles in his amazing abs contracted every time he flinched. He cleaned it up by saying, "Damn, I'm tired, can't stop...yawning."

"Oh yea. Working out?"

"*Trying* to. Gotta get a few bicep workout in before tomorrow, you know Spring Break is right around the corner."

I wanted to just die. This was my homeboy; I would do anything for him. The men I shot over him, the people I locked up because I wanted to protect him. His Mama was raped and murdered when he was ten years old and his father was booked and charged with her death. I was there for him, brought him into my Mama's home and always supported him. We went through high school together, graduated from the Police Academy together. He was the best man in my wedding, and now the Niggah turned out to be flaw, camouflaging-ass Niggah.

Working up enough nerve, I said, "Well, I'll holla before I get home. Much love."

"Love you, brothah." He hung up and started laughing. Tossing the phone he said, "*Suck that stupid Niggah from the head of my dick...yea, baby, umm hmm just...like. That. Yes!*"

I was shaking my head. Then it dawned on me, he never loved me, never respected me. Our entire friendship was a big lie.

A little plan forming in my head, I called my house phone. My wife froze, looking at it. Sean said, "Don't answer it."

"I got to; I always answer when he calls."

They smiled discreetly. "Well get it, just don't stop blowing me off." He sat up straight, putting a pillow behind his back. "In fact, it's turning me on, my so-called best friend's wife, giving me some head while he's on the phone."

She answered, gripping his dick, studying it, and then kissed the head. "Hey, baby."

"I miss you." Tears were falling down my face. I tried to will the pain away but I couldn't. I never cheated on her, and I wasn't about to start.

"I miss you too, Lennox."

"Oh, I'm not *baby* tonight?" I asked. She never called me Lennox.

"I'm just tired."

"Where are you?"

"Over my Mama's house." How she could lie so easily? I had to wonder, how long had she been cheating on me? Did it just happen? Or had this been an ongoing thing?

I smiled. "I'm at your mom's now, I don't see you." She stopped sucking Sean's dick and stared deeply into his eyes.

"You're at my Mom's house now?" Sean was alarmed. He mouthed, "Make up something," and she nodded her head. He was getting out of the bed, putting on his police uniform, his athletic body shimmying from the dim lights.

"Yea, where are you? In the back yard or in one of the bedrooms, I'll find you. I'm hanging up now, makes no sense to talk to you when you're here at Mom's house. What is she doing?"

"Oh, she's cooking a pot roast."

I opened the closet door slowly, my gun aimed, holding the cell to my ear with my shoulder, walking heel to toe towards my bedroom. "Sounds delicious."

"It is." She covered the receiver and whispered to Sean, "I don't know what to say. He's at Mom's house."

Sean seemed nervous. "I'm going to buy him something to eat. I'll somehow distract him. Probably call the precinct and have one of the fellahs radio him for backup."

"But he's off duty," my wife said, about to pull her hair from her scalp. I was in the doorway, aimed at Sean's back. My room was huge, so they still didn't notice me. They scrambled, putting on clothes, tidying up the place, setting up my wedding picture. Sean stuffed the condom and opened Magnum condom wrapper into his pocket, snatching up his badge, putting it on, and slid his pistol into the holster.

"Baby, are you there?" I asked, my eyes red.

"Yes. I had to leave really quickly; I left through mom's back gate. Gotta run to the store. Need feminine products."

*Fucking liar! You just went to the store last week and raked up on $120 worth of feminine shit!* "Ok, I'll see you when I get home."

"I love you, Lennox."

*I hate you, bitch!* "I love you too, Danielle." I hung up, stuffed the phone in my back pocket and when they turned to face me, both of them had heart failure.

"Dawg," said Sean, pleading, his hands raised. He was walking towards me. "I can explain."

Not wanting to hear excuses, I shot out the lamp and he froze, dropping to his knees. I had a heart of stone. "Famous last words. How do you explain fucking my wife?"

She was crying, sitting on the edge of the bed. Looking like the victim, trying to be the victim. "Baby, this isn't what you think it is."

She screamed when I shot the ceiling fan from the ceiling. I was an expert marksman. Shooting targets came second fiddle to me.

"Oh, *now* I'm baby. You called me 'Lennox' twice on the phone a few minutes ago. I was watching you two from the closet for the past thirty or so minutes."

They just stared at me. Sean reached out to me, his hand grazing my pants leg and I kicked him so hard in the face blood splattered this way and he flew that way, crashing into the foot of my bed. Moaning piteously, he lay there, holding his face, shuddering with fear.

"You know what? You two deserve each other; you're not worth my time. You're not worth my freedom. Sean, get the fuck out of my house. And Danielle. You get out, too! The clothes on your back, since I bought them, stay here. To the left—to the left out of my goddamn room, bitch!"

She stood up, running up to me. Embracing me, she showered my face with kisses and my lips automatically danced with hers, urgent and probing, wanting and needing. I was tasting Ted from her tongue. I held her, gripping the gun with my right hand, slowly gyrating our pelvises together. I didn't know if I should kick her ass or love her. I sucked on her neck and she begin rambling, "Oh, baby...you don't want to do this. I'm so sorry I shouldn't. Have. Done. This. To. You. It's not your fault. You *work* too much. You're never home..."

I looked deeply into her eyes, smiling, the sadness washing over me. I loved her with all my soul. I took vows. For better or for worse, 'til death do us part, yet I didn't remember the vows reading, 'til you suck my best friend's dick.

"I love you," I told her.

She relaxed. "I love you."

Impulsively, I slapped her so hard with the butt of my pistol she fell on her back, painfully falling on the floor. She was whimpering, crawled into the fetal position. I never hit a woman before, but I always told myself, hey, my Mama was a pricey Ho when I was growing up, when I found the woman of my dreams, she must a) be classy, b) respected and c) far from promiscuous with other men if it wasn't me, and she just failed all the choices.

Unzipping my pants, I pissed all over her, draining the rest of my urine on Sean's cut. It burned him. I started kicking him in the torso, the face, the chest. My rage boiled over. I snatched my wife by her hair and dragged her outside, throwing her into the grass. The sprinkler system was on, soaking her clothes. I snatched off her silk blouse, I paid for this, $590 from Bloomingdale's, because I wanted her to have the best; off came her silk skirt, $389 dollars, the matching pumps...I used my shirt to wipe the make-up from her face. I bought that shit from the Dadeland Mall with my hard-earned money.

My friends were filing out of their houses. A couple of my homeboys ran over and grabbed me. I spat at the bitch, becoming a savage. All my pain and hurt boiling over, I couldn't talk straight, sounded like I was speaking gibberish.

In a fit of rage I said, "You bitch! How could you...cheat on me, Ho! Get that bitch out of my front yard before I defile that slut!"

One of my friends, Jay, 5 feet 4, took her by the arm, and told Danielle, "Come with me and my wife. You can stay the night with us, until you find out where you're going."

His wife, Valletta, was at his side. She tried to calm everyone down. She said, sinisterly, "And you're sleeping with me, Jay. I don't trust this bitch around my husband!" She looked at Danielle, handing her a coat to cover her naked body. "If you so much as look at my man, Ho I'll fuck you up! I'm only doing this because I care about you!"

A couple hours later, I zipped up my pants, put on my police shirt with "Sergeant Pale" on the tag and grabbed my keys. I was due in to work at 5 a.m. I was late. Fuck it. Who cared? I had nothing to work for. I needed to engross myself with work so I didn't think about Danielle. Sean was still in the hospital recovering. Of course the police questioned him. I was present. But I knew Sean. Despite it all he wasn't a cowardly snitch, like most men I knew. He said he was robbed and when he came to my house for help, because the robbers took his wallet and cell phone, he sought out my wife for help. The robbers followed him to my house, and hoped to get more cash.

When they didn't have cash, they jumped on him and my wife. Miraculously, my wife confirmed the story and no one in my neighborhood spoke against it. They better not; I had enough dirt on half the people in this neighborhood to get them locked up for life without the possibility of parole. A few weeks later Danielle called me. It took everything in me to be civil. The more days that separated the actual act of infidelity, the better I felt. At work I totally avoided Sean. He had called me and wrote me countless emails and letters. Fuck him. Fuck him to hell.

"Will you sit with me?" she asked.

"Nope. Look Danielle. Didn't my lawyer call you yet?"

"Yes." A few beats of silence. I loved her. But she disrespected me. And there was no turning back. "I don't want a divorce."

"I do."

"I called a marriage counselor."

I laughed. "Dr. Ruth?"

"Funny. We should go and work on our marriage."

"You are unbelievable. Did you only cheat on me once, Danielle?"

It took her a minute. "No. For two years."

I was silent, my heart splitting in two. "With Sean?"

"With Sean."

I was angry. "*Why* Sean?"

"He was…convenient. Plus your mother…she caused all this…"

I blinked twice. "She *what*?"

"Your Mama doesn't want nothing and no one around you. She paid Sean and I handsomely to have a threesome with her. She sucked and fucked him and I to her heart's content." I had to close my eyes. "…I knew it was wrong but you worked day and night and no one comforted me. She played on that. So we *did* it. Don't blame me for the marriage falling apart. Blame your controlling mother…Sean sold you out for your mother's money…

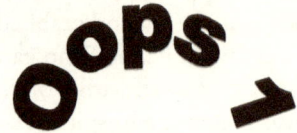

I worked all the time. I had a wife and a home to support. Nothing else in this world meant more to me then breaking my back for a woman who was my Queen. My wallet, bank account and house were hers. I put my all into my marriage. Now I had nothing.

Marriage was challenging, considering I was a white man married to a black woman. I went through all the "Oh, no you didn't marry a black woman!" stares at work and in public. But that didn't deter me from loving her and showing her public affection. Black men sneered at me in disgust and every time I turned my back they pounced on her as if she was a water buffalo and they needed nourishment. She remained loyal. She was a startling beauty: big ample breasts, perky nipples, Apple Bottom derriere, and chiseled Janet Jackson abs. She was a work out buff. She had short, croppy hair, loved poetry, loved eating the best foods and danced to the best music.

When I met her at the Muvico Movie Theater in Fort Lauderdale, Florida, just off of Sheridan West (traveling North on I-75), a couple months ago, she looked very vulnerable attending the *Mission Impossible 3* premiere by herself. I could tell she loved Tom Cruise. The stallion of black men trying to get her attention was amazing. The way certain black men grabbed her hand and she seemed to cringe. She told one of them, a tall basketball player type, "Look, *don't* touch me. I don't *know* you and I'm *not* your goddamn Mama!" He retreated without hesitation. I was laughing to myself, finding it all amusing. She lusted after a white man on a poster, so out of touch with reality because he was in Hollywood—still being ridiculed for the stunt he pulled on the Oprah Winfrey show—and she was in Florida. She knew he existed, but hadn't one iota that she existed.

Home girl looked good in tight snake-print pants, long leather boots with spiked heels with the cowboy golden spinners behind the backs. Her chandelier earrings sparkled with abandon. The long-sleeved gold blouse with a huge oval button holding her breasts in place for dear life was something I had never seen on a woman. Pretty classy, if you asked me. She definitely had junk in her trunk. I told myself: *Maybe tonight is my lucky night.* I was thirty-five, single, very handsome. My drinking buddies said I looked like a young Brad Pitt. I took that as a compliment. I actually won a Brad Pitt lookalike contest three months ago up in Aspen when I went skiing with some old college buddies.

Clad in nice blue Dockers pants, a pink IZOD shirt, and pink Banana Republic shoes, I made my way over to her.

I made small talk. Why not? The only thing she could possibly do was a) dismiss me—like most black women seemed to do, despite hearing, "Damn, you're cute, but I don't do snowballs…"—or b) give me a little tongue tag.

Here goes. "Movie seems like it'll be better than the first two installments."

She smiled at me, eyes sparkling. Hotdamn. She was a beauty. Definitely caused a ruckus in my briefs. My veins seemed to tighten when she smiled. She extended her hand.

"I'm Bianca. And *your* name is?"

I was salivating something terrible. "I'm Ted Oxford."

She grinned. "Like Ted Bundy from *Married with Children*," she joked, patting my shoulder. "Just kidding."

"Nah, I am not married and I don't have children."

She didn't believe me. "Good looking man such as yourself? Not Married? What about kids you don't know about?"

"Sister, I'm 35 years old. I can count on one hand how many women I slept with in my life time."

She was definitely interested. "Wow. White men own the world and the blondes with it and you can count on one hand how many you *slept* with?"

Now I was grinning. "Yes. Don't forget HIV runs rampant like the winter Olympics."

"Amen, Dustin Hoffman. No. No. *You* look like Brad Pitt."

"*Phew*. Dustin Hoffman over Brad *Pitt?* You had me about to search for Oceans Fourteen to get the hell away from you," I joked, smiling.

She touched my hand. "I'm a direct woman."

I gripped it. "Likewise."

She rubbed her thumb over my hand. "I take it your favorite color is pink."

I felt the chemistry building. "Yea. *Unusual* for a man, I know, but I don't live by the rules."

Her eyes drank me like Scotch. "I like that. Your zodiac sign is?"

My heart raced. "Pisces."

"So your birthday passed," she said, forgetting we were in a theatre.

"Yes. March 15th."

"I'm a Scorpio," she informed me.

I was enjoying her already. "Nice. Powerful and manipulative. I better stand guard."

We laughed easily. "Down, Buster. Favorite food?"

"Shrimp scampi."

She nodded her head. "Same here. No hotdogs and pork and beans for this bitch."

I was impressed. "Articulate, are we?"

She hugged me. "Very. Favorite singer?"

I felt good in her arms. "Well, Garth Brooks and a little bit of Janet Jackson, Tim McGraw and Faith Hill."

She pushed away from me playfully. "Garth is straight. Faith is cool. Janet is ok. You're a man so you like Janet because of…"

"Her tits. I can't lie. I'm straight forward."

"At least you're honest. My favorite artists are Nelly and The Dixie Chicks."

"Favorite song by the Chicks?"

"Wide Open Spaces. And I commend them for speaking out on cheating ass George Bush. They spoke for legions of black people in this country."

"Believe me I regret voting for a lying, oil driven man myself."

She snapped her fingers. I was confused. I figured it was some college thing. "Amen! I like you. You're not half bad."

"You're a hot cookie yourself."

"And your breath smells good. I can tell you don't do tobacco."

"Hell no. I do Tic Tacs and Jolly Ranchers. I can't *stand* women who smoke."

"I hear ya'!"

Here it goes. I went in for the kill. I was about to get shot down. I breathed in deeply, closing my eyes. "Are you here with anybody, sexy woman such as yourself?"

This is the part when I cringed. Go ahead. Give it to me. No. Because you're white. Your ass is flat. Black men have dicks. I do dicks. Not cocks. You smell nice but I heard crackers smell like dogs when they get wet.

"I'm flying solo, like Amelia Earhart."

"Care to join me for a movie. My treat."

"Sure. I would love to. Thought you'd never ask."

"Great." I extended my arm and she put her hand through, not at all embarrassed to be out with a sexy white man with blue eyes.

"Lead the way," she said, her nipples hardening. I couldn't help but look. She didn't strike me as a tough-talking, gum-snapping, head popping black chick that got rough and tough. She seemed really down to earth. I didn't smell a hint of cigarette smoke in her clothing, didn't see a hint of nicotine on her pearly white teeth. No caps and no fillings. Definitely two pluses. We might just get along great.

I wanted to spend some time with her. I suddenly didn't want to be alone. "Do you want something to eat?"

Her eyes sparkled brighter. "Yea, I am famished. But the cost of food here is sky high."

"No problem. I make $90,000 a year and I do a small gig as a security guard five nights a week. No kids and no wife. So why not?"

I studied her reaction when I mentioned my income. *Kaching* didn't register in her brown eyes. Thank God she wasn't a gold digger. I'd *never* tell her I was engaged before; that my fiancé died in a small charter plane cash three weeks after the singer Aaliyah perished. It took me three years to get over it. I turned to drugs to escape. Lost my friends who tried to help me and damn near lost my career as a carpenter and subcontractor. It took God to pull me through.

After paying eighteen dollars for tickets and another thirty bucks for two nachos, two large sodas and popcorn, she helped me carry the food into the theater. She led the way.

I couldn't keep my eyes off her magnificent ass. My little friend was hard as hell. Her ass bounced. She led me up the stairs and I tripped four times. I played it off. I wanted to tell her booty to stop staring at my eyes, but it seemed silly and childish.

She led us to the back of the theater. It was kind of empty anyways. Most of the people, white, sat in the front. Hardly anyone sat in the back.

I tripped again.

She looked back at me, smiling, her earrings dangling. "Are you ok, Ted?"

Had to find a quick lie. "Yea, I'm chipper."

She didn't believe me. Her eyes peered through me. "Are you sure?"

I looked guilty. "I'm positive." We talked through half of the movie, didn't really pay it attention. We found it easy to have a decent conversation. She didn't curse once. Good sign, because when I was mad I got furious and I cursed. I had a temper out of this world.

She told me, "I wasn't raised in the projects. I wouldn't know what one looked like. I was adopted when I was three months old by an Australian family. I was a crack baby, can you believe that?"

I chocked on my Coke. "What? A *crack* baby?" People shushed me. "…Are you serious?"

She was stern. "Yes. I was raised in the suburbs of Miami. Went to the best catholic and private schools. I graduated from Palmetto Senior High, though, a public school, with honors. I did four years in the Airforce. I did a tour in Tokyo and another in China. I got my Montgomery G.I. Bill and attended college. I went to USC off and on. I did another three years reserve. Once I got tired of wearing blue I finished law school, gave up on that dream, attending TV Production. I wanted to be a reporter. That dream failed, so now I work at Channel 7 news in Miami, as a sound editor. Hey, I get the best concert seats. I know I'm boring you."

"No, not at all. I'm impressed."

She kept looking at my crotch. My dick had been hard the entire time. I tried to ignore it, but it had a mind of its own.

She sipped the soda suggestively.

"Your thing is alive and kicking."

"Never mind my penis. Just *pretend* its not there."

She stuck out her breasts. "Girls like dick, that is so hard to do."

Wow! Like, totally wow! Did she say what I think she just said? Do I bite or do I deter? "I *love* pussy." We couldn't stop staring at each other. I felt the electricity. It was strong, the current licking at my eyes and face.

She licked her lips, setting the soda down. She massaged my phallus, sending shivers up my spine. I loved her touch, she was fire. Unzipping my pants, she went down on me. Pulled an Alanis Morrisette. Well, shit, did she speak eloquently also? She didn't even look around to see if the coast was clear. I loved it.

She ran her tongue up and down my shaft, finding my balls with ease. She sucked one ball, and then the other...expertly. I went crazy, holding in my moans. I was thrusting my hips, my toes causing damage on the inside of my shoes.

Sucking me with the power of her strong jaws, she could suck a golf ball through a straw. She damn sure knew what she was doing. No one had ever gone down on me in a theater. Especially not a black woman. She sucked my dick long and hard, taking my near ten inches as if they were five. I felt her tonsils, she played with the head, looking up into my eyes and working that tongue. I leaned my head back, savoring the moment. After an eternity she felt me tense up and I told her I had to come and I burst deep down her throat and she swallowed every salty drop. I looked at her with love in my eyes.

Sitting up, she fixed her blouse, sipped some soda and said, as calmly as she could, "Let's get out of here. Let's do the town."

I was in love. I couldn't let her get away. "I thought you'd never ask."

And do the town we did. She drove a Benz. I drove a pickup truck. She followed me back to my house in Homestead. Waterfront condos. And we sat and talked before going to South Beach. I played some Frank Sinatra. We talked some more, on our drive to the beach. I took my truck. We got close really fast. We were both loners, hopeless romantics. I found myself looking at her at the oddest moments. When we got out to the beach, crowded as hell, I paid twenty bucks to park in the garage by Ocean Drive. We walked all over the place. I bought her some clothes and a fancy straw hat. She bought me a Gucci outfit.

We ate, drank wine, danced at Club Deep and found ourselves wrestling in my bed hours later, pumping myself in and out of soft pussy. We were both tipsy and I became one with her nipples. She rode my dick wearing a straw hat, taking all of me. She rode me backwards, the Reverse Cowgirl, yelling into the darkness, her titties bouncing. I came inside her all night long. Not once did I think of condoms.

A month later, after baring our souls to each other (I shared photos of my dead fiancé with her) I knew I wanted to be her husband, but I never said anything. My pride got in the way. I didn't want to live without her. I wanted to share my life with her. She already had keys to my place. When she got off work she always came over. I sent flowers four times a week to her job. She introduced me to all her friends and her adoptive parents. They loved me.

I took her around the fellahs and they were so jealous of me, that I pulled a Queen. I proposed to her in front of her parents over dinner at my house a few days later. I caught her off guard. She sat there at the dining table clad in white. Just as sexy as she wanted to be. She gushed and accepted my proposal. We set a date. A few weeks later after planning our big day we married at my house. A small gathering with family and friends. Sixty people all together. This was truly the happiest day of my life. She sold her house and we pocketed the money. I put her name on everything I owned.

Then it happened. My demanding job pulled me away from my wife. People wanted this fixed and this contracted. I did a lot of roofs and my overnight job became a hazard. Everyone was quitting and I was the only one left so they asked me to work more nights, seven nights a week, from 8 PM until 2 AM. I said sure.

My wife didn't like it.

"Baby, why are you working so much?"

She needed things done around the house. I couldn't do it. I had to make the money. So she quit her job so she could always be at home. She came to my job cursing me out.

"You need to let the second job go! I need you *home*! You can't neglect your new wife, what the fuck, Ted!"

She was right, but I couldn't abandon my boss. I told my wife, "Just hold down the fort until I get home."

When I got home I fell asleep in the doorway. When I made love to her I fell asleep before the tip of my dick could touch her urgent walls. I was unintentionally neglecting my wife. She'd have breakfast cooked, but I was in a hurry after my shower. I grabbed the toast and was out the door and by the time I came home, dinner was colder than ice. I just trashed it, showered and jumped in the bed.

Before I knew it, it was July 15, 2006. And things hit the fan. I cursed her out. I had to work. I had to pay the bills. I loved her.

I got off work early Sunday night. My stomach was in knots. I almost fell asleep at the wheel.

When I pulled up in the drive way I turned off the ignition and I nearly crawled in the house. Up the stairs I went, walking to my room to hug my wife, who tolerated my shit.

When I got to the room door I froze. I saw her tits bouncing and my friend Dexter tagging the ass from the back. I felt bile rise in my throat. She was riding him, and he had her ass cheeks spread apart and his dick, way bigger than mine, filled her up. Her come, thick and white, was all over his nature.

"You like it, Bianca?"

"I love it, Dexter!" She got off him, sucked her cum off his dick, watching his nuts bounce. He covered his face, pumping himself inside her hot mouth. I guess she got bored because she took him out of her mouth and squeezed her tits on his hardened member. She tit fucked him. My heart died. He stood up in the bed, turned her back to him and entered her asshole, pushing her forward and tearing her hole to hell. She screamed out his name, saying she loved when he fucked her senseless, that she looked forward to him always sneaking in my house when I worked late nights and he take her to town.

She threw the ass back on his dick. Her ass jiggling. Dexter had a basketball player's build. He always got the bitches. He was my best friend.

When he came she turned and sucked shit and nut off his dick, swallowing, not even seeing me in the door way.

Seething with rage I went to the kitchen and put on a pot of grits. The minute it started boiling I snatched up the pot, ran up the stairs, burst in the door and was surprised they were gone. I heard giggling from the shower.

"I'm divorcing Ted. We can build a life together. What was I thinking marrying that punk! I mean, I don't listen to the Dixie Chicks. I just told his ass that so I could get in his wallet. I was never adopted. Can you believe he fell for that shit. My parents still live in the ghetto. I was never a suburban bitch…"

"I never him anyways," said Dexter. "Now get on your knees and suck on my dick, bitch."

"Ooh I love it when you talk dirty!"

I was betrayed. All her lies washed over me and created boulders in my heart. Opening the bathroom door, I snatched open the shower curtain and, startled, Bianca could only say, "Oops."

Fucking Oops? Dexter, trying to plead, said, "I can explain." Bianca looked frightened. She should be. The devil jumping out of my eyes I dumped hot grits on both of them. Shocked, Bianca screamed from the pain. Grits tore away at her pretty face. Fuck the bitch. I slapped her so hard across the face with the pot she flipped in the tub and fell on her knees, moaning piteously. Bet you they didn't teach her that flip in the Airforce! I stomped Dexter, who had grits on his face, dick and chest. I beat his ass with the pot and left him there bleeding.

I trusted him! He was my best friend and my best man and he fucked my wife? I got my revenge. Disoriented and my life blown up before my very eyes, I packed a bag, grabbed my keys and wallet and before I left I paid Dexter a visit.

"You go to the cops I tell your wife and son you fucked my wife. I tell her you been cheating on her for months and I lied for you. I'll help her take half the shit you own and custody of your child. I would advice you to not fuck with me."

And I was gone, back in my pick up truck, thinking about my dead fiancé, never to fuck with a black bitch ever again.

The next day I called my lawyer. "I want to file an annulment."

"Already, Ted?" Maybe you should consider a marriage counselor."

I was a beast. "*I want a fucking divorce!* She cheated on me. Infidelity. I want the *black* bitch gone out my life forever."

"Sure, Ted. I'll get right on it." When I hung up the phone I called Dexter's wife, Karen. She was a lively woman, always looked for the best in people. Her dumb ass just didn't know Dexter cheated on her for three years.

My heart bled. "Hey, sexy. Where's Dexter?"

"He's been gone all night. I'm tired of it. Where is he?"

Should I tell her? "Can I come over? I have to talk to you."

"You're always welcome here."

I was about to destroy a happy home. Mine was toppled Legos. "Your son there?"

"No. He's out of town."

"Good. By the way I can tell you where your husband is."

"Where?"

"I caught him fucking my wife last night. And it's been going on for weeks now."

She was silent. I heard crying. "Come over, Ted. I'm so sorry. I never liked the bitch."

"I'm alone, Karen. When my divorce is final I'm leaving town."

"Come over. Let me show you the trick I can do with my tonsils. He hasn't fucked me in months. Its time I put my pussy back in the habit. I know it's wrong, but please, Ted, I want some dick. Please come comfort me. I'll even change the locks so Dexter's keys fail him."

"Is that right?"

"Please come before I change my mind."

"I'll be right over."

*Oops that, bitch!*

# PH Balance

Believe me I wanted to scream. Scream as loud as I possibly could! For one, I lived in Keys Gate, behind Homestead Senior High School, paying $1,200 a month for a condo that was barely big enough for my pussy. Secondly, I wanted to scream because I was in love with a man who was gay! Yes, I said it. *G-A-Y, you ain't got no alibi you GAY!*

But the sad part was that he didn't know I loved him because we were best friends. It was odd that I had these big brown eyes and the vulnerability that made guys want to protect me but I gave off auras of insecurity because of the walls I had up, that said "Stay away bitch!" at 20 paces a minute—they didn't know how to approach me and very rarely did they proceed with caution...and when they did finally get in they fucked it up. And that's my biggest problem. Because I was so picky. I was very fond of saying "When it comes to me, what you see is what you get." But very few bother to look beyond my titties. I had issues with my weight. I wanted to lose 20 pounds. Like Beyonce did in *Dreamgirls*, yet after seeing plus-sized Jennifer Hudson tear it up, I couldn't lie, I had the sudden urge to stay thick. Men didn't think I was fat. They loved my huge ass, huge titties, small waist and pretty feet. One of my friends, well the man I was in love with, Mr. Y.M.C.A., brought me Janet's *US Weekly* magazine, HOW I LOST 60 POUNDS the headlines rang all in my face like a fat woman with carrot cake on cheat day. I got a little flustered.

He tried to make me laugh and it wasn't working. "Why are you upset?" he asked, sitting down on my sofa, throwing his Jordan sneaker-clad feet up on my low-table, knocking a few of my *Time* magazines on the floor and he didn't even bother to pick them up. See, that's why I never invited people to my house. People didn't treat your shit the way they wanted their shit to be treated. "Hell if Janet Jackson can drop 60 pounds in four months and look the way she looked on the B.E.T. Awards last night then we all got hope. Well, not me. I'm not fat, mind you. Plus I'm a man."

I rolled my eyes and sucked my teeth, putting my hands on my hips. "...Nothing against Janet, 'cause I *looove* some Miss Nasty—but that woman got a hell of a lot of money, a *personal* gym, *swimming* pool, a *personalized* meal plan where a trainer created all her meals right on down to the *calorie* and a personal trainer and let's not forget plastic surgery is also an option so yeah I don't use that as a reference point."

He just shook his head. "Just focus on changing your diet, sweetness." He was always understanding, when he wanted something.

"I can't leave Popeye's chicken alone, and my cheese and spinach, and my candied yams, *Chile* are you *kidding* me?"

I sat next to him and threw Janet across the room.

"I *feel* you, girl. I feel you, believe me. But if you want to drop the pounds you *gotta* do the work."

*Ok, Dr. Phil. And I can't stand his ass, either!* "I *tried*. When I ballooned last year I was so depressed. My tummy was Knots Landing all of a sudden. But I am down to about 125 pounds now and at 5'5 that's not too shabby—now if I could just completely flatten the tummy—hell a 6 pack would be lovely but I don't see it happening."

He smiled, pulling out a joint. I was trying to quit, he was making it very hard to do that. I loved weed just as much as I loved money, which was why my favorite color was green: money and weed!

The thug in him was coming out. I loved his thuggish side. He worked at Jackson Memorial Hospital. He was attending the University of Miami, trying to be a doctor, and the Niggah was doing a helluva good job.

He faced me. "Hit this weed with me," he said knowingly. Hard to believe this man never had pussy a day in his life, never even *thought* about it. Now don't get me wrong, he didn't act or look gay. He was so deep in the closet I think a pile of clothes were on top of him. He was very secretive, very private. He never put anyone in his private affairs, except for me. He had the world thinking he was going with Kamala, some clueless bitch, but they hadn't even so much as smelled each other's shit yet. Smokescreens always kept stinging sensations in the public's eye.

He was always there for me. Whenever I needed him he'd drop any and everything. When a booty call kicked me out of his car last year, fifty miles away from my home, my best friend got up out of a deep sleep, picked me up, told me to drive back to Miami (from Fort Lauderdale, Florida) because he was tired, and never asked me for gas. He has slept in my bed with me countless times and never touched me, never thought about it. But I damn sure wanted his dick because one day I walked in on him taking a piss and his dick was so huge I nearly fainted.

I was horny for this man, always have been. I looked him over, FUBU this and that. Caesar's waves in his hair. He was always meticulously trimmed and barbered. He always dressed in nice clothing without being too dressy. I loved his skin tone. He used Ambi and Oil of Olay. Pretty feet. I wanted to see them so I said, "Kick off your shoes, homeboy. Make yourself at home."

He kicked them off, lighting his joint, taking a puff. Puff, puff then he passed it to me. "Here you go, Jenna."

"I'm straight," I told him, turning my face. I didn't want weed. I wanted him! I wanted to be the first woman to give him some pussy and show him that "boy pussy" was fake and phony. God made Adam and Eve, not Adam and Steve...wait a minute, God did make Adam and Steve, my bad. He didn't condone what Adam and Steve did, I should say.

"Turn on some music, let's jam to some cuts."

Good idea. Plus I was in an upbeat mood. So I got up and turned on some music, clad in army attire, nothing overrated. Hat pulled low over my eyes. Some Brandy "Full Moon" came on.

"Nah," I said, turning her off. "I don't do Brandy."

"I hope you don't," he joked. "Put on some Tupac."

"Nah, I want to put on some Otis."

"Redding?" He looked at me with a shit-eating grin.

"Yea." I put it on. I danced around some, acting silly, girly. Holding his joint he joined me, snapping and shaking his ass. I told him, laughing out loud, "...Cute very cute—I'm not much of a dancer—I can fake it pretty well but I'll never be able to drop it like it's hot like one of those video girls—not that I think I'd want to."

He was grinning. "I like the way they drop it like it's hot. I want to drop it like it's hot!"

And he started dropping it like the video Hoes and I started clapping. He was doing a good job.

We looked at each other and I felt the electricity, and I wasn't trying to circumvent it, nor fight it. He turned away and went over to my bar, opening the top counter and pulling out some liquor. He poured some E&J into a small red plastic cup with a few ice cubes added for bonus. Then he poured in some orange juice. I thought it tasted nasty with OJ. Maybe with Coke, yea it would taste good but OJ? But he liked what he liked.

He stunned me when he took it to the head with one hefty swig. Something was bothering him. Trying to play it off, he danced back out to me, taking me into his arms, smiling, puffing the joint, red-eyed. "So you want me to show you how to drop it like its hot, lil Mama?" he asked, with a sexy voice. Was he coming on to me? Nah, he was gay, how could he? He hated fish; he loved sausages in his bread.

"IT DONT HURT TO TRY. I CAN BE YOUR SAFETY NET!" I screamed out in happiness, just feeling some of the effects of inhaling all this weed. I kissed his cheek, my pussy on fire.

He gave me the most sensual look, that made my panties recoil. "You keep talking like that and see where that lands you..."

I wouldn't give in. "I know where it'll land me, in a chair after I pull out yours when I take you out to eat."

He smiled. "A female, pulling out my chair. I thought it was the other way around?"

"It is, but hey sometimes it's good to think outside the box."

"You sound like a Taco Bell commercial."

"Shit, let's go get some."

"Hell no. I don't think so," he blurted. He kissed my forehead, pulling me closer to him. I felt the heat rise, and I wasn't wearing Degree deodorant, either. I felt hot, unnaturally so. My hips tingled, my breasts felt like being fondled by his smooth hands. Yea, my pussy and those hands would make such good dancing partners. "Tell me about your love life. We never really talked about it."

Ok. Now I knew what was going on. He was probing for information. But watch how I flipped the script on his funky ass.

"Are you gay, for real man? Because you got me hot."

He didn't flinch. "Yes, *very* gay. *Never* been with a woman. Always wondered what it was like. But never made the plunge."

"...You know I've only been on like 2 official dates in my 22 years of living. My first was to the movies when I was 14 years old. We fucked and I found out I should have kept my virginity, but the more we fucked the more I wanted some dick in my life, hey I'm being real. My second relationship was about 2 years ago. Dinner and dancing—yeah I'm pathetic—and we wound up fucking at his Mama's crib. She came home early, caught us, and threw me out. That's when I stopped dating Niggahs who were live-in sons with their parents. Someday I want to get married. Yeah, ok. I should also warn whoever seriously asks me to marry him in the future there is a strong possibility for multiple births in my family. Yeah I so go off topic."

"No problem with going off..." He was leaning towards my lips. "...topic." He was closer to my lips. "You're a sexy bitch." The sparkles in his eyes, that man-for-a-woman sparkle, that I-want-some-pussy-for-the-first-time sparkle. "I want to *fuck* you. Let's be real. Never had pussy and I'm 27 year old. But I got a lot of dick, and I want it knee-deep in your pussy. Sup, Ma, show a Niggah how to be a man." The lips connected. He gave me some good tongue. He was a bit uncomfortable, but he tried his best not to show it. But one thing was undeniable: his DICK WAS ROCK HARD!

I felt so good, like I had a high school crush. I couldn't believe this was happening to me, finally getting to fuck a man every woman in Little Haiti, my neighborhood in Miami, wanted to fuck but couldn't fuck because he fucked men in the ass, even though females didn't know it. Since he was the "pitcher" I wanted to show him how to pitch for the Pussy Leagues.

I was an open book. "I want you, Niggah. Take me, *please*."

He was very gentle. "I am gay because of what I went through as a kid, my brother used to touch all on me and make me do things. He was older and I always hated it, but I was so young and by the time he stopped it was too late, I had anger, I slept with men out of anger, I never asked to go through this, I tried to stop."

I held him, resting my head on his fabulous chest. He shook a little, hot tears falling from his eyes. Maybe it was the weed and alcohol, but I had a feeling he really wanted to confide in me and I was about to let him. "It's not your fault."

"Yes it is. I could have stopped him. But it got to the point where I started liking it; I wanted it to happen after a while. I hated it, I actually had feelings for my own brother, but I had to end it and when he went away to the military and never came back I was both happy and sad. Happy because he couldn't abuse me anymore but sad because I didn't get to feel the pleasure."

I was so glad he came over. "All I can say is wow—you've over come a lot—you are a good man and more importantly a strong black man and this world are sorely lacking those sad to say. I won't say I'm sorry for your struggles because everything you've gone through has helped shape the man you are today."

He looked at me with a smile. "It felt good to finally get that out; I never thought I'd ever talk about it. Yea. I don't feel so incredible, though. I'm not perfect. Plus I was a kid, roughly about 5 years old when this happened. But the one thing I'm glad I achieved is keeping my sanity through it all. Thanks for being so understanding and hearing me babbling on about this and that. Appreciate it."

I kissed his lips. "Babbling is defined as an utter meaningless sound—you are doing anything but babbling. Sanity is kinda nice—I can appreciate anyone with a working knowledge of sanity because mine is forever slipping; don't let the pretty face fool ya! I like that we're already trusting friends...and the fact that you look like a lost member of Jodeci is just a bonus—although you have gotten better with age. Yes that's the beauty of black men (and woman) they age very well."

"I can't take it," he admitted, taking off my hat, running his fingers through my hair. "I love your hair. I love women with real hair. I hate weave."

I had a weave! Oh, God! My hair wasn't real! I didn't want to lose this potential dick so I said, "My hair is real, got to be real, you feel me?"

He was rubbing my ass, kissing my neck, taking his time, pressing his huge dick against my stomach....I loved it, I wanted him to take me higher, take me to lands unknown...I couldn't believe this

Desperate for my affection, he got on his knees, hooked both his index fingers behind my panties and slacks and pulled them down to my ankles. He buried his tongue in my pussy, his FIRST TASTE of pussy, hell yea, Adam and Eve, Adam and Eve! He was hungry, like he had just discovered the fountain of youth, but this was the Fountain of Good Pussy and Fortune, his tongue probing and plucking. I damn near fell on my face.

I came so fast I leaned back and smiled. I was shivering, holding his head, tears falling down my face. *"I'm coming, baby!"*

"Lemme taste that shit."

Back in the hole he went with his experienced tongue. He sucked my pink walls and clitoris so fluidly I had multiple orgasms, he swallowed every salty drop.

I was already spent, didn't take much to please me.

But Daddy was hungry.

Standing up he slid that big, thick dick up into my wet pussy and we both had mouths agape.

He was stunned.

"I can't believe it feels like this!" he said excitedly. "Oh my God what have I been missing?"

We moved together, danced to some Otis Redding. Sitting on the Dock of his bay, watching his nuts bounce away, spending time! He was all that and then some;

I was so out of touch with reality that I couldn't believe this was happening. His dick filled me like a hand in a glove.

He held me close, showered my face with kisses, bumped groins...long dicked the pussy. Pushed it all the way in and paused, wiggling his hips. I was punching his chest.

We fucked through four songs.

All over the table, floor, washer and dryer.

I sucked his dick, slobbing all over it, taking it to the nuts....

I made him cum down my throat and when his dick started to get limp I sucked it some more, brought it back to life and told him, "Ready for round 2?"

"Hell yea!" was his eager response.

We were now in my bed, and he pushed my legs all the way back, grinding himself deeply inside me. Damn, Niggah!

Mirrors were all around us. Images bouncing in our eyes. Performing for an audience of two, getting creative with it.

After an eternity he tensed up, come build up from his toes and he started grunting and stuttering and his eyes rolled to the back of his head and he came deep inside me.

I felt the spurt on my walls.

I loved the sound of his voice, that I could make him feel this way for the first time in his life. *"Shit shit shit this feels so good baby goddamn pussy feels so good I want dis shit everyday this is my shiiiiit!"*

When it was over he lay on top of me.

A few days later, when he was gone I was on cloud nine. A few weeks later we fucked all over Dade County. He never touched another man again. A few months later I called him and told him he had a baby on the way. He came right over to my house with a bundle of roses, looking and smelling like a new man. Once I put the flowers in a vase, I turned to face him and he was on one knee. I was stunned, happy, and quiet. I started to cry. Marriage? I didn't think so, but he was a good man, went through a hard life. So what he fucked men in his past? Everyone had room to change, and he truly wanted to change.

We were open and honest with each other, talked about everything under the sun, and trusted each other, his Mama and family adored me. His Mama took me out, and she told me, over pasta at the Olive Garden, "Thanks for making my son a man."

"No problem," I told her.

Now he was in my face, making me want to pull my hair from my scalp. "Will you marry me?" he asked. "I want to be your husband, and I want to be a father to our child."

*No I wouldn't marry him! Fuck no! I couldn't! There was dick I wanted to get from a few other men. Yet HIV was out there and I didn't love this man, wanted to grow old with this man so I said* "Yes, baby. I would love to!"

I had never been so sure about anything in my life, but I knew I would be his wife. And that's how strong the Pussy is, *Strong enough for a woman, but PH Balanced for...a man.*

# Purple Panties 2

Who would have thought that I, Rosaline Cowart "Roz" would get caught up in a love triangle by an intelligent man who knew more about me than I knew about him or myself combined?

Depressed beyond my wildest dreams, I stood in the spacious bathroom, cautiously trying to get it together. I didn't really want to stay in this home with my man, well my ex man, but I knew I had to go, trying to keep the stinging tears from tired eyes. I turned on the tap water, let it run as cold as it could get and I splashed it on the little face I had left because the rest of my face was out on the living room floor by the couch. Little droplets raced down my face, spilled onto my breasts. I shook with pain. I didn't want to hurt my ex boyfriend. I really didn't intend on him finding out that I was sleeping with his god brother's wife. But I was, because I craved pussy like I craved dick. I was bisexual, shackled inside a lesbian lifestyle so many people disapprove of, but fuck people! The hell with society, who were they to tell me what to do with my body?

This was mine!

Turning off the water I turned on the radio in the bedroom and started taking my clothes out of the drawers while Brandy asked the listening audience "What About Us?" When she needed to be worried about that fifty million dollar lawsuit slapped in her face by the family of the very person she killed, or so I heard. You couldn't always believe what you heard on the news, especially when you're black. The media always made blacks look like sex freaks and incompetent hags, and make white sluts like Anna Nicole look like an angel when she was one of the biggest sluts in Hollywood.

Putting Hollywood entertainment out of my mind, I looked zombie-fied. I kept going over in my brain the fact that I called Tay—my ex boyfriend—another man's name—Pierre—and hadn't even realized it. And now that I was thinking about it, he did wince when I called him "Pierre." When it came down to the nitty gritty, of him finding out I slept with Pierre's wife, part of him *knew* that I had also cheated on him with his God brother Pierre, a man he loved and respected. Yea, I could admit that I fucked 'em both. But with Pierre it was more of a thrill. I was trying to understand why a stone cold lesbian would marry a man as opposed to being in love and truly happy with a woman.

So I gave him some trim and tried to assess the situation and wound up being dick whipped, tongue lashed and came all night long. I could certainly see why she married him, because Pierre was the Justin Slayer of the Hood. Now it was all out in the open, and he wouldn't even talk to me about it. I tried calling him on his cell when he stormed out of here to work. He declined my calls. I left him a recorded message. I assumed he erased them because they went unanswered. I felt guilty; it was eating away at me, consuming me. Because of the silence he was giving me. And Blowing Kisses in the Wind, Waiting for Him like Paula Abdul and her sappy ass song wasn't going to cut it with me because she released the song for money; I just wanted an understanding from my ex. He said he hated me. And he was moving out. I sacrificed a three year relationship with a caring and sensitive man for what? Thirty second pussy? Trashy dick from his God brother? Well, *trashy* wasn't the word to use, because Pierre had it going on. I couldn't get over the fact that he said he followed me the other night to his friend's house and personally saw me and his friend's wife rolling around on the couch, bumping pussy; sucking and licking, finger banging and appreciating. I felt so embarrassed right now. I wondered what was going through his head at that particular moment. Did he want to shoot us both? Did he feel betrayed? Did he get off when he watched two sexy women get off 'til the break of dawn? A million and one questions that may never get answered in this life time went through my mind because he wanted to leave, but this was his house, I should be the one leaving. Not him, he didn't deserve this kind of treatment.

My hair all over the place, I needed to take off this huge trench coat, which was open and showing off my bare breasts and purple panties. I loved those panties. The very satin panties me and Mya, Pierre's sensual wife, played in. I thought of her now, her sweet, sweet lips. Her red, red wine, and every time I drank from her wet opening I felt so, so fine. She was warm and fun, fiery and had the soul of a lioness in battle. She knew how to touch and tease me. She'd drove me crazy, draw me near orgasm every time she went down on me trying to shoot *Pearl Harbor Part II* with the film crew trapped in succulent lips and a slick tongue. But before I could send off the heat seeking missiles from the bubbling lava in the depths of my volcano, she'd stop cold turkey, sit back and watch me shiver, plead with her and beg. My orgasm fizzled into nothing, no BOOM Artillery as they say in the Army, no fireworks. I'd cry myself to sleep, wanting to touch myself and finish myself off but she wouldn't allow me.

The next day she'd do it again, get me bodied, hot and bothered, taste my love with the urgency of Diana Ross in need of a much needed number one hit and once her tongue found the *Da Vinci Code* in my clitoris and the code became the Force Being With me, I'd start climbing the mountain, soaring past the clouds, being wet by the moisture and she'd stop cold turkey before nature could yank out my orgasms. And again I would be mad, curse her, bitch at her and she'd tongue kiss me, hug me, rubbing my titties, my ass, stroking my Kitty Kat and she'd tell me, "Just hold out, I promise this will all be worth it."

Then the third day, we were at it again, kissing, tasting and bumping pelvises. She always looked me in the eyes, concerned about my pleasure. She always asked me questions. Did it feel good to you? Was there anything she needed for me to do? Did I need improvement in any areas? She was a pro; I always gave her the control.

Yet this time, when she spread thy pink walls of the flaming pussy and saw the Pink Panther dancing around chasing spots I started to shake with glee, I was about to pull my hair out, my toes curling to the point of cracking. My eyes rolled to the back of my head while I held her bobbing head. When I came, an explosion rocked me so speechless I couldn't even moan. The pleasure that washed over me was reminiscent of ocean waves across the sandy feet of two lovers running in the glow of the moonlight in search of finding their souls to open the haven so they could mate, becoming soul mates. And when it subsided and my body was no longer in an arch, reminding me of the *Exorcism of Emily Rose*, I would just hug her, tightly, and tell her how much I loved her. She said she loved me too, yet we had committed men in our lives, which prevented us from truly being together. She loved Pierre. I some-what loved Tay.

And now she still had Pierre. And I didn't have Tay.

Crying my ass off, I opened a suit case and threw in my folded clothes when the house phone rang. I froze, just staring at it. Complete silence. I didn't even flinch. I looked at it more fixedly, just waiting for the answering machine to pick up. But I couldn't wait, it could be Tay. So I rushed over to the nightstand, yanked it up and said, as calmly as I possibly could, "Hello."

Silence.

"Hello, damn it I'm *not* in the mood."

Sobbing. Heavy sobbing.

I was alarmed. "Tay, is that you?" My eyes bounced all over the objects in this room. "I'm sorry, baby, I didn't mean for you to get hurt."

Tears welled in my eyes, which kept surprising me because it took a lot for me to cry, yet I know what it felt like to be cheated on. I went through that years ago. Which was why I had conditioned myself to harden my heart against men?

Now my heart bled for Tay.

"It's not Tay," she said and I just blinked once, gripping the phone.

I couldn't keep the smile from my face.

"Mya?"

"Yes, baby. It's me. Can we talk?"

"Sure. You *know* we can talk. Where do you want to meet?"

"Downtown. Bayside. Bubba Gump Shrimp, we can talk there."

"When do you want me to meet you there?"

"*Now.* It's important."

I hung up. A tad bit disoriented, I put on a "Monika" kimono top with bold orange and black printed designs, six snake-print bangles on either wrist, I loved being...accessorized. A necklace with a huge diamond medallion that rested between my breasts, put my hair up in a bun, slid into some tight blue jeans. Quickly rushed into the bathroom and made up my face with Elizabeth Arden. Lorreal, Maybelline and Dark and Lovely would never grace my face.

I grabbed my beaded cornhusk bag, threw in a bottle of perfume, which I'd spray on me in the car, slid on some clogs, though they were played out but since when did I play by the rules and I put on huge chandelier earrings that dangled and tinkled.

I was a very beautiful 40 year old woman. In love with a woman who was younger than me—20 years younger.

I was out the door, headed for my Durango ten minutes later, after turning on the house alarm.

And yes.

I still had on the purple panties.


My heart hurting for Tay and the lives I helped destroy, I entered Bubba Gump Shrimp, a bustling restaurant, with a smile, looking around for Mya. She must not be here yet so I asked the waiter to get me a table for two, preferably in the back of the restaurant. Best to keep it discreet.

"Right this way, ma'am. You're looking rather dashing today," said the handsome young white male. I shook his hand, then he kissed mine.

"Thank you," I told him, glowing like the huge ball of fire above Bayside, one of the hugest tourist attractions in Miami.

A few men were checking me out, mumbling to themselves with secret smiles.

"I look ok?" I asked them, turning in a circle, running my hands over my attire.

"...*Yes, you look good...*"

"...*You're wearing that kimono, pretty lady...*"

"...*Your husband is a lucky man...*"

I shook their hands, feeling a bit festive and made my way to the table. Such the gentleman, the waiter pulled out my chair and I sat down, thanking him silently. He said, "Would you like a drink?"

"Why yes, a Sprite would do."

"Do you know what you want to order?"

"Grilled shrimp. Two orders. And bring the receipt ahead of time so I can pay it and get it over with."

"Coming right up, would you like anything else?"

"No, I'm ok. And thanks."

"I'll be right back with your drink, ma'am." When he pivoted, to go take care of my order Mya's eyes looked down at me. She smiled, leaning over and kissed my cheek.

"Hey, Roz. Have you been here long?"

I stood up and pulled out her chair. She looked ravishing. I loved the red cassimere sweater and the flowing skirt, which dangled into a split along her right leg. Her make-up, flawless. Every finger had jewelry. Her necklace, thin and glittering.

I got right down to business; I was a direct woman, in and out of the bedroom. "So what did you want to see me about?"

She was quiet for a few minutes. She nodded her head to a country song that I never heard before. "I left Pierre."

I was quiet. "Why?"

"I don't *love* him." She looked away from me, which told me she was lying. "It's not good to stay in a marriage when you don't love the person."

"Tell me the truth." I kept my voice warm and affectionate, just the way she liked. She looked at me, nervous. I held her hand.

"Anyways, how is your day going, Roz?" Her voice was strained, like she was holding something back.

"My day is...tolerable. I lost my man, of course."

She licked her top lip, averting her eyes again. She would not look at me. "That was inevitable, Roz."

"I didn't mean for Tay to get hurt."

"We all got hurt, girl. We all played a dangerous game and we lost. Tay lost everything he had in you."

"He'd get over it." My throat was stinging at the thought of such a good man going through all that heartache.

"You don't just deal with heartbreak over night, Girl." She looked at me, going in her purse and pulling out a stick of gum.

"Girl, let me get one."

She gave me a nasty look. "Go and buy your goddamn own, you took enough from me."

I didn't understand. "What did I take from you?"

"My life. You know we can't be together, even if we wanted too."

"But what about the plans we made."

"What plans?" She had selective amnesia.

"You know, leave our men and move to Polynesia."

"What black bitch you know lives in Polynesia? And you know what they say about plans."

"Plenty black people go to Polynesia."

"Name one."

She had me. "Girl, let's stop this game. I need you."

"Tay needed you, girl. I was in it for the sex; I am not going to toy around with you. It was fun while it lasted."

"It can still last, Mya."

"You sound desperate." Mya couldn't keep the contempt from her voice. "And you're getting older. You're twenty years older than me, I'm still young and I don't want to grow old with you."

Those words cut like a knife, tore through me like an ax.

"Where is all this coming from? Why would you come in public and hurt my feelings this way, maybe I don't know you as well as I thought."

"Look, Roz. Shit just hit the fan. Tay came over and told Pierre what was going on. There was a huge fight."

My mouth fell open in shock. "No, girl."

"Yes. Pierre told him that you slept with him as well, told him everything, girl. That you two fucked for months. Tay was in a fit of rage, he said he hated you and he would hate you forever, that he'd never forgive you."

I couldn't stop the tears from falling. I shuddered with pain. I never meant to hurt such a good man. It was probably women like me that turned good men into dogs, into the disrespectful beings they would eventually become, growing hearts of stone.

Tay was good with me, knew everything about me, from my favorite color to how I liked my food. He helped me out with my parents, always took my Mama food. He never asked for money. He never asked for anything. He was the most selfless man I knew. And now he was hurt.

I didn't know what to do. "I got to call him, girl."

She squeezed my hand. "You may not have the opportunity." Her voice and eyes trailed off.

I was guarded. "What are you talking about?"

"Well I left them fighting. I grabbed my keys and went to my neighbor's house and called the police. They were breaking dishes, cursing each other, screaming I hate you back and forth. A chair flew out the living room window; Tay took bricks and broke his windshield and shattered every window on our house. He was a monster; he said he loved you more than life itself.

Pierre said something and Tay rushed into the house, closed the door and two gunshots made me and the neighbors blink in stone silence. I was so scared, girl."

Her hands were trembling.

I didn't like the picture she was painting. She had to be lying. I was in serious denial. Tay would *never* shoot anyone. He *hated* guns. Well maybe Pierre shot him. I didn't know. I was about to explode so I said, frantically, "Girl what happened?"

She didn't waste any time. "Tay shot Pierre in the head. Then turned the gun on himself."

While I went through withdrawal of my own, a terrible ringing in my ears giving me headaches, Mya slid to the floor, covering her face, sobbing so hard everyone started to notice. She was screaming, saying over and over she was sorry, that she should have never allowed herself to get involved, she should have never betrayed herself, her marriage and Tay, who had always been good to her. "I warned you about wearing those panties, I told you not too but you were so..."

Some guy helped her off the floor, and showed genuine concern for her and she snatched her arm back, got in my face and pointed a bony finger.

She had fire in her eyes, made me shudder. "I *told* you not to wear those panties but *no*, you just *had* to wear them. Those purple panties created all this. I can't believe Pierre and Tay are dead. I got two funerals to attend, how will I explain this to his family, to my family, to Pierre's family? That us licking pussy brought about this hell!" She tossed her hair behind her head and stood erectly, gazing me in the eyes, forcing herself to hate me. No one uttered a word. Even the cops over at the opposite table lowered their heads.

She laughed bitterly, crossing her arms across her chest.

She said, matter-of-factly, "Don't call, write or stalk me. I got a restraining order against you. If you come within a hundred feet of me bitch you will be arrested. The love I had for you died the instant the gun went off and I lost my husband and my friend Tay. In life we pay for mistakes and bad decisions. Sometimes we can get over it, move on and try to forget it happened. But I *can't* forget I helped create this massacre. Go to hell, because I damn sure don't want to burn with you."

She snatched up her purse and I, dying inside, my world spinning, jumped up to my feet and grabbed her, pleading with her, begging her not to leave me. The cops looked sternly, but didn't move from the table.

I grabbed her in a bear hug. All the love I had in my heart for her snowballed me. I wound up kissing her luscious lips. They still felt warm and soft. I had to resist the urge to rub her pussy. I wanted it bouncing on my tongue while her clit slid against it. I wanted to watch her shiver when she came and moaned my name, telling me I was the most gorgeous woman in the world. I wanted us to slap asses with a dildo linking us together. I wanted to lick the sweat from her tight asshole and finger fuck her into a fierce orgasm. I wanted the old days back, when Tay didn't know I slept with another woman. I wanted to be her one and only, take her away from all this hell. I wanted Tay to be alive and well so he could find another woman, fall n love and forget I existed…

Now we gave each other some tongue, hugging and rubbing, our hearts mending and fencing…in front of everyone. I didn't care. I rubbed her ass, told her we'd get through this, that I couldn't live without her, shouldn't live without her and her lips didn't move anymore. Her arms dangled at her sides.

Biting my bottom lip, she slapped me and ran out of the restaurant, in tears. I, my hair disheveled, sank to my knees, my shoulders shaking, the tears ripping my soul apart and I couldn't contain the guilt and the shame that turned me to flames.

I wish to God I would have never worn those purple panties.

# Rayne in the Bedroom 2

Clever felt elated today. Her game of mastery and trickery in the sheets filled her with a certain glee that was only found inside the cavities of the greedy and the rich. The thought of the chase engulfed her like flames on hay. Today, of course, another challenge beckoned her. Looking over the framed photograph on the nightstand, she picked it up and kissed the woman clad in the floral dress. Her misty eyes clouding over, she set it down and turned to face him. With a secret grin, she said, "Honey, I want to live out my dreams."

Clad in a top hat of velvet and a smoke-colored suit, he responded, "Then *live* it."

She looked amused. "Edgar, is she *coming*?"

He blinked a few times, sighing. "Today, my name is Edgar? I like the name, Clever. Truly, you know what my real name is…

"Yes, I do. Edgar is so…fitting. This is girl number four. All in a week's time period!"

Edgar was amused. "Yes."

She looked at herself in the mirror. "But what about the photographs," she asked nonchalantly.

Sheepishly, he said, "They can stay. She just wants to be paid…"

She smiled—a reflection of her man. "Let the fantasy begin!"

"Begin, it shall, my lady."

"I can't wait!" she gushed.

Ah, the British accent worked wonders.

The new scapegoat sauntered into fabulous bedroom like a summer's breeze— sassy, classy and she wore those chandelier earrings that almost brushed her shoulders like old slaves back in the day with their brooms. Her face made up just right. Ah, he liked! She commanded attention from every piece of expensive Picasso, Da Vinci, and Van Gogh painting on the red walls. She especially loved the oriental carpet. *So divine*, she thought meaningfully.

*I'm going to break this man for his money. I'm 19 years old and I'm feisty. I went to the doctors and had my physical. I have to take my daily shot, which I forgot to do. And my throat is a little parched. Maybe I should ask for a tall glass of water.*

Mystified, Edgar asked, "And *your* name is?" The British accent did a number on the willing prostitute. She absolutely *loved* the Voice. They *all* loved the voice. This Hollywood-type beauty rubbed her gorgeous breasts seductively, licking her lips like Audrey Hepburn back in the early 19th century. She had long, black curly hair, full, sensual lips; her nipples were at least a half inch long, poking against the expensive satin fabric crafting the rest of her magnificent dress.

"I'm Desire!"

Edgar was jubilantly pleased. *"You're mad! You're gorgeous!"* He was rubbing his penis.

Desire looked down at the shape of his penis. *It's too small to be classified as a dick. And he wants to fuck me with that little ole thing. Maybe I should inquire about it; hell my mind wants to know. And my ass and hands do, too. I'm just being real. I want my money and then I'm acting funny.*

With breathless adoration, Desire brushed lint off the smoke-colored suit. "Love the choice of dress," Desire said enviously, calculatedly kissing his lips. With the skill of a seasoned veteran, his tongue danced in sync with hers. It wasn't one of those sloppy kisses, thank heavens. She could taste remnants of red wine and pistachios.

Desire was on fire, she wanted to ignite his flames and hoped infernos turned the sheets to ashes and her horniness to dust so she could lay, spent and then spend her hard earned money. *I must not forget the real reason why I'm here, though. And money isn't the* only *reason!*

She had to pay off her student loans. She attended City College in South Miami, Florida. It used to be located just across the street from the South Miami Metro Rail station. Now Baptist Hospital took over the glass and concrete building. She used to love the smallness of the inside floor. The college was one level with small classrooms. No more than ten people; the library was small, intimate, sweet and to the point, about three computers, tops. The Computer Lab itself had about forty computers.

*Now my financial advisor is always at my classroom door, calling me out into the hall. I think he likes me, and that's why he's forcing me to pay these loans! How could I? I work at Denny's at night, busting tables, taking tips and sometimes assholes come in there and they don't even* leave *tips. Or they slip out without paying and it comes out of* my *check. I live in a section 8 house. I don't have any kids because I can't have any, for a reason. I want a better life.*

Pushing all that to the back of her mind, Edgar took the time to turn on Barbra Streisand's *"Wet"* album. It was hard to break away from Desire's kisses. Such passion she had.

"You never told me your name," said Desire, walking over to him and kissing him again. The way he felt, the slickness of his tongue, the smell of his fragrance pushing her up and over her limitations dethroned thoughts of unease. He was holding her face like a fine piece of crystal, pressing his warm body up against hers. Her eyes danced over the Van Gogh painting of huge sunflowers, the Tiffany lamps, the Gucci watches and belt buckles and cologne on the dressers.

Barbra Streisand and Donna Summer were singing "No More Tears." She loved the song, never heard it before. She had all of Donna's albums so she knew her distinct voice. Her eyes fell on a few 5x7 photos of a lovely woman with green eyes sitting like Queens on the nightstand. She had on a summer dress, or did they call it floral dresses?

"Are you married?"

He pulled away from her, softly pushing her to the bed. Seduction danced in his eyes. He was rubbing himself.

"Checking the package, 'ey?" asked Desire, licking her lips.

She gave a grin that made Desire melt. "Yes."

She smiled. "Is that your wife in the photograph? You never said you were married."

Hesitated a bit. "Yes, that's my wife."

She wanted to initiate some freaky shit. "Turn her pictures to the bed, so she can see what I do to your dick."

"Fire, aren't you…And for the record my name is Edgar."

"Nice name…."

Edgar said, "Why thank you, madam."

Desire turned the photos so they were facing her. She undid her bra with one hand, the red Victoria let out the Secrets that bounced with a sudden joy. Edgar nearly came on himself. He pulled her dress down to the start of her belly button. He rolled his tongue around her soft, creamy black skin. She tasted like sugar.

"You taste sweet, like sugar…"

"I put real sugar in my edible lotion everyday so that I'm *always* sweet."

Edgar wanted this one to be his! "You're *mad*! I have a question for you."

"Shoot."

Edgar went in for the kill. "Have you ever slept with a woman?"

Desire's mouth fell open. "No. I'm *not* that way. I'm a woman, I don't *suck* pussy."

Edgar's eyes beamed. "Ok, I got you."

Desire grabbed her right tit and shook it. "Now let's get it on."

"Sure." He sucked on her breast like his tongue was dying of thirst, like a fish out of water just dying for a gentle drop of the ocean. Desire melted, reaching behind the nape of his neck, rubbing it. She wanted to take the hat off, but she didn't. He looked good with it on. He moved his hand over her breasts, his lips and tongue dancing with mound of flesh. Desire rolled her groin, lust tearing her up. She ran her hand behind her soft hair, smelled of strawberry Suave, and held it atop her head; strands falling into her face as she leaned her head back.

"Take your pants off, Edgar," she cooed.

"No can do. This is *your* moment; I just want to eat your pussy."

Desire was unnaturally quiet. She didn't *want* head. She wanted to get tagged from the back. She was an *anal* bitch. *Stick it in, fuck me hard, long and good. Make those nuts slap my ass like Kobe Bryant taking basketballs from Michael Jordan while Derek Jeter looks on with his bat.*

Desire told him how she wanted it. "I want to be fucked in the ass, baby. I want to swallow your cum; let your cream play tic tac toe on thy ole tongue. I hope your come doesn't taste funky! And I hope you washed your dick. You men have a habit of jacking off and letting your seeds dry up on your shaft because you're arrogant, territorial and cocky!"

Edgar was slowly losing interest. Prostitutes weren't supposed to be demanding or talkative. "I can do that. Mind if I use toys?"

Desire was unperturbed and appalled. "*No*! I want the real thing. Skin versus skin. I want your dick in my ass! Fuck the bullshit. And then I want my 500 bucks."

Edgar stood up. "Such a raunchy mouth you have! Online, when we met last night, before we set up this meeting, you told me you were a woman of impeccable taste. Judging from your raunchy word choice maybe that was a lie."

Desire was taken aback. "*A lie?*"

Edgar couldn't take it anymore. The slut had to go! "Yes, a lie. A fib, storytelling, liar, are those *enough* words for you?"

Desire's eyes widened with shock. "Your British Accent…it's gone. Like…it…was. Never there."

He smiled. "Well, if that's the case, then game over. My fantasy is *ruined.*"

Desire needed the money. She had to get him back in the habit. Suddenly the financial advisor popped in her head, taunting her about paying for her loans. "Your voice sounds somewhat feminine now. What's going on? Are you a feminine fag or something? Getting off on your sick games?"

Edgar's eyes widened. He was insulted. *This bitch has got to go!*

Desire covered her breasts with the satin sheet. "What?" She looked over and saw his Salem Lights cigarettes and a lighter. She took a cig, lit up and pulled on it, sucking the smoke into her lungs. She was stressed.

*I drove south on US1 from Kendall to this jerk's house. Traffic was crazy and half my hair do was messed up because it was raining. I had to study for midterms, and he says game over? That means no money! I can't pay on my loans. They are going to vault. I got to pay for my doctor's examination, and now I can't. Plus I owe forty bucks on my light bill, twenty more on my water and my Brinks security Alarm bill is due. Ninety dollars! And this man is playing with me.*

Desire apologized. "I'm sorry. You don't have to sex me; I'll do what you want." She blew smoke in the air. "I need the money, please understand. I'm just a little pressed for time."

"Light me a cig, Desire," he said, the accent returning, the eyes gleaming again.

*Spoiled freak!* "Sure." Desire held a cig up to his lips, then the flame under it. He puffed and appreciated.

"What do you want to do?" Desire asked.

Edgar didn't waste any time. "Eat you out, my lady."

She was hesitant. "Take your hat off, first," said Desire.

"Ok." He stood up, took a few steps back and took off the hat. Desire saw the hair net.

She was suddenly guarded. "That's a lot of hair," she said. He took off the net; the hair fell around his face.

"Oh my God," said Desire. "A man with hair. You look like a girl. Men aren't *supposed* to look like girls."

Off came the shirt. Desire chocked on smoke seeing two tits duck taped, making them look compressed. Snatching off the tape, Edgar winced painfully.

Desire was embarrassed. *"OH MY GOD YOU'RE THE WOMAN FROM THE PHOTOGRAPHS!* You were watching yourself," said Desire with shock.

Edgar took off the pants; the sock fell to the floor. Desire thought, *No wonder his dick looked small, he didn't have one. He was a female!* She took off her panties. Tossed them in Desire's face. Repulsed, she threw them across the room. Angry, Desire picked up some pillows and threw them at Edgar, or whoever this freak was. Cologne and perfume bottles crashed and broke open on the tile, the liquid spilling everywhere. Clever smiled. "Hi, my lady. And you said you didn't want any lesbian action."

Desire smiled. "For a reason." She took off the covers. So sexy she was. Clever was wet all over. She started rubbing her velvet softness; she cooed and moaned to herself.

"Go on, play with your pussy," said Clever, trying to seduce Desire.

"Such raunchy words. And you came down on me for cursing…But I got a surprise for you. Come, my lady, you can eat my pussy now!"

"I knew you'd see things my way." Clever opened the nightstand, took out five crisp one hundred dollar bills and gave to Desire. She held the money. On her knees she was, between Desire's beautiful legs. Her nose was two inches from Desire's private area.

Desire pulled out her nine inch dick, which was tucked between her legs, said, "FREEZE!" and Clever jumped out of the bed as if it was on fire.

Desire smiled sweetly, watching Clever tremble with anger.

Desire said, "*I got a secret.* I got to pay for my next dosage of hormone shots, actually. I forgot to take one before I left. Causes my voice to be feminine. It's no walk in the park intravenously shooting estrogen into your body. I was born a man. Fortunately, for me of course, I *knew* you were a woman. I just played the fantasy, isn't *that* what *you* paid for?"

Clever's world destroyed, devastated, she fell to her knees, screaming into her hands. Someone tapped her shoulder. Looking up, Desire was putting on her clothes. "I'm a woman, but I never said a *complete* woman. Now you understand why I'm so…anal retentive in the ole rectum region."

Clever felt sick. The room spun. *"Fuck you! Get out! Get out now!"*

Another tap on her shoulder. She froze. She slowly turned to face Rayne, who was filming the entire thing. Bringing her face from behind the small Sony digital camera. "Stop your games, or the Internet gets the tape. Oh, by the way, my son wants that Playstation 3. I think it cost about $500. How about buying it for him when it comes out. Better yet, give me a cool thousand bucks, for pain and suffering and you won't wind up in court."

Clever paid them, and Rayne, slapping palms with Desire/Steven, left out the room.

Clever closed her eyes…

Clad in her male disguise, Clever said, "Honey, I want to live out my dreams!"

Staring at her reflection, she said "Then live it," using the male British accent.

Clever asked, "Is she coming?"

"*No,*" he said emptily. Something died in him.

Clever forced herself to grin. "This would be girl number five. All in a week's time period!"

Edgar shouted, "No." She looked at herself in the mirror. Intently. Smiling evilly. "Desire wasn't a girl. She was a man in drag."

Clever looked blankly. "But what about the photographs," she asked nonchalantly.

He said coolly. "They can stay. Rayne just wants to be paid...paid a visit"

She smiled. "Let the fantasy begin!"

"But what fantasy will this be? Desire destroyed it."

Acid in her eyes. Clever said, "Rayne, Rayne go away, when I kill you; you will never come back another day."

Ah, the British accent worked wonders.

# Smoke and Mirrors

When I first met my wife, Gladys, she was the sexiest woman in the world! She had a voluptuous body and an even hotter pussy. Back then I thought I was a player, running game on all the bitches. In fact I never thought I'd fall in love let alone stop calling women a name they call themselves. Everyone wanted Frank Sinclair, which would be me. As much as I hated it, I was named after my dad, a real asshole who was drugged out, currently sleeping on a Downtown Miami bus stop bench by the courthouse.

My wife and I had a different type of relationship now. Depressingly sad, I lay in my bed, clad in silk boxers and a wife beater tank top T. The news of a few murders flashing in my face, I was waiting for my divorce to be final within the next few months. Where did I go wrong? Did I *not* love her enough? Did I not try hard enough? Yet all those questions I pulled from a bucket of oranges when the situation was a bag of spoiled apples. Unusual circumstances willed the divorce. Unfortunately, I didn't have a choice. And despite how I felt about her, no matter how much I *still* love her, love was the *only* thing I could possibly save from this union.

A union that shouldn't have even taken place. I drove a recently-restored '67 Chevy rolling on deep dished chromed rims. I couldn't live without my booming stereo system that made my trunk rattle like a few screws were loose. I sold cocaine and weed on the side, while holding down college and a full-time job. And during all this my wife turned on me, and became someone else. A stranger. She had the face of a super model and a body that would turn J. Lo into a lesbian. She had everyone from the crack heads to white-collar business men begging to fuck her. Her ass was so big, when she crossed the street Niggahs would hold up traffic just to watch her walk by. She loved it, thrived on it. I used to be *proud* to be her man; I never thought a woman could capture my heart. My father was a rolling stone; my grandfather was a rolling stone. So I was a goddamn boulder.

I fucked any and every bitch and I didn't care if she was married. I didn't care if my friend dated her. If my cousin went with her I didn't give a shit. Pussy was pussy and if the bitch gave it up to me then quite frankly the pussy was never his to begin with, so why get mad at me? I was a grimy Niggah when it came to money and pussy. I was feared by a lot of Niggahs in Miami-Dade, especially in Leisure and Liberty City. I'd walk into the USA Flee Market on NW 79th Street and even the big time dope boys gave me respect. I have shot at so many Niggahs that it just didn't make any sense. I had a rough life, bad upbringing. I didn't have the opportunities the kids in the suburbs had. After begging God for a few months to open the door of opportunity for me, and going to church to set it stone it never happened so I haven't gotten my knees dirty in years. I used to watch my Mama, Verona Sinclair, get dicked down every day by a different man with a different reputation. I was a little kid, watching her slang weed and snort coke just to make ends meet the rent and the light bill. I mentally took notes because she once told me this was how you got by in life. Hustling. For a few months on end she disappeared and I had to cook, clean and take care of myself. I took myself to the doctor, sometimes getting one of the older dope boys to pretend he was my father so my shots and immunizations were up to par. She always made sure the rent was paid and food was in the ice box. *That* I didn't have to worry about. I didn't take school seriously at all. I talked back to teachers and started letting the environment shape me. I duly listened to Elder black men in my neighborhood who told me that Niggahs were only good for three things: getting some pussy, playing a sport and staying out of jail.

We drink booze and we sold drugs, they continued to say. We whipped bitches asses to keep them in line and we protected our word and balls like they were an endangered species. I took all that to heart. I became it, slept on it, fucked and ate it. Even though Mama was a Ho, I loved and respected her no matter what. I *never* back talked her; never let her see me cry. She never talked down to me. When she saw me her eyes lit up. Mama sold her pussy up until she was found dead behind a restaurant on South Beach a few years ago, before I turned twenty. I was still bitter about that. Daddy had killed her because he got tired of her whoring around Dade County. But he never brought up the fact that he was an even bigger Ho than she was.

At her funeral I was distraught; I tore up every flower. I fought my Daddy and accused him of murder. Family pulled him from the church. I was in a blinding rage. I couldn't control myself. The police came and I denied the allegations. I wasn't a snitch. I didn't like crackers in my business. They didn't care about a prostitute anyways. The look on their pale faces told me that. Rumors circulated that Daddy had another kid somewhere. But he denied it and without any proof, what could I say? He was a prick. I hated him with a passion and he never showed me fatherly things. We never spoke. He never looked out for me. Funny, we lived in the same house and we didn't have any type of a relationship. I stopped giving a damn after I turned eleven years old. I gave up on a Daddy/Son relationship. I even asked God to erase his existence from my memory.

Some girl hugged me at Mama's funeral. In tears of her own she held me tight. She was clad in a floral dress and big red ribbons in her hair. Her name was Paula Jakes, a year younger than me. I didn't know *who* she was, pretty little thing. But all I could do think about my mother. How she suffered when she was alive; I wanted to know what drove her to prostitution, why she never told me about my grandparents. I had so much contempt. Yea, she vanished for months but I always knew she would come home. Now she never would. I could never see the sparkles in her eyes when she saw me. Angrily, I pushed Paula off me. She shook with fear. "Fuck you! I want my mother!" I spat icily. The preacher told me to stop cursing and I pushed the podium over and threw the Bible at him. "Tell God to stop cursing my goddamn life!" One of my dope boyfriends embraced me and I cried on his shoulder until my nose burned.

Little Paula ran off and hugged an old-looking man, who sat by a female police officer with the name Officer Brown on her name tag. I would *never* forget the woman because she stared at me with a wicked look on her face. I *knew* she was mad I was acting a complete fool at the funeral, but I didn't care. I didn't know how to process that type of pain, being the young age I was. It was too much for me to bear.

Years later, when I got married my wife Gladys helped me deal with my mother's death. I cursed her and called her outlandish names. She never got offended. She never turned her back on me. She let me vent and throw things. She always replaced the items when she got paid without asking me for anything. She never wanted my money. She had her own job, her own crib and her own car. She treated her pussy like it was a priceless antique; she made me work for her panties.

When I cheated on her she stopped calling me and she talked down to me. When I tried to slap her lippy ass she kicked me in my nuts, pulled my own gun on me and said, "Niggah, I'll shoot your sperm cells in the head just to make sure they die off like your no good ass if you try me." Goddamn it, I fell in love right there. She was a Gangster Bitch, without coming off looking like one. Suddenly, right then and there, what the Elder black men once taught me—that men were supposed to whip a woman's ass to keep her in line—went right out the window.

I became faithful. For the sake of our relationship I deleted all the booty call phone numbers. In fact I gave the phone away and got another phone. I didn't give out the number to anyone.

I totally reformed myself; against my will, I met her Mama, Janis Jakes, an oversized heart of gold. She looked real familiar, but we were from the same neighborhood so I probably saw her around in the grocery store or someplace like that. She treated a Niggah like a black man and not like an environmentally-shaped inept asshole. She treated me like a person, told me she detested the N-word. I told her to fuck off, but she told me, "Real men don't use that word, especially after learning the history of it."

You know me. I had to debate. So I told her, "Well, I *heard* you call another friend of yours a bitch. Hey, bitch. How are you, Ho? But I can't use the N-word? Please, Mama. *Save* it."

I won. She cooked for me. I could come and go as I pleased. She shared her daughter's baby pictures with me. She even showed me pictures of herself when she was young. The pictures look very nice. I appreciated her sharing them with me. I didn't *have* baby pictures. My parents never cared for photos. She gave me black books to read. Honestly, I hated reading, but her Mama was so laid back, so real and so down for being black. She represented what true black beauty was. Shockingly, I fell in love with books. They opened up a whole new world I never knew existed. When the fellahs on the dope corners saw me walking up the block reading they were stunned. "Niggah, you read books?" my good friend Harold asked, grabbing his dick and trying to stand in those loose, baggy jeans.

"Yea, man. This Sistah Souljah book the Coldest Winter Ever is the freshest thing I have ever read."

All seven dope boys looked at each other, and burst out laughing. "Stop playing," said Little Bishop, the youngest in the crew. A scar lining his face, he said, "Put that Sister Hoax shit down and let's sell a few birds. And make this money…"

I kept walking towards my crib, totally engrossed in the book. Sadly, I lost them as friends. They wanted a hustler, not a book worm. I didn't give a shit. What I acquired meant more than drugs, pussy and the block. I read Eric Jerome Dickey novels and E. Lynn Harris. I expanded my mind. I read *Call Her Miss Ross*, the unauthorized autobiography on evil, slutty ass Diana Ross. I read Sidney Sheldon and Terry McMillan. I actually hated *Waiting to Exhale*, the movie but I *loved* the book. My girl and her mother became my world.

I was raised in Brownsville. I went to school there, and fought there. I had a lot of bitterness about life. I used to hate the law. I used to hate the president. I used to hate black people. I used to hate the Cubans. And I used to hate myself.

My girl taught me how to love; I dropped out of high school, never finished. My girl talked me into going back.

"I got faith in you, baby, I'll help you. You can do it."

And she did help me. I got my G.E.D. I was so happy. If only my Mom could be here to see that.

I proposed to her when I turned 20 years old. I knew in my heart she would be the woman I'd grow old with. My wife never judged me. She taught me how to have empathy. After a year I left drugs alone, because her Mama worked for the police department. I also changed my friends. Gone were the dope boys and I enrolled in school and tried to become a better man. I had to learn how to deal with the past, how to let go of it and move on. My wife helped me with that. We actually saw a therapist and we went to group sessions twice a week. I discovered growth on a grand scale. I didn't bring a cloud of disrespect around my wife's mother's expensive bungalow in Earlington Heights, Florida (Miami).

But she started changing a few months after we tied the knot. She talked down to me and started cheating. Even though I could never prove it. She harbored a secret I had found out about one day when she left her Diary on the dresser. She never finished the journal entry, and on the top of the page were the words "funeral," "flowers," "stranger." I threw the shit on the floor. Initially, it didn't interest me, and I never thought about it again. Well, that was until she came home a few days later, crying her ass off. And as her faithful husband, going through the ups and downs of marriage, I had sat her down, comforted her, let her cry on my shoulders, and I asked her what was wrong.

"Did somebody do something to you?"

She remained quiet. She wouldn't open up to me.

I said, "Talk to me," rubbing her back, fondly.

With a burst of anguish, she pushed me. "You can't help, Frank! You're the problem!"

I was dumb-founded, shaking my head. "What did *I* do?"

She exploded. "EVERYTHING!" Leaving me confused, she ran off, slamming the front door behind her. She wouldn't come home for days. I would worry, sit up late and every time the phone rang I'd quickly answer. It was the bill collectors, family and friends. But *never* my wife. I was reverted back to the little child I was when Mama used to disappear. My world was suddenly cold and cruel. I used to cry in the dark, too afraid to turn on the light and see my own tears. My blood ran colder than ice. It got to the point where I stopped caring and *stopped* losing sleep. If she wanted to come home she knew where we lived. She had a key. I was a man, and I started worrying about myself.

Then the shock of a lifetime took my breath away. Her Mama tried luring me to bed. I fought with her all the time. She wanted me. I didn't understand her sudden interest. It took a few weeks to realize that maybe she always wanted to have sex with me. She groomed me very well, giving me books, and cooking for me. The signs were there but I guess I ignored them back then. Now I thought of them all the time. I eventually broke down and fucked her Mama in the ass a few months later, and then I got the pussy a week after. We had a regular affair. We met up to fuck and I left to go try to be a husband. Since my wife wasn't taking care of home her Mama took care of mine. I needed the love and the attention, even though once I came in the bitch's face my love ran down her chin like tears. Janis Jakes loved the dick. She had some bomb pussy and some smoking head.

I lost respect for Gladys. I lost respect for myself. She started smoking weed and snorting coke. Every Friday night she got intoxicated with her no-good, fire-in-the-pussy friends. She was bringing them into our home. She never listened to me when I said I didn't want them there. She disrespected me in front of them. And since I didn't want to break her fucking face I just packed a bag and got a hotel room, so I could get some sleep. I had to work in the mornings. I slowly started reverting to my old ways, threw my G.E.D. away, started selling dope again, sought out the familiar bitches, and treated my wife like shit. She was losing weight, big time, but I denied it. I tried not to think about it.

I tried moving out of the house, but she caught me on video tape fucking some bitch in the ass on South Beach. I loved fucking Hoes in the ass. It was tighter than the pussy. No homosexual shit with me. I actually *thought* about my late mother when it came to ass.

I remembered the day I walked in on some stranger pounding her in the ass. She was earning rent money. Mama loved dick inside of her, from the looks of it. She had a huge smile on her face, spreading her cheeks apart so homeboy could admire the sight from behind. I fell in love with it then, but of course I was only eight years old, and I didn't utter a sound. I tip-toed to Mama's closet, leaving the door slightly ajar and I watched her take dick for hours. I knew I was going to do girls like that myself. All that went through my mind when my wife threatened to bootleg the tape of me screwing the bitch on South Beach and sell DVD's and use it against me in court if I didn't become a faithful man. So I did. Reluctantly, she started controlling me. She controlled the relationship. I felt like the bitch.

Then one day I saw something that made me lose all respect for her forever. I was leaving the CITGO gas station on S.W. 268th Street—about thirty minutes away from my house—when I saw her arguing with a man across the street in the Pine Island Projects. I had slowly turned my Chevy up into the projects, turning down my music. What was my wife doing thirty minutes away from home? I had a valid excuse. My job sent me down there to drop off an employee.

I parked in front of an abandoned duplex and cut the engine. I rolled down the window and listened.

"You aren't shit, Niggah! Where's my money?" she asked, slapping him.

He punched at her but she pivoted on her heel and slapped him again. "Fuck you, Ho!" He got in her face; they were about the same size—skinny, toothpick-built people. They were on drugs.

"I am not giving you shit!" he stammered.

A crowd was gathering. I was heartbroken. Yea, I cheated on my wife, but I didn't expect to see all this. It was hard to believe this was the same woman I fell in love with. A woman who helped better myself and now she couldn't help better herself. She started smoking weed and snorting coke even more. Like my Mama, her beauty was going to hell. She was starting to look like a cracked out Grace Jones, the actress. Her ass was flat; her cheekbones looked sunken.

She was stubborn. "*I want my money!* I have been selling pussy for a year. I lie to my own husband, making him think I still work at Bellsouth when I got fired for having sex with half the company. I want my money."

He slapped her so hard she flipped on the ground. I bit my bottom lip, fire in my eyes. I wanted him to whip her ass. I couldn't lie! I didn't know what to think. But the more I sat in the car thinking about this entire so-called marriage, I realized something— that made something on the inside of me die: I only married her because she made me feel good. Because she had a banging body. Because I hit the pussy and it was good pussy. And because her Mama had money.

I turned on the car, rolled up the windows, crank up my music and got on the Turnpike North, heading for my house.

I smoked three blunts and drank some Paul Masson liquor when I got home. Depressed, stressed, and listening to Tupac Shakur. Wallowing in my sadness, I asked myself: What was I going to do with my life? Was this it? Was *this* what life was all about? Money, hoes, pussy, clubs and cars? At about 2 a.m. my wife came home. I pretended to be asleep. She waltzed in the bedroom and shook me until I opened my eyes. She turned on the light and I damn near went blind. She was naked, her sagging tits making my stomach turn. My eyes danced across the track marks on her arms. She was a druggie. I was pissed. I had actually known she started doing drugs, but I was in denial. I didn't want to believe it. I didn't want to think about it. So I worked harder, sold dope from here to West Palm Beach and involved myself in other people's business just so I wouldn't think about it.

I had put the sheet over my face. "I'm trying to sleep. Turn off the lights."

"I want to fuck," she said flatly. No emotion in her voice.

I was angry. "Hell no, Ho! I got to work in the morning."

She was defiant. She refused to back down. "I want some dick…give me some or else." She snatched the sheet from my face.

"Look, bitch." I jumped out the bed and punched the bitch in the face. She flew into the wall. I was naked, dick hanging. I had enough! I had to get out. I was drowning. Thank God we didn't have any kids together. She walked up to me and said, "You don't love me?"

I was in a Catch 22. I cared for her. I seriously had some type of connection with her, that went beyond thought and understanding…but I *wasn't* in love her. I cared about the illusion of a marriage—the *image*. I cared for her because she once believed in me.

"I'm fucked up," she went on. "I can't control my drug habit. I don't love myself. But I *can't* live without you," she said. "I got to tell you something," she went on, and I sat on the bed, burying my face in my hands. I was torn. I hated seeing her suffer. She reminded me of my Mama. In fact she looked like her, the way she looked when she was strung out, when the drugs talked for her, when she gave her sob stories. But this Ho was butt-booty ugly. She wasn't pretty anymore. People picked at her now. Kids thought Halloween kept coming early every time she went outside. How could I make love to her when she didn't turn me on?

I fed into her bullshit. "What do you have to tell me?"

"It's something I should have told you a long time ago. It's the source of my downfall. Why I can't stand myself—why I am so ashamed..."

*Damn, she'll do anything to get some money!* "What."

Indifferent, she stood up. "Gimme some money! I want to buy some weed and coke. My Niggah Stan sells heroine. I need a fix."

*I knew it! Money to support her habit!* "*That's* what you need to tell me?"

Her hands were twitching uncontrollably. "If you give me a hundred dollars—"

I was perplexedly thrown. "—A what?" I glared at her, my hands tight fists. She was insulting my intelligence.

"A hundred." She smacked her lips. It really repulsed me beyond understanding. "Look. My Mama isn't the bitch you were fucking behind my back."

I blinked once. "What? I *didn't* fuck your Mama!"

She glared at me with a satisfied smirk on her face. "Yes you did. I saw you through the window one time, fucking her in the ass."

Damn it! I remained quiet. Busted. Fuck it, I was a man, stand your damn ground. That was all I could do. "Gladys..."

She spat icily, "Janis is not my mother!"

## ~~Part 2:~~

I narrowed my eyes. *Damn, what* wouldn't *she say for money? This was all a game and I have to realize that.* "What are you talking about?"

She was laughing bitterly. "...My *real* Mama sold me!" Sparkles lit her sunken-looking eyes. My heart skipped a beat; I wanted to run out of the room. She intimidated me. "Yes, Sir! She needed money for crack; she was on it badly when she was pregnant with me."

She was lying. "What? Your Mama works in law enforcement, Miss Janis Jakes don't even look like she touched drugs a day in her natural life."

She challenged me. "It's true!" I could see her rib cage and her veins. She looked sick. She walked up to me and hugged me. I couldn't push her off. I sat on the edge of the bed and she was clinging to me. I cringed inside, like I turned to stone. I felt for her. Deep down I wanted to help her. After all she taught me empathy and she taught me how to love people enough to pray for them. I wanted to see her get well, even though I didn't want to remain her husband. She kissed my lips. I didn't move mine. She sat in my lap and my dick got hard. I couldn't help it. I was so used to her pussy my dick was like a dog—it got excited for the master every time. She slid on my dick. My mouth agape, the warmth engulfed me. Her desire pulsating with the same fire it had when I first got it a long time ago. She rode me, slowly, looking into my face. I closed my eyes tightly, about to throw up, but her drugged-out pussy was good.

She tried to persuade me. "Give...me some...money; you *know* you can't escape this pussy."

She was right! I couldn't. I grabbed her bony ass and fucked her long and hard, squeezing my torso muscles together and made myself nut in about three minutes. Sensation rocking me senseless, I stood up with haste, grabbed her hair in a closed fist and pulled her face to my dick. I wiped come all over her forehead, lips and chin. She licked it up, swallowing every drop. The nut felt good, I couldn't lie. Spent, she lay on the floor, looking up at me, twirling a curl of hair with a bony index finger. She was lost in thought. Fed up, I started emptying out my drawers, throwing my clothes on the floor.

"You're not gonna give me the money?"

I glared at her, disappointed in myself for falling in this sick game. Did I even *know* this woman? Who was she? What happened to my loving wife, that sweet woman who talked me into getting baptized and giving my life to God, the woman with the mother who introduced me to books?

"Hell no! And I'm leaving. It's *over*, I can't see you like this. We both fucked up, doing fucked up shit. I *don't* love you." *Yes I do, love you but not in love with you.*

She was hurt. "Ask me who my Mom was..."

Time to end this game. *"Fuck your Mama!"*

My wife stood up and snatched her purse from the dresser. She pulled out her wallet and opened it. There was a slit on the side. I saw her Driver's License. It read: Gladys Jakes-Sinclair. She pulled out another I.D. She gripped it, looking down at it.

"...People take secrets to the grave every day."

Suddenly, I was guarded. Backing up from her, I was silent.

"All this for a hundred bucks?" Something was not right.

She said, "I have been lying to you for years."

I swallowed hard. "About."

"My name isn't Gladys."

The breath caught in my throat. "Stay off those drugs!"

She smiled bitterly, fresh tears falling down her face. "I once hugged you so tightly, wanting to *love* you."

"We just had sex, damn. What *more* do you want? Money? Here!" I snatched opened the top nightstand drawer, took out a hundred dollar bill and threw it at her.

She took it and ripped it in two, tossing the bills over her head.

"BITCH! What kinda game are you playing?" I was on my feet, chocking her. I had laser beams in my eyes, sweat popped out of my pores, my dick swinging. She dug her nails in my face and I backed up, blood running down my cheek, dripping from my chin.

"I got on drugs because I couldn't do it! I couldn't let my Mama do it to me anymore."

I was a monster. "Do *what*? BITCH SPEAK ENGLISH!"

*"My Mama isn't a goddamn cop!"*

God! The LIES! "I *knew* I shouldn't have fucked your Mama. I *swear*, Gladys..."

*"MY NAME AIN'T GLADYS!"*

"She came on to *me*. Is *that* why you turned to drugs? Because I slept with your Mama?" My heart bled for her. I was dead ass wrong. I *shouldn't* have done that to her. I could just imagine how she felt when she looked in her Mama's window and saw me freaking Janis Jakes. Her Mama may have been overweight but she had good ass.

"Frank Sinclair, I was at your Mama's funeral...."

I fell into a deep silence, falling into a dark abyss so fast I nearly went blind. The room spun. I couldn't breathe. I had to hold the dresser.

"You're lying."

"Remember. The flowers on my dress. I tried to show you so much love. All I wanted to say was that I knew what you were going through. That I felt your pain. But you angrily pushed me. I was so embarrassed. I ran over and stood by an old man. He sat next to the woman who bought me from my real mother."

Images exploded in my head. The funeral. Of the little girl hugging me. Oh, God! My WIFE WAS THE LITTLE GIRL! I remember pushing her. The red ribbons in her long, resilient hair brought out her amazing eyes. The woman with the police uniform evilly stared at me. "Officer Brown" was on her name tag. What was going on here?

Then my wife's unfinished Diary entry on the dresser came to mind. The words "funeral," "flowers," "stranger." Now made it sense.

I slowly walked up to her. "Tell me everything. How could you have understood my pain? Your Mom is alive!"

She handed me the I.D. On it she was about 14 years old, and the name, "Paula Jakes."

She said, "I couldn't live with myself. My so-called adoptive mother *never* went to court to officially adopt me. She bought me for five hundred dollars. I was a newborn. I wasn't breathing on God's green earth for fifteen minutes before my Mama hawked me off. Janis Jakes raised me. *Janis* is an alias. That's *not* her real name. Her real name is Florida Brown. She worked for the police department for twenty years. She falsified documents…changed her identity and changed mine. My birth name was not Paula Jakes. My father I never met, but I saw him before. He lives right here in town."

"Who is your mother?"

"…Verona Sinclair. Frank, you're my oldest and only brother. You've been married to your sister."

My world exploding, I didn't believe her; I punched her so hard she flew into the wall. I started vomiting all over the floor. My stomach was coming up through my throat. I started punching holes in the walls. I couldn't believe this! Incest? Was she *crazy*? Was *this* why she turned to drugs? Because she was forced to keep this secret? Did Janis or Florida, whatever the bitch's name was, orchestrate this entire thing? Was my father also her father? Oh God! *It made sense!* The rumors of my father having another child were fucking true! Gladys, Paula, whatever her name was tried to hug me. Suddenly the connection between us made sense, like the final notch latched into place, locking our bloodline and our souls together, forever. I've been fucking my sister? MY GODDAMN SISTER? She shook with fear. The pain tore through us like fire. I embraced her, kissing her forehead. It wasn't *her* fault my mother sold her for crack. My mother, a woman I respected, despite her downfalls, used to disappear for months on end. She had a baby girl while she was gone; sold her to keep it hidden. My sister being raised by Florida did a number on me. The horror of the entire ordeal weakened me. All the times I prayed for a sibling, a brother or a sister, and I thought God didn't hear me. I looked at her and I was so sorry for hitting her, having sex with her and loving her. This wasn't fair. Why did people do this to human beings? She and I deserved to know the truth.

I made up my mind. "We're leaving town."

She was defiant. "I'm not going anywhere."

Against her will, I picked her up; kicking and screaming, I threw her on the bed, opened my closet and took out duct tape. I sealed her mouth closed; I duct taped her wrists together then her ankles. I picked her up and threw a blanket over her, running out to my car and throwing her in the back seat. It was now 4 a.m. I wasn't worried about work; I would never work there again. I would never see Miami again; my sister would never see Florida the bitch or the state ever again.

I hoped inside and I didn't bother locking my front door. I had lots of money in three bank accounts and about fifteen thousand under the spare tire in my trunk. I owned my house. I'd hire a moving company to ship my things to the state I would live in. North Carolina. I drove for hours, never going to sleep. My sister squirmed the entire time. I left her ass tied up. Fuck it! I was her guardian now. About fourteen hours later I arrived in North Carolina. About to fall asleep at the wheel, I then checked into a hotel. I carried my weak sister, who has pissed and shitted all over herself, into the room. I took out the yellow pages and called a drug rehab center. I told them I found my sister drugged up. They told me to bring her by. I took her. She was suffering from malnutrition. She had to be hospitalized. They put IV drips in her wrist, and she would be there for two months. While she was being nursed back to health I told doctors do not let her out of their sight. I paid them under the table with drug money for their loyalty. Battling feelings of guilt, and being ashamed that I didn't know I was married to my sister, I called a lawyer, told him the situation and I paid him a hefty retainer to discreetly have our marriage annulled. He did it quickly. In a few months we'd be divorced. I then called a moving company and had my things packed and shipped to my new home in Winston Salem, North Carolina. I also called a realtor and had my house put up for sale. A Cuban college student by the name of Hector bought it. $240,000 put into my bank account. I would provide for my sister.

I would be right by her side. She was well rested and after a few weeks she started gaining her weight back. I would stare at her for a long time. As each day passed and she got stronger and the drugs were pushed out of her body, she would start to look more and more like my mother. She had Mama's eyes, nose and chin; she had my Daddy's forehead and beautiful smile. I cried for a long time I silently prayed to God and got my faith back. The mustard seed was growing every day. We would talk and talk, now that the truth about us was out amongst ourselves we got really close. It was hard not to have romantic feelings for each other but we practiced it, and every day it got easier and easier to let those feelings go. After another two months I no longer had sexual feelings for my blood sister.

I was her big brother. For now what I said, went. I had to be her protector. She'd been hurt so much, back when I didn't know she was my sibling, back when she was a "*stranger*" at my, I meant our mother's "*funeral,*" with "*flowers*" on her dress. I told the Director of the Rehab Center that she would be there for at least two years.

"I'll be here every day to visit her, to see her progress," I said.

"We went through illegal channels to admit her, Frank," said Dave, the Director. He also did her paperwork. He used "Verona Sinclair" on her papers. I got her a fake I.D. and I knew a man who worked for the Social Security office back in Miami. It was costly, but I was a thug, a hustler, I made moves. He some kind of way got her a new social security card made. With that in mind, never to reveal this to anyone, I closed Dave's office door and handed him an envelope with three grand inside.

I stared into the Director's eyes, with a no-nonsense attitude. "Silence is golden."

"Why are you doing this to her?" He took the money.

"I never had the chance to save my mother." I smiled, tears falling down my face, having empathy for my sister. After all, she taught it to me. "But I have the chance to *save* my sister. And save her I will." My face got dark, thinking about Florida Brown. "Even if I have to kill for it. I will protect my sister at all costs."

The Director looked at me, with a grin.

He said, "Kill for it?"

I sat down in the chair, lowering my eyes to the desk. "I won't actually do that, but, you feel me, she's my blood."

"Yea, family is important."

We understood each other.


Now I was flipping through the TV channels, sitting in my room, boxes all around me. I needed to unpack, but I didn't have time for that. I was still trying to get used to the beautiful sights of Winston Salem, North Carolina.

A few murders flashed in my face from the TV. An image caught my attention. A police badge had black tape around the center.

"…Miami-Dade Police officer Janis Jakes-Brown was gunned down early this morning as she was leaving her Earlington Heights home…witnesses say a masked gunman ran up to her, just as she got in her Yukon Suburban, and opened fire. He shot her three times in the chest. And once in the head. No suspects in this heart-breaking crime have been found..."

Clad in black silk boxers and a wife beater tank top, I smiled to myself.

"Damn, who did her ass in? Karma, I tell you."

I let a Salem Light cig. I puffed on it, blowing smoke towards the ceiling fan. "Karma is a bad bitch!"

"And in related news, drug dealer Frank Sinclair, Sr., notorious in the drug world, was also found shot to death in a local Denny's restaurant on Biscayne Boulevard...The F.B.I. have been probing him for months are startled at his murder. Witnesses say a ski masked gun man, clad in a black cargo uniform, rushed inside, and shot him in the head. He allegedly threw a picture of Officer Brown on his table and fled the scene in an unmarked van..."

I was really laughing. *Goddam!* My dad got killed, too? Evil danced in my eyes as I sat in the darkness, with the glow of the tube illuminating me like a vampire.

Driving back to Miami to kill those sick bitches, for hurting me and my sister, was well worth it! I was stubbing out the cigarette. I was in so much pain. Janis watched me marry my only sister, and didn't stop it and she didn't tell us.

My Dad didn't stop it and didn't tell us.

They kept the secret, hoping it would never get out. I cried for my mother. I forgave her. I also forgave myself. The drugs had her mind gone, she was a victim. It was my Dad that got her hooked on drugs and introduced her to selling pussy. I cried for her being naïve. She was a fool in love. Willing to do anything to keep that man in her life, she put his needs above her own.

I wished I could have saved my mother, which is why I was saving my sister.

My sister was right. People die every day taking *secrets* to the grave. Janis was the prime example of that. Now I was another example. Because this was *one* secret even I was taking to my grave.

Sometimes murderers did get away, what do you think about that, Mr. John Walsh? I continued to ponder as *America's Most Wanted* came on, profiling serial killers. I had to look forward to my divorce.

I was losing a wife but I gained a sister, something irreplaceable. I had to get over loving her, though I would always love and care for her. I would always make sure she was ok.

I was her blood brother.

I laughed myself into a deep sleep.

I was my Sister's Keeper.

# The Kitty Chronicles

He didn't *want* me anymore. Me or my sweet Kitty. It was going to be hard putting this man out of my mind. After all, my Kitty has a mind of her own. I remembered just last week. Tommy, my husband—well, my soon-to-be-ex husband—picked me up from work. I left my car parked in the garage at my job. It'd be safe for the night. He took me to the Ramada Inn. When I walked in the Suite there were rose petals everywhere. Sade sung the "Sweetest Taboo" from the radio, the volume turned down low…the lights dimmed, candles flickering everywhere. Those smell good candles. My pussy was in heat and wanted the dick in the kitchen to *stand* it. My titties wanted to get right on down to business. Urgently, my husband picked me up and carried me to the sofa. He lay me down gently and took off my skirt with a hunger I'd never seen before…then my blouse slid past my breasts and navels locked under his teeth. He undid my bra. I lay there. Craving him. Wanting the Big Bang and then Quit It so I could sleep. I thought that's what *he* wanted. All we did was Bam Bam Bam Boom then its over. Never the slow stuff. Yet here we were, doing the slow stuff. How I loved this man! He finally listened to me. Thank, God!

He slowly munched on my velvet room, rolling his tongue across my pulsating, sensitive clitoris. He tongue kissed it for nearly a minute. I went wild, holding his head, my legs spread eagled. My hair in my face, I shivered with delight. He took his time, carefully sucking my work day from my body. Tiny nibbles on my nipples, tongue rolled on my belly button…he gently kissed my thighs, then sucking on my toes…I was self-conscious about the corn on my pinky toe but fuck it, he sucked it like corn on the cob. My stomach was in knots as I squirmed here and there. He was kissing my calves. He then rolled his tongue back to my pussy and ate and ate until I heard a burp.

"There, Daddy is full," he said, taking out his dick, jacking it slowly, making sure it was nice and hard. From the looks of it…Hmm, it was *ready* for Mama…

He did the unthinkable. He rubbed the head of his dick on my pussy like a painter swirling his brush in paint before the brush-to-canvas connection. Felt so good. He was looking down into my tired eyes. My face was a bit sweaty, a bit humid in here. I asked him to turn on the AC.

He said, "I kept it off for a reason…about to get hot in here."

Yes, sir. He continued playing with my pussy. Tommy was a good man from a good family. No, he *wasn't* rich but he was rich in character, treated his women like queens, and loved feminine acting women, women who loved being women. He was so unlike my first husband. My first husband left me for the…streets. It took forever to get over him. After months of blaming other people and lashing out at the very ones who I loved, I met my new husband. I used to compare him to my ex husband, and he hated me for it. It took a few months for me to stop. When I saw that he was there for me, I let down my guard. And when he tore this pussy up I let everything down. Now my new husband left me and my Kitty. He packed his shit and left before I got off work. He changed his cell number and moved with his sister in Alabama. He called my phone from a restricted number and told me he couldn't take not meeting my children, that I had *too* many secrets. I found this odd because I never hid *anything* from him. And I wasn't *comfortable* enough to introduce him to my family. I loved my family more than anything, and I just wanted to make sure that he was Mr. Right before I took such a big step. When I married him my grown kids didn't come to the wedding. They sent me *Get Well* cards and not a *Congratulations* Card. I read one Get Well card and one of my sons wrote, "Get Well soon because you marrying that man will never replace our father!" They thought I was a bitch for replacing their father but they were grown! They had to grow the fuck up and let go that Al Bundy *Married With Children* Dream go and find another dream because Mama would NEVER marry their father again. I had a right to be happy in my life.

Unfortunately, I already knew the *real* reason why he left. I happened to find out when I went to the hair salon to get my hair done yesterday, and it was still burning me up inside. You know how bitches talked. Well, let's just say I found out my soon-to-be-ex-husband cheated on me with a woman I would hate for the rest of my life. It was funny because, as I sat under the hair dryer, looking prim and proper, the bitches talked about me in the second person, making it seem like they were talking about someone else.

I lived in Miami, Florida—congested-ass Kendall, to be exact. This was an upgrade from the Rainbow City Projects I lived for ten years. Back *then*, I had to wash my clothes in the bathtub with my neighbor's water hose pulled through the bathroom window because I didn't have enough to keep my water bill paid. *Then*, roaches were my third and fourth cousins. *Then,* I had to ask people to take me here and there or catch the bus with tons of grocery bags in tow, while trying to rear four sons. *Then,* I used to cry myself to sleep because I was on welfare, couldn't afford to buy my kids anything, and I used my pussy to make ends meet in ways heads and tails on flipping quarters could never fathom. *Now,* I was rolling high. *Now,* I had a 9-5 job with a 401 (k) and benefits. *Now,* I could afford for my kids to live productive lives. *Now,* I drove a Mercedes Benz, paid for. Yet all of that couldn't bring my man back, a man who had been there for me left and right, but he couldn't truly open up and love me because he had too many walls surrounding the soul of his very existence. I was actually smoking my eighth cigarette, drinking the fourth cup of coffee, marveling over the nineteenth hour in the day because I couldn't sleep, nibbling on the same piece of garlic bread. The spaghetti had gone cold, the meatballs and the sauce looked like hot lava frozen over after the volcanic eruption. My smoothie was watery.

The Billie Dee Williams' poster taped to my wall—a poster that has been up for nearly eleven years, irked me.

Because, goddamn it, God didn't *make* men like him anymore. The poster was the only memory I brought with me when I moved into this $350,000 condo I got with my military voucher. I had a doctor's appointment at 0900 hours. I missed my Pap smear test last week and with my hectic work schedule I may have to cancel my doctor appointment and call the damn lawyer so I can file for divorce. I had to send some paperwork to Washington D.C. pertaining to my Army discharge. I did six years. And called it a quits. I used the service to elevate myself from the slums. I had to sign the rights to my kids over to my gregarious, too-sweet mother and she reared them while I slaved away making a living for my kids and at the same time doing a public service for a society that didn't give a rat's ass about me or my black children. I did a tour in Japan. I hated it. But it was better than living in Rainbow City!

Yes I was an adult woman, well into my forties when I was supposed to have my shit together. Hell, I didn't. Let's be real. I couldn't even keep a goddamn man! I needed a man to grow old with, someone I could love and nurture. Yet when I found Jimmy, who I dated for a month before I met my soon-to-be-ex husband, I couldn't stop trying to be his a) mother b) Mommie c) Mama and d) Provider. All of the above spelled I. A-M. A-L-O-N-E! And my kids! *Damn it!* My oldest son was a faggot. I didn't give a fuck about GLAAD— The Gay & Lesbian Alliance Against Defamation. If they come to my damn door I'ma shoot each and every one of the crummy assholes; my youngest son was an alleged rapist (now cleared of all charges, thank God). My third oldest son was a woman beater—he had a big problem with taking orders from women. This was *my* fault, he said, because I cursed and beat him so much. Now, any woman he dated that even looked like or *resembled* me he beat their asses—like he was getting back at me and the shit didn't hurt me at all. Just cost his ass a free trip to jail without a Get out of Jail Free Card. This wasn't Monopoly, but you couldn't tell his dumb ass anything. My knee baby was just so fucked up the psych ward didn't even want him. Strapping him to the bed was enough to make the hired help go insane. He actually sat on his ass all day counting tile— one, twooo, *three*, fo', five, six, se-ven, *eight*, NINE, ten blue tiles Mama!

My oldest son, Kendrick, got on my nerves! Always something with this bozo! Seriously. I wished I woulda followed my gut and aborted his ass, or swallowed him when I sucked his daddy's dick back in the day. I would have loved to feel his seed burning from my stomach acid, but I could never have that relief. I was stuck with his ass until the day I died. I knew he was gay ever since he was eight years old. Out of all the goddamn Smurfs on the old school popular cartoon, he loved VANITY SMURF, with his little scarf and SMURFETTE! He was Smurfette for Halloween. And he wondered why all the neighborhood Niggahs around his age started throwing rocks at his dumb ass. Then out of the blue he started loving Bugs Bunny. Bugs wore more drag queen shit then the homosexual transvestites tramping all up and down NW 79th Street in Liberty City, not too far from Club Boi, a gay club.

Just when you though he couldn't get any worse, he idolized the Snaggle Puss cartoon. Running around my house chanting, *"To the moon, even!"* drove me crazy. I threw my curling iron at him one morning and it hit him in the head. He looked at me like he lost his mind. I glared at him like I wanted the punk dead! Then He-Man burst onto the TV, with all his...muscles. His...Battle cat and his...Sword. "Mama, He-Man is cute," he once said and his brother threw a Tonka toy at him.

Then it was on to *Jem* is truly outrageous, a rock-n-roll Barbie looking cartoon that focused around music. I shook my head. By then I was at the boiling point. I was getting fed up. As a mother I couldn't explain how I felt to see my son acting like a woman. His brothers hated it. When he started walking around singing, 'She-ra She-ra....*I am Sheeee-raaaaa!"* from the popular cartoon—He Man's cousin—I jumped off the sofa and slapped him across the face with the force of a Tech 9. Startled, he ran to his room and I was right on his ass. I kicked down the door, Karate-kicked him on the floor, pounced on my sweet ass son and snatched his ass to his feet.

I couldn't breathe. "Now you listen here goddamn it! I gave birth to a son with a goddamn dick! Not a weak-pussy punk!" I was steamed, embarrassed to even go in public with my son. I was so upset. He was frightened. Being that he was a kid during the time, I could certainly understand that. I lightened up on him when he started to cry, covering his face, his fragile body shaking. What was a mother to do? I took my son into my arms and I held him, in tears of my own. Because his father was also a drag queen, selling his body for money.

My ex-husband left me for the streets and the horny men it catered too. All for the love of money. I never understood *what* happened to the man I loved. The man I woulda died for. The man I sometimes sold my Kitty Kat for. Somewhere along the line he went from praising me and my body to wanting to BE ME and *have* my body. He started wearing my panties, then my bras, then my socks. I had tried to work with him, because I was in some serious denial. We even went to counseling. But some things were better left alone. Some shit couldn't be counseled. You had to actually give it to Jesus and hoped he passed it on to God.

Now my oldest son was headed in the same path as his fruity-pebbles-eating Daddy. All my boys had the same father. I always wondered *why* my oldest son turned out to be such a fruit cake. Hell his favorite cereal was fruity pebbles and his favorite drink was anything with fuckin' fruit! It got so bad I stopped buying fruit for my kids. Hell I even went as far as not buying anything with the word FRUIT OF A LOOM on it. I was so serious.

Yet I couldn't think of my oldest son right now. He betrayed me in the worst way possible.

My second oldest son, Man Man, allegedly raped some ghetto trashy girl who teased him about the pussy. She led my son on for months. Had him thinking he was gonna get it. Wore those shorts up her ass, shook her ass at the local DJ's, tramping all up and down the block, dancing suggestively. Her fast ass would suck his dick and stop just before he came and told him, "Your orgasm will be stronger....just do it my way."

Mind you she was only 16. So was my son. The average 16 year old didn't talk or think like this, so I knew deep down in my heart adults in her environment told her about it. She taught my boy how to eat pussy. While I was thinking he was in school getting an education he was skipping school and beating me home before the school called me to tell me he didn't sign in. So when the rape thing came up I was furious! I tried to tear him a whole new asshole! I beat him with an extension cord until I saw blood. Then I beat him with a broom. Every time I thought I failed as a mother I'd beat his ass some more. I woke up out of a deep sleep, grabbed the cordless phone, went into his room while he slept and beat his muthafucking ass! Dumb bitch! How the fuck could you rape someone? I knew I raised you better than that! I felt helpless. I needed his father to help me, but he was too busy trying to be a woman with titties perkier than my own.

He always told me he didn't rape her. "She's lying on me!" he stammered helplessly, looking at me to save him. Sorry. When the crackers came for you a Niggah hadn't a fucking chance in AmeriKKKa. I tried to do right by him. I tried to put him on the right path. But he chose to do something else, hanging around those losers he called friends and they abandoned his ass when his face flashed on the TV. I didn't believe him because that was so cliché: I didn't do it. It wasn't me.

Man Man said he hated me, that he would never forgive me for not trusting him, for not believing in him. They had my son in the papers. They didn't give a damn about him being a minor; all they cared about was defaming another black child and destroying his life. I stood behind him, despite it all. He was my bad seed.

Then the bomb dropped. She showed up at my house while I was filming my knee son, Lenox, 14, making his Science project. We say "Knee son" down in these parts, meaning he's the third oldest. When Keonna, the one who my son raped, waltzed in my house without knocking, I set the camcorder down on the dining table, snapped to attention and told the girl, "I don't remember you knocking." She had some nerve!

She was a feisty lil' bitch. "Your son got me pregnant! And I will be putting him on child support. Shit, I'm set! Now I don't even gotta work if I don't want to."

I couldn't believe my ears. "What? You're *set*? My son ain't rich, bitch!"

She wagged her tongue at me. "So what! I can be like my Mama. She got nine kids, and she sits on her ass and collects about $800 a month from the government. I wanna do that. Fuck school. Your son better pay up. Or I will have Uncle Sam and his brother Uncle Cracker at this damn door to collect."

I wanted to shoot this bitch! "Have you *lost* your mind? Is that what you think life is about? Having babies at a young age and collecting checks?"

"*News fa-lasshhh, Lady!* Look around Rainbow City! Poverty! We can't even afford food to eat! My Mama gotta sell her body. Do you think that's fun? Watching all those crackers on TV with those perfect little lives and the Niggahs who did make it out forget where they come from yet want our ghetto dollars brandishing fake ass we-give-back-to-the-hood smiles. Fuck that!"

I was getting real tired of this. Lenox kept tending to his Science project, listening to every word. "Don't cuss in my house."

She laughed real really loud, waving her hands. Her huge Salt-N-Peppa earrings dangled. "House? Chile, please! This is a housing project. The lowest on the totem pole. White people got houses!"

*I'm sick of hearing about this white shit.* "Don't matter." I was deeply offended. I didn't have much but I loved what God did bless me with." "Don't cuss in my presence."

"Where is your...rapist son? Tell him I'm gonna call the Man and tell them he raped me again he don't start paying me for this baby in my womb."

"You haven't even had the baby yet."

She sassed me. "Don't matter honey! I want money. I got things to buy and niggahs to spend it on. I got the hottest piece of pussy in town! I gotta reputation to withhold."

I had enough. "Withhold? Or uphold?"

"Fuck you." She walked past me, trying to walk up the stairs. "Man Man WHERE ARE YOU RAPIST BOY!"

Rage flashing in my eyes, I grabbed her by the arm and snatched her into my face. I was silent for a moment. I wanted to double T this Ho right in the face! Double T or DDT, shit it was one of them. Old wrestling moves. I was old school. Defiantly, she snatched her arm back and pushed me on the floor. My head hit the dining table. My son's mouth fell open in shock. Yea, she's real big and bad now. Miss Bad Bitch. Ok, I got you. I saw where you were coming from.

Keeping my wits in check, I staggered to stand up but once I did, I brushed cookie crumbs off my pants suit, put my wig back on my nappy-need-a-perm head and got in her face. Now I was a little woman, about 5 feet 3. This Ho was about 5-9. She looked down at me, with pussy-puller shorts clinging to her ass. Her titties were barely covered by her Ice Cube halter top that looked ghetto made. Her feet were so black I nearly puked and she smelled like hard labor, and I wasn't talkin' about bean picking smells either. She smelled like ass and dick, like she just got through being fucked.

I said this one time. "That ain't my son baby."

She challenged me. "Your son *raped* me, Ho!"

Calmly, taking a deep breath, I looked at Lenox. With a smile. "Go in your room. Mommie about to have grown woman discussions out here."

He left with a humph! When he closed the door I slapped the bitch in the face and she fell to her knees. I snatched her by the little hair she did have and I slapped her again. "Look, bitch! Don't come in my house! You got a case against my son. He raped you; you aren't supposed to be here! But let me tell you one goddamn thing, I'll beat you and your crack head Mama's ass! Don't come in my crib with the bullshit, Ho now get the fuck out! My nerves are bad, I don't need this shit, and I can't even have peace in my life because ya'll keep bullshit at my damn door!"

I let her go. I wanted to kill the bitch with my bare hands!

She jumped up, snappily said, "I'm calling the cops," and waltzed to the door. She paused and looked back at me, some blood on her teeth. She smiled. "Your son really didn't rape me. I told him to stay away from other Hoes. But *no* he cheated on me so I put a rape charge on the dumb bitch! He will never see this baby; I don't want my child knowing this fucked up family!"

And she slammed the door behind her. I just smiled, because I had the Ho on video tape. I couldn't believe the audacity of these black bitches these days. You didn't get what you wanted so that meant you put bogus charges on other people's children, like I didn't love my son as much as her mother loved her. I took the tape down the prosecutor's office a few days later. I had to actually prepare myself. I really didn't want to talk to a man who thought he knew my son was guilty. Spent the last couple weeks defaming his character, making him out to be villainous monster. I actually believed that was it for my child, that his life would be ruined, that he wouldn't be able to get a job anymore, that doors would close in his face.

But the sun was beaming a little differently today.

The elevator released me on the third floor of a building in Downtown, Miami. I didn't know exactly where I was, but me and my huge K-mart knock-off purse got there with style. After going through the metal detector three times (too much jewelry and my clitoris piercing), I entered the prosecutor's office and walked up to his ditzy secretary, a pretty blonde-haired bitch with pricey clothes and her damn stilettos were killer, damn it I wanted those shoes. I should whip her ass and take them. Bitch couldn't beat me.

"Is Mr. Rodgers expecting you?" she asked me.

"Yes, he is. I have a 1 o'clock appointment."

She looked through the list before her. Damn it gotta do something.

I doubled over, holding her desk, moaning piteously.

She was alarmed, "Ma'am, are you ok?" She rushed over to help me.

I held up my hands. "I'm. Fine. Where's your bathroom, feels like I gotta vomit, oh God I don't feel. So. Hot."

"Right this way..." She told me to go down the hall and make the first left. I just shook my head. "And when you get back we'll get you in to see Mr. Rodgers."

"Thanks..." I walked down the hall and made the first right, walking past the bathroom and pausing at Mr. Rodger's office door. It was closed. I knocked on it with a smile, more than one way to skin a cat.

He answered. He was tall and handsome, even at 56 years old. Real butt munch. He frowned down at me, not even offering to shake my hand.

He smiled boyishly, brushing hair from his face. "Oh, its you."

I kissed at him and he wanted to puke. "Yes, it is."

"I hope you're not here to save your son. He's going down! The City of Miami wants a conviction."

I yawned, offending him. "Really? The white part of Miami or the ghetto part?"

He held up his hand and let me into his office. "Really."

I entered, taking into account the fancy certificates, the law degrees and the photos. He met a few famous people. There was an aristocratic vibe in the huge office. Overlooking the bums and the beggars below. He looked like the type who frowned down on the less fortunate and wouldn't even give a bum change.

I helped myself to some coffee.

"I have just enough for me to get through the day."

I sipped it. I liked it black, no cream and no sugar either. *Who gives a shit?*

"You won't make it through the rest of the day."

He sat on his desk, fiddling with his tie.

"Yes I will. I'm preparing to take your son to court."

My brows rose. "I should make the tax payers spend money."

He smiled again, taunting me. "Well, its money well spent."

I paused before him, pulling out a video tape and handing it to him.

"I find you will watch this. I made a duplicate."

He used a napkin to pick it up, like I had a disease. "What is this?"

"Your ticket to a half work day."

I set the coffee mug on his desk. "On second thought, fuck this nasty motherfucking coffee. Watch the video tape." I sashayed towards the office door. "My son and I will be expecting a phone call from you."

"With the court date, you surely will."

I looked back. "Yes, with a court date, Prosecutor."

"I'm looking forward to it."

"So am I." I slammed the door behind me.

Over the next few days my phone didn't ring at all. In fact the only communication I got from the Prosecutor was a letter sent to my house by messenger informing me that the charges against my son were dropped.

I showed my son the letter, and he was thankful he had his life back. I just hoped he learned from his ordeal.

Because I was his Mama. I had my own problems.

But that was all in the past. Pushing all of yesterday's memories to the side, and trying to forget my son was ever allegedly linked to anything. I couldn't get my ex boyfriend out of my mind. I drove to my doctor's appointment in complete silence, the Miami scenery zooming by like a huge blurry picture. Tears fell down my face; it took a lot for me to cry. But I couldn't understand why my man would cheat on me with a bitch I couldn't stand. I smoked cigarette after cigarette, trying to calm my nerves. They didn't help. I was just in a deep depressed state.

When I got to the doctor's office in Cutler Ridge, by the Southland Mall, I parked in the handicap spot, with no handicap sign on my rear view window, mind you, got out and locked the door. I was walking towards the building when my cell rung. It was Kendrick. Asking me where I was.

I got an attitude. "Why?"

The feminine voice tore me up.

"Mommie, we need to talk."

"About?"

"I'm in jail; I need you to bail me out."

I laughed so hard I had to hold my stomach. "All the tricking you do up and down 79ᵗʰ Street and you want me to bail you out?"

"Yes, Mommie."

"You're a grown man."

"A grown woman, I haven't been a man in fifteen years."

I was deeply hurt when he said that. "Did you go through with your sex change?"

"Yes I did, successfully. Now I'm one of you."

"You will never be one of me; you see I'm a real woman. And check this, bail yourself out of jail."

He began sniffling, in a way that always got to me. "So you're gonna leave me in here?"

Suddenly I didn't wanna go see the doctor, not in this frame of mind, this is why I needed to move out of Florida, leave my grown kids here by themselves because I had a life and my life was forever surrounded around doing shit for my inept, incompetent children.

"Why are you in jail anyways? Kendrick?"

"It's Keisha, and I'm in jail because an undercover cop said I was soliciting services."

"Good for him."

"We fucked, Mama and when he found out I was really a man he arrested me and denied everything."

"I'll be down to bail you out of jail."

"Are you bringing your boyfriend?"

Unlocking my car I thought about it. "Yes, I will bring him, now that I am thinking about it."

He was in Alabama with his sister; there was no way I could do that.

My son waltzed out of the Dade County Jail House like he was RuPaul. He looked flawless wearing a big pretty wig and his make-up was on point. Shit. He looked better than me, put my old ass to shame. His dress and high heels were to die for. He looked like a complete woman; everything on his svelte, voluptuous frame had been cosmetically altered. He took hormone shots so his voice sounded more feminine than Jennifer Love Hewitt. He had a huge ass, enormous tits and one look at him you would never guess he wasn't really a woman.

"Hey, Mommie, I knew you'd come through for me."

"Yea, good or bad you're my son."

He rolled his eyes, hugging me. "Oh, Mom! *You're* in denial. You'll get over it. I'm in the process of going to court to get my status here in the U.S. changed to 'female,' and have my name changed to 'Keisha James.'"

This burned me up but what could I do? He was a grown man, I meant woman, he had a legal right to do with his life what he wanted, but I was dead set against it.

"Whatever."

He got in my car and closed the door, snapping on the seat belt, turning my stereo to some house music. I turned the shit off.

"This is my car; don't switch my shit like you pay my car note."

"Mommie, quit it, can't we just get along like two girls?"

"Why won't you accept the fact that you are hurting me every time you say that to me, Kendrick?"

"Mommie, I'm not trying to hurt you." I could see the hurt on his face, he wasn't trying to hurt me, that much I did know but my son always wanted to fit in, which was why he turned out the way he did.

"But you did hurt me. And are we leaving the jail house today?"

I smiled at him, squeezing his hand. "Yea, we are. After you clarify something."

His eyes sparkled. "Yes, Mommie, anything."

I showed him a photograph I took from my purse and he smiled really big.

"That's Paul, such a handsome man, how do you know him Mommie?"

"Are you two seeing each other?"

"Yea, for the past eight months we were in a relationship."

My stomach did flips. "Did you tell him you were really a man?"

"Yea and it's like he fucked me that much more when I revealed it to him. He's my heart, my lover man. He hasn't called me in about two days." He looked at me. "I heard about this Tommy man you're seeing, so when are you gonna introduce him to the family?"

"Never. He dumped me a few days ago, moved to Alabama with his sister."

My son hugged me tight and I cried to myself, I missed Tommy. I really was hoping it worked out with him because I was getting older; I wanted someone I could grow old with, spoil and languish happily. And all of that blew up in my face.

He leaned back and held my hands. "How did you get a picture of my boyfriend?"

"Because his name wasn't Paul. His name was Tommy. You were dating my boyfriend the same time he was fucking me."

My son was so angry he punched my passenger side window from my car, glass shattering, blood everywhere. "I'll kill that Niggah!"

"No sense in getting mad, he moved out of town. I don't have his number or an address."

"Get me to the nearest drug store so I can clean myself up, then I wanna take you somewhere."

"Where are we going?"

"To Alabama."

# The King of Erotica 4

## The DeTHRONEment of a King

### FŘ∑AℲ

O

F

TH∑ :

O

A

T

H

Remember *The Oath of the Freak* in the King of Erotica 1: The Throne? Well, if you read all the books leading up to *this* one then you are **The Freak of the Oath**. If you cheated and read Book 2 or this one before reading them in order than you *aren't* a Freak of the Oath. You are lost until you read Book 1 and Book 2. If I had you from day one then you realize with a jolt that as the King of Erotica I don't give a shit about feelings and emotions. The King slays, he doesn't edit a goddamn thing and he doesn't give a fuck about what YOU gotta say about him. The more you talk the more I'm gonna *make* your ass talk. So get over it. As Dapharoah69 I don't care about Larry or the King of Erotica. He edits, so get over it. As Larry I am a humble sonofabitch. I give my last and don't expect it back. These books should challenge the alter ego in you. We all have many different sides. Some of you are too scared to be free. So you bash those who *are* free to build yourselves up. As I requested in BOOK 1, you have pledged The Oath of the Freak with yourself or a friend. You have read these books in private, in public and before bed at night. You have cried, laughed and gotten angry with me. You have taken cold showers, had hot flashes, jacked your dick, played with your dry-ass pussy and looked at your goddamn door knob differently. You have shaken your head and told yourself, "Oh no he didn't write that!" That's the Freak of the Oath. But don't claim the title as of yet. Just because you lick ass and listen to the rapper Plies doesn't make you a damn freak. You don't have to have sex to be a freak. A freak is simple. They talk about it, they *be* about it and they be *safe* about it. Freaks are erroneous fucks. If you're still hiding in the closet looking for her husband, if you still can't read "dick" or "pussy" without cringing then you are still holding on to your inhibitions and what the public thinks dictate your life and your decisions. If you're still having unprotected sex then you aren't the Freak of the Oath. You're playing with fire. If you're a married man fucking men behind your wife's back then you aren't a Freak of the Oath. If you're a married woman licking pussy behind your husband's back, then you aren't the Freak of the Oath. If you don't know your HIV/STD status you aren't the Freak of the Oath—1 in 4 people don't know they are infected with an STD. I don't give a damn about you rolling your eyes. Save a life. If you're purposely infecting people with STDs stop now and save a life. God is a God of understanding and forgiveness. If we were made in God's image then be as forgiven as God. Do *You* then do *your* part. If you cherish your lover without cheating you are the Freak of the Oath. If you love, nurture and have compassion for your wife I applaud you. Keep those whores from your home. They will wreck it. Keep your friends outta your private affairs. They will *run* it. Everyone has a goddamn past. Embrace your flaws and live for your inner beauty. Only then will you be the Freak of the Oath.

**I'm the King of Erotica**
**And I approved this message.**

# Fate Williams Revisited

Janis the Pearl loved Michelle Lakes-Williams. She was an upstanding citizen who paid her taxes on time, loved making people smile and had a fantastic career with the federal government. And let's not think about that gorgeous $450,000 home she owned. Michelle has certainly done well for herself. From poor, nappy-headed black girl to a career-driven woman with power and control left one to be desired. It was because of Michelle that Janis the Pearl decided to go back to school, after twenty years of doing nothing but mixing drinks at parties, and get her G.E.D. She could remember when she met Michelle. They were in junior high school. They liked and fought over the same boy. They both screwed the same boy. The boy played games. Janis the Pearl got tired of *sharing* the boy. So she quit the boy and befriended Michelle. Even in junior high school Michelle had a strong, intimidating presence. She knew what she wanted and how to get it.

They would remain good friends and get married together after they graduated high school. Janis eventually met a sailor from Detroit and Michelle met a man named Gin Williams, who was a very hardworking man. He was tall, chocolate and had the dreamiest eyes known to man. Janis the Pearl had a secret crush on the man and before they had a double wedding, Janis sucked Gin's dick in Michelle's bed while she was out shopping and gave him some good pussy.

"Since we're both getting married to different people," Janis said, her tits bouncing as she rode Gin's thick dick, "We might as well fuck. Kiss the single life good bye."

Gin, such the eager, whorish lover, didn't really love Michelle. He wanted a wife who would stay at home and cook and clean and do what he needed to run a successful household. He wouldn't trade in the women, he wouldn't trade in men sucking his dick on the down low and he wouldn't give a bitch his heart.

When they tied the knot, Janis to Earl and Michelle to Gin, they lived happily ever after. Not so. Michelle moved away and started her life with her husband, cutting Janis off completely. Janis gave birth to a beautiful baby girl. She would love and nurture her daughter more than her husband. Janis hated the fact that Michelle moved away from her. She hated the fact that the man she really did want was married to Michelle and the thought of Michelle enjoying that big dick depressed her.

She started losing weight and neglecting her nutrition. A wonderful wife in the beginning, she started slacking off. Her husband was never happy with her. She constantly complained about every little thing. She prided herself in her daughter. She gave her the nickname *Autumn's Rose*, because she was born at the start of Fall. She was a very gorgeous young woman. She had her father's cheeks, eyes and nose. Whatever her daughter wanted she gave her without question. Earl didn't like his daughter being spoiled. And to make matters worse, Earl's mother, Josephine, didn't like Janis, didn't attend the wedding and swore to everyone that Autumn's Rose wasn't her grandchild. This angered Earl and the rest of the family.

They lashed out at Josephine, telling her to stop being incredulous and, feeling betrayed, Josephine moved out of town, met a decent man, married him and never contacted her children again.

After Autumn's Rose got in the seventh grade, Earl decided that he'd had enough of the marriage. Rumor had it that Michelle moved back to Miami-Dade County but no one knew her whereabouts.

Between teaching Autumn's Rose about her developing body and her acquisitions about boys, she started the transition back to the single life while sitting back watching her soon-to-be-ex-husband frolic with a much younger woman, named Jonnie Bullard, who was about 20 years old and already knocked up with a baby. This angered Autumn's Rose. She felt betrayed. How could her parents divorce? Was it her fault? Was it something she did wrong?

"Mama, why did you just give up on Daddy?"

Janis was lying in her bed, with the covers over her naked body. She had been crying into the night and endless coffee cups. She needed nicotine and caffeine.

"He left me, Baby. He's divorcing me for that young girl."

"Who is she?" Autumn's Rose asked, vowing to find out.

"Her name is Jonnie Bullard. Her people are from the Bahamas. She lives not too far from here. As a matter of fact she attends our church."

Autumn's Rose closed her eyes. Before Janis knew it her daughter was in high school and doing very well for herself. She fell in love with a boy and Janis loved him very much. He was kind and decent and sweet. She hated Jonnie with a passion and when

Autumn's parents were officially divorced she was suicidal. But that quickly blew over. Before her daughter fell in deeper with her love for the young man, she lost a lot of sleep, wondering would she ever find her friend Michelle Lakes-Williams. She missed her very much. But she missed her husband Gin even more.

Janis got a rude awakening one day in church. Jonnie had come late and when she showed up, clad in the most gorgeous dress she'd ever seen and her hair done up in Shirley Temple curls, she had her new husband on her arm. Earl. Earl and Jonnie didn't acknowledge Janis when they walked by. Janis didn't even look at them. She tugged on her flowing skirt and ran her shaking hands through her hair. Church members gossiped and whispered their disapprovals. But Janis didn't care. Life went on.

Autumn glared at Jonnie. She sat on the back pew, fanning herself with a hand-held paper fan. In her heart was blackness. She wanted Jonnie to pay for destroying her family.

*Did she really destroy them? Or were my parents on the verge of breaking up before Jonnie came along? Either way Daddy should have never divorced mom. For better or for worse. 'Til death do you part. What happened to those vows?*

Jonnie stood up from the pew and whispered something to Earl. Earl smiled, kissed the rock on her ring finger and Jonnie disappeared to the restroom. Autumn looked at her mom across the room. Janis was talking with one of the men. She looked sad. She wiped a few tears away. Autumn stood up and went to the back of the church.

When she entered the restroom she bumped into Jonnie. "Excuse me, ma'am. I didn't mean to bump into you," said Jonnie, extending her hand. "I'm Jonnie."

"I'm...Pleasure," said Autumn, summing her up. *Whore. Slut. Home wrecker.*

"Nice to meet you." Jonnie turned to face herself in the mirror. "It's hot in here. Don't you agree?" Jonnie asked rhetorically, patting her curls and tilting her head like Ginger Rogers. "My dress is starting to stick to my skin. I feel rather...itchy. I shouldn't have worn cotton in the heat."

Attracted to her, Autumn's eyes danced all over her gorgeous body. Nice butt. Huge breasts. Heart-shaped lips. Gorgeous face. *Oh my God! Why am I looking at this woman like this?*

"Nice to meet you, too. And it's always hot in this stupid church! So are you *new* here?"

"No. I have been attending for some months now. I moved down here from good ole Savannah, Georgia!"

"I never *noticed* you," said Autumn. "Probably because I stay to myself. Are you married?"

Jonnie's eyes lit up. "Yes. To a man named Earl."

"Earl?" Autumn was shaking her head. "I don't know him. Does he have any children?"

Jonnie looked Autumn deep in the eyes from the reflection in the mirror and said, "No. He said he doesn't have any kids. And quite honestly I don't want to give him any."

The tears fell from Autumn's eyes. *He disowned me.*

Jonnie turned to face Autumn. "I should...get back to the service."

Autumn's lips were inches from Jonnie's. The chemistry built from their toes and mounted all over their breasts. Jonnie couldn't breathe and Autumn wanted to know what she tasted like. *If Daddy can have her then so can I. I got a plan. I hope it worked.* Jonnie reached up and touched Autumn's lips. They started to kiss, pouring into each other like the sunlight through the worn curtains. Like poetry they crafted prose and words and similes on their lips and passion dancing in their juices spilling into their panties.

Autumn told Jonnie to sit on the toilet. She pushed Jonnie's legs back and put her nose down between her legs, smelling her pussy. It smelled of perfume and some type of expensive lotion. She knew the fragrance was expensive because the smell lingered like butterflies in the sunlight. Jonnie couldn't breathe. She wanted Autumn and had wanted her ever since the first day he saw her in this church. She used to dream about her and desire her and need her when she played with her pussy, bringing herself to earth shattering heights. When Earl made love to her she thought of Autumn.

Autumn took off Jonnie's panties and tossed them on the floor. Jonnie held her legs back and let Autumn get a visual of her pretty pussy. Autumn dove into her, tasting her sweaty flesh, making her moan obscenities. Jonnie's legs trembled. Autumn was glorious. She knew just how to touch her. Earl ate her pussy like she was a piece of T-bone steak. He was good but he was too aggressive. Too strong. Too demanding. But with Autumn it was different.

"Do you love Earl?" Autumn asked, playing with her pussy. Her hand on her soul revived her, and she almost forgot her plan.

"No."

"Then why are you with him?"

"I needed a roof over my head...Damn, baby. You eat some good pussy."

"Leave..."

"What the fuck is going on in here!" came the boom from a familiar male voice. Autumn paused, and didn't dare get scared. Jonnie, on the other hand, was shaking out of her mind.

She tried to stand up but she fell back on the toilet. She bent over and took up her panties, putting them on. Autumn stood up and turned to face the man who denied her.

"*Hi*, Earl."

Jonnie was confused. "Do you know him?" she asked Autumn. "I need to know. Because the way you looked at him when you stood up and said his name is a bit unusual for two people who never met."

"Yes. I know him quite well."

Earl was so upset he couldn't breathe. He pushed past Autumn and took Jonnie by the neck and he squeezed as hard as he could.

"We just got married and you're cheating on me already?"

Autumn took him by the arm. "No, Earl. Don't hurt her. You could go to jail."

The thought of jail scared him, so he released her and took a few steps back. He was deeply heartbroken and devastated. Jonnie regained her composure, swallowing hard.

"Earl. I can explain."

"How do you explain this?"

"I was just..." Jonnie looked at Autumn with contempt in her eyes. "You lied. You *do* know Earl. How do you know him? Is he your ex boyfriend?"

"No," said Autumn with a smile. "I'm his daughter. The one he hid from you."

Jonnie started vomiting all over the floor.

*Mission Accomplished,* Autumn thought, walking out of the bathroom.

Earl filed for an annulment. He kicked Jonnie out of the house and Autumn never told her mother what happened in the bathroom at church. All Janis knew was that Earl's marriage blew up in his face in a matter of days.

Janis was pleased.

When Autumn's Rose graduated, she moved away from her mother. She wanted to branch out and do her own thing without Mommy holding her hand. No matter how Pearl protested, Autumn wasn't hearing it. She wanted to discover America. She went to college and focused on getting an education, amongst other things.

After four years she graduated with honors and felt good about her future. She had no desire to contact Earl. She didn't care to share with him anything she had going on in her life. Harboring the death of a very special person, she dedicated her life to getting over her loss, and getting through her pain. She vowed it on her life.

Now Janis sat in the Main Lobby at Miami Jackson Memorial Hospital, with tears in her eyes. She cried so hard her throat was sore. Michelle. Her good friend. Was dead. After all those years of looking for her and wanting to know if she was ok, Michelle had found her. Janis was mixing drinks at a friend's party that Michelle happened to be attending a few months ago. They ran into each other and they embraced and sobbed and ignored other party goers and they talked and talked and talked and got caught up in what one or the other was doing.

"Where's Gin?" asked Janis, her heart racing. *I can't wait to see him.*

Michelle said, sadly, "Gin died so long ago."

"Oh, Michelle," said Janis, hugging her.

*Good dick gone to waste.*

Now Janis mourned the loss of her friend. There was so much she wanted to tell Michelle but she felt the time wasn't right. She didn't know how to bring herself to tell her.

*We were just at a party together. We were having a good time.*

*I met Fate Williams, her daughter. She was a gorgeous girl.*

*I wished I knew where my daughter was and what she was doing. But she cut all ties with me and said she wanted to live her life and not worry about me.*

*She wrote me a letter and told me I was a pretty, smart woman and that I would survive without her.*

*Oh, Michelle. Now I don't have anybody.*

Michelle Williams lay on a medical gurney. Her body was being examined. When she dropped unconscious at her party the paramedics thought she was dead. But they felt a weak pulse. On the way to the hospital, while she was on a gurney in the back of the ambulance, she flat lined. A short, gracious-looking fellow initiated shock treatment. Each time the two pads touched Michelle her body jumped.

But nothing happened.

"She's dead," was all he said.

*Poisoning Mama was the best thing I could have done to her.* "Fate Williams" was on my I.D. from my job. I should have taken my credentials off while I was parking my car but I didn't have the energy. I worked too much. Then I had two sons who drove me absolutely nuts. Between keeping up with their grades and making sure they weren't into too much MySpace or Black Planet, supervising them to ensure they weren't trying experimental drugs and booze, monitoring what they watched on TV and put in their bellies, I didn't have much time for myself.

I entered the hospital. My tired eyes red, I decided to come see about my dead Mama alone. This was my cross to bear. Not Red's. Bad enough that one day God was going to judge me for killing the whorish bitch.

*All the years of abuse, all the taunting, all the lies and the pain she inflicted on me has gone to the grave with you, Bitch!*

I told my girlfriend Red to stay home and watch the boys.

*Good. After all these months of being together I haven't met any of Red's family. Was she ashamed of me? Was she trying to hide me like I was a four leaf clover amongst the well-cut green grass? I asked about her parents and a glow befell her face. She said her Mom's in a nursing home up in Toronto. And her father was a senile cop trying to hold onto his badge. She said she had two sisters and one brother. Yet she didn't have any photos of them. She claimed she lost all her photos in Hurricane Andrew back in 1992. I understood that. Because I lost a lot of things I could never get back in that storm as well.*

Slowly realizing that some folks in the Lobby had bigger problems than I faced, I hesitantly went to the front desk and told them my mother was rushed there. I wanted to run. Why did I come here anyway?

"Her name?" asked the gorgeous RN.

"Michelle Williams."

The fat woman's eyes lowered to the desk.

"What's wrong?" I asked.

"Come this way. You can speak to the doctor."

"I already know she's dead."

A few days later, Red was in a myriad of thoughts. She was working at the CVS store on South Beach. She was a Pharmaceutical Technician. Tears falling down her face, she took a break and walked out into the drizzling rain, heading for her car. Her cell phone rang. She looked at the caller I.D. flashing in her face.

*My baby. Fate Williams.*

Inhaling deeply, Red answered. "What's up, Baby."

"What's up, Baby? You say that like we don't have problems."

"I *know* we do, Fate. We have talked about this twenty-eight times today and you're still not satisfied."

"I wouldn't care if it was ninety four times to the square root of your asshole. You lied to me. Yes, I came back to you. Yes, I want our sons united. They do share the same Daddy; the man you stole from me back when we were in high school…Dunn McKinney was the love of my life!"

*Dunn McKinney…Dunn…Oh, God! Even the mention of your name pricks the love for you out of my heart and presents to my soul your passion we once shared. How I miss you, baby. I will never get over your death. I will always love you.*

Red placed her arms on the top of her car, leaning against it. She looked at the S Metro Bus slowly parading up 5th Street, past the Walgreen's.

"Get over it. That was over ten years ago, Gurl."

"When my clit extended an inch I wasn't a girl anymore. I became a woman."

"OK. I don't need Anatomy as given by Fate 101. And you're being a whiny brat."

"Well shut the fuck up 202 and tell me why did you lie?"

"You know why. And your Mom has died, Fate. We should talk about…"

"Like hell!"

"Baby, we should *talk* about it."

"Talk about *what*, Lolita Harvey? How she has hurt me?"

"She's dead, Fate. Damn. It's in God's hands now. And call me *Red*, Fate. Please."

"Oh. I'm sorry. Did I hit a nerve that happens to be in your skull and not your sweet tasting pussy? I'm *sorry*, Lianna Gregory. That is your *real* name."

Angrily, Red gripped the phone.

*Why does she say my fake name like that? I know why? When we started dating I told her my name was Lolita Harvey, when in fact my birth name is Lianna Gregory. I had fake I.D.'s made, fake certificates and all. I like Lolita better. I didn't want to be the girl I used to be in high school. That cookie cutter bitch that was too afraid to stand for anything.*

*Good thing I went to court and legally got my name changed, so there wasn't a need for the fake paperwork anymore. The courts authenticated it all. Why can't Fate understand that after my Baby Daddy was brutally shot to death, a huge part of me died with him? Why can't she understand that me and her both had his sons the same year, and that I wanted my son to know his brother?*

*I had to some kind of way worm my way into her life to make that happen and now that it has I can't change the outcome.*

"You know…"

"I know what, Red?"

"Your Mama…"

"My Mama *what*?"

Red unlocked her car and got inside, sticking the key in the ignition. She turned it on and turned on the AC, so she didn't sweat to death. The bass kicked in so hard it felt like her seat punched her in the back so she turned the tunes off.

"I know you miss her."

"I don't, Red."

Red watched a few fine black men walk by.

*Damn, they are fine as hell. If only I didn't enjoy eating pussy. I haven't had any dick in years. Not since my child's Daddy died.*

"So you aren't going to plan the funeral?"

"No. I mean, Yea. I don't know, Red. Mama has hurt me so much in my lifetime."

"She's dead, baby."

"*So!*"

"Baby, it's not good to hold onto your anger."

"Listen to Martha Stewart Living."

"Martha Stewart Living can go to hell. And I resent that shit."

"I resent your lies."

"Oh, *Boy*! Will you let me live that down?"

"I don't know. You came into my life under false pretenses. You had me thinking you were one person and you turned out to be someone else. I found out my ex boyfriend, my child's Dad, also fathered your son. They are brothers. You knew all along and I didn't have a clue. You then told me Mama shot and killed my Baby Daddy when she didn't have enough to buy his drugs. So yea I'm still pissed."

"Well, I guess this isn't a good time to tell you that I got a tattoo today."

"You *what*?"

"It's a really small one. I got a name."

Fate tried to laugh. "Does it say Fate Williams?"

"No, Fate. But it says something."

"Like what?"

"Let it go. I'll show you later."

"Tell me now!"

"No!"

"Fuck it then. I am not begging you."

"You need to let the past go, Gurl. Yea, I fucked up. But you said you forgave me."

"*Ha!*"

"I thought that when you moved back in with me you let all that go."

"You thought wrong. And just because you sucked on my pussy doesn't mean I'm over it."

Red shook her head, looking herself over in the rear-view mirror.

"Fate. Why do you argue and fight with me? What happened to that fun, loving Jamaican woman I fell in love with?"

"She's still here. She just doesn't trust you like she used to."

"Then why are we together?"

"Because, good or bad, this pussy belongs to you. Hell I tattooed *Red* above my clit. Yet you couldn't get my name tattooed on you. I still want to know what kind of new tat you have."

*Oh, no she didn't!* "Is that all I own? Your *pussy?* What about your heart?"

"My heart is incarcerated at the moment. And if my soul had daytime minutes I'd have to buy some more because right now I'm just too upset with you."

Red closed her eyes when Fate's mournful voice drifted through the phone. *Baby. Please don't cry. I know we won't get over our problems over night. I know I lied and deceived you. I know what your Mama has done to you. Abusing you. Emotionally destroying you. Even after she died your Mom has a hold on you, Baby. But you have to let it go or it will destroy you.*

"Red. I don't mean to take it out on you." Red pushed in the car lighter and whipped out a half-smoked joint. "…It's just a lot to deal with. I never expected her to die any time soon. I remember when I was a little girl. I used to beg God to kill the sadistic whore but he never did. And now she drops dead?"

The lighter popped out. Red took it by the black handle and pressed the glowing tip up to the joint. "God heard your plea." She pulled on it, holding the smoke in her lungs.

"God is *love.* I don't think it was him that killed Mama."

*I need a fifth of Hennessy.* "You're right. It was her time to go. Rumor has it that someone poisoned her…"

*With rat poison and weed killer,* Fate thought bitterly. "I heard that, too. I don't know who could have done such a thing. The cops are investigating everybody who was at the party. *Anyways.* I have to meet with Paul's Funeral Home tomorrow. I have to go over the arrangements."

Red's brows rose. "Can I be present?"

"No. I got it."

Red started to cough, beating her chest, her eyes watering. "What do you mean? I have a right to be included. We're in a committed relationship."

"Well this ship has sailed, Popeye. And I need to do this alone."

"Like hell. And what about the boys? They should be included as well."

"Goddamn, Red. Fine."

*She is really pissed off at me. Maybe I should eat her pussy from the back tonight and slide her favorite toy deep in her tight asshole the way she loved.*

"Do you hate me?"

"*No. I love you.*"

"Then include your family in the funeral arrangements."

"Ok. But I might wait until Wednesday."

*What? Hell, No, Fate!* "That's in two days. We already made plans. We're taking the boys to Haulover Beach and we're barbequing, Baby."

"Oh, Well. We have to cancel."

Red looked at her watch, running a hand over her low-hair cut. *My break is almost over.* "That's a negative, Houston. We are not canceling our plans because you want to plan your abusive mother's funeral."

"Says who?"

"Says *me*! I'm the Aggressor. I'm your Man."

"You're a woman with a fat pussy who happens to dress and act like a man. Big difference."

"Fate. *Please.*"

"Red, drop it. You can't always get what you want."

"You're a spoiled little bitch!"

"Tell it to my clit, bitch!"

"And you're sleeping on the couch."

"Bitch, it's a pullout bed and I'll be just fine sleeping on it."

Red's blood boiled. *There's no way you're canceling our date with the boys over your goddamn Mama!*

"And you're telling the boys you canceled our big day."

"YOU TELL THEM."

"Tell it to my clit, bitch!" Red hung up.

Gathering her wits, and stubbing out the rest of the joint, Red squeezed anti bacterial gel in her hands and rubbed them together. Reaching into her back pocket, she pulled out a folded note. She kissed it and attempted to open it but she didn't.

*Why doesn't Fate want to include me in the funeral arrangements? Aren't we a couple? Doesn't she love me and the boys? Am I truly enough for her? What if I'm not?* Red slowly opened the letter.

At Jackson Memorial Hospital, Michelle's body was being prepared for autopsy. Doctor James was talking to one of the nurses. They were holding a series of folders and having the police combing their asses. They wanted to know how Michelle Lakes-Williams died. The Feds also wanted to know. They vowed to get to the bottom of it.
    Would they?

*I love Fate more than I have ever loved anyone. I hated to admit it, but I loved her more than my child's Daddy, Dunn, also. I feel so connected to her. I can't live without her. She makes me happy, mad and sad in ways no one ever has. No one has ever captured my heart the way she had. Our love making is always an event.*
    *She makes me come in ways I never knew existed. Without her in my life how will I go on? She's the reason why I am so happy! She's my sunshine and my joy. So why are we arguing and fighting all the time?*

*What's up! I want to be in your world because I really feel God put us together.*

[Well Fate, if you felt that way then why are you trying to push me away?]

*I'm writing in text form, the way I do when we text with cell phones, because it's easier to say what I have to say and it's quicker to write.*

[I wish you would have verbally told me this. It means more when you say it, instead of being impersonal and writing it.]

*I have tried nothing like this before but I want to be happy so I'm willing to do this for the first time in my life to be in a relationship with someone I care about, which is YOU.*

[Ha! You want me? Are you sure? The way you talked down to me on the phone when I was at work? Commitment means thinking outside of the box and being faithful in thought, in your heart and soul. Yet you said your pussy belongs to me, and not your entire body. That doesn't sit well with me.]

*I want us to just accept each other for who we are. We are soul mates. We will last and finally get it right because we want to and because we are ready to start over fresh with no judgments of any kind, please.*

[No *judgments*, Fate? You didn't mean a word of this letter when you wrote it. When you moved back in with me you gave me this letter and you said you wanted to move on, yet when we spoke on the phone you keep throwing my mistakes in my face.]

*When I come to you I will trust you and I do trust you. I have and will make sure I put all my baggage behind me.*

[You didn't put the baggage behind you. I take it you didn't get a clue from Erykah Badu. Bag Lady. You g'on hurt your back. Carrying all those bags like that. Well, bitch. You're about to crowd my space. You're pushing me away. So you better pack light.]

*Thanks for going to therapy with me, to help me deal with my past. This truly allowed me to open up about my life and work on myself, and that made me a better person. A better mother. And a better lover.*

[Bullshit, Fate. Therapy helped temporarily. Now you slipped back to the state of mind you were in before therapy. A better lover? *Please.*]

*I don't know how much more of this I can take.*

[Honestly I don't know how much I can take, either. Maybe we've said and done too much. Let's call it a quits.]

Deeply upset, Red crumpled the letter in her hand.
    And tossed it out the window.
                £@®®¥

I was writing some thoughts down. How could I not? I had a lot on my mind. Maybe I was wasting my time. All this goddamn writing served what purpose, exactly? I didn't want to be an idiot. But they say writing could be therapeutic.

Yea, right.

*I inhale convulsions*
*igniting in Rome explosions*
*on my face I lay in ruins*
*reminiscent of elegant intrusions*
*Mama pushed me out her womb*
*and threw me out a few months after June*
*Why does Satan try to attack my stellar vessels*
*Boxed with chocolates: bite into my cerebrum*
*Many want my taut body*
*they want to taste the result of my mind's gate*
*open them to find my rates*
*too high for the Dow Jones*
*up three points*
*down the slope of my pussy by six*
*go to bed by nine*
*setting clocks...I can't tell time*
*Booker T Washington on my mind*
*sleeping on both sets of sheets*
*Hold an umbrella over my head as I teach*
*I inhale convulsions*
*On my face lay Rome in ruins*

I loved my lifestyle, even though I didn't ask for it and if I could change it all I would because, in some unexplainable way, I *did* want a husband and a family. But I know in my heart of hearts that will never, ever happen. Dick turned me off, quite frankly. And men were full of shit. These days they couldn't think past their little heads and when the little head decided to go ballistic and get all hard and Gangsta, men really showed their asses. And I didn't have time to babysit a grown ass man who was supposed to be the carvers of the earth. I didn't know what point I was trying to prove by writing that poem, but I did know I felt good when I wrote the last stroke on the "s" in "ruins."

Looking at my diamond-encrusted watch (a take-me-back-gift from Red, my Butch Bitch), I realized it was about 10:39 p.m.

I needed to check in on my son Renaldo and his brother (Red's son) Jameson (they share the same baby father, rest his soul) but I really didn't need to because I could hear them playing John Madden

'08 on Playstation 3. They lived and breathed that game console the way I used to breathe my Atari and Miss Pac Man and Pole Position back in the day. I turned on Patti Labelle. I didn't know what song played, but I did know she was just what I needed right now. My sons turned up the volume on the game a little louder. Oh, no!

Not over Patti!

I stood up, clad in night clothes and red furry slippers (shaped like the male penis) and beat on the wall. My breasts jiggled.

"Turn that shit down!"

"SORRY MOM!" They said in unison. But the sound didn't relent much. I waited about five minutes. Busying myself in the process with putting a few rollers in my hair, I thought about me and Red's phone conversation. She could be a bitch when she wanted to be. I didn't want to deal with Mama's funeral and I didn't want to talk about it. I still hated her. The sound of my children's video game didn't decrease and my anger did. I hated when my sons didn't pay me no mind. I opened the bedroom door, stamped down the hall, with my hand on my hip and kicked their door open. They were startled, dropping the joysticks on the floor.

"*Mom.*" Renaldo turned it down. He and Jameson had on Scooby-Do pajama pants and do-rags tied over their silky wavy hair.

Jameson gave him a secret look. I unplugged the game and slapped them both in the back of the head when they tried to get rowdy. I stood my ground. "Don't you two have school tomorrow?"

"Yes," they said together. I thought it was cute. They always said the same things.

"Why are you still up?" I hated that 50 Cent poster on the wall. He was aiming a pistol at the camera lens.

Renaldo challenged me. "Ma. I'm not sleepy. I'm not a little kid anymore. I want more freedom!"

Jameson was his back up. "*Yea.* And I don't want to go to sleep, either."

"Word?" I said, putting my hands on my hips.

"Mama, people don't say 'word' anymore," Renaldo corrected, standing up, stretching. He wrapped his arms around me and I saw Jameson in my peripheral trying to plug up the game.

"Yea. Get with the times," said Jameson. When he picked up the plug I back kicked him in the chest and he slammed into the wall.

"*Bed time!*"

"MAMA!" shouted Jameson. He called me "Mama" and he called Red "Ma."

"NOW!" I said more sternly. I meant business.

"Come on, bruh," said Renaldo in defeat. He crawled in his bed and pulled the covers up to his chest.

"…Let's go to bed. Red isn't home and Mom has to use the toy by herself."

My mouth fell open in shock. "What did you say?"

"Come on, Mom," said Jameson, snickering at my shock. "We are teenage boys. We chase girls and we know storks don't deliver babies. We hear you through the walls."

"And can you say yuck?" said Renaldo, covering his face.

I wanted to die. "GO TO BED!"

Embarrassed, I ran out of the room. They were laughing at me. I didn't care what anybody said. Knowing my sons have listened to me and Red get our groove on sickened me to my stomach. I never thought they would ever hear us through the walls.

I got to be more careful.

Sitting at my desk, a composition notebook open before me, my heart lay in ruins as if it was Rome. Mama tore down my Acropolis years ago, back when I was a little girl. She used to eat my pussy better than any man ate hers. I never understood why Mama wanted to destroy me. I never understood why God allowed the dumb bitch to give me my first orgasm when I was seven years old. I remember the day well. I didn't understand the feeling that came over my body. But I did know that I started to love when she ate my pussy and made me come and I didn't want it to stop. Not to mention she took my virginity with a banana when I was 13 years old.

I remember the day well.

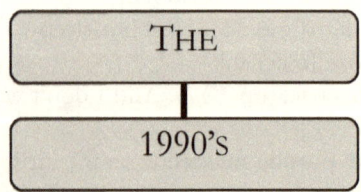

THE

1990's

*It was just after Easter, and I was going over to a friend's house. Initially, Mama said I could stay over for a few days, because she was going out of town. She worked for the federal government and we hardly spent time together. I didn't like being alone in the house all the time so Mama trusted my friends and allowed for me to stay over. But Mama had a dark side. She was starting to get jealous of me staying over. I wasn't allowed to talk to boys and when she caught them trying to tell me hello or good bye when I got out of school, she whipped my ass so badly when I got home I couldn't think straight.*

And let's not talk about the men who crept in and out of my room when I was growing up. She did this behind Daddy's back. I never understood why she allowed it to happen. Maybe she hated me that much. But after a while I stopped questioning it and I just let nature take its course.

Mama claimed I put people before her and it didn't sit well with her. When I got to my friend's house I wasn't there for an hour and Mama knocked on the door. In fact she pounded on it. Miss Rogers, my friend Gloria's mom, answered. She was a bit upset. Mama took one look at Miss Rogers and darkness fell over her face. Driving me home, she didn't say a word. I didn't say a word. I closed my eyes and sucked down my anger. I didn't want to go back home. The more time I spent away from Mama the better.

When we got home, Mama closed the door when I went into the kitchen.

"So that's why you want to stay over to Gloria's all the time."

I opened the refrigerator, ignoring her.

Mama poured a drink in the blender and some strawberry daiquiri. She turned it on and the whirl filled my ears. "You don't hear me talking to you?" she asked, turning the blender off.

My heart hammering through my chest, I tried to keep myself under control. She took out a small glass and filled it to the brim with her concoction.

"FATE!"

"Yes, Ma." I drank the milk from the carton. She snatched me by the hair and slapped me so hard the milk carton flew across the kitchen.

"You're letting that whore suck your pussy?"

I was disgusted. "No, Ma! Nothing like that is going on!"

"Did you ask could you drink my milk? Do you think I have time to keep running back and forth to the market to buy this and that?"

My throat constricted into my chest. A ball formed in my throat. "No, ma'am!"

She handed me the drink. "Drink it up."

I did. It tasted good. But I didn't know why she gave it to me.

"You're a whore! I'm glad your Daddy is dead. He wouldn't approve..."

"Approve of what, Mama? That you have destroyed me? That you have turned me into society's enemy?" I set the glass on the counter and wanted to pack my things and leave town and never talk to her again.

She sat on the table, looking me up and down, her eyes becoming the sinister creatures they were. She stared at me so lustfully I felt like I was naked.

"Get naked."

"No, Ma. I'm on my period."

"GET NAKED!"

I felt helpless and worthless. The way she talked to me reminded one of a homeless dog.

"Mama! No! I don't want you touching me anymore. I can't stand it. It grosses me out. I want a normal life. Can't you understand that? Is that too much to ask? There's a bulletin in school that says if anyone is touching me inappropriately to call the police. Maybe I should."

"Don't test me, bitch!"

"My teacher said I am a Queen. I'm not a bitch!"

"You're the Queen's feces. You know what they do with feces? They flush it, whore."

Mama, *don't* you love me?

"Why do you hate me?"

"I don't hate you. No. I hate myself."

I believe you do.

"Mama, why? I'm your daughter…"

"I should have had an abortion."

Hearing those words hurt me beyond reason.

"Why do you hurt me?"

Tears fell down my eyes. I really wanted an understanding. Why a grown woman would molest her own child. There has to be a sick bitch living in her pussy somewhere, controlling her needs through what she thought she wanted and desired. Mama tilted her head. "Your tears don't move me, Chile. Do you think the white man care about a black bitch's tears? They used to rape our women back in the slave days. Hell your great grandfather is a white man who used to own a plantation."

"Who cares, Mama? Don't tell me now!"

Her eyes were glowing coals.

"LISTEN!"

"No. For years I wanted to know my grandparents and you made up stories about them. Now you want to tell me?"

"Shut up, bitch! My Mama bared nine of the white man's babies. She was raped every time. She didn't have a chance. Mama sold me to the white man but after a few weeks they gave me back to her. She didn't wanna loose her six penances or her efficiency on the white man's property. My aunt, my Mom's sister, was forced to eat my Mama's pussy in front of white plantation owners for entertainment."

I had to lean on the counter. The room was spinning at the revelation.

"…She then had to suck them all off and swallow their seeds. 'Die in the belly of the whore!' they said together, playing their music and drinking their wine. When my aunt became pregnant, the white man cut her baby from her womb and hung her from a fucking tree. Where were your tears then, bitch? How do you think I feel knowing my father used to whip slaves, sell them as property and rape my mother for his own sick pleasures?"

*Oh, God! This is the first she's spoken of this. It helps me understand her and what she is doing to me a little better.*

*Mama went on, wiping water from her eyes. She refused to cry. She had up reinforced steel walls.* "I pay bills. Your job is to cook my food. Clean my house. Go to school and make good grades. Eat my pussy and make me come. And give me your body when I see fit. God put you here to be my sex slave, bitch!"

*I decided to stand up to her. Enough was enough.*

She can't make me suffer for another man's mistakes!

*"Show me in the Bible where it says it's all right for a mother to abuse her child."*

*"Sure!" She hopped up to her feet, opened the kitchen drawer and pulled out a huge Bible. Taking a black Sharpie, she opened the good book and wrote*

## FATE IS MY WHORE!
## SHE WAS PUT HERE AS MY SLAVE!

*She held the book up so my eyes could drink her edit. With no scruples, she guardedly walked over to me, one foot carefully crossing the other one, like a tight rope walker. She looked me over the way a master looked over his property. She then hugged me close, holding the Bible.*

*I was getting extremely tired. My eyes were getting heavy.*

*"You see...in the beginning was the Word. The Word was God and the Word was with God. And so were you."*

*She slowly pulled away and licked the tears from my face. I wanted to puke. Her saliva on me didn't sit well. I wiped it off and she slapped my hands.*

*I was about to give up and give in. I couldn't fight her any longer. If I told someone, what if they didn't believe me?*

*"Mama. I don't have anybody. All I have is you."*

*"Yes. All you have is me. You don't even have God. Read your History. Even Harriet Tubman returned to her master in the beginning. Yes, Child. She tried to taste a piece of heaven from the sugar bowl and was caught. She ran when her master got the raw hide. She hid in a pig pen. But she didn't have food, nothing to drink. Night fall was on the horizon. She knew what was to come when she returned, yet she did just that: went back. And that's the point you're at in your life. If you leave this house, where will you go? What will you eat or drink? God has forsaken you. He doesn't love you, Girl!"*

*She was right. I had nowhere else to go.* "I don't think God has forsaken me, Mama. Maybe you have but certainly not God. I love God above all else."

*The words were blows to her gut.* "You love God above all else?" *Mama taunted me, running her hand through my unruly hair.*

"Yes."

"The Bible says that?"

"Yes, Ma."

"The Bible also says you're my whore."

This crippled me to hear. My own mother treating me this way. How could a mother treat her child like she wasn't worth the very breath she breathed? "You wrote that, Mama."

"Because you saw me write it, correct?"

I whispered, "Yes."

"So you don't believe it?"

I was shaking my head feverishly. "No."

"Yet mortal man wrote the Bible, correct?"

"Yes." What was she getting at?

"Did you see mortal man write the scriptures and the verses?"

I looked deep into her evil eyes. "No, Mama."

"Yet you believe what is written? Have you contested the versus? Read them for yourself to see what they mean to you?"

"No."

"So why do you believe a man made Bible, believing in versus you never saw Paul or Matthew or John write? Yet you don't believe what I wrote, when you saw me write it?"

She had me.

"You're right, Mama. I still believe in the Bible. It's been read and studied and taught for decades."

I had a longing to sing. I heard slaves used to sing spirituals in the face of danger and it got them through. Maybe I should try it. So I opened my heart and I belted.

"... Jesus loves me, this I know...."

"For the Bible tells me so, 'ey, Fate?" Mama mocked me. "...Sing it with me. Yes, Jesus loves meee. Yes, Jesus loves me," I sung with Mama, tears dripping from my chin. "Yes. Jesus loves meee. For the Bible tells me so..."

"Fate. God doesn't love whores. God doesn't love white men who rape black women and give birth to innocent babies who grow up to be shamed. Where was God when my aunt's baby was cut from her womb? Where was He when four white men clad in fancy garments tied her to a huge tree in the back of the Big House and cut her hair from her scalp, spitting on her?"

I was horrified. The way Mama made the revelation filled my head with grotesque images. I didn't want those images, but she was planting them in my brain and they refused to leave. I shook with anger.

Mama hugged me. I cringed inside. My arms remained at my sides. They were unmoving. She then kissed my ear lobe. She started to sensually whisper, rubbing her body against mine.

"I can tell you what kind of blade they used. It was a bayonet used in the Danish Army many rains ago, Child. The blade was 137 mm..."

*Mama was tracing my arms with her fingertips, withdrawn into her story.*

*She said, "The blade thickness was 2.8mm...I know this, because my mother told me, right after she...tried to...touch..." Mama clammed up. "Never mind, Child. That's not important."*

*"I can't deal with this, Ma. I'm too young for this."*

*"If Booker T. Washington can give hoes to children big and strong enough to carry them in the late 1800s then you surely are old enough and strong enough to handle whatever I have to give you. They say God don't put on you more than you can handle."*

*"I'm not Booker T. And you don't believe in God."*

*"No. You're not Booker T. Listen...what do you want to be when you grow up?"*

*Was she serious? "A sniper. To assassinate whoever hurts me."*

*Mama rolled her eyes. "Funny. You know, to be a sniper takes skill. Determination." Mama was slowly walking around me, looking me up and down. "You have to dress like the white man, eat the white man's food, talk like the white man and believe in the white man's religion. Without those four things you will forever be labeled a nigger in this country."*

*"Ma..."*

*"Kiss me, Fate?"*

*"No...no, Mama," I stuttered. She reached under my dress and grabbed my panties. Her breath on my face she tried to pull them down. I let her.*

*"You say you're on your period?"*

*"Yes."*

*She gripped the string to my tampon and pulled it out, tossing it by the trash. "I love you."*

*"I doubt that you do...I will stop this..."*

*Mama took a few steps back and opened the fridge. She pulled out a banana and started to suck on it, as if it was a penis.*

*"I want fried chicken for dinner. Cook it naked, bitch. I don't want any garments touching your body. I might get jealous."*

*"No, Mama. I will not do this. I am not your slave. I've been that long enough."*

*Nothing I said registered in her brain.*

*I was shaking my head.* Saying "no" was like telling her "yes."

*"I want you humping my tongue while you cook the mashed potatoes. You got that?"*

I got to put a stop to this!

*"I am telling the police!"*

*Threatened, Mama ran up to me and backhanded me. I slammed into the fridge. That hurt. I fell to my knees. She pushed me on the floor, my head slamming on the tile. She got on top of me. She was trying to frisk me. Her breathing increased.*

*"You are mine. You won't tell anybody anything or I will kill them and kill you, you little cunt!" Her hands were on my pussy. She tried to feel the warmth and I squeezed my legs closed, being defiant. Once I did I remained still, too afraid to breathe or move. I feared her with everything in me.*

*"Disobedient children won't see the kingdom of heaven."*

*"And sick mother's will die and see eternal flames!"*

*Mama was brutally punching me in the gut. Holding my stomach, I have never felt so much pain in my life. She stood up and started kicking me.*

*Why did she hate me so much? What had she gone through in her life? She was taking out her anger on me and it wasn't fair! I didn't ask to be here! Hadn't she done enough to me?*

*Crawling in the fetal position, my head was spinning. I was moaning piteously. What was happening to me? Mama nearly looked like a ghost. I felt my legs opening. I saw her sucking the banana. "Don't worry, baby. This will be quick and pleasurable. The drink I concocted seems to be working. Life is full of shit. I should know. My Mama taught me that. When she, well, you know, took my virginity!"*

*Mama violated me with a banana. Taking my virginity. Or was it truly my virginity she took?*

*I lost that when I was a little girl.*

I had a lot on my mind. A helluva lot. I didn't even know why I went to therapy a while ago. I thought it would help to talk to a complete stranger about my abuse, but it didn't do anything because I had a lot of issues pulling me in every which direction. I didn't *love* myself. I didn't *care* about myself. Now that I was in my late 20's, I wanted to control my past. I could defend myself now and protect myself.

However, every time I tried to mentally go back and stop Mama from deflowering me it didn't help. Because she didn't really take my virginity in the kitchen with the banana.

I lost that back when I was eight years old, with the men Mama and Daddy had parading through our home. What I went through was a second virginity. Since mine was forcibly taken, I vowed in my mind that I would give myself to the person I loved when I was older and he or she would love and adore me and take his or her time with me. I did that with Dunn.

Red being there helped more than actually talking to the shrink. She would hold my hand, watch me lash out in anger and listened to me wail my scrutinized life helped me to release some of it. I couldn't forget what happened. Why should I? I was the one who went through it.

Mrs. Martinez, the therapist, with her pale, expensively perfumed skin and designer suits, told me that there were people in the world that had it much worse but I wasn't trying to hear that. Why did people say that? Why was I letting a Spanish woman tell me what was logical and what was surreal? It's almost like a person was minimizing my pain and magnifying a complete stranger's personal strife.

"Think about it, Fate. There are people who are going through much worse…"

In my mind Miss Martinez said, *"Oh, yea! Forget about your mother twitching your clit because Tom in Delaware had a Daddy who beat him until he saw blood."*

OK. I didn't want to sound mean but *fuck Tom!* I didn't *know* Tom! I didn't *understand* Tom! I never *met* Tom! *I* didn't know if he had *titties* or *sideburns*. Tom didn't even *know* I was alive! So *why* should I put my pains and my struggles aside for Tom or whoever else who had it *worse?* Looking at blotch marks didn't help. I thought I could move past it but something didn't feel right. I couldn't explain it. Mrs. Martinez told me there were no wrong answers, yet every time I looked at the blotch mark I saw one thing:

Mama abusing me.

Mrs. Martinez asked one thing that baffled me. Even Red had to hold her breath.

"When are you going to realize that the abuse you suffered wasn't your fault?"

I had looked at her. I released Red's hand.

"Mama said it was my fault." I felt like a little girl trapped in a cage.

"Fate. The day your mother abused you was the day you mentally stopped maturing. You are now an adult woman, yet you have the mind of a child."

"Bullshit, Mrs. Martinez! I'm grown!" I snapped, flipping a small table over. I sulked.

Mrs. Martinez challenged me. "You're *seven* years old. You are the little girl who had a mother who let men come into the room and deflower you over and over and over while compensating your mother. Your mother allowed these men to do the same things to *her*. Your father secretly authorized it. He was a pimp. *You* thought he was at work earning honest money yet he was accepting cash and favors in exchange for your security being broken in two and handed to you through sex, lies and orgasms too powerful for your body to handle at the time. Your mother was a part of a vicious cycle. Your great grandmother abused your mother!"

"SHUT UP!" I was starting to crack open. I stood up and rubbed my arms.

Mrs. Martinez was on a roll. "Your mother had to pay the price for those white slave owners using her for entertainment. You told me your mother once told you white men watched your grandma and other women eat each other. They suffered psychologically because of it. They never recovered."

*Shut up, bitch! What do you know!*

Red reached up and squeezed my leg.

Mrs. Martinez flipped her glasses into her reddish hair.

"...*Perpetrators* always say it's the victim's fault. They shouldn't have looked at me. They shouldn't have worn those get up shorts. They shouldn't have kissed my cheek. They asked for it! I'm sorry! An eight year old girl asking an adult to have sex is absurd."

Red nodded in agreement. She remained quiet and didn't say anything. Making silent assumptions, Mrs. Martinez sipped her Evian water.

"Even if the child does ask for sex the adult has to be an adult and say 'No' and seek help for the child. Therapy, in some cases. Because the child is reenacting what they saw their parents or other adults doing and they become curious. They were probably exposed to adults having sex in porn movies and they want to know. Kids are very impressionable. *You* were a child. Your mother's flesh and blood daughter. She wanted control. She thought she could get away with it. You were a lab rat. Her abuse was a needle. Stick you and see what you do. Poke you and see what you say! She had distorted thinking. *When are you going to forgive yourself for what happened?*"

Red looked at me and I was at a loss for words.

When I left the office with Red, I never returned again. I was too confused. I was worse off than I was when I first came.

*When are you going to forgive yourself for what happened?*

Then on top of that I was in love with Red. I hid this from our sessions, since it was solely based on helping me deal with abuse. I *loved* her with everything in me. But she has lied to me. I had a big problem with that. Despite the letter I wrote her (and I hated expressing myself) she turned out to be the girl I was in love with back in high school. I was still coping with that.

And if that wasn't enough my Mama died on me. I didn't *want* to poison her but I had no choice. She once drugged me. She blended the drug with strawberry daiquiri and gave it to me. Then she told me about what my Aunt and grandma faced in the air of oppression. I still shuddered, thinking about my aunt being tied to a huge tree at the Big House (the Master's Mansion) and those sick bitches cut her baby out of her womb.

Good riddance, Mama! Part of me mourned her. But the other part, the part she molested and shaped and molded, detested her. Rumor has it that she dropped dead at her birthday party. Janis the Pearl served drinks, and for some reason that lady spooked me. Something didn't sit right with her. When I told her I was Michelle's daughter her eyes lit up and her attention span was directly placed on me.

*God, please forgive me for killing Mama. I had to, Lord. You know what that woman put me through. I had to protect myself. I had to protect my son.*

I was standing up, about to go shower when Red walked in the room. She didn't look at me and I didn't look at her. *Well, fuck you too, bitch!* Taking off her white lab coat, she hung it up in the well-organized closet, with her well-structured ass, and took off her dress pants. She hung those up, too. She was humming a Sam Cooke cut.

Infuriated, I walked into the bathroom and turned on the shower. If she wasn't talking to me I wasn't talking to her. That simple. I turned on the hot and cold water and took off my sleeping clothes. I looked my body over in the mirror. Why did women love looking at their bodies in the mirror? What did the glass possess that the male eye didn't quite capture? I put my hand under the water and made sure it wasn't too hot or too cold.

It was just right.

Before I could get in the tub Red hugged me from behind, planting her warm lips on my neck. I felt good in her arms, but she lied to me and despite what I wrote in the letter, I was thinking of taking it back.

"I love you, Fate. I will help you get through this."

"And how are you gonna do that?"

"I will show you the tattoo I got."

"Really." *It's a start. Trying to re-evaluate our trust.*

"But first...you said your pussy is my pussy, right?"

"Yes. But I have to shower..."

"Sit down on the toilet."

"Ok, Miss Thing." *Damn, she looked like Gerald Levert. Baby suck on my Private Line. You can call it any time!*

Red spread my legs apart. She was massaging my thighs, taking her time. I loved when she did this. She never rushed when she munched on my vaginal walls and made them feel like sushi.

She ran her tongue over my pussy, my clit pulsating. I was about to explode.

While she ate me out and steam formed in the bathroom, she was saying, "The tat is on my neck." It was very small. Between focusing on my nut and enjoying her tongue lashing, I read it.

*What the hell does "Autumn Rose" mean?*

The next day I was dressed in a nice pants suit Red bought me. Renaldo wore a shorts set that matched Jameson's. They looked very handsome with their neatly cut hair. They were putting coolers in the truck and Red was grabbing the beer and putting it in the truck as well. She never let me lift heavy stuff or open doors. She wanted to be the Man and I let her because that's what I loved.

Jameson came into the house and called my name. I was in the kitchen, putting the finishing touches on the sandwiches. I cooked the chicken and marinated the ribs over night. So when we got to the beach Red could man the grill and I could look cute in my bathing suit and look forward to buying Janet Jackson's new line of lingerie coming out Early 2010 called "Pleasure Principle."

"Ma!"

"*Yes*, Jameson."

Red kissed my cheek, looking at her son with a huge smile. She rubbed his head.

"There's a woman here to speak to you."

"Who?" asked Red, her guard going up. Red didn't trust strangers showing up at the door unannounced.

"She said she is a friend of your mother's."

Oh. OK. "Invite her in. Bring her to the kitchen."

Red busied herself.

"OK, Mom. I'll go get her."

"What lady is here?" asked Red.

"Baby, I don't have a clue. Mom had a lot of friends. She did work for the government. I may be getting a lot of visitor's between now and the funeral."

"You better get ready for it."

The short, stocky woman followed Jameson through the living room. She clutched her purse. "What a lovely home," she said, looking over the boy.

*He is so handsome.* She paused when she saw a few photos hanging on the walls. The two women looked so gorgeous.

They were very photogenic. Her heart leapt with joy. She loved photographs, she always has. Jameson studied her briefly.

"Ma'am, the kitchen is this way," said Jameson, taking her hand. "Are you ok?"

It took her a moment to get her thoughts together.

"No. Michelle was a very dear friend. I can't believe she's gone."

"She's in a better place. At least that's what Mom tells me."

"And she's right."

Jameson pulled her into the kitchen.

Fate Williams recognized her. "Oh, *hey*! How are you?" She hugged the woman. *You look just like your mother and father!* "I could be doing better. I am so overwhelmed. I came here intending on giving my get wells and my condolences and I was thrown into the shock of my life."

"Why, Janis the Pearl? That is your name, right?"

"Yes. That is my name. I'm glad that you remember."

"So what truly brings you by?"

Janis paced the kitchen. She was deep in thought. "Something troubles me, Girl."

"Ok. What?"

"Family. Ever since your Mom died I've been thinking about family. What it means to have them. Why family hurt each other before their friends do."

"Tell me about it." Fate sat at the table, thinking about her horrible past. "My parents let me down."

"In a way I let my daughter down, too. We haven't spoken in years. She graduated high school and wanted to do things on her own. She didn't want my help." Janis had huge tears in her glassy eyes, but they didn't fall.

"Have you tried to get in touch with her?"

"No. I don't even know where to begin."

"Try your heart."

Janis sat at the table with Fate. She took her hands. "I don't even know where to begin. My heart is in disarray. I made a lot of mistakes. Granted, I never hurt my daughter. Never. Not once in her life."

"Then why doesn't she call you?"

"She is upset that I focused on her father, my husband at the time, more than her. But she never went without anything. I fed her, bathed her and bought her what she wanted. I even helped with her schooling and taught her things a woman should know." Janis set her purse on the table.

"My Mama never taught me womanly things." Fate's face grew dark and Janis shuddered.

*What are you trying to tell me?* Janis thought silently.

Janis stood up from the table and walked over to the counter. She saw a few sandwiches that needed to be finished. She turned on the tap water and rinsed her hands. She took a paper napkin and dried them. She picked up the Mayo and a butter knife.

"Maybe it wasn't meant for my daughter to always be in my life, Fate. Obviously you weren't made to always be in your Mom's life. She died at her birthday party."

Fate appreciated her finishing the sandwiches. She really didn't feel like making anymore. She wanted to go to the beach with her family and enjoy the rest of the day while she prepped her mother's funeral. Fate stood up, the chair sliding back audibly. Stretching, she walked over to Janis, her heels clicking against the checkered marble floor.

"*Fate.* You and Red look so happy together. I envy that. I haven't had a man in my bed in years. When my husband died I couldn't bring myself to remarry, date or give away his body. It's so hard!"

"I understand that. You truly loved him…

"Yes, I did. My second husband, I should say. I loved him more than my first husband Earl."

"How so?" Fate asked.

"Earl left me for another woman. Her name was Jonnie. I never forgave him for abandoning me and leaving me with a daughter. My child blamed me for the split."

"Divorce is hard on children. They feel it's their fault," Fate said knowingly.

"That is true. But it's not their fault that adults can't get it right," Janis said.

"I agree, Janis."

"I hope you and Red get it right," Janis said. "I don't support gay marriage, but one look at the boy who led me to the kitchen showed me that he is truly happy. Who am I to judge? I wish you and Red all the luck in the world!"

"Thanks. Red and I are happy. We have our problems."

She looked over her shoulder and made sure Red was still out back, loading the truck. Red hated Fate telling her business to anyone. She felt very strongly about that. "I don't really trust her like I used to.'

"Why?" Janis put a piece of bread on top of the ham and she grabbed a sandwich bag, putting the sandwich inside. She set it off to the side by the nine other ones.

"She lied about who she was. In the beginning I thought her name was Lolita Harvey. It turns out her name is Lianna Gregory. We went to school together. Why would she do that? Yes, we talked about it and I understand her reasoning, but when you lie about something as small as your name, I have to wonder what else she lied about."

Janis touched her shoulder. "Get over that, Child. Life is too short. OK, she lied about her name. But look around. You two share a home. Those two boys are gorgeous!"

Fate beamed. "Thank you, Janis."

Janis asked, "Have you met her family?"

Fate said, "No."

Janis thought about it for a moment. "You *should*. If she loves you she will share you in every aspect of her life. I'm not trying to pry. But if she's hiding you and your son then something is seriously wrong."

Fate was shaking her head. "I don't think she's hiding me…"

"What do you call it? I know if my daughter Autumn's Rose hid me I would be greatly saddened."

"As you should be. I know with…" Fate's eyes widened.

*Autumn's Rose? Where have I heard that name before?*

Red opened the backdoor and peaked in. Janis was making another sandwich.

"I'm sorry for interrupting."

"No problem, Baby," said Fate, hoping Red didn't hear any of their conversation.

"Hi, ma'am," Red said.

Janis looked over her shoulder. "How are you?"

"Thanks for helping Fate make the sandwiches."

Janis turned back to the jar of Mayo.

"The pleasure is all mine."

She smiled.

Fate waited until Red walked back to the truck. She saw the boys running behind her, trying to tackle her. They loved Red. It melted her heart to see her family bonding.

"Fate. I think you should inquire about meeting Red's parents. Does she have any brothers and sisters? What is her father's name?"

"You're right. I will ask to meet her family."

*Where have I heard Autumn's Rose? I heard that name before. It's right on the tip of my tongue.*

*Where have I heard that name before?*

Red came into the kitchen again, closing the back door. Beads of sweat were on her face. She smiled, watching Fate walk up to her. She looked so elegant, so sensual.

They embraced. "You feel good in my arms," said Red, her heart fluttering.

"And you feel good in mine."

"I want to marry you."

"Really?"

"Yes. I know we can survive, baby. I love you and I will bend over backwards taking care of you and our sons."

Janis opened a huge bag of chips, trying to be quiet, and filled a few sandwich bags. Fate looked at the back of Janis's head. Janis looked over her shoulder and nodded. Red's back was to Janis.

Fate shook her head "No."

Janis turned around, crossing her arms, leaning against the counter. She picked up a marker and a notebook. She flipped it open and scribbled something.

"Fate. Will you marry me?" Red asked, kissing her neck. Fate melted from her touch, like a hot poker through butter. Fate kissed Red's neck, running her tongue across her new tattoo.

Fate then bit the bottom of Red's earlobe, her pussy getting wetter by the second. Fate slowly pulled away, her eyes landing on the tattoo. The breath caught in her throat, but she played it off and pretended that she had to sneeze.

The tattoo.

Autumn's Rose.

*Oh, God! Janis the Pearl is Red's mother!*

Janis held up the notebook when Fate looked at her. Fate was shaking her head, stuck in the middle of a game. Red wasn't to be trusted. Everything she has ever told her was turning out to be well contrived lies. Why would Red do such a thing to a woman she claimed she was in love with? It made absolutely no sense to her and her heart was turning black because of it.

*Now we can't be together. I don't want to be in this house. I don't want her touching me. Janis said her daughter's name was "Autumn's Rose." Coincidence? Or sick, twisted game Red was playing, using human lives and human emotions to her sick advantage?*

Fate read the note Janis scribbled.

### Ask to meet her family, Fate.
### She's hiding you and your son.

*No, she's not hiding me. What does she know? But she is my elder and elders know the drill. They been there and done that. What if Janis is right? What if Red is ashamed of being a lesbian and don't want her family to meet me? After all, Red met my Mama. Mama didn't like her but they still laid eyes on each other. They at least tried to be civil with each other. Red met my son. My son loves her. I really don't know anything about Red. Except that we share the same Baby Daddy.*

Janis closed the notebook.

Fate had an idea.

"Baby. If we get married I want your parents to come," Fate said lovingly, her heart torn.

"You know they can't come."

"*Sure* they can, Baby. I got a confession to make. I did something behind your back that might upset you."

Red pulled away from her. "What did you do?"

"I called Orlando. I checked into that nursing home your Mama is in…"

"OK…" Red was getting scared.

"They said Sasha Lloyd isn't registered there. I also called California, to check on your Daddy. They said he's doing well."

Red smiled. *My Dad is dead.* "Is that right?"

"Yes," said Fate. "I bought a plane ticket for Orlando. I'm going to find your mother. I want to meet her. Then I am flying to Cali to meet your handsome Daddy…"

"I won't let you."

"I'm grown."

"I don't want you meeting them."

"But I want to. And I'm taking my son."

Red slapped Fate so hard she held her face. Janis looked up from the sandwich, but didn't turn around.

Red sunk to her knees, holding Fate's legs.

"You struck me for the last time."

"Fate, please."

"You know I was abused greatly in my life. And you do this to me?"

"Baby."

"When you hit the one you love it's automatically over. My Mama is dead. She hit me enough."

Red broke open. "Please…"

"When I get back from meeting your Mama and senile policeman Daddy I will pack my things and leave."

"Fate."

"My plane leaves today. I bought the tickets while you were packing the truck."

"But what about our picnic?"

"Stand up, Red. Please. Company is here."

"Can you please leave and go home," Red told Janis.

Fate said, "She can stay. I don't want her to leave. She is my mother's friend…She will always be welcome in this home. She didn't do anything to you."

Defeated, Red stood up. She tried to hug Fate.

"I will marry you under one condition."

"Name it."

"I want to meet your parents."

"Baby…"

"Why are you hiding me? Are you ashamed of being with me?"

"Baby, that's not it."

"We've been together for a long time and not once have I met any of your family. Do you have cousins?"

"Yes."

"Where do they live?"

"They live in Wisconsin."

Fate laughed, walking past her. She stood beside Janis.

Red eyed her evilly, shaking her head. *Send her home. I don't like discussing my business with strangers present. You know I hate that shit, Fate. She won't leave me. I'll suck the lining outta that pussy. She won't go anywhere. I'll beat that pussy with my tongue and dildo 'til she rolls over and go to sleep.*

*Then I'll fuck her in the ass the way she liked. She loves dildos in that asshole. And I love fucking her in it. I love bouncing in that pussy. Making her skeet in my mouth. Making her take this tongue.*

"They don't live in Wisconsin, Red."

"They do."

"What does Autumn's Rose mean?" Fate asked and Janis stopped breathing. "The tattoo on your neck. *Who* gave you the name?"

"My great grandma. She loved me so much. She said I reminded her of a Rose in Autumn."

Janis chocked.

Fate said, "Do you want something to drink, my friend?"

Janis looked at her. "No."

The look in Fate's eyes told Janis that she knew Red was her daughter.

*Fate knows!*

Janis silently walked over to her purse.

"Red. If I don't meet your folks we are not getting married."

"OK. We will meet them."

"Really? Where is your Mom institutionalized?"

"In Orlando."

"Liar."

"She is."

"Try Ontario. Isn't *that* where you told me she was institutionalized?"

Red's heart stopped. *She's catching me in all of my lies. Why didn't I realize it? Orlando?*

*Orlando should have been my first clue.*

Janis was pulling out her wallet. She quietly looked it over, tears falling down her face. Fate asked, "Why is your Mom in a nursing home? Why didn't you bring her here to live? You are in good health. She birthed you and raised you and I'm sure she did everything for you."

"She…"

"The truth, Red!"

"OK. I hated my mother. She loved my Daddy, Earl, more than she loved me."

*No, baby. No. I didn't love him more than you. I just wanted to be there for my husband the way a wife should. I didn't love him though. I loved Gin, Michelle's husband.*

"Are you sure?"

"Yes." Red walked up to Fate, taking her hands. Tears spilt from her eyes.

*She's trembling*, thought Fate. *She's telling the truth. Finally. She trembles when she tells the truth about emotional things.*

"When my Dad divorced Mom I blamed her. Maybe she didn't love him enough. Maybe she could have done something better, whatever that something was. He started dating a much younger woman. Her name was Jonnie. I *hated* her. She went to our church. Dad eventually married her. I used to watch Mom in church, amongst gossip, trying to pretend like it didn't bother her and it did."

Fate shook curls from her face. Janis opened her wallet.

"No one knows why Daddy left Jonnie. But I know."

Janis paused, holding her breath.

"Why did your Daddy leave?" asked Fate, looking past Red at Janis. Janis turned and stood behind Red, her daughter, the missing link in her life has been found.

"I had sex with Jonnie."

Fate's and Janis's mouth fell open.

"I didn't want Dad with her. I thought that if I broke them up Dad would go back to Mom and rebuild the family. I ate her pussy in the church bathroom, on the toilet. Daddy walked in and caught us. He had lied to her and told Jonnie he didn't have any children…"

Janis held her neck. *Why would he say that? Why would he deny Lianna Gregory?*

"So where is your Mom, truly? And where is your Dad?"

"Earl is dead. He's been dead for years. And my Mom…I don't know where she is. After I graduated high school I hit the road and never looked back."

Renaldo and Jameson silently came through the back door. They sat at the table, and didn't say a word. Something wasn't right with their Moms and they wanted to know.

"So your Mom never met your son?"

"Yes. She met Jameson. I had him the year I graduated. But once I left, I cut all ties. She hasn't seen him since."

Fate looked at her boys. Janis was looking at Jameson, her grandson. She was overwhelmed with joy. She always wondered how he was doing and what he looked like. Now she knew. Jameson was uncomfortable. *Why is that old lady looking at me crazy?* He wondered. But he decided to let it go. Didn't really concern him.

Renaldo said, "Are we leaving anytime soon, Mama? I waited all week to go to Haulover Beach with the family."

"Trip is off," Fate said and Jameson and Renaldo started getting upset. They silently fumed.

Red said, "OK. I told you everything. Can we please leave?"

"Red. Turn around and face your truth."

Red was confused.

"What?"

"The truth is behind you. You always tell me to look forward, never look back. Well, sometimes you have to look back to see your future. Look back. It'll make sense."

Red turned around and saw her boys. She smiled. "I love my sons."

Janis said, "I love Jameson."

Red said, "You don't even know my son."

"But I know you…"

"Woman you don't fucking know me!"

Fate said, "Don't curse Janis!"

"She doesn't know me. Who is this woman? I never saw her before in my life!"

"Think long and hard about it. Don't deny me three times, Girl. When you do you will suffer the wrath of God."

"This Looney toon bitch needs to get out of my goddamn house!"

Janis handed her a photo. It was folded and turned backward.

"Jameson looks just like Dunn," Janis said.

Red said, "How do you know Dunn?"

"Open the picture."

Red opened the picture.

She was sitting on her mother's lap. She looked up, shaking her head.

"How did you get this picture of me and my Mom? This was taken over fourteen year ago."

Fate extended her hand to Janis.

Janis shook it. Red was taken aback.

"Nice to meet you Janis Gregory. I finally meet Red's mother."

Red started to take a few steps back, shaking her head in denial. "No. *Noo*. No. she's *not* my Mom."

Janis took off the wig and set it on the table.

She picked up a paper towel and wiped off some of the makeup.

"*Hi*, Lianna. It's been years. I thought I would never see you or my grandson ever again."

Red covered her face.

Jameson and Renaldo stared at her. Jameson said, "You're my Grandma? You mean to tell me that you aren't really in a nursing home in Ontario, like Mom always told me?"

"Yes, son. I am your grandmother and I love you very much."

Jameson hugged her. "I thought I would never meet you."

Renaldo glared at Red. "You are a liar. I don't want to talk to you ever again in my life."

Fate was in tears. Red walked up to him and Renaldo ran behind his mother. "You keep the lying wrench away from me, Mama. I want to go. I don't wanna live here anymore."

"I love you, Renaldo, like my own son," Red pleaded desperately.

"I wanna go with Fate and Janis," said Jameson. "I don't trust you right now, mom. You whip me for lying yet you are the biggest liar I've ever seen in my life."

"I lied to protect you," said Red, ripping the picture in two. "I had to lie. I didn't want her in my life. She loved Earl more than she loved me."

Fate said, "Red. It's over. I hold no malice. I will take my things and go."

Jameson said, "I'm going, too. I'm going with Fate."

The demon came out of Red. "You're staying with me. I'm your mother."

Jameson ran at his mom, swinging fists. His hand hit her in the face and Janis grabbed him, but Jameson was a beast. "Why are you breaking up our home, Mama?" Jameson asked Red, in tears. He didn't want his family divided. Red tried to hug Fate and Fate walked away from her. "I will never marry you. I still love you. I always will. But our relationship is a lie."

"*Fate!*"

Fate said, "Janis, watch the boys. I gotta get out of here. I can't deal with this. I still have to plan my Mom's funeral. How can I do that with all the lies being told to me by those I love the most?"

Janis said, "Take all the time you need. I've been without my grandson Jameson long enough."

"You are leaving my son here, Mama," said Red. She got in her face. "If you take my child I will call the police."

"I'm glad Fate opened her eyes about you, Lianna."

"It's *Red*."

"It would have never worked. What's done in the dark would have come out eventually."

"You made sure it did."

"I have to tell you something. And I know it will hurt. But I have to tell you."

"What?"

Fate sat at the table, her face buried in her hands. Her soul cracked open. Renaldo was rubbing his Mom's back and Jameson was trying to kiss her forehead.

"Before Michelle married Gin, something happened."

"What, Mama? What happened?"

"You can't marry Fate if you wanted to."

"Why, Mama?"

"Earl isn't your biological father…"

Fate looked at Janis, with her mouth hanging open. "Janis. Are you sure?"

"Yes. I am. I was a different woman twenty plus years ago. I was young and naïve. When I met your Mom we fought over the same boy. We eventually became friends. But when she met Gin he was gorgeous! I wanted him to myself."

Red was shaking her head.

"I slept with him in Michelle's bed one day when she was shopping. I was already engaged to Earl and Michelle to Gin. We had a double wedding a few days later. When I learned I was pregnant with Lianna, I didn't tell Earl. Because it wasn't his. I had sex with him a few more times before I lied and said I was pregnant with his baby. Michelle and Gin left town before I could say anything. And I kept it between me and God."

"Are you saying…?" Fate stood up, walking over to Janis. "No. You're not saying…"

Red said, "She's lying, she has to be."

Janis said, "I wouldn't lie about something this deep. Fate. And Lianna. You two are biological sisters. You've been dating your own half sister."

Her world destroyed, Fate ran out the back door, jumped in the truck and sped up the block.

*God! God! God! Please tell me she's lying!*

*She's not,* a voice said in her conscious. *She's not lying at all!*

Her cell rang. Fate, parking at a nearby Hotel, looked at the Caller I.D. It was Paul's Funeral Home. "I can't deal with that. Not today. Not ever. Red is my sister? Are you kidding me? Janis fucked my father before he married Mom? I can't believe this is happening. God why do you keep dealing me shit? Do you hate me? Or does Satan love me? Am I cursed, Lord?"

Fate turned off the truck and rests her head on the steering wheel.

"What do I do now?"

The cell rang again.

She answered. "Yes."

It was Red. "Come back. I don't care if we're sisters."

"I CARE! It's bad enough my own Mama molested me and now you're telling me to pretend like we're not blood relatives?"

"But we didn't know."

"You're right. We didn't know. But now we do. Do I look like a V.C. Andrews novel? *Petals in the Wind? Flowers in the Attic?*"

"No, but baby I love you…"

"We can't be together! God is playing a trick on us! Punishing us for the crimes committed by our parents! I don't know if I'm coming or going! This can't be happening!"

"Baby, please don't cry!"

Click.

A few hours later, Fate was back in her old apartment. Again. From another lie that was told. Why couldn't people be honest? Why did people cheat and make children and hide them? Didn't the parent realize that maybe one day the unknown siblings would meet up and might like each other? When Janis learned she was pregnant from her Mom's-then-husband she should have came clean. And because of her mistake, *life* caused Red and Fate to meet in high school. Then again in Goodfellahs. And they fell in love and fucked all over the place.

*Gross! Why did God allow this to happen? It wasn't God's fault. Sure it was! No, it was Gin and Janis's fault. But God allowed it. Satan influenced it. God just let it happen. Free Will. Every Human has the power of Free Will. Fuck Free Will. Everyone has choices to make in life. They make them. They have to live with them. No one can escape it, no matter how hard they try. Decisions must be made!*

Fate went into her bedroom and turned on the light. The stale stench was enough to make her gag. She hadn't been there in a very long time. Disoriented, she looked around the dusty room, inhaling, her heart broken in two. She saw the Bible on the dresser. She walked over to it, picking it up.

She thought of the Book of Job. She turned to it, ripping out the pages.

She put them in a neat pile on the dresser. Going into the bathroom, she set the Bible in the tub. Taking out the alcohol, she poured the liquid all over the book. She took out a book of matches from the drawer under the sink and she struck it, the flame dancing before her eyes. She dropped it, the Bible going up in flames. She wiped tears from her eyes.

It was done.

Around nine thirty p.m., Fate was done reading about Job. He lost his land, his kids and was plagued with diseases. But he never gave up on his faith. *Then why does it feel like faith and God is slipping through my fingers?*

There was a knock on her front door. "Who is it?" Fate turned her cell phone off so she knew that deep down it could be Red, checking on her. Or maybe it was Janis. *Couldn't* be Janis. Janis never has been to her apartment before. Yawning, Fate walked to the door and answered it.

"Hi, baby. Long time no see."

Fate's face lost its color. "Oh my *God!* OH MY GOD!"

"No, it's not God. It's me, Michelle. Your mother!"

Fate closed her eyes. *This must be a trick.*

A tired smile on her blotchy face, Michelle theatrically entered the apartment and closed the door. "But you died."

"Yes. I did. In the back of the ambulance I flat lined. But I was revived, Fate."

Fate was stuttering. "I *poisoned* you…I wanted you dead! I had to save you from yourself." Fate was crying. *No! She's back! She is back to destroy me, to try to rape me again. God, why are you doing this?*

"You didn't put enough poison, Child. You should have seen the doctor's face when I started breathing and the levels on the EKG machine started to beep. They called it a miracle."

Fate's lips trembled with fear. "Mama…"

Michelle was trying to hug her daughter, Fate ran over to the dining table, and picked up a knife, her hands shaking uncontrollably.

Michelle smiled deceptively. "Mama is back…Don't you miss me?"

Huge tears fell down her face. "No, Mama. I don't. Get out! Get out!"

"Sure. I'll leave. But, believe me, Fate. You will see me again."

Michelle put on a pair of rubber gloves. "I don't want my fingerprints in this apartment. I don't want the authorities knowing I'm alive quite yet."

Fate set the knife down. Michelle slowly walked up to her. "Were you going to cut me?" she asked.

"I will if I have to."

Michelle picked up the knife and studied it. It was a very small, compact knife. The blade was a little rusty and dull. She ran her tongue over it, making Fate's stomach turn.

"I don't think you want to do that. You're in enough trouble. I'll let you stay free for right now." Michelle walked behind Fate and put the knife to her neck. "You will give me some pussy when I want it. You will be my little whore. Remember, the Bible says you were put here to be my sex slave. Nothing has changed. If you don't adhere to my demands you will go to prison. I will go to every police and tell them you poisoned me. You got that, bitch?" Michelle asked, running her tongue on the back of Fate's neck.

Fate held in her grief. She refused to cry, but tell that to her pussy because it was suddenly like a leaking faucet. Michelle opened the door and left it open. Fate listened to her heels click down the hallway.

*Mama is alive!*

Fate covered her face, sobbing. *She's not dead! She will go to the police and report me. I will go to prison and I will never see my son! I should have known I couldn't escape her claws. What was I thinking?*

She wiped her face, getting herself together. Her house phone rang but she chose to ignore it. She thought about what her mother said.

*Damn, what do I do now?*


Red was face to face with her mother. She sent the boys over to their friend's house down the street. She didn't want them hearing what she was about to say. "You destroyed my home, bitch!"

Janis handled the words effectively, careful not to get upset. "You were the one who cut me off, moving away. You were never the same when Dunn died."

"OK, but that doesn't justify the lies you've told."

Janis laughed. "Lies? I told lies? We all lie, girl. In our own little ways we all lie to get what we want."

"If you say so. Maybe some of what you're saying is true. But you know what this is about, don't you? So *Gin* is my father and not Earl. How cold hearted can you get? You actually let me grow up thinking another man fathered me. You tricked Earl's family into thinking I was a part of their bloodline. You lied with a straight face. What kind of woman does that?"

"What kind of woman sucks pussy?"

Red swallowed hard. "I resent that, Mama," Red said, insulted. She shook her head. "You're *not* a perfect woman."

"I know I'm not. God knows I've had my share of mishaps. As far as your biological father is concerned, I had to lie. I didn't want to hurt Michelle. How could I just come out and tell you?"

"It was easy, Ma. You preach the honesty rule, yet you are anything but honest."

"I had my reasons."

Red's eyes widened. "What were they?"

"How was I supposed to know you'd turn out to be a pussy licker? I had no goddamn clue! Was I to know you and your sister would meet up?"

"Mama! I mean Janis! Listen to yourself."

"I am…"

Red grabbed her by the arms. "You destroyed my life."

"I didn't destroy your life. *You* destroyed your life."

"I can't believe you're not taking accountability for what you've done. If you would have been honest I would have known Fate was my half sister."

Janis slapped Red's hands off her arms, walking past her. "I'm going home."

Red grabbed her above the elbow and yanked her into her face. "Oh, no, bitch! You're not going anywhere. Time to face the music, bitch."

"Watch your…"

Red smacked her mother and Janis kicked at her, falling to her knees. Red was backing up into the counter, covering her face. She couldn't keep it together. "I don't understand you, bitch. You are playing games with human lives."

"And so are you! You have lied to Fate, making her think I was in a nursing home in Ontario. I could barely say the word."

"I had to lie to her. I didn't want her ever meeting you."

"Why?"

"I don't know, Ma. I just wanted to do things on my own. I wanted to live my own life."

The door bell rang.

"I thought I told my boys to go over their friend's house. I'm not in the emotional mood to deal with them right now."

The door bell sounded again.

"GO BACK TO YOUR FRIEND'S HOUSE!"

The door bell sounded four times.

"Goddamn it, I am going to break my foot off in their asses."

"You are not going to touch my grandson."

Red said, "Bitch *get* outta my house. He's my son."

"And he's my grandchild. I am already pissed that you excluded me from his life."

"Don't get used to it. I'm going to burn you out of his life next. At least I know who my child's father is."

Red stamped through the living room. Janis was on her ass, grabbing her by the arm. Red was snatching it away.

The door bell sounded yet again.

"And you have a key. Why are you ringing the door bell? I am going to beat both your asses…Stop grabbing me, Janis."

"Please don't hit them. They didn't do anything wrong."

"This is my household. I will run it how I see fit."

"The answer is not in violence."

"Whipping their motherfucking asses isn't violence…its discipline!"

"Red, please!"

Red pushed her mother on the floor. The pain shooting through Janis's knees blindsided her. She wouldn't give up on her daughter. She would weather the anger and stick it through. She refused to let the devil win over her daughter. She vowed it on her life.

"I am going to kick some ass!" She snatched open the door and the color left Red's face.

"Hi, doll. It's me, Michelle."

The room was spinning.

"Oh my God! You are supposed to be dead. I know I'm seeing a ghost."

Michelle walked into the house, closing the door behind her.

"I assure you, bitch. I am not dead."

Janis looked up in shock. "Oh my God. You're alive."

"Well don't look so excited."

Darkness enveloped Red's home. Her white Dodge pickup truck sat serenely in the drive way. A few lizards crawled along the thick bark of the oak tree, a masked man leaning against the side of the house, breathing hard. He never took his eyes off Red and Michelle arguing. He saw them through the living room window.

He smiled.

Fate picked up the phone and called the police. When the phone rang she quickly hung it up. "No, girl. Get it together. Don't incriminate yourself. Mama's too sophisticated to go right to the police. She would milk this situation to her advantage. What does she want? Something had to give. Something was not right. I can't believe the nightmare isn't over. God, why am I going through this?"

She sat on the sofa, smoking cigarette after cigarette. She wolfed down some liquor, and tried turning on music. It didn't help. She tried exercising to Carmen Electra's aerobics video. In it she was in Las Vegas, performing her routine. She tried to concentrate but she couldn't. She was given two devastating blows. One, Red was her half sister.

And two, her mother wasn't dead

Red had to sit down to gather herself. Janis stood up, using the low table for balance. She was getting old. She wasn't as strong as she used to be. "You're alive…but, but you dropped dead at your party."

Michelle smiled, running her shaking hands up and over her hips.

"I dropped, yes. But I didn't die, obviously. I breathe the same air as you." Michelle looked at Red. "Hi, whore."

Red jumped up to her feet. "Get out. I don't care how you managed to survive. Get out."

"Make me."

Janis held up her hands. "Please. So much is happening. I am still trying to grasp the idea that you're alive."

Red was in Michelle's face. She took her by the arm and Michelle kicked her in the shin. "Look, bitch. I just came back from shaking Satan's hand in hell. He told me he wasn't ready for my induction. I have another purpose to fill."

"Get out," Red said, running over to the closet. Opening it, she took the Gat from the shoe box. She aimed at Michelle, meaning business. "I'm not Fate. You're not going to touch me, bitch."

Janis lowered herself to the Lazy Boy. She was getting migraines, and she had to press on her forehead.

"What are you gonna do? Soot me?"

"Yes."

"In front of your mother."

Janis looked up. "Red, *please*."

"So does Michelle know the truth?"

Michelle looked at Janis. "Know the truth about what?"

Red said, "The truth about Earl not being my father."

"What are you talking about?"

Red said, "Gin is my father. Mama slept with him before he married you. Fate is my sister.

Michelle said, "This has got to be a sick joke." The air seemed to leave her body.

Red still couldn't believe it. "Oh, no. Tell her, Ma! It's not a joke at all."

"It's true," Janis began. "I made some huge mistakes back then."

"I would say you did. You fucked my man at the time and smiled in my face?"

"And you molested your own daughter, bitch. I know you're not trying to preach to me."

"Yes I am! And you can't prove that I molested my daughter. It's her word against mine. If Michael Jackson told you he loved pussy would you believe it? Just because he said its true doesn't make it true. You dumb bitch. You'd believe my pussy was flour if you fried your chicken right. You fucked Gin, now that is a fact. I trusted you."

"The same way your daughter Fate trusted you. And you violated her time and time again. I didn't even have a clue. But now I know, and I can't believe you would do this to your own child."

"Fate the *victim*. The bitch tried to poison me and all of you seem to forget that. How could you? I didn't ask to be treated that way."

"And Fate didn't ask to go through all that abuse," Red stammered, keeping her aim. Her palms were starting to sweat.

"I tell you what. Let's make a deal."

"I don't make deals with the Devil," said Red.

Janis said, "Michelle, just leave. What's done is done. Fate is a big girl. Obviously you couldn't break her. You tried to destroy her but her spirit remained intact."

"I want to make a deal. Red. Leave my daughter alone. Stay outta her life."

"And if I don't?"

"You and Fate will be going to prison for murder."

Red lowered the gun.

Outside of the house it started to rain. Water engulfed everything it touched. The branches on the oak trees shook wildly from the strong wind. Footprints were in the mud, leading to the front door. They stopped just before the truck.

The masked man was gone.

"I can't leave Fate alone. We didn't know we were sisters. And how do we know Mom was telling the truth? What if Gin really isn't my father?"

Janis said, "Gin is your father, baby. I'm sure of it. I wouldn't make something like this up."

"Yes you would! You hate the fact that I'm a lesbian," she went on, setting the Gat on the low table. "I believe you will say whatever you have to say to keep us apart. Why are you so against my lifestyle? I don't bring it around you. I don't bring it around my family."

"Yet you prance around my grandson, hugging and kissing on another woman," Michelle said, sitting on the couch, crossing her legs. "You're confusing the boys. You are letting them know that it's all right to fuck other women."

"No I'm not."

"Face it. You're a lesbian, a gay bitch."

Janis said, "You can't talk about my child."

Michelle stood up and walked over to Janis. "We have been friends for years."

Janis looked up at her. "OK."

"And you betrayed me. You are walking on thin ice."

Janis slowly stood up. "Now wait a minute. Wake up, Susie."

"Bitch my name is Michelle."

"I don't have to take your rebuttals."

"I didn't ask you to. You slept with my husband before we got married? I'm still stuck on *that* part."

Janis thought about it for a while. She hated confrontations, but she wasn't about to back down and look like a pussy in front of her daughter. "It was years ago. Just accept the fact that you weren't the queen bitch you thought you were."

"So were you jealous?" Michelle asked, fiddling with her bra.

"Of what?"

"Me? You had to be jealous. If you weren't you wouldn't have slept with my man."

"Ha. And why do you have on rubber gloves?"

"Mind your business."

"I'm not minding shit. I wanna know. Why are you wearing those gloves? You are starting to worry me. You're a sick bitch."

Michelle was getting darker by the second.

"Shut up."

"What did you go through in your life? If I would have known you were a fruit cake I wouldn't have befriended you. I don't even know what Gin saw in you."

Lightning and thunder boomed. Michelle smiled to herself, something in her soul dying.

"He saw a real woman."

"He saw himself, probably. Both of you were sick. I can't believe you would harm your daughter."

"You're talking like you're a perfect woman."

"I'm more perfect that you."

"SHUT UP!"

"Were you raped as a kid? Something made you snap and turn into the whore you are."

Michelle whipped out the rusty blade, snatched Janis by the hair and sliced her neck from ear to ear.

She dropped the knife on the floor.

Red was nailed to the floor. She couldn't move. "Oh my God! You killed my mother!" Janis lay twitching on the floor, grabbing at her neck. Blood spurted on the floor. Michelle looked at her, tilting her head. She then looked at Red, walking over to her, her heels clicking against the tile.

"I remember something, something you don't know. To reply to something your mother said, yes. I was raped as a kid. Brutally. I only passed to my child what my mother taught me."

"I can't believe…" Red was wiping tears out of her eyes. She thought she hated her mother. That was until she was cut with a blunt knife. She realized then she would die for her mother.

"You know what? I'm not gonna talk about the past. Let's talk business. That knife has Fate's prints all over it. You will stay away from her. If you go around her or even phone her I will go to the cops. I will let them know you knew she poisoned me. You aided and abetted a murderer. I will tell them she killed Janis."

"But you killed my mom. In my face. I swear to God. I will find a way out of this. And when I do I will kill you myself."

"Ah, baby. You feel passionate about that, don't you? I would advise you to stay away from my daughter. That's my pussy, you feel me? I promise to treat her the way she needs to be treated. You can't hang with the puppet master, bitch. You are a butterfly amongst killer bees. You can't compare to me. Don't try." She patted Red's shoulder. "I suggest you hop in your truck and get the fuck outta my face."

"I'm not leaving my mom…"

Michelle picked up Red's cell phone and dialed 9-1-1. When the operator answered, she said, "I would like to report a murder…"

Red snatched the phone out of her hand and hung it up, dropping it on the floor. She crushed it with her foot.

"Please, don't do this to Fate. You've hurt her enough."

"I know, sweetie. And with you outta the picture, we can begin to make memorable Kodak moments."

"Kodak moments? Why would she want a moment alone with you? Haven't you given her enough bad memories?"

"Good or bad she's still my child."

"I don't understand freaks like you…"

Michelle tilted her head back and laughed. "What is it you inept whore? Are you jealous?"

Red smirked. "Jealous. Of a woman who raped her own daughter and boasts about it? You are sick and deranged. You need to be locked up in a mental institution."

Michelle was slowly walking up to Red. "You are jealous. Jealous, jealous, jealous. Look at you. You look like a man. Fate loves pussy…yes she does. Want me to tell you how she makes Mama come all over."

"Shut up!"

"Oh, yeah." Michelle paused in her face, licking her lips. "Fate begs for it. Oh, Mama. Lick my pussy. Make me come. Make me come. She begs and begs…"

"SHUT UP!"

"And begs and begs and begs oh yea Mama slide that dildo in my tight asshole, work my walls like you're hanging Picasso, you nasty bitch!"

"SHUT UP!"

Michelle turned on her heel, her hair whipping behind her head. "No one saved me when I was being destroyed. I was somebody's daughter. I was a fucking kid. No one protected me. SO DON'T TALK TO ME ABOUT PROTECTION!" she barked viciously. "DON'T ASK ME TO GIVE A FUCK! EVERYONE TALKS ABOUT THE VICTIM, VICTIM, GODDAMN VICTIM BUT DO YOU SONSOFBITCHES STOP TO REALIZE THAT THE PERPETRATOR WAS ONCE A GODDAMN VICTIM!"

"Michelle…"

Michelle paused, raising her head, her shoulders slumping. "I never wanted to hurt my girl. But the little girl in me still lives. She cries, breathes and she is me. She doesn't love; feel emotion and she doesn't trust. She wants to be safe but doesn't know how to. My mother did so much to me I lost sanity. I was near insane when I got pregnant with Fate."

Red was staring at Michelle's backside. "Michelle, I know you've been hurt…who am I to judge you?"

"Believe me, Red, I wanted to be a good mother. Trust me, I did. I did everything I could to stay a complete woman. But men broke me and my child's father was scum and he denounced the core of my soul and somewhere in me I died. I was insolent and void. I didn't comprehend human emotion. The little girl in me wants to be free…free to grow, to prosper and to endure. But how can she?"

Michelle turned to face the barrel of Red's gun.

Red was shaking. "I sympathize. Believe me, I do. You didn't have help or therapy and you grew into a destructive system. But, you see, I *love* Fate. I will not let anyone hurt her ever again. You are still hurting and you are taking that hurt out on your child. Do you feel no shame Michelle?"

Michelle gritted her teeth. "Fate is your fucking sister."

Red spewed, "And she's your fucking daughter."

"Bite me, Bitch. Does it look like I care about what you have to say? Does this look like As the World Turns. THIS IS REAL LIFE, WHORE! Why should I listen to a woman who sucks her own sister's cunt? The shit you talk is real salty. No wonder Fate looks like she suffers from malnutrition. You are sucking the nutrients from her clit you thirty bitch! Let's clock your tea, shall we. Isn't that how you gay bitches talk?" Michelle went on, tossing her weave behind her head. Red wouldn't break away from her demanding gaze.

"What's the tea, bitch?" Michelle mocked. "Well I'm a Moet kind of bitch. I like the best. I have the goddamn best. Women like you play the Captain Save a Ho role. You throw your cash, money and dildos like goddamn confetti, trying to save whores that don't want to be saved. Does it look like I'm scared of that goddamn gun, bitch? I work for the Feds. I shoot guns all the goddamn time." Michelle licked the opening of the pistol. "Mmm…tastes like Fate's…"

Red lowered the gun to Michelle's heart. And pulled the trigger. Michelle, in a state of shock, was thrown into the wall, her arms and hands up and over her head. Red held her stomach, backing into the low-table, nearly falling to the floor. Michelle was making gurgling sounds, slowly sliding to the floor, leaving behind a trail of blood on the wall. Indecisive, Red stuffed the gun in her waist line and slowly walked over to her mother.

She dropped to her knees, taking her mom into her hands. *Oh my God, Mom! I'm so, so sorry. It wasn't supposed to be like this.* Crushed, she rocked back and forth, her life over. She felt it. She knew it would never be the same.

How could it be? Two murders happened in her home tonight.

"Mom…I love…" Red swallowed the words.

Red was in her truck, punching the steering wheel. She was on the turnpike, mashing down on the gas pedal. She stopped by her friend's house and asked her would she keep the boys away from the house. She made up a lie and said that she set up roach bombs all over the place, and she didn't want them anywhere around them. Her friend said sure.

*They'll be safe there.*

She turned off the radio, the rain picking up harder. She didn't care. "I can't believe this. She killed my mother. How could she? I can get out of this. I know I can. I can call the police and tell them she killed my mother and I shot her in self defense. Yea. Yea, they had to believe that. They had to. I can't go to prison. And I won't!"

She opened the glove box, maneuvering around a slow-traveling SUV. She took out her other cell and called Fate.

"What, bitch?"

"Baby…please. Listen to me."

"About *what?* You're my sister. We can't be together. Mother is alive. Everything is going wrong."

Red omitted the part about Michelle killing Janis. And she didn't think about shooting Michelle. Good for nothing bitch.

"Can I see you?"

"Will you give up? Leave me alone."

"I love you."

"I don't."

"So you don't feel anything for me?"

"NO!"

"Well fuck you!"

"No, fuck you! I have too much going on. If you died tonight I wouldn't give a fuck! I can't stand you anymore. Everyone in my life lies to me! I can't deal with this."

Michelle managed to crawl over to the couch and climb on it, blood gushing all over the place. She has never experienced so much pain in her life. She prayed to God so hard in her mind she was sick to the stomach. She reached over and tried to light a cigarette. It fell from her lips, into the blood, the lighter falling on the floor.

She stared at Janis's body, pleased with her handy work. She felt nothing inside anymore. She didn't care about life, love and liberty. *Good thing I am dying.* She thought back to her birthday party. She remembered Fate brought her a Rum and Coke, smiling in her face like everything was all right. She tried to extract another cigarette from the pack, her hands trembling, her energy seeping rapidly from her body. The room was getting blurry, the pain even greater. Michelle closed her eyes.

She never opened them.

Red felt betrayed. *She doesn't love me. I knew it. She is no better than her mother. She's probably mentally fucked up. Who wouldn't be? Michelle fucked the girl so much she doesn't know if she's coming or going. I wanted to love Fate. She is my world. But not anymore. God dealt a devastating blow. Fate is my sister. My mother is dead. I can't believe this. Fate doesn't want me. I didn't know we were related. Why can't we go on pretending that we aren't sisters?*

Red saw an accident approaching. She started to brake, but the brake pedal went all the way to the floor. At 85 mph, the truck sped towards four state trooper cars.

Red screamed for dear life, covering her face.

Fate tried calling Red, but she didn't answer. She wanted to see the boys. Something in her heart wouldn't let her relax until she spoke to them. Fate shook her head, pacing the living room. She tried calling Red again but she didn't answer. Now she was getting fed up.

"OK, bitch. I know you're mad at me. Yes, I do love you. Yes, I wanna be with you. But I had to lie and tell you those things so you can get over me. We can never be. We are blood. We have the same father. I can't lay up with you knowing this. I would be no better than my Mom if I continue fucking you. I would be guilty of incest. I can't fuck my own sister. The forbidden fruit from the Tree of Life has been bitten. Eve has been cast from the Garden of Eden. Now we must reap the consequences."

"I love you. For some reason my heart won't let you go…"

Fate hung up the phone, turning on the TV.

*Baby I love you. But it's over.*

*Everything has changed.*

Renaldo was getting out of the shower, drying off his exhausted body. He took a moment to put on his boxer briefs and T-shirt. He smiled, thinking about his mother. He wondered what she was up to. Krishna, Red's friend, had come into the room, looking him over.

"Hey, Renaldo."

"Sup, Krishna."

"Have you seen Jameson?"

"No. I just got out of the shower."

"That's weird. One minute he was in the kitchen making a sandwich and the next minute he vanished."

"Maybe he's…"

Jameson walked into the room, slapping palms with Renaldo. "Where were you?"

"I took a walk to clear my head. It ain't everyday you find out you had a grandma you didn't know existed."

Krishna rubbed his head. "I understand. Red told me all about it. Why don't you go take a shower and get ready for bed?"

Jameson said, "That sounds like a good idea."


Fate was channel surfing. How could she focus on TV when her life was in shambles? Her mother was alive and was blackmailing her. Red wanted to continue a relationship that has become forbidden. She didn't know where her sons were. Her house phone rang and she answered, just as a Breaking News Report interrupted an episode of *The Golden Girls.*

"Hello."

"Hi, Ma!"

Fate smiled. "Baby, what's up? Where are you?"

"I'm at Krishna's house."


A short, stocky man entered the local bar on Oakland Park Boulevard. He ran his hands through his unruly hair, sitting at the back table. Four huge plasma TV's blared in his face. Good. The news was on. He took out his cell phone and made a call.

"Yo…when do I get my money?"

A sexy waitress paused at his table, holding a note pad. She flashed a smile, thrusting forward her perky tits stuffed in a light blue uniform.

"Hi'ya handsome!"

*Real airheaded bitch.* "Hey…"

"Welcome to Jerry's. Can I get you something to drink?"

"A shot of Vodka, light ice. Straight."

"Can I see your I.D.?"

He stood, grabbing his dick. "Access denied, bitch."

"Well you don't have to be rude about it. I'll go get your Vodka."

"Thank you…"

He waited until she stamped off. "OK, I'm back. So when do I get my money?"

"I'll get it to you tomorrow," the caller said, hanging up.

Jameson was in the shower. He lathered his body with soap, refusing to use a wash cloth. Shampoo in his head, he smiled. His cell phone rang but he ignored it. It was probably Vanessa, with her fine ass. He already got the pussy a few times. He even fucked her sister. Yea, he loved being a horny teenager. Life got no bigger than the Ho's.

Well, maybe life did get bigger. He was happy that his grandma came into his life. She was gorgeous! Her name was Janis, from what he understood. He wanted to know everything about her. He wanted to know her favorite color and her favorite foods. Where she was born and where she was raised. Did she have other kids? Why didn't his mom tell him he had a grandma? He knew his Mom was talking to her, and when tomorrow came he could go see her and talk to her and get to know her and she would tell him old stories of when she was a little girl.

Yes, that's exactly what was going to happen. He looked out the bathroom window. It faced his mother's house.

He frowned when he noticed that her truck was gone. *Ma? Where are you?*


Fate clutched the phone. "Have you showered?"

"Yes, Ma. And I rubbed the stick deodorant under my arms, and used my hand to massage it in."

"Good. Where is Jameson?"

"In the shower."

"I still don't understand why Red took ya'll to Krishna's house."

"She didn't want us at the house with all the drama that's going on."

"So you know what's going on?"

"Not really. Jameson knows, but he won't tell me. He said he'd protect me, that it's best if I didn't know. I do know that his grandma Janis is in his life. And I think that is so cool. Finding out you have a grandma you didn't know you had. I'm jealous."

"I know."

"I miss Grandma Michelle. When's her funeral? Have you planned it yet?"

"No, Baby. Not yet."

"Why? I know it's hard, Mama. But we all gotta go."

*I haven't planned it yet because the bitch is still alive.*

"I know, baby."

"I don't think I wanna go. It's gonna be hard telling her good bye."

She closed her eyes. "*Look*, get some rest. I'll come get you two in the morning. I'm tired."

"OK, Ma. I love you. Good night."

She kissed through the phone.

The waitress brought the man his Vodka. He thanked her with a killer smile, slipping her a twenty with his phone number on it. "Do you want to order something to eat?"

"No. The drink will do."

She was smiling at him, her hands pressed down on the table. She licked her lips.

"Well, if you change your mind."

"I'll be sure to let my dick know."

"You're so direct. I like that!" Her nipple were erect, her pussy wet. He inhaled. He could smell it in the air. *I betcha that pussy is pinky tight!*

He focused on an old episode of *Friends*. He laughed when he saw Lisa Kudrow. *She's the entire show*, he figured.

The show was interrupted by a Breaking News report. The anchor woman looked vexed.

*This just in. A speeding Dodge truck slammed into state trooper cars, killing three armed officers before careening over a banister.*

Poor officers. Awww. Poor, *poor* officers!

*The truck, said to be driven by a woman, slammed into the road below, blowing up instantly.*

Fucked up way to die, he thought gruesomely.

*We have footage from the scene, and parents, if you have children viewer discretion is advised...*

His eyes widened. "Oh my God!"

*That's the truck I rigged.*

Fate was about to turn off the TV when an anchor woman said:

*This just in. A speeding Dodge truck slammed into state trooper cars...*

She shook her head. "Thank God it isn't anyone I know..."

She stood up, heading for the bedroom. When she got inside, she picked up the remote, pointing at the TV. The same breaking news report was on. She didn't have time to mingle in other people's problems. She had to work tomorrow, and when she got off she was going to get her boys and sit them down and tell them the truth.

They deserved to know that she and Red were sisters. They would be devastated, but she wanted them to hear it from her.

*We have footage from the scene, and parents, if you have children viewer discretion is advised...*

Fate sat on the bed. Before she could press the "Off" button, she froze, her blood curdling. Bile rose in her throat and she jumped off the bed, in a fit of tears. Her world exploded, blinding her. All logic and reason suddenly became null and void.

"Oh my God! RED RED! NOO OH MY GOD THAT'S RED'S TRUCK!"

She grabbed her purse and keys and ran out the front door, closing it behind her.

Jameson and Renaldo were watching TV. Krishna, taking off her apron, smiled at them. They were in the Den.

"I think its bed time, you guys. You have to go to school tomorrow."

Renaldo sneered. "Man!"

Jameson patted his shoulder. "Come on, Bruh. We gotta go to bed. Wouldn't want to be late for school."

"Actually, I do wanna be late."

Krishna picked up the remote. Jameson's cell phone rang. He looked at the number and frowned.

Krishna was taking Renaldo's hand, trying to pull him into the living room.

*Oh my God! Red's truck just plummeted off the Turnpike! I can't let him see that.*

Renaldo was laughing. "I can walk on my own, Jeez. You're about to pull my arm out of its socket."

Krishna played it off, her heart hammering.

Jameson waited until they vanished. He answered the phone.

"Hello." His back was facing the TV.

"Yo. Those brakes I rigged for you..."

Jameson sat back on the couch, smiling. "I will pay you. I'm just glad you did it. I didn't want my Mom jumping in her truck trying to leave. She needs to talk to my grandma. Having her brakes rigged was the insurance policy. She hopped in her truck she would know the brakes were out so she would go back inside and finish talking to her mother. I want us to be a family."

"Bruh…"

"So you will get the two thousand I promised. I know where Mama keeps her stash. Plan failed anyway, her truck is gone."

"Bruh? I hate to tell you, but are you close to a television set?"

"Yea…"

"Turn it to the news…"

He turned to face the TV. "Hell, the news is already on…"

He watched quietly.

When a picture of his mother popped on TV, and then the visual switched to her burning truck he threw the phone at the TV, shouting so loud Krishna stormed into the room, Renaldo behind him.

"Bro! What's wrong?"

"Mama is dead! Oh my God! I fucked up, bruh! I just wanted her to talk to Grandma! I paid to have her brakes rigged. And now Red is dead! My Mama is dead!"

Renaldo fell to his knees, with his face in his hands.

Krishna couldn't believe her ears.

F ate arrived at Krishna's house. She had to get to her boys and tell them before they saw it on the news. She hopped out of her car, heading for the front door. She knocked on it, her skin crawling. She was shuddering, and the tears wouldn't stop falling.

*My baby is dead! She died thinking that I didn't love her anymore. Oh my God! Can this situation get any worse?*

When Renaldo opened the front door, he wrapped his arms around his mother.

"Mama! Something terrible has happened! Red died in a car accident!"

"I know, baby. I just heard…"

Jameson was digging up the carpet in the living room, blaming himself. Fate looked at him, pushing Renaldo to the side. "Why are you blaming yourself?"

"Mom!" He engulfed Fate, digging his claws into her blouse. "I did it! I didn't mean to! I just wanted them to talk…"

"Who, what…slow down…"

"I paid to have Red's brakes rigged. All I was doing was trying to ensure that she didn't leave the house. I wanted her to talk to Grandma. That's all. I didn't mean to kill Mama!"

Fate was stunned. Krishna remained quiet.

The man stood up, grabbing his phone. The waitress seemed to drop from the ceiling.

"Where are you going?"

"Away from here."

He had never run so fast in his life.

*Fuck the money! I don't wanna go to jail. Thank God this phone isn't registered in my name. I stole it from some dude at the Mall Earlier.*

*Nothing can be traced to me.*

# Jadish Houston 3

My world exploding, I hesitantly sat in my car and leaned back against the seat. I couldn't stop crying, my heart beating out of my chest. Silently, I guardedly stared at the house before me. The place owned by a man who shattered *my* glass house. The house owned by a man that destroyed every logical nerve in my being. A house owned by a man I used to love. A house owned by a man that had a few of my pictures on the walls. Now I have become a stranger in the photos on his dusty mantel. I was now the stranger in *all* the photos. I didn't know who the hell he was anymore. Had I ever known him? I loved him so much. I could recount the times, when I was a young, impressionable girl, he would wipe my tears. He helped Daddy teach me to ride a bike. Daddy was mean, always spanking me for falling and scrapping my knees. But my God Daddy would be right there, brushing off my buttocks or my knees, telling me to "Get up and try, try again." In the blink of an eye everything has changed. Everything I have ever wished, hoped and dreamed has become hogwash. My pre-school graduation picture and my first grade class picture were on his dresser. Pictures of my first cheerleading try outs were in his photo album. My lungs felt like flames and my stomach was the identical twin. I held my legs but they continued to shake. It was hot in this car but I welcomed the heat. My panties stuck to my pussy with both sweat and lust. Lust for a man who used to be my Godfather. Lust for a man I *used* to trust. Lust for a man my father once brought in our home when I was a little girl. I loved him like an Uncle. I used to tell him my most intimate thoughts and his ears became my diary. I even let him *read* my diary without shame. He told me I was beautiful. He told me to watch out for men who would promise me the world just to get a shot of coochie. He told me that men were vicious creatures. They wanted what they wanted and didn't care *who* they hurt. He also told me to never trust those closest to me. They would hurt you first. And that's exactly what he did. Hurt me first. Why didn't I listen?

Who would have known that I *should* have been watching *him*? That's what happened when you were young and naïve. When you have blinders on, you look for the good in people. You become a sitting duck. I've been wounded from the pump shot gun of Tommy's selfishness. His sickness was blinding. He taught me the ups and downs of love in ways Daddy used to hide from me. I appreciated Tommy for telling me that I shouldn't marry the first piece of dick I get. He told me to live and learn and find out what worked best for me.

Daddy wanted me to be his little girl forever. How long did he expect me to keep my legs closed? Forever? Tommy said I would grow into a beautiful woman. He watched me sprout like a rose.

Betrayed, I punched the dash board. Dried blood was on my bottom lip. Yes, the blood from Tommy's dick. I tried to *bite* it off. I should have cut it off. Goddamn it, Tommy! Why? I was thinking this entire time I was a virgin. I prided myself on being one of the *few* girls that kept the cherry bush set up in my pussy and thought I would let my George Washington chop it down or dig it up, whichever way he preferred, when I got married. It didn't quite work out that way. And what hurts the most was that I put my husband Sax through two years of emotional hell. I punished him for *Tommy's* mistake. Wait a minute. Raping me wasn't a mistake. Why was I minimizing what my God Daddy did? Was I in denial?

I put my husband through unconscionable hell. I wouldn't let him get the pussy because I was distraught over the nightmares I used to have. In it, an evil man with a big red X over his face was chasing me to the Red sea. I now knew I was the woman being deflowered in the middle of the ocean floor. Why hadn't I seen the signs before? Did I *not* remember anything about my graduation night? The night Tommy had his way with me. I hoped he enjoyed it because he would never touch me again. I hoped he died. I couldn't believe a man I trusted like an Uncle would unabashedly destroy me and rob my future husband of taking my purity.

I thought back to a conversation my husband and I had years before this grueling moment. I had begged him to tell me why he got in a fight with Tommy when he took me and my family out to eat. He told me Tommy fucked me on my graduation night and I was so taken aback I instantly shut down and started defending the man and Sax was right, right, right!

I closed my eyes and silently prayed to God.

*Lord, please forgive me for punishing my husband. You sent me a very sweet man who was a virgin himself and innocent and pure and I spit him back in your face because the taste in my mouth reminded me of what I thought I had. It overshadowed every logical nerve in my body. All Sax wanted was love and acceptance and I gave him hell and it's unapologetic wrath. What kind of woman jacks her man's dick on his honeymoon and didn't make love to him? I didn't give him me, all of me. I gave him some of me. The selfish part of me. The part of me I have tried to erase for so many years and have been unsuccessful in doing so. But now I want to correct the wrongs and give myself to my husband.*

*If I can get past Tommy's betrayal.*

*In Lord Jesus name I pray.*

*Amen!*

I have never *willingly* given myself to a man. I used to sit back in high school and watch the boys pick out vulnerable girls and fuck them and their reputations to hell. I didn't want to be one of them so I never put myself in the position to become victimized by boys with testosterone problems. My girlfriends didn't have an ounce of class. They gave away free pussy like the boys paid for it. Where was their self-esteem? Where was the self-confidence? I remember, during high school, I stayed over to Sasha's house. We were about fifteen and she told me her parents were out of town. Initially she told me it was going to be me and her chilling and eating popcorn and lusting over Denzel Washington movie posters. I especially loved *Ricochet*.

I had told my parents I would be staying the night with Sasha, since her parents grew up with my Mama. Hesitantly, Daddy told me to make sure I had the dishes washed. Tommy, who was sitting at the table drinking a cold brew, looked at me and smiled and I melted. It took a while for him to look away and I couldn't stop lusting over his gorgeous smile. Once I was done with the dishes and cleaning my room Tommy drove me over to Sasha's. When I got out of the car and grabbed my night sack I kissed Tommy's cheek and he left.

The instant I knocked on the door Sasha whipped it open and snatched me inside.

"Why are you pulling on me like that?" I asked, confused.

She closed the door, hugging me.

"I have my reasons. Glad you could make it, Girl."

I looked around. I saw her clothing thrown everywhere. Her shoes were all over the place. The TV was on an old episode of *Good*

*Times* and the sound was muted. I smelled something cooking from the kitchen. I sniffed. Chitterlings? Maybe, but I did know that it smelled like shit.

Sasha was picking up her clothing in a hurry and stuffing them in the hall closet.

"Help, Girl."

"*Hell*, no." I looked at her like she was crazy. I still didn't know what was going on and I wasn't sure if I wanted to know. "I'm your house guest. *Not* housekeeping."

Shaking my head in disgust, I tossed my bag on the couch. A roach ran from by the pillow and I jumped behind the end-table, making shrieking noises and she laughed at me.

"They probably came from outside. It rained earlier and they seek shelter in the living room."

*Right*, bitch. You had roaches for years. And don't blame it on the neighbors, either because you haven't had a neighbor in three years. *Why do black people blame the climate for their roach problems?* I threw some salt in the game. "It looks dry as hell to me outside."

She kicked three pair of her shoes in the closet. Then she tried to push the door closed but she had too much stuff in there.

She was struggling. "*Help* me, Girl."

*Like hell.* "I'm cool. I'll *watch*."

She tried her best to get it closed. She even pressed her body against the door and she gave it all she had until *finally* it closed and she sunk to her knees, sighing with relief.

She had on her mother's dress and pumps. She overdid it with her mother's make-up. I didn't understand *why* she dressed that way, since she dressed like a bum in school. Holes in her jeans never did anything for her front crooked tooth. She had a teaspoon of nappy hair and it didn't do anything for those god-awful shoes she wore that smelled like spoiled milk. Hell, the silly bitch didn't even have enough hair to get the famous Halle Berry or Toni Braxton look.

She stood up and stretched. "Bob, Sam and Micro are coming over, Girl. We gotta get ready for them. The finest niggahs in school are coming to stay the night with us. Isn't that exciting?"

I wanted to whip her ass. What was this? A sex party? "Uh, no. I didn't come over here for that...you said it would be me and you." I glared at her.

"It is. For *now*. Plus I'm pussyphobic. I break out in hives when I'm around another woman for too long. I like dick, not fish, you feel me, Gurl? No offense."

I didn't want those boys around me. They fucked any and everything on two legs. I wouldn't be surprised if they fucked each other. Birds of a feather flocked together. Or, as my Grandma once said, *"Gays masturbate and lick it from the one eyed snake."*

"I'm not offended and I happen to like fish sandwiches. With a lot of tartar sauce."

She chocked on her saliva and she held her burning throat.

"You eat fish?" she asked, short of breath.

"*Duh*, bitch. I *love* catfish."

The color left her face. She avoided my eyes and started moving away from me, like I had a disease and that offended the hell out of me.

"Oh," she went on, chuckling. The color returned to her face. "*Fish*, fish. I got you. You eat *real* fish sandwiches."

I was even more confused. She was acting like a ditzy bitch.

"What are you on tonight because you are acting dumb as hell."

She rolled her eyes. "*Anyways*, Chile. Check this. *Hoes* are already talking about me and you. Half the school wants Bob and Micro. They are the stars of the football team. When you rush over a thousand yards you deserve to get all the pussy you want..."

I gave her a confused look. "And *why* are you telling me this?"

She was patting my shoulder and pushing me up the stairs.

"Because I heard Tonna wants to fight you. You know she likes Micro and he is going around telling everyone he wants to eat your pussy and give you some dick."

"Like hell. Not in this lifetime."

She led me into her Mom's huge room. About five or six nice dresses were on her mom's bed. I liked the green one with the green floral bust.

"*Pick* a dress. We don't have much time. Verona and Lily are coming over, too."

Now see. Now the game stopped. "I don't like Lily. I heard she fucked half the basketball team."

"So *what*. Don't hate. She is giving her pussy some experience. Men don't want inexperienced twat. They want their women skilled enough to pay the bills with the flick of the clit." We were laughing. She was so silly.

She went on, warming to her subject. "So when Lily marries Ted, when he makes it to the NBA, she'll know how to hold him down with her pussy-popping skills, Chile...He's her meal ticket. You know she put holes in the condoms so she can get pregnant and be set for life. Who wants to live in the projects forever?"

"I feel you. But I don't know about having a man's baby just to hold on to him. I don't believe in being deceitful. Eventually it blows up in your face."

I could have been talking to a pig. *Oink, oink, oink, oink.* Nothing I said registered in her brain. She picked up the red dress and held it up to my body. "That looks good on you."

I pushed it away from me. I hated the color red. Yuck. I think of my period when I see red. Plus I used to wear red pants to school when I was on my period, especially the days Mom couldn't afford maxi pads. "I like the *green* one."

She tossed the red dress on the bed like she never liked it. I took off my black skirt and red blouse and she snatched off my bra and I was startled. *But you don't do fish, 'ey?* My breasts were bare and I didn't like other women looking at my bazookas.

"Take off your panties," she said, handing me a pair of green pumps. "It's best if you stay naked underneath the dress so when the boys come they can eat your pussy without the hassles."

Oh, no. It's not going to be *that* kind of party.

"Eat my pussy? *Wait,* what kinda…"

She was determined. "Put on the fucking dress. You walk around school keeping your pussy guarded like Michael Jackson's room. Give it up. This is high school. Let's fuck now and tomorrow we can worry about everything else."

*I guess you think you tell me what to do.* "I don't…"

"We're young once. Do you want to turn sixty years old with a shriveled up pussy you never used?"

*Ugh!* "Girl. Don't say it like that."

"All right then, The Mummy. Let's get to it. Let Micro dig Nefertiti outta your asshole and slide it in your mouth to taste the tombs of the Sphinx Pyramid. I heard he has a big, juicy dick!"

She walked over to her Mom's nightstand and picked up a blue cup. She handed it to me.

"What is this?" I asked, wanting to puke. I felt my pussy shut down. I suddenly wanted to go home and crawl under my blankets and die.

"Liquor."

She picked up the other cup and wolfed it down. I didn't want to look amateurish in front of her so I wolfed it down, too. I cringed then gagged. It burned my throat. What the hell.

"Girl, that's what you call that good shit."

"It's nasty."

She was staring at me. I was confused.

"What?" I asked.

"Feel it yet?"

"Feel what?"

"That's my special blend. Grey Goose and weed."

"Weed?" I wanted to gag.

"Hell yea. Drunk and high is the way to go. Ever get fucked high on weed? That's what you call 3D dimensional dick."

She put the dress over my head and was pulling it down. It fit perfectly. I helped her situate it on my body, silently thinking about what she said. About turning 60 and never being with a man. I did want to know what sex was all about.

Daddy fucked Mama in the ass every night. He wanted the ass more than her vagina. I found that weird but every time Mama said, "Plow that ass like Frederick Douglass planting okra!" I shut right up and gave it to God. I heard them through their bedroom door all the time and they didn't try to be quiet about it either.

Sasha told me to sit down on the bed and I did, still trying to take this all in. She pulled my hair into a bun and then put her mother's long curly wig on my head. It was a little itchy. I looked in the mirror. I looked hot. Damn. Maybe I needed to let go and have fun. It didn't make sense to hold on to my virginity and not experience sex at it's greatest.

She took out her Mom's make-up bag and she artfully coated my lips with light green lipstick.

"Oh, Girl. You're hot! Watch out Iman!"

She pulled out the dark green rouge and blush. She coated my cheekbones with some glitter. I was watching her the entire time, her breath smelling like ass but who was I to rain on her parade? Might run some more roaches into her house for cover. I still couldn't believe she said that. She was so worried about my pussy and my image when she needed to focus on brushing her goddamn teeth but I didn't say anything because I didn't want to hurt her feelings. Nappy headed bitch.

She looked fabulous but her breath was like going over to Madonna's house and finding feces on the low-table next to the caviar. I chuckled at the thought.

"What's so funny?" she asked, the rush of her breath making me wince. *Goddamn, bitch! Gargle!*

"Nothing." I could barely get the word out.

"Something must be funny. You keep chuckling."

"I can't be to my thoughts?"

"You need to be thinking about how you're gonna give Bob that *ass.*"

"You make it sound so gross."

"Girl, sex is a *business.* Find your pension and hope it's a hefty 401 (k) plan. Mama taught me that."

"That's why I'm going to college. To care for myself. Plus your Mama is weird. Why would she let a married man screw her and he doesn't even pay ¼ of her bills?"

She didn't like the comment. "That's her..."

"Where's *her* hefty 401 (k)?"

Sasha's eyes flashed dangerously. "*Listen* Abigail Adams. Find you a John Adams and hope he becomes the President of the United States."

"No."

She looked me over with a smile. "*Look* in the mirror. Your transformation is complete."

I stood up and closed my eyes, wondering was I making a mistake. I slowly opened them and I saw a gorgeous young woman with green lips and the dress brought out the rhinestones in the pumps. I was gorgeous. Wow. *I should go lock myself in my room and fuck myself.* I couldn't stop smiling. Why was I staring at the door knob?

I hugged her. "I love it."

"Are you sure you like it? You're not just saying that?"

"I mean it." I pulled away from her, taking up my bag. I pulled out two peppermints. I popped one in my mouth.

"Give me one. I brushed my teeth earlier but this candy will keep it cool."

*What did you brush your teeth with? Shitty diapers? And you need that peppermint more than I do.*

Just then the doorbell rang.

I followed Sasha down stairs and when she answered the door I saw Bob and Micro. They took one look at us and fell in love. Micro and Bob grabbed my hands and Sasha tucked her chin back.

"Excuse me? All this right here and you ignore me for Jadish?"

Sam crept up behind her, pulling her into his embrace. He was sucking on her neck and she was trying her best to get the dress off. Micro closed the door and looked at Bob.

"Damn, Jadish. You are hot, Gurl."

I couldn't take my eyes off him. He looked really good. He was dressed in a black shirt and black slacks with black boots. Bob was trying to kiss me, feeling on my booty and I didn't feel good about it so I pulled away from them and Micro pulled me back and Bob got behind me, trying to take off the dress.

I felt uncomfortable. Micro pulled out my titty and was trying to suck on it and Bob pulled up the back of my dress and was breathing all over my neck. He pulled down his zipper and pulled out his dick and I turned and slapped him.

"No, man. I am going home!"

Bob snatched me by the wig and Micro ripped off my dress. Sasha was naked. Sam bent her over the low-table and sex filled the air. She loved every inch of his dick.

I couldn't go down like this. I didn't want to be a Ho. Not like this. I didn't want my first time to be with boys who took first times for granted.

Bob brutally head butted me and a rush of pain and nausea fell upon me. The force of the blow knocked me to my knees. I had never known pain like that before in my life. Micro picked me up and threw me on the chair, positioning himself between my legs.

He was a beast. "If you don't give up the pussy we'll take it."

I tried to kick at him but my head hurt so badly it felt like I was dying. Bob put his dick up to my lips and tried to force it in but I wouldn't budge and he was slapping me in the face with his dick and it hurt.

"Suck it!"

"No," I mumbled. I wouldn't let them break my spirit. *God please help me! Help me, Lord. You said you will never leave my side. What is going on? What have I ever done wrong?*

"SUCK IT!"

I turned my head away from his penis and he turned my face back to it and he pissed in my face and I was flapping my arms and trying to stand up as urine soaked in my hair and the dress.

Micro kissed all over my titties, tasting the piss. He smiled, rolling his tongue all over my nipple. And Bob pulled my legs back. I felt a cool breeze blow across my pussy and Micro looked at me evilly and said, "I'm making you a woman tonight, Ho."

"No, please, Micro. Sasha…Sasha, help me…"

She didn't hear me. Her moaning and obscenities reached peak levels and I knew then this was all planned. It was all a set-up.

Sasha wasn't really my friend and now Micro was going to rape me.

Micro wiped Bob's piss all over my pussy and he buried his face in it. Bob joined him. I couldn't move. It felt good but at the same time I didn't want this done to me. I wanted Mom! I knew then I would never spend the night outside of my home, where I felt safe.

Bob and Micro tongue kissed each other and then two tongues started slithering all over my pussy. Bob pushed my legs back and I felt weak.

Micro then tried to kiss me and I bit his lips and he raised his fist and just as it started to plummet towards my face Tommy grabbed his hand and snatched him off me.

Thank *God.*

Daddy grabbed Bob by the throat and threw him so hard he flew through the living room window. The sound of shattering glass made me scream. His body lay still by a row of cherry bushes. Sasha was in shock. While Tommy beat Micro under the low-table, blood seeping from his nose and lips, Sasha tried to flee and Daddy snatched her by the wig and it came off. She ran up the stairs and he was behind her. When she reached the top of the stairs Daddy picked her up and threw her down the stairs, her head slamming into the pedestal. Her body remained still.

I lay there, trying to take it all in. I was praying to God and wondering why the room was turning black. My breathing came in spurts and I felt vulnerable to the sudden pleasure that came over me. The darkness seemed like a nice place to lay and to sleep. Yea. I tried to keep my eyes open and Daddy was in my face. He was tapping my cheek. "Baby...Are you ok? Baby!"

His voice turned into vicious wails and screams. "BABY! WAKE UP! BABY!"

His voice seemed distant. I smiled at him and his tears fell on my face and he pulled me into his arms and I saw Tommy standing behind him, shaking his head in denial. I felt my body immobilizing. Daddy opened the front door and rushed to his truck.

I blacked out.

I felt elatedly good. The cold air enveloped me like a second skin. I was weak. I inhaled deeply. I felt something in my nose. It was hard and uncomfortable. I opened and closed my hands. Something was in my right hand. I couldn't raise it. Something had a grip on it. OK. My left hand worked. I slowly opened my eyes and it took a minute for the room to come into focus.

Daddy was sitting in a chair, holding my hand tightly. He was snoring loudly. Mom was sleeping on the chair over by the TV, wrapped in my old Big Bird blanket. Why did that make me smile? Tommy was sprawled on the floor under another blanket.

Where was I?

"Dad...Dad..." My voice horribly cracked.

Mom opened her eyes and looked at me and when she realized I was blinking she jumped up to her feet, screaming with joy. "My *baby*!"

Daddy and Tommy were startled.

"She's awake! She's awake!"

Mama pushed Dad out of the way and she threw her frail body on mine, showering my face with tears and kisses. Tommy hugged Daddy and they pat each other's back.

"What happened to me?" I asked Mom. I could not remember anything.

She was studying me. "You were almost raped."

I was quiet. "Raped?" I grew pensive, tears forming in my eyes. "Somebody *raped* me?"

Tommy took my hand. "No. Your Dad and I got there in a knick of time."

"Daddy!" I called out for him. A few nurses rushed into the room and a doctor, holding a clip board was behind them.

Dad hugged me and I wouldn't let him go.

A police woman asked me some questions and I told her all I could remember. Not that it did much because Daddy told her, "Please let her rest."

"Its protocol," said the white cop with the prettiest hair and the bluest eyes I'd ever seen.

"I don't give a fuck about protocol. My daughter was almost raped. And if they would have succeeded I would have murdered the motherfuckers and you woulda been asking me the goddamn questions now get the fuck outta my daughter's fucking room!"

"I understand you're angry. I would be, too, if it was my child," said the cop. "But I have to do my job, Sir."

"Well hurry up. Then let her sleep."

I answered a gazillion questions. Once I was done she left. Two nurses checked the EKG machine and the third nurse flashed a little light in my eyes to see if I responded to it. She scribbled down something on her folder and the doctor told them to leave. Mama was telling me that Micro was in intensive care in the very same hospital I was in and that Bob suffered a head concussion. Before I could question her any further, the doctor asked me how did I feel and I told him I felt like Frederick Douglass planting okra and the blood left Mom's face and Tommy and Daddy chocked and I was smiling.

"I see you have your sense of humor," the doctor told me. "Whatever *that* means."

"Ask Daddy," I told him. "Mama tells him about Frederick Douglass and his okra every night through the walls."

Mama covered her face and Tommy pointed at Daddy, laughing at him. The doctor got the hint and he quietly sped out of the room. I asked Mom how Bob suffered a concussion. Tommy looked at Daddy and Dad told me, "He tried to rape you. Micro, also. Tommy and I got there and saved you. I threw him out of the window. The glass cut up his face pretty badly."

"Is he ok?" Not that I cared.

Tommy said, "He's in a coma."

Everything was happening too fast. I was still trying to formulate in my brain exactly what happened. I remembered Sasha wanted me to stay the night. She told me that Bob, Sam and Micro were coming over. She dressed me up in a green dress and she did my make-up. I remembered Micro and Bob grabbed my hands and they tried to force me to have sex. OK. It was all coming back to me.

"What happened to Sam?" I asked Mom.

"He's ok. But as for Sasha, she was treated for minor injuries and I pressed charges against her for luring you to her home to have sex with her male friends."

I was antsy. "She's my friend. She wouldn't hurt me."

Tommy said, "She lured you there with the intention of being raped."

I tried to sit up. "How dare you!" I steamed. "She's my friend! Don't bash her in my face!"

Tommy looked hurt. "Jadish. It's true…"

Daddy put his hand on Tommy's shoulder and shook his head. Tommy nodded and moved to the back of the room.

"Baby," said Mama, trying to calm me down. I tried to attack Tommy. He was lying. He better watch his mouth!

Daddy said, "Jadish. Please. Calm down."

Hesitantly, I settled down.

Tommy said, "I hate to tell you this but Sasha dressed you up in that dress and make-up so your body could be sacrificed. She set you up to be raped by two horny school boys."

"Mom!" I called out in fear and she kissed me and held me until I fell asleep again. This was too much for me to handle. *Why* would Sasha do this to me?

A few hours later the doctor discharged me. I wasn't talking much and Mom helped me wash up in the bathroom. When I put on a pair of pants and a white blouse, Mom pulled my hair into a bun. I thought about when Sasha put my hair in a bun, just before she put her Mom's wig on my head. Nausea filled my stomach. I took my hair from the bun and let it hang.

"No, Mama. I don't want my hair like that."

"Why?" she asked.

"Sasha put my hair like this before her friends came over to rape me."

She understood.

Mom and Daddy were in the back seat arguing over who was going to cook dinner and Tommy drove. I had on my seat belt, riding in silence. Tommy would occasionally look at me but I didn't recognize or acknowledge him.

"Are you still mad at me?" he asked.

I sucked my teeth.

"I'm sorry, baby girl. I don't want you to be upset with me. I was only telling you the truth about Sasha."

Mom and Dad were yelling at the top of their lungs. I could hardly hear Tommy.

In my hands were papers. The doctor wanted me to see a psychologist and I told my parents I didn't want to talk about the situation with a stranger and they said they wouldn't force me. They told me they would handle the legal part of the attempted rape and they wanted me to focus on getting well and returning to school.

"Jadish."

"What?" I whispered harshly, wiping tears from my eyes. "What do you want?"

Mom and Daddy talked over the music. They were heated with each other.

Dad said, "You are *gonna* cook. I can't cook tonight. I'm tired."

"And I'm tired too, goddamn it and you need to cook sometimes. Motherfucker I'm not a robot!"

Tommy said, "I told you the truth."

"Bashing Sasha is not the truth."

"Listen. Your Dad and I went out tonight. We stopped by the pizza parlor and we ordered a large pepperoni."

"OK."

"A few girls came in. Your Dad and I checked them out. But they were too young. One of them, I think her name is Lily…" The color left my face. "Told another girl in the group that a girl was going to be deflowered at Sasha's house. Initially *your* Dad and I didn't think nothing of it. Lily then told the other two girls 'Jadish has been a virgin long enough. Micro and Bob just arrived at Sasha's house. They are going to rape her.'"

I was so quiet I seeped with anger. I hated Lily so much. She never liked me. And to think Sasha was in on the plot. Why would she do that to me? I prided myself on keeping my virginity.

And after tonight I would keep my virginity until I got married.

Tommy grew quiet when he saw I squeezed my hands into fists.

"I'm sorry."

I didn't say anything. Life went on. I told my parents to keep me in the same school. Bob never recovered from intensive care and he died. Daddy was charged but in court he won his case. He protected his daughter from being raped by two men who beat her and urinated on her and humiliated her. Even Bob's parents couldn't do anything. They actually shook my father's hand after his victory, not that Daddy gloated. He loved all people and taking a life would be on his conscious forever.

Bob's parents were so in shock that their son tried to rape me (and the fact that he died) that they decided to move out of town. Micro recovered. Charges were brought against him and Sasha and he wound up getting three years in a juvenile detention center. Sasha got probation and was withdrawn from the school. Her parents stopped talking to my family and we were now bitter enemies.

Micro was kicked off the football team and slandered in school. My business traveled but I didn't care. I kept my head high and I still went to school. I didn't care what anybody had to say. Tommy helped me get through the ordeal. He was easy to talk to and he told me him and Daddy would always protect me.

I wound up going to see the shrink. It wasn't bad at all. The psychologist's name was Advance Stevens, a frail-looking white woman with huge freckles and curly red hair. Over the next few months she helped me deal with what happened through essay writing and role playing and she loved holding a mirror up in my face before and after our sessions ended.

I started to gain my self-esteem and self-confidence back. I felt like a new person. I knew in my heart I would never trust people the way I used to.

Boys tried to go with me in school. They treated me like flowers. They tried to nurture and protect me and everyday a different boy bought me chocolates or roses or brought me a teddy bear.

My sexuality kicked in, despite the attempted rape. I wanted to know what it felt like to have sex but every time I came close to doing it I chickened out. I thought something was wrong with me. I used to suck on a little dick or let the boys eat the pussy but I have never been penetrated. I didn't know that my virginity would be taken from the same man who saved me from being raped.

I was married now and I hadn't even let my husband fuck me yet and it's been over two years and I didn't know how to move beyond the apprehension. There were brief sexual encounters. We would be licking and tasting but I was too afraid to go any further.

Despite Tommy drugging me on my graduation night and fucking me all night long, to his heart's delight, he secretly prided himself on being the first to get the pussy and I didn't have any knowledge. I should have known! I thought back to that unfortunate morning. The day after graduation.

I had awakened with blood everywhere and my body on fire. I didn't know what to think or what to say. Where did the blood come from? I looked at my arms and legs but I didn't see a cut. After throwing up in the toilet, I called Tommy. He always came to the rescue. I told him that I didn't feel good, that I saw blood everywhere and he was like my knight in shining armor. He showed up in his polished green Buick and he looked after me. He brought me some changing clothes and he stayed in the room until I showered and was dressed up like a doll. I loved the way he used to look at me.

He didn't give me the I-wanna-fuck-you stare like most guys in my neighborhood. But the gleam in the corners of his hazel eyes reminded me of love. I knew then he was in love with me but I didn't know I was face to face with the man who raped me. I felt so foolish for thinking I was still a virgin. It would take a lot to forgive myself for what happened. I blamed myself for what Tommy did. Did I lead him on? Did I give him signals? No. I *never* looked at Tommy in a sexual way.

Breaking the silence was my ringing cell phone. I was still parked in Tommy's front yard and I knew I had to go but I wanted to burn his house down. I felt so betrayed.

I answered and it was Daddy.

"Hey, pop." I faked it, trying to sound upbeat and my insides felt like tropical depressions.

"*Hi*, Baby. How is your day going?"

I turned the key in the ignition. I smiled, tears falling from my eyes.

*Help me, Daddy! Your best friend raped me on my graduation night! How do I tell you? I wanna kill him! Damn it! Why do I feel so murderous?*

"My day is magnificent."

"Magnificent?" he asked skeptically. I heard Al Green in the background. *Let's stay Together.* Very nice song. But right now I wasn't a nice bitch. My whole world just blew up in my face.

"Yea." I put the gear in reverse and backed into the road. "Magnificent."

"Darling, you don't use words like that. Something is wrong."

"Mr. Lenny Houston. I do feel that way."

"Baby I know you better than you know those panties you're wearing."

"That wasn't a very good summation, Daddy."

"Get over yourself. Can you take a joke? But you feel magnificent, right? Your voice betrays your feelings. What is it? Just tell me."

He intimidated me. "I'm good, Pa."

"Pa?" He was chuckling. And it wasn't pleasant. "You never call me 'Pa.' Do I look Spanish? Pa? I'm Daddy! I love being black."

"Don't we all."

I put the car in drive and sped up the block.

"Why are your tires biting into the pavement like that, Jadish? Are you ok? Where are you?"

"Dad, I'm good." The tears fell harder. I slowly braked at the approaching stop sign. I put the car in park, pressed "mute" and I threw my head on the steering wheel. I hurt so much my shoulders were shaking. The heat didn't help matters and everything I felt for Tommy was compromised.

"Why, Tommy? Why did you rape me? Why did you do this to me? I trusted you!"

"Jadish?"

I sucked in air and my nose was stopped up. I sat back against the seat and I smelled my pussy in the air. It was still in heat. I was remembering Tommy's dick in my mouth a few minutes ago, when I was secretly picking him for information. And to think my husband Sax knew all along what had happened on my graduation night. He told me that but I wouldn't listen. I guess I was in denial about it all.

But I wasn't in denial about it anymore. Question was: what was I going to do about it? Would I call the authorities? Would that be beneficial? Would I feel better? I have already been violated by a sinister man. Would he do another woman like that? Had he done another woman (or women) like that? I couldn't have been the goddamn first?

I pressed "unmute."

"Daddy, where is Sax?"

"He's next to me. Are you ok?'"

I smiled. Someone blew their horn at me and I put the car in "drive" and started up the block doing the 35 M.P.H. speed limit.

He put Sax on the phone. Sax could remember the first day he saw the woman who was to be his loving wife. They were going to the University of Miami. College.

Both led an individual life that was going nowhere. He was leaving the Convocation Building and he saw her in a plaid skirt and white shirt. Women laughed at her style of dress but she was unlike anything he'd ever seen. He was directly behind her, inhaling deeply, trying to get a whiff of her womanly scent. What kind of perfume did she wear? It was soft and invitingly gorgeous. It made him smile. Her earrings weren't elaborate. And her shoes were simple. She had tripped and he caught her just before her chin slammed on the concrete step. They had been inseparable ever since. Now Sax frowned. He didn't want to talk to his wife. His loving wife. The woman who sat on her pussy like it was a bank account reserved for a rainy day.

He was happily married to the woman of his dreams. Sex came with the package. Sure, it wasn't everything but goddamn, it's been two years and she hasn't let him fuck or make love.

Why?

He knew why!

He was indirectly being punished for Tommy's betrayal. He knew Tommy fucked his girl when she graduated high school.

Giving her all those drinks.

Each laced with GHB.

He knew it.

But he couldn't prove it.

Sax glanced at Jadish's humble, broad-shouldered father. Should I tell him that his best friend fucked his daughter and left her bleeding?

Sax cleared his throat, taking the cell phone and putting it to his ear.

"Hey, Jadish."

"Why do you sound so down?"

*Because you're my wife. And you'd rather fuck yourself with bedroom door knobs than your own husband.*

"I'm good," he lied.

"I have something special planned for you."

He closed his eyes.

*I heard that before.*

A very tall, handsome man boarded a plane in Chicago. He carried a leather attaché case and he stayed to himself. Freshly clad in a business suit with red tie, the ladies swooned over him. He had on thick shades, making it impossible to see his eyes and his shoes gleamed just as brightly as his moderate jewelry. On his finger was a wedding ring. He found his appropriate seat and put his attaché case under it. He sat down and sighed. He hated flying. But he had business to handle in Miami, Florida.

He snapped for the stewardess, who stuck out her bubble ass and perky tits and licked her lips as she approached him.

"I'm happily married," he said and her tits and ass deflated instantly.

She then had an attitude. She didn't like being rejected.

*Fag!*

"Can I get a coke?"

"When the plane gets in the air…" He handed her a five dollar bill, changing her mind. "Coming right up. Try to keep it inconspicuous."

*All Hoes loved money.* He winked at her. He had no plans on being inconspicuous. He was a grown man. Fuck the lames. Indifferently, he pulled out his Blackberry. He called his wife. The phone rang for what seemed an eternity. *Answer the phone.* It went to voice mail. He hung up, calling the number again. This time she answered.

"Hey, baby"

*She acts like we're doing ok.* "Hi. How are you?"

"I'm feeding our son."

"Cool. I won't be long. I just wanted to say that whatever happens, just know that I love you."

"Whatever. Our son needs me. Bye."

She hung up.

He then clicked a few buttons and a name popped up. He smiled when each glorious letter shined in his handsome face.

*I can't wait to see you, Bruh.*

Tommy was in his bathroom, crying from the pain. His dick burned. *Goddamn,* Jadish. He didn't mean to hurt you.
He picked up the phone to call the paramedics.

What do you have planned? Another church Bake Sale?"
    Jadish rolled her eyes. He was getting an attitude. He has been Attitude Country for the past few months.
    "No, man. *You're* so silly."
    *I'm so horny but you won't fuck me.* "I'm just Sax."
    "Baby I hear it in your voice. Something's wrong. What are you not telling me?"
    "I'm good, Jadish. And you know we're having problems in our marriage."
    Lenny's brows rose. He held his breath, listening. They couldn't be having problems because if they were she was *not* moving back into the house. Daughter or no daughter. Make your own way in the world and stay out of his way. He was fucking his wife butt booty ass naked the day she turned 18 and left and he'd be damned if she jeopardized his pussy any time soon.
    "Baby, is this about sex again. It's like all you think about."
    "JADISH!" he exploded, infuriated. Lenny was startled. He wondered what was going on.
    "Why are you yelling at my daughter?"
    Sax didn't give a shit. He felt like they were trying to double team him and he didn't like being pushed into a corner.
    "Can you stay outta of me and my wife's business, Lenny? Thank you."
    Lenny averted his face.
    Sax had enough. "All I think about is sex? We have been married for two plus years. You haven't let me make love to you. I am a man. You haven't made me a complete man yet and there's *nothing* you or your goddamn father can say about it."
    Against his better judgment, Lenny was quiet. He certainly understood. He been there done that before. When he married Jadish's mother Paulette, she was 19 years old at the time. He was gang banging. She was wishy-washy with the pussy in the beginning. But once he got it he was hooked. Lenny wondered why Jadish hadn't had sex with her husband yet. He used to talk to his wife about it all the time. No one knew. But Paulette told him and Sax, "Just don't

pressure my daughter. Don't force her because the more you force it the more resistant she will be."

That was an understatement.

"Baby…Just be patient. Tonight I planned a special dinner and everything for us."

"What about my dick? It wants to eat, too. And not any head. I wanna be inside you."

Sax shook with anger and frustration. He never cheated on his wife but every day women threw good pussy at him and he turned it down because he was faithful to this stuck up bitch-of-a-wife. And what thanks did he get? Misery. This was crazy. He lived once and he did not WANT TO DIE A GODDAMN VIRGIN AND HE WOULDN'T!

*Even if I gotta pay for pussy.*

"I love you."

Sax was quiet, wiping his eyes. Men didn't cry.

"I love you too. I won't be home tonight. I'm staying at your parent's house."

He hung up in her face.

Completely devastated over Tommy, Jadish pulled up into her driveway. She understood her husband was just mad and he was ego tripping.

She unlocked her door and took a quick shower, getting Tommy's blood off her. Once she was done, she dried off and put lotion on her body. She eyed the door knob, went over to it and she attempted to put her dripping pussy on it but she decided against it. Tonight, masturbation stopped. The touch of her hand would be replaced with her husband's. The veil had been lifted. The burden was gone. She could now fuck her husband for the first time.

And she couldn't wait…

When Sax's father-in-law pulled up in his drive way Sax's eyes swooped over to the worn-down two door Mustang sitting on four cinder blocks. Sax smiled. He loved old cars. "Nice car. Every time I come over here I look at it."

Lenny worried about Sax. He knew what he was going through. Lenny cut the engine. "I wish I could fix it up, but I know nothing about it."

Sax looked at him. "I do."

Lenny was chuckling, his Adam's apple moving. Yea, right Sax. "About fixing it up?"

Sax smiled. He loved cars as much as he loved his wife. "*Hell* yea."

Lenny was skeptical. "Yea, right. Show me."

Sax felt the challenge. "Sure." He got out of the car and walked over to it, his hand on his chin. He observed it and started to walk around it, analyzing. Hmm. He pulled a small notepad from his back pocket and a pen from his work shirt. His dad-in-law stood in the background, smiling.

"Do you have the yellow pages, sir?"

"Yea, I do. Come inside. Plus your mama-in-law cooked some stewed chicken and cornbread and rice. And we know you're going to attack the pot." Lenny's big ass was rubbing his stomach, anticipating the meal. Sax followed him into the house. Thinking of leaving his wife.

For good.

Tommy staggered from his home, with a towel pressed hard on his dick. He tried to keep his pants pulled up. He debated calling the paramedics but he didn't. He didn't want to be embarrassed. Blood was dried in his hair. He remembered Jadish ferociously beating him in the head with a frying pan. He'd looked in the mirror. Wasn't too bad. Nothing iodine couldn't get rid of.

A black man carried out on stretcher with his dick half bitten off wasn't the image he wanted to project in his neighborhood. Well, not half bitten off. Just Jadish's teeth marks were in it. He felt like shit. She knew the truth and suddenly he feared his life. Jadish's father used to be a Gangsta, a feared one at that. He knew people who still owed him favors and would do *anything* for him if he decided to get back into it. What if Jadish went to him and told him what happened. He'd be a dead man. And he had his whole life to live, things he wanted to accomplish was his main goal. He couldn't let anybody stop it.

*I should leave town!*

He got in his car and his hands shook while putting the key in the ignition. Turning it on, he continued to put pressure on his dick until the blood clotted and he drove himself to Miami Jackson Memorial Hospital. He had a few friends who worked there. One was a doctor and the other was a RN.

His cell phone rang.

Lenny's name flashed from the screen.

Jadish lit some candles. She had them strategically placed all over the house. A few in the kitchen. On the stove she warmed up the meal she had cooked for her man. Fried chicken. Cream corn. Asparagus and vegetable rice. She pulled out her good China. Smiling exotically, she thought of her husband's dreamy eyes and her pussy was wet and she was slowly rubbing her tits and her fingers suddenly gained weight and dropped to her clit and she was massaging her vaginal walls, cooing into the air. She grinded on her fingers, the wetness electrifying her thirst for her man.

*I should do something different. Yea, I think I will. This is a big night for me and my husband. I am going to give him so much pussy he won't know what hit him.*

Smiling, she used her pussy juices and with her index finger she wrote *Jadish* on the plate. She clipped a few roses and set them nicely on the edge of the it.

She felt so giddy. But part of her wondered about Tommy. Was he OK? What the hell! He raped you and you're having empathy flashes for him? Get a grip, Chile. *Who gives a rat's ass about Tommy!* I trusted him. But I love him. *But he violated you.* But he's a giving man. *Shut up, Conscious!* She turned on some Mary J. Blige's "We Ride." She loved Mary. Mary spoke for all women of color, all women in the struggle. She sang for the women who have been up and down. That's what Mary J. Blige meant to her.

And she would share that with her husband.

He took off his shades when the plane was flying into Miami. He pressed some keys on his Blackberry and the name that flashed in his gorgeous face made his heart skip a beat.

*Saxophone Jenkins.*

Jadish was washing a few dishes when the house phone rang."Must be my baby. Seeing if I'm home. I *knew* he would come."

She dried her hands with a dish towel and turned off the water. Walking past the dining table, she picked up the remote and turned down Mary to a dangerously low level. She paused at the end table and looked at her wedding photo for a second. Sax was so fine.

*And he's all mine. I'm gonna make him suck honey off my pussy while fucking me in the ass with a dildo. Hell, yea. I wanna do it all. I'ma kinky bitch and I can finally break free of those nightmares and reclaim my life.*

She took up the phone. "Jadish speaking."

"Hey, Girl."

She narrowed her eyes. "*Who* is this?"

"Philippe."

"Oh my God! *Hey*, boy! How is the family?"

"We're good. Is Sax around? I need to holla at him."

"He's at my Dad's house. Call his cell phone. And call me back. I miss you, man. And did your wife like those pictures I sent her of Sax and I?"

"Girl, it's all she talked about. Now she wants me to take her to Cancun, Mexico."

"You should. Give her some on the beach."

Philippe closed his eyes and thought, *Yea. Not in this lifetime.*

"Cool. We'll do that. I'll be in touch."

"Ok and you…"

He hung up in her face, leaning back on the seat.

The airplane continued to travel without any turbulence.

Tommy rushed through the sliding doors in the Emergency area of the hospital. He was screaming and a few nurses rushed him.

"Sir, what is it?"

"My penis! Someone tried to bite it off."

Several patients were very upset. How did he get to go before them and they were there before he arrived?

Tommy thought about Lenny.

Sax saw Miss. Paulette enter the room from the kitchen. She had on a simple black dress and an apron tied around her hip. She smiled when she saw her handsome, sexy ass son-in-law.

*Jadish looks exactly like her mother.*

She embraced him. "*Hey*, Son."

"Hi, Miss Paulette."

"I didn't know you were here?"

Sax frowned. "Yea. I am."

Lenny cleared his throat and Paulette brushed Sax to the side and she hugged her man. Kissing his lips, he was feeling on her booty and Sax was laughing.

"Ya'll are so nasty," he joked.

"We're in love," Lenny said. He looked into his wife's eyes. "Sax is going to fix up the Mustang."

She looked back at him. "Oh, yea? Good luck. Half of the parts are hard to find. Plus so many bushes and weeds are growing throughout it you might find a few snakes in the carburetor and under the engine. I wouldn't mess with that car if I was you, Son."

Sax opened the phone book. "Really?" he asked rhetorically.

"Yea," Lenny went on, hugging his wife. "We called all over the place for parts."

Sax found a phone number. He took out his cell and called it.

The other line beeped with *Philippe Laagers* in the screen but he didn't see it.

"Bob's Junk Yard."

"Yes, how are you, Sir?"

"Who are you talking to?" Lenny wondered.

Paulette said, "No stores have the parts, Son."

"I know," Sax said. He held up his hand at them. They tucked their chins back with a smile.

"What parts do you have for an '85 Mustang?"

"I have them all. Pricey but affordable."

"Good. How soon can I come by and check it out?"

Lenny's eyes were wide.

Paulette said, "Who *are* you talking to?"

"You can come tonight. We close at about 7 p.m. It's 6 o'clock now."

"Lenny and I will probably be by tomorrow morning." Sax put a thumb up with questionable eyes. Smiling, Lenny put two thumbs up confirming the scheduled date.

"Cool. And your name is?"

He looked into Paulette's eyes. "Sax."

Tommy was told to take off his clothes and to put on the polka dot gown. As part of an emergency measure, one of the doctors put antiseptic and a bandage around his penis. The bleeding stopped. The doctor told him the wounds weren't life threatening, and he'd live. He could still urinate, have sex and do what he do with his penis. He could breathe again. Tommy smiled, but on the inside he was a wreck.

*What was I thinking? I can't believe I drugged Jadish's drink and raped her. Was I not in control? Should I go to Lenny myself and tell him the truth? Should I call the police and tell them what happened?* He felt safe right now. The hospital had skin-tight security so he didn't worry about anything. Did Jadish tell Lenny what happened? This burned him up because he just had to know.

*Oh, God. The suspense is killing me. I don't wanna say too much if Jadish didn't say anything yet. If she keeps quiet I will keep quiet.*

He picked up the hospital phone and called Lenny's cell.

God please don't let the shit hit the fan.

He sighed. His room door opened and two uniformed cops walked inside.

"Are you Tommy?"

The American Airlines plane landed in Miami at approximately 7:40 p.m. When he grabbed his attaché case, he put back on his glasses. He had serious jet lag.

He slid his Blackberry into his pocket and made his way towards the Budget Car rental place. With Sax on his mind.

"Hello, how are you, Sir?" the woman said, wearing a God-awful black dress. Her hair was thrown into a bun, and thick braces were on yellowing teeth.

"I'm good. I'm here to pick up a rental car."

"Have you already made a reservation?"

He pulled out his I.D. from his wallet. "Yea."

She took it and began typing his information into the computer. His Blackberry rang. He looked at the caller I.D.

It was his wife.

He slid the phone back in his pocket.

Sax was eating some food. He told Jadish's mother that the reason why he didn't want a lot of food was because Jadish cooked for him. And part of him wanted to go home to his own house and be with his wife.

*If only she fucks me. It's going on two and a half years. How many Niggahs would have stayed with their wives if they refused to give up the panties? Not many. Hell, if any I should say.*

Lenny sat in the Lazy Boy, barking at ESPN. Sax set the plate down. "I'll be back. Gotta use the bathroom."

Lenny was so into the sports channel that he didn't hear him.

Sax thought about Jadish. He wanted to go home but his heart wasn't right.

*I need a diversion. I can't go home and be with a woman who doesn't even respect me. I have been a gentleman. I never rushed her or tried to force her. But she refuses to love me. I want to have sex. I don't wanna die a lonely virgin who didn't get three minutes playing time in some pussy. Coach, put me in the game. I'm tired of giving my ass to the bench. The bench has fucked me more than I fucked my wife. I want to run out of bounds on that pussy.*

*Coach, give her my balls so I can give her an orgasm.*

Sax opened the front door, without telling his In-laws good-bye, and the house phone rang. He noticed that his mom-in-law was in the bathroom and Lenny refused to move. So he left the door ajar, walking through the living room. He looked at the caller I.D.

It read *Miami Jackson Memorial Hospital*. He answered.

Tommy asked, "Where is Lenny," as the cops stood by the bed with note pads and smiles.

*OK, they aren't here to arrest me. If they were they would be looking at me sternly.*

Sax looked at Lenny. "He's...out."

Tommy hung up.

Sax stared at the phone.

*Why is Tommy calling from the hospital?*

Sax left, getting in his car.

Jadish was in the bathroom. The bubbles went flat and the bath water has turned cold. She drained the tub, ran more warm water and put in some Mr. Bubbles. Sax loved bubbles crackling on his nuts.

He once told her that. It was something that followed him since childhood. She smiled, lighting more candles. The ones she lit previously have burned out. Particularly because they were too little. She should have bought the more expensive ones.

Sitting on the toilet, she glanced at the small boom box. Zhane's CD was on cue. "La La La" would be the first song she wanted him to hear. There was an envelope entitled "Mr. Jenkins" leaning against the tub.

Picking up the scented envelope, she slowly took out the letter, smelling the light perfume and pussy radiating from the page. Setting the envelope on the sink, she unfolded the note and read it over. Making sure there were no misspellings or mistakes.

Everything had to be perfect.

*Hello, baby! How are you doing today? I hope this little "note" found you in the best of health and good spirits. I know you're fed up with the fact that you haven't boned your wife yet. Bitter pill to swallow, I know. But this is only temporary. I compiled a little list, which I'm typing right now. You have to do everything on the list so lie back in the tub, relax, smile and be to yourself and your thoughts. Forget about church today, even though it's Sunday. We need alone time. Please don't fight me on this. While you relax, I want you to think about your past. Do you remember how we first me? Do you remember the first words we said to each other? I can remember when you first smiled. I nearly fell down the stairs at the Convocation Building on the University of Miami College campus. Do you remember that? Do you remember our bond? Reflect. The glow and the warmth of the candles should dig silence in your head, allowing you to open-mindedly engulf everything you feel for me. The incense and the gentle smell should open the deepest part of you, a part you thought was forever sealed, and you should let what comes out walk out so you can examine it and hope it makes you a better person. It should allow you to flow with what I'm doing for you. The bubbles in the tub and the warmth of the water, mixed with some edible oil should make your skin soft and collaborate with your being able to allow yourself to let your special Day engross you. I went all out for this day, pulled out all the stops. I know you work 6 days a week and you come home drained and tired. Today is your day, baby.*

*Let go your inhibitions. Let go of your problems. Forget that people exist in the world. When you hear my voice let the universe cease to exist. The only two people that exist are you and I. The bathroom is the Meditation, Release Room. Utilize it. Let go of imposing bills. I'm cutting your phones off. The special request goes as listed below:*

5) *Open the envelope titled: Mr. Jenkins, leaning against the wall on the front of the tub. You should be facing it.*

6) *Secondly, listen the Zhane songs "La La La," and "Off my Mind." Listen to the words. That's how I feel about you.*

7) *Then listen to Mary J Blige's "Beautiful Ones." And "All I have to Say." "Beautiful Ones" embody everything I feel for you. When I hear this song I think about you.*

8) *Then put in the PM Dawn CD and listen to "Die Without you" from the Boomerang soundtrack. This used to be my "cry" song. When I was depressed I'd play this to cry to.*

*I know in my heart you are my soul mate. Life is too short for all the fighting and arguing and fussing and alienation.*

*By now you should know you have a beautiful best friend who thinks the world of you and would do anything for you.*

*Sincerely,*

*Jadish Houston. Your wife.*

Yes. It was perfect.
    She picked up her cell phone and called him.

Sax pulled up into Tommy's front yard and killed the engine. Getting out, he closed the door and looked over the home. Something wasn't right. He felt it. Walking up the sidewalk, he approached the front door. He knocked. Nothing. The house was dark, the glow of the TV came from his bedroom. He tried the knob. The door opened. His phone rang and he answered it.

"Hey, Sax. Where are you?"

"I had to make a stop. I'm coming." Wish I was coming in your pussy, you selfish bitch! "Just keep the food warm. I'll be there."

"OK. I love you. Tonight changes everything, Sax."

*Surely does. Because I'm leaving you.*

*Right after I eat dinner.*

Tommy was looking at the cops. "What brings you by?"

"One of the doctors said that someone tried to bite your penis off."

The short, blonde-haired cop asked, "Who was she? What exactly happened?"

*So Jadish didn't squeal.*

*Good.*

Sax went inside, closing and locking the door. Why did Tommy call from a hospital? The question has burned through his mind. He turned on the living room lamp. The place was a mess. Empty beer cans here and there. Overflowing ash trays. *Ugh! A grown man shouldn't be living this filthy!*

He looked in the dining room and an open bottle of lotion lay on the floor. One of the dining room chairs was angled about four feet away from the table.

He went into Tommy's room, snooping. The room hadn't been cleaned. Tommy was a slob.

He opened the nightstand and looked through open condom wrappers and other bullshit. He opened the bottom cabinet and saw photo albums.

He took one of them out and opened it.

He frowned at the red X's crossed over the faces.

"Oh my *God!* Jadish dreamed of a man with a big red X over his face chasing her."

*It now made sense.*

Jadish looked at her watch. It was going on 8 p.m. Where were you, Sax? She could only warm up the food so many times. She was starting to get the point. Sax wasn't coming home. Her heart burned. She hoped she didn't prepare all that food for nothing. Get a clue, Jadish. The man wants to fuck his wife, not eat any food.

What if he's with another woman?

Nah. He's with my Daddy. She picked up the phone and called her father. He didn't answer. She called again. Her Mom answered.

"Hey, Baby."

"Hi, Mom. Is Sax there?"

"Yes. He's eating. I'll go get him. Hold on."

*I knew I could trust him. He's a very sweet man. And I have been unfair to him. He has a right to make love to his wife. I've been so plagued with nightmares that it didn't make sense. Now it's over. Tommy will pay for what he did to me.*

She sat on the couch and turned on the TV. Deciding to watch an episode of *Extreme Makeover. Damn, Ma. What's taking you so long?*

"Baby, I'm back...Sax is gone."

Tears filling her eyes, she hung up the phone.

Sax closed the photo album, setting it on the bed. He grabbed his keys and went back out into the living room. Just as he walked past the low table something caught his eye. He walked over to the lotion bottle and got on one knee, looking it over.

He tried to ignore the uneaten KFC on the table, and three ashtrays overflowing with more cigarette butts.

He blinked a few times. A frying pan with dried blood on it was on the floor next to an empty Coke bottle.

*Tommy hates Coke. He never drinks Coke.*

*Jadish lives for Coca-Cola products...*

*Why is blood on the floor, chair, frying pan and the bottle?*

And why was one of Jadish's earrings glittering under the chair?

Sax called the hospital from his cell phone. He went through a series of automated prompts, which got on his nerves. He pressed "0" for Operator.

"I wish to speak with a Tommy Bullard."

"Is he an employee or patient?"

"A patient."

"Hold, please..."

"OK." Why was Tommy admitted into the hospital? Did Lenny know?

What was going on? He knew the frying pan, Coke bottle and his wife's earring told a story.

What was it? He would get to the bottom of it.

"Yes. He's a patient here..."

Sax held his chest. "What room number is he in?"

"Room 567."

"Thank you."

He hung up, running out of the house.

Lenny turned off the TV, standing up. He felt a weird sensation in his gut but before he could give it much thought it dissipated into nothingness.

"Why would Sax leave without telling us good bye?"

"He probably went home to his wife."

"Yea, I suppose. But that's not like him to just up and leave. Especially after we spent the day together fishing and shit."

"What did you catch?"

"Some panties, high heels and fledgling clits," he joked and she didn't find it funny.

"Watch it, Lenny."

He hugged her. "Ah, Baby. I'm just playing. You know this is your dick."

"Whatever."

Lenny kissed her lips and squeezed her ass. She melted from his touch. She gave him some tongue.

"I'm about to shower," she said. "Wanna join me?"

"Yea. Get the water started."

She kissed his cheek, walking towards the bathroom. The phone rang. Why did Miami Jackson Memorial Hospital come up on the Caller I.D. screen? He picked up the phone.

"Hello."

"Hey, Lenny."

"Tommy?"

"Yea, Man. What's up with you?"

"I'm about to go hop in the shower with my wife. Why are you…?"

"Well, go handle your business. I'm at a party, having a good time. Brandisha's here."

Lenny narrowed his eyes. "Really?"

Tommy laughed nervously. "Yea. She says *hi.*"

"Let me talk to her feisty ass."

"She just walked off. But I just called to see how you are doing."

"Cool." Lenny hung up. He sat on the chair, thinking to himself. Why did Tommy call him from a hospital? Easy. He said he was at a party. At a hospital? Yes. OK, if that were true, then why did he say Brandisha said "Hi?" Maybe she did. Well, she must be a ghost because Brandisha died two years ago from breast cancer.

So how in the hell did she say "Hi?"

*Tommy, what's going on?*

Sax called Lenny. It took him a moment to answer.

"Hey, Son."

"Have you heard about Tommy being admitted into the hospital?"

Lenny jumped up from the chair. "My boy is in the hospital?"

"Yes. Room 567."

"Thanks for letting me know."

Lenny hung up, and went into the bathroom with his wife.

Jadish was in the shower, soap all over her body. She was so distraught, she failed to think logically. She didn't want to lose her sexy husband, but in her heart she knew it was already too late. Too much has been done. It was beyond repair. She threw away the food and she trashed the candles. She ripped up the note.

*He doesn't love my anymore. And it's all my fault.*

She was scrubbing the perfume and expensive lotion from her body. She felt like a fool.

*I started this mess. He's a good man.*

*I should have known he wouldn't wait forever!*

Lenny entered his bathroom, enveloped in warm, moist steam. He pulled back the shower curtain, looking over his wife. She had soapy bath foam trailing her curvaceous body. He took a moment to look her over.

"Are you getting inside?" she asked, licking her lips. She faced him, her tits perky and ready for the taking.

"I gotta step out for a minute. I want some…ice cream."

She frowned at him. "Ice cream?" She narrowed her eyes. "This time of night?"

"Yes, Baby."

"Ok, Joseph Jackson. Who is she?"

"No, Baby. It's not a she. I want some ice cream."

She slapped him with the soapy rag. "There's ice cream in the freezer, jack ass."

"I don't want nuts in my ice cream."

She chocked, smiling. "OK, boo. But hurry back."

"I'll hurry back, Baby. I promise."

She wrapped her arms around him, sucking on his neck. He pushed back a tad. "You're getting my clothes wet."

"I'm putting hickies all over your neck so a bitch knows you're taken…"

His eyes rolled to the back of his head.

Thirty-eight minutes later, Sax pressed the elevator button. Once it opened, he boarded it and pressed "5". He hated elevators. His heart pounding, he closed his eyes. Something wasn't right in his soul. Why was Jadish's earring under Tommy's chair?

Why?

Two cops were leaving as Sax walked into Tommy's room. When Tommy saw Sax he grew wearily quiet.

"Hey, Tommy." Sax threw a teddy bear at him.

Tommy caught it.

"I guess I should say thanks."

"Nah, you don't have to. Nice wrap on your head. Somebody hit you with a frying pan?"

Tommy was quiet, looking over the bear. "I always liked Curious George."

"That's why I bought the Curious George teddy. Figured you were…curious."

"Why are you here?"

"Talk to me, Tommy," Sax said, sitting down in the chair. He turned off the TV.

"About?"

"Um, life. Let's connect as boys. In the beginning we got off to a slow start."

"Yea. Until you blamed me for the cob webs and tumble weeds in your bedroom."

"I didn't blame you."

"Sure you did. You think me and Jadish got something going on."

"Do you? Is there something I should know?"

"You can't handle a woman of Jadish's caliber."

"Oh, yea?"

"A woman like that you have to fuck daily, to keep her tamed."

"And how do you know?"

"I don't, shit. I would like to know."

Sax was brooding. "I'm not gonna let you get to me."

"Well, the door knob gets to your wife. Tell me something, Sax."

"Shoot."

"Something is wrong when your wife will fuck a door knob and not her husband."

"It's deeper than that."

"Really."

"Yes. It's like those huge red X's on the faces in your picture book."

Tommy grew pensive then. "How do you know?"

"I just left your house."

"You went through my shit?"

"*Yea.* Figured you needed a house keeper. I mean, my wife's earring was under your dining room chair. And an open lotion bottle was on the floor."

"Stay outta my crib."

"Why was her earring...?"

"Like I said, a woman like that needs to be fucked daily..."

"And you say that because..."

"Let's just say Jadish has been watching High School Musical."

"Meaning..."

"She keeps her...head in the game. Ask her. She sucked my dick today, and man let me tell you, Sax was the last thing on her mind..."

A trail of cool air blew over Sax's neck. But he didn't think about it because, angrily, he stood up. About to bash Tommy's head in.

"Why are you trying me, Tommy? Should I go get the cops? Bring them back in here? So we can all talk?"

Tommy was suddenly guarded. "Why should I do that?"

"Because you drugged my wife on her graduation night. You fucked her senseless, Tommy. Come on, Man. Let's not play around anymore."

Tommy cringed inside.

*Damn it! He does know! I gotta do damage control.*
*I can't afford for this to get out.*

"I didn't do no such thing, Sax."

Sax sat on the edge of the bed, smiling down at him. "Oh, yea? Why did she wake up with blood all over her? Why was she having those nightmares, of the man with a big red X over his face chasing her through open fields and her high school before he raped her in the middle of the ocean floor after the Red Sea split?"

"Sax, you're accusing me of something unconscionable."

Sax played around with the strap on Tommy's medical gown. "You're right. It was unconscionable what you did. She trusted you. You've been in love with her for years, haven't you? How have you groomed her?"

"Groomed her?"

"Yea. How did you groom her?" Sax stood up, toying with his cell phone.

"I don't know what you're talking about."

"Let me use words from the NiggahCology Dictionary. How did you fatten the Hen before you slaughtered her for Thanksgiving?"

"Sax you're starting to piss me off."

"I know how, Tommy. You were there for her. You offered her your shoulder to cry on. You granted her things her Daddy disapproved of. You read her diary and supported her decisions. You told her she was beautiful and she could do anything."

Tommy was weakening. He wanted to bash Sax's head in. He was in the danger zone and he better trek cautiously.

"Shut up, Sax!"

"Am I right? You warned her of the big bad men in the world. If they promised her the stars grip her panties and run like hell. But what you didn't tell her was that you would be the one to destroy her. You selfishly fucked my wife all night long while she was unconscious, and you should pay."

"It's your word against mine."

"I'm going to tell her."

"She won't believe you..."

"Why shouldn't she?"

"You're just mad because I fucked her and you haven't. Dumb Niggah. You been married to her for over two years and all you did was scratch and sniff the pussy. You virginal asshole."

"You're pissing me off, Rapist."

"So how do you explain Jadish's earring on my dining room floor? She sucked my dick. She knew to bring the pussy to Daddy. Poor, poor Sax. She made me come so fast she swallowed my shit, moaning my name. Begging me to fuck her from the back. But I thought about you and told her I couldn't... You'll die a lonely virgin. How pathetic! You're a bitch ass Niggah. As Puff Daddy says, I don't have time for your Bitchassness, Dawg. I should make you suck my dick, Punk!"

Sax was so upset he walked over to the EKG machine and snatched the cords from the wall. Tommy tried to lash out at him, but Sax punched him in the rib cage, jumping in the bed. They were wallowing, both falling on the floor.

The cool trail of air stopped flowing on Sax's neck. Two nurses ran into the room, both males, and one grabbed Sax and the other grabbed Tommy. "Call Security on his ass," Tommy shouted. "Putting your hands on me."

"No, call the police," said Sax, trying to push the nurse off him. "He raped my fucking wife, you sack of shit!"

"You two need to calm down," said the thick, stocky nurse. "Larry" was on his name tag. He pushed Sax to one side of the room. The other nurse, "James," pushed Tommy to the other side of the room.

Tommy said, "I am going to shoot your ass, Niggah!"

"Oh, yea? I should shoot your rapist ass, you sick bitch. Why did you rape my wife motherfucker?"

James said, "Calm down you two. I'm not getting in the middle of this, but I will call security on you man if you jump on the patient again."

Sax said, "No need. I'm going to talk to the police."

Sax walked out of the room, burning with rage.

*So, Jadish…you sucked Tommy's dick?*

Jadish was on the sofa, Maxwell singing into her ears. But she didn't know it because she was sound asleep, the candles on the end table slowly burning out.

And the TV flashing in her face.

Sax was burning rubber in his car. When he turned onto the 836— West Expressway, he whipped out his cell phone. Tears were in his eyes but he refused to cry. The nerve of Tommy! He had to be lying on his wife. Jadish would never give him head. She wouldn't touch him with a ten foot pole. Or would she? You couldn't put anything past a bitch these days. If it quacked the pussy would duck it.

He attempted to call his wife but he hung up, putting the phone on the seat. He didn't know how he felt. Tommy's words replayed in his head.

*You virginal asshole.*

*So how do you explain Jadish's earring on my dining room floor?*

*She sucked my dick. She knew to bring the pussy to Daddy.*

*Poor, poor Sax. She made me come so fast she swallowed my shit, moaning my name. Begging me to fuck her from the back. But I thought about you and told her I couldn't…*

*You'll die a lonely virgin.*

*How pathetic!*

*You're a bitch ass Niggah. As Puff Daddy says, I don't have time for your Bitchassness, Dawg.*

*I should make you suck my dick, Punk!*

"Jadish, I hope to God he's lying. Because if he isn't, then I am leaving you forever."

Just then the phone rang.

He answered it with an attitude.

"WHAT?"

"Damn, Homie. It's *Philippe*."

Sax was ecstatic. He slowly put on the brakes, changing lanes. "Oh my God! Is that my Dawg? My Niggah? My Homie from college?"

"Yea, Man. It's me. Long time."

Sax was about to burst with joy. "Hell, yea! It's been a long time. Where are you?"

"I'm in the Marriot Hotel by the Dadeland Mall."

"You're in town? And you didn't call me?"

"I called your wife, but she said you were out," he said.

"Man I'm coming to see you right now!"

"Where are you?"

"I'll see you in about twenty minutes. What room are you in?"

"Call me when you arrive. I'm at the bar. Let's have some drinks and get caught up on everything."

"I'm on my way, Niggah. Goddamn! My motherfucking Homie is in town."

Sax hung up. Smiling.

Tommy was being checked by Dr. Williams, an old, black man from South Carolina.

"Well, you're in good health, Tommy."

"Thanks."

"I would advise you to take it easy. Your head is fine. We ran a CAT scan. Everything looks normal. As for your penis. There wasn't any damage. May I make a suggestion?"

"Yes, Doctor."

"Treat the ladies with respect. If you don't...you may not get teeth next time."

They chuckled. Lenny walked into the room, with a small purple, suede bag in his hand. A bottle of E&J protruded from it.

Lenny shook Tommy's hand. "Sup, Niggah."

The Dr. said, "If you will excuse me..." and he left the room.

Sax pulled up into the Marriot Hotel and a valet parked his car. Graciously he thanked the man and made his way to the front lobby. A very gorgeous black woman greeted him. "Where's your bar?"

She smiled. "Donna, can you watch the front desk." She shook Sax's hand. "Follow me. I'll show you where it is."

Sax looked at her ass the entire time.

When they got there, Sax's mouth fell open. What a bar. It was very clean and classy and he especially drooled over that because a clean bar was like a clean pussy. Pussy always came to clean bars and he had a clean bar to stick in pussy and that pussy could come, come, come all over the bar, the floors of the nuts and drip down his asshole to keep it consoled, soothed and satisfied.

Suffice it to say, this bar was a little dark, but the dimming of the lights made it look mysterious.

Loving her perfume, Sax shook her hand. It was soft. "Thanks."

"No problem," she said, tugging on her skirt. She looked at him a little too long. Smiling again, Sax pivoted on his heel, walking over to the bartender. The last thing she saw was the gleam from his wedding ring.

*Damn! He's married!*

Sax sat on a stool, looking around. There were about twenty or so people present, and most of them had on suits and classy dresses. Very adult. Sax liked it. He looked over his shoulder and saw an empty table, towards the back.

*Maybe he went to the bathroom.*

Sax stood up, walking over to the table. He thought about his life and his wife. He loved Jadish so much. But she had to learn that when you found love you nurtured it, you didn't become a selfish bitch. He waited two plus years to make love to his wife. Not his girlfriend. Not his fiancé. But his wife! And he couldn't wait any longer.

He sat down at the table and folded his hands, lowering his head. He bit back tears, a fire erupting in the pit of his stomach. His skin was hypersensitive. Everybody and everything was turning him on. Temptation called his name everywhere he went.

*I don't know how much more of this shit I can take.*

Checking his watch, he was startled when he saw Philippe sitting in front of him, smiling.

"Is that my boy Sax?"

Sax gushed with excitement. "Oh my God!" They slapped palms, jumped up to their feet and embraced, patting each other's back. *In five seconds Philippe has shown me more love and affection than my wife has in two plus years, Lord.*

"It's been years, bruh!" Philippe loved his cologne. *What kind of fragrance are you wearing, Sax?*

*Don't let me go, Philippe.* "I haven't seen you since we graduated college."

Reluctantly, they pulled away, looking each other over. They could not break the gaze. Philippe had arrestingly gorgeous eyes. Pupils that ignited his irises and made for good *aqueous* humor.

"Well damn, bruh," said Philippe, his eyes sparkling. "You put on a few pounds."

"Well, you know," Sax joked, chuckling. "I'm a man now." *And you look good yourself.*

Philippe let the words settle in his ears. "Yes you are. At least it's not fat."

"I know, right! I acquired muscle, and I do watch what I eat." *Except when I'm eating pussy, but my wife is acting stank with that as well.*

"I do that sometimes myself, even though my wife love piling on the food."

"You don't look a day over 20, bruh."

"Well, I'm reaching the thirty mark in a couple years. A Niggah isn't looking forward to pushing up daisies anytime soon."

"Don't even mention daisies. You remind me that I'm right behind you pushing up roses."

Philippe shook his hand. "Ha, ha…how about a drink. My treat."

They tightened their grip, not letting each other's hand go. "Ok. Because I need one." Sax's voice lost its luster and Philippe noticed.

Philippe searched Sax's face. "Are you ok, bruh?"

Sax averted his face. *Can't give anything away. He's in town for a few days. I can't burden him with my problems. Why should I?* "Yea, I'm good. So how's your wife."

Philippe lowered his head and faked a smile. *What do I say?* "She's ok."

"Go order the drinks and we'll get caught up," Sax said, sitting down.

"All right. What do you want?" Philippe asked, pulling out his wallet loaded with plastic Visa cards.

"Buy the whole bottle of Grey Goose."

"Got'cha."

Philippe made his way to the bar and Sax lowered his head.

*I stood up my wife. What kind of husband was I? I'm in pain. She stood me up for years. Making me think we were going to make love and she chickens out because of those nightmares. But now that the secret is out, now that she knows that Tommy slipped drugs in her drink and raped her, maybe we can get back on track. Nah. Psychologically my wife is probably fucked up and we need to seek professional help.*

*But she won't do it.*

And Philippe. He looks as good as ever. That's my best friend right there. I love the hell out of him. We met in college, when he was going through a divorce at 19 years old. He was married to an older woman who treated him more like her son than her husband. He had a good job and she was on public assistance with four grown children older than Philippe. She only married him for his money. I was passing by the little park by the University Metro Rail Station when I saw him. The University of Miami loomed behind me. He was sitting on a bench with his head hanging low. What gravitated me towards him was the sadness on his face.

Why was the brothah so sad?

"Are you ok, bruh?" I asked, sitting by him.

His eyes were red. He had Grey Goose in a McDonald's cup, and from the looks of it he was intoxicated.

"No. I'm not, man. And who are you?" he asked, glaring at me.

I extended my hand. "I'm Sax. I go to school here."

"So do I," he said, reluctantly shaking my hand. "I would suggest you leave."

"Why?"

"I'm not in the best of moods, bruh. I'm getting divorced."

"You are?"

He turned away from me. "Yea."

"How old are you?"

"Nineteen," he answered, sighing.

"Damn. And you're married already?"

"It's complicated."

"I would imagine."

"Have you ever been in love?" he asked with an attitude, glaring at me maliciously.

"I can't say that I have. Women are weird asses and I can't figure them out."

He chuckled. "Isn't that the truth? I was married for eight months. She's 43. And she has four grown sons who are twenty-eight, twenty-nine and thirty."

My eyes bulged out of my head. "Wow. So you're the nineteen year old step Daddy running shit."

He laughed, and that's what I wanted to see. "She runs me. She runs my paycheck, she runs my car and she is so demanding. If I don't do what she says she doesn't cook or clean up and her sons rally against me, trying to jump on me. I fought them three times already."

"That's not love, bruh. When you have to go through that, love is gone."

"That's why I'm getting a divorce…so you go to school here?"

"Yea."

"Cool, how long have you been going here?"

*"I started this year."*

*"Me, too. Do you live in the dorms?"*

*"No. I'm from here so I don't have to."*

*"Do you have a number I can reach you?"*

*And we exchanged numbers.*

Sax smiled when Philippe set the bottle on the table, and two small glasses loaded with ice. "You were daydreaming?" Philippe asked chummily.

"Yea. Are you going to ask me what about?"

"No." Philippe sat down, taking off his suit jacket. His chest was a lot fuller than it was in college, when all the women chased after him. Every day Philippe had new pussy on his tongue or on his dick. When Sax and Philippe finally did get an apartment together during their second year of college, Sax had to buy ear plugs because Philippe was fucking Hoes regularly.

*And I still haven't had sex yet.*

Lenny sat in the chair next to Tommy. Tommy, lying in the bed, with his street clothing on, sighed and said, "I had a bad accident, man."

"So that's why you didn't call me and let me know you're in the hospital?"

Tommy wouldn't look him in the eyes. "Yes. I didn't want you to worry."

"Now I'm as worried as ever. Was your car totaled?"

"Yes," Tommy lied.

"So that explains why you lied about being at a party at the hospital…"

"I'm sorry, man. I lied because I didn't want you stressing out over me."

"That's my decision, and you're my best friend. My family loves you and whatever they love I gotta protect at all costs."

Lenny lowered his head, holding back his grief. A lot was churning through his mind and he didn't know what to think about anything. "How long have we been road dogs?"

"A very long time," said Lenny.

"Seems like centuries."

"You are the only man I ever brought around my family. I love you like a brother. In a lot of ways you are my brother. We have always had each other's back. We have always been there for each other. We could tell each other any and everything, no matter how big or small, no matter how good or bad." Lenny looked up, his eyes tired and red. "Want something to drink? I bought some E&J."

"Sure."

Lenny opened the huge paper bag and pulled out two plastic cups. He set the ice in the sink, ripping open the bag. He put in three ice cubes and poured Tommy something to drink. He handed it to him.

"Thanks."

"No problem."

Lenny poured himself something to drink and replaced the cap on the bottle. Sliding the bottle back into the purple velvet bag, he then put it in the paper bag on the floor.

He set his drink on the little counter behind him. "Are they letting you go home tonight?"

"Yea. Even though my head is killing me." Tommy wolfed down the drink, and wanted more. Lenny handed him the other cup. Lenny didn't want the drink anymore, Tommy could have it. Tommy wolfed it down.

"Are you sure you're ok, Man?"

"Yes, Lenny." Tommy turned on the TV.

"I know you like a book."

"Depends on what book you're reading. I'm not the Color Purple tonight. Cellie has left the building."

"Ha. Dear Tommy? What book are you?"

"Dear Lenny. I'm *The Silence of the Lambs.*"

"Oooh. Hannibal."

"Yea."

"I gotta get out of here. I have an angry wife at home who keeps blowing up my phone. I told her I was going out to get ice cream."

"And you haven't gotten it?" Tommy asked, laughing.

Lenny fell silent for a brief moment. "No. I said that so I could come see why you're in the hospital. I didn't want her worrying about you."

Tommy's brows rose. "Does Jadish know I'm in here?"

"No," Lenny said. "I didn't tell her."

Tommy was relieved. "Good. Good."

Lenny cupped Tommy's hand. "So I'll see you tomorrow. You are checking out tonight, right?"

"Yea."

"Here," said Lenny, handing him the bottle of E&J. "You can keep this. Drink up. I can't drink all this shit, plus I'm driving home."

"Thanks, man."

Lenny was walking to his car, thinking to himself. *Why didn't my best friend call me the second he got to the hospital? That isn't like him. I know this man more than I know myself. I used to be a goon, I know these things. I know the streets; I can be a goblin when I wanna be. I will tote those guns; I will blast those lights if something isn't clear to see.*

Lenny reached his car and unlocked it. When he opened the door his eyes landed on another car and his mouth fell open.

It was Tommy's car.

And it wasn't totaled.

*I hate motherfucking liars!*

Sax and Philippe had one too many drinks. They were laughing, talking about the happenings in the news. A few people left the bar, heading to their rooms. And once the clock struck ten p.m. they were the last two in the bar.

"So, why didn't you bring your wife down here to great ole Miami?" Sax asked, popping peanuts in his mouth.

"She's back at home, holding it down. She gotta handle our affairs there."

Sax was silently chewing. "So…how's your son? I know he's getting big."

"Yea, he is."

Sax swallowed the peanuts. "I bet he looks just like his Daddy."

"Yea he does. I talked to him earlier. He wants to talk to you."

"Well, call him up!"

"He's sleeping. He has school tomorrow, remember."

"Oh, yea. I remember back in the days Mama made me go to bed at 9 p.m. every night, even on weekends."

"Taught you how to be punctual didn't it?"

"Yea…"

Philippe had a thought. "How's Jadish? I called her tonight, asking for you."

Sax's frown crashed on the table, literally. He hesitated with his answer. "She's…selfish."

They fell quiet. "Selfish, *how?*"

Sax was laughing, but inside his heart was slowly corroding. "I've been married over two years and she still hasn't made love to me."

Philippe's eyes were wide. "What? Are you fucking me right now?"

"I wish I was. Then maybe I'll finally get some ass."

"She hasn't made love to you, man?"

"No." Sax drank his seventh glass of Grey Goose and wanted another. His eyes were narrowed and he felt good to finally get that out.

"So what did you do on your honeymoon?"

"The selfish bitch jacked my dick, made me come and rolled over and went to sleep."

"Why? I didn't take Jadish for the selfish type."

"Don't get me wrong. She's a very compassionate woman. But when it comes to her pussy she's the Queen of the Damned."

"Man…so Akasha ain't coming off the pussy."

"Basically." *Akasha was one of the characters from Anne Rice's Queen of the Damned book.* "And Aaliyah's dead so there goes Jadish's pussy."

"Well, I have a confession to make," Philippe said, looking into Sax's eyes.

"What?"

"My wife and I are getting a divorce."

"Wow. Oh my God. Man. Why?" Sax sat up straight, pouring another drink. He refilled Philippe's glass.

"She's in love with someone she met in high school. An old flame has rekindled in her loins and she wants him. He calls her up and says he has Cancer and it's like she dropped me and our son to rush to his aide, and somewhere along the line they made love and she wants to be with him until his dying day."

Sax was stunned. "Whoa."

"Yea. She traded in our wedding vows for the leukemia patient."

"Wow, man. So I guess we're both…"

"In the same boat. I haven't made love to my wife in ten months. Ten, dawg. I'm faithful to her. Back in college I wasn't faithful at all. I fucked women left and right."

"I know. I was late to half my classes the next morning because of it. A Niggah couldn't sleep because the bitches were 'Ahh, yea, fuck me in the ass, Daddy!' all damn night…"

"You're a trip, Homie."

"I'm in love with a woman who won't let me fuck. Isn't that one of the quirks of marriage? To get pleased at home so you don't have to pay for pussy in the streets?"

"That's what I heard. But men pay for it whether they like it or not."

"I haven't."

"When you pay their rent, lights and water and buy the grocery and buy the gas to cut the lawn and fill up your woman's tank, you're paying for pussy."

"Damn, man. Never thought about it like that…well, I'm done paying. I may be filing for divorce. And I haven't told Jadish yet."

"When are you going to tell her?"

"I might let the lawyer tell her."

"That's the best way to handle it. My lawyer worked out the legalities and everything. I'm letting my wife keep the house so my son keeps a roof over his head and we will split custody."

"Man I know this will be hard on your son."

"It's even harder on me, because I feel like a failure."

Sax took his hands. "What? Why do you feel like a failure?"

"I lost my family. A man isn't a man unless he can build a home and run his household successfully, like a successful business. Sure, sometimes the NASDAQ will drop or crash, but his home is his home and as long as his woman and child is happy and content under one roof then he succeeded. But I failed."

"You're an incredible husband, Dawg. And you are an equally incredible father. Your son loves you. You taught him how to read before he even started Pre-K."

"I surely did."

"And you always treated your wife with love, kindness and respect. I remember when I saw you two get married. Remember?"

"Yea."

"You were glowing, man. You were so happy to be divorced from the older bitch that ran your life that you could barely contain yourself. Your wife has an education and grew up middle class. It doesn't mean she's better than anyone else, it just shows that not all black women grow up in the ghetto."

Philippe rubbed his thumbs over the top of Sax's hands. "Thank you, man. I needed to be reassured…"

"So don't ever say you failed. Your wife failed you. Women want a good man and when they get one they fuck it up with baggage they should have given to the Goodwill before they got married."

"True. And now I'm losing my wife. And I wanna make love. And I can't…"

"I have wants and needs and desires…"

"And fantasies and my wants I have never needed because I never got what I needed and now I am a walking, horny toad and all I want to do is fuck something."

"I want to fuck something my damn self."

"What are you waiting for?"

"What are you waiting for?"

Philippe licked his lips. "The right person."

"But H.I.V. is out there and STD's and I don't have time for all those doctor check ups, unless it's to check my cholesterol."

"I'm getting sleepy, Homie."

"Ok. I gotta get home to Jadish. She cooked me some fancy dinner tonight."

"And you didn't go?"

"No. She stood me up for two plus years. Tonight, she saw just what that felt like."

Philippe stood up, having a little trouble keeping balance.

Sax wrapped his arm around Philippe's waist, helping him to the elevator. *He feels good next to me,* Sax thought quietly.

"I got you, Dawg. What room number are you in?"

"Room 269."

"OK. I'll help you. Then I gotta be getting home."

Philippe's heart dropped. "Thanks, man. I appreciate that."

Sax shook his head. "What are best friends for?"

"Tell that to my wife."

Sax laughed, pressing the elevator button. "Tell that to mine. With her selfish ass."

The elevator doors opened.

Lenny entered his home and closed the door and his wife slapped him.

"Are you cheating on me?" she asked, looking a wreck. She'd been crying and she was about to explode.

"No, baby."

She was punching at him. "Where's the ice cream, liar? I thought you wanted ice cream! Who is she? Oh my God, Lenny! I have been nothing but obedient to you and you go out and…"

Lenny hugged his wife. "Baby, calm down. There isn't another woman. I went to see Tommy in the hospital. He was in a bad car accident."

"Oh my God! Tommy! Is he ok?"

"Yes. I just left there. I stopped by the store and bought him some things and I sat and talked to him for a while. He's being released tonight."

"I'm sorry, baby."

"I forgive you, Honey. I'm man enough to handle you. That's why I married you."

She kissed her husband. "What's in the bag?"

"I had to buy some rat poison. I saw a rat behind the washer."

"Make sure you kill it."

*I already have.*

Jadish awakened with a start. She looked at her watch. It was a little past 11:30 p.m. She stood up, stretching. The TV was blaring so she turned it off.

"Sax!" she called out but there was no answer. Annoyed, she went to the bedroom and he wasn't there. "He still hasn't come home. What have I done? Is it too late? Did I lose my husband?"

Her eyes fell down on the door knob, the one that brought her so much pleasure. There was a magnetic force inside the metal, beckoning her to spread her ass cheeks and back up against it so it could slide up inside her pussy. She actually smiled thinking about it. Running her fingers across the brass, she shook her head and decided against it.

*Tonight I leave the door knob behind and I fuck my husband. I will finally give my husband his pussy. No more door knobs. I have to stop being selfish and nurture my man. He deserves it. After all I did make vows to love him, to cherish him and to nurse him during sickness and in health.*

She called his cell phone.

Tommy was checked out of the hospital. He walked to his car, disoriented. Lenny couldn't find out about what he did to Jadish. He couldn't lose his best friend and he didn't want to go to prison or be labeled a sex offender. When he reached his car he unlocked the door and got inside.

It took him a minute to gather his thoughts. He was rubbing his face, his legs trembling. He really couldn't afford to go to jail. Maybe he should talk to Jadish. What if she called the police when he showed up. No, Tommy. Stay away. Leave her be. She needed to calm down and rethink things. Maybe time and patience was what everybody needed. Yea. That had to be the answer. Let sleeping dogs lie.

*What can I do? I have to do something.*
*If I don't I could be looking at serious prison time.*
He knew what he had to do now.

When Sax got off the elevator, the phone buzzed in his pocket. Philippe said, "Aren't you going to answer that? That's probably your wife."

"I'm getting divorced, remember. I don't have a wife."

Philippe said, "Whatever you decide to do I got your back."

The phone stopped ringing in his pocket.

Deeply disheartened, Jadish threw the phone on the floor. *He's not answering the phone. He's probably mad with me. Oh, Baby. Come home. So I can make it up to you. I can be there for you in that lovingly special way. I can finally make love to you and give you all of me. I can make you a man tonight. For two plus years you've been just a male, now you can be a man and come deep inside your wife.*

*We'll go half on a baby.*

Philippe's head was swimming, but he knew where he was. Feeling the cool air from the AC somewhat mellowed him. The lights on the ceiling fan were very bright. He was glad to be back in his room, where he felt safe. Sax released him, standing up straight. He checked his watch.

"I gotta go, bruh…" His head felt light, and his legs were about to give out. *Oh, God. Can I even drive in this condition? I don't wanna leave Philippe. He's the one bright spot in my life. Maybe I should stay here. Maybe I shouldn't.*

*No.*

*I shouldn't.*

*Because if I don't leave I am going to fuck the shit out of him.*

*Wait, Sax. What are you saying?*

*I'm saying this: I'm in love with Philippe, and I don't know how to tell him.*

*No, you're not. You're just hurt. You're not thinking logically. You are making rash decisions based on the weakness of your flesh.*

*No, I'm not.*

*Yes, you are. You need to leave, go home to your wife and beg for her pussy if you have to.*

*No. Why should I beg for pussy when she's my wife? It should be easy as 1-2-3.*

"I can't let you drive drunken, bruh," Philippe said, taking his hand. Sax looked down at it, his heart hammering. He could barely catch his breath.

*Stop touching me, Niggah. I love the softness of your hand. I love everything about you. I wanna taste that ass.* "I gotta try to get home."

Philippe snatched Sax's keys, and dropped them inside his pants. They pressed against his dick. Philippe pulled Sax closer to him, breathing his air. He could not take his eyes off him. The flames were ignited. The fire was building. "I can't let you, man. What if you get in a crash or something, then I can't live with myself knowing I let you walk out of my hotel door without attempting to stop you. If something happens to you I will go crazy."

"Why will you go crazy? Life goes on."

Tears built in Philippe's eyes. He hated expressing himself. Every time he expressed himself to his selfish wife she laughed at him and made him feel foolish. *Please don't make me feel foolish, Sax!* "I don't want life to go on without you, baby."

*I love your height, your face, and your sincerity.* "I don't want to live without you, either…"

*Go for the juggler, Philippe. Do it, Niggah. He's right here in front of you. He's the reason you boarded a plane spur of the moment and came to Miami. Sax is the reason you don't want to be with your wife anymore. So go for it, goddamn it!* "Stay with me tonight…if not the entire night, just stay for a little while. Be my singing group Jodeci. Let me be your group member, Devante Swing."

Sax was falling deeper into a vortex. *I love the sparkle of your eyes; I love the sun of your smile. The way your dimples form when you lick your lips. The way your lips bend over the tip of the glass when you're drinking.*

"I gotta go, man. Jadish is waiting. Thanks for your concern."

Abruptly, Sax yanked his hand back and turned to face the door.

*I gotta get out of here. Run, Sax, Run! Bubba Gump wants your shrimp and you don't have a shrimp boat, Niggah. You want Jenny, but she's at home, biologically named Jadish Houston. And she has sweet, sweet nectar between her legs. That gushy stuff that makes you a man.*

His tie loosened, Philippe walked in front of him, blocking the door. "Look me in the eyes and tell me you truly want to leave."

"Man, trust me. I don't wanna leave but I have to go. I have to get home to my wife. I made her wait enough. I love her."

"But she doesn't love you. If she loved you, why wouldn't she make love to you on your honeymoon?"

"Because she was making me suffer for another man's mistake."

"That's not love," Philippe said, his lips getting closer to Sax's.

"What is it then?"

"Selfishness. Baggage."

*God, move this man from in front of the door. If his lips touch me I am going to beat his ass to a pulp. I have to do that, Lord. Because I want my dick so far in his ass I want him screaming from the excitement.*

Sax looked away from him. "I'm not going to rush home. I will drive slowly. Why should I rush home to a loveless home? My wife will never make love to me. I will officially die a virgin."

Philippe said, "Sax…Look at me."

"No."

"Come on, Man. Don't do me like this."

"Just leave Jadish out of your mouth."

"I can't. I respect her, yes. But she doesn't respect you, Sax."

"Please!"

Philippe stroked Sax's cheek. "Aren't we boys?"

"Yes, man." *Lord, his touch is setting me on fire. I want his fingers in my mouth.* "Get your hand off me, goddamn it!" *I'm sorry, Philippe. I didn't mean to yell at you. But I will never tell you that.*

Initially hurt, Philippe walked past him, and paused by the bed, taking off his jacket. He dropped it on the floor.

Philippe was shaking his head. *What was I thinking,* Philippe wondered bitterly. *He doesn't want me. Sax isn't even bisexual. I'm the weird one. I shouldn't push my lifestyle on him. And even though I'm not out the closet and my wife doesn't know, I love him too much to lose him.*

Sax closed his eyes, biting back tears. *I can't cry. I'm a man. I have to fight temptation. Philippe is a very gorgeous man. I can't lie. I fantasized about him years ago in college. I once masturbated while I called out his name, but I never acted on those feelings. I was never abused as a kid. I was never raped or anything like that. I had a good life and a very good upbringing. So why did I want to make love to my male best friend?*

Philippe cleared his throat. "Sax, please. Look at me."

Slowly, Sax opened his eyes. He was surprised that the ceiling fan lights were turned down very low. He turned to look at Philippe and his mouth fell open. Philippe stood there.

Clad in his boxers.

H is clothes were at his feet. He was smiling, his eyes sparkling. He'd rubbed baby oil all over his amazing chest, his nipples erect and mouth watering. He looked like a helpless dog searching for food and never finding it.

Sax was blown away.

"*Philippe…*" *I want him, Lord. Forgive me, Father. I have to have him. Just once. Just for tonight. One night, God. One time. The recital and the encore all in one nutshell.*

Desperately, Philippe wrapped his trembling arms around Sax and their lips anxiously and awkwardly touched…then they fell into each other like well-mixed paint. Sax felt vulnerable, melting underneath Philippe's sweet touch. He taste good, the inside of his mouth warm. Sax greedily held Philippe's buttocks, and his tongue dipped from his mouth and trailed his neck. He gave him a few passion marks, taking his time. Careful not to rush or appear needy.

Philippe took Jadish's prize. "If your wife won't give you some ass then I will," Philippe said, smiling inside. "I will give you what you've desired all night long, baby. I am your ocean, give me the shore."

The flood gates inside Sax's flesh burst open. He could no longer contain himself. A sudden sexual knight in shining armor, Sax picked him up and walked to the bed. He was tired of being Repunzel. He was tired of being trapped in the tower. He was going to let down his zipper and explore. He wanted to know what his feet felt like on new soil. He wanted to blaze new terrains and slay new jungles.

Sax gently lay Philippe down and used his teeth to take off his boxers. When Sax saw his penis he was hesitant. He cracked a smile.

*My God! I've never been this hard for my wife. My dick is on brick status. I can actually feel it throbbing in my briefs.*

Then reality struck.

Sax stopped smiling. "What am I doing?" he asked, sitting on the bed, his head hanging low.

"What's wrong?" Philippe asked, putting a pillow under his head.

*I've broken my vows, Lord. I've betrayed you and my wife. I should be stoned do death.* "I've never been with a man before. Where is all this coming from?"

"Maybe it comes from your heart."

Sax looked back at him and couldn't help but smile when he looked in his heavenly eyes.

*But I love him, God. How long have I loved him, who knows? But why was being with another man wrong? Was it really wrong, God? You said in the Bible you want us happy. Well, my wife hasn't made me happy. Philippe has made me happy. I want to cry when I look at him. I want to tell him all my joys, pains and sorrows when he blinks. And now I want to feel his warmth, his tightness.* "Maybe I'm just hurt because my wife doesn't accept my true worth."

"Maybe she doesn't know how to calculate your true worth…"

Sax said, "I should go. I already went too far."

Philippe sat up, unbuckling Sax's pants. "Then I will take over."

Philippe pulled out Sax's humongous dick and slowly put it in his mouth, slurping and pulling expertly. Sax died in his stroking ability. His eyes rolling to the back of his head, he licked his lips, spreading his legs as far as they'd go. He couldn't believe Philippe felt like this.

*Work it, baby. It's yours if you want it. My wife abandoned it. Shit. Abandoned? She never really had it inside of her.*

So what was he truly missing from his wife? A thought? A dream? A fantasy? They were moaning together and kissing seconds later. They couldn't keep their hands off each other and why should they? They were both on the verge of divorce. They both wanted and needed each other. Sax actually relaxed, telling himself that if Philippe hadn't come to town he probably would have chocked Jadish for toying and boxing his emotions like Barbie dolls, to be consumed commercially. Sax was rubbing, needing and desiring his best friend in ways he never knew existed.

"I wanna fuck, Philippe. I wanna lose my virginity, tonight. I can't take it anymore. Too much is built up inside of me. I am about to loose it, baby…"

Sax lovingly turned Philippe on his stomach and got on his knees. He admired the view from the back.

*I can't believe a man is this beautiful. Philippe, you are so gorgeous to me. I love your body. I want to explore. I want to do to you what my wife didn't let me do to her. You're going to love it. I will spend all night stroking you, fucking you, massaging you and tasting you if I have to. I just don't want you to leave me.*

*Stay with me.*

Spreading his ass cheeks, he slowly ate Philippe out, bringing him pleasure. He loosened him up, getting him to match his rhythm. Philippe couldn't believe that it was finally happening.

After years of imagining what it was like, he now found out.

Sax slowly put the tip of his dick on Philippe's warm opening, pushing inside him slowly and cautiously. Philippe bit the pillow, slowly pressing his ass back.

Once Philippe's butt cheeks connected with Sax's torso they rocked and fucked the next few hours away, trapped in their secret sexual bliss. Sax pretended the outside world didn't exist. He needed nourishing and Philippe made him feel godly, made him feel whole.

*What have I been missing*, he pondered, thrusting himself inside Philippe. *He feels so good. I love this man. I want this man every day. I'm addicted to his body already.*

Philippe was receiving him without packing slips.

Sax flipped Philippe on his back, his dick still inside of him. They looked into each other's eyes and continued to rock the boat in unison. Philippe wrapped his legs around Sax's waist, holding his amazing ass.

"I love you," Philippe said.

Sax gave him some tongue. "I love you, too…"    "You feel so incredible. Just the way I imagined."

"Imagine no more, baby…Kiss my lips."

They kissed, slowly building themselves into a crescendo of lust. Sax didn't want the night to end. Philippe pushed all thoughts of his wife from his brain. If this was wrong, Lord they didn't want to be right. Selfish pleasures overshadowed logic and thought. Sax suckled on Philippe's nipple, softly biting it. Philippe was grinding all over Sax's thick stick, about to explode all over himself. They were face to face, breathing and panting...huffing and puffing.

"I'm about to come, Philippe."

"Come inside me."

Sax's body locked up. Philippe's warmth took him captive, kidnapping his spirit and gave him relief. Sax felt himself throbbing, his seeds pumping inside Philippe's warm flesh. He screamed out from the pleasure, not believing it felt like this. He was sweating so hard he lay on top of Philippe and they fell asleep in each other's arms.

In love.

There was a knock at my door. I didn't know who it was, and whoever it was they were going to get cursed out. For one, they didn't call. I liked for people to call me BEFORE they come over. Not AFTER they arrive. What if I was sucking Sax's dick? Do you think a doorbell will stop me?

I was already upset. Past upset. Sax hasn't called me. I tried calling him again and nothing. My father called me and I didn't answer. Mama called me and I ignored it. I wanted to hear from my husband. I couldn't find him and this worried me because he has never been this late coming home. Never.

I checked my hair in the mirror. I didn't bother with putting on a coat to cover my lingerie. Why should I? This was my house.

I opened the door, shaking my hair behind my head and when my eyes landed on Tommy I had heart failure trying to slam the door.

But he grabbed it.

"Jadish, *please*. I need to talk to you."

"Talk to me about what?" I stammered, pressing my body against the door, using everything I could muster to push it closed. But Tommy was too strong.

"Baby, please."

"Baby? I hate you! Get away from me."

"Please, allow me to explain."

"Explain what?"

He pushed it so hard I fell on my ass, disoriented. He came inside, closing the door. He stood there with a box of chocolates and a dozen roses. Bitch. He knew I loved chocolate and roses. But I loved my virginity more and he raped me on my graduation night. On the night everything came together for me. When I was celebrating my achievement with my friends he plotted the demise of my pussy. He took that from me and I didn't have a clue. I remembered waking up with blood everywhere and my body on fire. Maybe I did know what happened. Maybe I was just in denial.

He extended his hand, but I averted my face.

"Can I help you off the floor?"

"I feel safe on the floor. Away from you!" I spat icily. My heart beat out of my chest. I was so afraid of this man. I feared him to the point I think I was starting to break out in hives.

"Jadish."

I staggered to stand up. He had sad eyes. I loved this man. He was my God daddy. How could he betray me? I was having a hard time with this. I wasn't going to be able to eat or sleep. Because of Tommy I made my husband suffer.

"What do you want, Tommy?"

He handed me the roses and chocolate. Absent-mindedly I accepted the flowers. I tossed them by the front door. He watched them separate from the bunch.

"Forgive me."

"Forgive you for what?"

"What I did, Jadish."

"I want you to say it. Tell me what I should forgive you for."

"For having sex…"

"Having sex? That's what you call it?" I asked, putting my hands on my hips. Tears fell from my eyes. It really felt like I was against the world. Like I stood on my own. I had a husband and a father. But I felt so disconnected from them. Like somebody turned my computer off and no information surged through my fucking hard drive. That's how I felt right now.

"Yes, Jadish."

I had to sit down, my face in my hands. I was rocking back and forth. "When you say 'having sex,' that means it was an act agreed upon by two consenting human beings." My head snapped up. He walked up to me, sitting on the low-table, careful not to make me cut his ass. "You consented. I didn't. Did you have fun, Tommy?"

"No, Jadish. I was being greedy. I was in love with you and I didn't know how to tell you."

"You were in love with whom? You?"

I saw the love in his eyes. It was undeniable. I couldn't turn from it. I loved him, too. But in an Uncle kind of way. I used to be in love with him, back when I was a teenager and I didn't know love from the hole in my pussy. But now, too much has been done.

"Please…I'm not trying to pressure you."

*Girl, good or bad he's your god father. He has been there for you during some trying times in your life.*

*But he put drugs in my drink and when I was out of it he fucked me left and right. How do you explain that?*

*Forgive the man. Men are creeps. You know that. Men are uncontrollable motherfuckers. You know that, too.*

*Sax is perfect.*

*Sax is falling out of love with you.*

"Jadish. Did you hear me?"

I broke open. I couldn't take it. "I should tell my father."

"Please, keep this between us."

"Keep what between us, Man? I still want to hear you say it."

"Fine. I was so in love with you I thought you'd reject me if I came out and told you I wanted you to one day be my wife. I watched you from a kid grow up, develop and mature before my very eyes. You were like those roses. Red with love. I wanted you. I desired you. I wanted to take you to your prom…"

I was stunned he felt that way. "So I guess being there for me when I was young, giving me what I wanted and giving me money was your way of grooming me before you pounced."

"No."

"YES! They call that grooming the victim. You groomed me well. I can't look past the fact that…FUCK! You still haven't said what you've done!" I jumped up to my feet and slapped him so hard his head snapped back. He closed his eyes, sucking down the pain.

"Go ahead. Shoot me, lash out at me. I'm in love with you. I've already lost you."

"SAY IT! SAY WHAT YOU DID TO ME! WHAT DO YOU WANT ME TO FORGIVE YOU FOR?"

"I loved…"

"Tommy!" I snatched him by the shirt and he stood up, standing face to face with me. Our lips were inches apart. My body cried out for him. I felt the heat radiating from his skin. Why did I let him in? Why didn't I call the police the instant I saw his face? Why was I in a catch 22? Why didn't I want to see him suffer?

What do I do, God! You forgave me so many times. Sax has forgiven me so many times. We're not perfect.

I inhaled deeply. "Tommy. Tell me what you did. Without all the *I love you* and *I did it because*…I want to hear you say it. Be a man. Own up to what you did. Be like Ilyana Vanzant and acknowledge your mishap."

He inhaled also, looking at me. He took both my hands and I melted. My pussy was so wet my panties threw a block party on my clit and invited my ass cheeks for drinks because no matter how much shit they go through my ass cheeks are loyal motherfuckers. They always come back together.

"Fine, Jadish. I watched you in your cap and gown. Your smile set me on fire. Your eyes held me hostage. The sight of your amazing body made me lose it. I got you a martini and when no one was looking I slipped crushed pills inside, stirring it with a miniature red straw. I handed it to you. You took it to the head. I urged you to have another drink. I put another crushed pill in it. Slowly but surely I lured you from the party. I told you to go to your room. You did. I beat you there. When you came inside I closed and locked the door. I was already naked. I had rose petals on your bed. You were zonked you didn't see the lit scented candles. I slowly took you into my arms. You were disoriented. You started moaning piteously, saying you had a head ache. I gently lay you down…"

I couldn't believe I was hearing this. Why did my heart skip a beat? Nowhere in this did he say he was a beast, that he rushed and fucked me and left. He had rose petals on the bed?

He kissed both my hands. "I then…"

I leaned up to him and our lips touched. Sax didn't want me; I didn't want myself if Sax left me. He didn't come home and Tommy was my God father. But for some reason my body responded to Tommy in ways it hadn't for Sax. Maybe my body had a memory cell. Maybe it remembered Tommy gave me my first string of dick. Our tongues danced slowly. He was awkward, opening his eyes. He didn't trust me. He cringed inside, backing up.

"No, Jadish. I can't do this to you. I violated you. I am an asshole. I'm a sick individual and I should be dragged in the street and shot."

He pivoted on his heels and raced to the door. Scooping up the roses, he opened the door and I pushed it closed, grabbing him by the shirt. I pushed him on the floor and I got in his lap, pulling my titties from my bra. They sat there like two famished fat bitches ready for some goddamn cake.

"Jadish. Please…let me go."

"Make love to me. Recreate in this room what you did in my room on my graduation night."

"I can't…I am trying to atone for what I've done. I don't want to go to prison. But if you do call the cops then I will accept my fate."

I brought my quivering lips to his, and we tasted my tears. Gradually his hands explored my body, his fingers firm and polite. He was being a gentleman. He closed his eyes, finally relaxing. My pussy was so wet a huge wet spot was on his pants.

He picked me up and carried me to the couch. He gently laid me on it. I spread my legs and he got on his knees, tasting my pussy. He took his time. While he tongue fucked me he pushed both my legs back, grabbing one of the roses with his other hand. He pulled his tongue out, and told me to hold my legs back.

"Don't let them go."

He went into the kitchen and I quivered. I was about to pull my hair out. If Sax was here this was what I wanted him to do. But he couldn't hold his temper in place. He didn't come home. What if he's fucking another bitch? I couldn't even be mad at him if he was and I'd forgive him, this once.

Tommy appeared with a bottle. He got on his knees and removed the cap. Setting the cap on the table, he poured the virgin olive oil all over my pussy. Now this was hot. He slowly massaged it in, careful to drape my clit with it. Wow. What a feeling. This has never been done to me before.

"I'm sorry, Jadish. I shouldn't have done that to you. But I want to do it right."

"Baby, I'm tired of getting head. I want to make love."

"I want to taste you."

"TOMMY FUCK ME NOW!"

He smiled, standing up and unzipping his pants. He pulled them below his waist, his dick hard and ready. I looked for my teeth marks. Could he make love to me after I tried to bite his dick off?

He got on his knees and told me to spread my lips. I did with urgency. Into my pussy he dove. Swimming for the Olympic gold and finding the silver metal on my pussy.

I held him, indulging in his powerful arms, his powerful hips. He moved like pistons. I enjoyed every second. Dick felt like this?

Oh my God! I didn't know it would feel so incredible, so wonderful. I spread my legs and he pushed them back, like a huge V on my couch. The olive oil gave his dick the lubrication, and it was then I thought about a condom. God, what was I doing?

*Girl, he's in the pussy now. Just enjoy it.*

"Jadish…you feel so good, baby…goddamn, baby…"

"Get it, Tommy. Get it, baby."

"…What about Sax?"

"Fuck Sax. Just fuck me and shut up."

"Your wish is my command."

Tommy was excited; finally getting to make love to a woman he's been in love with for years. Jadish trusted him again. She had to.

Part of him didn't want to go up in her pussy raw but this was Jadish. A girl who kept her legs closed all through high school. A girl who was almost raped by friends and he and Lenny saved her.

"Jadish, I'm about to come. I don't want to come yet. It's too soon…"

He tried to pull out but she wrapped her legs around him and held him there. The minute she did her body tensed up and she twirled her hips for dear life.

It built up in her body, swirling in her loins, tossing in her skull, burying in her pussy and she exploded, coming all over Tommy's dick the instant he started to come deep inside her, her pussy receiving the nutrients and her tight walls remembering the scent.

She was panting, her eyes wide open. Her mouth ajar. It felt so good she couldn't talk.

*This feels better than my door knob*, she thought jubilantly. *When Sax comes home we're fucking every day. I know he'll love it.*

*Girl, you can never tell him you just fucked Tommy.*

Sax and Philippe lay side by side. Listening to Sade. The covers pulled up to the start of their abdomens. Philippe was gently stroking Sax's upper thigh. Sax loved his touch. He wanted to call Jadish but he made up in his mind that he was getting a divorce.

"So where do we go from here?"

"Nowhere," said Sax, turning to look in his eyes. "I don't want to leave here yet. I can stay here forever."

Philippe smiled. "*Really?*"

"Yes. Thank you."

Philippe kissed his lips. "For what?" He rolled over, opening the nightstand. Pulling out a rolled blunt, he closed the drawer and lit it.

Sax kissed his forehead. "For taking my virginity. For letting me play in your body. For making me come. You felt so good."

Pulling on the blunt, Philippe looked at it for a brief second, passing it to his lover.

"I didn't *take* your virginity, bruh," Philippe said with love and admiration in his voice. "I simply pulled back the curtain on your virginity and showed you the man you are. The incredible, committed and loyal man you are. Jadish doesn't deserve you, bruh. What woman makes her husband wait two plus years to make love? No man would have stuck around for that, unless she was battling cancer or something. And you were the best lover I ever had."

Sax beamed like the morning sun. A huge cloud of smoke gravitated around their spent bodies. Philippe pulled hungrily on the blunt once more, setting it in the ash tray. Sax tongue kissed him, getting a contact high. They talked between lip locks. "I'm curious." Kiss, kiss. "How many men have you been with?"

Kiss, kiss. "*Two*," Philippe said truthfully. Sax believed him. They have always been honest with each other about everything.

Sax smiled, pulling away. "So I'm number three."

"No. You're number two…And you were the *best*! You are everything I ever imagined."

"I have loved you for years, Philippe. I misplaced it as brotherly love."

"How did you know it wasn't brotherly love?"

"Because I used to get hard when you came around. I knew then. I just never said anything."

"I know. I did, too. I was too scared of losing you as a friend."

"I wouldn't have turned on you."

"I know that now. But back then I was terrified. I didn't even like gay people. And when I turned out to be bisexual, I thought I was the weird one."

"You're not weird. But we both have wives."

"And I have a son."

"So what are we going to do? I'm not ready to come out and I never will.

"Me, either. I mean, I respect those who have. I respect those who keep it real and they are who they are but I have to think about my job, my reputation. I do want to leave my wife and be with you."

"I do, too. You have always made me feel so good about myself. You always believed in me and offered me advice and hope."

"And I always will."

Sax kissed his lips. "I hope you're ready."

"Ready for what?"

Sax turned him on his stomach and began to taste him all over. Philippe's cell phone rang.

I couldn't believe it. I just fucked Tommy. Bitch, were you crazy? Was I that vulnerable that I had to give in to the man who raped me? Was this normal? Was I normal? I just violated my own self. I stood up, running my shaking hands through my hair. I truly didn't know what to do or what to say. Should I cut his ass? No, how could I? I got on my knees every night and asked God to forgive me for my mishaps. So why couldn't I forgive Tommy? If I wanted God to forgive me I had to forgive others. But I thought I could forgive on my own time and on my own terms.

*I just cheated on Sax. What is going on with me?*

Tommy was pulling up his pants, quiet. He refused to look at me. He was shaking his head, cursing himself.

"What's wrong, Tommy?" *Bitch, did you care what was wrong with him? Tell him to get out! Call the police! Have him arrested.*

*No, girl. You're talking through your obvious hurt.*

*Bitch, you can't be too hurt. You just fucked him without a rubber, a Jimmy, a condom or whatever you wanted to call it.*

*Oh, Well. He had some good dick.*

*Are you insane?*

"I have to go, Jadish."

"No, Tommy. Stay…Are you hungry?"

"A little. But it's cool." He was walking to the door. "I'll grab some McDonald's."

"Don't be silly. Go sit to the dining table. I'll warm you up some food I cooked for Sax tonight."

"Where's Sax?"

"He never came home. I think he wants a divorce."

Quietly, Tommy slipped out the door when Jadish opened the fridge.

Driving home the entire episode played out in Tommy's head. He was deadly tired, yawning what seemed every five minutes. He didn't understand why he was so tired. Maybe because he had a long night. A night of worrying, praying and dreading. He worried about Lenny. Maybe he shouldn't have drunk the liquor his best friend bought. He smiled to himself, trying to manage his automobile on the road. Small specks of rain fell on the windshield. His cell phone rang. He looked at it and it was Jadish. He kissed the phone, and put it in the glove box. Tonight had been wonderful. It would be a night he would never forget. He loved her. Yes, she forgave him. But he didn't understand why she gave in to him. If she would have stabbed him he would have accepted it. He was dead ass wrong for drugging her drink. He was dead ass wrong for violating her trust. She trusted him and he took full advantage because he thought he could get away with it.

*God, forgive me Lord. I was wrong. I made a bad decision. I was out of pocket and out of line. But I'm a man and I have weaknesses. I am not perfect.*

*God I'm asking you to forgive me. Why am I so tired? I am getting painfully sleepy. I need to pull over on the side of the road. Yea.*

*I'll do that.*

Tommy slowly braked, pulling over to the shoulder of the road. He turned off the engine and turned off the lights.

"I'll just get a little rest. I'll drive home in an hour or so." He set the alarm on his phone for an hour. He set it on the dash and leaned the seat back as far as it'd go.

"It's better to be safe than sorry."

As the passing cars continued to zoom by him, Tommy fell asleep within minutes, silently praying to God to forgive him for raping Jadish.

The woman of his dreams.

The next day Sax was heading to the shower in the hotel room. Looking at his watch, he realized he was late for work. But he didn't care. He loved his job and he loved his co-workers and his boss. But he loved Philippe more and now that Philippe opened the Candy Shop in his ass, he wanted to taste all the flavors. Philippe had hooked up his Xbox 360 to the TV and was playing *Halo*, a game he loved. Sax wasn't one for games, just football games on ESPN.

Sax smiled, grabbing a towel from the chair by the small dining table. "I don't know how I'm going to tell Jadish I want a divorce," he said, eyeing Philippe. He was pressing buttons so fast it made his head spin.

Philippe was heavily engrossed in combat. "I don't know how I'm going to leave my family, bruh," Philippe said. He pressed "pause," looking at a half naked Sax. His eyes raked his body, carefully noting his amazing ass, his plump dick and his beefy thighs. His calve muscles were just irresistible. "I do know I love you and I want to be with you."

"And I want to be with you." Sax walked over to him, kissing him. They melted into each other again.

"Go shower."

Sax said, "Ok."

Philippe answered his ringing phone.

"Hello." He resumed the video game.

"Dad!"

"Hey, Son."

He was sniffling. "Tell me it isn't true."

Philippe turned off the game without saving it. His son was more important. "What isn't true?" He narrowed his eyes.

"Mommie said you are leaving us."

His heart dropped. "No, son. I am not leaving you. But I don't…"

*How do you tell your son his Mama doesn't make you happy anymore? Why did she tell him about our impending divorce without me present? Silly bitch! She's already trying to come between me and my son and I'll be damned if she comes out the victor!*

"But you promised to always be there for me."

"And I will."

"But Mama said you're moving out."

"Son, it's for the best."

"NOO, Daddy! What did I do?"

His heart exploded. "Son. It's not your fault."

"YES IT IS! You're leaving me! I hate you, Daddy! You promised!"

"Son…"

"If you leave me I will never talk to you again."

"You're young, Son. I don't expect you to understand…"

"I'm eleven years old, Daddy! I understand perfectly. You found another woman and you don't want us."

"It's not like that."

"Go to hell!"

His son hung up in his face.


Sax was bathing. On the sink counter his phone buzzed and he answered it. "*Yo!*"

"Why didn't you come home last night?"

"I couldn't face you, Jadish."

"Why? And is that the shower I hear in the background?"

"Yes, Jadish. It's the shower."

"Oh my God! You cheated on me! How could you!" She broke down and he felt guilty.

"I'm sorry, Jadish. I am going to be a man about it. Yes, I did cheat on you."

"But you made a vow…"

"Yes, I did, and you forfeited on the fine lines before I slept with somebody else."

"So now you don't want me? Is that it? You hate me now? I mean nothing to you?"

"Baby. I *do* love you. But you wouldn't make love to me. You made me feel terrible inside. You walked on my manhood. No, it's not all about sex, but two plus years is sheer lunacy. I can't believe I stayed that long."

"Please come home. Let's talk about this."

"I'll be home soon. And when I get there I'm packing my stuff and I'm leaving."

"Why, Sax! Why are you doing...?"

"I have to go."

"Who is she?"

*It's not a she, baby. It's a he. Philippe. And I want and need to be with him. And we already decided that we would be together. We were going to get an apartment together and make love all day and get to know each other deeper all night. It's a done deal. I'm just waiting to sign divorce papers. Nothing was going to stop us from being together.*

*We just had to keep it on the low low.*

He hung up the phone.

*Before I lose my mind.*

Philippe couldn't stop crying. He wasn't a water bucket, but he never dreamed of hurting his son. He lay on the bed, rubbing his temples. Next to him was a pen and a pad. He shook his head, sitting up. He smoked the last of the joint. Did he really want to leave his family?

Yes.

And he would leave them. He *had* to go. People had to stop using the children as an excuse to stay inside a loveless marriage.

Plenty of adults raised successful children while divorced. Hell his Mama has been doing that for years. She never complained so why should he? Children had to stay in a child's place. They didn't dictate what he did and who he did it with.

*I got to leave. I can't stay with my family. I don't love my wife.*

He picked up the pen and scribbled a note.

Jadish sunk to her knees, sobbing. Her nose stopped up instantly. She had to breathe through her mouth. Her skin crawled and her pulse quickened. She wanted to break something. She opened her counter and shattered her dishes. She screamed to release steam.

"It's all my fault! I did this to him! I drove him to the arms of another woman."

She threw her good China against the wall, basking in the symphony of misery that trickled into her ears.

"I cheated on him, too. We both did something unforgivable. I can't believe I lost my husband. Another woman will enjoy his body and I haven't even enjoyed it yet. She already has leverage over me. Who is the bitch? I'll gut the Ho!"

She vowed it on her life.

Tommy was out of it. The alarm continued to go off, but he didn't move. The sun rose above his car, rays beaming down on his skin. He was clammy and unprepossessing. Cars traveled to and fro. His mouth was ajar. His eyes open to the world. His pupils stale and dry. His eye lashes, curly and disdained. Ants crawled along the hood. Bugs flapped all around the car.

The grass was wet with the morning's dew.

Tommy was dead.

Lenny hugged his wife, thinking about Tommy. He didn't understand him. Well, he used to think that he did. But obviously he didn't know Tommy as well as he'd thought. Why would he lie and say he was at a party at the hospital? Why would he say a dead woman told him to say "Hi?" Was it to cover up the fact that he was actually the one admitted into the hospital?

Lenny kissed his wife's cheek and decided to let it go for now.

He already did what he had to do. And he was cool with that.

*Next time Jadish…make sure you press the mute button when you say Tommy raped you and you didn't know how to tell me.*

*Plus I overheard Tommy and Sax's argument at the hospital.*

*I was standing at the door the entire time.*

*Devastated.*

*Holding a bottle of E&J.*

*Loaded with rat poison.*

Sax came out of the bathroom. He thought about calling the auto parts store so he could pick up the parts for Lenny's Mustang. He forgot all about it.

*I'll do it later. Just because I'm divorcing his daughter didn't mean I turned my back on them.*

*They have become my family as well. I love Jadish's parents.*

"Philippe…" Sax grabbed a toothbrush. He did a quick job on his teeth then gargled. He had to see Philippe.

Turning off the water he checked himself over in the mirror. He was fully clothed, ready to go to work.

He walked out into the room. The TV was on.

"Philippe…"

*Oh, he probably stepped out to grab a bite to eat.*

Sax sat down, putting on his shoes. He smiled to himself, thinking about his man. His baby.

"Why did he wait this long to make a move. I wish he would have done this years ago. But do I truly want him? Or am I infatuated? Nah. Must be lust mixed with love. Had to be."

Sax looked forward to his new life. That was short lived.

He frowned when he realized the drawers were open and empty. The suit cases were gone.

"What the fuck? Did he leave? Without telling me bye?"

He felt like a cheap hooker that wasn't compensated. He snatched up his cell and called him.

"How could he just up and leave? Nah, bruh. You don't treat Sax like a piece of meat. Little bitch!"

When his eyes fell on the note on his pillow he hung up the phone. The note was in Philippe's handwriting.

*I love you. I love you like I have never loved any other man. You fulfilled a fantasy, a dream I long ago had. I actually asked God to let me have one night with you years ago. I think Satan heard my prayer, because my son called me this morning and told me to go to hell. He told me I made him a promise that I would never leave him. And, yes, I love you, bruh. I would die for you. But my son comes first. I have to make him feel safe and secure. He's a Mini Me. I can't make him with his mother then turn and leave. It's more complicated than I thought. I'm going back home to work it out with my wife.*

*Please work it out with yours. We will never be. We could never be. You felt wonderful last night. Your body against mine reminded me of doves in flight. They flap and they fly. They gawk and they sigh. But eventually wings get tired. Famished, they must land to reevaluate the next travel plan. South for the Winter or East in the Spring? You tell me, bruh. I'm not ready to leave my family and exchange my house, life, and child for a life living in the shadows. That's for the trees and the sun when it changes course in the sky. Whether that sky is sunny, blue or dark. Clouds have the type of wetness that either cleanses or floods. My job is done. I was to come and show you something. To pull back the velvet ropes and show you the man you are after your first sexual experience with someone who truly loves you for you. I want you to go home and patch it up with Jadish. You both hurt each other. I should be on the plane by the time your pupils slid across the last word on this page. I prayed to God about it. My conscious told me to go save my family.*

*I have to save my son. I made him a promise.*

*I'm a man of my word.*

*P.S. What we did and what we shared stays in the Marriot Hotel. I will never destroy your reputation. I will never cause you harm. Please don't destroy mine. If you do, I will man up and own it. But I know you're too good a man to destroy a life. I should know. You were married to Jadish Houston for two plus years, saving a woman who wasn't ready to be saved. But now that she knows of Tommy's deception, maybe you two can truly be happy. Now's the time to go home and get your pussy once and for all. I love you. I love Jadish. Us sleeping together was meant for one thing. Mending. Healing. Fixing. Building bridges. I love you. You love me. I love my son. You love my son. You're his God father. You want him happy. You want him nurtured. We must build our village and raise my child. You. Me. My wife. Jadish. We were two vulnerable black men coming together to make beautiful Love, not War. Please Inspector Gadget this letter when done reading. And even if you keep it, please keep this sacred and private. I want to cherish feeling you inside me. It's not for public consumption. It's not meant for office fodder. I trust you, the way you trusted me last night to show your virginity the door.*

*I love you.*

*P.*

Sax closed the letter and stood up. He read over it a few times, understanding why Philippe left. He couldn't blame him. Sax was at the hospital the day little Phil, Jr. was born. He held him and took pictures with him. Philippe was on cloud nine. Nothing was bigger than his son. There have been times Philippe and Sax stayed up for hours on the phone talking about his son. His expectations. His dreams. Sax was very envious, one day wanting a son of his own.

*I will never have a son. I'm divorcing you, Jadish.*

He took out his lighter and opened the letter. He held it up, tears falling. He was burning the evidence. He was burning his love. He was burning his infidelity. As long as the letter existed, the infidelity on both their parts was immortal. It lived on. It was the Last Emperor. It was life threatening. It could destroy lives.

Sax walked out of the room, wallet and keys in hand.

The letter turned to charred ancient ruins seconds later.

There was a knock on Jadish's door. She had showered, changed clothes and decided to pull herself together. She was done crying. She couldn't change what happened. When she opened the door five men in suits stood before her, holding roses and huge teddy bears. She melted into a smile. A small band walked past her, standing in her living room, clad in silk suits. They played Blackstreet's "Don't Leave." Jadish loved that song.

"*Oh my God!* What is this?"

The men set up the roses and set the teddy bears on the living room couch. One of the men handed her a bottle of Dom and two flute glasses.

In the glass was a ring and a small note.

Her hands shaking she took out the note and read it.

*I love you.*
*Let's get married again.*
*Sax.*

# Booty-Do Revisited

*God, I don't even know if I'm coming or going! I'm about to lose it. I'm about to go crazy. There's only so much a woman can take and right now my heart isn't the limit and love seems to be spending outside of my budget. My entire soul has been compromised because love has blown up in my face.*

Hot tears streaming down her beautiful face, Georgia, sitting on the floor in her huge walk-in closet, looked over her beloved school screenplay. She remembered when she wrote it. She was sixteen years old and she was going through something in her life. She had just lost her virginity with a disrespectful asshole named Eduardo Rodriguez. She thought she was in love with him. She waited her whole life to give her body to a knight in shining armor and when she did, after saying he was, she found out that he had sex with half the girls in school. She was nothing but a traffic stop. Her name was slandered and scandalized.

Other boys approached her, trying to get in her panties. They didn't respect her. She had to fight other women to get her respect back and she did. Her red light didn't last long enough to make Eduardo stay with her. And when her clit gave him the green light he did just that: left her.

Eduardo then had sex with her close cousin, Priscilla. He told Priscilla, during their sexual romance, that she felt better than Georgia. That Georgia was a prude compared to Priscilla's feistiness.

When Georgia found out through the rumor mill that Eduardo Rodriguez fucked her cousin she was so upset and betrayed she jumped on Priscilla during her Sweet 16 party, stabbing her with a huge kitchen knife in front of other family members. Once the shockwave swarmed throughout the event, she turned the knife on Eduardo, stabbing him so deeply in his arm he almost bled to death on the way to the hospital. Priscilla was in the same paramedic truck with him.

When her parents lashed out at her in confusion and anger, she ran and locked herself in the bathroom.

*If only they understood what Eduardo and Priscilla did to me, then they wouldn't be so quick to jump on me.*

"Open this door, Georgia!" her father raged, pounding on the door. Her Asian mother was calling her all kind of names.

"How could you stab your own cousin? You little bitch open this fucking door!"

"LEAVE ME ALONE!" Georgia spewed, opening the medicine cabinet.

*Eduardo didn't love me. He loved Priscilla. They went behind my back and had sex. I am so embarrassed. No one will ever love me. How could my cousin betray me?*

"Georgia." Her father pounded on the door again, the door about to break free. "Open the door!"

"I DON'T WANT TO LIVE ANYMORE! FUCK PRISCILLA! SHE FUCKED MY BOYFRIEND BEHIND MY BACK!"

"Baby," her mother reasoned, touching her husband's arm. He settled down. "Open the door. We can talk about this…"

Georgia sunk to her knees, eyeing the bottle in her hands. The razor was by her legs. Her hair hanging in her face, she started to perspire.

*Eduardo lied to me. He told me what I wanted to hear just to fuck me. He got what he wanted. People bash me in school. The boys think I'm easy. I hate life. I hate love. I hate men. I hate myself.*

Georgia opened the pills and poured them into her mouth. She struggled to swallow them. The bitter taste in her mouth nearly made her gag. Once she swallowed them, she took the razor and slashed her wrists. She lay in the fetal position and welcomed the pain. She welcomed the embarrassment. In her mind she saw herself stabbing her cousin and Eduardo. She kept her eyes closed tightly.

*Good bye Mom and Dad. Good bye to everybody. I won't be missed. No one will mourn me. Death is the only option.*

"Georgia…" Her father listened. Nothing. Her mother called out her name, knocking.

Nothing. "Why is it so quiet in there?" he asked his wife.

Before she could answer they heard banging sounds.

"What's that?" he asked, looking confused. Other family members started forming a crowd behind them.

"Oh, *God!* BABY, OPEN THAT DOOR! GEORGIA! NO, BABY!" her mother was covering her face, backing up from the door.

Scared for his child, her father kicked in the door. When he saw Georgia twitching on the floor, blood everywhere, he picked her up, screaming at the top of his lungs, and he ran past family and put her in his truck.

Her mother was right behind him. Before she could open the door he sped off. He put the pedal to the metal getting her to the hospital, her mother speeding behind them in her car, her heart hammering. Georgia pulled through. She would spend two weeks in the hospital. Her parents were right by her side. They didn't care that Eduardo made it and that Priscilla pulled through. Georgia had to go to counseling. She didn't love herself. She didn't want to live. She wanted to die. She didn't want to go to school. She didn't want boyfriends. She didn't want the very air she breathed. Her parents convinced her to go on living, that they would love her and be there for her. They told her to finish school and Georgia, after a lot of hesitation, agreed.

She vowed that if she gave her body to another man he would have to be in love with her, cherish her and be there for her when she wanted. He couldn't have eyes for another woman. She vowed to never get close to another female.

But God had a different plan for her. Her father had a friend who was in the Marines with him. He had a daughter named Princess Webster. Mr. Webster was a warm, intimidating man. She met him and Princess during her junior year at Spellman College. She liked Princess instantly and they started to hang out and be there for each other and stay up on the phone talking about fashion, boys and life. She felt in her heart that she would not make Princess pay for Priscilla's mistakes. Not all women were whores. When Georgia met Ed her life changed forever. In the beginning he dogged her, talked shit to her and he used to hit on her. She didn't know what it was about his eyes and the warmth of his smile, but as she got to know him and finding out that he went through a lot of emotional abuse as a kid, she grew closer to him. She never gave up. Ed asked her to marry him over pasta at an Italian restaurant. She said yes, despite everything he'd put her through. They were married two weeks later. Princess couldn't attend the wedding because she didn't believe in them.

Thank God for Princess Webster's father. He single-handedly got a hold of Ed and beat some sense into him. Ed was like the son he never had, and he got it together after marrying her and showed her that he could be loving and sensitive and attentive and caring.

*Now Ed is in love with another woman. Call your lawyer and get a divorce. Thank God Ed and I don't have children together, even though we were going to start trying in a few weeks. He wanted a son and he told me he didn't want to die and not leave behind a child to carry on his name. I wanted to give him what his heart desired. Now I never will.*

Tears fell on the play. Several words looked smeared. This was the play that won her rave reviews and a scholarship to Spellman College. *If it wasn't for this screenplay, I would have never gone to college. I didn't even want to go to college. I just wanted a high school diploma because my Daddy never earned one and Mama did, but she never put it to use or use it to its full potential and I wanted to be different. I wanted to be better than my parents. This play did just that.*

That was the play her parents were proud of. That was the play her high school would use for future reference for other drama students. That was the play Priscilla and Eduardo attended and loved.

That was the play that changed her life for the better and gave her high self-esteem and self-confidence she didn't have growing up in a loveless home with an overbearing father and a mother who let her husband walk all over her like floor mats.

That was the play that detailed a lonely wife who cooked dinner and was having an imaginary phone conversation with a friend to keep her mind off of what she didn't have in her life. The very same play she reenacted when she caught Princess and her husband having sex in her guest bathroom the morning after Ed's very successful and much hyped and talked about party. Georgia remembered that morning well. It has played over and over in her mind like a movie she hated.

She remembered standing at the guest bedroom door, her hands flatly pressed on the paneling…her eyes locked on Princess sucking her man's dick in ways she never had…while he sat on the toilet. Loving it. Needing it. Craving it. In ways he never craved Georgia.

Georgia didn't see the Bob Marley pictures on the wall that were gifts from her mother, when she attended a reggae festival in Jamaica six years before. She didn't see the black carpet she bought online from Indonesia a few years ago and paid over $75 to have shipped UPS to her house. She didn't see Ed's $3,500 big screen TV mounted in the wall, a TV she has, with Ed and friends, watched numerous Super Bowls and NBA Championships on. Her heart crashed and burned when Ed ran his hands through her hair and was moaning her name and his deeply rooted love and affection he claimed he always had for her. This was before they closed and locked the bathroom door. Georgia was about to go crazy. Her world, her home life, her household and everything she invested exploded in her eyes and reconstructed her face.

Georgia moved like a zombie across the room. She pressed her hands on the door, silently sobbing. She turned her face to the side, and put her ear to the door. She heard them moaning in unison. She heard the suction sounds of Princess's lips on her man's dick.

*"I gotta pee," Princess said to Ed.*

The door opened a tad. It wasn't locked! Oh, God! Did she really want to see what lied behind the door?

She opened it slightly, enough for her to peek inside. She saw Ed eating Princess's pussy. She was sitting on the toilet, pissing into it. Ed took some of her urine and wiped it on her nipples. She wanted to puke.

*Burst in! Kill them both! Do it, Georgia! Kill them! Do something, bitch! Stop acting helpless and show these two fucks that no one crossed you. You made a vow to yourself, after what Priscilla and Eduardo did to you. You wouldn't love a man unless he loved you for you and he couldn't have eyes for another woman.*

Her soul died when Ed got on the floor, guiding Princess's pussy on his dick. She took his Nike hat from his head and slanted it on her head. Georgia softly closed the door and ran down stairs, vowing to kill them. But in her heart she had a conflict. She was in love. She loved her husband. She loved Princess like a sister. What would she do? Before Georgia caught Princess and Ed having sex, she was initially walking up the stairs. She was on her way up to tell Princess that she wanted to cook her breakfast. She knew Princess had the Hennessy and Coke drink at the party and she was out of it.

She wanted to make sure she was ok. She looked out for her friends when they stayed over and that rarely happened because the only person she and Ed allowed in their home was Princess.

On her part, she knew that allowance came from her loyalty to her friend. On Ed's part, she had to wonder was it because he truly wanted to fuck Princess?

*No time for that now. I gotta do something. I can't go on pretending like I don't know what's going on between them. That's why Princess ducked me for months. She didn't take my calls. She didn't return them, either. She totally avoided me. If she would have been a woman and come to me on the morning she fucked him would have made all the difference. Friendship over dick.*

Georgia shook with rage putting her play, which was neatly and meticulously formatted on 8.5"x11" paper, back in the suit case and returning it to the top of the closet.

*Why did I cook that morning and pretend to be talking on the phone? Why did I redo my play, a play I did on stage in high school?*

*Why didn't I stab the bitch when I caught her crawling out of my kitchen? Do to her what I did to Priscilla?*

Georgia was in the shower, wondering why Tina, Thomas's wife, didn't show up. Her cell phone vibrated on the sink counter. Wrapping a towel around her, she got out, the shower still running, and answered it amongst steam.

"Hello."

"Hey, Girl. I know you think I forgot about you."

"Hey, Tina. How could I?"

"I won't be coming over. I can't meet the woman who is pregnant from my husband. I will probably gut the bitch."

*Believe me; I want to gut her ass myself. She fucked my husband, Girl.*

"She's gone, anyway. I don't know where she went. And right now, I got my own dilemmas. I don't have time to be getting involved with other people's problems."

"What's wrong?"

"Nothing." *Ed cheated on me with the bitch that is pregnant with your husband's baby.* "Look. I'm in the shower. Call me later."

"OK. And Georgia?"

"Yes?"

"Thanks for the organizer. I appreciate the gift."

*Organizer? Bitch, what fucking organizer? I didn't buy you anything.*

"No problem, Gurl. Bye."

Click.

A few hours later, Georgia quietly sauntered into *Johnny's Fuci-Fino's Sport's Bar and Grill* on *Oakland Park Boulevard*, and hesitantly sat at the bar. She had tried to call Ed, but he didn't answer. She also tried to call Princess, wondering did she go to Thomas and tell him who she really was.

*The girl is in love. That much I will admit. I don't know what kind of magic Thomas had on his dick, but Princess is hooked on him. I have never seen her so happy. And she's pregnant from Thomas. That's another thing. What is she going to do? Thomas is still married. And why didn't Tina show up? I waited on her and she never came over to meet Princess. Not that it mattered. Princess bolted on me to go after Thomas.*

Gorgeous in an ankle-length dress with a lily in her curly hair, she smacked her lips and decided that she made a mistake coming to a bar to alleviate her inner turmoil.

*Why did I put that lily in my hair? Ed used to love when I put flowers in my hair. He said it brought out my eyes. He used to stroke my hair and say he loved me. I used to die from his touch. Now I don't want him looking, touching or thinking about me.*

It was after 6 p.m. and Happy Hour was from 4-7. She didn't care about the free buffet, either. She wasn't hungry and she didn't have a craving for food. Her craving went deeper than well-prepared dishes. Her craving tied in to her husband and trying to love a man who didn't love her. The place had great dining; drinking, people, laughs, fun, and dancing yet her heart didn't want to be there.

*Then why did I even come?* She loved coming to that particular sports bar because it wasn't like all the others. It was very people-friendly and it catered to her needs in ways she wished her husband would.

*Maybe I should go home. I really don't feel like being around people. Not today.*

She wasn't like most women yet she needed and desired and wanted a solution to her burgeoning problems. Looking at her pricey watch, she tossed her bang from her lightly made-up face and looked around. There were a lot of black folks in there doing what they did best: trying to take each other home and fuck each other's lights out.

She grooved to Marvin Gaye. "Let's Get it On."

*I don't think so,* Georgia thought.

A few men tried to hit on her but she wasn't interested. A tall fellah grabbed her hand, trying to get his game on and she shot her buzzer before the game winning shot.

"I'm married. Release me or catch a rape beef."

He had never run so fast in his life. She rolled her eyes, and set her small Chanel purse on the counter, lowering her head.

*I love him. God, I took vows. I meant them, too. Did he? Why did he turn on me? I can't believe this. And Princess. God. I love that girl so much. With everything in me. She's my partner in crime. I trusted her with all of my secrets and my fears. I know all of hers. I know she is afraid of the dark. I know she hates being alone. I know she was picked on throughout her twelve years of school and when she was a teenager she used sex to validate herself and that quickly turned into a profitable business.*

*Why would she turn on me and take my husband?*

"Ma'am," said the bartender, looking as good as he want to be. "Can I get you something to drink?"

Marvin Gaye ended and Barry White started. She loved that song. She and Ed made love to it a million times. I Wanna Do it Good to Ya. *God.* Shoot me. Snatch my hair out.

"Ma'am…"

She focused on him with a frown. "Oh, sorry. Yes. Give me a Husband on the Rocks."

"I'm sorry?" he was shaking his head, placing his hands flat on the counter.

A few other women were trying to get his attention but he only had eyes for the pretty lady who was obviously going through something painful.

She wiped tears away. "Never mind."

"I'll get you something to cheer you up," he said. "I'll make you something you have never had before."

"What will that be? You'll make a Good Man? Make that, since you fucking men think you know what women has never had. I never had a backstabbing best friend who fucks her friend's man. She's pregnant with another man's child."

"Wow. You are really going through something."

Georgia jumped up to her feet, grabbing her purse.

"I shouldn't have come here. I need to call my lawyer. Why am I telling you this?"

He held up his hands. "Wait, ma'am."

"This was a mistake. I'm so sorry. And don't wait on me. You won't ever see me again in this bar. And this is my favorite place in Fort Lauderdale…"

She rushed out of the bar, running to her car.

*God. I'm about to lose it.*

*Get me home before I go completely ballistic.*

Heartbroken, Georgia lay in her bed hours later, her soul shattered into a million little fragile pieces. She couldn't think straight. On her nightstand, next to Ed's picture (He was so handsome. Lord, his smile radiated, even after all these years) were empty beer cans.

Georgia didn't drink. In fact she hated people who did. She couldn't stand people who put their problems in beer bottles. She detested people who went to bars and told all of their business, right on down to bra and dick sizes, to the bartender and *he* didn't even know how to get himself out of a bind.

*That's why I left Johnny's. I was turning into one of them. A lonely woman who couldn't decipher men from pigs.*

Yet she has succumbed to doing just that: drinking away her derision for her husband's decisions. She was paying for her husband's mistakes. His lack of judgment has left her hearing impaired. She wasn't trying to understand anything about him any longer.

*But I have to. I'm his wife. We are still married. Is it me? Did I do something wrong? Did I suck his dick right? Didn't I swallow him enough? Didn't I let him come inside of me the way he loved? Wasn't I his bitch in the sack? Didn't I roll his joints fast enough? Didn't I cook fried chicken for his friends on game days? Wasn't I faithful enough, Lord. Why have you and my husband forsaken me?*

Cigarette butts were all over the floor. Georgia didn't smoke. Now she was. She was too stressed. She tried playing with herself, thinking about her husband but before she could insert the dildo she dropped it and the lube on the floor and she started crying so hard her nose stopped up. How could he betray her? How could he give himself to another woman? How could he look her in the face, smiling and laughing, like everything was alright? Didn't he have a heart and a soul? Hadn't they been through enough together?

It was a few minutes past 1 a.m. Ed still hadn't come home.

*Where are you? With Princess? No, you can't be. She is probably with Thomas, where she belongs. Stay far, far away from here.*

She was listening to every sad song imaginable. She had erased all of the songs on her iPod and she downloaded the sad shit. Aretha. Patti. Whitney. Janet. Beyonce. Scratch Beyonce. She's *too* young. A grown woman of Georgia's stature didn't need to be listening to little girls giving it to Mama and wearing Freakum dresses to get back at a man. Every woman didn't have that kind of dress in the back of their closets. Hell, she had clothes she couldn't fit all through the closet. And getting a new man was not the answer. When you were a whore, sure, you could go out and fuck whoever you wanted. But when you're married and you wholeheartedly stood before God and family and told a man how much you loved, adored and admired him, then the stakes were higher. If her marriage was on the Dow Jones the stock market would have crashed the minute she realized Ed's phone switched to vibrate status. It would have exploded when she realized she was a married woman and a Freakum dress would not bring her husband back. No, she hasn't thrown him out and no, his shit was still in the armoire, dressers and in the closet. But in her heart and in her mind, body and soul Ed was out on his natural ass. And he wouldn't be coming back.

*Where are you, Ed? Why are you not home yet? The least you could have done was call me. I am so worried about you. Well, maybe I'm not.*

*I already know the deal. I know what's going on, but you're a man and men think they have all the fucking sense and when it comes to sex and their dicks they don't have the sense of a freaking bird.*

*You are in love, yes I know. Your heart isn't pure, which is another matter I won't get into. When are you going to be real with yourself?*

This was unusual. He always came home around 9 p.m. He never stayed out late. And when he happened to get off work late he always phoned her and insured that he was ok. She reached over and picked up her cell phone. She closed her eyes. Should she call him? Nah. She wouldn't. She had her pride. Husband or not she wouldn't sweat him. Why should she sweat him anyway?

*He's in love with an ex prostitute.*

Ed was in a myriad of thoughts. Inside his heart was a Hurricane and it spelled disaster. He wanted a woman who was in love with another man.

*I can't live without Princess. I love her. But how do I tell my wife that I don't want her anymore. How do I tell her that I love her like a sister?*

He was driving his Mustang along Campbell Drive. He has passed the Big Lots store. He could barely keep his eyes open. If he lost Princess he didn't want to live. She was his soul mate.

*But does she know it? Does Princess know she is my missing rib?* He knew it in his heart and in his soul and he would fight Satan for her love and her time and her devotion. The thought of another man getting the pussy killed him inside.

*I know it's late. It's after 1 a.m. But I couldn't come home after work. How could I? I have been camped out at the Motel 6. I watched Princess throw herself into Thomas's arms. She's pregnant with his child. How could she ignore my love for her and go with another man? Hell, how could I cheat on my wife?*

*Why did I drink myself into a stupor? Why didn't I call my wife and tell her I was going to get home late. Why didn't I give a fuck? Niggah, the least you can do is call Georgia. She's a loyal woman. She has never hurt you.*

*So what? And?*

Ed phoned Georgia, softly braking at a stop light. No other cars were on the road.

*How do I tell you I don't love you?*

The cell phone vibrated on Georgia's nightstand. She was fast asleep, Toni Braxton's "Seven Whole Days" playing.

Georgia was holding Ed's picture in her arms. The Bible opened and on the floor. The phone vibrated off the nightstand and onto the floor. A few seconds later it stopped vibrating.

Ed parked his car next to Georgia's Toyota Camry.

*She's home.*

He looked at his room window. The lights were out. *She's sleeping.*

Unlocking the door, he slowly walked inside, the cool air hitting him in the face. Closing and locking the door, he activated the alarm.

Making his way upstairs, he paused. *Princess. I need you. Make love to me. Have my children. Replace Georgia in this house. I don't want Georgia living here anymore. Why am I such an asshole?*

Ed entered his room. Music was playing at a moderately considerate tone. The glow of the moon illuminated Georgia's gorgeous face.

*I love you like a sister now. I think I always loved you that way.*

He took off his leather coat and his jeans. *I don't even want to lay next to you.* He crawled in the bed next to her. He noticed it. She held his picture in his arms. *She's so in love with me. How do I get her to understand?*

He put his arm around her and went to sleep.

When his arm went around Georgia she inhaled, and her eyes opened.

*Please. Stop touching me. Get your arm from around me. I hate you.*

*I know you wish I was Princess.*

Georgia was sitting at the dining table, across from Ed the morning after. On the table was her wallet, the cordless phone and her purse.

*Stupid prick. He sits there like nothing has changed. Everything has changed. Nothing is the same.*

The silence fell on their ears and they didn't know what to do or how to deal with it. Ed was thinking about Princess.

*I wonder what she ate for breakfast. Is she happy? What is she wearing? I want to buy her roses. I want to massage her feet. I want to taste her sweet pussy and make her titties chameleons to what I feel inside.*

He wanted her slithering all over his chiseled body, riding his dick. He wanted to make her come day in and day out. He wanted to wax on and wax off the pussy but how could he? She was avoiding him. She refused to talk to him. She didn't take his phone calls. She ducked and dodged him when he went over to her father's house. Didn't she love him as much as he loved her?

*What are you thinking?* Georgia wondered, sipping some water. Her throat was parched and her heart with it.

*Or do I already know. You're thinking about my best friend. My best girl. Princess. The woman who fucked my husband. She was supposed to be my girl. My ace. Which is why I should have never trusted a bitch around my always-hard husband? He couldn't go throughout the day without whacking off to porno tapes. If I heard Janet Jacme moaning one more time, "Put it in my ass, Niggah," I will freaking scream!*

"Baby." He spooned rice and beans into his mouth, careful not to drop food on his white pants.

Her brows rose.

*I'm not your baby. And I don't want to have your baby anymore.*

"Yes, Ed?"

He gave her a heartwarming smile. It did nothing for her. "You haven't said anything since we've been sitting here."

*Want to talk about business? Hmm, ok. Stock is up three points in Princess's pussy.* "Is there something you want to talk about?"

He wiped his lips with a napkin. "Yes. Us. You. What's going on with *you*?"

*You fucked Princess in my home! That's what's going on with me and both of you looked me in the fucking face and lied about it! Prick!*

"I'm fine, Ed."

"I'm fine, Ed," he mocked. "Since when did you call me Ed? You always call me *baby*."

*Bitch, fuck you!* "Not tonight." She toyed with her food, her head hanging low.

"Baby. Something is wrong."

Her head snapped up. "Ed. *Please.* Just drop it, ok? It's not that big of a deal and I really don't feel like dealing with it or talking about it."

"I'm your husband."

*He remembers! Gee golly wow!* "Oh, you remember."

He slammed the fork on the table and the table shook. Georgia wasn't rattled and she wasn't intimidated.

"Slamming forks isn't going to get me to talk."

*What is her malfunction?* "What will get you to talk, Georgia?"

*Stab yourself in the eyes and fart out my alimony. That'll do, Ed!* "Leaving me the fuck alone."

He released a large gush of air. He wasn't hungry any longer. She spoiled his appetite. "I can't do that. I'm your husband."

"You say that like it's a badge of honor."

He looked into her eyes. She averted her face. "It is."

"I don't think so, Ed."

"STOP SAYING MY NAME LIKE THAT!" he exploded.

Defiantly, she threw water on him. It splashed in his face, and dripped from his puffy cheeks. "I can say what the fuck I want."

"Don't make me slap your ass. I'm the man of the house."

"With the two ton balls. Yea, yeah, yeah. Don't I know it? Poor, poor Ed. He does what he wants, when he wants and how he wants. He stays out all night and crawls in the bed after 1 something in the morning and think by wrapping his arm around me I am going to let it slide. And when I try to do something for myself you tell me that I'm being selfish."

*Damn it! Princess would never talk to me like I'm a peasant. She's making it easier for me to leave her.* "Right now you are."

She shook her head, glaring at him. "I'm selfish? I cook your food, wash your clothes and let you fuck me to your heart's content. But as of late we haven't fucked because you fucked up, Ed."

"How did I do that?"

"When we fucked around three a.m. this morning, my heart wasn't in it. I cringed the entire time."

His ego took a nosedive. "Really?"

"Yes, really. You were so into my pussy you called me something I don't approve of. And I don't understand why you called me that."

"What? Calling you my whore? My dirty little slut? In the bedroom you are those things to me. As long as you're my dirty little harlot in the sheets but a lady in the streets that shouldn't even be a problem."

"But it is a problem, man."

"Why? What do I look like saying, my dirty angel? Or 'Oh, yea, baby! Take this penis. Yea. Let me screw you in the booty.' That doesn't move me. I want to grab those ass cheeks and be like 'Ho, take this dick! Throw that pussy back on my shit, bitch!'"

She was repulsed. She was waving her hands.

"Not at the dinner table, man."

"It's *my* table."

"It's our table. I *bought* it, motherfucker!" They stared each other down like Gladiators. "And I don't want to eat my food imagining your dick in my ass, Man. Have some fucking respect."

"You're barely touching your food."

"Because you won't shut up. And for the record I don't have a problem with you calling me names in the bed."

"Then what's the problem?"

"Your mouth wrote a check your dick can't cash."

"Meaning?"

"What do you think it means? It has meant the same thing for months."

"You aren't making any sense."

"Oh, Ed. It makes perfect sense."

"I'm tired of this…" He stood up, stretching. "I'm going to work."

"Sure. Go ahead. Go to work, Plumber."

"Plumber? I am not a *plumber*."

"Sure you are. I heard you lay good pipe."

He was suddenly guarded. "Baby…"

"It's Georgia, and I am no longer your baby. Nor do I want to ever have your motherfucking child, dumb ass!"

He was angry. "You're going to have my child. You know how much I want one…"

"This is why I'll never have your kid, bitch. When you came inside me this morning, you called me 'Princess.'"

The blood left his face.


Thomas and Princess were lying together in bed. Their legs intertwined and their toes wiggling all over each other. She was laying on his chest, listening to his heart beat. She smiled, biting back tears. She was in love with this man and he loved her.

"So what are we going to do?"

"We are leaving town, Baby," he said. "My wife filed for divorce today and when I'm served the papers I will sign them. She double-crossed me anyway."

"How?"

He kissed her forehead. He tried to forget about it but the more he thought about her deception the angrier he became.

"Do you want to know why I'm not a father?"

"Why?"

He was silent. Maybe he shouldn't talk about it. Yes, he loved Princess and yes he was happy that she was pregnant with his kid, but he wasn't used to people wanting to know his problems. He was too busy helping others with theirs.

"Maybe I shouldn't say."

Princess kissed his lips. She still could feel Thomas's dick in her. His come had long ago dried on her titties and on her ass.

"Tell me."

"OK. Here goes. She was taking birth control pills the entire time, preventing herself from getting pregnant. She was convincing me that she was trying. I thought it was me. Maybe I was shooting blanks. But when she revealed those pills to me I was crushed."

"How could she do that to you?"

The force of Georgia's words knocked the earth from beneath him. He had to sit down and shake his head for a second. *Damn it. Damn it. I fucked up. I fucked up badly.*

*Gotta do damage control.*

Ed reached across the table and took Georgia's hands. He rubbed the top of them with his hairy thumbs.

*Damn. How could I have slipped and called her Princess? I wonder what she's thinking. Thank God she doesn't know that Princess and I had sex. She's all I ever think about.*

She pulled her hands away and ran a shaky palm through her hair. He didn't understand what was going on.

"You smell nice, Ed," she said. "I see you're using Dove soap now."

He smiled, remembering when he first used it. It was when he fucked Princess in the shower in the guest room a day after his party. Princess had the hottest piece of pussy in Dade County. From day one he always wanted her. He really wanted to date Princess but she wouldn't give him the time of day. And being married to a woman he didn't love was the true crime but he could learn to love her.

"Ed."

He snapped out of the daydream. "Oh, yea. I use the soap now. Smells good, huh?"

"Yup. When did you start using it?"

"A few weeks ago."

"A few *months* ago?"

"Weeks."

"It's funny. When I wanted you to use the soap you vehemently denounced it. And now you are using it? What was the catalyst?" Georgia's eyes rose. "Something I should know?"

"No, baby. I use the soap now. Big deal."

"You're right. It is a big damn deal. And call me Georgia. I am not your baby anymore, Ed. I haven't been your baby in months. *Tell* me. What made you start using it?"

*Princess.* "You."

"*Me?*"

"Yes. I got tired of you bringing it up so I started using it. There. Happy?"

"No. I'm *not.*"

"What can I do to make it better?"

"Nothing, Ed." She stood up from the table and he rose also, walking around the table and wrapping his arms around her. She clammed up and he felt it.

He slowly pulled away from her. He slid his hands in his pockets to hide the fact that they were shaking.

"You just cringed when I hugged you."

"I did? I didn't notice."

"*Yes* you did. Now I know something is wrong."

"It is, Man. It is."

"What?"

*I can't hide it anymore.* "Let's just say the morning you started using Dove soap I found your wet boxers by the shower."

"OK." He was shaking his head. "And?"

"Princess's earring was next to it. The morning after your party."

*God! She knows!*

In good spirits, Princess was holding Thomas's hand while he drove his Monte Carlo over to Georgia's house. She couldn't believe her good fortune, that God has blessed her and changed her life. In the blink of an eye her life has been shifted heavenward, showing her everything she has been missing. The only problem was that Tina now knew she was pregnant with Thomas's child. Was she ready to deal with the nuclear fallout? Maybe. Maybe not.

Plus she still harbored a secret hurt for allowing herself to sleep with Ed behind Georgia's back.

*I should tell Thomas? No. I can't. I can't do that to him. I'm pregnant and I am happy. I want to be with him and I can't risk losing him again. I can't breathe without him. I can't hurt Georgia. I can't do it to her. She's so sweet. But the hooker in me wanted Ed's money.*

Who knew that the man she once cursed out was the father of her child? Who knew that her prostitution days were finally gone? It wouldn't even be hard to let go because true love has pushed all desire to be with other men from her heart and soul.

She told herself that she would read the Bible and go to church and nurture the good things that were happening to her. The times she slept with men and charged them for it would forever be a part of her. She would always remember the misery she faced when giving up her body for money to feed a sick need to be loved and to feel special.

Thomas smiled, turning up the radio. An old Aretha Franklin cut was on. "Giving Him something He can Feel."

He could remember his mom and dad used to dance to this song when he was growing up. He used to sit on the couch; eating his candy and watching them love each other and stroke each other's hair.

He told himself that when he was older he would treat his woman the same way.

Ed and Georgia weren't looking at each other. He has made several attempts to talk to her but Georgia shut down. What he didn't know was that she relived what she went through with Eduardo. All the hurt, all the pain and embarrassment was getting to her, slowly breaking her down. Her eyes were out of focus. *Does Princess feel better than me, Ed? This is my fault. I should have left you years ago. But no. I believed in forgiveness, giving you a second chance.*

"Georgia, Baby." He reached over and took her hand, squeezing it fondly.

She didn't squeeze it back. "What, Ed."

"We can make this work."

"How?" She looked at him, trying to keep the sting from her words. "How are we going to make this work? You cheated on me with my best friend. I feel betrayed, man."

He leaned over and kissed her cheek and she wiped it off. "I don't want my cheek smelling like Princess's pussy."

His mouth fell open. "Baby, you're being unreasonable."

She glared at him. "Unreasonable? You stick your trashy dick in another whore and I'm being unreasonable?"

"Yes. Baby, I'm not perfect."

"No, you're not. But you have common sense."

"Georgia."

"Am I packing my shit or are you going to pack yours?"

"What are you saying?"

She snatched her hand back, turning her back on him, pressing her feet on the floor. Her head hanging low, she remembered. Slitting her wrist after swallowing the pills. Her father kicking down the bathroom door. Rushing her to the hospital.

"I want you to pack your things. If you don't, then I will. I will go live with my cousin until I decide if I want to divorce you or not."

Ed jumped out of bed and raced around it, getting in her face. "You can't leave me."

She picked up the phone and called Princess. It rung a few times. Ed sat on the chair, looking into his wife's face. Too much has been done to turn back. Georgia couldn't stand the sight of him. Men were liars. They couldn't be trusted. They were pricks. *I gotta get out of here. I can't stay another second. He can have the house, everything. Maybe he'll give it to Princess. How could she betray me? I loved her. I would give her the world. She was my sister from another mother.*

"What's up, Georgia?"

"Could you come over? I want to ask you something."

"Are you ok?" Princess asked, tapping Thomas's leg. He looked into her face, wondering who was on the phone.

"Yes. I'm good. Can you come over now? I would appreciate it very much. And bring Thomas."

Ed lowered his head.

"I'm so glad you found true love. You deserve it, Girl."

Princess kissed Thomas's lips. "Thank you. We're on our way."

Georgia kissed through the phone, tears falling from her cheeks. "See you soon."

She slowly replaced the receiver.


Tina was on the phone with her lawyer. She wanted to get the divorce over with. Sure, part of her loved Thomas. But the other part didn't want to give him children. The thought of it killed her inside. She had an explosive career as a Journalist. She didn't have time to walk around barefoot and pregnant. She didn't have time to play desperate housewife. She didn't feel like being at his beck and call. So sure she took birth control pills and didn't tell him. Why not? Who said you had to tell your man every damn thing about you. Sometimes you had to keep things to yourself. Sometimes you had to put yourself first. Sometimes it had to be all about you and not your man because when it was all about your man they bragged about it to their friends, they talked bad about you and let their boys know that "Hey, she does what I want her to do," and she burst his fragile, egotistical bubble.

"So how long will the divorce take?"

"When he signs the divorce decree it will take up to six months."

"Why so long?"

"Well, its very heart wrenching. Assets have to be split up, bank accounts frozen until the judge works out the legalities. If you own houses and cars, the judge also deals with that."

*I just want it to be over.* "He can *have* everything. I just want him out of my life. I don't want to be attached to him at all."

"But what about your son?"

Tina thought about it all of three seconds. Her mind wasn't changing. "He's *not* the father."

"But he signed the birth certificate."

Tina frowned. *Lawyers are always trying to milk your piggy banks!* "Because he felt he had to. He was in love with me. But he's not the father. I tricked him in the beginning and made him think he was."

"I'll look into that for you. Don't just walk away from everything. You said he cheated on you, right?"

Tina needed a tonic. "Yes."

"And you said this Princess girl is pregnant with his child?"

Tina burned up just thinking about it. *The whore needs to die a horrible death!* Tina's heart blackened, and in her mind she wished every ill, inconceivable thought against Thomas and Princess. "Yes."

"Well let's play *our* cards right. The proof is in the pudding. If Princess's baby comes out and DNA proves *he's* the father then, *baby*, you walk away with alimony, the house and his car and the bank accounts, too. Adultery is frowned on."

Tina thought about it. Yea. I'll be damned if I see another whore living in *my* house.

Tina's eyes clouded over with evil. "I agree. Let's do that."

"Can you get them to take a paternity test?"

Tina thought about it. *I don't know about this.* "I doubt it."

"I got you, Tina. I'll have the judge subpoena the test. That way if they refuse it makes them look bad, holds them in contempt of court and they could be facing jail time."

Tina said, "OK. I'm in."


Princess looked over her dress, tugging on the waist part. Thomas hugged her, kissing her lips.

"I can't believe you're mine."

"This feels like a dream."

"And you're pregnant with *my* baby. I am *so* excited about becoming a father." He held her booty, giving her some tongue.

"I can't wait to give you a son or a daughter."

Thomas reached past her and rung the door bell. He kissed Princess's neck, drawing heat from her titties.

The door opened and Georgia smiled at her. She hugged Thomas, kissing his cheek.

"Hey, cousin! You look happy."

He looked at Princess, winking. "I am."

Georgia reluctantly hugged Princess. "Hey, Girl."

Princess felt the tension. *What's wrong with my girl?*

"Hi, Georgia." They pulled away from each other.

"Come on in. I hope I didn't disturb you all."

"No, cousin. You can never disturb me," said Thomas, coming inside. He saw Ed smoking a blunt, sitting on the couch.

"Hey, Ed!" Thomas said, giving him some skin.

"Hey, Dawg…" He held up the joint. "Wanna hit this?" Ed seemed to be in another world.

"*Hell*, yea…" Thomas pulled on the joint, holding it in his lungs. "What is this?" he asked with a strained voice.

"That's Louisiana Kush, Dawg. Chronic don't have shit on this!"

"I heard about this shit…"

"So Princess is pregnant with your baby, 'ey?"

Thomas sat next to him, blowing smoke in the air. "Yea. I'm so excited, Dawg."

"Oh, yea?" Ed asked, torn up inside that Princess carried another man's baby.

Princess barely looked at Ed. "Hi, Ed," she whispered.

Ed's eyes sparkled like diamonds. This crushed Georgia. She held her stomach, sitting at the dining table. "I called you all over for a reason," said Georgia. *Keep it together, Chile.* "Can we all sit to the table? I have some Grey Goose and some plastic cups and ice cubes. Princess, I got you some orange juice."

"Thanks, Girl," said Princess, taking Thomas's hand and pulling him to the table. When Ed looked at her Princess gave Thomas the best tongue of his life, pissing Ed off.

Georgia had a huge smile on her face, glaring at her husband. Ed sat down, trying to keep his anger under control.

The door bell rang. Princess said, "I'll get it, since I'm closer to the front door."

"Who could that be?" Georgia asked, thinking about the possibilities.

Princess ran her hands through her hair, opening the door.

She was face to face with a very beautiful woman.

"Is Georgia here?" she asked, clad in leather pants and a leather jacket and the most expensive heels she'd ever seen.

"Yea." She extended her hand. "I'm Princess."

The Leather Bitch stared into her eyes.

"And I'm Tina. Thomas's wife. Nice to finally put a face with the dream he had so many months ago."

The smile was frozen on Princess's face.

"So we finally meet, Miss Webster," said Tina, eyeing her from head to toe. Princess put her guard up, breathing Tina's cheap perfume. Rubbing her tummy, Princess said, "Yes. We finally meet."

"So I understand you and Thomas are quite the odd couple."

Princess tilted her head, scowling a tad. "I wouldn't call us the odd couple."

"Sure I would. A recovering prostitute and a soon-to-be divorced creep. I think that qualifies you for Odd Couple of the year."

"And what about you?" asked Princess. "I heard you swallow more than just birth control pills."

Tina rolled her eyes, her failures in her marriage evident and written on her face in a way her make-up failed to do. Dandruff flakes were on her collar and this grossed Princess out. "Watch it."

"I did. I watched him hold me, kiss me and protect me at night. I watched him smile, laugh and shed tears of joy when we finally found our way back to each other."

"I guess I should look around to make sure Ashton Kutcher ain't punking me."

Princess tried to slam the door in her face and Tina pushed it open. "Face me. Be a woman!" Tina said and Princess spun on her heel, walking to the kitchen.

"Who's at the door?" Georgia asked, and Tina grabbed Princess above the elbow and Princess snatched her arm back.

"Look, bitch. I don't suck pussy. So don't grab me like you lost your mind."

Dropping his napkin, Thomas stood up and pulled Princess behind him. "Why are you here?"

Tina opened her leather attaché case and pulled out a manila folder, wiggling it in his face. "These papers got more gun powder than Iraq."

"Are you trying to be funny?"

"No. I want a divorce. Just sign the goddamn papers and we can all be happy."

"I am already happy. Princess is unlike any woman I've ever met."

"Do you say that to all the whores you buy?"

Insulted, Princess tried to get to Tina but Ed stood up, placing a friendly hand on Tina's shoulder. "Can we all talk like adults. Princess is pregnant."

Georgia said, "Tina, sit down for a minute."

"I just want Thomas to sign the papers," Tina said, tears falling from her eyes. "He cheated on me with swine. I thought pigs belonged in a pig pen."

"Bitch you got one more time to insult me," Princess said, sitting down in the chair. She was opening and closing her hands into fists.

Tina dropped the papers on the table. "Sign them."

"After I read over them I will."

"You can read them now!"

Georgia stood up, walking to the fridge. She needed a stiff drink. It seemed that divorce was the big theme tonight.

"I want my lawyer present."

Tina wasn't hearing him. *"Sign them now."*

Thomas hated being embarrassed in front of family and friends. "Bitch, fuck off! I'm a grown man!"

Tina raised her hand to slap him but she refrained. *I'm going to make him look like a pussy in front of a pussy ass bitch!* "I don't want you!"

"And I hate you, whore! Go swallow some more birth control pills and hide the fact that you are a deceitful bitch!"

Thomas sneered, throwing the divorce papers across the room. Ed's mouth fell open. Georgia, an open beer in her grasp, sat back at the table and said, "Look, Tina. We all need to talk. All parties here are guilty of something. No one in this dining room is exempt. We all need to calm down. We're acting like children." When she said it she wanted to take it back. Georgia wanted to bash Princess's head in and watch the bitch bleed to death.

Tina ran her hands through her hair, shaking. She was about to explode. Princess stood up and walked over to the dining room window, looking outside. Thomas looked over his shoulder, making sure she was all right.

Ed didn't know what to do. Part of him wanted to hold Princess and protect her and kiss her face and tell her that he wanted to spend his life with her but another part of him respected Thomas.

Georgia set the beer down. "Princess. Why."

Princess looked at her. "Why, what?" *Damn, I hope she hasn't figured it out. God, no. Please don't let that be the case. I'm so not ready to reveal it. I can't deal with it. I'm pregnant for God's sake and if anything messes up my chances of being with Thomas I'd rather die.*

Georgia slowly stood up, cautiously walking over to her friend. She looked her over, trying to find the words. She hurt inside. "Why did you do it? I loved you like a sister. I thought I could *trust* you."

Thomas said, "Georgia, *she's* pregnant. She is dealing with *enough* stress." Thomas wondered what she was talking about. His mind worked overtime.

Georgia looked at him blankly. She felt nothing inside for anyone at the moment. "Do you *love* her?"

Thomas said, "Yes. I will die for her. She carries my child." He wasn't too sure of it. He was still getting over the fact that the woman he fought turned out to be the love of his life.

Georgia was skeptical. You didn't meet somebody and boom, fall in love. Love wasn't a nuclear bomb. "You don't *know* that."

Everyone fell silent. Ed's mouth fell open. Thomas looked at Princess.

Tina said, "If this was Maury Pouvich, he would open the DNA test and say 'Thomas, you are *not* the father...'"

Thomas snapped on her. He wrapped his hands around Tina's neck and tried to rip out her esophagus. Ed grabbed his arm, and used all the strength he could muster to pull him off. Princess simply looked out the window and Georgia snatched Princess by the arm. Tina sat down, trying to catch her breath. "That's all you can do when I tell you the truth, Thomas? Is attack me?"

Thomas was so infuriated he wanted to bash her face in. "*Fuck* you, bitch! You're turning me really bitter really fast."

Once Ed calmed Tina and Thomas down, Georgia took Princess's hand, fondly squeezing it. She smiled. Princess smiled. Georgia asked, "*Why* did you fuck my husband the morning after Ed's party?"

Princess's mouth fell open. *No, no! This can't be happening, God! Please, not now. Please let this be a trick, Lord. PLEASE! Oh my God! I love my Girl, and now she thinks I betrayed her. Hell, I did betray her.* "Girl. I'm sorry. It was a mistake." *A mistake! Bitch! A mistake? I had distorted thinking.*

Tina said, "I guess when you and Thomas fucked, *that* was a mistake too. Tramps, I tell you. Thomas I hope you're happy."

"TINA!" Georgia spewed, shutting her up. Georgia got in Princess's face. "Talk to me. I was your best friend. We have gone through thick and thin together. And you do this to me. Face me. Grab your titties and face me, damn it!"

Princess was breaking apart at the seams. "Georgia, *please...*"

Shocked beyond his wildest dreams, Thomas said, "When did you sleep with Ed?" You could hear the hurt in his voice. If it was one thing Thomas believed in it was Georgia's and Ed's marriage. He rooted for them. He could remember when they got married. He attended. He remembered what he bought them: sexy underwear for their honeymoon.

Ed said, "You two don't have to gang up on her."

"Oh, God," said Tina. "What a love triangle this is. Now Ed loves the prostitute."

Princess rubbed her arms, wanting to run. "I can't do this." She sped past Georgia and Georgia was on her ass. When Princess whipped open the front door Georgia pushed it closed, standing in front of it. "Don't run. Talk to me. How did you suck his dick?" Georgia sunk to her knees, holding Princess's hips. "Were you this close from it? His boxers on my guest bathroom floor and your earring by the toilet?"

"Georgia, please…"

"How did it taste? Did his dick taste better than Thomas's? Or what about his brother? He paid for it, didn't he? Didn't you try to steal Thomas's phone number out of his brother's phone when ya'll had sex in your Daddy's house? Maybe I should call him and let him know you ran a whore ring from under his roof!"

Thomas rushed over to Princess, burning up inside. He didn't know who to believe or what to say. The rug felt pulled from beneath his feet. "Is this true? You fucked my *brother*?"

"Seems like this tramp can't keep her lips closed…Is this who you want to spend your life with, Thomas? You messed up our happy home for the Whore of Babylon?"

Thomas said, "Did you sleep with Ed?"

Princess said, "Yes."

"And when were you going to tell me, Princess?"

"Everything is happening so fast! I was going to tell you!"

Tina looked at Thomas. "I want a paternity test of that baby. You will get a subpoena. I am going to prove that you committed adultery and when I do I am cleaning your ass out."

Princess watched Georgia stand up. "Princess. Who's the father of that baby? Is it Ed?" Georgia watched Thomas cringe inside. "Or is it Thomas?"

Princess tried to hug Thomas but he backed away from her, shaking his head. "Answer the question, Princess. Who's the father?"

"Thomas. We can talk about this in private."

"Seems like doing shit in private is what got you in a world of shit. Can you not control your pussy, whore?" Tina asked, clearly devastated.

Princess said, "I gotta go!" She opened the door, rushing outside. Her heels clicked against the sidewalk, heading for the car. She had the keys in her purse. Thomas could find his way home.

"Princess!" Ed called out, running behind her. He wanted to wrap his arms around her and protect her from the cold world.

"GET AWAY FROM ME!" *Oh, God! I'm losing everything. Every bed I made I gotta lay in. I only have one body. I can't do this. Who is the father of my child?*

Georgia brutally snatched Princess by the hair. They started fighting. Georgia slapped Princess so hard she fell to her knees, the pain from the sidewalk making her mouth fall open. She kicked Princess in the chin, and she fell back, her head slamming into the pavement. She moaned piteously. Georgia started remembering. Eduardo. Her cousin. Fucking him. The suicide attempt. The knife. The party. The family.

"You fucked my husband in my house, you trifling bitch!"

Thunder boomed and out of nowhere it started to rain. Tina tripped over her own feet trying to get a piece of Princess. Once she did, she kicked Princess in the face and she fell back on the wet grass. Staggering to her feet, Georgia and Tina double-teamed Princess, their feet crashing into her skull, titties and face. Blood began to openly pour into the lawn. Princess had never known so much pain in her life.

She began twitching where she lay, her legs thumping against the ground. Crazed, Tina had completely lost it. She blamed Princess for taking her husband; she blamed Princess for all of her faults as well. In her own sick way, Princess was to blame for everything that has gone wrong in Tina's life. At least that's what she told herself.

When Tina picked up a cinder block, trying to smash it into Princess's face, Thomas grabbed Tina and she turned and dug her nails into his face.

Thomas punched her so hard in the nose Tina lay unconscious on the grass. Georgia was kicking Princess in the side. "I hate you, bitch!" She was a monster. "I loved you! I trusted you! And you took my husband!"

Pain skyrocketed throughout Princess's body. She curled in the fetal position, blood pouring from between her legs. She started screaming, holding her stomach as the rain continued to pour. Thomas panicked.

"Oh, no! No! The baby!" he yelled, about to lose his mind.

All the blood left Georgia's face.

*What have I done?*

Terrified, Ed picked up Princess, rushing to his car. She was heavy but he didn't care. He'd carry her all the way to the hospital if he had to.

He didn't bother with calling 9-1-1. She might be dead by the time they arrived. They always took their time to answer calls in the black neighborhood of Florida City.

"Hold on, baby! Hold on!"

Thomas ran behind Ed. "I'm going with you. I'll drive." Thomas heart beat out of his chest, his breathing coming in short spurts.

When it dawned on Georgia that Princess could lose her baby she ran inside the house and grabbed her car keys. Her head spun so fast she nearly vomited on her carpet.

"What have I done, Lord? My anger has gotten the best of me. God, I don't want the baby to die."

It may be too late.

Princess ached all over. She was distraught, clearly out of her natural mind. She did know that lights sporadically passed over her face. The truck was silent. She felt Ed stroking her face. He was rocking back and forth, scared out of his mind. Tears dripped from his chin and onto her face. Thomas kept looking at them through the rear-view mirror. He blamed himself. He shouldn't have cheated on his wife. He shouldn't have brought Princess into his life when he wasn't even divorced yet. What was he thinking? Did he truly love Princess? He battled his emotions. He didn't know what he wanted. Everything happened so fast. Everything was so convenient. His father once taught him that if a foundation wasn't met then a relationship couldn't be built. The house would topple like sticks. The debris would be washed out to sea with the current. Why didn't he listen? Now Princess might be losing the baby. His baby.

Or Ed's baby.

Ed was sitting in the Lobby at Jackson South, on 152$^{nd}$ Street. Princess's Daddy wasn't a happy camper. Once Georgia explained to him everything that has been going on he was in shock. Thomas was trying to focus on the news but he couldn't. His eyes were so red you couldn't see his pupils. Georgia was pacing around, the Pepsi soda going warm in her hand. She tried to sip it but she felt like throwing it up. They have been waiting for six hours, and nothing. When Thomas went to the circulation desk, asking for a check up on Princess, the nurse didn't offer him any information. Ed was about to go crazy. He loved Princess with all of his heart.

Georgia decided to sit down. She wondered about Tina. She was brought to the very hospital by the ambulance. For some reason she really didn't care if she was all right or not. She worried about the baby.

Ed looked at Georgia. "I hope you're happy."

"No, Ed, I'm not," Georgia snapped, a few people listening in on their conversation since there wasn't anything exciting on TV.

Thomas said, "Ed, no one is happy about this."

Princess's father stood up, walking outside. He wasn't in the right frame of mind to hear their bickering. His daughter was pregnant and he didn't have a clue. Finding all this out in one night did a number on him.

"You should have thought about that before ya'll gang up on a pregnant woman. Now she could lose her baby."

"I feel bad, man. Trust me I do. I love Princess."

"Really?" said Ed, standing up and getting in his face. "*Really?* You love her?"

Thomas looked up at him, trying to remain calm. "I am confused, Ed."

"Confused?"

Georgia said, "So am I. I'm losing my husband. I'm losing my marriage. I don't know if I'll ever forgive you and Princess for what you did."

"OK, Georgia. I fucked up. There. Move on. Princess is in the hospital. Because of you and your uncontrollable anger."

"I had to make her pay."

"And you see what payments can do, right?"

"Don't try to chastise me in front of people."

"Fuck you, Georgia!"

Her mouth fell open. She couldn't believe her marriage has resorted to this. "Whatever, Ed."

A tall doctor, early forties, suddenly appeared, trying to get Georgia's attention. When he finally did, she rushed over to him, looking scared. Thomas ran outside to get Princess's father. Ed's heart seemed to stop beating.

"Doctor…how is she?"

Before he could answer Princess's overbearing father rushed into the hospital, and up to him, with Thomas at his side.

"How is my daughter?"

Dr. Beckman reached out and took his hands.

"There is never an easy way to say this…"

"Say what?" he snapped, about to go crazy.

"Doctor…" Georgia's legs were shaking so bad she had to sit down. Ed's heart fell out of his chest.

"I'm sorry. Princess…neither she *nor* her baby made it."

Princess's father grabbed Georgia by the neck and started squeezing. "YOU BITCH! YOU FUCKING BITCH! YOU KILLED MY DAUGHTER!"

Thomas grabbed him, on the verge of breakdown himself. Ed grabbed Georgia and pulled her outside. Georgia was weeping so hard she couldn't breathe. She was in denial. God, Princess couldn't be dead. And the baby, too. God, help her. Save her. God why was this happening. As Ed put Georgia in the car, closing the door, Princess's father broke free of Thomas's embrace and he sprinted outside. Looking around wildly, he didn't see the security guards running at him. When he saw Ed's car he picked up a brick and ran full throttle for the car. He threw the brick through the windshield, and it hit Georgia in the face. Glass cut her across the cheek and neck. He dived into the windshield, chocking her to death. Blood was everywhere. Ed opened the door, grabbing him by the arm, trying to pull him out. Security guards intervened. Once they pulled him out of the car, he wouldn't stop screaming. Georgia was losing a large amount of blood.

Police officers thundered from the hospital. They apprehended Princess's father and Georgia.

They read them their rights.

They were co-defendants. Georgia and Tina. They were whisked into a public nightmare. Their faces splashed across every newspaper across the country. On the TV their lives played out. They were being talked about in businesses and hospitals. Both of the women, once very good friends, were pitted against each other. They were looking at life in prison for the murder of Princess Webster and her unborn child. Princess's father wasn't fit emotionally to come to the trial. Temporarily, he checked himself into a mental ward. He said he would kill Tina and Georgia if he hadn't. He was under 24 hour surveillance.

Georgia's lawyer was a recently graduating scholar from Yale. Coming from a family high on the pedigree chain, she was white, blonde and knew her shit. Georgia paid out the ass to get her on the case. But from how it looked, Liliana Gray said, point blank, "We have to enter a plea. Because if you fight this you will lose. Thomas and Ed are testifying against you. Both of these men were obviously in love with your ex best friend and their passion alone, their hurt and grave pain will be enough to get you convicted."

"I don't want to plea. I want to go all the way through with it. I wasn't in my right frame of mind. And I hate spending time in jail. It's horrible in there."

"I will see to it."

"I hope so. I want to win. She shouldn't have taken my husband," Georgia spat icily. Tina, sitting next to her, was trapped within herself. She was already raped in jail and she was threatened. Big Pussy Dropper told her that if she snitched her out she would die a horrible death. Tina knew she was being punished, and she couldn't believe she lost custody of her son. The Department of Children and Families was set to find a deserving family for the boy if she was found guilty. And even if she by some twist of fate beat the charges, the Department would keep the child with an adoptive family until they saw Tina fit.

Liliana sat next to Georgia, opening her brief case. She pulled out some files and set them on the table. The courtroom was filled to capacity. Several news programs were interrupted across the country with this harrowing tale. When the Honorable Judge James came from his chambers, the bailiff told everyone to "rise."

Everyone did. He was a burly man with a thick mustache and an overbearing, piercing gaze.

He sat down and began his opening remarks.

Georgia couldn't sleep. A week has passed and nothing went right in court. Watching Ed testify against her devastated her. Hadn't he betrayed her enough? When Ed looked her in the eyes and said, "Georgia and Tina stomped her on the ground, in the rain. I stood helpless, like I couldn't do anything…" Georgia lost it. She jumped up to her feet screaming.

"You fucked that slut! You were my husband! What happens to you for your infidelity?"

The judge ferociously beat his gavel.

"Order, Georgia! ORDER! One more outburst in my courtroom and I will hold you in contempt of court."

Reluctantly, Georgia sat down, covering her face. Tina didn't say anything. She already entered her guilty plea. There wasn't anything she could do. She wasn't going to be like Georgia and publicly embarrass herself.

Princess's doctor testified. Pictures were shown of her brutalized face. The members of the jury cringed, some of them lowering their eyes. Georgia turned away from them, sobbing. Tina put a huge smile on her face, shocking the entire courtroom.

*I'm glad she's dead, bitch!*

The day had come for the verdict. Georgia kept her fingers crossed. She was still dazed that she threw her life away. Everything that she was as a woman, everything that she accomplished has gone up in smoke. Ed sat behind her, refusing to talk to her. He didn't even acknowledge her.

*You're making me suffer. You killed the one woman I loved with my heart. I would never know if she was carrying my child. You robbed me of that, Georgia. I never knew you had blackness in your heart.*

Thomas didn't say much. During the entire trial, he didn't say one word. He didn't talk to family. With his brother present, he didn't talk to him, either. He didn't talk to friends. He quit his job. A thick beard has grown on his face. He was slowly letting himself go. When the "Guilty" verdicts were read Georgia had gone deaf. A loud sound filled her ears and she covered her face, screaming. Tina remained quiet. She smiled, standing up. Police men handcuffed them.

Georgia and Tina got life in prison, without the possibility of parole.

# On the Low Low 2

Now see, I was mad! Deeply upset. I was so damn pissed off my bladder jerked and it wasn't pretty. I was going through a bitter divorce from a very selfish man. I never imagined that my wedding day so many moons ago would turn into the onslaught it has become. I have been separated from my husband, Terrance Jo'Shawn, for about nine months, with his punk ass. How could he fuck my brother and not tell me? Hell, how could my brother betray me like that? Fucking my husband in my bed when I worked. I thought I could trust him, like any big sister would.

I bought his broke ass things and I was there for him. He's the only man that I knew who had a good job and was broke an hour after he got paid. I could have been a cruel bitch and spread his business, but it would make me look bad. I was raised better than that and I really didn't want my girlfriends knowing I married a gay man who really wanted my brother and not me. How could I have been so stupid? You read about this type of shit in books and in Terry McMillan's life, but not in mine. Ugh! I swear! I had the best pussy in town, yet my husband left me for the best piece of ass in the United States. Who knew my brother loved a banana in his tail pipe instead of in banana pudding?

Thank God we didn't have kids. If I had a son or daughter I would have to tell them their father was gay. And who gave a shit about Clay Aiken coming out on People magazine saying I'm Gay with his newborn son? I didn't believe in gay people raising children. That was just me. Who would be the daddy? Seriously?

Before I go any further I should say how I caught my husband playing around dookey chutes. I had come home months ago to my man waiting for me, or so I thought. We kissed and all that jazz. I didn't even know that he was fucking my brother prior to me coming home. My brother was hiding in the guest bathroom, half naked, his heart beating out of his chest. Of course I was the dumb bitch. The joke was on me. So my husband told me to go shower and I did. I was washing my body, playing with my pussy, trying to get a quick nut so when he pulverized my pussy with his incredible cock it would take me a long ass time to come the second time.

When I come I come harder than 50 Cent riding a tricycle balancing Ja Rule on his magic Stick. My knees buckling, my weave was wet from the shower. I didn't care. I was about to get the royal fuck down from my husband and sweat my hair out anyway.

I turned off the shower and I heard my man fucking my brother through the wall. I was so in shock I stood there for a minute, hoping it was a porno tape. And even if it was a porno, why would my man have gay flicks?

I sat on the toilet, about to pull my hair out. I heard them. Oh, yea. Feels good. Fuck me, Terrance and all that jazz. I couldn't move, I was nailed to the floor, my life blowing up in my face like a bad face lift. By the time I walked out of the bathroom, leaving the towel on the floor my brother was long gone. I went in the guest bathroom and smelled sex in the air. They didn't clean up very well. I wondered where my man was. I looked for him. He was in the kitchen, with a towel wrapped around his waist, looking good enough to eat. But I wasn't hungry. My eyes were so red I couldn't cry. Why should I cry over a gay ass motherfucker? If he would have told me before I married him that he experimented with men I would have still married him because he was compassionate, kind and loving and you never knew what a person went through in his life that turned him towards guys. He treated elders like Gods, held gainful employment, and fucked a good meal when he cooked it the way he got this pussy in the sack. But since he decided for me, choosing to lie to me, taking his vows under false pretenses, all wouldn't be fair in the game of divorce.

Absent-mindedly, he poured me a cup of coffee. I held the Styrofoam cup, simmering. I refused to look at him. It took everything in me not to gut his dumb ass. He smiled like everything was all right. Was he really that heartless? Was it that easy for him to lie? Did he think about me when he fucked my brother? Did they bash me? I thought he was my partner as well as my best friend. I guessed I was wrong. He tried to hug me and I walked past him, groaning.

"Baby, I wanna make love to you."

I paused by the stove, setting the cup by a huge bowl of fake fruit. The fake bowl seemed symbolic to my fake ass husband.

*Baby, I wanna make love to you.* "You do?"

"Yes." He traced invisible shapes on my cheek. Felt so good, but I had to force myself to become stone. If I gave in to him it would mean that I condoned what he did in the darkness. Didn't he understand that what's done in the dark will come to the light?

He took me in his arms, and I welcomed it, reminding myself of what I *wouldn't* be missing when I left him. Should I leave him? Shouldn't I stay and try to work it out? How could I work it out with someone who didn't even love me? That would be a complete waste of time to even try to save something he ruined when he slid his dick inside my brother. He kissed my neck and I was self-consciously rubbing his back. My pussy was wet. I tried to go numb but I *couldn't*. I loved the way he touched me. I was obsessed with his body and his hands. This body loved him and oh how my heart missed him like a Janet song.

*Kick his ass! Kick his ass!*

"Let's do something different," I told him, my tits bouncing as I opened the cupboard and took out the duct tape. He was getting excited. I didn't know what I had in mind, but I did want to immobilize the bastard so I could do what I had to do. And it wasn't going to be pretty. Not by a long shot.

"Damn! You wanna get freaky?"

I giggled like a white girl. "Yea-uh! Sure, why not?"

"Add some spice in our life!"

"Sit in the dinette chair…"

He sat down, putting both wrists on the arms. I ducked taped them one by one. I then duct taped his ankles together. I started sucking on his dick and his head leaned back with pleasure. His dick grew in my mouth, and it tasted so sweet.

I stood up and went into my bedroom. I told him I'd be back. I took the blindfold from his side of the bed and waltzed my hot, upset ass back into the kitchen. I blindfolded him. I straddled his waist, lowering my pussy on his dick, tossing my hair like Hurricane Ike.

He moaned obscenities. His dick filled me up like a glove, taking me away once again. Every time he fucked me it was an odyssey, an epic adventure of hair pulls, toe curling and ass slapping.

I held his head, bouncing on that dick, like a real bitch. I was Heather Hunter and he was Sean Michaels.

"Baby I'm about to come!" he said. I stopped riding him, standing up. He tried to break free of the tape to finish him off and I sucked my pussy off his dick.

"Suck it, baby…make that dick spit."

"You want to come on Mama's pretty face?"

His hips were moving a mile a minute. His scent, heavenly, just the way I loved.

"YES!"

"Oh, yea! Give it to me!"

"I'm coming!"

When his come spurted from the head of his dick, I snatched up the huge coffee pot and dumped it all over him, scorching his faggot ass.

*Die, bitch! You cheated on me with my brother in my house then suffer the consequences!*

Experiencing excruciating pain, he savagely tried to break free of the duct tape, trying to get out of the chair. He fell on his face, his ass in the air. He twitched on the floor like a fish outta water and I didn't feel a twinge of remorse. Why should I? I'd rather be gouged with hot coffee than go out and knowingly cheat on my man.

I brutally beat him in the head with the glass pot, the pot cracking in four different places.

"YOU BEEN FUCKING MY BROTHER, FAGGOT!"

He laid still, his body unmoving. I stared at him, dropping the pot.

I lowered myself to my knees, sobbing over his body. Was he dead? Did I care? I hope he had some decent insurance because I wasn't paying for his burial. And when I was done I called the police and told them if they didn't get his faggot ass out of my house I was going to call Miss. Bobbitt and cut up another dick.

BITCH! That was months ago. I couldn't say that I was glad for winding up in the slammer. I had to do two months and I was on three years' probation. The only reason why I didn't get three years for assault and other charges was because Terrance felt guilty for being caught and he asked them to go easy on me. I didn't care, honestly. My brother skipped town and refused to talk to me. I didn't lose any sleep. The day was coming when he had to face me and deal with the aftermath. I was going to royally fuck him, and not in the way he liked. Terrance and I were in court when he made the "go easy on her" remark. Angrily, I jumped up from my chair and shouted, "If you didn't go easy on my brother's asshole, why go easy on me? You don't think I'm woman enough? I'm not *tough* enough?"

My lawyer told me to calm down and the judge was going through a divorce herself so she didn't say too much. Terrace, half of his face fucked up for life, refused to say anything else. He had to go to physical therapy, and he had to see a shrink. Initially, the courts recommended that we go to marriage counseling but there wasn't enough marriage counseling in the world that would make me forget a dick in his goddamn mouth and ass. So the court ruled that possibility out. Bottom line: my marriage was over. And they were all going to laugh at me. The hating bitches who said it wouldn't last.

Now I was getting my life back together. My divorce would be final next week and I couldn't wait. There was no love lost between us, but there would be no love gained with his stinky ass around me.

I walked away with the house, the car and a nice severance package from our business transaction of a marriage. Shortly after my court room drama I met a man named Andrew at the grocery store. He seemed promising. I asked him where did he work and he said he was a corrections officer. It was all good. I did see a nice pair of pumps and a few wigs I wanted from the Mall. I think I just found my cash cow. We hooked up, fucked in his van and we started seriously dating. It didn't last very long. I put my all into the relationship, but he didn't.

It was what it was.


MySpace has come into my life. I sat behind the computer, looking at those fine ass men! Damn! The candy store was right in my face. Shopping for dick has never been so easy. Part of me missed my soon-to-be-ex husband, but my heart told me the separation was necessary. I didn't want to be with a man who didn't love me. Terrance and his ordeals have drained me and the only thing I needed a man for was to suck this pussy like a Tootsie pop and fuck me to sleep. I could handle the rest when I sent his ass home. I wasn't ready to be a kept woman. I wasn't interested in one woman men. Fuck it. I was going to do me and do me well.

Sending messages to all those hunks online was a cinch! In ten minutes I must have sent out eleven of them. Online now icons flashed under their default pictures. In no time I got a response.

Hell, I was bending over in my main profile picture, clad in pink high heels and a huge afro wig. What Niggah wouldn't look at all that ass and get at me? They better get into it because time was limited.

I read the message from someone who called himself the Pussy Bandit. Hey! Get right on down to business, shall we!

SUP WITH YOU, PRETTY LADY? I
AM DIGGING THAT PROFILE PICTURE.
BUT CAN I DIG YOU? I AIN'T G'ON LIE.
I JUST WANNA FUCK, SO WHAT'S UP?

Hell, yea! There was nothing wrong with a little premarital sex. My blood boiling from the anticipation of getting my boots knocked, I thought up a quick response. I sent him a message back.

I WANNA DO THE DAMN THING.
SO WHAT'S UP. SHOOT ME A NUMBER OR SOMETHING AND WE
CAN MAKE THIS HAPPEN.

I decided to hook up with The Pussy Bandit's fine ass. He had a gorgeous face, fabulous chest and I remembered I played with myself while looking at his photos. On his Top Friend list were big booty Ho's. Ego problems, Sir? I didn't care. Just as long as he fucked me good, licked my pussy and my crack then we would be fine. When I called him (finally) I asked him why he didn't smile in any of his pictures. He told me he didn't like smiling, that people ran him over and assumed he was nice when he did so I was like "OK, we gotta meet." I was fresh out of a relationship with Andrew.

Men and I weren't hitting it. I was still waiting for my divorce to be final. Andrew was too controlling, too contrived and lied more than Eddie Murphy in *Beverly Hills Cop*. And the bad part about it was that he lied with a straight face.

I should have known that fucking a corrections officer wasn't going to cut it.

I got all dolled up. I shaved my pussy with a dull ass razor, to give it that…edge and I wiped baby oil all over my lower half so it shined when I pulled down my panties. Nah. I'd let him use his teeth to take off my panties. Maybe I should clit ball. Clit ball meant leave the panties at home and let the fabric of my clothing brush the kitty and keep it purring. I wanted to call my girlfriends and tell them of my new find. But I quickly decided against it because I didn't need them Clit Blocking. Clit Blocking was when they found out about your man and went behind your back trying to fuck him.

Mama called me and told me that she wanted to take me out but I declined because my pussy was hot and my breasts wanted to be out and about some action so I pulled up my panty hose, crawled into a long, flowing black skirt with ruffles on the ass and a breathtaking black blouse with golden Chinese art on the sleeves. I had to put Mama on speaker phone so I could use my hands.

"Baby, we should really go out to the Olive Garden."

To top off my outfit, I rubbed cocoa butter on my face and decided against make-up.

"I don't like the Olive Garden, Ma. I'm black, not Italian."

"I know you're not Italian, dumb ass. I'm just saying…let's go out. Mother and daughter bonding. We haven't done that in such a long time. Plus you're getting divorced. You don't need to be alone."

"But I am alone, Ma. And I'm a big girl. I can take care of myself."

"Whatever. Look, I'm about to go. I gotta quilt I need to finish knitting."

"I got you, Ma. I love you. Bye."

I hung up.

The reason why I chose to leave the make-up alone was because I wanted to show his fine ass that I didn't need the pyrotechnics of make-up to pull a man.

It was that simple.

I should have asked his name. I wasn't about to call him the Pussy Bandit.

What if he couldn't fuck? I didn't wanna jinx the dick so I kept my eyes wide shut.

My lips were chapped. I took a trick from my cousin Melissa Jackson's playbook and wiped pussy all over my lips, so I didn't have to bother with lip-gloss.

OK. I looked the finished product over in the mirror. Ah. Yes. I'm the shit, believe that, Ho. So I locked my house, my purse under my arm and I smelled pussy on my lips all the way to his crib. I chewed some Winter Fresh, to give it some attitude. I heard on the radio that people needed to register to vote. I knew I was. I'd rather see Obama than George Bush in the Presidential seat. When I got to the Pussy Bandit's home I parked by two garbage cans. His place wasn't anything extraordinary, but I actually liked it. Cozy little place. OK. I could fuck in there. I could tell he did his own landscaping. His car, a Chrysler, was polished to a shine. The tires gleamed like diamonds. The expensive rims glittered like gold. There was a rose garden growing under the window, and as I approached the door I heard some Erykah Badu. So the brothah had some flavor. Hell, yeah.

When I got to the door I pulled the compact mirror from my purse and looked myself over. I could have done something different with the hair but why do *that* when I only came over here to get my hair pulled while he fucked me? I wasn't auditioning for America's Top Model.

Before I could knock my cell rang. I loved running my trap on the phone so I answered, wishing I stopped by my cousin Sted's house in Florida City and bought a few dime bags of weed.

"Yes, Ma…"

"Can I use your washing machine?"

"Why, Ma? Don't you have your *own*? Sure you do. I bought you the most expensive dryer and washer combo Best Buy had to offer…"

"Yes! But I wanna wash my clothes over your house because my light bill has gone up a hundred dollars."

I stomped my foot, my hand on my hip. "So you want to run mine up? No, Ma!"

She sighed audibly. "Come on, Girl! It's not fair! I'm your Mama and I…I have been there for you and taken good care of you; and when you were growing up you didn't want for anything. And I paid for your Prom and bought you your first car. As a matter of fact you are still driving it around town like you're grand and I can't wash my clothes at your house, Girl? God don't like ugly…"

"And God don't like you washing your Granny panties in my washer, Ma! The *last* time you washed clothes at my house your thick, synthetic bloomers stalled my shit and smoke set off the smoke detector. You waste detergent all over the floor, didn't bother to clean it and you secretly washed my *brother's* clothes without telling me and you *know* I can't *stand* his ass. You violated my trust and I don't want you doing that to me again, Ma!"

"He's your brother, good or bad. I didn't raise my children to be at odds and ends with each other."

"You should have said that before my brother fucked my man! Did you raise him to be gay? I don't remember pussy looking like a dick."

"Girl, watch your mouth. He's my son."

"And you love him more than me."

"I love you both equally."

"*Imagine* coming home and finding your man playing Barry White. You think he's naked for you and your brother is hiding in the guest bathroom, having just had sex with your goddamn husband, faking like he was taking a shower. Are you *serious*? Then on top of *that* I heard them through the bathroom wall, trying to keep it all quiet and shit. He didn't *remember* that *our* bathroom was on the *opposite* side of those cheap tiled walls." Tears fell down my face. It still hurt to think about it. "...I was devastated! And then I meet *Andrew* and dumped his sorry ass because he *also* fucked my brother and he had the nerve to *lie* about it."

"That's hasn't been proven. I'm not going to let anybody bash my son. Not even my own daughter."

"Oh, *yea*? It hasn't been proven? Then *why* was Andrew wearing my brother's draws? I bought my brother that underwear for his birthday a couple years back and Andrew came home with them on. He mistakenly put on the wrong draws after he fucked my faggot ass brother. So for that reason I don't want you washing clothes at my house because I know you're going to try to wash my brother's clothes."

"Baby, *please*. Can I wash clothes at your house? I don't have time for all this back and forth. My nerves are bad and I'm wearing my bad wig so my head tingles when I think too much. Goddamn!"

I waved my hand. "All right, all right. Come by in a few hours and I'll wash your clothes."

"Too late. I just poured in the Tide with Bleach. And you didn't tell me you knew how to bake peach cobbler. You got a lot of food in your fridge. How did you get all of this food, they don't load the food stamp card until the first of the month and it's the middle of August..."

I tucked my chin back. "I'm grown. I stopped explaining myself when I got my first taste of dick. Good bye, Ma. And keep my house clean!"

I hung up.

I knocked on the door because I didn't see a door bell. I was already hell bent on that because I wasn't trying to chip my nails by knocking.

When I got my acrylics done by the Asians my fingers were accidental prone. I paid over $40 dollars for my nails and I'd beat a bitch's ass over them.

No one came to the door. I knocked again, holding my purse, sucking my teeth.

Again, nothing. OK.

Was anybody home? Did I make a blank trip?

I called his ass on my cell and he answered. The music blared through the receiver and I yanked my head back from the phone.

"HELLO?" he was screaming.

"I'm at your door," I said politely.

"WHAT? I CAN'T HEAR YOU! HELLO!" he said louder.

"I'm at the door," I said more sternly.

"WHAT?"

"MAN I'M AT THE DOOR!"

"WHAT! STOP PLAYING ON THE PHONE!"

"I'M NOT PLAYING MOTHERFUCKER ANSWER THE DOOR!"

"YOU'RE BREAKING UP, *WHAT?*"

Fed up, I bammed on the door, my nail snapping on my index finger. It popped me on the forehead.

Damn it! God*damn* it! After a few moments, he turned down the music. He opened the door, smiling like a Cheshire Cat. He engulfed me like we were long lost friends, his dick pressed against my pussy.

"Hey, Girl! I didn't *know* you were out here."

I closed my eyes, inhaling, my pussy getting dryer than the sun.

I *now* knew why he didn't smile.


I stared at Gumby with a fake smile. He extended his hand and I shook it, wanting to run. He was a gorgeous man, but his grill? Oh my God! He probably didn't have a dental plan with his current employer. My clit seemed to pull back deeper into my body.

"Would you like to come in for a drink?" He was trying to grab my hand and I was snatching it back, clearly annoyed.

"*No,* Gumby…I meant, no, no I'm ok. My Mom called. She wants to wash clothes at my house and…I gotta get home."

Gumby smiled again. Ugh, God! Shoot me. I half covered my face. I wasn't trying to be rude but his mouth made his face look like shit. I didn't want to play this game anymore, Gumby. Game Over. You win.

"She can wash clothes over here. Damn you're fine. I know you can't wait to take this dick," he went on, his breath smelling like somebody bathed his tongue in pure shit. He wore baggy jeans, with his boxers in plain view.

He started slowly walking around me, checking me out like I was in a police line up. When I saw the shit stains on the back of his boxers it was a wrap. Now if you knew you wasn't going to wipe your ass at least wear black underwear. I was about to puke. One of his nipples were shorter than the other, he had jacked feet and he had so much dirt behind his nails you'd swear he was clawing through dirt.

"No, I don't want my mother washing clothes over here…she doesn't know you like that."

He kissed my cheek and it took everything in me not to spray Lysol disinfectant spray on my face to kill the germs. Ugh, man!

"She can get to know me."

He was trying to touch my booty and I slapped his hands. He didn't have any finesse. I guess I was getting what I asked for. "You're gonna be my bitch. Goddamn, how did I get so lucky?"

I looked behind him.

He had two other men inside.


They were snickering, looking at me. They wore baggy jeans and Young Joc T-shirts that were about eight sizes too big. I hated when men didn't wear clothes that fit their asses. Plus his house was filthy. The air trailing up my nose wasn't very flattering. And if his house smelled like baby shit then his dick had to smell worse.

Empty Colt 45 beer cans were on the floor. Who the hell drank Colt 45? Roaches were crawling along the wall beside him, like they were getting ready to bungee jump. Now I had to go. I was running to my car, my heels clicking against the side walk. I hit the alarm button and the car unlocked. I couldn't believe I drove an hour across town to get my clit pierced with his tongue and I wound up coming face to face with Gumby.

MOTHERFUCKER! So now I'm in my car, speeding on the expressway. I was shaking my head, cursing myself out. Could you believe the nerve of that man? Shitty breath, dirty underwear and an unclean house were three things a black man should never do. I didn't think men were capable of shit like that. For real. He had more gums than teeth. If I wanted some goddamn gum I'd buy some Bubble Yum, for real. That fine ass man with baby teeth. I *knew* the Tooth Fairy must have gone out of business because he didn't shed his childhood teeth. Ugh. I should have known it was too good to be true. Why did God ruin such a glorious body with too many gums and little reptilian teeth? My cell rang and I refused to answer. It was him. Gumby. I put it on silent. He kept calling me back to back. By the time I got off the turnpike forty minutes later, I had thirty five missed calls from him. I was just happy to be home, looking forward to my divorce. Shunning away online and grocery store men forever.

Now if only I could get Mama to take her ass home.

# Oops 2

My name was Ted Oxford. And I was depressed. Nothing in my life seemed to be going right. I longed for my childhood. A time in my life my parents' home was filled with bluegrass music, apple pies and good Caucasian cooking. I didn't have to pay bills, I didn't have grown man problems and I didn't have to work a 9-5 job to keep the water on and food on the table. Things seemed to be so much simpler than they were now. I was a cut-around-the-edges white man who loved all kinds of music, people and places. Completing my physical package were blue, piercing eyes that made women buckle at the knees, a nice body and Southern views imposed on me by myself and the standards I set back when I was a teenager in high school. I was never the playboy type, and I was never into environmental issues. I could give a rat's butt about global warming and I could care less about bums begging for change. If they could blink, shit and fart they could work. That was my theory. And even though the singing group Everclear sings a song saying "You don't know what it's like," unless you walked a mile in their shoes, I didn't want to *wear* their shoes because their shoes were too big and *my* shoes were expensive and I didn't care to get a toe fungus behind those who walked five hundred miles and wanted to walk five hundred more to prove a fucking point. By many accords, I thought I had life figured out. I thought I knew it all. I used to pride myself on this, being able to solve a murder mystery on TV in record time. Growing up, I played Hide and go Seek with my friends and nothing and nobody got past me. My uncle Paul, my Mom's loving brother (they were closer than white on rice) used to watch us from her living room window. He was a quiet man, who never got into much. He didn't like my father very much, but he always treated him with respect. Paul once told me I had cat eyes and a dog's sense of smell. I would lure you from the darkness like I was rays of sunshine in Summer. He also told me I was very intelligent. That when he was younger he was equally smart, but when he went to jail for trying to shoot one of his ex girlfriends (for cheating on him), all of that intelligence went out of the window. He lost his job, lost his reputation and he moved in with Mama, since she was the oldest child, and focused on family.

I was in Pre Calc by the time I reached the ninth grade. My way with numbers would stun you. That's why I was now trying to go to accountant school. And with my impending divorce from my wife, I would now have a lot of time on my hands to do so. Why not enroll in college to preoccupy myself?

Most of my peers hated my high I.Q. And because of it I was sometimes ousted from the group, becoming the outsider. When they did this I felt alone and abandoned and deserted and I developed thick rhinoceros skin that was unperturbed. When I was a lad, my loving Christian mother, Stacy Oxford, born and raised in Illinois and my father, Phillip Oxford, used to brag about me to their friends. "I have a smart son," Papa used to say. "Nothing gets over his head."

And he was right. When our home was broken into when I was ten years old, my parents were devastated. So was I, considering my favorite sweater had been pissed on by said robber. My valuables were gone, couches over turned and insulation ripped from the roof. My uncle Paul had been kidnapped for ransom. I knew this as fact because the robber left a half-assed scribbled note on the dining room table, next to a magazine. My parents called the police, as they should have. But something didn't sit well with me. Why would my sweater have warm piss on it? It hadn't dried up, it was still wet and it was still warm. When the police arrived I sat out in the living room with them and my parents. Mama cried her heart out, Frank Sinatra playing at a low volume from the stereo. Daddy was aggravated. Not only was he upset about the break in, and the robber taking over $700 of his money from his drawer, but he hated Frank Sinatra and he wanted to put on his favorite bluegrass CD.

The two cops weren't very "seasoned," as I liked to say. They seemed to be zonked, like they were on drugs. The taller white guy, named Officer Ways, had a huge mustache and you couldn't see his lips when he spoke. His eyes narrowed too much and he obviously was chewing on tobacco. His breath reeked of something foul. It turned my stomach and made me want to barf. Officer Simms, a five feet 4 inch midget of sorts, kept cutting his eyes over to my mother, questioning her. At first I dismissed it as standard procedure. But every time Mama's ample tits shook Officer Simms was asking another question, as if giving himself an excuse to look at them. His hard on, suppressed with a folder, was evident. I dismissed myself, because I didn't really have a place in grown folks business, as Papa liked to say.

It was when I stood up, yawning, that my eyes cut over to the hallway closet. The door was ajar and I saw a pair of eyes glittering. I didn't make a sound, I didn't blink. I pretended like I didn't see them. I sat back down and said, "I'm tired."

Mama signaled for me to come over to her. When I sat in her lap, her sparkling blue eyes shined down on me. "Are you tired?"

"Yes," I said, Daddy rubbing my head. "I'm very tired."

"Well go on up to bed," Papa said, picking up his beer from the low-table.

I looked at the cops. "Thank you for responding to my parents call so quickly."

Officer Simms grinned. "He looks like a little detective," he said offhandedly, Officer Ways agreeing.

Mama beamed, despite her grief. Papa smiled.

"I will make a good detective," I said, taking Officer Ways' pen from his uniform shirt pocket. I took his pad and I said, "I am going to write something and let's see if you all can guess what it is."

"Son," said Papa, not in the mood for games.

Mama said, "Honey, it's ok. He's just a child. We should encourage him."

Papa grunted in defeat. I wrote something and handed it to Officer Simms. When he read it he sat up stiffly, handing the pad to Officer Ways. Officer Ways was confused. He didn't understand Officer Simms reaction. Now my parents were alarmed, but tried their best to hide it from their faces. Officer Simms looked at Officer Ways.

"Well, I think our work is done here," Officer Simms said, standing up. He picked up his hat from the end table and put it over his blonde, unruly hair.

"If you all have any questions or wish to give some more information…" Officer Ways handed them a slip of paper with his writing on it. "Don't hesitate to call."

Somber, Papa's eyes clouded over. "So that's it? Our home gets broken into and you do *nothing?*"

Unshielded, Mama began weeping. I hated to see her cry. It unconventionally cracked my soul in unexplainable ways.

"We'll be in touch," said Officer Simms, hurriedly heading for the front door. He took a pack of cigs from his pocket, extracted one and lit up. Officer Ways was behind him. When Officer Simms opened the front door, Officer Ways snatched the closet door open, quickly and expertly drawing his pistol.

Fire was in his eyes. "FREEZE! DON'T MOVE!"

The perpetrator was so caught off guard he couldn't blink, smile, fall or react. Mama and Papa couldn't believe their eyes. The perpetrator was handcuffed. I studied him. He had a ski mask over his face, was about five feet 7 and had blondish hair peeking from under the skull cap. His black pants were rugged, his black fleece jacket a little on the worn-out side and his tennis shoes had mud caked on the bottom.

After his rights were read, Officer Simms looked at me. "Son. You are going to make a great detective one day. I can truly see nothing gets over your head."

Papa hugged me. "That's my son."

Mama said, "We're pressing charges. But before you haul the creep away, I just want to see who it is."

Mama snatched the ski mask off his face. Her mouth fell open in shock. Papa had to sit down and my world became an appendage.

"Do you know him?" Officer Simms asked.

"Yes," I said. "That's my Mama's brother Paul."

The last thing I remembered, before Papa whisked me to my room, was Mama taking the lamp and brutally slamming it over Paul's head, instantly knocking him unconscious.

That was many years ago. Now I was a grown man trapped in a situation I didn't know how to control. Silently driving in my truck, I was on my way to my best friend's wife's house. I called her earlier and let her know what her husband Dexter had been doing behind her back with my wife. I was still numb inside, feeling betrayed by two people I loved and trusted most in the world. My wife Bianca and my best friend Dexter. When I met my soon-to-be-ex-wife at the Muvico Theatres in Fort Lauderdale (I was going to see the Tom Cruise flick *Mission Impossible 3*), I really thought I had found someone genuine. She was the most beautiful woman in the entire establishment. When I lay eyes on her, I knew then that Papa telling me nothing went over my head had to be correct. She had an Apple Bottom ass, Janet Jackson wash board abs, ample breasts and perky nipples. She had short, croppy hair, loved poetry and loved eating the best foods. She turned heads, I tell you. Clad in tight snakeskin print pants, long leather boots with spiked heels and cowboy golden spinners on the back, long-sleeved gold blouse with a huge oval button holding her tits in place, I was in love. Initially, I wasn't going to say anything to her. She seemed stuck up. Plus my wearing a pink IZOD shirt, blue Dockers pants and pink banana Republic shoes didn't sit too well with me. I thought she would turn me away. But she didn't.

I didn't even think I had a chance in hell with her. Being that I was a white man, I tended not to believe the rumors I heard about black women from my colleagues.

All of the rumors skyrocketed in my skull, watching her in motion.

- They were finger-snapping, head rolling trolls who was all about money and being independent.
- They loved weave and make-up more than life itself.
- Fried chicken was the ritual.
- They all went to the clubs on Saturday and then to church on Sunday.
- They liked big cocks and were size queens.
- They had two or more Baby Daddies
- They spent their child support checks on anything but the children.

One of my friends who worked security with me, Kamal, told me, "You better be careful. Black women buy their own diamonds and they buy their own rings now."

I used to laugh it off, brushing it off as stereotyping.

Now my world was destroyed. I was still in love with Bianca, but I was caught between a rock and a hard place. Since I've been a work-o-holic, she has been sneaking my best friend into the house, fucking him senseless in my bed, on my sheets. My insolence got the best of me. Their images sped through my brain like Speed Racer…I nearly ran off the road thinking about it, punching the dash board didn't help matters and blaming God was irrelevant.

Boom.

There I was. In my doorway. Frozen. Dexter was tagging Bianca from the back. Bile rose in my throat. She was inefficaciously riding his dick…Dexter was selfishly dancing inside her declination…spreading her ass cheeks apart. His dick was light years bigger than mine. I felt insecure in my own home watching my own best friend, my partner in crime fuck my wife. She started to come. Thick, gooey nut was all over the shaft of his condom-less dick.

"You like it, Bianca?" he asked seductively.

"I love it Dexter." Getting off him, she sucked her come off his dick. I had heart failure. She then tit fucked him. After that ended, he stood up and slid his dick deep in her ass. She went haywire, saying she loved when he fucked her in the ass. She loved when she snuck him in my home to have sex. Seething with rage I raced downstairs and put on a pot of grits. The minute it started boiling I snatched the pot off the stove, ran up stairs and burst into the room. They were in the shower.

After Dexter said he never liked me and issued sexual demands from my wife, I snatched open the shower curtain and all she could say was "Oops." I dumped grits on them. As the grits ate away at her pretty face, I beat Dexter to a pulp with the pot and my feet. When I married Bianca he was my best man. And it all blew up in my face.

I guess I had to blame myself. I believed everything she said when we met without investigating any of it. She told me I looked like Brad Pitt. I was flattered. She also said she was a direct woman, that her zodiac sign was Scorpio. I told her I loved shrimp scampi and she nodded her head, saying "Same here." Why didn't I notice that? If I would have said "Spaghetti," she would have said, "Same here." She said "Wide Open Spaces" was her favorite song from the Dixie Chicks, yet couldn't sing three words of the song after we got married. She also told me that she wasn't raised in the projects. She wouldn't know what one looked like. She said she was adopted when she was 3 months old by an Australian family. She was a crack baby. I had chocked on my Coke soda. She had me emotionally from that point on. She knew just how to lure me in. And it worked. She then said she was raised in the suburb of Miami, but never said which one. She went to the best catholic and private schools. She graduated from Palmetto Senior High with honors and did four years in the Airforce, did a tour in Tokyo and another in China. She got the Montgomery G.I. Bill and attended college. She went to USC off and on. She did another 3 years in the Airforce Reserves. Once she got tired of wearing blue she finished law school, gave up on that dream, and got into TV Production. She wanted to be an anchor woman. That dream failed. She said she (at the time) worked at Channel 7 News as a sound editor.

She was everything I wanted in a woman. After she sucked my dick in the back of the theatre and swallowed my come, I still didn't see her for what she was. I was blinded by the head she gave.

What classy woman sucked dick in a theatre and swallowed instead of spit?

She didn't know my ball bag from a sack of grocery at the time. But I was so alone, so tired of sleeping alone in bed that I didn't care. Things intensified.

She drove her Benz back to my crib and we went out to South Beach. We wined and dined, went to Club Deep and hours later I beat the dust off the pussy in my bed, which became her bed shortly after when we married. I sent her flowers four times a week, gave her keys to my place and she introduced me to her friends and adoptive parents. I would later propose to her in front of her family and she would accept. They ate my food, tarnishing my image and they drink up my liquor bashing me, then once I did get home they smiled in my face like everything was ok. I was the dumb cracker. I was the man who believed in his woman and his friends. I was the empathetic fool who loved sports but loved life even more. I was the man who would give the coat off my back to protect a woman's high heels from getting water on them.

But the day I caught them together in the shower, she told Dexter, "I'm divorcing Ted. We (meaning she and Dexter) can build a life together. What was I thinking marrying that punk? I mean I don't listen to the Dixie Chicks. I just told his ass that so I can get in his wallet. I was never adopted. Can you believe he fell for that shit? My parents still live in the ghetto. I was never a suburban chick."

What was I to do?


I turned off the truck when I parked in Karen's driveway. She was Dexter's wife. She was expecting me. I was having second thoughts. Two wrongs didn't make it right. I was better than this but I was one hurt motherfucker. Logic was the last thing on my mind. When I initially called her and told her of her husband's infidelity she told me that her husband hadn't fucked her in months. She told me to come over and take care of her sexually. Since Dexter fucked my wife I was going to fuck his. We were both consenting adults, why not? I was mad, angry and vulnerable. I needed a woman's touch. I needed Karen more than she realized. She said she'd even change the locks so Dexter's keys failed him.

I licked my lips, knocking on the door. For a moment I didn't hear anything. I knocked again and Karen answered, clad in a bathrobe. Her skin was milky white. We were of the same breed. *God, she's so beautiful.* We looked in each other's eyes and saw the hurt and the betrayal. *I need you, Karen. But I don't want to appear desperate.* She wrapped her arms around me and openly sobbed. *Let it out, Baby. I'm here. And once you're done I am going to give you the best cock of your life.* I held her and refused to cry over an unfaithful bitch. *Bianca can rot in hell!* I was shaking where I stood. Karen's skin felt good against mine. She smelled of light lotion, and her perfume was gentle and sweet.

She didn't want to let me go. "Come inside," she said, pulling away from me. I walked past her. She put her hair in a ponytail, her eyes casting to the tile. She closed the door and rested her hands on it.

*I know you're hurting, Karen. So am I. What are we to do? I know why I'm here. But do I want pussy that badly? Well, yea. Getting pussy was always the brass ring. But you are a very dear friend. And you have always been there for me over the years. Maybe this was bigger than sex.*

I was reluctantly looking around. On the low table was her wedding picture. She'd torn Dexter out of it. His image lay in shreds on the floor.

"Karen…" I walked up behind her, carefully putting my hands on her shoulders. She looked over them, faintly smiling. She felt so soft.

"Yes."

"We don't have to do this."

She faced me, giving me some tongue. "I always wanted to do this. I've wanted to kiss you for years"

"Why didn't you?" I asked, unsure of what she said. Women always gave false hopes and blinking dreams when they were hurt.

Our lips danced in unison. I was on fire and I didn't want to be smothered. I was about to combust. I felt the smoke rising in my loins and pushing the blood to the head of my cock. Her breathing increased, and she released little moans that turned me on. I held my breath. She was a beautiful woman. Why would Dexter cheat on her with my wife?

She untied the robe and it fell to the floor. She looked into my eyes and seemed to be hesitant.

"What's wrong?"

"I guess I can't be upset at my husband for his betrayal."

"Why do you say that?" I asked, taking off my shirt. I wasn't leaving here until I fucked his wife.

"It's my fault," she said, falling to her knees, her face in her hands. "I loved him so much."

"And I did, too. He was my best friend."

"It's deeper than that."

I got on my knees in front of her. "Look at me."

"No."

"Karen." I lifted her face. Her eyes were dull and sad. I wanted to protect her.

"Yes."

"Kiss me."

"I don't know…" I stood up, taking her by the arm. When she stood up I picked her up and lay her on the couch. I spread her legs and started to taste her pussy. She exploded with jubilancy. She shook out of her skin. I spread her salty pink walls and thumbed her clit while I pushed my aching tongue in and out of her twat. She sunk her nails into the leather of the chair.

"Yes, Ted. I love it."

I ran my tongue all over her thighs, carefully pleasing her. I was erasing her hurt and alleviating her pain. This wasn't the first time I was there for her. Even though we never had sex, we were always attracted to each other. I just never went across the line because Dexter was my best friend and I would never betray him by fucking his wife. I was there for her when she came to me, one day last year, and told me she didn't want to be married to him anymore. That her family disowned her when she married the "Nigger." She loved her family. They were the core of her universe. But I defended my boy and told her she could marry anybody she chooses and if she lost her family because of it then oh, well. Life went on and life was bigger than friends and family.

Suffice it to say her parents cut her off. She went through depression. Dexter came to me in tears, not understanding why his wife turned to the liquor bottle. She closed up. She would not tell him. He grew further and further apart from her. He told me he didn't want to be married to a woman who didn't trust him enough to confide in him. I should have seen the signs then, but I was in serious denial.

Pushing the memories away, she held my head, telling me to suck her clitoris. I gracefully obliged. I told her to hold her legs back. I sucked all over the pussy, loving her scent, loving her taste. If my tongue was a cock her pussy would be a chanticleer.

After an eternity I felt her body tense. I smiled, chewing on her walls. She was trying to push me away. I took my tongue out of her and put my dick so far up in her pussy she gasped for air, wide-eyed. I slowly grinded in her tunnel as she continued to rise above the clouds in search of the mountains. They weren't there. Just a ledge. The waves crashed below and her clit was man overboard, drowning in the seas. I wanted the clouds. She wanted the waves. Swoosh, I pinned her legs as far back as they'd go and I gave her every inch of my cock. Holding my back, she was moaning my name in ways she never called out for Dexter. So I took her higher, dancing in her dripping pussy like a game of tic-tac-toe. She wanted the X and my dick formed an O with her cunt. My cock sliding in and out, I started fucking her harder, giving her what she wanted. I was tired of playing around. I was getting a divorce. I lost my wife. I lost my best friend. I wanted her pussy to heal me, take me past the hurt and the pain and show me the way. Show me the light. Show me how to get up and get beyond deceitful people. I needed her pussy because I hated my wife. Her pussy was the deterrent. Her pussy was everything I needed and wanted. I was a man. I needed pussy to heal my open sores. I needed pussy to get me through the day. When I had a bad time I played in pussy. Most men called up the "boys" and played a game of ball. Fuck the boys. Give me some pussy. Her pussy was the Band-aid. Heal my wounds. Her come would be the antiseptic. Heal my sore heart.

When she came I felt her pussy throbbing on my dick. It felt like a hand was gripping and releasing. I pushed it all the way in and froze, looking deep in her eyes with our mouths agape. Her breath was hot on my face. I had to pull out because, I didn't know what it was, but I started to come. I didn't want to come in her.

We lay next to each other, drenched in sweat. I was ready for round two. She was ready to shower. She faced me, playing with my navel. I rubbed her arm, looking at her.

"I have a confession to make."

"Yes. What is it?"

"I am a family-oriented woman."

"That's your confession?"

She laughed and so did I. "No, that's not it. But it's part of it. When my parents cut me off I could not live with myself. Ever since I was a little girl, I loved having family around. I was always different."

"Different how?"

"I included my family in everything I did. They supported everything, except my love for blacks."

"So they are racist."

"Very."

"So how did they take it when you got married?"

"They cut me off. You know that. They didn't even come to the wedding, and that hurt. My Dad said he wasn't going to give me away to a nigger. Mama told me to die with him and go to hell. She said that if I had mixed kids she would have nothing to do with them."

"So why are you telling me this?"

"You are a good man, Ted. You always have been. Ever since the first time you listened to me vent I've had strong feelings for you. Dexter doesn't listen. He dictates. He tells you what he wants and that's what he expects."

"But you knew that before you married him."

She was massaging my head. That felt good.

"He wasn't that bad when we got married. He was stubborn, yes. But not over the top rude." She grew silent, struggling with her words. "I love you, Ted," she finally admitted and I held my breath. I felt like an episode of *General Hospital*. "And I want to be with you."

"We're rebounding, Karen. And you know that. This is too convenient."

"Who gives a damn? I know what I want."

"And how do you know that? You only recently found out your husband is cheating on you with my wife."

"Actually…"

"Actually, *nothing*, Karen. You are confused. You are stunned. You don't know if you're coming or going."

She was trapped in her own existence. "I do know I love you. That's why I took action."

*Took action? What is she talking about?* "In what way?"

She sat up and got between my legs, foreign territory. She took my arms and wrapped them around her…her body was so warm. Her skin was so soft.

"Like I said. When I lost my family I think I died inside. And I wanted them back. I loved Dexter, yes but I had to do something that would make everybody happy. So I played Devil's Advocate."

"OK."

"You worked long hours. Bianca was always over here talking about it to my husband, like you and I used to talk. We got our secrets, Dexter and Bianca had theirs. I set them up to meet one on one. I would call her over, and then I would call Dexter. I would tell them I needed help with so and so. So by the time they got here I was long gone and they were alone."

I didn't like was she was insinuating.

She stood up, taking her hair loose. She gave a smile, a sad smile. "My plan worked."

*What are you talking about?* "How?" I slowly stood up, facing her.

She was rubbing my arms. "They weren't initially cheating on you. I wanted my family. So I kept setting them up to meet by chance. Bianca was hurting because you worked long hours and sometimes I cursed her out. I treated Dexter like shit. He didn't fuck me in months because I told him I didn't want to have sex. I kept faking my period and a head ache. I drove them two together."

"YOU WHAT?"

"And now Dexter and I are getting divorced. I knew they were cheating on us before you walked in on it. I wanted an excuse to divorce him so we could be together and my family would accept me. If they saw two whites married in Holy Matrimony my father would walk me down the aisle and give you me. My mother would be there and all my brothers and sisters. Being married to a black man has driven a wedge between my family and I. I can't deal with it. I want a happy marriage and my family to share it with me."

"Do you realize what you're saying to me? You are playing God. And here I blamed my wife. Yes, she is to blame but I didn't know about these chance meetings. I thought you cared for me as your friend."

Desperately, she hugged me. "I do."

I pushed her on the floor, spitting in her face. She was disgusted. *"You motherfucker!"*

I exploded. "You bitch! Did you think it would be that simple? Did you think I would pick you up with my white horse and ride off into the sunset? You destroyed two marriages with your selfishness and greed. You love your family so much you would ruin your marriage? You would drive Dexter into the arms of my wife? He was probably hurt because you kept faking headaches and periods. I know Dexter like the back of my hand. You tell him no too many times he's gonna go out and fuck another woman. You made sure my wife was available."

"I'm sorry," she said, standing up. Shaking her head, she wiped saliva from her face. "Sometimes you gotta do what you gotta do."

"I can't believe I'm hearing this."

"*Believe* it." She was approaching me. "We will be happy together and my family will love you."

"You're sick."

"I called my father this morning and told him my husband cheated on me. I also told him I met a good man. I told him all about you. He wants to meet you."

I said it slowly. "*You* are insane!"

She touched my arm and I slapped her. She held her jaw, looking at me sadly. "I'm sorry."

"Stay away from me. I can't believe you would do this to me. I guess you think you're the only one who is supposed to be happy in this life. I lost my wife. She was my earth. I rotated on her axis. You talk about racism but you're one yourself."

"I love all people."

"You love all people as chess pieces on your chess board. You castle the rooks and blind the queen to get to a King. I don't want to be a stalemate move on your game board. Do you hear me?"

"We can learn to love each other."

"I'm leaving."

I walked past her and opened the door. I heard two clicks and I froze.

"If you walk out of that door I will kill you."

The cool breeze blew across my face. I closed my eyes, sucking in air. I could smell the earth. I also smelled rain in the air.

"Come back inside, Ted."

"Why should I? You're going to shoot me anyway."

"I will if I have to."

"Why are you doing this?"

"I want my family back. Ever since I married Dexter my life has gone downhill."

"You made the choice. No one put a gun to your head."

She pressed the gun against my temple. "I'm pressing one against your head. Come back inside."

"Guns don't scare me, Karen." They scared the living shit out of me, but I wouldn't show it on my face.

"They should."

"I'm leaving, Karen. I can't be a scapegoat in your scheme. I really thought you were a friend."

"I am your friend. I just want a husband and a family and..."

"You had that with Dexter. You traded it in for selfishness."

I turned to face her. I didn't want to meet her demanding gaze. She looked weak standing there with the gun. Guns were not her thing. Her arms shook like Julia Roberts in Sleeping with the Enemy. I shook my head, putting both hands on the gun.

"You don't want to do this. You really don't want to shoot me. If you do you will go to jail and you won't have anything. Your world will cease to exist. Dexter left you for my wife. I fucked his ass up, too. Right now he should be checking into a hospital. I threw hot grits on him and Bianca."

"You did?"

"Yes. I did. And I come here thinking I was going to get revenge on him by sleeping with you and I find out you was the Master Puppeteer."

I took the gun from her and took out the bullets. She hugged me. "Please. I need my mom, my dad and my siblings. I want you, Ted. We can divorce our lovers and get married and have one big happy, kosher ending."

"A kosher ending. For whom? This is absurd. Are you crazy?"

"TED!"

I knocked her unconscious with the butt of the gun and looked at her body as it slumped to the floor.

I openly sobbed because I wasn't a violent man. I didn't like causing another person harm. But I had no choice. She was a sick bitch. There wasn't anybody here to watch me cry. No one was here to ridicule me…or to criticize me.

Fitting. Stuffing the gun in my pocket I walked to my truck. I got inside, put the key in the ignition and turned it on. It cranked silently. Putting it in reverse, I backed out the drive way. I put it in drive when I got in the middle of the road. I drove off. I was going through with my divorce. I was going to move out of town. I was going to pack my things and be done with it. I would never get married again. I wasn't going to go that route. Love didn't live here. Love didn't live with friends. I couldn't trust anybody after this ordeal. Karen. Sweet Karen. The orchestrator of my doom. The catalyst.

After tonight they were all dead in my life. Forever.

# THE WEDDING 2
## FRANCINE'S ANGER

She was quietly riding in the back of the cab, trying to convince herself that, despite what Samuel had done to Chandra, she still loved him. Feeling like a zombie, she asked the cab driver, Manuel, for a cigarette. He smiled at her through the rear view mirror, handing her one. Manuel turned on the windshield wipers. It was starting to rain. He cleared his throat. "Pretty women shouldn't smoke," he said, brushing cookie crumbs from his jacket. "Doesn't make you look good."

Absent-mindedly lighting her cigarette, she hungrily pulled on it. "Well, I'm not pretty today. I'm a pissed bitch in a wedding dress…"

He humored her. "Getting married I see? You wear your wedding dress to the church in a cab? Why? Shouldn't you be in a limo?"

She rolled her eyes, pulling on the cig again. "For one I am getting married in my home. And *fuck* limos. They're *too* costly." She looked at him more fixedly. "Why all the questions?"

He turned onto Florida's Turnpike, South. "I was just asking." He glanced at the meter. "You don't have to get so uptight about it, Lady. Jesus. Breathe."

She was offended. "Just because you gave me a cigarette doesn't mean I'm spilling the beans about my life. And you need to drive this cab and stop trying to sniff my panties. You're not driving Miss fucking Daisy, goddamn it! I don't care what you say or do—don't look at me like you lost your dog. All you men are the same—you meet a pretty girl and the first thing you think about is our pussies." She was heated. Crossing her shaved legs, she said as politely as she could. "Now get me to the church...I meant to my house. I'm running late..."

*Well fuck you, bitch!* he thought gravely. He was annoyed. He hated lippy broads.

"Look, for you to be engaged you are an uptight..."

She flashed angrily. "Don't say it, don't go there. If you call me a *bitch* I will curse your ass out. You don't fucking know me to be bringing the bullshit. Where's the goddamn customer service?"

He sucked in stale-clad air. "Whatever..."

"You must not be getting any at home," she stammered, directing her anger on him. "That's why you're trying to talk up on this. Look, dude. I have a sour taste in my mouth when it comes to men. If your money ain't right you're talking French to me."

"Don't worry about what I'm doing in my home..." he snuffed, shaking his head. He was embarrassed. "And I wouldn't pay for your snatch if it was the last piece on earth."

"I'm about to *snatch* your ass by that fake ass toupee if you don't shut the fuck up..."

Her cell phone rang, saving him from a verbal beat down.

Glancing at the caller I.D. she said to herself, "Damn..."

She answered. "Where are you?" Francine's iron-fisted mother asked with an attitude, walking away from a group of people at her daughter's house. She walked into one of the massive bedrooms and closed the door. She sat on the edge of the bed, her mind moving a mile a minute.

"I'm on my way back to my house." She smoked the cigarette, crossing her legs. A heel dangled from her big toe.

"How are you getting here?" she asked, sitting on the edge of the bed.

Francine reached over the seat and stubbed out the cig in the ash tray. "In a cab."

Manuel said, "You ..."

She slapped him in the back of the head and put a finger over her lips. He brooded like a child.

"A *cab*? Have you lost your *mind*?" her mother asked, jumping up to her eight-inch-heels.

Francine rubbed her lips together, smoothing over her lipstick. She didn't have time for the bullshit.

"Nah. But you lost yours. This is supposed to be my wedding day."

"I knew something was wrong with you today. I felt it. You have two families sitting in your house, waiting to see a marriage and you get cold feet and skedaddle out of here like you're going to a Van Halen concert."

"Van Halen? Who the fuck is *that*? And I don't give a fuck about two families sitting there, eating my fucking food, running up my light and water bills, sneaking eight, nine plates of food home for relatives I never heard of. Don't talk to me about family…"

"You…"

Francine interrupted. "When I get there, meet me in my bedroom. I have to talk to you about something. If you're not there you can get your ass outta my house. I am getting tired of you. Get your own goddamn life and stay outta mine. Today's the day I tell a bitch off, and you're first on the roster."

"Who in the hell are you talking to?"

"*You*! I'm a grown woman. If you don't like what I have to say GET THE FUCK OUTTA MY HOUSE!"

Click.

Francine called Chandra. There was no answer. *Damn, girl. Are you okay? Answer the phone. I'm getting worried about you. I know you're going through a lot and it doesn't seem like you'll make it through. But baby girl we've weathered the storm together and I won't abandon you now. We are friends till the end. I will never turn my back on you!*

"Seems like you're having problems," Manuel said.

"Damn. Are you *still* alive? You haven't died yet?" Francine shot icily.

Manuel laughed. "I love women like you."

She sucked her teeth, averting her face. She watched the scenery zoom by, looking more like blurs. Ghosts with untold stories. She wondered did any of those ghosts have a sick fiancé who deceived her. *Sure*, Samuel got her best friend pregnant behind her back, put a gun to her head and her stomach and made her do drugs, but what did she do? She loved his money more than she loved him. Everything they owned was split down the center. Leaving would be hard. Most black women would have cut his ass off. But for her it wasn't that simple. She tried calling Chandra again.

It went straight to voice mail.

Chandra tightened the rubber band around her upper arm, hot tears streaming down her face. Finding a hit at the hotel proved to be impossible. Luckily, when she got dressed and went to the bar, the bartender mentioned to a tall, black man that he had a supply of heroine. She eavesdropped.

When the tall guy walked off she made her move. She paid him handsomely, using Francine's money and now, sitting in her room, dead to the world, she inserted the syringe into a fat vein, her eyes fluttering to the back of her head.

She lay back against the wall, staring blankly into her reflection. Nowhere on her beautiful face was the sweet, innocent woman she used to be. Samuel had drugged her, raped her and pumped her body full of heroine so by the time she came to, she craved a drug she didn't know about.

Then she found out she was pregnant. He was very possessive and controlling. Beat her ass from sun up to sun down when Francine thought he was working. Made her have sex with him. Supplied her drug use. He was jealous of Francine being best friends with her. He tried to destroy Chandra before Francine could ever find out.

So she could *never* find out.

But now Francine knew. Shame on Francine's mother—Satan's bastard child—for taking Samuel's side. She was a very deceitful, controlling woman. She never cut Francine a break. No matter what Francine did it was never good enough. Or she could do better. Or she should have done this.

It would drive anyone mad.

Her body felt like it was on fire, her heart pounding. She knew she was destroying her child, but what could she do? She didn't knowingly do drugs, a sick man slipped GHB in her alcohol and spent a few hours carefully injecting heroine into her veins.

Now she had a habit, one she couldn't break. The room suddenly turned black and her head spun. Moaning piteously, she lies down and fell into a deep sleep.

Francine hung up the phone.

"She's probably sleeping," she told herself.

Thirty minutes later, Manuel pulled up in front of her house. Everyone was still there. Vehicles galore.

She threw Manuel three 20's and got out, closing the door. A few people noticed her and started to smile.

"There she goes."

Francine ignored them, and made her way to the back wooden gate. Unlatching it, she went to the back door and noticed people in her kitchen eating her food.

*Niggahs, I tell you!* she thought bitterly. *Didn't nobody tell them to go into my kitchen and start eating food!*

She made her way up the back staircase, leading to the balcony. When she arrived, she opened her bedroom door, slipped inside and closed it.

She lowered her head, sucking in air. She shook with revulsion, tears spilling from her gorgeous eyes like rain from clouds. She hurt for herself. She hurt for Chandra. She hurt for her not-going-to-happen marriage.

"Yes, I am marrying him," she told herself.

"I can't wait until you do. This has gone on long enough."

Startled, Francine tugged on her dress. Turning to face her mother.

Samuel looked himself over in the guest room. His brother Prado, as handsome as ever, said, "Bruh, you're killing that Steve Harvey suit."

Samuel was flattered, rubbing his goatee.

"*Really*, bruh?"

Prado brushed off the back of his brother's jacket. "Hell, yea. But of course I do it better."

Samuel shrugged his shoulders. "*Right…*"

They shared a laugh. Prado fired up a blunt and poured a small glass of Grey Goose.

"Pour me some. I'm about to marry Francine."

Prado, the blunt between his thick, luscious lips, poured a second shot, handing it to his brother.

"*Thanks.*" Samuel killed it, slamming the glass on the nightstand with force. Smacking his lips, the pleasurable burn ignited his eyes with zeal. "Pass the Dutch, bruh…"

Prado was in a sneezing fit, his eyes watering.

"Damn. This is some good shit, bruh." He passed the blunt, thinking about Francine. He couldn't get her off his mind. Never has he met a woman that captured his heart the way she had.

Samuel hit the joint, holding the smoke in his lungs until his body reacted with coughing.

He poured another drink.

"Cold feet, bruh?" Prado asked, turning on some Young Jeezy. He kept the volume low.

*Hell yea my feet are cold. No, no they're not. They're blocks of ice. I will lose everything if Chandra opens her mouth. I have to make sure the canary doesn't sing!*

"Nah. I'm ready. I thought she wasn't going to marry me. I love her. I can't live without her."

Prado loved her, but he would never tell his brother. He would keep it a secret. He could still taste Francine's pussy on his tongue. It smelled so good and fresh. He could still feel her lips all over his dick. He would cherish that for the rest of his life. Part of him was jealous Samuel was marrying Francine.

"She loves you, too," said Prado, frowning a little. It hurt him to say the words. He couldn't blame her. She was playing it safe, marrying a man with money.

Samuel's eyes sparkled. "She does?" Samuel asked, unsure of himself.

Prado hugged his brother, angry inside.

"Yea. She does."

Francine looked at her mother, the woman who gave her life. The woman who controlled her, the woman she could *never* please. *She's a jealous bitch!* She thought about Chandra and what she was going through. A sweet woman thrown into a nightmarish game of lies and betrayal by two people she trusted most in the world.

Chandra was vibrant and colorful. Full of life and God. She cherished church and family. She loved her friends and was a darling. People loved her instantly when they met her.

Now she's a manufactured heroine addict with no idea on how to save herself.

Now she was pregnant with Samuel's child. She chain-smoked, didn't keep herself up and she bites her nails. She hadn't an iota of God or religion in her mental frame of mind.

And Francine had to rectify that. She owed her best friend that much.

"I don't want you to be my Maid of Honor anymore," Francine said, waiting to bash her face in. She was counting from ten to one in her mind, keeping her wits in check.

Mama was furious. "What?" She huffed, snapping her fingers like she'd gone crazy. "I have on this fabulous dress and I called all my girlfriends, Chile. They are here and want to see me sport my Dolce and Gabana pumps, Chile. *Please.* You must have gotten drunk or something." Francine tucked her chin back. "Girl, give me some of what you're on so I can act out of whack with you. Ain't nothing and nobody stopping me from modeling this amazing dress."

"This is a wedding, not America's Next Top Bitch. Tyra Banks isn't the emcee and fuck that ugly ass dress!"

Mama tucked her chin back. She just about had it. Image was everything to her and Francine just destroyed it.

Dangerously, she said, "You will not talk to me…"

The little girl inside Francine called out to her.

*Don't upset Mama! She will whip you. She will talk down to you. Please, Francine…she will lock you in the closet again when she doesn't get her way! She will call all your friends and tell them you're a bitch and tell all your business.*

Francine held her stomach, bile rising in her throat. Frightened, she stood her ground.

*Francine, don't do it. Don't talk back to your mother.*

Exploding inside, Francine walked into her Mama's face, her hands on her hips.

"Don't look at me like that, Ma. You don't fucking scare me anymore."

*Francine! Please! PLEASE! She is going to lock you in the closet! And leave you there all night to fight the darkness! Like she did when you were nine years old!*

"Ever since I was a little girl I always tried to make you happy. I did whatever you said. You used to lock me inside the closet for hours. If I didn't clean your house right you locked me in the closet. If boys talked to me you'd whip me until you drew blood. I remember when your cousin called you and said I had lost my virginity…"

"Your point…"

"SHUT UP! And you snatched me by my braids and shoved a hot sauce bottle up my pussy! What kind of mother does that to her child? I couldn't piss straight for weeks. I lied to the doctor for you and told him I tried to masturbate with said bottle just to keep you out of jail. And it turned out that your cousin lied. I hadn't lost my virginity yet…"

"Grow up. You're still singing that sad OH GOD LIFE IS UNFAIR song and quite frankly you remind me of Patti Labelle trying to will another hit. *Ain't* interested."

Francine gritted her teeth.

"I'm sick of you…"

"Take some Advil."

"I'm no longer scared of you."

"Whoopee!"

"Go to hell, Mama! Burn for an eternity. I can't deal with this anymore."

"I should have had an abortion. I was sick of you years ago…"

Hurt beyond belief, Francine pushed her mother against the wall and snatched her by the hair. Her mother was shocked by her attack.

"What in the living fuck did you and Samuel do to my best friend?"

Mama footed her in the shin and she doubled over. Mama kicked at her and Francine, tired of being locked inside the little girl in her heart, grabbed her foot and snatched the dick-loving bitch to her knees. They tussled.

"She's a druggie bitch!"

"Oh, yea! You and Samuel orchestrated the entire thing! How could you do such a thing, Mama?"

They slammed into the closet door, painfully pulling each other's hair. Neither would relent. The room door opened and Prado rushed inside, grabbing Francine and Samuel grabbed her mother.

"What is going on in here?" asked Samuel, wanting answers.

Francine said, "Get the bitch out of my house or I will kill her. I no longer have love for the trifling bitch."

Samuel could hardly hold his mother-in-law. She growled, flinging her arms towards her daughter. Huge tears ran from her eyes.

"You two can get over this," said Prado, pushing Francine to the bed, putting his weight on her. She was a beast.

"GET THE BITCH OUT MY HOUSE NOW OR THE WEDDING IS OFF!"

Samuel looked at his mother-n-law and said, "You have to leave…"

"But she knows…"

"OUT!"

"LISTEN TO ME, SAMUEL!"

"BITCH GET THE FUCK OUT BEFORE I THROW YOU OUT!"

Mama was defeated. She swallowed her words, looking them all over for a brief second. She huffed. Mama stamped from the room, slamming the door closed.

Francine said, "Prado. *Get* off me."

Prado stood up, fixing his suit.

Samuel helped her off the bed.

"Tell everyone we are about to get married. I'll be out there in a second. Leave me to myself right now."

Samuel said, "Are you sure?"

She faked a smile. It hurt her to look at him.

"*Yes*, darling. I can't wait to be your wife. I just don't want my mother being a part of my big day. In fact she is no longer welcome in this house…"

Samuel said, "I understand. No argument from me."

"I hope not. I'm calling the police and getting a restraining order. Her purpose in my life has been fulfilled. I'm a woman now, and I will not live the next thirty years being controlled by that bitch!"

Prado kissed her cheek and her panties were wet. "You look beautiful, by the way…"

She touched Prado's cheek. "Thanks," she said appreciatively.

Samuel kissed her lips.

And she felt nothing.

The music cued up and everyone smiled, clapped and a few people said, "Well it's about damn time!" Samuel took his place at the altar. His mother and father stood behind him. He smiled so big sunlight seemed to pierce through his teeth.

Samuel, Sr. was proud of his son and all he accomplished. He showed off, holding his cane and hugging his wife.

Samuel inhaled; *thankful* Chandra didn't get to Francine. He was ecstatic that maybe she'd overdose and be rid of her all together. Maybe the baby would die with her.

He wanted to control who and what came around his wife. Give her a false security; make her think it's all about her. But in all actuality, he wore the briefs and the fucking pants. He built his fortune from the ground up. He'd be damned if a woman compromised it all.

He was like Tru TV. Not reality. Actuality!

Prado was in the bathroom, torn inside. When he heard the music playing his heart shattered into a million pieces. Never to be put back together again. He never cried over anything, let alone a bitch. Jay Z said he had 99 problems but a bitch ain't one. Prado used to say the same exact shit. Now a woman was a problem, a woman that was his habit. Licking his lips, he savored the faint taste and smell of Francine's pussy. When the marriage was final he'd never wash his lips again. If he died right now he'd be the happiest man alive. He had the opportunity to make her come on his tongue. He was blessed to feel her warmth…He loved breathing her and touching her on her wedding day, when she was about to give herself to his brother.

He loved Francine with all his heart and to lose her to Samuel killed him inside. He could still remember what she wore when he first laid eyes on her. His brother was in school, and he brought Francine to the house. Prado was a promising child football star living in his brother's shadow of Honor Rolls and newspaper articles.

She wore a lovely red dress, with her flowing, long black hair tinted and swept from her face. She introduced herself to his parents. They were overjoyed that a pretty little thing fancied their son. When she met Prado he was enraptured. He took a rose from his mother's vase and plucked the stem, sliding the rose in her hair. Samuel didn't like that very much but he kept quiet. Staring at his reflection in the mirror, he hated the man looking back at him.

YOU'RE A FAILURE! YOU LOST! SAMUEL HAS THE WOMAN OF YOUR DREAMS!

Prado then started fucking women without a care in the world. Every woman he compared to Francine. Every time a woman got pregnant with his child he harbored a secret hurt because he only wanted Francine having his baby.

And now that would never be.

SAMUEL HAS YOUR GIRL. NAH. SHE WAS NEVER YOUR GIRL. WHY DID YOU FALL IN LOVE WITH YOUR BROTHER'S FIANCE? YOU LOST!

Prado punched the mirror so hard the glass shattered into the sink and onto the counter and floor.

Francine said into the house phone, "Yes. Is it completed now?"

"Yes, Francine. Everything is taken care of."

Francine smiled. "Good. Because tonight is my honeymoon. Everything has to be perfect."

"Congratulations on your wedding," the woman said through the phone.

Francine hung up.

She sang, *"Goingggg to my living room because I'm goingggg to get maaarrieed!"*

Prado paused behind his brother, hugging his mother.

"I like the leopard-print jacket, Ma. Dad, must have cost you out the ass…"

They shared a chuckle.

Samuel said, "I'm glad you're my best man."

Prado hugged him. "I'm glad to be here, bruh."

Samuel pats his back. "Thank you…"

"No problem, bruh."

Prado, hiding his hurt, looked his brother over.

*I'm not happy about this at all. Francine, good bye. I will always love you.*

When Francine appeared, clad in the most gorgeous dress known to man, everyone rose to their feet with applause. Prado refused to look at her. He stared ahead, holding his breath. He refused to take another breath of air.

He wanted to die.

Samuel's breath caught in his throat. That wasn't the same dress he'd just seen her wear.

Samuel's mother, Mrs. Lester, held her pearls. His father smiled.

"She's wearing my dress," said Mrs. Lester. "And she looks amazing in it."

"No, honey," said Mr. Lester, eyeing Samuel with a secret smile that made his heart flutter. "She looks *better* than you ever did in that dress."

Looking into Samuel's joyous eyes, she stamped Mr. Lester's foot and he frowned in pain.

"Watch it. Or I won't spank you while you suck my high heels…" she whispered conspiratorially.

Samuel said, wanting to puke, "Ma…not here," with a smile, looking at his father coyly. Prado closed his eyes.

Francine smiled, her hair in a series of curls. She retouched her make-up. Nothing was overdone. She wiped half the shit off her face. Lord knew her heart hammered with both anticipation and excitement for what she was about to do. She made a last minute decision to wear Mrs. Lester's dress. After all it was in the back of the guest closet. She remembered Mrs. Lester had it cleaned and, once it was done, she called Francine and asked her to pick it up from the cleaners. Francine had done so, but when she got to Mrs. Lester's house she wasn't home. So she put it in the guest room closet.

Now she looked radiant. Nowhere on her face was any sign that she'd just whipped her Mama's ass. Nowhere did it say Chandra was pregnant with Samuel's baby. Prado turned to face Francine.

He smiled so big he couldn't stand it. *She's wearing Mama's dress.*

She was the most beautiful woman he'd ever seen. Wow. Prado looked at Samuel and slapped palms with him.

*I can't believe God let this angel escape heaven. Looking at her turns me to mist. I just want to envelope Paris, and touch the metal of the Eiffel Tower.*

*God, I want to be Moscow while she becomes my Kremlin!*

"She is gorgeous," Prado said.

Samuel couldn't wait for the honey moon.

Mr. Lester noticed no one walked her down the aisle. Before he could, Prado walked past him and up to Francine.

Samuel smiled.

"Since your Dad isn't here, mind if I walked you down the aisle?" Prado asked, kissing her hand.

She said, "Sure. I can't wait to become Mrs. Lester."

Prado respected her decision.

He had to let her go.


Francine took Samuel's hands. He nearly shook with glee. Prado was happy for his brother. He knew deep down he had to let her go. Couldn't get mad over something that wasn't his.

Pastor Reynolds opened his Bible and said, "We are gathered here today to join two individuals together in Holy Matrimony…"

Francine kissed Samuel's lips.

"I love you," she said flatly.

He responded with a breathy, "I'll die for you."

Prado held his brother's shoulder.

Mr. and Mrs. Lester were pleased. A photographer walked here and there snapping professional photos.

"Marriage is sacred and should be cherished," the Pastor said. "It seems these days people get married for all the wrong reasons. Whether it's because of good finances or good sex, building a foundation on deceit and lies corrodes a marriage into the untimely hell of divorce."

"Amen," said Francine, eyeing Samuel, who seemed uncomfortable.

The Pastor closed the Bible. "Francine and Samuel, are you two getting married for the right reasons?"

Samuel looked Francine in the eyes. "Yes."

Francine looked Prado in the eyes, squeezing Samuel's hands tightly. *Don't ruin my big day, Prado! You better keep your fucking mouth closed about our little secret rendezvous. I'll be your Karyn White forever if you shut your jaws.*

"Yes, Pastor."

"Is there anyone here today who wishes for these two not to be united as husband and wife? Here's your chance to speak. Speak now or forever hold your peace."

Everyone looked around.

Prado sucked in air and thought to himself.

*I will forever hold my peace. Congratulations, Francine and Samuel.*

His heart hurt.

"May I have the rings," said the Pastor and a very vibrant, handsome little boy by the name of George walked up the aisle, wearing a light blue suit.

People clapped and whispered love and adoration.

George walked up to the beaming Pastor.

Succinctly, Francine said, "Um. Wait, before we go any further. I want to say a few words to my husband to be."

Samuel smiled like the sun.

Francine looked him deeply in the eyes.

"I love you beyond anything. And sometimes love conquers all. Through all the ups and downs love shows a person a road past the crossroads. A door out of hell. A place beyond nightmares and unfaithfulness."

"I love you too, Francine," said Samuel. "I will love and honor you. You are my alpha and omega. I want no other woman but you. You complete me."

Francine turned to Mr. and Mrs. Lester. "I adore you two. You have been married for decades. I hope to share that many decades with your son. I love him. I will die for him. He treats me like a lady and opens doors for me. He appreciates me, doesn't talk down to me and treats me like his equal."

Samuel was the happiest man alive.

Mrs. Lester, huge tears flowing, touched Francine's face. "You have always been a woman about action. Polished military veteran, you wear many hats. I am proud to say you're now becoming my daughter-n-law who I love and admire as if you're my own flesh and blood."

Mr. Lester said, "Samuel got it right. I just pray my other son finds peace, joy and happiness."

Francine hugged Mr. Lester. "He did find peace and love."

Francine walked over to an open microphone and she said, "I wrote a poem for my husband to be."

Prado was about to run out of the room. Everyone seemed to have found happiness and not him. He had children he had to be a father to. He had to get his life together.

Francine said, "I wrote a poem. Called two hearts…"
Her beautifully-shaped lips inches from the microphone she said:

> *Love is like seeds*
> *water it with hope*
> *And pray for life.*
> *Life is like love*
> *shower it with bashfulness*
> *and sing for peace.*
> *I love love like love love life*
> *shower me with praise*
> *and hope for life*
> *To sing you a song.*
> *I love my husband like love is seeds*
> *I will water him with hope*
> *and pray for life.*

Amongst applause and praise, the poem moved the Lester's beyond anything reprehensible. Francine stepped down and walked towards Samuel with a huge smile and was so optimistic about her future being a married woman. Mrs. Lester.

Samuel made his way to his amazing fiancé and extended his arms. Francine walked right by him and wrapped her arms around Prado, sending a shockwave throughout her home.

"Prado, will you be my husband?"

Prado couldn't believe it. He held her tight, showering her face with kisses. *Oh my God! Oh my God! OH MY GOD! There is a God! Thank you, Lord! I won! I fucking won! FINALLY! Samuel lost!*

"Yes. YES!" He couldn't keep the joy from his voice. He nearly had heart failure.

Samuel felt betrayed.

Francine said, "Pastor, you are right. I loved Samuel because he had money. He was the polished son. He was my first boyfriend, my first everything. I loved him when he was down and out, broke and unpolished. Before he started his business, one I helped build with my own two hands and half the paychecks I had ever gotten."

She pulled Prado to the open microphone and she looked into his eyes. "That poem I wrote for you. I realized last night how much I was in love with you. You open doors for me and treat me as your equal. Samuel never opened a door for me in his life or pulled out a chair for me."

"Francine, are you sure? I want to be your husband, oh God I do…"

"*Yes*. I'm sure. But I haven't been totally honest. Before I take the ring and let you put it on my finger, you have to be a better father to your children. I love you for you. You are everything I hoped a man to be. You're smart and funny. You have flaws that you never hide or sugarcoat. You don't bash people. You love life. Samuel finds the bad in everyone, but you, Prado, you look for the good. I admire your strength and your courage."

"Francine, I have always loved you. In life I have always been let down and disappointed. My own family talks about me and call me outlandish names. I was never as good as Samuel. He did everything right and I was always wrong."

Some people were on their feet, clasping their hands together. Mrs. Lester shook her head, hugging her husband. The look on her face told Samuel that she always knew Francine loved Prado.

Mr. Lester said, "I guess Prado did get it right."

Mrs. Lester walked over to them and she took Francine's hand. She stared at her for a moment. "Francine. I'm glad you listened to the Pastor. About marrying for the right reasons. My husband and I have a confession to make."

Prado lowered his head. He smiled and tried to hide it. His life was about to change.

Mrs. Lester went on, the camera man walking over by them, filming. "I wrote everything the Pastor said today. About love and life. My husband and I were indirectly letting you know that we were aware of your love for Prado."

Mr. Lester nodded at Prado, placing his hand firmly on Samuel's shoulder. Not looking in his face at all.

Mrs. Lester went on. "…To have a decades-old marriage like me and my husband is rare. Black people these days seemed focused on clubs, sex and breasts jiggling in 50 Cent videos. They look to rappers for love and think its fine to marry a woman because her body is sexy or marry a man because he has a hefty retainer from his employers. What happens when the sex diminishes and he loses his job?"

Francine said, "I understand…"

"No you don't. What happens? I will tell you. When the money and good sex is gone then you want to file for divorce. Your foundation has been met and you want out. You want to find another dumb man or woman to marry so you can rebuild your foundation, meet it and walk away pleasured and your pocket's filled. Gold diggers work this way. I knew why you chose to keep it safe and marry Samuel. He was your first. You never really dated and you thought you were supposed to marry the first man you gave yourself to. But, honey," Mrs. Lester went on, wiping tears from Francine's face, "I will tell you the day Prado fell in love with you."

Francine looked over her shoulder at Prado, extending her hand. He cupped and kissed it.

Samuel was brooding. All his anger silently recreated his DNA.

"It was the very first day Samuel brought you home to us. Prado snapped the stem from a rose and he so lovingly put the flower in your hair. Prado had never been so happy, and you were a complete stranger to us. He talked about you day in and day out. Always asking his brother Samuel about Francine. That's the same way his father looked at me the day we met so many years ago. Samuel never had the eyes Prado had and still has for you. I'm glad you found your way home to your true heart's content. Welcome to the family, Mrs. Prado Lester."

Mrs. Lester took Prado's hand and kissed his lips.

"We're proud of you. God is giving you a chance to make it right with your life and your kids by doing what a man should do: honor and protect his family. Don't throw it back in his face the way Samuel has."

"I love you, Ma," said Prado, feeling like he had his family back.

Mrs. Lester held Francine and Prado's hand, leading them back to the altar. They stood in front of Samuel. Samuel took a few steps back and silently watched Prado slide the ring on Francine's finger. Francine smiled and slid the ring on Prado's finger. Five minutes later the Pastor said, "Now I pronounce you husband and wife. You may kiss your bride."

Prado kissed Francine with a longing and yearning he had never before experienced in his life.

Samuel was pain-stricken. He had stood by and watched this fiasco long enough. His parents deceived him. Prado, his own brother, stole his woman. She was now married to his fucking brother.

Samuel walked past his parents and punched Prado so hard in the face he flipped over the podium, slamming into the Pastor.

He was a beast. He ripped every flower and people starting gasping. A few ran out of the house.

Samuel snatched Francine by the arm and yanked the slut into his face.

"You led me on! You never loved me, Francine? How could…"

Francine said, "I deceived you? I did?" She was shrieking with anger.

Samuel said, "Yes! You married my brother in MY FUCKING HOUSE?"

"This is *my* house, too. Our name is on the papers, you sack of shit. I hate you." She snatched her arm back, getting in his face. "You are the biggest prick I have ever laid eyes on, Samuel."

He said, "I always treated you good. I have never lied to you about anything."

Mr. Lester held his wife, realizing there was some untold story about to unfold.

Prado regained his composure. His mother took some napkins from the table and wiped the blood from his face.

"I'm fine, Mama." He glared at Samuel. Waiting to pounce.

Francine said, "Oh, yea? You never lied? Then *why* is Chandra pregnant with your goddamn baby you sick, twisted freak? Why did you pump drugs into her body? And why, oh Lord please tell me why, you fucked my mother behind my back?"

Samuel lowered his head in shame.

Defeated.

Chandra was dreaming of red lollipops swiveling over a white light. They smiled at her, waving their arms wildly. Then the butterflies burst from a blue spot on her face. She loved the beauty of them, the rare thought of being high as Saturn drove her mad. She rolled over on the bed, smiling.

Francine's mother slid another syringe into Chandra's arm, injecting more heroine. Tossing Francine's cell phone on the bed, she felt alienated. Her daughter attacked her. Over this drugged out cunt! Clad in the dress she wanted to show off, she snatched the extensions from her hair and threw them into the trash.

*I was always jealous of you and my daughter's friendship. Even though you two are the same age you were there for her in ways I never was. I hate you for that. She is MY DAUGHTER! I'm glad your life is slipping through the cracks. Even though it's unfortunate Samuel drugged you and now you are an addict, I helped him. I supplied the heroine. I got him the syringes from my job, since I work at a hospital. No one will take me from my daughter. Without you here Francine and I can recover.*

*All mothers and daughters fight. I got to get through to Francine and make her realize that family is number one.*

*Too bad you'll be too fucked up to see our reunion.*

"Room Service!" the French maid called out, slowly entering the room. "It looks a mess in here. Aye aye. This is going to be a long day." She started to pull the sheets from the bed and a body rolled from under it.

"*Madam.* Oh, I'm *sorry.* I didn't know anyone was in the room."

The maid, Matilda, looked at her more closely. She was gasping for air.

"Oh my God!" She looked around and noticed syringes all over the floor.

"She's on drugs. God, not on my shift! Why today, Lord?"

She looked at the covers and noticed a lot of blood. The woman was moaning piteously, hair plastered to her face.

She was perspiring.

"My...my..." She was making gurgling noises.

"I'm calling 9-1-1..."

"My baby...is...coming. To. Early. Help."

More gurgling sounds.

Matilda called 9-1-1. "Please, hurry. A drug addict is in labor she says her baby is coming too early. Yes, ma'am I'm at 564 Biscayne Boulevard, the James Hotel. By Bayside. Thank you. I stay here with her."

A few police men walked into the living room, looking around for someone. People were wondering what was going on. The wedding had been a disaster. Samuel was disillusioned, wanting to retreat into his body. Mr. Lester was rendered speechless. Mrs. Lester walked away from Samuel, averting her face and turning her back on him forever.

Francine snapped at the cops. "There he goes. Samuel. The man who pumped drugs into my best friend."

The cops, with mean looks on their faces, made their way towards Samuel.

When they got up to him the tall white cop said, as politely as she could, "You have the right to remain silent..."

The short, black cop hand cuffed him.

Prado was driving Francine in his car. They were on their way to the James Hotel to check on Chandra. "So where do you want to go for the honeymoon?"

Francine held his hand. "I'm not going anywhere until I admit Chandra into a detox program or something. She's pregnant with your niece or nephew."

"I *still* can't believe he drugged her and all that shit." Anger flashed in his eyes. "Maybe I really didn't know him."

Francine said, "No. I was the one who never knew your brother."

"And what about money? I got a little something. Maybe we can admit Chandra into a program and then fly to Cancun, Mexico for a few days. To get over the shock of everything that's happened."

"I got money. I called the bank before I married you from the house phone and had every red penny wired from all three of our bank accounts to my bank account at Washington Mutual. Samuel doesn't have dime. And from the looks of it he's going to prison for a very long time. I recorded Chandra on tape. She told me everything, even implicating my mother. The cops will be arresting her phony ass real soon. I can pay for Chandra's care with that money. Since he robbed her of life I robbed him of his money."

Prado, turning down Anita Baker on the radio, turned onto I-95 and said, "How is that possible? You got all the money?"

"Yep. I'm on all the bank accounts. And I'm also part owner of his house. I own 51 percent of it. He signed that into the papers."

Prado said, "Wow. I guess Karma is about to teach him a lesson."

"He taught himself a lesson."

They saw the hotel from the Interstate.

Francine said, "We're coming, baby…"

*Nobody will every hurt you again, Chandra. I vow on my life. Best friends forever!*

Samuel was led through the downtown Miami police precinct. Depressed, he avoided the stares. A few men who were being fingerprinted eyed him. They wondered what his story was. A man in a suit being jailed. What did he do?

An hour later Samuel was fingerprinted and booked.

He had court the next morning.

Chandra was in the intensive care unit, hooked up to an EKG machine, an IV drip and two doctors overlooking her. She was unconscious.

Dr. Gristle said, "I have never seen anything like this…"

Dr. Hanks, a short, white man in his fifties, said, "That makes two of us. She's in critical condition. Lost a lot of blood."

Dr. Gristle looked over a chart. "And the baby?"

Dr. Hanks said, "...We did an emergency C-section. Had to try to save Chandra's life. Very risky at 27 weeks. The baby was only 5 pounds, barely five pounds I should say."

Dr. Gristle said, "Wow. My heart goes out to her."

"The cops are supposed to be stopping by. But what can they do? She's out of it, and I don't know if she'll pull through in this state."

"My heart goes out to the baby. How could she do drugs knowing she was pregnant?"

When they left the room, Chandra flat lined.

Never to open her eyes again.

Francine and Prado got off the elevator and approached the room. A team of Coroners and a few cops were there. Francine said, "Uh-huh. Somebody is dead or something on this floor."

Prado said, "Hope it isn't anybody we know."

Francine said, "Probably one of these drug-loving tourists."

When she said it she thought about Chandra.

"Oh, God! They're in her room!"

Her heart dropped in her stomach. And Prado covered his face in shock.

*Samuel, what have you done?*

Francine pushed Prado out of the way, screaming into the room. She startled the Coroners and the police. The hotel Manager jumped behind the bed.

A crime scene investigation team stopped snapping photos and halted dusting for prints. Another team of investigators put on some rubber gloves and started combing the room, taking things and putting them in plastic bags.

*"Where is she? Where is Chandra?"*

Two cops apprehended her but she started to fall to the floor and kick at them, flinging her arms.

"WHERE IS CHANDRA? WHERE IS MY BESTFRIEND! WHAT HAPPENED HERE?"

Officer Taylor took her by the arm and said, "Who are you in relation..."

"Where is Chandra? Where is she, goddamn it?"

Officer Taylor, taking off his hat said, "Chandra died in the hospital five minutes ago…"

Francine grabbed her husband and fainted. Prado held her as she fell towards the floor.

Prado thought to himself, *Samuel. You will pay.*

*A* nurse was writing on a chart. She smiled down at the little bundle of joy. Sadly, he was in an incubator, fighting for his life. Her heart went out to him. "God will protect you," the nurse said with passion. "God will watch over you. Your mother did drugs, little one. I'm calling you Super Man. Because you're a super baby."

She touched the incubator. "You'll get stronger everyday. Those drugs will be flushed out of your system. Huh, what did you say little one? Who am I? I'm family. No, Chandra isn't related to me but she's best friends with my daughter Francine."

Mama smiled victoriously. "Correction, she *was* best friends with Francine. She's one dead little bitch. She actually thought I was going to let her live! I lost my daughter, so I took her from Francine as well. She'll be forgotten in a few weeks. No one will remember her name. She will be just another druggie bitch stuck on heroine."

She scribbled on the chart, and left the room.

Samuel lay in his bunk, tears wetting his face. He couldn't let his Bunkie see his tears. He wiped them away, wondering how long he was going to be in there. He would use his lawyers and every resource in his power to get out. Yea. He had money. And money bought everyone, including judges.

"Yo," said his fat Bunkie, looking down from the top bed.

"The name's Samuel, playah."

"Yo. What time is Chow?"

"Who knows?"

"You should know. I want to eat. A Niggah is hungry, you feel me?"

"No, I don't."

"What are you in for?"

He thought about it. "I'm in here for pimping a bitch."

"Playa, playa! So that means you got money?"

"I'm ok."

The fat man jumped down off the bed, grabbed the small golf pencil, and stuck it under Samuel's neck. He was breathing in Samuel's face.

"Since you got money, pay me not to fuck you in the ass. I am getting life. I might as well start by fucking you, bitch."

"I will never…"

He pushed the pencil just under the larynx.

"Think about it. Pay for your life. I want money. I'm doing life! I don't have a family. I have nothing. Mama burned to death in her car. Daddy shot himself in the head."

"I will not…"

The Fat Dude was pulling down Samuel's pants. Samuel tried to yell and the Fat Dude pushed the pencil deep in Samuel's neck. Samuel was twitching on the bed.

The Fat Dude fucked him until Samuel drew his last breath.

"How are you?" Roderick asked, pacing the Interrogation Room at the downtown precinct.

"I'm fine." She lit a cigarette. "Why am I here?"

"You should know. Your daughter Francine said you had something to do with Chandra's death."

She chuckled. "She is disillusioned. She doesn't know if she's coming or going."

"But she knows you are involved with Chandra's murder."

"She overdosed."

"It would appear so." The cop looked at the Plexiglas, frowning.

She fixed her hair, crossing her legs. "I didn't do anything."

"So you didn't help Samuel drug Chandra?"

"No."

"When was the last time you seen her?"

"A few days ago."

"Was she happy, sad or shooting up dope?"

"All of the above." She pulled on the cigarette, refusing to cooperate.

"You can make this easier for yourself."

"How? And when is my lawyer coming?"

"Just admit it. We'll give you probation."

"You think you're slick. Why should I plead guilty to anything when I'm not guilty? She was a drugged out bitch. It's my daughter's word against mine."

"Really?"

"Yes," she said, challenging the overzealous cop. "Chandra's dead. She can't talk."

"The dead can talk, if they want to." He sat in the chair across from her, taking a cigarette. "Do you mind?"

"No."

"Chandra told me you drugged her."

"She didn't tell you shit. You're trying to intimidate me."

He leaned over and picked up a wrapped gift. He put it on the desk and slid it to her.

"What's this?"

"An early Christmas gift."

She opened it, humoring him. She took out all the tissue paper. She was laughing. "What is this?"

"You'll see."

She took out her weave. Her face hit the floor. There was also a tape recorder.

"We recovered your hair in the room Chandra was in at the hotel. We ran DNA. You were a perfect match."

"This doesn't..."

"Yes it does. It proves you were in the room when she overdosed. We suppressed tapes from the hotel. It showed you arriving in a Dodge truck. We have you taking the elevator to her room. We seized the camera in the hallway leading to Chandra's room. You're seen going into her room. Oh, yea. Press play."

She pressed play.

She heard Chandra's voice.

"Ah. The dead talks, baby. You are under arrest..."

Mama closed her eyes, defeated.

# The Golden Masks Freaks

Naygee was on the airplane, twenty thousand feet above Florida. Looking out of the window, he enjoyed the view. The homes looked like Legos cities from afar. Rivers and small little lakes crossed through the land like alleys behind buildings. Breathing a sigh of relief, he thought about calling his wife. But he quickly decided against it because he told her he wanted a divorce when she wouldn't go down on him. It wasn't that he upped and left her. No. He wasn't that cold hearted. He loved her more than the law allowed. He bought her what she wanted, gave her what she needed, fucked her the way she wanted to be fucked, gave her his paychecks when he got paid and played her Bible Boy in church. But he's been asking her to give him some head and be his dirty slut in the sheets for a year, but she kept throwing the Bible at him. It pushed him away, considering he was an atheist. She never met his needs, never did the things he wanted and when her parents came over they treated him like a

Hebrew Slave. Enough was enough he figured, so he told her he was leaving, packed a few bags and left her a broken mess as the door closed behind him. Smiling, he closed the blind and leaned back on the seat. *Melissa. I'ma beat that pussy out the frame. I can't wait to see you, with your freaky ass. I want you to tit fuck this dick again. Damn, girl. You're the shit.*

He was extremely tired. He couldn't get Melissa Jackson off his mind. She was the freakiest bitch he'd ever seen. She turned him out without him telling her. Couldn't blow her head up. With a bitch like Melissa, who needed new pussy when she had that good shit? Pulling the thick comforter over his lap, he dry jacked his dick, carefully looking around, making sure no one watched.

He came in a matter of minutes.


A yellow taxi with 305-888-8899 on the doors pulled up into a rain-swept drive way. The driver turned, looking at the handsome customer. A fifty dollar bill was slipped into his hand and a wink of the eye arrested his attention, but he played it off because he was a faggot on the low, sometimes liking it deep in the ass and he was on the clock (with Vodka on his hot breath) and wouldn't be getting off till three a.m. so he didn't have time for a bunch of penile fights.

"Thanks, bruh," the customer said, grabbing his leather bag, smelling of expensive soap and FCUK cologne.

The driver eyed him with a smile. "No problem, bruh. You be safe."

"You, too."

The driver put the car in gear, backing out of the drive way.

The customer looked over the house before him with a huge smile, his eyes sparkling. Glancing at his watch, he realized it was getting late. He'd go inside and shower.

He was thinking about the bed.


I was very in tune with my sexuality. Most women couldn't say that. How could you be called a "woman" yet you weren't woman enough to sometimes be called out your name. Shit, when a man called me a bitch it was normally after I emptied his wallet while I was riding his dick. Yes, ma'am. Give him a shot of pussy to keep his mind off the gold and you'd be the California Gold Rush every time he comes and his ass rolled over and went to sleep. He'd wake up broke as a joke. I wasn't a lesbian, but if a pussy looked scrumptious I'd suck a bitch's clit into remission. I loved the smell of pussy on my lips. If you haven't tasted your cunt yet then what the hell you were waiting for?

Pussy did the body good, the hell with those milk slogans. Bitch, Got Pussy? Check, please! If a woman was fine enough I'd dig in her twat and rub her juice on my lips. Which reminded me, when I ran out of lip gloss I'd rub my juices on my lips, saved me about ninety dollars a year. Call me what you wanna, I really didn't give a damn. But give me, me and get the hell on. And leave a fifty on the nightstand, because a bitch had bills to pay and every little bit helped.

I wasn't a greedy chick. I had my share of "moments" with the girls. I called them "lesbian tendencies." Because when it came down to it I'd pick a thick dick over a dripping snatch any day. But I liked what I liked.

I've deep throated a dick or two and I've let two women suck my pussy and everywhere in between. Are you Freaky Deaky? I asked them and they told me they were so when I asked them to eat my ass and let me taste it from their tongues they seemed to be a bit stagnant. I rode a bitch's face while her husband fucked me in the ass.

I've made him pull it out and I tasted it. I then kissed his bitch while thumbing his balls. I've fucked the mail man for a hundred dollars, seduced the UPS guy and shipped my clit Fed Ex. The Best Buy Home Installer guy wanted to marry me after I made him jack off and swallow his own come, the Home Depot cabinet installers ran a train on this pussy and my Mama's ex husband fucked me with the plunger because there was a blockage in my loins that Drain-o couldn't suffice. I couldn't lie, Mama's ex boyfriend had a little dick, but sometimes your pussy needed a break from being long dicked. I got tired of banging my head against the wall, shit. Sometimes my cunt wanted some short strokes. Let me stop airing my dirty laundry for all to see. Some things I had to keep to myself.

Illegally changing lanes, I smiled to myself, thinking about New York. I haven't been home for two hours and already I was back on the road.

I had the time of my life in New York, and seeing Janet Jackson on 106 and Park (and getting to hug her) was a treat. I think that's the single most beautiful thing that has ever happened to me. To smell Janet's perfume up close and personal. Outside of that, meeting my thug friend in a department store in Manhattan was another treat. Putting candle wax on his dick and sucking his essence through the shaft like yogurt was the thrill of a lifetime.

I still couldn't believe he let me fuck him in the ass. He didn't have any inhibitions and that was a good thing. He was still a man when we both came. I was a piece of Down South Pussy in the City that Never Slept and the city will never forget Melissa Jackson. I left my stamp of approval, and any bitch that fucked him after I left would read "Melissa's Pussy was here" on his dick when they gave him some head. That's a good way to keep my name in their…mouths. Ho's paled in comparison to me. Fucking him after my breathtaking performance was virtually impossible.

Part of me felt like shit because a few months ago, I turned my church into a lustful playground. At the time I thought I was dying of Cancer and I figured hey, if I was going to die I might as well pussy pop all over the back of the church and pussy pop was what I did. I was clad in a robe with a golden mask on my face. It was so freaky. I could still remember the briefing from Big Daddy Good Dick. You'd swear you were entering the matrix with all of their "rules." Since that day I haven't been right. I stopped believing in organized religion, and I stayed away from the building. I had to change my phone number because several Golden Mask participants wanted round two and three and my pussy wasn't built to back track. My pussy didn't do piss recalls when I squatted on the toilet so why should it do a church recall? What's done was done and life went the hell on.

It started to rain the minute I got on the Turnpike. Realizing that I left my Sun Pass home, I had to now pay the toll. Damn, Melissa. What were you thinking? Money didn't grow on trees. Tolls seemed to be going up a mile a minute and with rising gas prices and George W. Bush being the bitch he was, I couldn't afford half the shit being sold in stores let alone paying the toll. Patting my weave, I checked over my face in the rear view mirror. I looked a mess. So I opened my knock off Chanel purse I bought from the Indoor Flea Market in Perrine and pulled out some lipstick. Licking my lips, I held the steering wheel with my left ankle, rolling the small clip on the bottom of the tube and ran the thick red stick over my dick-sucking lips. Rolling them together, I tossed the lipstick back into my purse, smiling, making sure I didn't have any on my teeth. The last thing I needed was lettuce or lipstick on my teeth when I sucked a mean dick. Good dick deserved bright teeth so I did the damn thing. Taking control of the wheel, I signaled "left," getting into the left lane. I just passed Coral Way. I still had a ways to go before I got to the airport.

Thank God traffic wasn't the fat bitch it could be. Some days the bitch could be eating cheesecake and drinking Twinkie juice, congesting every lane and every road on the 826, but *tonight* was refreshing because her fat ass was on a diet, Jenny Craig was closed and the lanes were free of vehicles. It started raining harder, and the flash of lightning scared me a bit. I ignored it, of course. Lightning wasn't that bad—BOOM! *Goddamn* it! You see, Lord! You just scared the holy *shit* outta me! Damn! Now my nerves were bad. I needed a cigarette. Nah. Fuck it. I needed a joint to calm down.

BOOM!

Thunder rocked the streets. I covered my face, one eye on the road, my car swerving. *Get a grip, Melissa! Don't panic, Chile.* My heart racing, I was about to panic anyway. Where did all this lighting and thunder come from? A few cars sped past me.

*God forgive me for my sins! I know I'm a freaky bitch and you know I keeps it real with you and myself, Lord. I don't fake the funk and you told me to come to you as I am so here I am, Lord. I am a whore, but I'm a pricey whore. But lightning scares the living shit outta me and I know I fall short of your grace but I don't wanna die on this slippery ass road, Lord and I do wanna make it to the airport because when Naygee steps off that plane I hope he brought his snake with him because I'm gonna go Samuel L. Jackson on his dick and put his snake in the plane of my pussy. I love you, Lord. Talk to you soon. Muah. Amen. And a hallelujah good night!*

I didn't know why I was about to jump out my skin. I had to take deep breaths to calm down. I always got righteous when God made it thunder. I looked through my purse for my cigarettes. They were behind my iPod. Taking the pack, I shook it. It was empty. Damn. I gotta re-up on the cigs. I was slipping like some good pussy. A bitch like me kept some cigarettes.

With all the pussy I've been giving away, now wasn't the time to be all prim and proper when lightning and thunder scared my ass.

Turning on the radio, I channel surfed. Nothing of interest was on. Mariah Carey. Oh, No, Chile. That's one ditzy bitch. Next. Paula Abdul. "Straight Up." Come on now, radio stations! This wasn't the '80s. Next. Rhianna's long forehead ass yodeled all over this cut. Next. Under my Umbrella-eh-eh-eh wasn't cutting it tonight. Fuck it. I turned it off. I slowed up a bit when a Buick cut me off without signaling. I tucked my chin back. I blew the horn, cursing his ass out. He didn't hear me with the windows up. I grabbed my purse and put it on the back seat. On the passenger seat were two fabulous novels by sexy ass black men I've come to love. I love my black authors. Ty B. Moore's *Liar's Truth* gave Eric Jerome Dickey a run for his money and Michael Mayhem's *Yes…My Retarded Ass Signed Up* novel was glorious. Thinking about his fine ass made my titties rejoice and my nipples repent. I had to rub my pussy a little bit, looking at his picture, trying to keep my eyes on the road. Niggah was gorgeous. I loved military men. Come Search and destroy this pussy and cause it some…*mayhem*, Michael. Now I was horny. What did a bitch do? Simple.

It was time to play with myself. Spreading my clean-shaven legs, my hot pussy skirt inched up these juicy thighs. Trying to control my breathing, I slowed in speed, the speed-o-meter dropping to 45 M.P.H. but my booty hole remained idle. I loved it in the ass, but right now I didn't have time for ass play.

Desperately wanting to be fucked, I unbuttoned my cream-colored blouse and my tits tumbled free like spilt marbles. I grabbed the left one, suckling on my erect nipple, gently biting it with my teeth. Sensation shot through my body like heat seekers. I knew I was in my car being lewd and lascivious, but if these seats were made for fucking, then fucking's what I'll do… and one day these seats are going to walk all over this pussy because Mama didn't have on any boots, I didn't feel like taking off my stilettos and I looked light years better than Nancy Sinatra.

I noticed a few men in a huge truck were on the side of me, honking their horns, trying to get my attention. Men were always messing up my free time. I turned on the stereo to block their asses out. A bitch needed alone time, and since I was an exhibitionist, fuck men because it was time to get right on down to pleasuring myself. I started to sweat as the smell of my twat filled the air. Turning on the AC, I got a contact high. I did this with weed sometimes. Rolled the windows up and put the AC on full blast. My scent mixed well with the strawberry air freshener dangling from my rear view mirror. I gasped collectively, rubbing myself. It felt so good my legs drummed together.

I glanced at Michael Mayhem's book cover, sliding two fingers into my pulsating hole. Call me your dirty bitch, Michael! Come and give it to Mama. My tits bouncing, I rubbed myself for dear life like I was a camper trying to turn some twigs into smoke and flames. I was cold; Mama needed a heater in this pussy.

I leaned back on the seat, the men getting closer to my car. *Ya'll better not hit my shit! I hope you got some good insurance!* I loved these leather seats because I was slipping and sliding in sweat and pussy juice. I grabbed the baby oil from the cup holder, popped the top and squirted it all over my body, rubbing it into my tits. I felt it trail down my body, mixing with my well-cut pubic hair. I was really sliding now. I just had to get a taste of the strawberry, so I sucked my cunt down my throat with an appreciative smack of the lips. My foot pressing slightly on the accelerator, I was playing with myself again, thinking about the quickest way to come.

I wanted a nut and I wanted it now! I got it. Impulsively, I reached over and opened my glove box, S.W. 8th Street approaching on the Turnpike. That wasn't my destination, so I could get on with the regularly scheduled programming. I quickly pulled out my vibrator, leaving the glove box open.

I looked to the left, eying the horny men. They were waving, smiling and looking so fucking childish. One of them had a camera phone, recording me.

He couldn't see anything. My pussy was shielded by the car door. I wanted a soundtrack so I turned on my CD player and pressed "play."

The mixed CD began to play. Amerie's "That's what I'm Talking About" boomed. I loved this song, plus she's a pretty bitch.

I inserted the tip of the nine inch cock inside me, grinding it the rest of the way in. Oooh, yeaaa, damn it.

That's what I was talking about, Amerie! My mouth ajar, my eyes were narrowed, as I prepared to take this plastic dick. Maybe I should talk dirty to it.

*Give* it to me, you *plastic* fucker! *Fuck me like you never fucked me before!* I'm your bitch; I loved plastic more than cash right now because your thickness was rocking my ass to sleep. Yes. Yes. Yes. Fuck me, Baby. Make Mama come all over this plastic cock! The heat from my pussy was so intense it was about to melt the dildo like it's a doll. Fuck me, Chucky! This pussy wants to play. I'll be your friend till the end! Hi-dee Ho, bitch! Ah, yes! Let Mama spread her legs wider. What? You want me to put a pump-clad foot on the dash board? Sure. I did what you said; now get in this pussy like a broke Niggah getting in a dime bag of weed.

Spread my pink walls apart like weed on some Swisher Sweet paper. Lick this cunt, bitch and roll your flame under my clit. Oh, yea! I was about to come! Oh, god! I love you, Your Plastic Majesty!

My pussy is clamping on your rod!

AHHHHH I'M COMINGGGGG GOD THIS FEELS SO GOOD! YES YES YES! HERBAL ESSENSE THIS PUSSY!

When my orgasm subsided, I smiled, sucking my come off the dildo. Tasted good.

It was thick, which told me I needed to drink more fluids and eat more fruits, like pineapples, oranges and grapes. I was a freaky bitch, on her way to pick up a freaky niggah from the airport.

As far as the truck full of guys who watched me, they got a free show. But my exit was coming up, and from the looks of it we would be out of sight out of mind in about two minutes. Bye, boys!

It's been nice.

I braked, pulling over to the side of the road. Cars zooming by me, I buttoned my blouse and fixed my skirt. Replacing the dildo into the glove box, I closed and locked it. I felt rejuvenated. Interrupting me, my cell rang and I answered. It was Naygee. My titties tingled just thinking about his juicy steak.

"Are you coming?"

I put the car in "drive" and entered traffic. More and more cars were coming out of nowhere.

"Yes. Has the plane landed?"

"We're circling the airport now."

"Damn."

I mashed on the gas pedal, approaching the 836, which would take me past the airport to the exit I needed. I think it's called LeJune Road or some shit like that. I'll know it when I see it.

"I can't wait to see you."

I blushed. "And I can't wait to see you."

"I left my wife, Melissa."

See, now I was mad. Why couldn't we just meet up and leave the strings on the puppets?

Did I look like an episode of *Sesame Street*, Naygee?

The only thing he could do was stuff his Snufflelufugus in my Big Bird and call it a goddamn day. I wasn't trying to keep him.

There were still men I wanted to fuck and one dick never stopped a show. My pussy didn't start and stop with him.

If you read Page 3 of my Pussy Manual it clearly stated the following things:

My pussy came in

*French. Creole. Spanish. German. Chinese. Afrikaans. English.*

If you experience troubleshooting with my clit write the manufacture and fax a copy of the original warranty. There was a mandatory three hundred dollar fee. If the warranty has expired, there was a re-certification fee of one hundred dollars, plus tips when you ate this pussy again. I didn't care how good he was, I would never be tied down to a piece of cock.

"Did you hear me?"

"Yes, I heard you. Anyways, I'm almost there. I can't wait to see you."

"The plane is landing now."

He entered the home, closing and locking the door. He turned on the light switch by the front door, smiling.

His eyes glittered as he moved about the living room. Lovely sofas, beautiful throw pillows and a light red carpet caught his attention.

It was an Asian meets African-American feel. He ran his hand over a 5x7 photo of a gorgeous woman. In it she wore an ankle-length dress and her hair was pinned atop her head.

He turned to put his bags on the floor. Entering the kitchen he opened the fridge, grabbing a Heineken. He used the back of a cigarette lighter to pop the difficult top. Tossing the top in the trash, he took a hefty swig, wiping his thick lips. When he went back into the living room, he noticed it. A glittering China cabinet, with one thing in the center.

He smiled, shaking his head.

I was standing at the American Airlines corridor. The place bustled with activity. I just had to be cute, pulling my hair into a bun. You never knew who you were going to meet.

Someone tapped my shoulder and I looked at her. She was about five feet 8, cute little bitch, with nice titties.

"Hi."

"Hi," I said obtrusively, rolling eyes and popping my gum. "Can I help you?"

She touched my arm. "I just love your pumps."

*Bitch, don't touch me!* "Thank you."

"Where did you buy them, I would love to get a pair?"

*Like I'm really gonna tell you!* "Amazon.com." I lied smoothly. "Type in 'stilettos,' and viola, you can choose from the list."

She was appreciative. "Thank you. I'm Dana. I just flew in from Atlanta."

"And I'm Pauline." We shook hands. "I'm waiting for my lesbian lover."

She gave me the once over. "You're *gay?*"

"Gayer than the Flintstones."

She rushed off, mumbling "Ugh!" under her breath.

"Ugh you too, bitch!" I yelled after her. Several fellahs were chuckling, checking me out.

One walked behind me, looking at my ass. I farted so loud he averted his face, clearly turned off. Must have been the grilled cheese I bought when I got here. Shit, Mama always taught me it was better out than in.

I was just about to sit down when I saw him. Naygee. He turned the corner, throwing his arms up. Yes. He was still the same gorgeous specimen I sucked up on an airplane on the way to New York days ago. He still had the green bandana wrapped around his forehead and he looked gorgeous in black suede baggy jeans, fresh Jordan sneakers and a huge Plies T-shirt.

"Hi, Ma," he said, taking me into his arms.

"Hi, Naygee. I told you I'd be here."

He gave me some tongue. He moaned, grinding his hips on mine. We hunched standing up. I didn't care. I got off on people looking.

Taking his hand, I said, "Did you bring any bags?"

He looked deep into my eyes. "Nah. I just brought the bag I'm carrying."

"Well, let's go."

I had to squeeze my ass cheeks together because I had to fart.

When I got home an hour later, I closed and locked the door when he dropped his bag, settling on the sofa. He kicked off his shoes.

"You have a nice pad." He was looking around, liking my set up. "Damn, that's a big ass plasma TV!"

I took off my blouse, my tits bare. I always lounged naked in my crib. "I know. It cost a pretty penny, too."

He pulled off his shirt, his killer abs well cut. He unbuckled his belt, pulling it off. I sat by him. We looked at each other, not saying another word.

I was glad that he came. I wasn't trying to keep him, but he was fine as wine and I wanted some Kool-Aid all of a sudden.

I looked past him at the China cabinet, my heart dropping. Oh my God!

I jumped up to my feet as if my couch was on fire. Where is it?

Naygee touched my arm. "What's wrong, Ma?"

"It's gone!"

"What's gone?" he asked, trying to figure out what the hell I was talking about.

Before I could say it a tall, stocky figure walked out of my kitchen, pausing in front of me. He was naked, his dick hanging like Tarzan.

He wore the Golden Mask. Naygee stood up, clearly disgusted at the sight of another man's dick. I was turned on. Who the hell was this man in my home standing in my living room like Santa Claus sent me an early gift? A big red bow was tied on his dick. He had the perfect body.

He was walking up to me.

"Melissa, why didn't you tell me your man was here?" Naygee asked, putting on his shirt. He looked like he was about to vomit. But the strangest thing happened. Naygee kept looking at the stranger's dick. What straight man looked at another man's package? Like he owned my house, the stranger swiftly walked past me, snatched the shirt and threw it across the room. Naygee steamed, taking a few steps back, like he was about to swing. I carefully watched him. He was looking at homeboy's package again, trying to keep up the disgusted attitude.

The stranger paused in front of me, sinking to his knees. He took my skirt and pulled it down, my booty cheeks free and jiggling, baby. He inhaled my womanly scent from the skirt, running his tongue over the leather. He then pulled my pussy to the slit in the mask and his tongue began ravaging me. This felt so good. He took his time, his fingers embedded in my skin. The pain mixed with the pleasure and I welcomed it with open arms. I held his head for balance, Naygee's dick hard. Naygee tried to look away, but I saw his eyes watching, probing and studying. He began rubbing himself, sitting back on the sofa.

"Fuck it, I'll watch," he said, spreading his legs. "I surrender…but you better keep this shit quiet. What goes on in here stays in here…"

My Stranger Man told me to hump his tongue. Where had I heard that voice before? He talked like the rapper Bustah Rhymes. I grabbed his head and shivered when his tongue slid across my clit. He was lean and strong, my toes tingling with pleasure.

I was about to come already. I bit down on my tongue to stall it. I didn't want to come yet.

He picked me up and carried me to the couch like a lily. Laying me next to Naygee, he spread my legs and then spread my wet pussy lips. I looked at Naygee, reaching for his dick. He unzipped his pants, pulling it out. I gripped it, slightly jacking it. This had to be heaven because I hadn't known hell to be this virtuous.

The Stranger ate me out again, like my pussy was a plum. Naygee wanted in on the action so he got on his knees, and began tasting me also. He tongue kissed the stranger, making me shudder. This was hot. Two men (who were strangers to each other) were kissing my clit at the same time. Naygee finger fucked my asshole while the stranger fingered my cunt. I couldn't stand it.

The Stranger sat next to me and he raised a finger.

"I want you and Naygee to suck my dick," he said and I looked at Naygee. He struggled with himself.

"I don't know, dawg," he said. "Eating pussy with you was where I drew the line."

"Shut up and suck this dick, Niggah. Melissa, get on your motherfucking knees and suck this nut out. Make my dick spit."

"Yes!" I got on my knees and took his juicy dick into my mouth. My knees were tired, but that's ok. "Are you Freaky Deaky?" I asked him.

"Hell yes!"

I reached over and grabbed Naygee's dick. I sucked on it, rolling my tongue around like it was a juicy lollypop. I wanted to put them together so I asked the stranger to stand up and he did. I put both dicks in my mouth, handling it like the bitch I was. I was twirling my hips. My tits were shaking for dear life. I was so wet. I smelled my pussy in the air. I released the dicks and rubbed some juices on my hands. I then spread my pussy jizz on both dicks, massaging it in. It was time to suck them again.

Before I could, the stranger sat down, his legs cocked open. He was so sexy. I took him into my mouth and Naygee got on his knees next to me. The stranger reached up and pulled Naygee's lips down to the head of his pulsating dick.

Veins traveled like intersections all over the beautiful member.

Naygee and I tongue kissed the head of his dick, Naygee taking it into his mouth. He chocked a lot, and his teeth kept grazing the dick.

I was lost for words. Where did I know the stranger from? His body looked like familiar territory, so I paid close attention to it.

While Naygee necked his dick, I stood up and slapped Naygee's booty cheeks. He had a nice tush.

"Are you Freaky Deaky, Naygee?"

"Hell, yea!" he announced.

"I can't hear you!" I grabbed the paddle on my low-table and spanked his ass.

"HELL YEA!"

I got on my knees and spread his cheeks apart. I tasted the chocolate. His ass smelled so good and it was clean. I loved cleaned asses.

The stranger stood up and got behind Naygee, eating with me.

He used his big, hairy hands to hold Naygee's booty cheeks apart so we could both eat Thanksgiving dinner early.

He was nasty like me. Naygee grinded his hole on our tongues, lost for words. I looked at the stranger and he looked at me.

"Take the mask off my face."

I slowly took it off, my mouth falling open. My Bronx bred niggah has found me. The man I met in Manhattan. Melvin.

I was stunned into silence. He looked as gorgeous as ever. I must be one lucky girl. I had two fine ass men in my living room ready to fuck the brakes off my pussy and each other. Naygee stared at him, a small smile playing on his lips.

He stood up, looking into his eyes. We all hugged each other, rubbing each other's genitals. I kissed Melvin, the urgency in my body catapulting past Olympic heights.

I then kissed Naygee, while Melvin rubbed my pussy with his left hand and rubbed Naygee's ass with his right hand. We were both moaning when Melvin finger fucked us both.

He had his index finger deep inside Naygee and his other index finger in my pussy. We looked at each other with a pleasurable longing I had never experienced before. Melvin wanted to run the show. He asked me to put on the Golden Mask and I did. He took Naygee's shirt and tied it around Naygee's eyes. He then pulled a condom from his bag on the side of the chair and put it on.

He took out a small container of lube, spread Naygee's cheeks and squirted it at the start of the crack of his ass, the liquid trailing over his hole. He massaged it in. He pushed Naygee on the chair, pushing his legs back. I helped him hold them in place. Melvin slowly inserted his dick, Naygee's mouth hanging open. Damn this was hot.

After he slowly inserted it, Melvin slow grinded, so Naygee's hole could get used to the beef. Didn't make sense to open Wendy's drive-thru if the menu wasn't established.

Once Naygee's walls slid against the thickness of Melvin's rod, Melvin went to town, fucking the shit outta him. I let Naygee's legs go, straddling his hips. Just because he was taking dick didn't mean he couldn't suck on my pussy. I held the couch, lowering my wet opening on those lips. He was moaning so loud I nearly went deaf.

"Damn, Son! Damn, shit, Niggah! Get it, Daddy! Goddamn, this shit feels good!"

Naygee blindly ate my pussy, Melvin kissing my back. Naygee's legs were behind his arms, and I reached back and grabbed both his feet for balance. My eyes rolling to the back of my head, I was starting to sweat. The mask was hot on my face.

Melvin sucked on the back of my neck, getting deeper inside Naygee. He grabbed me by the hair and snatched my head back, giving me some tongue.

"Are you Freaky Deaky?" Melvin asked me, stealing my line. This turned me off a tad. When I asked a man was he Freaky Deaky that was my catalyst because I was Queen bitch!

"Yes, I'm Freaky Deaky."

"ARE YOU FREAKY DEAKY?"

"YES!"

Melvin pulled out and turned me to face him. He took off the condom, and shoved his dick down my throat. I gagged, but being the pro that I was I recuperated lovingly. His dick was scratching my tonsils and I loved it.

He took the mask from my face and aligned the hole in the eye of the mask with my pussy. He put his dick through the eye, and into my warm center and I died. He told me to hold the mask and I did.

Naygee slipped on a condom and got behind Melvin.

"It's my turn."

Naygee went up in Melvin without all the slow stuff and Melvin's body cringed from the pain. Naygee was more Gangsta with it, grabbing that ass and plowing him like he was planting watermelon seeds. We were tangled in our three way fuck, and I didn't want it to end.

Melvin and Naygee forgot about me and Melvin pulled out, while keeping Naygee deep inside him and they fucked all over my living room. Naygee had some skills. He made Melvin come without touching himself. I wiped up Melvin's come, lubing my fingers. I then lay in front of Melvin's lips and coated my pussy like Pepto Bismol. Melvin munched the cooch, ordering a side Caesar salad from my clit. I couldn't stand it.

Naygee had to come. His sweaty body jerked, and he pulled out, snatching off the condom like a porn star. He stood on the couch and come dripped all over me and Melvin and we were wiping it up, sucking it off each other's fingers and faces. I loved the way Naygee made it rain and cleared this pussy out. I looked over the mountain for the rainbow and got nothing but Melvin's tongue, back inside me, searching for the lost gold and finding the Leprechaun and he was one mad motherfucker because he asked "Where's me Gold?" and I answered the instant my pussy locked up and exploded all over Melvin's thick fingers, falling into a deep sleep.

The Golden Mask on top of my titties.

I felt myself breathing, but my eyes were still closed. Inhaling, it was cold as hell in my room but the bed felt so comfortable I didn't dare move. I reached over and pat the bed but I didn't feel anyone.

I opened one eye, but the room was dark. The glow of my clock lit my face. It was 6 a.m. I reached over and fumbled for the lamp. I had to sit up, took great effort. I turned on the lamp and was surprised I was in a red night gown. Did I shower? Because I felt refreshed. Damn. I slept for hours on end. I called Naygee's name. But he didn't answer.

I called Melvin's name, but he didn't answer. That's weird. Where were they? Hmm, they were probably fucking in the living room. Two hot and bothered black men on the DownLo were to be desired. Black love was a beautiful thing, in my opinion.

I stood up and walked around the house. I looked in the kitchen. Nothing. I looked in the bathroom, the back yard and the garage. Nothing. Melvin's stuff was gone. Naygee's stuff, too.

I picked up the house phone and called Naygee.

I heard the busy signal. "MSN Zero One. The mobile customer you are trying to reach does not answer."

I must have the wrong number. I called it again.

The same thing.

Damn it! His phone was off.

I called Melvin's number. I got the same thing. I called his home in New York. The prompt informed me that the number had been changed to an unlisted number. I lowered myself on the couch, trying to understand this. Two men who didn't know each other came to my house and fucked me to sleep and when I woke up there was no place like home because Todo was nowhere to be seen and Dorothy was crying because the house fell on the Wicked Witch of the East and I was a lonely bitch.

"What the fuck is going on?" I lit a cigarette, blowing smoke in the air. I looked at the China Cabinet.

The Golden Mask was back inside, sitting gloriously in the center.

Sparkling.

# First Nut 2

I have a story to tell. It's a story I have kept hidden for years. I lived in fear. I never exposed the fear or tried to understand it. Why should I? If I couldn't get rid of it why should I try to get rid of it? My sexuality was another matter. I felt like a monster. I felt like a weird fool because I had feelings for men. I love men. I couldn't help it. I've tried to dissect it. I tried looking at it under a microscope and in front of a telescope and I saw nothing but stars twinkling and atoms splitting. Was I born with it? Was it hereditary? Did it have something to do with genetics? I didn't think so. I wasn't born a gay man. And people who say I was can kiss my ass. You couldn't tell me about me. If my father would have never emotionally and sexually fucked me up I wouldn't have turned out like this. In my heart I knew this and couldn't anybody tell me different.

In my opinion this gay lifestyle was a learned trait. There's no way someone was born a gay man. Some people justified their sexuality by saying, "Ah. I was born this way," but how do they know? When my gay friend Bob told me he was born gay I was like "Whatever." This was a touchy topic. Even when I debated it with friends it has resulted in fights. I never got my ass whipped, but I've seen people's faces get bashed in for not believing that people were born gay. This was equivalent to religion. Did you believe in Allah, Jehovah, Buddha, Gandhi or some angel? Sexuality and religion has become two of the most diverse, complicated topics in the world. People were passionate about what they believed in. Go to Iraq and say "Do it in the name of Allah," and people would be blowing themselves up by the thousands. Say "I am gay," and you might catch some bullets in your ass.

When babies were born what did they know? They didn't know what a penis looked like, they didn't know they had assholes and they didn't know how to spell their names. This was why they're taught to say their A-B-C's and 1-2-3's For understanding. For balance. That's a learned behavior. So what about sex, sexuality and fear? What about love, deception and liars? If I was born *knowing* I liked men then why wasn't I born knowing how to tie my shoe, ride a bike or drive a car? Why were those things taught behaviors? Ding, ding, ding. You get my point.

But would mother? She has long suspected me of being gay. I never brought women around and she's seen me with more men than anything. No, I never brought the lifestyle around her house but come on. I didn't want kids and I didn't care to. I couldn't even take care of myself. I still lived in my parent's home. I still depended on them. And even though I worked at a retail department store (I got fucked tonight in the warehouse, and the dick was good), I still asked my parents for money and nine times out of ten they gave it to me. My mother was a business woman focused on her career and my father has been raping me for years. How did I tell her? I didn't know how and now she looked at me, as we sat in the living room, and she said, "Tell Mama about your first nut."

The request was a little over the top. Why would I discuss this with Mama? I felt weird even listening to it.

"Son, did you hear me?"

Why would she want to know about my first nut? It wasn't a pleasant memory and I didn't care to ever talk about it.

"So you're going to ignore me? I hate to be ignored. You know that's a pet peeve of mine."

Bad enough it engulfed me when I had dreams. Every time I looked at my father I remembered the pain he inflicted on me. Every time I heard his voice I figured it was my fault he did what he did. I had to pay the price. I was sacrificed. I didn't want to discuss this with her. How could I tell her that her husband, my father, raped me for years? How could I tell her that his abuse was a recycled entity he carried down from his own father and probably his father's father? I was ashamed enough. I didn't even like being a bisexual man. I hated the monster he turned me into. How could I explain to her he used to teach me how to kiss, how to caress and how to take him like a man?

Mama was determined to get me to talk to her.

"Baby...talk to me. I know something is there." She poured another drink. She tilted the glass towards me and I nodded. Maybe I did need a drink. And I needed one now!

I watched her pour some liquor into a small glass and then she put in three ice cubes. "Mama, drop it."

She handed me the drink. "You can talk to me," she said depressingly, like she was hinting at something.

"I can't, Ma. It hurts." I wolfed it down, the ice tinkling in the glass. I slammed the glass on the low-table. "Can I have more?"

She thought about it. "Sure."

"Fill it up."

"But you're not a heavy drinker."

"But I'm a heavy thinker and I have a lot on my mind."

She filled up the glass. "Talk to me, Son."

"Mom. No. It hurts too much."

She handed me the drink. "Why does it hurt? What hurts? Who caused the hurt?"

"Mama." I wolfed the drink down my throat. It burned, my watery eyes narrowing. I needed a blunt.

"Son. I know you're keeping secrets. I know you are. I've known for years"

"You are wrong." I jumped up to my feet. I was about to run. I had to run. Gradually my head was feeling light, like I was losing a grip on reality. If I uttered the product of my heart's discontentment it would destroy the fabric of the family. And I know she was one for image. She basked in the spot light. Being a political woman, she was into public perceptions, caring about what they thought. If I told Mama my secret it would crush her.

I started to leave the living room.

"Son. Please. Sit down and talk to me. Please. I am here to help you. Not hurt you."

I put my hands on the wall, next to Mama and Dad's wedding picture. In it Dad stood erect, like his penis once had. Ready to destroy me. Of course he brainwashed and groomed me. He made me think all fathers did this to their sons and I was so young and naïve I believed it. Why was I so dumb? Why? I was so powerless. I felt hopeless. I couldn't defend myself. And now every time I lay down with a man I thought about Dad. I recreated what he'd done. I didn't want kids of my own because I was scared. What if I harmed my child? I would kill myself.

"Mama I never wanted it to happen."

She was behind me. Handing me another drink. I took a moment to get it. Tears fell from my eyes. She was rubbing my back. I felt her breath on my face. "Drink it, Son. It'll help."

I slowly looked at her. I was losing it. I was about to click on a bitch. I didn't have to reveal the source of my pain. God had his reasons for allowing Satan to play hockey with my life. Satan was probably laughing at me.

*Drop it!* "Mama. No. I don't want to."

"Son. You can tell me about your first nut. I know all about it."

"Stop playing with my mind. Maybe I shouldn't have drunk that liquor so fast."

"Your first nut was with my husband. Your father…"

I closed my eyes. *She knows!* "Mama, you're off base. How could you…"

"Son. No sense in denying it. I knew for years."

"Nothing happened."

"Why do you think I poured myself into my work? Why do you think I hated and dreaded being home?"

I looked at her. I took the drink. I killed it. I threw the glass across the room. It slammed into Dad's picture.

"I know you're angry. I would be, too."

"How did you find out? Did he tell you? Did he say it was my fault?"

"No, son. No one told me. I saw it. I saw him kissing you one day. I dismissed it as father and son bonding. But then a week later I was standing in the door way. I saw him inside you. I saw it all. I was so shocked something snapped in my head. I died inside. I lost it. I started working harder. I couldn't believe my husband would do this to you."

"So you chose to sweep it under the rug. You are my mother and you didn't protect me."

"Son, I had a career. I couldn't let this get out. Do you know what this would have done for my political career? I would have been dragged through the mud."

"DRAGGED?"

She wiped tears from her eyes, drinking from the bottle. I snatched it and threw it at her. It missed her face by inches. She grabbed me, trying to make me understand but there was no way I could. She just admitted to me that she saw my father deflower me. She saw it all. And all she cared about was what the public had to say. So what! I was her son!

"Son. Listen."

I pushed her off me. I hated putting my hands on a woman that gave me life. But I had to. I was tired of people touching me and I didn't want them to.

"Listen to what?" I stormed past her. I had to get some air. She grabbed my arm and I tried to punch her. I was scared. I felt trapped. I was suffocating.

She was a beast. "SON!"

I was a lion. "Let me go!"

"You don't understand. I couldn't tell anyone. I couldn't call the police. It would all come out."

*What will come out? My rape? I'm getting the impression that there's more to this story!* "Yes it would, Ma. And you were supposed to stand right by my side, look the media in the face and protect me. For my well being you were supposed to throw all that political bullshit out the window. I can't *believe* you. You're still worried about public opinion. This is worse than when I asked to meet my grandparents."

---

"You can't meet them. They are dead."

"Really?"

"Yes. They were bad people. They treated me like filth. I didn't want you to meet them."

"I want to. But of course I can't because you say they are dead and gone. But that's irrelevant. I can't get past the you-watched-your-husband-rape-me part. Are you sick?"

"Son, no. Just let it go. It's the past. You're a grown man."

Could you believe her? "And I'm supposed to forget it?"

"Yes. Let it go. Look how long you kept it a secret?"

"I gotta go. I can't be in this house. I will call the police myself. I can't go on like this. I'm trapped in a gay lifestyle and I can't break free because your husband, my Dad taught it to me."

"YOU CAN'T CALL THE POLICE! IT WILL ALL COME OUT!"

"What will come out? My rape?'

She studied me, wiping tears from her eyes. She wasn't the aristocratic bitch she normally was. Gone was her ruggedness. Gone was the toughness. What stood before me was a caricature. A woman I no longer respected. I was so angry I didn't think I loved her.

Mama said, "Wait right here. I have to tell you everything then maybe you'll understand."

"Tell me what?"

She vanished up the stairs. I sunk to my knees and stared at my lap. My own mother. Stood by and put her career before her own child. She gave me life and she watched that man snatch it away. All those years I thought I was keeping it from her because I didn't want her to feel she failed as a parent. And all this time SHE KNEW! BITCH!

She slowly came down the stairs holding an envelope. It was a manila one. She played around with it. Her heels clicked on the tile walking up to me. She refused to meet my eyes.

"It will all come out, Son."

She handed me the envelope.

"It's best if you heard it from me. It's time. You're old enough. You deserve to know the truth.

Before I could open it the front door opened.

Daddy walked inside.

He smiled when he saw us. He walked over to Mom and kissed her cheek. It was like she got shocked. She jumped out of her skin, standing behind me. He looked strangely at us.

"Something is going on," he said, barely above a whisper. "What is it?"

Mama said, "Nothing."

I said, "She's lying. Something is going on."

He smiled at me, rubbing my head. "That's my boy."

I slapped his hand off me. "I hate you."

He grew quiet. Looking from me to her and back to me. Looking himself in the mirror, he was shaking his head. He saw the glass shattered by his shattered picture. The broken liquor bottle silenced him.

"You two got in a fight. Son, did you raise your hand to my wife?"

"No, but you raised your hand to me."

"Son, what are you talking about?"

Mama said, "I should have confronted you years ago. But I cared more about the image of family. My political career came before my family."

"Confronted me?" He shook his head again.

"For raping our son."

He turned and refused to face us.

"Look at me, Dad," I said, opening the manila envelope, suspense killed me. I had to know what was going on inside.

"Why did you lie to your mother?"

"Ha! I lied?" I asked, pulling out the papers. There were about five of them. I looked at the first one.

Mama said, "I'm sorry baby. Now you see. It'll all come out."

My face turned ashen. I couldn't breathe. I dropped them on the floor, looking at her.

"I'm adopted?"

Dad turned to face me.

Mom said, "Yes."

I couldn't believe my ears. She had to be lying. She told me she gave birth to me on June 5, 1977. It was all a lie? Was she serious? The official adoption forms and certificate was on the floor enshrining my feet. So she had to be telling the truth.

"Dad! You knew I was adopted. Is that why you abused me?"

"Son…"

"According to these papers we aren't related. I can't believe this. In one night I lost my family, but in all actuality I lost my family years ago. Both of you are sick individuals. Mom wanted a political career.

So she shunned my feelings and emotions to have it. She saw you rape me, Mr. Dad. She saw you with her own eyes."

"She didn't."

"I did," she went on. There was a knock at the door.

Dad answered it. He was face to face with uniformed police men.

Mama said, "They are here for you, *husband.*"

"And for you, too," the shorter cop said, frowning. "Both of you are under arrest."

I didn't know what would become of my life. People called me gay yet no one understood what I have gone through. No one saw the vehicle my fake Daddy drove to get me to the destination. I didn't want this, I didn't ask for this. They say God didn't put on you no more than you could bear but who wanted to bear this? I was a monster. Or so I thought. I didn't love myself. Maybe I should start. I had a feeling this big ole house would be mine. And I would take it. All Mama's jewelry I would pawn it, but why? Diamonds and gold couldn't erase what was done to me. I picked up a phone book and called the first shrink's office I could find. Once I made an appointment I picked up the Bible and turned it to the book of Psalms.

*God help me.* And I knew in my heart he would.

# RAYNE IN THE BEDROOM 3

*My fantasy is ruined! How can it end like this? How dare a transsexual pose as a real woman in my home? How could the fledgling he/she pull out his penis in my face, just when I was about to eat her pussy? She didn't have a pussy at all. I can't believe the horror of a penis in my face! I hate dick! I haven't had a dick inside me since I was 19, and even when I did take said dick I poisoned him in the end because he told all his college friends. I am so grossed out. And to think Rayne was behind this. It wasn't my fault I tricked her into letting me suck her pussy. I love pussy more than men. Yes, I am a woman of impeccable standards. I slash the dots on the I's and I explode the crosses on the t's. I made my own rules and broke them. I was sexual by nature. I was one way in public, attending Catholic Church, hosting Bake sales, mingling with the common folk and doing what society expected of me. But inside my expensive home, I was another way. I was the lesbian Dr. Jekyll and Mr. Hyde. I used toys to make myself come and rode dildos to my sheer delight. I hated real dicks but I loved the plastic ones. The difference between a real dick and a fake one were the batteries. I would masturbate with fruit and eat them to a polish. I would suck oranges and rub the stinging citrus all over my pussy. I would sleep while the citrus dried on my twat* and awaken around 4 a.m. and fuck myself senseless on the Web cam. Women around the world have watched me work my pussy into the orgasm phase. I have watched them. Typing demands on the keyboard became their utter failure. If I told her to wipe piss on her tit and suck it off she would. Just to get a taste of Hollywood. But this wasn't the red carpet. This was sex. This was dominance. This was power. I never showed my face online. The internet could be a miserable vessel if you let it. I loved wearing fancy wigs and dressing like a boy. I got off on the trickery. I got off on tricking women into lesbian action for years. It was something I've been doing since I was a promising teenager. It was something I did after I got heartbroken by a man. I painfully remember when I first thought about it. I was dating a man named June. He had long, curly eyelashes and the creamiest black skin. He had an amazing body and the way he walked reminded one of poetry. He was a Ladies Man, but at the time I didn't care. He had the most heavenly eyes. The way he smiled parted my heart into beats never seen by my pulse. He came into my life a promising rose and left a dandelion. He tricked me into thinking he loved me, only to lay up with a male friend of his and make love to him the way a man made love to his woman. I remember standing in the forest watching them. I was taking a walk that night when my parents fell asleep. I was rubbing my arms, the breezy air blowing my hair into a frenzy. I'd spoken to June earlier that day and he told me he was going out of town to visit his grand mother. I didn't have any control over that so I didn't care. I told him to give her my best. He said he would. When I saw the forest I wanted to run. Because it was after ten p.m. and it was very dark. But something lured me to it. So I went. When I passed a huge oak tree I saw June's car. It was rocking. The lights were off. I slowly walked up to it, my heart thumping. I saw a male's face pressed against the driver side window. I walked closer. I heard the cursing and the moaning. This ass is good. Fuck this dick. I'm gonna come deep inside you. I was nailed to the grassy terrain. I cried for dear life. I was shaking my head, pounding on the windshield. The rocking stopped. The heavy breathing died. June was so shocked he couldn't move. His male lover ducked his head. But it was too late. I'd already seen his face. I started to scream and he got out of the car, his penis swinging. I didn't want it by me. It was suddenly a strange creature and I didn't care for it. I didn't want to feel it, touch it or taste it. My love had been cracked like swollen sea shells. Over by a huge root sticking from a tree I saw a brick. With all my might I picked it up and swung at his face and missed. I threw it at the windshield and it shattered. It hit his lover in the face and blood was everywhere. I covered my face, running off. "DON'T TELL ANYONE, CLEVER!" came the insightful call from behind me. But I didn't care. I didn't even want to tell myself. I was so in love I tried to commit suicide. I used to pray about it, begging the Good Lord to erase my blood line from the world and bury me a love sick fool. I would cry for weeks. My grades declined. My uptight, anal parents would whip my tail for bad grades but I welcomed the pain. Daddy noticed the change in me and wanted to know what was wrong but I closed up inside. I turned ugly and dark and gothic. I started wearing black nail polish and black lipstick. My hair once down to my ass I cut with sheers. It now hung just past my ears. I asked God to take my heart and get rid of it. But he gave me something else once I put on one of Daddy's suits. A split personality. Somewhere inside me I snapped. I would begin to talk to myself in the mirror. Changing my voice like I was from Brazil. Or was it France? It was one of those overseas countries. I would do this day in and day out when I didn't have school. I would sit at the sowing machine and alter his smoke-colored suit so it fit me.

Thinking about June I wanted revenge. So this was how I got it. I befriended his mother behind his back. She was a timid little bitch, stuck on her divine looks. She used to stare at herself in the mirror for hours, asking the mirror who was the sexiest of 'em all. I remember I stole money from mother's expensive purse and caught the public bus to the local grocery store. I bought June's mother a chocolate cake and took it to her. When she saw me her lips parted in a very confusing way. She was clad in a floral dress with flowers all over it. I loved the way the satin at the bottom grazed her calves when she walked. She tossed her hair about her head, looking like an innocent bird.

After she accepted my cake she asked could she brush my hair. I said, "Yes."

"Who are you anyway? Are you here to see one of my sons?"

"No, ma'am. I don't even know your sons," I lied, anger surging all over my face.

"Then why are you here? Why did you bring me a chocolate cake?"

"Because I'm new in the neighborhood and I thought I'd extend a greeting, since the outside of your house is heaven."

She blushed. "Why thank you. I tend my gardens every day. It keeps me busy...would you like to come inside?"

"Sure," I said, nervous as hell. But I kept my cool. I was the enemy. You could never get too cozy with the enemy.

I had to remember my purpose and my mission. I had to get back at June for making me fall in love with his bisexual ass.

There was no way he could get away with it. Not on my life or his life. And right now his life was a bucket of peons.

Entering her home was awkward. Up until then I had never been inside anybody's home but my own. My parents forbade it. I could never tell them I was at June's home. Hell, they had never heard of or met June. My parents said I wasn't allowed to have boyfriends. So I never brought them around.

I took into account the Italian feel in the room. Italian chairs and beige Italian throw pillows. An old, yellowing black and white picture hung above the mantel.

*"You have such long, long hair," she said, smiling at me. She sat on the sofa and I sat on the floor, between her legs. I could smell her pussy but I didn't say anything. I was a teen ager. She was an adult. I was into other men and women around my own age.*

*"Thank you."*

*She was brushing my hair lovingly, humming a famous tune I couldn't name. "I always wanted a daughter."*

*"Why didn't you try for one?"*

*She thought about it. "Because I have three sons. They run wild in the streets then come home when the sun goes down to rest. I guess I'm content with that."*

*"Are you really?"*

*She smiled again. She had a lovely smile. "Yes."*

*"Are you married?" I asked, looking around her living room with both awe and jubilancy.*

*"Yes. I'm married," she spat rather quickly. My pulse quickened thinking about it. Her fingers betrayed her words. There wasn't a ring on her finger. Even the faded marking wasn't there. I tried to understand why she fibbed. Was she embarrassed that she was a single mother trying to raise little rascals? Who knew? Some women thought their pussies started and stopped life and all it did was give you pleasure or a kid or two. Nothing more. Nothing less.*

*The floor beneath my buttocks was uncomfortable. I shifted a little, wanting to go home. I just wanted to bring her a cake and analyze the inside of her home.*

Retrospection interweaving her thoughts, Clever smiled, thinking back to that time. When she tricked her first lover into doing something he wasn't aware of. June paid dearly for cheating on her. Oh, yes. He did. And when she gave him the receipt for her endeavors he wouldn't know what hit him. But she knew what hit him. She wanted him to suffer. She wanted to play her tricks and make him squeal with misery. Oh, Yes. Thinking about it, she wanted a tonic but she decided against it. Now was not the time to drink and think. Rubbing her pussy, she inhaled deeply, the scent igniting in her heart vengeance and in her soul revenge…

*June's mother was brushing my hair rather lovingly. I was uncomfortable now and I wanted to leave. I thought about Daddy's suit and wearing it. I wanted to be a man again. To talk like one and walk around my room like one. Practice made perfect.*

*Before I could say anything the front door opened and June walked inside. I lowered my head so he couldn't see my face. He slammed the door and the pictures on the walls shook. I was too afraid to look up. I didn't want to be found out. I wanted this all to be a trick, a game. The fantasy was to cunningly destroy his mental state and give him an image that wasn't there. I felt it pulsating through my veins.*

*He didn't even speak or find out who I was. He ran up to his room in tears. His mother didn't even seem interested in why he shed tears. She was more into brushing my hair. What was wrong with that picture? Why didn't the maternal instinct wash over her face? Why didn't she demand that her son tell her what's wrong? What kind of mother was she?*

*"Could you do me a favor?" I asked, testing the waters. How else would I find out if the lake was a damn or the sea?*

*"Yes?"*

*"Could you cut the cake? I have a taste for chocolate and I'm famished."*

*"Yes. I could do that. How about some supper?"*

*"Yes. I would like that."*

*"It isn't cooked yet. It would take a while."*

*I looked at her, my eyes sparkling like diamonds.*

*"Take all the time you need."*


*When she left I stood up and explored the house. I wanted to know where her bedroom was. I walked down the hallway and saw an open door. It was the only room on the floor. Once I went inside I took into account a dim light coming from the closet. I walked to it. I pushed the door open, my heart terrorizing my chest. I shouldn't be in there but I had to get June.*

*I saw the clothing and I smiled.*


*There was a knock on June's door. He answered it, his eyes red with sadness. He took one look at me and said, "Who are you?"*

*"I'm Tom. I'm a friend of your lover's."*

*"Did he send you here?'*

*I thought about it. "Yes."*

*"I don't know why. He left me. He blames me for Clever destroying his face."*

*"He blames Clever?"*

*"Yes. She threw the brick through my car windshield and it destroyed his dashing good looks."*

*"Oh..."*

*"Why are you here?"*

*"To help solve the problem. He asked me to."*

*June was confused. He looked me up and down, obviously liking what he saw.*

*"Well, the only way to help me..."*

*I caught the bait. "What way would that be?"*

He pulled me in the room and closed the door. He was rubbing my buttocks, giving me some tongue. I fell into his charm. I died inside his heat.

"You like the boys, huh?" I asked him.

"Yes," he said breathlessly, unzipping his pants. "Get on your knees."

"Would that make you happy? Is that what you fantasize?"

"Yes…"

I got on my knees and took him into my mouth. My lips were clumsy and untrustworthy. I had never done this before and it was hot that I was trying. He loved it nonetheless, falling on the bed. I was on top of him, sucking him dry, putting my heart into it with a rookie spirit.

"I love it…"

"I do, too."

"Take off the hat…"

"Do you really want it off?"

"Yes."

I sat up and took off the hat. His eyes popped from his head. I then took my hair from the stocking cap and shook it free. He sat up and I stood up, taking off his daddy's suit jacket and shirt. He was in denial.

"Thought a boy was sucking on you, 'ey?"

"This has to be a game. How did you get in my house?"

"Easy. I bought your Mama a chocolate cake."

"What?"

"She was brushing my hair when you flew through the front door."

"Get out, Clever. You have caused my life enough hassle."

"I caused your life a hassle? You cheated on me and you blame me?"

He was apologetic then. But it was too little too late. "I am sorry, Clever. I really am. Please. I can't deal with this right now. It's bad enough I'm bisexual and I can never be free with it. I will have to live a fantasy for the rest of my life because I may lose my mother. If she found out I had wings and became a fairy she would disown me…"

I thought about his words. He would have to live a fantasy. Well, bozo! I will have to live a fantasy as well. Just like you tricked me into thinking you loved me and it was all a lie, all a game I will do the same thing to whoever I encounter in life. I will get off on their naivety. I will be a flesh blood hound and suck them dry. Just like you did to me.

"Have some chocolate cake, my dear," I said and he looked at me blankly.

"What cake?"

"The one I baked for your mother," I lied. "Have a piece. If you can have a piece with her and ask God to forgive you and to forgive yourself I will leave amicably and I will never bother you again."

"Are you serious? If I eat some cake then it's all over?" he asked, not believing me.

*I glared into his eyes. "It will be all over. I promise. I will leave and never return. I will act like we don't know each other. I will never tell anyone you love men. I will take it to my grave."*

*We shook on it. He left me standing in the room and I put back on his father's coat. Checking myself in the mirror, I looked down and noticed his mom's make-up. Piking up her lipstick, I coated my lips and said, "I hope you like the cake."*

*I looked at the clock and shook my head. I had to be getting home soon. I slowly grabbed my shoes and crept out the room. I had to see if he was holding up his end of the bargain.*

*When I got to the kitchen I stood there watching him clutch his throat. Falling to his knees he began to foam at the mouth.*

*When his eyes landed on me he tried to lash out and I laughed, my eyes locked on the ceiling.*

*"Die, gay boy. Die a horrible death. I told you if you ate the cake it would all be over. Didn't I promise you that?" I was slowly walking up to his twitching body, his legs thumping one of the dining room chairs amongst other things.*

*"Did you like the chocolate cake?" I asked, pausing by the stove. I picked up the rest of the cake and got on my knees.*

*I smashed the plate into his face. Blood spurted in my face. Licking my lips, I used my fingers to wipe up his blood and I taste it. Yummy. Blood was the best form of revenge.*

*Finally, when the house phone rang his body lay lifeless, his foot resting on top of his mother's face. She lay sprawled underneath the table, her legs carefully bent at the knees. She looked peaceful. I was laughing again, crawling over to her. I grabbed her legs and pulled her to me. Resting her head in my lap, I began to stroke her hair, the way she stroked mine.*

*"So your son gave you some cake. I'm glad you both liked it. What I didn't tell you was that it was laced with poison…"*

*I closed my eyes, sweeping my palms over her eyes.*

*Closing them.*

*Like my heart.*

Depressingly, Clever unflinchingly sat on the long leather settee in her bedroom, her world in shambles. She stared at the flashing TV. On the floor was her wig. On the bed was the smoke-colored suit. Behind her was the glow of the computer screen.

Standing up, she stretched. It felt so good. Walking over to the closet she opened it. Looking around at the various clothes, she smiled, resting a finger on her temple.

Looking over her shoulder she stared at the rotary phone, next to her photo on the nightstand. She picked up the phone and dialed a series of numbers. The dial of the phone snapped back to the "0" position with a snap. The phone started ringing and she sighed. She looked at her diamond watch and sat on the edge of the bed, debating…plotting.

When the person answered the phone she was elated.

Very.

A few months later, Rayne was sitting in her living room, watching her son talk on the phone with his girlfriend. Watching him with the phone, she reminded herself that she had to call her friend Diana because she said somebody she knew was found dead in a bushy terrain in Ft. Lauderdale and Rayne really didn't care because her family lived in her neighborhood and it wasn't one of them. And her kids were ok. So she wasn't interested at the moment. She remembered the voice mail. "Girl it happened about four months ago and we're just finding out about it now…" Rayne didn't care.

Smiling, she marveled at how her son matured. He was certainly turning into a fine young man. He looked just like his dumb ass father. In fact she couldn't get over the man because every time she looked in her son eyes she saw him. Looking back at her. Taunting her. Out of her mind was Clever and the nightmare of finding out she was really a woman dressed as a man. But she had gotten revenge by calling her transvestite friend and putting the joke on Clever. Part of her felt good about it, but the other part of her was disappointed that she would try to be a prostitute anyway. She just wanted the best for her kids and she would do anything for them. Most mothers would get two jobs but Rayne didn't want two jobs. Despite having kids she did have her own life and she had to love herself before she loved anyone else. Times were hard and men weren't fathers to their kids. Women had to pick up the slack, pick up the burden and pick up the tab. They had to pay for it all. They had to nurse their children's tears when they asked where Daddy was and she couldn't give them an accurate answer. That was her life. Cleaning up her Baby Daddy's mess, straightening his damn lies. She would never love again. She didn't need a man. She would focus on her kids and she would give it to God. She would buy a toy and give herself an orgasm a night and when she came down off her high she would feel great. She wouldn't need a man then.

Her son was laughing at something his girlfriend said and she stood up, looking at a Britney Spears video on TV. Pop tart. She liked her. Britney was her favorite entertainer.

"Son I am going to bed."

"Ok. But can I ask you something?" he asked, handsome in a Phat Farm shirt and black pants.

"Sure."

"Can I go out?"

"Yes, Son. Just be home by 12 midnight. You have school tomorrow."

"Bet that up, Ma," he said, standing up, clutching his cell phone. He hugged his mom, kissed her cheek and she retired for the evening...

"Lock the door behind you."

He did so.

Rayne lay in her bed and she closed her eyes. She had a long day. First she cleaned her house and cleaned out the dusty shed in the back. There was so much grime it sent her sinuses into a hissy fit. Then she took out the frozen pork chops so they could thaw. She then played with her pussy, had an orgasm and saw to her kids.

When they were squared away she went jogging around the neighborhood. But the funniest thing happened. When she was jogging home a black car kept following her. It had illegal tints and she feared her life. She ran up to her door, looking back and the window was lowered.

She looked at him and he looked at her.

It was her son's dad.

"What do you want?"

"I want to be a better father to my son..."

Rayne rolled her eyes, pulled her hair into a ponytail and she walked coolly up to his car.

"It's a little too late for that."

"It's never too late, Rayne."

"I don't even know why I'm wasting my time."

"Because you love me." He reached out of the window and touched her hand and she snatched it away.

"Every time we fuck you think we are supposed to get back together. It's just sex and nothing more and I haven't touched you in ions, man."

"I miss you," he said, clearly playing a game with her and she knew it. The man couldn't talk without lying. He always caused her trouble. Drama always seemed to find him and once a week a different thug shot at his ass, trying to take him out. He was a liar and a cheat.

"I'm going inside," she said, pivoting on her heel.

He parked the car in the drive way. When he opened the door, he rushed inside her home and locked the door.

God why won't he leave me alone? I don't want him. Don't he have other bitches?

He was knocking at the door and she peaked through the curtain. "WHAT?"

"Rayne, let's talk…"

She closed her eyes, sighing. She loved him so much and that was the problem. He knew she loved him and he played it to the tooth and nail and she was tired of it. It would be the same old shit, different day. Different problems. Different bullshit.

She closed the curtain and turned on the stereo, turning the volume as high as it would go.

He knocked louder but she didn't hear it.

She started to dance around the living room, putting him out of her mind. Her pussy wet, she thought about the tattoo he had on the small of his back. It said "Rayne." She shivered thinking about it. She used to love eating his ass and staring at her name. He was a freaky man. No he wasn't gay but he loved her tongue and finger deep in his asshole and she used to love giving it to him just the way he liked.

*Those days are gone…*

It was 2 a.m. when she opened her eyes and saw him standing in her room. The lamp was on and her son smiled down at her, standing next to his father.

"What is he doing in here?" she asked with an attitude. "GET OUT!"

"But Mom," her son said, his sad eyes weakening her. "He wants to talk to you. He doesn't mean any harm. Why do you hate him so much?"

"Because he cheated on me."

"But mom. You teach me to forgive and forget."

"It's different when your father is a sleaze bucket."

Snatching the covers from her body she pointed at him. "GET OUT!"

He looked sad. He rubbed his chin, looking at his son. "Leave us to talk," he whispered to his son, barely audible.

Her son smiled. "Sure, Dad…" and he closed the door.

Rayne was looking at her son's father. "Get out. I don't want to talk to you."

He walked up to her and touched her shoulder and she pushed him on the bed. He closed his eyes, holding in his anger.

Rayne said, "What do you want to talk about?"

He opened his eyes. She was falling for them. They seemed a little…different and distant. She sat next to him and said, "What do you want? Why are you here? There is a reason you show up on my doorstep unannounced. Is everything ok with you?"

He sat up and looked into her eyes. Their lips were getting closer.

*Oh, God. I am about to fuck him!*

When their lips touched she melted into his arms, feeling like a wounded bird, needing therapy so she could fly away, fly, fly away…

He lay her down and took off her panties. He inhaled her scent and kissed her pussy. Gave it some tongue.

"We are not getting…back…together," she promised, holding his head.

She loved the do-rag on his head, hiding his waves. She loved his chest and she wanted to see it but when she tried to take off his shirt he grabbed her hand and raised a finger.

He continued to eat, tasting the salt…running his lips over her passion…wanting her to come so he could taste it. He stuck his tongue so far in her pussy she jumped with jubilancy.

"Yes, Baby…yummy…eat my pussy, Daddy…"

He pushed her legs back and stuck his tongue inside her deeper, her skin starting to break out in sweats…he ate for dear life, like a starving lion without his cubs…like the clouds without air and rain, he needed to be fulfilled.

Her body tensed up and she said she had to come and he sucked on her clit, rubbing her wet pussy with her legs bent back even with her ears and she shrieked, her muscles contracting…pushing her…aiding her into silence.

"Wow," she said, looking at him with love in his eyes. She hadn't seen the man in years and with him back in her life (momentarily) he seemed diffcrent. He was once a man with a lot of weight. He lost a lot of it, toning himself up. She wanted to get him out of his clothes, but if she did that he would think they were trying to make it work and she didn't want him back.

"I wanna taste you," Rayne said, patting the bed. "Lay on your stomach. I want to eat you.…taste your skin…"

He lay on his stomach and she straddled his thigh. He rests his head on his hands and she raised the back of his shirt, kissing his back, loving the feel of his skin…softer than she remembered it.

He was twirling his ass, which was fuller than it used to be. She loved how he toned up.

*He must be working out.*

She ran her tongue from the top of his back, down his spine…to the tattoo of her name…

The tattoo of her name always brought her joy. She closed her eyes and inhaled, sitting up. She couldn't open her eyes.

*He is with the same old games. I can't be pulled back in. He has gotten over me. Because he took my name off the small of his back.*

*It's gone.*

"This isn't a good idea," Rayne said, getting back to her senses. She had to stand firm in her decisions. Once a man fucked up she didn't back step. She couldn't do it over. She wouldn't give him a second chance. Why should she? He would do the same deceitful things to her over and over and she didn't have time for it. He hurt her enough.

"Didn't you hear me?" Rayne asked him and he turned over, staring into her eyes with a smile.

"What kind of game are you playing?"

He shook his head in the negative and she said, "Yes you are! You're playing with me…

He stood up and picked up a piece of construction paper from her dresser and a black marker.

"Oh, God. You want to play charades?"

He shook his head yes with a smile.

"No, Man. Grow up! I can't believe I fell for your bullshit again. When will I learn?"

He drew a square…she was falling for it. She did like charades. She used to play that game with her mother.

"I don't know…it's a square…"

He drew a C.

"Umm, damn…A square…the letter C…"

He put a huge X over the box and the C.

"DAMN, MAN! GET OUT!"

He drew two stick figures holding hands…

"Man…when I guess this shit then get out!"

He drew an EKG machine, with a line zig-zagging across it.

"Love…live…"

"Yes!" he whispered. He wrote "Live" at the top of the paper. He drew an eye ball…

Rayne was biting her lip. "Eyeball…I see. I see live…no, that doesn't make sense…I…"

"Yes…" he whispered again. "I…live…"

He drew a courtroom. It was a little rusty but she knew what it was.

"Courtroom…a place of just…"

He gave her the thumbs up. He wrote "just" on the paper…

He then drew a stick figure in a bed…

"Sleeping…"

He drew pictures over the stick figure's head…

"Dreams…"

"YES YES YES!" he screamed. "I JUST WANT TO LIVE OUT MY DREAMS!"

Rayne looked at him. "Huh? Why are you yelling at me?"

He pulled a small shiny gun from his crotch.

"Hi, Rayne!"

"Um…" Her heart pounding, she slowly stood up from the bed. She was shaking her head. "Why do you have a gun? Are you going to kill me? What did I do to you? You weren't a good father to your son! Is that my fault?"

"Yes," he said, but his voice didn't sound like a man. It sounded like a woman.

Rayne narrowed her eyes. "Why are you talking like a chick? You're scaring me…"

He said, "Look into my eyes Rayne…and tell me where you know me from…"

"You're my son's father! I know…"

He said, "I once paid you $500…I once ate your pussy…but I was dressed as a man…remember…you tricked me and sent that transvestite to my home and you tarnished my fantasy forever!"

Rayne began shaking, covering her face. "Oh my God! No, no, *noooooo* what are you saying to me…?"

"I am not you son's father. I am not the man you used to love. I am an illusion. I am an image. I am what you want to see…Isn't that what you did to me? Sent a man with tits to my home, knowing I was a lesbian and I hated dick of any kind. You sold me an image. An illusion…"

"But…you look just like my son's father, Clever! This can't be happening…"

"I will tell you how I did it! I killed your son's father months ago. We met at a bar and I lured him back to my home and we made out on the bed I ate your pussy on…When he came I stabbed him to death. Do you know how long it took me to pull him to my Buick? I drove to Ft. Lauderdale and I dumped him in the bushes…"

"Oh, God! Diana was trying to tell me someone I knew was murdered…but I didn't listen…Oh my God!"

"Before I had sex with him I took pictures of him. Of, yes. Pictures of everything. I gave them to my plastic surgeon. What a marvelous job he did. He then got rid of my breasts…He redid my nose and teeth…He did everything in his power to make me look like your son's father. This took three months total. I went through a lot of pain…but it was well worth it, bitch! I had to make you pay for what you did to me, you dirty WHORE!"

"But you sound like him…"

I have been taking hormones for months. So my voice is that of a man now. On top of that I studied your son's father, from the video I have of him. He has a very unique speaking pattern. I studied it. And now…"

Clever extended her arms. "I present to you a man who is about to kill you."

Clever closed her eyes and Rayne started screaming when the gun went off.

Rayne shook, pissing on herself. The wet spot beneath her was warm and stinky. She refused to open her eyes.

Oh God I'm losing a lot of blood!

She opened her eyes and saw her son holding the gun. He was screaming, falling to his knees. "Daddy! I didn't mean to shoot you! But you had a gun aimed at my mother…I'm so sorry Daddy! Wake up, please, DAD! Don't die please Daddy don't leave me! Why were you trying to shoot Mama?"

Rayne slowly stood up and walked over to her son. Taking the gun, she hugged him and he shook with fear in her arms. He just killed a man he thought was his father.

*How do I tell him that the dead bitch on the floor isn't his father? How do I say it? Will he believe me if I told him? What if he thinks I was making it up? How do I let him know that his father died months ago, and his body was dumped as alligator food in Ft. Lauderdale?*

*I can never tell him. I have to give him an image, an illusion…like Clever gave me. What a sick bitch*

*I have to protect my son. Rest in peace, Baby Daddy…*

# Rock Star

My name was Quintet James. And I had something on my heart. *Party like a Rock star* blasted from the sufficient stereo system in my need-to-clean-it living room. I got shit everywhere, I tell you. Angry about not paying my water bill on time (and the water company cut it off, it's Friday night, and they didn't open until Monday morning, which meant I was without water for the entire weekend, so *not* cool) and forgetting to take out the turkey wings to thaw so I could make my Mama's favorite dish, complete with white steamy rice and well-seasoned squash, the Florida sunshine was starting to fade like my favorite pair of tight blue jeans, when I accidentally poured in bleach a few hours ago. I could have sworn I was washing white jeans. But I had forgotten I had earlier in the day washed and folded them. I didn't hang up my jeans. Why bother, when I was going to wear them anyways throughout the week. Which brought me to my closet? I needed to clean that also.

I headed up the hallway, towards my room, my sanctuary. Passing articulately-framed photos of Mama, daddy and my three sisters, Lisa, Stacey and Dash Gregory…I've since pushed my family away…I had my reasons…sometimes, when you were faced with life altering decisions, you tend to push loved ones away because you didn't want to hurt them, because you needed to deal with things on your own, because you didn't need a bunch of people yapping all up in your face, claiming they understood what you went through when they weren't even going through the source of your pain and suffering. And I loved my family, thrived for my family. But I changed my address and phone number months ago, moved from Philadelphia down to Florida without so much as a post card, a good bye or a see ya' later.

For a reason.

Fresh in my mind were blogs I read on Myspace. I was fond of Mercury Chyld, the Ogre poet and Legendary. I loved poetry; poetry got me through the day. I had about eight of Langston Hughes' collection of poems behind me on the ceiling-to-floor book shelf holding an array of books ranging from *Along Came a Spider* and *The Bluest Eye* to Hirohito and the Making of Modern Japan to A.H.M. Jones' *Sparta*.

I thought about Audrey Michelle's "ATM" poem while I looked around the semi darkness of a room I suddenly didn't want to be in.

My closet. I opened the door. From the fading Miami sunlight I could faintly see clothes, neatly folded, everywhere. Files were here and there and the three filing cabinets sat off in the corner of the closet. Awards I've won throughout my life hang on the wall, 189 pair of shoes carefully lined the top of my huge walk-in closet...I needed to go through all this shit and get rid of what I didn't need. And donate some of the clothes I outgrew or didn't wear anymore to the Goodwill so less fortunate people could rock what I used to look good in.

I turned on the bedroom lights by clapping my hands; yea I still got the played out The Clapper. Lights come on. Voila. Dust city appears in places and on things I never knew existed. I needed to dust the TV, dust the dresser, my armoire, which holds my perfumes and big screen TV and lap top. I should have bought a Dell Laptop because this E Machines piece-of-shit I bought, after camping out in the Best Buy electronics store line all night long, broke down after two fucking weeks.

I tried to fight the sensation but I sneezed, my allergies kicking my hind part. I was a woman who lived by the mood. I smelled like Britney Spears, her perfume, *Curious*, had me pissed the hell off. When was I going to understand that buying perfume because Elizabeth Taylor or Celine Dion graced the bottles didn't merit good shit? Smelled like hot shit.

White Diamonds gave me a headache so I stopped wearing it years ago. And when I wore Celine I damn near broke out in hives trying to brush that stinky shit off me. My mother, Sue, loved Celine, her music, her Vegas show and her stank ass perfume. She always came over to my house, located in Homestead, not to far from the Super Wal-Mart, smelling like clouds of singer Celine's perfume.

I sighed, yawning. It was going on 7 p.m. I had a party to go to, but I really didn't feel up to it. Which was a stark contradiction because I loved parties, lived for them, breathed parties. This brings me to my story. Leaving to Inhale.

I read Terry McMillan's book *Waiting to Exhale*. Yes, I saw the movie. Yes, I loved it, the book better but she missed out on some parts. Sometimes women didn't give a good goddamn about men and their shit. Yea, the book was snappy and witty but they didn't have a bitch like me in there.

I met Benjamin last week. He came into the store, I worked at Scotts Unlimited, a retail store. Fortunately, I was the manager. He had a job application. Looking at him I told myself, damn, he's fine. I remembered seeing him somewhere before. He seemed confident, too goddamn confident. He had a swagger that told me, Yea I'ma get this marketing job because I was 6 feet 8 inches with a horse dick and big feet. Yea, baby!

I approached him, clad superbly and beautifully in a long skirt with slight split up the right leg. High heeled pumps that screamed make-over more than business. My hair piled atop my head with Janet Jackson ala 1993 That's the Way Love Goes Curls. I rocked this look longer than today's fucked-up breed partied like a rock star.

We shook hands. "How are you? And you are..."

"Benjamin," he told me, sizing me up like he worked for McDonalds and I was a Tony Romas chick with a side of Pollo Tropical. He then kissed my hand and I said, "I'm Quintet...Keep it business."

He challenged me. "I plan on it." His eyes fucked me from here to Kingdom Come but my eyes didn't fuck him past the front desk. Men like him I loved to diffuse. On second thought, maybe I should give him a dose of the funky stuff, wouldn't want him leaving out of here with a purple belly, meaning hungry...

I decided to play this man like a flute and I only played the clarinet. "You're punctual, fifteen minutes before the interview."

He looked dumb-founded. "Interview...I was, uh...just returning the job application."

*Damn! Play along. Some things went over a man's head faster than my lips over their bulging mushroom heads when I'm sucking dick. Save all that shit for Maury Povich. I just wanna get in your briefs and see what kinda water hose you use to water the lawns of the woman's pussy.*

*Let the games begin!* "I am the manager. Also the hiring manager. I wear many...hats. None of them say Magnum, but you..." I licked my lips. "...get my drift..."

He met my eyes eagerly. "Then I'm all yours."

"Nah, I think that's your mother's job." My voice dropped a couple notches. Nosey bitches worked here, always in my mouth, always in my goddamn business. I didn't really fuck men who worked here because every woman who worked here each fucked the men who worked here four times over. And there was nothing worse than bad dick than familiar dick.

I held up my hand, directing him to go to my office...and he proceeded to walk towards the corridor that took us to the back offices. I looked at Stacey, who was ringing up merchandise and giving me the thumbs up and an inconspicuous look. I nodded my head and watched his booty as we made our way to my office.

When we got there I closed the door and advised him to have a seat. He sat down, he did have good manners and he said, "Well thanks for your time. Thanks for the interview. I do need it."

"No problem." I took off my jacket and revealed a cream colored blouse that made my tits look huge. I sat down, released a large gush of air and said, "I had a long day." He eyed my tits like a little uncontrollable boy. "Very long day." I faked a yawn.

He looked concerned. "In what way?"

I looked at him. "Interviews. Lots and lots of...uh, interviews."

He was skeptical now. Wrinkles on his forehead, homeboy was doing some serious thinking. Don't think too hard, might burst a vein.

"Why did you give me one before reviewing my application?"

I said, "Looks like you could use a break."

"A break. I can handle myself."

*Ok, girl. This one has a quick temper and hates when someone compromised his manhood. Ok, change gears, pump brakes...slow it down, girl bring it down a notch. Ok, ok. Challenge. He looked like the type of man who had it bad or rough, either way it was badly rough...*

"I am sure you can. But a sister is trying to give you some help."

He frowned. "Some help."

"What are you, a goddamn parrot?"

"Nah, woman I am trying to..."

"Polly wants a cracker?" I asked with my little girl voice I used when I wanted to sucker someone.

Take the bait, Niggah. "Nah, I need a job. Don't play with me." Yes, he took it.

"I don't think I can play with you. How long have you been out of work?"

He snubbed my words with an audible, "Fuck you! I have a job!"

"Oh, yeah? Where do you work?"

"I work; um...I work for...I got my own business."

"*Where's* your resume?"

"You didn't ask for one."

"And you don't have a job, because if you did, any real business man or working man, neither applies to you, should already waltz in here with resume in hand, or in a portfolio and it don't even look like you can afford a portfolio let alone the Xerox paper to print your resume on."

"Look, you're pushing me." He had fire in his eyes.

Well, I had fire in *mine*. Fuck it; I got an inferno in my pupils. "Are you reliable?"

"More reliable than you are."

I played with files on my desk that I needed to shred. "Maybe this job isn't for you."

"Maybe that tired ass Janet weave isn't working for you." My mouth fell open. "Or is it a wig? I don't see it connecting to any follicles on your face, bitch!"

Ok, he was mad. Maybe I shouldn't have played this game. Brothah had it bad, made me feel kind of bad. Kind of. That meant I was having very little empathy.

"Can you handle the position if I gave it to you?"

He fell silent, swallowed the next word he was about to say. I wanted to slap the shit out of him for calling me a bitch. He looked like a homo and I wasn't talking about homosapien but I kept my mouth closed. If Tevin Campbell could turn out to be gay after making me wet with "Tell Me what you Want me to Do" and "Shh," and "I'm Ready," then I wouldn't put nothing past these men!

"I surely can, between having eight kids from eight different women and I'm only 23 I need a break. Child support and all." He looked proud. He looked down at his dick and played it off by brushing off imaginary dust. "I don't see my kids much." He looked up into my eyes and I shuddered. He was drop dead gorgeous. If a black Brad Pitt applied for a job it'd be Benjamin.

My pussy released tilted cups I didn't know it had and my panties got the tidal wave of its life. I felt my clitoris crying, that's how wet I was. His sternness and his cockiness turned me on full throttle.

I was shocked. "Eight kids...eight different women?"

He looked pleased at my reaction. That's funny. My pussy wasn't sending out party invites at this notable revelation. The once teeming-with-life Sahara Desert was starting to turn to rock and rubble. And that wasn't good at all.

"Yea, I was young."

*This motherfucker talks like he's 60 years old.* "You're *still* young."

He had piercing eyes. "I'ma man. I do what I have to do."

It sounded insulting. "I can tell." Time to teach him a lesson. A valuable lesson. I hated myself for even contemplating this mass deception.

I licked my lips. "What will you do for a job? We pay $19.50 an hour." His eyes enlarged with his dick, I could see it pulsating behind his slacks and it was huge. "If I hire you, how do I know you won't turn out to be a liability?"

I guess I was about to find out how many licks it took to get to the center of the Tootsie Pop and all I wanted was a Blow Pop.

Standing up he walked up to my desk, undoing the buttons on his jacket slowly. Looking deeply into my eyes he smiled a shit-eating grin that turned me to poop. I shook in the seat. I turned in my chair and spread my legs, rubbing my breasts. On his knees he went, pushing up my skirt, looking over my pussy and realized I had on crotchless panties. The crotch less panties were the best way to go, fuck thongs. Thongs gave my asshole rashes Preparation H couldn't heal.

Full of charm and grace, he massaged my thighs and I tilted my head back. I never thought of being a black woman abusing my authority, misusing my power but men have been doing this shit for years. If you could count the number of women and men who sucked a little dick or gave up a little ass for a job there wouldn't be enough rooms in the continental U.S that could hold them all. I should know, I sucked a little to get my position. I sucked my way into a hefty 401 (k), an off the chain pension, medical and dental. And I got to fire a bitch who looked at me the wrong way, dressed past company standards or showed up to work late.

He was fired up. Breathlessly, he looked up at me.

"You wanted this good dick the entire time, didn't you?"

*Hell yes yes yes!* "...Hell, no, Niggah!"

He laughed. "Sure you did. I got eleven inches, cut, three inches in diameter. I'm known to knock a woman's period on."

*Damn!* "You ain't gotta to lie, Craig you ain't gotta to lie!" We were laughing at my favorite line from Ice Cube's *Friday* movie.

"Do I get the job?" he asked, trying to seduce me.

*Hell nah!* "Rubbing me like teddy bears isn't going to convince me." I closed my eyes, taking his head and pulling those delicious lips up to my womanly embraced lips with the field of exotic hair, curly and moist. He slowly ran his tongue all over it, his head bobbing. I damn near screamed at the pleasure. He separated the pink curtains with his tongue and used his lips to tongue kiss my clit. God!

I looked down at him doing his thing. He used his fingers to separate, divide and conquer parts of my pussy I didn't know I had. He made it feel like I had three G-spots. Wow.

Abruptly, making me jump out of my skin, the telephone rang and I answered, urging him to eat quietly, no talking at the dinner table, ya' feel me? "Yes...hmmm mmmm, I'm doing just...peachy...yea, eat my *pussy*....yeah, girl this fine ass Niggah is chopping me up....yea, Benjamin suck right there....oh, yes girl sorry....can I call you back...? A girl gotta do what she gotta do...Ciao!"

I dropped the phone on the floor and before I could fall back into the groove the door opened but I didn't stop neither did Benjamin and when my higher up said, "What in the living hell are you doing? You are fired, clear your things..." I solemnly urged Ben to keep eating, and he did, unperturbed, and I said to my higher up, "First....damn, baby eat it, baby...you are going to keep your mouth shut..." I pushed back in the chair and it took everything in me to stand up. I was weak in the knees and even lighter in the ass.

Thinking lucidly, I crawled on top of my desk, my big booty on display, looking like a vixen, pussy all in Ben's face, and I knocked the lamp, books and my non-working company computer on the floor. Sparks were everywhere and I didn't care.

"Secondly, if you fire me your wife will find out I sucked you up for this job; third, close the door and fourth I expect a brand new computer by tomorrow or you will be on the 6 o'clock news for sexual harassment. Now have a good day..."

The door closed, he left in defeat. *Good ridden, beyotch!* Always good to hold something over the perpetrator's...head

It took a little minute for me to realize that Ben was ass naked. He had a huge dick. I took this time to survey all this land before my very eyes. Perky nipples, incredible chest. Tattoos everywhere. The tat "freak" on his neck. Thick lips, long, thick fingers. A nice ass. Homeboy had back for ribs and a few T-bone steaks.

I had to keep it together. I almost forgot what my real mission was here. I couldn't forget it. Mama always said good dick made you do good things you wouldn't care to do if it was bad dick.

Lord. My hands and knees were throbbing...He got on top of the desk, sliding his thick dick deep inside me. I gasped for dear life, looking back at him. I wanted to tell him to put on a rubber but I didn't feel like it. It didn't look like he had anything...and as for me, you know...uh, whatever.

He was full of fire, urgent and aggressive. Slapping my ass he started grinding inside me, slowly, controlling. I came instantly. All over him. He smiled then, grinning all in my face. He leaned forward and ran his tongue across my shoulders, sucked on the back of my neck as my ass and his dick played tennis.

Taking control of this ship, the way any real man should do, he pulled my curls; they fell all about my face, making me look more desperate than I intended to look. Never appear to be desperate for men. They would take that shit and run with it and nine times outta ten the dick wasn't even worth the inches God wasted on him. Some men had a nine inch brain and a small dick. Other men had a big ass dick and a six inch brain. Meaning men with a mind would fuck you to sleep with that little morsel-of-a-dick and men with a big dick would fuck you to a pack of Benson and Hedges menthol Lights because you need to smoke about six to figure out why a man with such a big dick can't fucking use it to its fullest potential. And if you really wanted to get technical roll a blunt and smoke it to the head before you let a big dick, can't-use-it man sex you up because weed + His Sexless ass = I'm high. So it didn't matter.

Men weren't designed to do shit but conquer the world and multiply the earth and the woman and her sweet tasting pussy was the catalyst, the start and the end and the goddamn captain of the ship. Eve was the start of destruction, not man. People get the game all fucked up.

And with this man in my face I couldn't breathe. I was being taken into pure ecstasy. Maybe this wasn't a good time to tell him I had genital herpes, which I was still bitter about it. Maybe I should tell him that I was going to infect every man that I possibly could. But not just any man, only the creeps, the bad fathers, the molesters and the rapists, the men who made eight kids with eight different women, men like him didn't deserve to be healthy. Men like him that played me back in the day. Men like him who broke my heart and sold it to their homeboys, allowing them to come into my life when I was vulnerable...opening doors for them to dig in my pussy like Timbuktu. Men who used and abused me, men who were savaged and cold-hearted. Men who took my money and spent it on other bitches. Men, who aided and abetted my own inner insecurity, took my beauty and handed me snowflakes when I was in Ice Land.

He pulled me up to him, hugging me from the back...he humped my woman hood like he never humped it before, his dick filling me up like O.J's hand in a glove...I was climbing the mountain as another earthquake started to send tremors up and down my spine...I was now in the river, it was taking me up the creek, past the damns and crevices, along the lakes and ponds, over the cliff of the Niagra and into the oceans, past Titanics and men overboard...God, past ski boats and floaters...I was about to fly, fly out of the water, drenched with sweat as my pussy told me, with an attitude, "Girl we about to cry again."

That male cockiness shining through. "You like it, baby?"

I could barely talk. "I love it!"

He pressed for more. Than I was willing to give. "I got the job?"

We were sweating profusely. I was in heaven; I didn't want it to end.

I was stuttering something terrible…"No, not yet…keep convincing me…" *I'm sorry, I wasn't gonna hire you. This was a game, and when you were in the game of deception you didn't follow the rules!*

And he did. Convince me, that was. By the time we both came together I sent him out of my office with his clothes barely on and let him know that I would call him with the date he could start working. I sat in my chair, breathing so hard I thought I was flushed.

I thought about my boss then. With his fat ass. A few years before, he was one of the finest men in town. But after a bad marriage, child support payments, getting drunk every night and excessive fucking and partying, he was reduced, well, he inflated past expectations.

I picked up the phone, and called him. He didn't answer. I called him again, getting annoyed. I knew he wasn't avoiding me. I knew his address, where he worked out at (as much as we fucked there) and I knew the wife's job number, cell phone and what route she drove to work.

Dusting my TV I smiled. That was three months ago. I put in a transfer. I left that job in Philly and was sent down here to Homestead. I know Benjamin was brooding with anger to find out I got a quick fuck at his expense. Maybe I was wrong, and I knew I was for having sex with an asshole when I had genital herpes.

But that should teach people. You didn't just fuck anybody, just because I had a fine body and a pretty face didn't mean I didn't have a disease. And on top of that I had H.I.V. Living that wild life back in the day led me to making hastily bad decisions. Mistakes were second to none, but bad decisions opened the door for reckless living.

My belief window was never met over time. I had sex to fit in. I wanted to teach people about my wrongs, but I kept meeting bad men. I didn't ask for H.I.V. *God*, no! But Mama warned me about going to the clubs. I didn't listen. A hard head made a soft ass! I thought I knew it all. And one day when I was 20, someone poked me on the arm with something sharp when I was maneuvering through the dancing, sweaty crowd at the club. I ignored it, thought it was a bug bite. Turned out it was a needle infected with H.I.V. blood. Someone had it out for me, and after I got checked out and the doctor told me I had H.I.V. I thought about that "bug bite" in the club. I was devastated. I couldn't function; I couldn't eat, drink or sleep. I cried for the next two weeks, going to work and cussing people, firing people for no reason and cussing the boss. I called his wife and told her we fucked and she filed for divorce. I pushed everyone away! It would turn out to be Cindy who poked me with the needle. She was a girl I met the year before who was married to a man I slept with behind her back. She wanted to get back at me, because her man infected her with a disease another bitch gave him, so she got back at me by passing on her death sentence. She's currently serving time for what she did. But before we even went to court I found that Ho and I beat her ass so bad with a stick she couldn't move by the time the paramedics got there. And I wouldn't have known it was her that infected me if it wasn't for my ex fuck buddy, her man, who came to me and told me she admitted to him what she did.

Now I tried to put this all out of my mind. I dusted the dressers and the mirrors, tears falling down my face. I still needed to do something, and I had no choice. I had to do what's right. When the doctor told me I had herpes he advised me to stop having sex immediately and to call any and everyone I fucked. Ha. Fat chance! But I told him I would, even though I knew in my heart I never would. I walked over to my purse and took out my cell. I contemplated calling him. I should, I should have a long time ago.

I was having a plethora of feelings. Mixed feelings finding their way out of the loop to become individual thoughts.

Empty inside.

I sat on the recliner by my bed and dialed the numbers. All ten numbers. It rung. My stomach dropped.

I closed my eyes when I heard his voice.

"He...Hello."

I was quiet, very silent.

"Anybody there?" he asked. His voice didn't sound the same. It was devoid of that fire I liked the day we met.

I forced myself to say it. My throat suddenly got dry.

"Hello Benjamin."

There was a long breath drawn. He was quiet. For a long time.

My heart sped up, maybe this was a mistake.

"I met a lot of women, half of them I will never remember. But I know this voice; a voice I met months ago, a woman who I thought would give me a job. And she did. She gave me a good job. And you know what that is?

The job of taking medications. The job of staying healthy. I've become a better man, I've become a leader. I teach my kids about the dangers of the world. I got a good job with the American Red Cross. I make more than that $19.50 you were supposedly going to pay me. I am healthy and strong.

I am alive and kicking. I am not even bitter, I'm not angry. Because your deception made me a warrior.

I teach kids all across the country about women like you. But I don't bad mouth you. I wish you well in life; I knew this phone call would come one day. If you ever need anything, just ask.

I won't stoop to your level. And when you go to bed tonight tell yourself one thing, you turned me from an irresponsible, sex-crazed fool into a real black man who finally took control of his life and kids and I married my high school Sweetheart. Good bye."

"Benjamin…I apologize, please forgive me."

He laughed playfully. And it was the weirdest thing. It was devoid of venom and betrayal. He sounded happy. That fire was back in his voice and it rendered me speechless.

He said, "I forgive you. And I forget you."

And the line disconnected.

I didn't know how long I have been crying. But I knew it has been days. I grabbed God's Bible and hugged it, flames licking through my soul. I cried and screamed, snot all in my nose to the point I couldn't breathe. I was wrong, dead wrong but I did my part. I thought I was hurting that man because I felt he wasn't worthy of a healthy life, and it turned out that I destroyed myself.

And days later, as the "Party like a Rock Star" song came back on, I turned over in my bed, my hair disheveled. I told myself that the reason dust was all over my room was because I was dreading picking up the telephone, for months, and calling Benjamin and telling him of my deception. It made me lazy, uncooperative and crazed.

I didn't take responsibility for my actions; I didn't want to accept it. I felt I didn't have to, that I was put here to punish bad men, even though I was a bad woman. I had to learn to forgive myself.

And now that I called him I had to call one other person. The Pastor's son, who was a part of a Golden Masks Orgy with me some months ago. We did it in the church.

I thought back to Roll Call.

# ~~From the King of Erotica 1~~
# ~~The Golden Masks.~~

*Well goddamn! This bitch is what James Brown would call Super Bad. Watch it now! I might have to make this one mine.*

"You look new," said the Inductor. The Pastor's Son.

His laptop open on the podium before him.

"I am." Elegance with long shaved legs shining from fluorescent lighting, nine inch stiletto heels gleaming. She licked her lips, tasting her lipstick. Her nipples erect, she stuck out her tits, beautiful in a Gucci dress and matching pumps.

"And you are?"

"Take It In the Ass Only."

He checked her profile on the lap top beside him. Model material. "You may enter."

She gave an attitude of model Naomi Campbell standards.

"Thank you. No one will touch my pussy, right?"

He looked around discreetly, coming around the podium. He got on his knees and kissed her pussy. Standing up, she smiled, pinching his cheek. "No one will touch it, but damn I just wanted to kiss it."

She wasn't impressed; in fact she shoulda pissed in his face.

"Can I go now?"

"Remember, follow the goddamn rules."

She smiled, silently farting as she went down the hallway.

Too much pasta last night.

*Damn, I got to take a shit. Oh, well. Too late for that. They still can't touch my pussy. I mean business, too. Somebody's getting a...shitty dick today!*

*And I don't care.*

*Bad men had to pay. And oh, yeah. I had H.I.V. and genital herpes. But I don't have to say all that now do I?*

# The Dawn Of
# The King of Erotica 6

I have a friend named Messy Sletty. She's a sexy bitch. She had nice titties given to her by an underground plastic surgeon, a huge bubble ass that saw more Botox injections than Beyonce's face and dick-sucking lips. She had it all, but she was a broke whore. How could you have it all as a broke bitch? It took money to get what you got and more money to maintain it. This bitch talked about everybody but her damn self. She had a husband. All he wanted was for her to be faithful and to suck his dick when he wanted and she could have everything, including the mirror on the wall telling her she's the fairest of 'em all and the keys to his Benz. But she didn't suck dick and when she bitched at him for not eating her pussy he dumped a 32 ounce bottle of Old English on her weave and he dropped her like a bad habit and this bitch had the gall to come over to my crib and ask for fifty dollars. Hmm. I didn't suck dick for free and I damn sure didn't let a man dig in my pussy free of charge. My pussy wasn't voting for Obama, my pussy didn't need "Change." Sorry, baby. My pussy needed money so if I gave her fifty dollars that would mean I fucked my man for free because I gave Messy Sletty the money I made from taking his big dick. I looked at this ditzy bitch like get a clue. Go get your ex husband back and suck his dick. I was tired of these women saying oh I didn't suck dick yet you wanted your man to take a bullet for you. If you couldn't take come from his dick with your lips why should he take a bullet for you dumb Ho's. You didn't want another woman taking your man then keep his stubborn ass by getting your knees dirty. Suck his dick like you never liked a testicle before. My clue to you was simple. Go find a good man. Give him some good head, some good ass and some good pussy…cook him a good meal, pour Crystal Louisiana Hot sauce on his steak and double fry the onions. Tell him he's a handsome sonofabitch and that he has some good tongue and over-the-top stellar dick skills. Once you do all of the above he will call you his bitch but treat you like his Queen. But this is the fine print: make sure he has a career…not a goddamn 7-11 job. You didn't want to be sucking, cooking and fucking for a man who made minimum wage and wasn't guaranteed a definite forty hours a week. Sorry, baby. That's where I draw the line and when I draw it I wasn't standing in line for welfare, food stamps or a WIC coupon for some free goddamn milk. I appreciate the man for his goals and for breaking the "white man is holding me down!" mold by getting a job but all work ain't good work and you'll be one pissed bitch if you settle for the bag boy at the supermarket and he gets ten hours next week and he couldn't even buy you a pair of fucking panties from the Kmart Clearance rack.

Got Milk.

No, Bitch. Check, Please.

**Think like a Niggah continued
In The King of Erotica 6:
Battle Plans
March of 2010**

**And the King of Erotica 7
~~Weapons of M(ASS)~~
~~Destruction,~~
Changed to "PHAROAH"
my autobiography
Coming July of 2010**

*Demetrius Mozell and the King of Erotica*
*Best friends for life.*
*The IMPROV Coconut Grove*

The KING of Erotica 5 has ended,
But THE KING OF EROTICA IS
Available NOW
In HARD COVER and PAPERBACK
www.barrnesandnoble.com
www.BN.com
www.Amazon.com Europe. France
Japan, Germany, Canada,
The United Kingdom and the U.S. of A.

*The KING of Erotica book 6*
*Get it now*
*www.BN.com*
*www.Amazon.com*
*www.barnesandnoble.com*
**PHAROAH,**
*The KING of Erotica Book 7*
*Dapharoah/Larry's autobiography*
*Coming 6.26.20.10*
*His 33rd Birthday*

www.ingramcontent.com/pod-product-compliance
Lightning Source LLC
Chambersburg PA
CBHW032030120726
47901CB00001BA/12

* 9 7 8 0 5 7 8 0 5 4 0 1 8 *